HORSE FLESH

A NOVEL BY TINA SUGARMAN

Clink
Street

London | New York

Published by Clink Street Publishing 2016

ISBN: 978-1-911110-51-4 paperback
978-1-911110-52-1 ebook

DISCLAIMER

This is a work of fiction. Any similarities in the book to real people, horses, organisations, or exact locations is purely coincidental.

However, what happens to the horses, as depicted in this novel, is real.

ACKNOWLEDGEMENTS

My thanks to my family for their inspiration, especially my husband, Matthew, who was with me almost every step of the way, offering help and encouragement. My thanks too, to Juliette, our beautiful Maine Coon cat, who kept me company in the attic on many a rainy day while I was writing this book. Also, I would like to thank Sam and Debbie, for turning my handwritten manuscript into something people can actually read, Ben Sugarman for his assistance with the front cover, Sadie Sugarman for her invaluable final edit and the folk at Authoright for making it possible for the book to reach a wider audience.

Last, but not least, my grateful thanks to the many Standardbred racehorses who have given me and our family so much pleasure over the years. Many of our experiences: the triumphs and the tragedies, the courageous horses and colourful characters we came across along the way, are reflected in this book.

This book is dedicated to all the horses I have known, but especially the Standardbred racehorse, whose friendly, trusting nature, in my experience, is second to none in the equine world.

ONTARIO, CANADA

Storm clouds were rolling in from the west, blotting out the sun and promising relief from the stifling heat. Heart of Darkness, the fastest standardbred filly in Canada, stood as still as a statue, her slender body silhouetted in the eerie light, her ears pricked, her nostrils scenting the air. A deep rumble of thunder and a flash of lightning on the horizon sent her spinning round her paddock. She put on a spectacular show.

It failed to impress her trainer.

"Bitch!" was Jim Mercer's heartfelt comment as the filly flew past him for the fifth time, tail up in the air. She was getting herself more and more worked up and if he didn't catch her soon, she was going to blow her chances of winning the Diamond Stakes final that night.

"Goddam bitch!" Mercer repeated, turning round and limping into the barn, sweating profusely. He wrenched the barn phone of its hook and dialled his wife.

"Get Evie. I need 'er right now. It's an emergency!" he shouted down the phone.

"Evie? She's at Art Camp!" he heard his wife protest weakly.

"Then get 'er out o' there!" Mercer yelled. "She's the only one that can catch the filly. We can't afford to blow a hundred grand purse, Pam, not the way things have been going lately!"

In the barn next door, the tension was also rising, Dave Bodinski was anxiously listening out for the chug of Scotty McCoy's old Ford engine. If Scotty didn't get back in the next few minutes, it'd be too late.

"Scotty?" Dave shouted, hearing a truck door slam.

"Okay I'm here!" Scotty panted, his stocky frame appearing at the barn door, clutching a shopping bag.

"D'you get it all?" Dave asked tersely.

"Three boxes o' baking soda, one carton of cake sugar and a half a dozen o' them big bottles o' Gatorade. . . the blue kind jus' like you said," Scotty replied, his face pink with exertion.

"Let's move it!" Dave urged, grabbing the bag. "She's in the fourth, right? We don't got a lotta time!"

Two minutes later, Scotty's entry in the Diamond Stakes, the filly Raiders

Moon, was standing demurely in the wash stall, while Dave manipulated a long length of plastic tubing up her nostril, down her throat and into her stomach.

"Pour it in," Dave directed impatiently, fitting a funnel to the free end of the tube and pointing to a full bucket of opaque blue liquid. "She'll go two, maybe three seconds faster with this inside of her," he added confidently. "She could fuckin' win the whole thing!"

"You reckon?" Scotty exclaimed. Then reality set in. "Come on! She ain't never gonna beat Mercer's filly."

"Heart of Darkness is pretty fuckin' good," Dave acknowledged, pulling the tube out of Raiders Moon's left nostril.

"Yeah! She ain't never lost!" Scotty agreed fervently.

"But your filly'll be right there tonight," Dave promised, tossing the tube aside. "No sweat!"

"You're the best, Dave!" Scotty told him gratefully.

Dave Bodinski, the baking soda king, had failed math at school, but he had no problem figuring out how to play the Exacta in the Diamond Stakes, the fourth race of the night. He aimed to put Raiders Moon on top with every horse in the race, going all out on the 2–6 combo: Heart of Darkness to win with Raiders Moon second. He was planning to make a killing, enough to get him out of the hole he was in. Nervously, he fingered his wallet. A miserable five hundred bucks was all he had to show for a whole year pumping gas, after paying the judges their lunatic fines. Adrenal Cortex wasn't even a chemical for God's sake, it was natural! However, if he pulled this off, he'd be back in the horse business again. He'd be getting his friend Scotty out of a jam, too. Raiders Moon hadn't won a race all season and her owner was breathing down Scotty's neck. But if there was one thing guaranteed to help a tie-up mare, it was baking soda, baking soda and more baking soda! No question about it, he assured himself. He'd be a winner tonight.

The first Friday in July was a big night at Iroquois Downs Raceway. By 8 p.m. an enthusiastic crowd had gathered in the grandstand. Dark clouds loomed overhead. The humidity index was at an all time high. Rumours of betting scandals were rife. But none of that could deter the punters on a night when the best young standardbreds in Canada were strutting their stuff. The first three races had been won by favourites, making the betting public happy.

Up in the air conditioned drivers' room, leading driver Theo Vettore stared blankly at the pair of aces in his hand, his mind occupied with figuring out the shortest route to the winner's circle in the next race, the $100,000 Diamond Pace. Theo was twenty-three, tall, slim and muscular, perfectly designed for the way he made his living: driving standardbred racehorses at speeds approaching sixty klicks an hour, wearing only a helmet for protection and separated from the wheels of his opponents by a whisker. Theo had the physique of a dancer, yet no horse, however bullheaded, had wrested the lines away from his powerful hands. Strength, grace and Italian good looks made him a magnate for lovesick girl grooms, though they knew they had no chance with him.

Theo Vettore, known in racing circles as 'the V Man', was out of their league.

A game of cards was the perfect solution to life in the drivers' room between races: short and sweet! No need to say too much, just deal the cards and take your chances. Theo's companion at the card table, 'Moose' Rankin from Moose Jaw, Saskatchewan, took a drag on his cigarette.

"You in or out?" Moose asked lazily. "I gotta be out on the track in two minutes."

"I'm in. Hit me again!" Theo replied, throwing a five-dollar bill on the pile.

The door opened a crack. Moose quickly stubbed out his cigarette. Anyone caught smoking got an automatic fifty-dollar fine, the last thing Moose needed. All the drivers resented the judges and their petty rules except the phlegmatic Ned Beazer, who played it safe both on and off the track. What did the judges imagine, that the racing game was fuckin' Sunday School? Theo thought angrily.

It was only Pete Summers at the door. He was on a no-hoper in the next race, the 6 horse, Raiders Moon.

"I'll see ya an' I'll raise ya," Moose drawled, re-lighting his cigarette, then hastily stubbing it out again. Down in the Race Barn, the Paddock Judge's rallying cry rang out.

"Fourth race! Get 'em ready, men!"

Theo Vettore threw his cards on the table.

"I'm outa here!" he gasped, taking the stairs three at a time.

SAINTE MARIE

At that precise moment, in his hilltop home in the eastern Caribbean, André Fontainbleu was holding a dinner party for the top politicians on the island: all of them recipients of his donations to their political campaigns. How simple it had been to ensure their co-operation, he thought, feeling only contempt for their willingness to compromise their integrity so cheaply. Meanwhile, his timeshare empire on the island and his offshore gaming enterprises were both prospering, free from the prying eyes of regulation.

Cries went up from the diners at the sight of the green flash which followed the setting of the sun. André Fontainbleu didn't see it, didn't care. He knew it was an illusion. Illusions were for other people, not for him.

At Iroquois Downs, the fillies for the fourth race were slowly making their way out onto the track, their flanks gleaming with sweat. Theo made a bee-line for the 2 horse, Heart of Darkness, who had a startling white star on her forehead and a long full mane. Along with the glamour came a ton of courage. She'd need that courage tonight. She was racing against the top three year old fillies in North America.

"She's the best!" her trainer, Jim Mercer, growled as he handed over the lines, increasing the pressure Theo was already feeling. Theo merely nodded. He swung himself effortlessly onto the race bike, the place he felt most at home in all the world.

Out on the track, the spotlight played on him and Heart of Darkness for a brief moment. Then the filly took off on him, her neck arched, her feet dancing on the stone dust track. He glanced at the odds board. She was even money. Suddenly he felt high, a natural high that was almost as good as the drugs he did on occasion. The only cloud on his horizon was the $35,000 he owed the mysterious individual known as the Scorpion. Theo had never met him and never wanted to either. The name fit him all too well: deadly with a sting in the tail. He shuddered. $35,000! How had his cocaine habit gotten so totally out of control? He stifled the thought. For now, he needed to focus on the race ahead. He eyed the competition, careful not to speak to any of the other drivers. The judges, who watched their every move, would assume they were plotting to get a long shot home. Moose's filly, Gypsy Queen, was the one to beat. But except for the two outsiders, Jolie Dame and Raiders Moon, it was a strong field.

The sky darkened. Two minutes to post! Floodlights were beaming down onto the racetrack, creating the illusion of a bright sunny day. Seagulls from Lake Ontario swooped over the infield and perched on the grandstand roof, their raucous cries filling the air. Black thunderclouds looked ready to drop their load as crowds of people clutching their tickets rushed down to the rail, anxious not to miss the start of the feature race.

Dave Bodinski slunk out with them, checked his tickets and gulped. The teller had messed up! Instead of doubling up Raiders Moon with the favourite to win, he'd doubled her up with the 10 horse, Jolie Dame, a rank outsider. Praying his eyes were deceiving him he checked again. But there it was 10–6, clear as day. Cursing loudly, he fought his way back through the throng. Less than one minute to post! Three people ahead of him in the line. He'd never make it, he thought despairingly.

Out on the racetrack, the wings of the starting car opened.

"Turn your horses, gentlemen, please," the suit in the car said. At those words, Theo's heart started pumping fast. Adrenalin flooded his body and brain. His senses became super clear, his reaction time instantaneous. Ten horses were lined up behind the car, noses on the gate. As the vehicle picked up speed, the sound of the revving engine was drowned out by the rattle of sulkies and the drumming of hoofbeats. A split second before the car sped away, Theo glanced swiftly to his left. The horse on the rail wasn't keeping up. To his right, he could see Moose getting ready to leave with Gypsy Queen. Theo made a split second decision. He urged his filly on. All around him he heard whips cracking and drivers screaming. He paid no heed. He made the top before the turn. To his surprise, instead of taking over the lead, Moose slipped into second place, behind him.

The crowd roared with delight, drowning out the call.

Dave Bodinski couldn't hear a word. As short as he was, with a wall of people in front of him, he couldn't see anything either. It looked like he was stuck with the tickets. Right after he'd told his story to the teller, the starting bell had rung, making exchange impossible. Though he could hardly bear to watch the race, he doggedly fought his way down to the rail. Raiders Moon had got away last and was sitting at the back of the bus. He was well and truly fucked, Dave thought despairingly.

At the half mile point, the timer flashed 55.2. Time to back it off, Theo decided, giving Heart of Darkness the message. As the pace slowed, drivers behind him began edging their horses out. Glancing back, Theo was surprised to see the 10 horse, Jolie Dame, powering up on the outside. What on earth was Ned Beazer playing at? Jolie Dame was 50-1!

"I'm the power here, Bud!" Theo roared, loosening up on the lines. Heart of Darkness lurched forward and Jolie Dame fell back, but not very far. She was sitting outside Gypsy Queen now, trapping Theo's main rival, Moose Rankin, along the rail. Theo grinned to himself. Anyone who wanted to challenge him now would have to take the long way around and go three wide. As for Gypsy Queen, she was literally breathing down Theo's neck, banging her head on his helmet. She needed out bad. Theo grinned again. He was enjoying this!

As they rounded the last turn into the stretch, Theo cracked the wheel disc with his whip. The sound set Heart of Darkness alight but to his astonishment, the long shot Jolie Dame reappeared beside him, matching him stride for stride down the lane. As they fought head to head for the top, Gypsy Queen pushed through on the inside, sandwiching Heart of Darkness between the other two fillies like a piece of pastrami between two slices of bread. They were only 100 feet from the wire now. It felt like 500. Theo's filly still had her head in front. Just! Then out of the corner of his eye, he saw a horse on the far outside, moving like an express train with Pete Summers at the helm screaming like a banshee. It was the 6 horse, Raiders Moon. The caller's voice was rising hysterically.

"They're coming down to the wire! Four of them across the track! Heart of Darkness, Gypsy Queen, Jolie Dame and on the far outside Raiders Moon! Too close to call! Photograph! Photograph! Hold all tickets. I repeat, hold all tickets!"

From his vantage point down by the rail, Dave Bodinski had seen and heard everything but he had no idea who'd won. He ran around quizzing complete strangers. No one had a clue. All four fillies were still on the racetrack so even the drivers didn't know for sure. Dave kept his eyes glued to the tote board. He wasn't religious, but clutching his ticket, he prayed. Thanks to the idiot teller, the only way he'd make any real money was on the 10–6 combo, Raiders Moon to win with Jolie Dame second, the most unlikely of the lot. Ten agonizing minutes later, the results of the fourth race finally appeared on the board. The number 6 appeared first, then the number 10. Dave groaned. Exacta meant exactly that. The horses had to be in the correct order. His tickets were worthless pieces of paper now.

There was a sudden murmur from the crowd. The numbers 6 and 10 were flashing on and off.

"Attention! The judges have declared a dead heat. There will be a payout on both horses to win. Exacta payout on 6 and 10 in either order!"

"I'm a winner!" Dave screamed, punching his fist in the air. "I'm a fuckin' winner!" All around him, people were ripping up their tickets, cursing. Dave did a rapid calculation in his head. Every one of his $2 tickets was worth $1200. Unbelievable! His mind reeled at the high numbers. Then it sunk in…He was rich. He was a fuckin' millionaire!

Well, he realized, not quite a millionaire but $24,000 was enough to put him back in the horse business.

With a clash of thunder, the storm broke, drenching the spectators. The mood turned ugly. Losers were crowding around the winner's circle in the rain, booing and shouting obscenities. Jolie Dame and Raiders Moon hadn't just beaten the favourite, they'd beaten the best three year old filly in Canada and the darling of the betting public. They'd felt she simply could not lose and had bet the bank on her. Dave hung back watching a bemused local bigwig clutch the trophy to his chest, unwilling to hand it over to either trainer, as both had won. In the end, the two of them, an ecstatic Scotty McCoy and a smirking Andy Price, worked it out by holding it between them in a rare show of trainer co-operation.

The commotion around the winner's circle had not escaped the eagle eyes of the judges, perched high above the grandstand. Two floors below them, newboy Alastair McTavish, recently appointed as Director of Iroquois Downs Raceway, was gazing down at the scene with an increasing feeling of unease. Al was an imposing 6 feet 3 inches with the kind of presence that demands respect. At 58, he didn't have a single grey hair, though he was thinning on top. Even though it was his first week on the job, he recognized trouble when he saw it. He reached for the red phone, his direct link to the presiding judge. John Jewells was a no-nonsense type who had trained at the famous judge school in Arizona, known locally as Jewells' School.

"What's going on down there, John?" Al McTavish boomed.

Jewells ducked the question.

"What can I do for you, Director McTavish?" he asked.

"I'm a little concerned about that last race," Al persisted.

"Already on it. Got the Mutuals Manager looking for any suspicious betting patterns. Probably nothing in it, but you never know." Thirty seconds later, the presiding judge had an intriguing fact to ponder. Twenty $2 tickets had indeed been punched sequentially for the winning combination. It was a highly unusual sized bet for two long shots.

"Instruct the teller to check each winning exacta ticket," Jewells told the Mutuals Manager. "If anyone tries to cash in all or part of that sequence, hold them on any excuse."

"You betcha, John."

John Jewells, tight lipped, picked up his own red phone, his direct line to the Paddock Judge, a Mr. T. Roberts, who controlled the Race Barn like an army sergeant. On any given night, there were over a hundred horses, almost twice that many horsemen and a few dozen drivers to keep in order. Roberts thrived on it. Despite the torrential downpour, he was on the case, rallying the troops, determined that the fifth race would leave the Race Barn on time.

"Automatic hundred-dollar fine for any trainer late for post parade! Let's get moving!" Mr. Roberts shouted. "We go in thirty seconds with the fifth, men. Get 'em ready! Mr. Hall! Where the hell are you with your horse? Get 'im out there now, and I mean NOW!"

The ring of his red phone interrupted the Paddock Judge's diatribe in mid stream.

"Mr. Roberts. It's John here." No one was on first name terms with the Paddock Judge.

"Yes sir!" Mr. Roberts replied eagerly.

"I want to talk to McCoy, Price and Rankin in that order, right away."

"Mr. Rankin's in the fifth sir."

"Get me the other two. I'll talk to Rankin when he comes back in."

"Yes sir!" Mr. Roberts replied slamming down the phone.

"Lead 'em out, men! Mr. McCoy, Mr. Price. Judges want to talk to you!"

Scotty McCoy's outraged tone echoed down the phone line when the judges suggested that he'd been stiffing Raiders Moon in her previous races.

"I never stiffed a horse in my life," he declared, puffing himself up in self-righteous indignation. "She was tying up! Ask my vet. He's been treatin' her for it."

Andy Price too had an airtight explanation, "I only got the filly ten days ago," he declared. "She came down from Quebec. It's her first start for me. You accusing me of doin' too good with her or what?"

Moose Rankin came in after the fifth race soaking wet, splattered with mud and in a foul mood, having finished last.

"Lazer told me to give Gypsy Queen a covered up trip," Moose said scowling at the phone. "Ned Beazer did the job on me. I'm sick about it!" The judges reluctantly took him at his word. They all agreed a hot head like Moose Rankin was the last driver any sane person would pick to pull off a betting coup. None of them felt it necessary to question the leading driver, Theo Vettore. He was always trying to win.

"Which leaves only Pete Summers," John Jewells told Al. "But it's the first time he's driven Raiders Moon, so we can't pin it on him."

The judges were still scrutinizing the tape of the fourth when the presiding judge's phone rang. It was the Mutuals Manager.

"Looks like we got your man, John. Listen to this! He's a trainer just come back from suspension, a Dave Bodinski."

"Hold off payment. Tell him we need more I/D and to come back in the morning. Tell him he'll have to see the judges first, but it's just pro forma," Jewells replied.

"Pro what?" the Mutuals Manager asked uncertainly.

"Routine," Jewells replied irritably.

"Gotcha," the manager said, sounding relieved.

Everything appeared to hinge on the judges' interview with Dave Bodinski the following day. But a call back from the Mutuals Manager clouded the issue somewhat.

"You'd better hear this for yourself," he told John Jewells.

"I remember the guy!" a flustered teller confessed. "He accused me of punching in the wrong numbers. Made a big stink about it! But it was too late to do anything. The starting bell had gone off."

Pretty soon the judges had a more urgent problem on their hands. The drivers had got together and were refusing to go out for the seventh race, claiming that conditions were too dangerous. It was true enough. The worst storm to hit Ontario in a decade was showing no signs of abating. Visibility was close to zero. Mr. Roberts, the Paddock Judge, was desperately searching through his rule books for guidance on extreme weather conditions.

Taking advantage of the lull, Moose Rankin collared Theo Vettore in the drivers' room.

"What the fuck were you playing at in the fourth, cutting the mile like that?" Moose hissed, "I thought your filly didn't like the front end."

"She doesn't," Theo replied sullenly. "I figured you'd cut it, you moron!"

"Listen to me," Moose exclaimed, lighting his cigarette and glancing over at Theo, his eyes half closed. "You're in big trouble. I heard the guys in dark glasses bet the bank on the exacta tonight and it sure as hell included you. Your horse was fucking even money!"

"She lost! It happens!" Theo retorted.

Moose didn't reply. He just drew his finger across his own throat, then pointed to Theo. The sound of rain drumming on the roof was deafening. Theo swallowed hard but said nothing.

"Attention horsemen!" the Paddock Judge's voice rang out. "Under rule 147, section 3, the stewards have decided to abandon the rest of tonight's programme due to dangerous racing conditions. I repeat, racing has been abandoned due to inclement weather."

"Roberts doesn't get to yell at us any more tonight," Moose said happily, turning to Theo.

There was no one there.

"Encore du vin, Monsieur?" a voice murmured at André's Fontainbleu's elbow. He motioned the waiter away. He had caught sight of the young Frenchman he had recently hired standing at attention, keeping a discreet distance from the dinner table conversation. When André raised a finger, Henri approached and spoke, sotto voce, in his ear.

"Ze young lady, she is waiting for you, *Monsieur,*" Henri said.

André Fontainbleu picked up his fork. The twinkle of silver on glass produced the desired effect. His guests fell silent.

"I regret, but always, business calls," he announced charmingly, rising to his feet and turning away from the Caribbean Sea, the backdrop for dinner.

The Australian girl was waiting downstairs, gazing up at the soaring ceiling and glittering candelabra. He ran his eyes over her slim figure, her full breasts. She was young, barely twenty at a guess and suitably virginal. According to his sources, she had been marooned on the island when her boat was caught in a freak storm. June was generally a calm month. Unlike the rest of the crew, she apparently wanted to stay on. As she wasn't independently wealthy, she needed a work permit, a lengthy bureaucratic process on Sainte Marie unless one knew who to bribe. That is where André Fontainbleu came in, provided, *naturellement*, that the woman in question was young and attractive.

There was a determined set to this girl's jaw, but he had no doubt that common sense would prevail, after he had laid out his terms. One weekend, that was what he required. Her body was the only thing she had to offer in return. The feeling of power was intoxicating. As he walked down the spiral staircase to greet her, he caught her eye and imagined undressing her. She blushed but she held his gaze without faltering. Her long dark hair revived bitter sweet memories. But that was long ago. This was going to be easy like everything else on this island. Almost too easy. Despite, or perhaps because of, his age, he was still attractive to women. The touch of silver in his crop of dark curls reassured them. It gave him a fatherly air. Also, the power and the money drew them in.

It promised to be a pleasant weekend, a very pleasant weekend indeed!

CORNERED

Theo sprinted to his car, through the pouring rain. He fumbled with the key, shaking like a leaf. He knew all about those guys in dark glasses. If they thought he hadn't done his best to win, however untrue that was, he'd be in big trouble. He'd been feeling pretty low about losing with Heart of Darkness. That now seemed insignificant. Somehow he got out of the horsemen's parking lot without running into anything. Then he hit the road. The rain was cascading down like Niagara Falls. It had grounded every sane driver, so he was alone out there. The windshield wipers simply couldn't cope with the torrent, but he desperately needed to put some distance between him and the racetrack. Moose had scared the shit out of him! Things were getting way too complicated at Iroquois Downs. There was plenty to worry about driving in a horse race without all that. He took the Indian Trail. It was slow going, as the road meandered through the bush. But Theo struggled on, using the blurred, watery house lights that appeared from time to time to guide him. At length he reached open country and a straight road. The rain was easing up. He breathed a sigh of relief. He was almost home. Ferme Victoire, his Uncle Bernie's place, was just around the corner.

His relief was short lived. A pair of headlights materialized out of thin air. He had a fleeting glimpse of a vast combine harvester coming straight at him, as he slammed on the brakes. He put his hand down on the horn and held it there, but the headlights kept on coming. Was the maniac at the wheel deaf as well as blind? And what the hell was it doing out at this time of night, in this weather? Suddenly he knew. A split second later, another set of lights shone in his rear view mirror, half blinding him.

He was trapped! He had to get off the road! He swung left and instantly regretted his decision. An ugly looking barbed wire fence lay on top of a steep bank. He swerved to the right. His tires squealed in protest, but he put his foot down hard on the accelerator and prayed. There was a deafening crash. The air around him exploded. Theo watched, fascinated, as tiny air bubbles floated slowly across his line of vision. The car rocked violently, then landed right side up. Everything stopped. His headlights were shining on a sea of green corn. It was eerily quiet. The passenger door was pressing right up against his right arm. But by some miracle, he was still in one piece.

He forced his way out and glanced up at the road. What he saw there made his heart stop. Two massive guys were silhouetted in the headlights streaming from a long black limousine that looked like a hearse. But the men looked nothing like undertakers. They were wielding powerful flashlights which, in their hands, looked like lethal weapons. But it was the sight of the long knives hanging from their belts which really scared him. He didn't wait to find out more. He pushed his way through corn stalks, floundering on the heavy ground, ankle deep in mud. He'd heard stories about these guys, terrifying stories. He struggled on, his progress maddeningly slow, his imagination running riot. But despite his urgent need to put in as much distance as possible between him and them, he could feel that he was running out of steam. He and his cousin Lara had been in plenty of scrapes as kids, but this was no game!

He hunkered down, listening intently.

Smash! Bang! They were trashing his car, breaking the windows, slashing the tires. The headlights dimmed, then died. A piece of Theo died with it. Apart from his race bike, the car was the only thing he owned. Bastards, he cursed silently, afraid to make a sound.

Suddenly everything went quiet again, a silence filled with menace. Now they were through with the car, they'd come after him, he guessed. He froze, peering through the rows of corn, hearing nothing, seeing even less. After what felt like an eternity, a powerful engine no hearse would ever possess roared into life, its dark outline menacing, even from a safe distance. This was no ordinary vehicle, Theo realized. Its front end was built like a battering ram. He shuddered as it rolled away down the road, its red tail lights glowing in the dark.

Theo rose cautiously to his feet and looked about him, wondering what to do next. There was no sense going back to his car. It was a total write off. As he squelched through the mud to higher ground at the edge of the field, he realized the rain had stopped. He sat down and emptied the water out of his shoes. What now? he asked himself.

Dave Bodinski waited for a break between cloudbursts before setting off for home, a one-bedroom walk-up on Erinsville's east side. It didn't bother him so much that he had to go see the judges in the morning. He and Scotty McCoy had to sing from the same hymn book, is all. But the rumour running around the Race Barn about some guys losing a big bet in the fourth, that had bothered him. Big time! He knew in his gut that Raiders Moon's win had a lot to do with it and, thanks to the judges practically arresting him in the grandstand, there was a big fat finger pointing directly at him. Every couple of minutes he took a peek in his rear view mirror, looking out for a guy on his tail, even though he had no idea what he'd do if he was being followed.

To his relief, he reached his building without incident. On his way up the stairs, the phone started ringing. He unlocked his front door in record time and ran inside, but the phone cut out, right after he picked up. Normally he'd have cared less, but he had to wonder. Who'd be calling at this time of night? And why? When no one called back, he assumed the worst.

He locked all the windows and double bolted the front door. He was thankful that his apartment was on the second floor. It gave him a sporting chance. He decided to take Scotty McCoy with him to cash in the tickets. Scotty wasn't big, but he was stronger than he looked. He was bull headed too. If anyone tried to jump them, Scotty wouldn't take it lying down. Hoping for the best, Dave switched off his phone and barricaded himself in the bedroom. He fell into a fitful doze, listening to the sound of the rain on the window panes.

The road was far too dangerous, Theo realized. He went in the opposite direction, walking along the narrow ridge of grass on the edge of the field, listening intently to every sound, trying to ignore the sinister rustling in the corn stalks. He was doing okay till an owl hooted in his ear. Eventually the corn field gave way to bush. He hesitated for a moment. Then he began fighting his way through the undergrowth, feeling very much alone. The moon, his only source of light, had disappeared behind the clouds. If he'd got it right, his uncle's farm wasn't far off. If not…he'd just have to hole up in the woods and wait till dawn. He'd reckoned without the coyotes. The first howl, too close for comfort, sent shivers down his spine. It was quickly joined by others. A deer came bounding towards him, nearly running him down. The pack was on the hunt. The clouds rolled back and he made out the shadowy forms of the coyotes snaking in and out of the trees, their eyes glinting. They were after something. He just hoped it wasn't him!

For the fifth time that night, Scotty McCoy left the pay phone and made his way back to his barn. He was cold, wet and worried sick. Where was Dave when he needed him? Raiders Moon wasn't acting right. If she got any worse, he'd be forced to call the vet and that was the last thing he wanted to do right now. It was like calling the police after you'd committed a crime. Nevertheless, after looking over the mare one more time, Scotty knew he had to bite the bullet. Things had gone too far. Even Dave couldn't help him now.

Coyotes didn't generally attack people, but they'd take a puppy or a pet cat in a heartbeat. Better safe than sorry, Theo reasoned, getting down on his hands and knees and groping around for something to throw at them. Eventually, his fingers closed on a dead branch. Pretty soon he spotted the coyotes' intended quarry: a clutch of round eyed baby raccoons, trying to shimmy up a tree trunk, the picture of innocence. As the pack edged forward, he brandished his tree branch, yelling at the top of his lungs. To his relief, the coyotes turned tail and ran. Ousting them gave him a much needed boost, but when he looked around for the raccoons they had disappeared. There's gratitude for you, he thought.

A hundred metres further on, the outline of his uncle's hay barn loomed up, its reassuring light shining like a beacon through the mist. He was almost home! Then the barn light cut out, plunging him into darkness. Minutes ticked by. Theo was afraid to make a move. Was this an ordinary power cut, or were the Undertakers out there somewhere, waiting for him?

Rain hit veterinarian Jay Winterflood smack in the face the moment he left the comfort of his truck. Getting to Scotty McCoy's barn was like fording a swollen river, something he'd had plenty of practice at on the Cree Reserve in Quebec, where he had spent the first fifteen years of his life.

Inside the barn, a man was sprawled on a rickety chair, half asleep. He jumped up when he saw Jay.

"Doc!" he exclaimed.

"Scotty McCoy?" Jay asked. Scotty nodded.

"She's bad, Doc, real bad," he said hurrying over to one of the stalls and opening the door. The horse inside was obviously in distress. She'd backed herself into a corner. Her head was almost touching the floor and her flanks were heaving. There was a chill in the air which had nothing to do with the temperature. It clung to the hay bales stacked in the aisleway and lingered on the upturned jog carts and the harness bags hanging from the rafters. Involuntarily Jay shivered.

"I don't understand it!" Scotty said, scratching his head. "She raced great tonight. She won!"

"How long has she been like this?" Jay asked, gesturing at the cowpat-like manure strewn around her stall.

Scotty hung his head. "Two, three hours," he confessed. "I figured she'd come out of it, see."

"I need to know exactly what she was given today," Jay said gravely.

"Nothing!" Scotty replied indignantly.

"If you want me to save your mare, you'd better tell me the truth!"

"Three boxes of baking soda," Scotty mumbled. "An' a box o' cake sugar."

"You know," Jay said, "you guys think that baking soda is harmless."

"I never used it before!" Scotty cut in.

"And in small doses, it is harmless," Jay continued "But you can see now, used in excess, it can have a devastating effect."

"You take cash?" Scotty asked, evidently anxious to put a stop to the lecture.

"You need to bring her into the clinic right away," Jay said firmly. "My preliminary diagnosis is intestinal distress and extreme dehydration. I can't treat her here."

"The clinic!" Scotty exclaimed, looking horrified. "They killed the last one I sent in there. Stuck me with a bill for three grand anyway."

"Not on my watch," Jay replied. "I'll meet you there in twenty minutes." He picked up his bag. "I'm hoping we won't have to operate," he added, walking towards the door.

"Operate!" Scotty repeated. Time was slipping away, Jay could feel it. He was blessed and cursed by an uncanny ability, a sixth sense. The gift had come to him from his mother's people. It made most Canadians uneasy, so he'd learned to keep it to himself.

"I don't want no trouble, Doc!" Scotty said.

"Load her up," Jay replied, losing patience. "The sooner I start treatment the better her chances."

"You mean she might not make it?" Scotty asked, looking terrified.

"I'm not making any promises," Jay replied grimly, heading out into the downpour.

The house was pitch black. Even the porch light was out. Clawing his way through the dark, Theo clambered up the porch steps, trying to avoid the one that creaked, a legacy from his teenage days. Uncle Bernie used to leave an emergency key in a flowerpot. He groped his way towards it and felt around. To his surprise, it was still there, buried in the earth. Gingerly, he opened the heavy front door only to be bombarded by the thud of boots and blinded by a flashlight. This time there was nowhere to run. He was cornered!

"Theo?" he heard Uncle Bernie's voice ask uncertainly. "What's going on? It's two o'clock in the morning! Look at you!" he exclaimed. "Marta!" he called out. "It's alright! It's only Theo."

A few minutes later Theo was sitting at the kitchen table wrapped in a horse blanket, drinking hot milk with a slug of brandy. Shadows cast by the candlelight were dancing on the walls. The electricity was still out.

"You look very bad," Marta pronounced. "Tell him Bernie. It is true, yes?"

"You got yourself in some kind of trouble?" Bernie asked, looking worried to death.

"I'll tell you," Theo replied shakily, finishing off the brandy. "I'll tell you the whole sorry story. You're not going to believe this!"

André Fontainbleu was sitting in his private study watching the video he had secretly made of him and Anya making love earlier that night. He was pleased with his performance. Two females had given him pleasure tonight: Anya and the filly, Jolie Dame.

TCO2

The next day Director Al McTavish was driving into Iroquois Downs listening to the local radio, when he heard some worrying news.

"This is your local station with today's news and weather at the top of the hour. A single car accident occurred on the Indian Trail last night. From the skid marks on the tarmac, police believe the driver lost control of his car and left the road. The car ended up in a cornfield. The vehicle is registered in the name of Theo Vettore, leading driver at Iroquois Downs Raceway. We understand Mr. Vettore was unhurt, though suffering from a few scrapes and bruises…"

Al McTavish switched off the radio. He'd heard enough. Another piece of bad publicity for the racetrack. That's all I need, he thought, as he pulled into Iroquois Downs' empty parking lot. The sky had cleared overnight and the only evidence of the storm was the pools of water lying on the asphalt, steaming in the morning sun. It was going to be another hot day. After shuffling papers for a couple of hours, Al rode the elevator to the judge's office on the seventh floor.

"Got any news for me yet, John?" he asked, peering through the doorway. From the look on Judge Jewells' face, Al surmised the news wasn't good. He went and perched himself awkwardly on the only other chair in the room, the so called prisoner's chair. That was where horsemen accused of wrong doing sat, facing Judge Jewells on his leather throne.

"No evidence, had to let 'im go," Jewells revealed, his mouth set in a virtual straight line. So Dave Bodinski had got away with daylight robbery, Al thought. It was disappointing to say the least. His gaze strayed to the racetrack far below where a few lone horsemen were still exercising their horses. There was so much that needed changing, Al reflected, on so many fronts: the low handle, resulting in slashed purses, the lack of funds to fix the decaying buildings. There wasn't a shred of commercialism in the entire enterprise.

"What do we do now?" Al asked.

"If you're serious," Jewells replied looking him in the eye, as if to gauge his fortitude, "then you gotta get rid of the baking soda boys!"

"Baking soda!" Al laughed. "Is that all they're using? It doesn't sound so bad."

"Take it from me," Jewells replied emphatically, "If you want to clean up racing around here, you have to put a stop to soda. It's far too easy for the horsemen to cheat."

"So you think those two mares last night…" Al said, catching on.

"Must've had a huge dose of it, yes," the judge nodded. "Take a look at their previous efforts," he added with a grim smile, tossing over the previous night's race programme.

"I never would have picked either of them to win if I was a betting man," Al acknowledged, feeling a little bewildered.

"Take a look at Jolie Dame," the judge directed. "Proof positive."

Al frowned.

"She's from Quebec," Jewells said, fixing Al with a penetrating stare.

Wilting under Jewells' stern gaze, Al wracked his brains. But he still had no idea what the judge meant.

"They've got black box testing in Quebec," Jewells said in an irritated tone, as if explaining that two and two equalled four. "Had it for a while, TCO2 scores are closely monitored. Stops the baking soda boys in their tracks."

"Ah," Al said finally getting it. "So you think Price gave Jolie Dame baking soda? You think that's why she improved so much down here?"

"Don't think it, know it! Can't do anything about it of course," Jewells said with genuine regret.

"Well, it seems to me, we'll have to find a way to test for baking soda at Iroquois Downs," Al replied, relieved that there was such a simple solution.

"Not so fast! It's not cheap. Where are you going to get the money? Besides there'll be a lot of resistance from the horsemen."

"And?" Al prompted.

"Good chance they'll go on strike."

Al frowned.

"Refuse to race," Jewells clarified, assuming Al wasn't keeping up.

"A strike. That's all I need," Al groaned. What have I got myself into here? he wondered. But he didn't intend to give up at the first hurdle. His good friend and longtime business associate Phil Harman had convinced him to take on this job knowing it would appeal to Al's sense of justice and fair play. Phil was counting on him to clean up racing at Iroquois Downs and Al was determined not to let him down.

"Leaving the money aside for now," he began, ignoring Judge Jewells' pursed lips, "I need your input on getting the trainers on board."

"Trainers!" the judge said contemptuously. "The winners are crooks and the losers haven't figured out how to beat the system yet."

"Nevertheless," Al argued, "we need to neutralize them if we're going to be able to accomplish anything here. We can't afford a strike. There's little enough money as it is."

"Got any ideas?" the judge asked.

"Not yet," Al admitted. "How about you?"

"None!" the judge replied sourly. And on that note Al departed. As he rode the elevator down to his office, he couldn't help feeling a sneaking admiration for this Dave Bodinski character. Just sitting on that stool was enough to make a guy feel guilty and want to confess all. But Bodinski had faced Judge Jewells and come out of it smelling like a rose. In Al's limited experience, horsemen were a pretty clever bunch. Anyone who didn't take that into account would get nowhere with reforming a lost cause like Iroquois Downs. When he got back to his office, Al grabbed a cup of coffee and dialled McTavish Construction. Since his appointment as Director of Racing at Iroquois Downs, he had handed over the day to day running of his building company to his daughter, Billie. It still felt odd not to be there himself every morning.

"Good morning, sir. I'll put you through to Miss McTavish right away," the operator said.

"Dad!" Billie McTavish exclaimed. "I'm glad you called. I wanted to get your take on that housing development, the one on Appleby Line."

"There's something I want you to do first," Al said.

"Okay," she replied, a little unwillingly, he thought.

"I need you to find out everything you can about baking soda."

"Baking soda?" Billie asked. "You baking a cake or something? You don't ever cook!" When Al didn't reply, her tone changed to one of concern, "Is your stomach bothering you, Dad?"

"No! Nothing like that!" Al replied hastily. "Believe it or not they use it on horses. It stops them tying up."

"I'm not even going to try to go there," Billie laughed. "Just tell me what you want to know, okay?" Al pictured her: the look of exasperation mingled with amusement on her face, the mane of brown wavy hair.

"I want you to find out if there have been any studies about the effects of high levels of baking soda, adverse or otherwise, on racehorses," he said.

"Okay!" Billie replied immediately. She sounded like she couldn't wait to get started now.

"Plus," he put in quickly before she could get off the line, "I need to know how you test for it and how much testing will cost."

"Fill me in here, Dad."

"They're testing for soda in Quebec," he explained. "Start from there. How soon can you get back to me on all this?"

"If I google it," Billie replied, "about an hour."

Al didn't have any real understanding of how googling worked. Like the majority of his generation, he'd been reluctant to use the internet. However, he'd learned that in Billie's hands at least, it produced excellent results. While he was waiting for his daughter to get back to him, he put in a call to Jim Mercer, one of the horsemen's representatives, intending to feel him out on the baking soda issue. But all Mercer wanted to talk about was Theo Vettore's accident the night before.

"They made it sound like Vettore was out on a drunk," Mercer retorted angrily, when Al introduced himself. "That's a damn lie! Everyone knows what's going on at the track! And what are you guys doing about it? Nothing!"

When Al asked him to elaborate, Mercer got even hotter under the collar.

"Don't give me that!" he shouted.

"Give you what?" Al replied feeling a little outraged himself. The guy wasn't giving him a chance.

"I haven't got time for this!" Mercer muttered. He must have put the phone down, because all Al heard after that was a loud dial tone.

'Well, that went well,' Al thought, gazing out of the window. It was so hot, the air was shimmering. The other rep, Bob Summers, was supposed to be the nice guy. But he wasn't answering his phone. It looked liked this job wasn't going to be so easy. Then Billie called.

"You're not going to believe this!" she said exuberantly. "There's a veterinarian doing a study, wait…here it is…a Doctor Jay Winterflood – that's such a great name! – anyhow, he's written a paper on the effects of sodium bicarbonate on the equine athlete…"

"That's…," Al interrupted.

"Baking soda, yes," Billy confirmed. "Also known as cooking soda, bicarbonate of soda, sodium hydrogen carbonate…or, if you want to get really technical, the chemical compound is NaH…"

"Stop!" Al begged, his head spinning.

"CO_3," Billie continued. "And listen to this. Doctor Winterflood is based right here in Erinsville…at the equine clinic!"

That's my girl, Al thought happily.

"Perfect," he said.

"What's wrong? You don't sound very pleased," she replied, her disappointment obvious.

"Oh, I just got my head chewed off by someone," he explained hastily. "Nothing to do with you, Billie. You did a great job. How about the cost?"

"Of testing, you mean? I already asked Jeff. He's got a lot of contacts in the States. He'll be able to get us a good price," she said, recovering somewhat.

"Your friend Jeff Lamare," Al smiled into the phone. "He's got his fingers in so many pies!"

"He's a dotcom millionaire!" Billie corrected a little huffily. "And he'd be doing this as a favour to me, actually. It's got nothing to do with his internet business."

Billie acted a bit like a porcupine at times – all prickles and humped back, Al reflected. But she was fiercely loyal to those she cared about and she'd never let him down yet. Did all fathers appreciate their daughters as much as he did? he wondered. His only disappointment was that neither of his sons had expressed any interest in taking over the family firm. However, Billie made up for both of them.

"Thank him," Al said humbly. "And Billie…"

"Yes?"

"The next meeting is in two weeks' time."

"Okay," she said doubtfully. She had the capacity to put a score of different meanings into that word.

"I'd like to have everything ready to go by then."

"Okay!" she replied, suddenly business like. "Leave it with me, Dad. I'll see what I can do." The magic phrase, which nearly always brought results, had been uttered. Al leaned back in his chair and relaxed for the first time since Heart of Darkness' humiliating defeat by two long shots the night before.

After the weekend Al put in a call to Phil Harman to get a read on the political side of things. He had to leave a message on Phil's answering machine. The next day, Phil called him back.

"What's up?" Phil asked.

"How about I tell you over lunch at your favourite restaurant tomorrow?" Al suggested brightly.

"No good. I got a lot on this week," Phil replied.

"How about next week then?" Al asked.

"Sounds like a plan. Long as you're paying, pal!" Phil laughed.

The Australian girl was lying on the terrace of André Fontainbleu's hilltop fortress, soaking up the sunshine. Other than a large pair of sunglasses, she was wearing only the briefest of bikinis.

André Fontainbleu, whose dark brown eyes had never needed protection, even from the harsh Caribbean sun, was resting his hand on her bare belly, palm down, fingers outstretched, in a habitual gesture of possession, pleased to observe the bruising on her breasts, testimony to the violence of their love making, just hours before.

The clinking of silverware and glass and the discreet scraping of chairs informed him that lunch was ready to be served.

"Get dressed," he said roughly, tossing a towel at the girl. "After we eat, we shall go to Bailey's Boatyard!"

She opened her eyes and stared up at him. The flicker of resentment was still there. It meant nothing. He was holding all the cards. That afternoon he showed her the boat he was offering her: a wreck that had cost him nothing, washed up on the shore like the girl herself, another consequence of the storm. Afterwards, he drove slowly back up the mountain to the Hermitage, which was his personal, private sanctuary, bought dearly with blood and tears (not his own, of course).

"You can leave now if you wish," he told her, the sun in his eyes reducing her to a dark silhouette.

"Leave?" she asked, with no attempt to hide her surprise.

"Why, yes," he replied, sure of himself now, reading her easily. The combination of arousal and confusion, with just a *soupçon* of surrender, interested him.

"What if…," she asked, her voice breaking. "What if I was to stay?"

She was so young, he thought without a trace of empathy. The weekend was already a week. But it was not convenient for him to take on any surplus baggage at present.

A LUNCH APPOINTMENT

The Old Mill was the priciest restaurant in the Erinsville area. Phil had expensive tastes. But Al considered that lunch was a small price to pay for Phil's expert advice. In over two decades, Phil hadn't steered him wrong yet. Al was profoundly grateful. He was keenly aware that things could have turned out very differently, had it not been for Phil's guiding hand.

Phil had first approached him at a time when Al's company was struggling to survive. Al was a hard worker but he was no politician. McTavish Construction's bids for government contracts were missing by a mile. Phil was a wheeler dealer who knew all the right people at City Hall. Phil's ace bids and McTavish Construction's quality workmanship had proved to be a winning combination, making a small fortune for both of them.

"How's things?" Phil asked, joining him at the table, looking suntanned and relaxed.

"What have you been up to?" Al countered.

"Let's get a couple of beers," Phil suggested, loosening his tie. The years had been kind to Phil. Perhaps, Al thought, it was because his friend had never married. His eyes were still the same shade of brilliant blue as the day they'd met. Unlike Phil, Al hadn't found the time for too many vacations over the years. Phil was always off to some exotic place or other. He had it made! The drinks arrived.

"Shoot!" Phil said taking a swig of beer. Al laid out his plan for introducing TCO2 testing at Iroquois Downs.

"Okay," Phil said, running a hand through his hair, which was long and floppy and gave him a youthful air, despite a few grey hairs. Al was a short back and sides man, himself. "You got two problems. First, there's no money for testing. Second, the horsemen will hate the idea."

"That's it in a nutshell," Al agreed, feeling things were pretty hopeless.

The steak arrived, the most expensive dish on the menu.

"You deliver the horsemen and I'll get you the money somehow," Phil said confidently, his knife poised over the meat.

"How?" Al asked.

"Usual channels…leave it to me," Phil replied cheerfully, waving his fork at Al. "You going to the Maple Leaf game on Sunday?" he added.

"I haven't decided," Al confessed.

"Meaning that wife of yours doesn't want to go," Phil diagnosed astutely. Unfortunately, it was all too true. "If she changes her mind, it's not too late to get tickets. Just give me a call, I've got the best seats in the park!"

"Sounds good," Al smiled. Phil was a useful man to know, he'd discovered over the years. Where would he be without him? However, this latest caper, Iroquois Downs, wasn't working out too well so far. It looked like Al had landed in the middle of a hornet's nest. He said as much to Phil.

"Listen," his friend said, dropping his voice and leaning across the table. "The racetrack's up for grabs, you have to know that! It's right next to the highway."

"Prime building land," Al agreed soberly, picturing the backstretch sprouting high rises.

"Look what they're doing in the US," Phil said.

"You mean casinos?"

"You could have Slots at Iroquois Downs too. The place could be a mini Las Vegas," Phil declared, taking out a wad of cash, peeling off a couple of bills and tossing them onto the table. "That'll take care of the tip," he smiled, rising to his feet. So that was why Phil had encouraged him to get involved with Iroquois Downs, Al realized belatedly. His friend was always one step ahead of him.

"Hey! I do believe you're getting attached to the old place!" Phil exclaimed.

"I'd dearly like to turn things around, yes," Al replied earnestly.

"Then you know what you have to do," Phil said "And I'm right behind you, pal." Al wondered where Phil really stood on the issue of Iroquois Downs Raceway.

Only time would tell.

THE MEETING

Ten days later as Al McTavish rode the elevator to the sixth floor of Iroquois Downs grandstand, he mentally prepared himself. A tricky and unpredictable morning lay ahead. When he entered the boardroom, he counted heads. Everyone was present, except for Judge Jewells, the man chairing the meeting.

The people on Al's team, from Finance, Publicity and Admin, gave him a friendly wave. He spotted the horsemen's representatives, Jim Mercer and Bob Summers, sitting at the table looking a little dishevelled, with glum faces. They were the only men in the room who weren't wearing ties. Over by the window, a pair of pasty faced guys in dark suits were avidly sipping coffee from paper cups. They'd be from the Provincial Racing Commission, Al surmised, the body responsible for policing the harness racing industry. He walked over and introduced himself.

Then the door opened and the presiding judge, John Jewells, strode into the room. Jewells immediately called the meeting to order, banging his fist on the table and giving those still on their feet a withering glance.

"We have a new Director at Iroquois Downs," he fired off, pointing at Al. "Director McTavish has called this meeting to put a stop to cheating." Only the horsemen's reps looked startled. Everyone else was in the know. "You all saw the shambles at the fillies' Diamond Stakes final a couple of weeks back," Jewells continued. "Two long shots winning in a dead heat! But there's gonna be no more cheating at Iroquois Downs from now on. That means no more baking soda, for anyone not keeping up! There's a simple solution. Test for it. They've been doing that in Quebec for months now. If the French can do it, we can damn well do it here, too!" With that, Jewells shut his mouth like a trap and glared defiantly around the room. Everyone started talking at once.

"One at a time and address the Chair please," Jewells roared, bringing his fist down onto the table with such force that it shook. Immediately, order was restored. Al kept a low profile, watching and listening to reactions from the various quarters. Predictably there was outrage from the horsemen, enthusiasm from the Provincial Racing Commission, caution from Finance and excitement from Publicity, who could hardly wait to break the good news to the media. "Over to you, Mr. Director," Judge Jewells trumpeted after everyone else had had their say.

"I'd like to thank you all for coming here today," Al began graciously, receiving a scowl from Jim Mercer. "Before we go any further, I'd like to share something with you." He gave a nod to Admin, who began distributing sets of stapled sheets. "It's a research paper," Al explained. "By a prominent veterinarian at Erinsville Equine Clinic. I suggest you read it over carefully before we discuss this any further." Silence descended, broken only by the ripple of pages being turned. Mercer picked his up, took one look and threw it down on the table. Al took a cigar out of his pocket. "Anyone got a light?" Al asked. No one did. Eventually everyone was done reading, or in Mercer's case, done staring at the table.

"Judge Jewells, I'd value your opinion on this," Al said, knowing precisely what his opinion would be. They had already discussed it at length.

"Well," a beetle browed Jewells said, looking across at Al, "I think I can summarize this pretty simply. According to Dr. Winterflood, there's no harm in using baking soda in moderation. But at higher levels, it can cause gastrointestinal distress and in rare cases, death."

"It can cause cardiac arrest," one of the PRC men exclaimed. "It says it right here on page four!" Dr. Winterflood's paper had evidently touched a raw nerve.

"Time for a prayer?" Judge Jewells responded with a twisted smile. "I'd suggest, 'Please God, if I come back in another life, don't let it be as a standardbred racehorse', not that I'm a religious man." A horrified silence followed.

"Our members aren't criminals," Bob Summers protested.

The other PRC man spoke up. "Certainly we need to decide what levels of baking soda are safe," he said soberly. "We don't want to be responsible for horses dying at Iroquois Downs."

"What do we need another test for?" Mercer challenged. "We got enough of them already!" He looked over at Bob Summers, who stared up at the ceiling.

Al could tell that Jim Mercer was getting pumped up. Before he could detonate, he jumped in with a rhetorical question. "What do we have to lose?" he asked.

"The goodwill of the horsemen who put on the show," Mercer shouted, red faced. "Where would you be without us? I'm up at 6 a.m. every day, so are the rest of the guys. Don't get to bed before midnight on race nights. I hardly see my family! I'm out there in the cold freezing my ass off all winter. I don't ever get a holiday, not that I'm asking for one…"

You could have cut the air with a knife.

"Look . . . er, Jim," Al said. "We all value the contribution the horsemen make. But the handle is falling. Aside from major stakes events, the public is staying away." He paused to let that fact sink in. "It won't help the horsemen if we have to cut purse money back again. If things get any worse, we could even be forced to close the place down."

"They'll never do that!" Bob Summers exclaimed. "Iroquois Downs is the top harness racing track in Canada!"

"It's a major racetrack, yes," Al conceded. "But it's costing our government a small fortune. We can't justify this kind of expense indefinitely. We have to get the handle up somehow!"

Bob looked beat, but Mercer wasn't giving up so easily.

"This paper doesn't change a thing!" he retorted angrily. "You can't do this without proper negotiation. We're going to have to call a strike." Mercer's threat was hardly a surprise.

"Go right ahead," Al said coolly. "But if the press gets a hold of this…" he picked up Winterflood's paper, "the public won't have a shred of sympathy for the horsemen. They'll just feel sorry for the horses. The animal rights groups will be crawling all over us. We've got enough controversy already with the betting ring scandal. So, go ahead and strike. You'll be digging your own graves!" Mercer glowered and said nothing. Not so, Bob Summers.

"If you think you can push us around, you're dead wrong! We ain't just gonna roll over an' play dead," he declared, looking at Mercer for support.

"That's right!" Mercer agreed.

"Okay, what are you saying, Bob?" Al asked wearily. Were they going to be here all day? he wondered. He had already played his trump card.

"You gotta give us a package. Something we can take back to our members," Bob said, not unreasonably. It dawned on Al that Bob might actually be on his side.

"What's your idea here?" Al asked.

"Give us a bigger percentage," Bob suggested.

"The percentages are set by the politicians. It's not in my control," Al explained. Bob hung his head. Judge Jewells jumped in.

"You're just going to have to convince the horsemen that this is in their best interests, aren't you?" he said, his tone leaving no room for discussion.

"Pie in the sky!" Mercer shouted.

"You gotta give us more than vague promises," Bob said, "or…," he paused.

Right on cue, Mercer jumped up off his chair.

"We're ready to walk out right now!" he threatened. The two PRC men exchanged nervous glances. Al waded in.

"Fellows, let's not get too excited here. There are no guarantees but…you all know what's going on south of the border."

"You mean Slots?" Bob asked incredulously. "Here? At Iroquois Downs?"

"There could be a great deal at stake here," Al replied, noncommittally.

"If this is a come-on . . ." Mercer growled.

"No promises," Al said. "But if we can get things cleaned up around here, then anything's possible."

"I dunno," Bob replied uncertainly. "What d'you think, Jim?"

"Not good enough!" Mercer snapped.

"It's the best I can do," Al said. "Take it or leave it."

Mercer leaned over towards Bob Summers. A muttered discussion followed, inaudible to Al.

"We're going to have to consult our members," Bob said at last, "but I reckon we gotta try to get the job done."

Mercer threw his cap on the table.

"The hell we will," he cursed roundly. There was an awkward silence.

"Anyone have a better idea?" Judge Jewells asked. No one spoke. "Then I'll take a vote. Let's have a show of hands: those for the motion to introduce TCO2 testing?"

Not surprisingly Mercer was the lone dissenter.

"The ayes have it. Motion carried," Jewells declared. Al stuck his cigar in his mouth.

"Here," Jewells said, tossing him a lighter. "Can't bear to see you sucking on that thing a moment longer. Meeting is closed," the judge added hastily. Everyone but Al and the judge filed out. Mercer was the last to leave, his face like thunder.

"We've been lynched today!" he muttered. The judge waited until the door slammed shut behind him.

"A good morning's work," he declared approvingly. "It'll all come to nothing, of course," he added.

Al stared at him, astonished.

"The guys with deep pockets will challenge the test in the courts, get the judgments against them overturned on some technicality and make fools of us all. Besides, there's no money for it," Jewells said.

"Don't worry about the money," Al reassured him, puffing on his cigar. "As for the courts. . . we'll just have to hope for the best."

"Better put that thing out," Jewells warned, with a hint of a smile, "before the smoke alarms go off!" It occurred to Al that he'd found an ally in the irascible Judge Jewells and maybe in Bob Summers, too.

Right now he needed all the friends he could get.

The instant rumours began to circulate about the introduction of a TCO2 test for soda, trainers began to take evasive action. Keith Lazer got on the internet and ordered a supply of Human Growth Hormone. It claimed to cure almost every common ailment suffered by the standardbred racehorse, including tying up. Lazer decided to give it a try. There was currently no test for HGH. Tom "Cowboy" Larson had never needed baking soda. His secret weapon was stashed away in the cattle barn. Baking soda had never been Jim Mercer's crutch either. He was contemptuous of trainers who depended on it. Training a horse a double-header a day was a simple, effective way of dealing with the problem. If the animal couldn't stand up to that, Jim reasoned, it wouldn't have been much of a success anyhow. He didn't believe in mollycoddling racehorses. Trainer Andy Price immediately had a council of war with Doc Meecham. To his relief, the doc came up with a long list of legal remedies for tying up. They didn't come cheap, but they were effective. Andy told jealous trainers that his success was all down to his No. 1 groom, Crawfish Brown. No one believed him but what did Andy care? Keith Lazer was still top trainer, but Andy Price was hard on his heels.

In the end, the horsemen approved TCO2 testing by a small margin. The politicians came up with the money, as Phil had promised. To Al's great joy, a month after the meeting, TCO2 testing began at Iroquois Downs Raceway.

CAUGHT

Alastair McTavish was in the winner's circle. Flanked by his wife and daughter, he was struggling to hold aloft a heavy gold cup. The roar of the crowd was deafening. He awoke to the roar of the vacuum cleaner and realized that sadly, it had been a dream. His wife Sofia was cleaning again. Sunlight was streaming in through the bedroom window of 210, Laurel Drive. It was 8 o'clock on a still August morning in Erinsville, Ontario. Al's first thought was the phone call he'd received from an exuberant Judge Jewells earlier in the week.

"Looks like we've caught our first fish," the judge had reported. "Trainer named Scotty McCoy." The hearing was at 11 a.m. today.

Half an hour later, after grabbing a quick cup of coffee, Al was on his way out of the house. Walter, a three month old Maine Coon kitten, was waiting in the hall. When Al opened the door, Walter dashed through it and scampered over to the tall maple tree in the front yard. He ran up the trunk then turned around and stared down at Al with his large green eyes. July's humidity had given way to the clear skies of August. It was Al's favourite time of year.

The Mercedes was waiting for him in the garage, like an athlete begging for exercise. Al drove with the top down, enjoying the warmth of the sun and the scent of newly mown grass wafting over him. The car had been a present to himself when he'd handed over control of his construction company to his daughter. He was not used to such luxuries. He sometimes wondered if he'd lost his mind spending so much money on a car. But he guessed he'd probably never have another excuse to blow fifty thousand dollars on mere transportation. Neither of his two sons had shown any interest in the business. In the breach, Billie had proved to be far more capable than he could ever have imagined. His one fear was that she would get bored and want to take McTavish Construction nationwide. Al had always been content to be a big fish in a small pond. Swimming with the sharks did not appeal to him. But he knew that Billie's restless mind could not be contained in Erinsville forever.

The radio was blasting out ear splitting beat music. Al hit the CD button. As the soaring notes of Italian opera rang out, he settled back and prepared to enjoy the ride to Iroquois Downs Raceway. He took the scenic route down

Appleby Line, which cut through horse farms and meadows. The road was lined with wildflowers. The big open sky was a brilliant blue. Soon, too soon, he was entering the vast treeless expanse of grey asphalt that fronted Iroquois Downs Raceway.

He went up to his office and waited for news.

Scotty McCoy was shaking as he took to his seat on the so called prisoner's chair in the judge's office. The hearing was about to begin.

It had been a truly terrible week for Scotty. On Monday, he'd lost his three best horses to a rival trainer. On Wednesday his wife had packed her bags and taken off with the groom to God knew where. And today, he was up in front of the serial killer: Judge Jewells.

The hearing was short and to the point.

"Raider's Moon and Annabel's Fancy," the judge stated. "Can you confirm that you were the trainer of these two horses as of August seventh, Mr. McCoy?" Scotty nodded. "Speak up, man!" Judge Jewells exclaimed.

"Yes sir," Scotty answered gruffly.

"Each horse was over the limit on TCO2, by a significant margin," Jewells said sternly, frowning so deeply that his eyebrows were virtually meeting. "Can you explain that, McCoy?"

"No sir!" Scotty exclaimed, "I just added the odd spoonful of baking soda to their feed. I can't understand it myself."

"So you admit administering baking soda to the horses in question?" Jewells said exultantly, evidently feeling he'd scored a point.

"Not enough to show up in any test!" Scotty protested, feeling flustered. He thought he'd been so careful. The timing of the black box testing had come as a complete surprise to him and everyone else he knew. The Race Barn had erupted in panic after Mr. Roberts had made the announcement. When the vets moved in to draw blood from the horses that were in the first race, trainers began leaving the Race Barn in droves, taking their horses with them. There were six scratches in the second race alone. Scotty had been slow to react. By the time he realized what was happening, it was too late. He had no choice but to sit tight and hope for the best, taking comfort from the fact that Dave had put far less soda in the drenches than normal.

"Step outside while we confer," the judge said. Ten minutes later, Scotty was invited back into the room. "Here's our ruling," the judge declared, looking at Scotty like a turkey vulture spotting a piece of road kill. "Automatic suspension of your trainer's licence for twelve months. A fine of two thousand five hundred dollars, for each horse."

Scotty's heart sank down to his boots. It didn't have far to go. Scotty wasn't very tall. Five grand, he thought, panic rising in his chest. Where am I going to find that kind of money?

"Can I appeal?" he asked.

"You have the right to appeal, yes," Jewells informed him. "But you'd have to challenge the accuracy of the test used."

Scotty had no spare cash and no lawyer. Who was he fooling? He'd never be able to appeal. It wasn't fair. He knew of people who used all kinds of illegal stuff on their horses and got away with it, trainers like Keith Lazer. The guy was a fuckin' chemist!

"Do I get time off for good behavior?" he asked.

"This isn't a jail sentence, Mr. McCoy," the judge said drily. "But your licence won't be renewed until you've paid off your fines in full, after the twelve months have passed of course. Until then, you are banned from all racetracks in Ontario. There's a reciprocal agreement with the rest of Canada and the US by the way, in case you were thinking of going somewhere else." Was he imagining it or did the judge look disappointed? Probably sorry it wasn't a hanging matter, Scotty decided. Better not say anything. It'd only make things worse. He trudged down the stairs to the ground floor. A year's ban! There'd be no sense in going to the yearling sale now. Not that he'd ever bought a yearling, but he'd miss the buzz and the chance to swap stories and sample the food that breeders served up to lure customers.

As he walked across the parking lot to his old Ford truck, he couldn't quite take in the whopping fine they'd stuck him with. He'd have to try to cobble the cash together somehow. Maybe get his old job back at Erinsville General. They were always short of cleaners at the hospital and the nurses liked him. Or he and his wife could move in with his sister to save on rent. Then he remembered he didn't have a wife anymore. There'd be no winter racing for him this year. No hot suppers in the track kitchen. No horse's breath hanging like smoke in the freezing air. He'd miss the spring stakes season, too. And the two year olds. He'd miss their first races, when he and his friend Dave Bodinski exchanged bets on which one of them was going to win the Diamond Stakes Championship.

"I'll be back!" Scotty swore to himself as he drove off. "Those sons of bitches ain't gonna keep me down forever!"

Two weeks went by. Al McTavish waited in vain for the next positive TCO2 test. Meanwhile, the trainers known as 'the big four,' Lazer, Price, Mercer and Larson continued to win most of the races, their performances apparently unaffected by the baking soda ban. It was puzzling, but Al was hoping for the best.

THE BET

On a calm evening in late August, Theo Vettore's cousin, Lara Vachon, was standing down by the rail beside Iroquois Downs' oval track, waiting and watching as Theo put Southview Sabre through his paces. It was 7 p.m. The plan was to take Southview Sabre a slow warm-up mile, but speed him up for the last eighth. Any hint of trouble and Lara was going to scratch her boy from the race and take him home.

On the night Theo had stumbled into Ferme Victoire afraid for his life, Lara had been on a vigil at Rivers Training centre, soaking Southview Sabre's red hot right front foot in a tub of ice water. Lara treated all the horses she trained like her children, not that she had any of her own yet. She was only twenty-eight, after all. Unlike most trainers, Lara did not have the luxury of picking out yearlings at the Annual Sale. Instead, she took on whatever her father Bernie Vachon decided to give her: well bred fillies with broodmare potential or colts who hadn't found a buyer. Once in Lara's barn, they were under her protection. She gave them as much time as they needed to get to the races and treated them all with equal affection, regardless of their talent (or the lack of it) on the racetrack.

As Southview Sabre flew past the tote board, looking like a ghost in the dusk, Lara anxiously scrutinized him for any sign on lameness, any break in the horse's rhythm. She found none. A pus pocket trapped deep inside his hoof had plagued Southview Sabre for weeks, unknown to anyone. After Dr. Winterflood had lanced it, the lameness disappeared overnight.

The track lights kicked in, flooding the scene with colour: the green number pad flapping at the horse's ribcage, the red and black of Theo's racing jacket and the pale blue sulky with its white wheel discs spinning. Though his warm up run was over, Southview Sabre showed no sign of wanting to slow down. He sailed by a horse flashing four white stockings. Hurriedly, Lara consulted her overnight sheet. It was Mountain Boy, the 3 horse in the second.

As both drivers swung their charges through a 180° turn and headed back to the Race Barn, a figure huddled in the shadows at the edge of the track sprang into life. A greater contrast between equine athleticism and human imperfection would have been hard to find.

Lara recognized him immediately.

As the man shuffled forward and reached out for Mountain Boy's bridle, she shuddered involuntarily. She had made the mistake of hiring Crawfish Brown as a groom a couple of years back, in an act of charity. But she had discovered to her cost that despite his pitiful appearance, Crawfish was no saint. His left leg was crooked. His left eye was offset and half closed. He was missing several teeth and he always had a plug of tobacco in his mouth. The only time he went anywhere near water was when he was bathing the horses. But that wasn't the real problem. Crawfish had generally showed up for work on time, unless he'd been out on a binge the night before. He was fairly good tempered, especially on pay day. He was conscientious too, unless he wanted to get away early. He was polite to Lara, unless he had a particular grudge to air. He was loyal, until Lara rumbled him, or as Crawfish put it, asked him to do a lot of things which weren't a groom's responsibility. . .

She came out of her reverie just in time to avoid being knocked flat by Southview Sabre, who was throwing his head around like he'd had the time of his life out there. Hastily, she grabbed the bridle before she was decapitated.

"'E was okay?" she asked anxiously.

"He went his last eighth in thirteen seconds! That good enough for you?" Theo replied with a smile, handing her the lines. "I gotta go," he added, a frown furrowing his brow.

"*Eh bien*! Go!" Lara said, glancing at the tote board clock and wondering why Theo was in such a hurry. Post time for the first race was twenty-five minutes away.

Inside the Race Barn, even though they were right next to one another, Crawfish ignored Lara. He busied himself, attaching his horse tightly to the cross tie chains, as if the meek Mountain Boy was going to try and make a break for it. Lara couldn't help noticing that, unusually, Crawfish appeared to have spruced himself up for the races. He was wearing a T-shirt without a rip in it, baggy black sweat pants which did their best to cover a pair of filthy, torn trainers and a lurid yellow baseball cap at war with his straggly brown hair, which she happened to know he cut with a razor, rather than getting a proper haircut. As for a visit to the dentist to fix his missing teeth, that was about as likely as a trip to the moon. Crawfish prided himself on being self sufficient. Lara steeled herself not to feel guilty about firing him. She had to put the welfare of the horses first, she reminded herself firmly.

Theo reappeared just as Lara was putting Southview Sabre's bridle on, prior to race two. It was a struggle as the horse kept throwing his head around. His eyes were on fire.

"Easy now, boy," Theo said, holding onto the horse's nose and steadying him. "Can't wait to get at it, eh? Listen," he added as Lara slipped the bit into the horse's mouth. "I put three grand on him to win."

"You did what?" Lara hissed. "You do not bet!"

"Hey! Lighten up!" Theo replied. "I got 12-1 online. After this race, God willing, I'll be a free man."

"But zey will zink I 'ave been cheating wiz 'im!" Lara said, feeling outraged. "'Ow could you do zis to me, Theo?"

"You want me to end up dead?" Theo muttered. Lara gulped. "How's his foot?" Theo added nervously.

"I am not telling you," Lara replied angrily, glancing at Crawfish Brown in the next stall. She was certain he'd overheard their conversation. If so, everyone in the Race Barn would soon know all about it.

"Hey! What d'you think you're doing? You've hooked the lines up to the head halter, instead of the bit, you dumb idiot!" trainer Tom Larson growled at Crawfish, as Mountain Boy's driver appeared.

"Can't get it right all the time," Crawfish grumbled, hurriedly fixing the mistake.

"What are you standing there grinning for? Lead 'im out!" Larson shouted. Crawfish jumped to it. But Lara noticed him hanging back after Mountain Boy had left the Race Barn, his left eyelid blinking rapidly. Her heart sank. Wherever Crawfish was, trouble was sure to follow.

Outside the Race Barn, a crowd of horsemen had gathered to watch the running of the second race. Lara joined them, her heart beating faster. What if she'd got it wrong? What if Southview Sabre was no good tonight? There was so much at stake, not just for the horse, but for her cousin as well. She understood Theo needed to get the money from somewhere to clear his debts. But why did her horse have to be involved?

As the starting car sped away, Theo grabbed the lead and opened up four lengths. The move did not go unnoticed.

"I got the first eighth in thirteen seconds," trainer Keith Lazer exclaimed, staring at his stopwatch.

"Arrogant bastard," Tony Hall exclaimed.

"He's as good as won!" Crawfish said excitedly. He was clutching a betting ticket, evidently dreaming of cashing it in.

"My horse is getting a great trip!" Tom Cowboy Larsen said happily, watching Mountain Boy narrow the gap with the leader. "Jesus!" he added, ripping his Stetson off his head. "What's that fool Harper think he's doing?" Mountain Boy's driver, Harry Harper, had brought his horse up to challenge Theo for the lead. The horse's white stockings were pumping like pistons. Lara uttered a sigh of relief when Mountain Boy got to the top. A grudge match was the last thing her horse needed. To her consternation, Theo immediately swung Southview Sabre out to retake the lead and the two horses pulled away, fighting it out head to head. Suddenly Mountain Boy fell back. The crowd screamed. Mountain Boy had dropped like a stone, catapulting Harry Harper up and over the horse's head. The driver landed hard and lay still. Unaware of the mayhem behind him, Theo carried on. Not for long!

"Accident! Accident!" the track announcer called out urgently. "Stop your horses!" With a heavy heart, Lara watched as one of the outriders set off at a gallop, urging her pony on to intercept Theo, who was now fifteen or twenty lengths ahead of the pack. The other drivers were finally slowing down. The racetrack was suddenly crowded with horsemen, running to help the injured.

Harry Harper and Mountain Boy lay strewn across the track, both of them ominously still. The vet ran over to Mountain Boy, who lay on the stone dust track, looking like he was made out of stone himself. Soon afterwards, Harry Harper got to his feet, looking a little dazed, to much cheering and clapping. Mountain Boy was stirring too. Tom Larson plonked himself down on the horse's head and immediately began bawling Crawfish out.

"Get this sulky off 'im before he comes to, you retard!" he cursed. "This is all your fault! Take a good look at that hopple hanger! No wonder he fell. It's popped right out of the keeper. What d'you think I gave you that tape for eh?" Crawfish stood motionless, his face working, as if he had a great deal to say but was afraid to voice it. "You're damn lucky he's only winded," Larson continued angrily. "You could've fuckin' killed him!"

"That's it! I quit," Crawfish declared, throwing down the bath bucket he'd been carrying and shuffling off.

"Hey! Come back 'ere," Larson said. "I ain't done with you yet!"

Crawfish kept right on going. Leaving Larson in the lurch did little to make up for a thoroughly disappointing evening. But it did cheer him up, just a bit.

The fact that he could have won by half a dozen lengths was mere salt in the wound for Theo Vettore. He was screwed. He threw Southview Sabre's lines at his cousin and stalked off, ignoring Lara's well meant, sympathetic comments. What was the use? He'd played his only card and, by default, he had lost. He still owed the thirty-five thousand. Part of him felt like cutting loose and heading home early. But with the drivers' championship up for grabs, he opted to stay. The "collectors" would be coming around to harass him soon enough. There was no escaping them.

At last the races were over. Theo changed out of his driving suit into jeans and T-shirt. As an afterthought he threw on a leather jacket. Ten drives and not a single win. What a night it had been! The Race Barn was almost empty. The last security guard had left his post and gone home, allowing two sinister looking individuals to walk through the gate separating the betting public from the Race Barn. They looked like a pair of bouncers on steroids and they were watching Theo's every move.

"Well if it isn't Mr. Vettore," one of them said, sidling up to him. Rationally, Theo knew he was worth more to them alive than dead. But what if they decided to make an example of him? Suddenly he felt terrified.

"How about we go to the cafeteria and talk this over?" he suggested, feeling light headed. One of the bouncers shook his head.

"Nothin' doing," he grunted.

Bouncer number two took Theo firmly by the elbow.

"We'll talk outside," he said. Theo looked around for help. Lara was long gone. There was no one around who knew or cared about his problem. He was alone with the collectors. Maybe it was better that way. Did he really want the whole world to know he was a cocaine addict who couldn't even pay for his habit?

"Let's take a look at yer car," bouncer number one suggested, walking him towards the parking lot. "Maybe it's worth something, eh?"

The tight knot in Theo's cheek relaxed. Maybe he could stall them, convince them he'd get a loan, pay later. Unfortunately, his insurance company was dragging its feet, contesting the claim for his accident even though he'd paid thousands in premiums. He was still driving a rental car. The plates were a dead giveaway, easily spotted under the glare of the lights. The parking lot was deserted, he noted nervously. Everyone else had gone home.

Suddenly the floodlights shut down and everything went black. One of the thugs grabbed him from behind and forced his left arm back, twisting it violently. Theo tried to cry out, but rough hands blindfolded and gagged him in two seconds flat, then threw him, face up, onto the ground. He heard footsteps approaching. A moment later he felt something heavy pressing down onto his head: a work boot. The rubber tread dug into his temple. He could smell his own sweat mingled with the overpowering stink of garlic.

"Message from the Scorpion for Mr. Vettore," a man's harsh voice reverberated in his ear. It was a voice Theo had never heard before, but was never likely to forget. "He appreciates your custom, but he's not a charitable institution. When you come round, remember this is a warning. Next time, it'll be for real."

There was an ominous silence, during which Theo fought for breath, his heart hammering in his chest. What with the boot pressing down on his face and the gag in his mouth, he felt like he was going to suffocate right there on the tarmac. Rigid with fear, he waited. The attack began with no warning. Helpless and blind, he had no choice but to silently endure the rain of blows on his head and body, unable to make a sound, let alone defend himself. To his surprise, what he felt mostly wasn't fear or pain. It was anger. Anger at himself for letting this happen. The humiliation! The King of the Track brought down so low! Then he passed out.

When he came to, he was alone. The blindfold was off. So was the gag. When he tried to get up, the pain made him dizzy and sick. So he lay still, staring up at the big blobs of light shining in the night sky. The throbbing in his head was loud and insistent, like the march of boots coming ever closer. He tried to call out, but his mouth wasn't working. His face felt like was twice its normal size. Each time he took a breath, pain shot through his rib cage like a red hot needle. He watched the stars above him until his eyelids swelled shut.

Then he lay quietly in the dark on the hard asphalt, waiting for the sun to rise.

5 a.m. The stars had faded. There was a faint glow on the horizon and the promise of another warm day. Reggie Blair, sole proprietor of Supreme Horse Feeds, liked to make an early start when he delivered to Iroquois Downs Raceway. That way, he avoided rush hour on the backstretch. After 6 a.m. the barn area was crowded with horses making their way to the exercise tracks. Horsemen were always anxious to get done early and beat the heat.

Reggie Blair's shock of blond hair made him look younger than he was.

But at thirty-eight, he didn't have a girlfriend, let alone a wife, a loss he felt keenly, especially when he was sitting home alone doing the books of a night. In the semi-darkness, he headed for Andy Price's barn. Since the introduction of black box testing, Price had bought so many different feeds and supplements for his horses that Reggie could hardly keep up with it all. It was good for business, but it took up a lot of his time. And time was money. After Andy Price, with a lighter load, he took his regular early morning route around the backstretch of Iroquois Downs, dropping off sacks of heavy western oats, bags of sweet feed dripping with molasses, tubs of vitamins and apple treats, carrots in orange string bags, red salt blocks and a dozen other specialty items essential to the well-being of the standardbred racehorse. He even kept a few bags of wood shavings in his truck, in case one of the smaller trainers had run out of bedding.

By 7 a.m. Reggie's feed van was empty. Time to load up again and go out to the training centres. He headed for the stable gate, waving to the security guard in her box as he passed. The huge parking lot was empty except for a sleek black sedan that Reggie didn't recognize. Then he did a double take. He'd seen something lying on the ground beside the car: a heap of clothes, or a horse blanket perhaps. It was difficult to tell in the early morning light. The long shadows might be playing tricks on his eyes. Intrigued, Reggie drove across the tarmac, his truck lurching back and forth over the uneven surface. When he got up close he gasped and slammed on the brakes.

"Jesus Christ! What the hell" he exclaimed, jumping down from the cab. It wasn't a pile of clothes. It looked like a body. But who was it? Reggie felt sick. The guy was a mess! His face was swelled right up, like it had been stung by a swarm of bees. His jaw hung loose. There was blood everywhere. Reggie feared he was looking at a corpse. Then he realized the man was trying to speak. Reckoning the guy would be frightened by any sudden movement after what he'd been through, Reggie did his best to move quietly.

"'S alright. 'S only Reggie. Let's see who y'are now," he said reassuringly, reaching inside the torn, sodden jacket. He pulled out an Iroquois Downs Driving licence and gasped. He recognized the man in the photo instantly.

"Jesus!" Reggie exclaimed, looking down at the tortured face, the body wracked with pain. He couldn't believe it was the V Man. But it was him alright! He ran back to the truck and immediately alerted track security. Then he called emergency services and asked for an ambulance. But the woman on the other end of the line kept asking questions.

"Can you give me your exact location, sir?"

"Iroquois Downs parking lot," Reggie replied, watching a half conscious Vettore gasp for air.

"I'm sorry sir. I need an address."

"It's a racetrack on First Line." There was a long silence on the other end of the phone. "Just send the fuckin' ambulance," Reggie muttered angrily.

"I can't find that address, sir. Can you see your fire number?"

Reggie, standing in the middle of acres of asphalt quarter of a mile from the entrance could only splutter. "No!"

"Can the patient make his own way to the Emergency Room?"

"Listen to me you dumb bitch!" Reggie shouted, losing it completely. "The guy's unconscious and can't move!" Before she was half done reprimanding him, he cut her off. She'd landed him in a hell of a fix. Track security were nowhere to be seen. He could hear Vettore groaning. Reggie Blair was in the prime of his life. He heaved feed sacks around all day long. He did things himself, his own way. He didn't intend to wait who knew how long for the emergency crew to figure out his location. After checking that Vettore was able to move his legs, he improvised a stretcher from one of the wooden palettes he stacked the feed on. He laid a bag of wood shavings on top and covered the whole thing with a horse blanket. Then came the tricky part: getting the patient onto the stretcher. But five minutes later, Reggie Blair was driving like the wind.

As the sun climbed higher in a blue August sky, Reggie hurtled down Highway 501, weaving his way through early morning commuter traffic and the convoys of long haul trucks. He couldn't check on his passenger, because he'd had to put Vettore in the back of the van where the feed got stacked. In any case, Reggie was fully occupied dodging the truckers. They were travelling nose to tail like a herd of circus elephants, occasionally blocking the highway completely by lining up three abreast. What with the honking of horns and the hiss of brakes, he felt like he was back driving at Erinsville Speedway, where all manner of dirty tricks were common practice. He was torn between fear and fury. In the end, fury won out. He rolled down the window of his van and gestured wildly.

"Friggin' sons of bitches!" he screamed, his face contorted with rage. A man driving a Beco Bananas truck looked down with contempt at the feed van from the lofty height of his cab. Reggie could see him speaking into his walkie talkie, no doubt hatching some sinister plot to 'fix' him, further down the road. The whine of a police car's siren put paid to the truckers' fun. Reggie picked up the live cover and followed the police car all the way to the exit, ignoring the signs 'SLOW DOWN AND BE SAFE' and 'SPEED KILLS.' He reached Erinsville in fifteen minutes flat, a record. He just prayed this wasn't going into any police record books. But thankfully the officers were either hot on the trail of a gang of international criminals (or so desperate for a cup of coffee!) that they didn't give him a second glance.

He pulled up outside the lofty grey building that housed the best medical facility in the area: Erinsville General. The Emergency Room lay beyond two large swing doors. Reggie eyed the entrance and concluded he could make it into ER without any help from anyone. He climbed into the back of the van, took a look at Vettore and was relieved to see that he was still breathing. In fact, he appeared to be resting comfortably on Reggie's horse blanket, cushioned by the bag of shavings. Reggie wondered briefly what the hospital would make of it, not that he gave a damn. Manoeuvring his way through the swing doors while carrying the stretcher proved to be more difficult than he had thought. The bag caught on one of the door handles and ripped open. A little trickle of wood shavings started to leak out. Ignoring it, Reggie made a beeline for reception. Luckily the nurse on duty wasted no time. She summoned the emergency team, which whisked Theo away, still on the make-shift stretcher. A neat trail of wood chips marked the route. Reggie was about to follow it, but he heard an imperious voice calling him back.

"Sir! I need the patient's details. Now!"

It was the reception nurse. Her brown hair was pulled back in a severe pony tail. A jutting chin and striking black eyes, which appeared to be boring into Reggie's head, completed the picture. It looked like he had no choice but to obey her. Also, he wanted his horse blanket back. It was old but it had senti-mental value. Emblazoned on it were the words Bronze Stakes Winner, the only one he'd ever won. He couldn't exactly blame the nurse for waylaying him. She was just trying to do her job. But his heart sank when he saw the mountain of paperwork on her desk.

"Name!" the nurse ordered, pen poised.

"Mine or his?" he parried.

"The patient's will do for now," she replied, adding ominously, "I'll get to you later."

She struggled over the spelling of Vettore. He came up empty on health number, but eventually they were done.

"Sign here, please," the nurse sighed. "And print your name and phone number."

To his dismay Reggie saw a janitor sweeping up the trail of wood shavings he'd been hoping to follow. The man looked vaguely familiar. He got up off his chair, but the nurse, a Nurse Elton, he saw from the name tag pinned to her chest, held up a large hand and stopped him in his tracks. She should have been a traffic cop, he thought. She was wasted here.

"Relationship to patient?" the dragon asked. He was floored by the question. What exactly was his relationship to Vettore? He hardly knew him, couldn't stomach the guy's arrogant manner, but he had watched him win night after night and would love to have had him drive one of his horses. "Relative?" Nurse Elton suggested. Reggie sniffed.

"He's no relation to me," he replied.

She waited a second or two while Reggie tried to think of the right answer.

"Partner?" she prompted.

Reggie coloured scarlet to the roots of his hair.

"Me? Are you crazy? I was on my way out of Iroquois Downs and I found 'im like this, in the damn parking lot."

"Did you two have any kind of disagreement?" Nurse Elton enquired.

"Put down whatever you want!" Reggie hissed. "This'll be the last time I try to help someone in trouble. Where is he anyhow? I want my horse blanket back!"

"If you were Mr. Vettore's partner," the nurse replied sweetly, "I could tell you. Otherwise, I'm afraid you'll have to wait for a family member." Reggie couldn't bring himself to pretend he was in a gay relationship with that arrogant bastard, not even for his precious Bronze Stake blanket. As he made for the exit he figured out the score. He'd lost a whole morning's work, been put down by a female dragon and it looked like his horse blanket was gone. On the plus side, he'd had some excitement, been in on a news scoop and came out of it as a bit of a hero. On the whole, he was pleased with himself. Then he heard a familiar voice calling after him. It was the janitor, carrying a sack of freshly swept shavings. Reggie suddenly realized why the man had looked so familiar. He hadn't seen Scotty McCoy since the baking soda fiasco. But McCoy was a good sort, he'd settled up with him before he left in disgrace.

"This yours?" Scotty asked, holding up a red and gold blanket. "They were gonna throw it out."

"Son of a gun," Reggie grinned. "I owe you one, Scotty! Big time!"

On the second floor of the hospital, Surgeon George Aldright, was looking over Theo Vettore's X-rays. The injuries (cracked ribs, a broken jaw, a bruised kidney and concussion, not to mention three smashed fingers) were serious but not life threatening. However, he'd need a nose job once he'd recovered sufficiently to stand up to the operation. If he'd been in a motorcycle accident, George wouldn't have felt so shocked. They showed up at ER every week, unfortunately. But to come across someone bruised and broken as the victim of gratuitous violence was virtually unprecedented in Erinsville. The townsfolk were, for the most part, a peaceable lot and lacking the yawning gap between rich and poor, they seemed to rub along together pretty well.

Since moving here from the UK some ten years earlier, lured by better pay and conditions with relatively low house prices, George Aldright had discovered many wonderful things about Ontario: its distinct four seasons for example (a relief from rainy Britain), a health service that wasn't broken but actually worked, room to wander in the many provincial parks and wild places, not to mention the lack of a class system. What George missed, naturally, were regular family get togethers and comforting British rituals like cricket at Lords, the Henley Regatta and Rugby at Twickenham. He'd been hoping his favourite niece, Caroline, would be popping over to Canada sometime this summer. But she'd landed a new job and couldn't get away. With no children of their own, he and his wife had been free to go anywhere they wanted. Workwise, it had been a good decision.

The man, Vettore, would have to be put together again somehow. George was looking forward to the challenge. The procedures would be fairly straightforward, he guessed, but with just a hint of possible complications. Enough to keep boredom at bay.

RESTITUTION

For the first forty-eight hours after the attack, Theo had been in a drug induced haze designed to help him cope with pain. Now however, he was slowly coming back to life. His cousin Lara visited him whenever she could, as did his parents. His Aunt Marta sat by his bedside, reading him stories from *Horseman's World* in French. Though Theo couldn't speak the language, he understood it well enough. He had left Montreal at the age of five, when the whole family had moved to Ontario. His cousin Lara had been ten, so learning English had been more of a challenge for her. Theo's girlfriend had come to see him once, then disappeared. Rumour had it she had defected to the leading trainer, Keith Lazer.

Bernie had been staying away too, but eventually Theo's uncle made an appearance. After he had chased everyone else out of the room, Bernie closed the door firmly and began pacing up and down until Theo felt positively dizzy.

"Theodore!" Bernie finally exclaimed. Uh oh, Theo thought nervously. Trouble! "People, they are telling me stories about you," Bernie continued. "I wish to know if they are true...*Eh bien*, Theodore, speak."

Theo knew better than to plead ignorance. That had never worked out well in the past. His uncle would only come down on him all the harder when he found out he'd been lying. Reluctantly he confessed all, feeling it had happened to another person, in another place. His uncle looked relieved, then extremely anxious.

"My poor sister, your mama, must never hear of this," he whispered in Theo's ear. "Me. . . I shall take care of everything! Now that I know the truth, I shall pay off the dealers, somehow...but you must swear to me on your life that you will never touch this...poison...again." Theo promised. "When the doctors, they say you are well enough, you come to Ferme Victoire and you work for me," Bernie added.

"Work?" Theo queried, his enthusiasm for the plan waning somewhat.

"*Mais oui*! I help you...you help me. It is how do you say...reciprocity, yes?" Theo was in no position to refuse.

Later on in the week he had another visitor: a man with grey hair and a nose like a toucan's beak.

"Well well, Mr. Vettore," the man pronounced gleefully, rubbing his hands together. "And how are you today?" Theo was floored. He'd never clapped eyes on the man in his life. And with that strong British accent, he was certain he'd have remembered him.

"Who are you?" he asked.

"Just wanted to take a look at your nose. See if it's ready."

"My nose?" The man was crazy. Plainly! "Ready for what?" Theo added, feeling panicky as the man came closer.

"Nothing to worry about. Ah yes. We'll be able to operate in a day or two. The swelling has come down nicely."

"Operate?"

"Nose job, Mr. Vettore. You don't want to spend the rest of your life looking like a punch drunk fighter do you? I'm Dr. Aldright by the way. You probably don't remember me…morphine can do that to you."

"Oh," Theo said.

"You're going to need physiotherapy after this. I have just the man for you…er…actually she's a woman, but I don't suppose you'll mind that too much." With that, he breezed off, leaving Theo in a bit of a daze.

A few days later, Bernie Vachon saw a silver sedan coming down the driveway of Ferme Victoire. Curiosity gave way to apprehension, when he opened the front door and was confronted by a pair of men in black leather jackets. He knew who they were immediately. He had been expecting them, but it was still a shock to see them in the flesh.

He led them into his study. They laid out their terms at once, conducting the whole affair in a businesslike manner. But Bernie was not deceived. He understood the terms were non negotiable. He agreed to everything they asked without hesitation, thankful that Marta, who was visiting Theo in hospital, was not around to witness his capitulation. So far, he had kept her in the dark about Theo's addiction to cocaine. One of them needed to be able to sleep at night. The agreement required him to purchase a timeshare in a villa on the Caribbean island of Sainte Marie for thirty-five thousand U.S. dollars. He had two weeks to find the money. Transfer of the funds was to take place on September 25th. Bernie had to be there to sign the papers.

The date coincided precisely with the Annual Yearling Sale, a critical time for Ferme Victoire's finances to say nothing of its reputation. Bernie had the strangest feeling that the timing was deliberate. Missing the sale was like being stabbed in the heart, yet he made the sacrifice willingly for his dear sister's sake, and for Theo also, just a little. The boy should be given a second chance by someone. And the parents, what could they do? Only watch and weep. At least Marta would be getting a pleasant surprise. One day he would have to tell her the truth. On his death bed, perhaps.

The day before the yearling sale Bernie and his wife boarded a plane south, leaving everything in Lara's hands. Knowing nothing of her husband's real intentions, Marta had insisted on coming along, pleased that Bernie was taking a break from the stress of the sale. If only she knew the truth, Bernie thought, sighing deeply. They were held up for twenty-four hours in Miami, waiting for a lightning storm to pass. The pilot eventually took off like a drunken sailor, battling the sudden gusts of wind. Marta had Bernie's hand in a death grip, the way she had clasped it during the birth of their daughter, Lara. Bernie closed his eyes and prayed to God to save them, silently cursing his nephew in French, for his wicked ways. Then the island appeared below them: a host of waving palm trees in white capped blue water. They touched down as the sun was setting, to fervent applause from the grateful passengers. Stage one was over. Now for stage two, Bernie thought nervously, preparing to disembark.

The Australian girl had a name: Anya Papandreos. She had even told him her life story. André Fontainbleu wasn't certain it was true. If he cared enough, he could have easily found out. But caring was for other people. Not for him. His flight was at 4:30 p.m. It was not necessary to tell her, she had already guessed that he was leaving. She came into the bedroom, waving the phone at him.

"What's going on?" she asked, sounding astonished. "I just called the bank, someone's put thirty-five thousand dollars in the account I just opened."

"It is nothing," André Fontaine said. Mere petty cash, he thought to himself, a harmless exchange from one client to another. He took her by the shoulders. "You know I'm going away for a while." She nodded. "You cannot stay here."

"At the Hermitage, you mean?" she asked anxiously.

"You can of course remain on the island if you wish," he clarified.

"Yes," she breathed, looking relieved.

"In that case you will need this money."

"It was you? You did this?"

"It will be put to good use, I am sure," he replied easily.

"The boat, you mean?" she asked, a tiny frown appearing on her forehead.

"The wreck!" he corrected, "you cannot do all the work yourself. It is impossible!"

"I don't see it that way!"

"In a month," he said, brushing her protest aside, "they will ask you to leave the boatyard. The season begins very soon. They will need the berth."

"I can't let you do this for me," she pleaded.

"You see it is so simple," he explained, feeling a little exasperated with her. "You pay other people to repair the boat. Quickly! *Eh voila*, you are ready for the tourists."

She fell silent. He watched her struggle, aware that she was trying to find a way out. But she would take the money. They always did.

"I'd need a partner," she said at last. The intensity of his disappointment troubled him. But only for an instant.

"So find one!" he replied. Was she unable to think for herself at all?

"Pete," she said, brightening. "He's in Melbourne, but I know he'd come out here if I asked him."

"Then ask him!" he snapped, losing patience. "The thirty-five thousand dollars is yours. You can do whatever you want!"

"It's so much money," she began hesitantly. He held her by the shoulders again. "I'm never going to be able to pay it all back," she added

"No?" he murmured in her ear, his right hand pulling up her flimsy little skirt, making his contempt obvious.

"I'm not a whore!" she exploded.

It was the first time he had forced himself on her, taken her against her will and, he was certain, against her better judgment. But she did not resist him for long. Afterwards, he noticed the tears of rage and frustration in her eyes. It gave him the greatest pleasure. He wanted her to have something to remember him by, to leave her with a lasting impression she would not easily forget.

He did not intend to see her again.

FALL

Sitting in his pickup truck waiting for his daughter Evie, Jim Mercer silently cursed his wife Pam and Theo Vettore in equal measure. They had both let him down. It was getting dark. At the last possible minute, Pam had cried off helping out in the Race Barn that night. Gusts of wind were ripping the last leaves off the trees, sending them bowling down the street. Okay, Mercer conceded, marrying a pole dancer hadn't been one of his best decisions. However, the Vettore fiasco was not his fault. Ever since Vettore had been put out of action, Heart of Darkness had been going steadily downhill. Moose Rankin couldn't hold a candle to the V Man. The Moose had dreamed up a dozen ways to get the filly beat. Which one would it be this time? Mercer wondered wearily, putting his hand down on the horn and holding it there.

The front door opened and Evie came running out.

"I just know Heart of Darkness is going to win tonight!" she announced as she clambered up onto the front seat.

"Buckle up," Mercer said gruffly, pulling out of the driveway. "Who told you that, your mother?"

"Uh uh," Evie replied shaking her head. "Hearts did!"

"I see. The horse told you," Mercer said, trying to keep a straight face. Wasn't she getting too old for this kind of thing? She was thirteen, after all.

"You don't believe me," Evie replied reproachfully.

"No, I do!" Mercer insisted. She was all smiles after that. It was merciful he reflected, as he took Highway 501 west, that Evie seemed able to live in her own private world, oblivious to the fact that her parent's marriage was falling apart right before her eyes. He wasn't a hundred percent sure that Evie was even his. She was a double for her mother looks wise, so it was impossible to tell. But that was all water under the bridge now. His main problem was Pam herself. She was getting itchy feet again. He recognized the signs. The first time it had happened was when Evie had started school. Pam had been left at a total loose end. Eventually she had reluctantly agreed to come work in the barn. There at least he was able to keep eye on her, though God knows what the help thought of her. With her tight jeans and skimpy tops, she looked more like a hooker than a groom. He was thankful that with winter coming on again, she'd have to cover up.

"You're scaring me!" he heard Evie exclaim. He realized belatedly that he'd been driving too fast.

"It's okay," he reassured her.

"It's not okay!" she contradicted him. "You're mad at Mom 'cos she didn't come along. I just know it!"

"Your mother can take the night off if she feels like it," Mercer stated mildly.

"You don't get it do you, Dad?" Evie said. "She's going out! And she's coming back late. Really late! I thought you knew!"

"It doesn't matter," he muttered.

"Are you and Mom splitting up?" Evie asked. "My friend Katy says her parents are getting divorced." Mercer took a deep breath.

"Listen," he said. "I want you to know that whatever happens, this house will be your home. I'm not leaving."

"Okay," Evie replied, looking a little happier.

When Mercer arrived at the track he was relieved to see that, wonder of wonders, Stinker the groom had actually done his job. Heart of Darkness was harnessed up and ready to go.

"Where's Pam tonight?" Stinker asked innocently.

"Go get Gold Digger ready," Mercer growled. "I'm taking her next."

Out on the racetrack, grey clouds were racing across the night sky. As Mercer took Heart of Darkness her warm up mile, he tried to figure out what to tell Moose about how to race her tonight. All he'd ever had to do when Vettore was driving was hand him the lines. Mercer had enough trouble with blacksmiths, vets and half baked grooms without having to figure out driving tactics, too. The racetrack was rock hard tonight. There was no cushion on it at all. They should have watered it, he thought uneasily. But Heart of Darkness was the soundest horse in his barn. She could handle it, no problem, he reassured himself. He spent the next hour fidgeting with the equipment and glancing nervously at his watch. It was her last race of the season. After this, whatever happened, he could relax.

He gave Moose his instructions, then joined Evie and Stinker down by the rail. The fillies were lined up behind the starting car in perfect formation, their hooves beating like a thousand drums. Mercer kept his eyes glued on Heart of Darkness. I want a little speed, but not too much, he silently willed the Moose. Unfortunately, Moose didn't get the message. Heart of Darkness sped off like she'd been shot out of a cannon. The timer flashed 27 seconds for the quarter.

"She's winning!" Evie cried excitedly. Mercer watched intently, deaf to the cheering crowd and the announcer's patter.

"54 flat! Way to go!" Stinker shouted in his ear, startling him as Heart of Darkness reached the halfway point. She was five lengths ahead of the horse sitting second.

"Is she going too quick?" Evie asked, sounding a little worried.

"Could be," Mercer nodded. The third quarter was a mere thirty seconds, enabling the horses behind to close the gap. It was a long, long stretch, Mercer thought grimly, and the wind was blowing right into the horses' faces now. But Moose hadn't lifted his whip. Not yet.

Half way down the lane, Ned Beazer brought his filly up to challenge. Behind them, the laggards were staggering towards the finish line, defeated by the wind. Moose brought his whip down hard on his filly's back. To Mercer's dismay, Heart of Darkness lost her rhythm. Her head dipped. She's going down, he thought, images of bust sulkies and broken bones filling his head. Then he saw Moose pull back sharply on the lines. Heart of Darkness's head came up and, without missing a beat, she hit the pace again. It had all happened in an instant but in that brief moment she'd given up the lead.

"Come on Hearts!" Evie screamed, climbing the fence to get a better view. Just before the wire, Heart of Darkness stuck her head in front. The race was over. She had won!

"Phew!" Mercer exclaimed, wiping the sweat from his brow. The losing horses were still streaming past them. "Come down off there!" he yelled at Evie.

The three of them made a mad dash for the winner's circle. The next few minutes were a blur for Mercer. Afterwards, he remembered Moose's idiotic smile and the flash of the camera, but little else.

"I want a picture! Please, Dad," Evie said, dangling her carrots under Hearts' nose.

"Okay," Mercer said. "But just the one. Get the sulky off," he snapped at Stinker, who was daydreaming. "Gold Digger's racing in the next!"

Heart of Darkness' work was done, but she didn't seem to know it. She was tossing her head and acting like she wanted to take off and fly. She was far too much for Evie to handle. Pam had picked one hell of a night to let him down, he thought angrily.

"I want to bathe her, Dad!" Evie was clamouring, "I got the water all ready."

Mercer jerked Hearts to a stop and looked down at his daughter.

"Listen to me," he said. "Go get your bucket. I'm taking her to the test barn. You can give her a bath there. And Evie…"

"Yes, Dad?"

"Calm down, okay?"

Gold Digger finished sixth in a very slow time. She'd make a good broodmare, Mercer decided, and produce nice big foals. But that's all she was good for. Hopefully, the owners would see sense. Back inside the Race Barn, he heard his name being called over the public address system. "Jim Mercer to the test barn right away!"

"I'll take Gold Digger," Stinker offered looking scared. "You better go!"

What were they going to do, complain about him employing child labour? Mercer thought feeling annoyed. Evie was thirteen, she was allowed to have a groom's licence.

"Dad, thank goodness you've come!" Evie exclaimed when she saw him. "Something really bad's happened. I can't get her hobble off. She won't let me pick her leg up."

"Is that all?" Mercer asked, glancing at the equipment stacked neatly in the corner. "I'll soon get that off her!" He strode over to Heart's left front leg. A few minutes later, having tried every trick in the book, he was forced to admit defeat. Something was very wrong.

"I'll go get the vet," he told Evie, "you stay here." These things happened in the standardbred business. No sense in crying over it. But his best filly…"I'll be back," he said. He'd caught a glimpse of the new track vet, Dr. Jay Winterflood, slipping out of a side door.

"Hey Doc!" he shouted. Everyone in the vicinity turned around and looked in his direction. Grooms, busy bathing their charges, paused, sponges in hand. Drivers quit tapping their whips on the ground for a moment and stared. Trainers, caught in the midst of adjusting and re-adjusting their horses' equipment, froze for an instant, sensing trouble. Winterflood turned around too. He was tall and lanky and with his high cheekbones, he looked like he'd stepped out of a cowboy movie, one where the Indians played a major part, Mercer thought uneasily.

"Ya talkin' to me?" Winterflood asked matter of factly.

He sounded just like any Canadian, Mercer realized, feeling relieved. "Gotta filly I need you to take a look at," he replied, jerking his thumb towards the spit box.

"I'll be there in a coupl'a shakes. Gotta watch 'em post parade."

Mercer resigned himself to a wait. In his first month on the job, the vet had gained quite a reputation for scratching horses lame. The trainers were up in arms about it and he'd heard management wasn't happy either. A late scratch lowered the betting totals which meant purses might go down, yet again. When Winterflood reappeared, he walked into the Paddock Judge's office. He was followed by Tony Hall, his cap pulled right down over his eyes, looking a picture of misery. A few minutes later the Paddock Judge got on the blower.

"Number six, Abadabado, is scratched from the fifth race. Lame in post parade," he announced.

Winterflood was back.

"Let's take a look at that filly of yours," he said, marching off towards the test barn. His diagnosis wasn't encouraging.

"Could be a fractured coffin bone," he pronounced after running his hands over the filly's right foot.

"Oh God," Mercer groaned. It was the worst possible news.

"Give her a few days' stall rest, then get her X-rayed," Winterflood suggested. "I'll give her a shot of bute," he added.

"Not necessary," Mercer replied grumpily, preparing to lead Heart of Darkness off. She'd come out of it soon enough, he thought, trying to convince himself it wasn't anything too serious.

"Dad!" Evie exclaimed, her eyes blazing. "You always say that!" she added reproachfully. She flung her arms protectively around the filly's neck. "Please Dad," she implored.

"Okay. Give her the bute, Doc," he agreed finally, shamed into it. Evie looked a lot happier, as well she might, getting the better of him like that. She was no pushover, he acknowledged grudgingly. Perhaps she was his daughter, after all.

Dr. Jay Winterflood sped off home as soon as the last race was over and done with. He drove through the silent village of Indian Falls then took the road south. When he reached open country, stars were shining in a dark, moonlit sky. He stared at the road ahead, trying to shake off his frustration. It had been another thankless night at Iroquois Downs. He should never have let Al McTavish talk him into taking a job which put him at the sharp end of harness racing, without the power to change anything. As soon as he decently could, he was going to resign as track vet. What was he really accomplishing by spotting lame horses anyway? Picking on trainers who didn't have an illegal pain killer? What was required was a whole new way of doing things: sophisticated testing and a policy of zero tolerance. But that was a pipe dream in the current reality. Dreamers had no place in the world in which he now lived. He had learned that lesson a very long time ago.

His ability to connect with horses, to feel everything the animals were feeling, was a positive menace in this job. As he walked through the Race Barn, it was obvious to him when a horse was in trouble. The body language, the expression in the eyes, told him the whole story. Why couldn't anyone else see it? Heart of Darkness' trainer genuinely hadn't believed his diagnosis. But the contrast between Mercer and his daughter was extraordinary. Mercer's face looked like it had been fashioned by the elements. His nose jutted out like a rock and his hair must have been shaved by a barber who'd only had half his mind on the job. The girl had sensitivity written all over her. A bond had instantly formed between them, a silent language which only they understood, as unexpected as coming across a friend in a strange town or finding an ally behind enemy lines.

He knew he needed to find another way of making a living. Yes, he had a wife, a farm with a mortgage on it and a baby on the way. But that didn't mean he had to abandon all his principles. By all accounts things were worse, not better, since the introduction of TCO2 testing. The trainers were using something much more deadly than baking soda now. But what? Whatever it was, it wasn't showing up in any of the lab tests. Why? He puzzled over it all the way home.

There was a candle burning in the window. Helena would be waiting up for him, as usual. He stepped into the house, relishing the warmth and the scent of wood smoke. Helena had fallen asleep on the rug beside the fire. She was curled up like a cat, feet tucked into moccasins, cozied up in the old fashioned nightdress she'd found in the attic the week they'd moved in. Her long dark hair was braided for sleep. He had no wish to share his burden with her. Instead, he reached down, gently pulled off the clasp and set her hair free. She stirred.

"Come to bed, Jay," she murmured. Then her eyes opened wide. "Something's wrong." she declared. Jay sighed. He couldn't hide anything from this woman.

"Not sure I can handle this job for much longer," he confessed. Helena was on her feet in an instant.

"Come to bed," she said again. "I'll make you feel better. I promise." If only it was that simple, he thought. But he followed her willingly. He'd have to figure this one out some other time. He was just too goddam tired to think clearly tonight.

BLAST FROM THE PAST

A cold wind was blowing, sending the bare branches of the trees into a frenzy as Reggie Blair pulled into Rivers Training centre. The grass in the paddocks was still green, but it wouldn't stay that way for much longer, Reggie Blair thought, as he parked his feed van outside Jim Mercer's barn. He began unloading feed, slinging the heavy sacks up onto one shoulder, running the gauntlet of the wind which was coming at him in fierce gusts at times stopping him in his tracks. When he was done with the delivery he headed over to Mercer's office, a tub of Muscle Power tucked under one arm. Mercer was on the phone. Reggie sat himself down and waited.

"We got two choices. Give her six months off and try her again, or retire her to the broodmare ranks," Mercer said. "It'd be a long haul I guess... Nope...not a great outlook Doc Meecham said...okey doke." He put the phone down.

"Well that's that!" he told Reggie, a look of resignation on his face.

"Which one is it this time?" Reggie asked knowing full well it was Heart of Darkness. That particular item had been on the bush telegraph for quite a while and had by now lost its fizz. Mercer gestured at the many win photos of Heart of Darkness that were pinned to the wall.

"Won every stake as a two year old. No one could touch her. She made a hundred eighty-seven thousand dollars that year. She'll make a decent enough broodmare...providin' she gets in foal," he said, then his voice dropped. "They don't wanna keep 'er. Told me to breed her and sell her on. You interested Reggie?"

"Too rich for my blood," Reggie laughed. Just then, Mercer's daughter Evie appeared at the office door.

"Food truck's here," she announced cheerfully. "What d'you want, Dad? Oh, hi Mr. Blair."

"Just a coffee," Mercer replied.

"I'll take a soup," Reggie said, handing her a ten-dollar bill.

"That'll be way too much," she said. "I'll bring you back the change."

After she left Reggie sat back in his chair.

"They grow up fast don't they?" he said, feeling the trite remark hardly covered the change in Evie's manner. She was no longer a child.

There was a knock at the door.

"What d'you need, Stinker?" Mercer growled.

"That creep's come around again," Stinker replied, "askin' for you."

"Well, tell him to go to hell!"

"He won't listen to me," Stinker said in a rare show of humility.

"Okay!" Mercer exclaimed, heaving himself to his feet. "I'll have to deal with this myself, I s'pose."

Jim Mercer recognized the man wobbling around on his bicycle right away. It was hard to say which looked more decrepit, Crawfish or his wheels. Mercer didn't invite either of them in.

"Got any jobs going?" Crawfish asked, taking off his cap and revealing a mass of dusty brown hair.

"I told you before. I don't need anyone right now," Mercer replied firmly. The nerve of him coming looking for his old job back, he thought. He noticed a crafty expression steal over Crawfish's face, but he was totally unprepared for what came next.

"I seen yer wife," Crawfish pronounced. Mercer stiffened. "She's a sly one, ain't she? I seen 'er down at that Tamale Bar…drinkin' and a-carryin' on."

"I told you…I don't need any help!" Mercer shouted, turning away. He felt furious. The Hot Tamale was a strip joint. What was Pam thinking? Damn her!

"You don't need to worry, Mr. Mercer," Crawfish said earnestly. "If I was to work for you again, I'd never breathe a word, honest!"

"You'll never work for me…never!" Mercer declared. He prayed none of the grooms had overheard the conversation. Conversation! It wasn't a conversation. The son of a bitch was trying to blackmail him. He reached into his pants pocket.

"Here's two hundred bucks!" he said, forcing himself to talk in a normal voice. "Don't show your face around here ever again, understood?" he added, handing over the money. Out of the corner of his eye, he could see Evie making her way back to the barn. Crawfish took the bills and folded them neatly, then tucked them into his shirt pocket.

"She's a pretty one, your little girl, ain't she?" he said dreamily. "Looks a lot like her ma, don't she?" He made Mercer's skin crawl.

"Get outa here," he hissed, finally losing patience.

"Yessir, Mr. Mercer," Crawfish replied, hastily mounting his bicycle and pedalling off.

It had been a good morning. A brilliant morning, Crawfish decided as he biked past the paddocks out onto the road which led back to his lonely room in the Iroquois Downs grooms' quarters. He'd scored big!

Reggie took the soup and set it down on the floor.

A short time later, Mercer returned and quickly downed his coffee. "When's Vettore coming back?" he asked. "You heard anythin' definite yet Reggie?" Reggie shook his head.

"No idea," he replied. "Shocking what happened to him, eh?"

"Could've been worse, I s'pose," Mercer said.

"Worse?" Reggie exclaimed in disbelief.

"You're too young to remember," Mercer replied gruffly.

"Remember what?" Reggie asked, leaning forward.

"Long time ago," Mercer muttered. "Up in Montreal."

"You can't stop there," Reggie said fretfully, aching to know the score. Mercer's eyes, he observed, seemed to be misting over.

"He was just a young fella," Mercer said huskily. "And I pray to God nothing like that ever happens to me or anyone else I know." Reggie was unnerved by this uncharacteristic display of emotion on Mercer's part. "He was a junkie, so maybe I shouldn't feel too sorry for 'im," Mercer added, recovering somewhat. "They beat 'im half senseless...then...no...I can't say it...not even to you, Reggie," he said, choking up again. "See, after they were done with him, he couldn't do nothing, couldn't even make love to his wife!"

Reggie's jaw dropped.

"Maybe he'd've been better off dead," Mercer concluded. "Damn good horseman, too."

"Jesus H Christ," Reggie exclaimed. "Best to stay a million miles away from those guys," he added with a nervous laugh.

"How's the soup?" Mercer enquired, changing the subject abruptly.

"Okay," Reggie gulped. "If you've a taste for battery acid, that is! I'll be off," he said, getting to his feet.

"You can take that crap with you!" Mercer told him, pointing to the tub of Muscle Power. "Find some other poor sucker, eh?"

"Andy Price is givin' it a try!" Reggie replied defensively.

"I wouldn't take it if you gave it to me for free," Mercer said shortly.

Reggie made himself scarce. On his way out, he took a peek at Heart of

Darkness. She was a looker alright, with her long tumbling mane and her doe eyes, but he wasn't tempted. Broodmares were a long haul...even worse than yearlings. A stud with strong bone like Mr President, that's what she needed. When he stepped outside, the wind whipped his cap off and it went flying over the barn roof. He dumped his soup carton into a passing wheel-barrow and jumped into his van, glad to get away from the gale out there. He decided to pay a visit to his local co-op and pick up some cold weather gear, maybe splash out on a pair of padded overalls.

Winter was on its way.

THE COLDEST SEASON

Roy McClean's convenience store, The Happy Shopper, sold everything from newspapers to nuts. Located just a few minutes from Iroquois Downs Raceway, there was plenty of passing trade. It started snowing as Roy began unloading the packs of firelighters and bags of logs he had bought for resale. Winter in Ontario wore Roy down. That's when he missed England the most: going down to the pub for a pint, sitting beside a roaring fire, surrounded by a bunch of blokes he'd grown up with, safe from the wind and rain outdoors. Yet, here he was in Canada, with another winter about to start.

When he got back inside, the phone was ringing. His wife Nora answered it. She'd gone back to her normal hair colour, a dull brown, but he knew it wouldn't last. She'd been studying hair dye leaflets all week.

"It's for you-hoo!" Nora trilled, handing him the phone.

"Gotta price on that cold and flu for you," the salesman told him, his voice crackling down the line. "Is it snowing down your way, too?"

"I'll take a case," Roy said. It felt like five minutes since he'd been bringing out the barbecues and hanging baskets. The summer season was a short one in Ontario.

"How about some Arm and Hammer?" the salesman asked hopefully.

"Don't need any. But I'll take a couple of cases of Chlorox," Roy replied. Since the new TCO2 test had been introduced at Iroquois Downs, sales of baking soda had plummeted at The Happy Shopper. However, along with ginseng tonic, sales of bleach were soaring, something Roy found hard to understand. The trainers who bought it didn't look like house-proud types.

It was getting dark. He decided to take Nora to the Cherokee Inn tonight. It wasn't quite like the pubs back home, but it came pretty close.

At Rivers Training centre, Dave Bodinski had spent most of the day getting all six of his horses reshod with borium, those magical little beads of metal that gave traction on an icy track like studs on football boots. Every hour Dave led a freshly shod horse back to its stall and brought one back to Jeremiah Hostetler's blacksmith's shop. Each time the air felt colder. As the afternoon wore on, snowflakes drifted down from an overcast sky. When darkness fell, the snow began to stick.

When Dave was ten years old, he'd climbed over the high fence in his back yard and landed in the barn area of Merryvale Raceway, an exciting place compared to home. Dave had always been sure he'd make it big in the horse business one day. So far things hadn't worked out that way. But training horses even in the freezing cold, beat pumping gas any day of the week. As he topped up the water buckets for the night, he wondered what Keith Lazer was using now. Lazer was winning everything. Whatever it was, Dave would have loved to get his hands on it. Unfortunately, he wasn't in the club.

Judge Jewells read Dr. Jay Winterflood's letter of resignation with jubilation. Now that the do gooder had fallen on his sword, the handle would no longer be dragged down by the vet's infernal late scratches. Perhaps, now, purses might actually go in the right direction: up!

Who did Winterflood think he was, anyhow, Mother Teresa?

Winter did not trouble André Fontainbleu. In the Caribbean, it was a time of pure pleasure; long, warm, sunny days and translucent water. As for the fools who visited the island, escaping winter's clutches for a handful of days each year, he felt only contempt for them as he watched them gambol along the beaches, picking up shells like overgrown children.

His online gambling operation had doubled profits in the last six months and cash was pouring in from cocaine sales in Canada. He had decided to purchase one of the new super yachts in order to compete in the annual Round the island race, which was held in Sainte Marie each February.

He had to get rid of the money somehow.

A NEW YEAR

January 19th: Jim Mercer was sitting in his office-cum-tack room, perusing the New Year's edition of *Horseman's World*, when he heard the roar of Jean Claude's truck.

"Shipper's here," he shouted, leaping to his feet. "Jimmy! Stinker! Get those mares out." Mercer's barn was jam-packed with new two year olds in training now, and his mind was set firmly on the future. Time to let go of the past, he decided, going out to greet the driver, a Quebecer from Montreal.

As Heart of Darkness stepped out into the freezing air, a tremor of excitement ran through her. She had been a prisoner in her stall for weeks. Forgetting herself, she gave a little leap of excitement. The tug of a lead shank and a twinge in her right foot brought her swiftly back to earth. But the sight of the shipping truck sent her into a panic. Twirling in tight circles on the icy tarmac, she called out for her stable mate, Gold Digger.

"*Oo la la*!" Jean Claude said. "We 'ave trouble now I sink."

"The other mare'll be out in a minute," Mercer said. "Jimmy!" he yelled, "Hurry it up!" As the minutes passed, Heart of Darkness took another leap skywards. Then, out of the corner of his eye, Mercer saw a man on a bicycle coming down the lane way. It was Crawfish Brown. Mercer felt like he was going to have a blood pressure attack right there on the tarmac. He noticed three of the grooms were standing there, sniggering and nudging each other.

"What the hell are you staring at? Go and help Jimmy!" Mercer said irritably. A few minutes later, Gold Digger sauntered out of the barn, looking like butter wouldn't melt in her mouth. Crawfish took a plug of tobacco out of his pocket and began chewing, still perched up on his bicycle.

"Ain't that the one I used to take care of?" he asked. Mercer turned his back on him and watched Gold Digger's bulky frame march up the ramp. To his relief, Heart of Darkness put her head down and followed meekly after her.

"Best filly I ever had. I'll miss 'er, that's for sure," Mercer said, filled with regret.

"Don't worry. Zey will be safe wiz me," Jean Claude replied reassuringly. "Soon, in one 'our, zey will be at Ferme Victoire."

"I's still lookin' for a job, Mister Mercer," Crawfish piped up. Mercer scowled.

"'E could come wiz me," Jean Claude offered. "Per'aps zey look for 'elp at zee farm, yes?"

"Great idea!" Mercer replied, jumping at the chance to get rid of his tormentor. "Get off your bike, Crawfish," he commanded. "You can ride in the cab with Jean Claude. Jimmy! Get that bike stowed on the roof. Give 'im a hand there, Stinker."

Crawfish hesitated, then reluctantly fell in with the plan.

Five minutes later, Mercer watched the truck pull away. Up on the roof, the bicycle was swaying precariously. Stinker had done a slipshod job as usual, not that Mercer gave a damn. In fact, he sincerely hoped it and Crawfish would smash themselves to oblivion, not that it was likely unfortunately. But at least he had gained a small reprieve and he could now look forward to a bit of peace, without worrying about Crawfish showing up and dropping a bombshell about his wife in front of Evie, or one of the owners. He took a deep breath of cold air. At least half a dozen of his two year olds, the top string, were looking pretty good. They were giving him a chance to start over. That was what the horse business was all about.

FERME VICTOIRE

As Theo Vettore watched Jean Claude's van coming down Ferme Victoire's driveway, he felt a surge of excitement. It was the main event of the day. But who was he fooling? It was the main event of the month! Since his accident nothing of any importance had happened to him, unless he counted his fingers having to be re-broken because they hadn't set straight the first time. He'd been away from the racetrack for five months now. He felt like he was becoming invisible. He probably was, he decided; to the trainers anyhow. Moose Rankin had taken over the top spot in the drivers' rankings and here he was, stuck out in the middle of nowhere. Running a breeding farm was his uncle's dream, not his. In six weeks' time he'd be out of this place. He couldn't wait.

"Ow's eet going?" Jean Claude called out, jumping down from the cab. "*Ca va mieux, maintenant?*" To Theo's astonishment, Crawfish Brown crawled out after him.

"Hey, what's he doing here?" Theo asked suspiciously.

"I's lookin' for work," Crawfish said.

"Your uncle, 'e need someone per'aps?" Jean Claude asked. Theo shrugged.

"No idea," he replied, feeling torn. He couldn't stand Crawfish. On the other hand, they were so short of help on the farm, he was being worked off his feet.

"Gimme a try, boss," Crawfish pleaded.

"Okay. One week, then we'll see," Theo agreed, hoping someone better would have shown up by then. "Make yourself useful," he added, as Jean Claude appeared with a mare who looked like a sumo wrestler. Crawfish jumped to it.

When Heart of Darkness came flying down the ramp, Theo felt like crying. The sight of her brought back so many memories.

"She looks great," he said, his voice breaking.

"What 'appened to you?" Jean Claude asked gently. "I 'ear many zings but…"

Theo hesitated. He hadn't told anyone about it, outside of the family. His aunt and uncle were snatching a week in the islands before the hectic foaling season started, so he felt more alone than ever. Could he trust Jean Claude to be discreet? he wondered anxiously. In the end, he poured out the whole story. He had to talk to someone! Jean Claude listened to what he had to say without uttering a word. He went about the business of closing up the doors on his truck. Then he turned back to Theo.

"I 'ear many zings about zis diable, zis devil," Jean Claude said quietly. "Bad zings…one time 'e used to do 'is dirty business in Montreal. But 'e never show 'is face there no more."

"Why?"

"Because 'e knows zey will kill him!"

"For real?" Theo exclaimed, a wild hope rising in his heart.

"Stay away from ze Scorpion, Monsieur Vettore," Jean Claude pronounced gravely. "A few broken bones, pah! Zat is nothing…"

"Nothing? Compared to what?" Theo asked indignantly. Self pity would get him nowhere, he knew, but he couldn't help it sometimes.

"Listen…" Jean Claude said sympathetically. "Now you feel, 'ow you say, 'low down, yes? But you are still ze king…and soon ze king will take back 'is crown, *n'est ce pas*?" With that, he leapt onto the roof of the van and carefully lowered Crawfish's old bicycle. Then he was on his way.

Why was it, Theo wondered, that all the doctors, the physios, the anxious relatives and the awkward phone calls from his fellow horsemen had hardly touched him. But talking to Jean Claude had turned his mind around. It was New Year, a chance to put all this behind him and start fresh. No more cocaine, he promised himself. Never again!

That evening Theo took his usual tour of the barns at Ferme Victoire before calling it a day. It was a clear night. No snow. But a raw wind was blowing. He turned up his coat collar and dug his bare hands further into his pockets.

"Must've left my gloves in the damn tack room again," he muttered.

He slid open the barn door and turned on the fluorescent lights. The horses blinked, reacting to the sudden change from dark to light. It was a familiar sight to Theo now. The horses seemed so vulnerable at night. He was in the broodmare barn, some of them due to foal in a month's time, each of them displaying the bulge in the belly that betrayed the presence of a healthy foal growing inside them. After two months of cold weather, their coats were as thick and luxurious as a hibernating bear's. Theo went down the shed row, inspecting the water buckets, checking the hay. They all reacted in their own way to his presence. Some stood at attention. Others stretched lazily. One or two turned their backs on him, ears pinned back. He knew them well enough by now to recognize any significant changes that could be a sign of trouble brewing. The shed row was long. There were fifty-one mares in all. Finally, he was satisfied all was well and he turned out the lights. Except for the rustling of straw, there was silence.

The lights in the big house were out. Theo had the place to himself.

He stopped off at the foaling barn, which at present was being used as an overflow facility for the maiden mares, horses recently returned from the racetrack to the broodmare ranks. They looked bored, he thought, bored and lonely, standing in the enormous stalls designed for a mother and foal. No doubt the mares missed the racetrack every bit as much as he did. They had a one way ticket. But he was counting on making a comeback. He would have been back driving weeks ago, half healed or not, if it hadn't been for his promise to his uncle. He couldn't refuse him, not after all Bernie had done for him. He left the barn door half open. It was good for the mares to get some fresh air, even on a cold night like this. God knows what viruses the two new arrivals had brought with them. The last thing he needed was a barn full of sick horses.

Theo's final call was to the stallion in residence, Night Raider. His excellent pedigree, record breaking performance on the racetrack and multi-million dollar earnings were all prominently displayed on a plaque outside the barn. Night Raider had sired hundreds of babies and scores of top racehorses. Two of his sons had become sires in their own right. That had made broodmare owners beat a path to his door. When Theo stepped inside the barn, he heard a whicker of welcome. Night Raider wasn't a big horse, but he was perfectly balanced, with an exquisitely formed head and alert, intelligent eyes. When Theo turned on the light, the stallion pricked up his ears and circled his large stall. Then he arched his neck and kicked out at the wall with his hind legs, obviously pleased to have a visitor.

At times, what with all the broodmares and babies he was responsible for, Theo felt like he was presiding over a maternity ward and nursery school. As the only unattached male on the farm (leaving aside Crawfish!), Night Raider had become Theo's friend and even his confidante. Theo felt he understood the source of the stallion's moodiness and frustration. He and Night Raider had a lot in common right now. Both were penned up in their bachelor pads. They were out of the limelight and separated from the female companionship they both craved. The horse carried a fair bit more weight than he had done in his racing days. But his potency was legendary. Theo tossed in an extra scoop of grain. The old fellow needed to keep his strength up. In six weeks' time, the breeding season would begin.

"Live it up!" he told him, as the stallion dived into his feed tub. If only his own life were that simple, Theo thought, heading for the warmth of his small apartment over the garage. It was 9 p.m. when Theo closed his front door, sat down at the kitchen table and confronted the thing he'd been running away from all day. It was hard for him to believe that the sight of a small packet of white powder could send him into such a tailspin. One sniff of it and he'd be back on a course of self destruction. He knew he should trash it. Instead, he left it lying on the table while he made himself a cup of strong black coffee.

11 p.m. Brilliant stars in a clear night sky. Not a breath of wind. Theo Vettore stripped down to his T-shirt running at top speed to nowhere in particular, preceded by clouds of white as his breath froze in the sub zero air. The thud of his footsteps. A stallion's answering scream. Theo stopped in his tracks, hesitating. Why shouldn't the horse have a few minutes of freedom? he thought. Moments later, Night Raider was galloping around his paddock, bucking wildly. After a while he froze, his ears up, his head erect, his upper lip curled back. A scent was drifting across from the foaling barn, irresistible to any stud: the scent of a mare in heat!

Theo was having a problem making it up onto the roof of the broodmare barn. He decided to try the old bank barn instead. He found a foothold in its stone wall and reached the top easily. He balanced himself on the narrow apex, stretched out his arms and walked giddily from one end to the other. As he gazed over the rooftops to the stars, he knew nothing could defeat him now.

Night Raider cleared the paddock fence effortlessly. Nostrils flaring, ears flicking back and forth to catch the slightest sound, he high stepped his way to the nearest barn. A mare's low nicker drew him in through the half open door. The breeding season had begun earlier than expected.

It was a great deal more difficult climbing down than up, Theo discovered. After half an hour of fumbling around in the dark, he finally made it on to solid ground. His first thought was to escort Night Raider back to his stall. They'd both had a little fun. It was time for bed. It took a while for Theo to accept that the stallion had left his large tree lined paddock. Much less time for him to sprint over to the barn, where he discovered him right away. The mares were in a state of high excitement.

Theo's relief at finding the stallion unhurt was somewhat spoiled by the fact that he was now sharing one of the large stalls with a dark beauty who had a white star on her forehead. It was Heart of Darkness! Theo didn't blame the stallion for being interested in her. He just prayed nothing untoward had happened. He noted that the mare next door, a big strong girl built like a truck, had a smug look on her face. He led a reluctant Night Raider back to his quarters hoping for the best. He closed the doors to the foaling barn firmly behind him. There was no thought in Theo's mind of telling his uncle what had happened, not with Bernie's fiery temper. He decided to lie low and hope for the best. In a few weeks' time he would be back at the track. As he opened the door to his apartment over the garage, he failed to notice Crawfish Brown's face, his eyes opened wide, staring up at him.

Theo's first thought when his alarm went off the next morning was hardly original: Black coffee! He stepped into the tiny kitchen and did a double take. Crawfish Brown was sitting at the kitchen table, looking like a malevolent gnome.

"How the fuck d'you get in here?" Theo asked.

Crawfish Brown slowly turned his head and fixed his good eye on Theo.

"I seen you," he said. "I seen wot you did las' night...wi' dat stud."

Theo noticed that Crawfish's left eye was blinking uncontrollably.

"Wanna cup of coffee?" Theo asked, stalling for time by switching on the kettle.

"Nope!" Crawfish replied. He sounds so damn sure of himself, Theo thought. He drank his coffee leaning up against the sink. Sharing a table with Crawfish wasn't something he could face right now. The guy stank. . . in every possible way. Gradually Theo's head cleared.

"Okay," he said. "What's your drift?"

Crawfish coughed, then spat tobacco juice across the room, narrowly missing Theo's left hand, which was resting on the counter top. He muttered something inaudible. Theo waited, listening to the ticking of the kitchen clock.

"Tell yer wot, you giv' me six hundred bucks and I never seen nothin' last night!" Crawfish offered.

"Five hundred if you quit," Theo replied quickly, anxious to get rid of the guy before his uncle returned.

"We got us a deal," Crawfish mumbled, pocketing the cash. "I was gonna quit anyways," he added viciously, slamming the door behind him.

Just like that, Theo realized, his precious fresh start to the year was over and done. He was furious with himself. He couldn't believe he'd been stupid enough to take the bait the Scorpion had dangled in front of him. He'd probably landed his uncle in the drink with Night Raider, too, after all Bernie had done to try to help him. He felt sick about it.

What was wrong with him?

SAINTE MARIE

After the last tourist had disembarked from the Sea Princess, Anya went down below decks and counted their takings.

"Hey Pete!" she called out excitedly, sticking her head out of the cabin. "We took fifteen hundred dollars this week!" A giant red sun was sinking into the sea and on the island of perpetual summer it was still a warm 70°F.

"Never mind that! Come and have a beer!" Pete replied cheerfully. Anya had known Pete forever, since primary in fact. He'd come all the way from Australia on her say so, just like that!

"Hey! Watch it. You'll drink up all the profits," she warned.

"This is way better than Melbourne," the Aussie replied, ignoring her and cracking open a beer. Maybe he was right, she thought. Being marooned on this island hadn't turned out so bad. Certainly Pete looked pretty happy here. But she still missed home. She'd have never left Melbourne and followed her parents to Greece, if she had known that they were going to try and marry her off to some guy she hardly knew and spend the rest of her life in the city of Thessaloniki: talk about wishful thinking!

Too bad all the best guys are gay, she thought wistfully. Pete was 6' 2" with blond good looks, easy going, too. Still, she comforted herself, with her record she'd have blown it for sure if he'd been boyfriend material. Certainly, hooking up with a sugar daddy hadn't worked out brilliantly. In fact, it had been a pretty big mistake. But at the time, she'd been right up against it. She had every intention of repaying André Fontainbleu the whole thirty-five thousand, however long it took her. It was a matter of pride. Pete didn't agree. But what did he know?

Better stick to boats, she told herself. The Sea Princess did whatever she was asked to do. Plus, she never talked back. As long as she was regularly maintained, she was A-OK. Dependable, too. Anya had yet to meet a man like that.

"What are you up to tonight, then?" she asked Pete, sipping her beer.

"I reckoned I'd go to Bed."

"As in..."

"The nightclub, yeah," Pete confirmed. "You?"

"Not a lot. I might scrub the deck or something."

"Sounds terrible! Why don't you come along?"

"You know, I just might," she replied.

A full moon was rising up out of the sea. The stars were unfamiliar, not a sign of the Southern Cross. But even with all its problems life on the island was still as close to perfect as she was likely to find, in this hemisphere at least.

FERME VICTOIRE

Nestled in his favourite armchair beside the fire, Bernie Vachon picked up the March issue of *Horseman's World*, smiling at Night Raiders picture on its front cover. He had eaten an excellent lunch and had left the veterinarian who was checking the mares in the capable hands of his new farm manager. Sighing deeply, he stretched out, luxuriating in the peace at Ferme Victoire. The house was much quieter now that Theo had finally moved out. After taking a short nap, Bernie intended to read the article about his stallion. The timing, the beginning of the breeding season, was perfect. To his dismay, he heard a loud knock at the back door. A few moments later, Marta ushered Dr. Winterflood into the room. Bernie smelled trouble. Why the house visit? he wondered. The vet was generally far too busy for fireside chats. Winterflood came straight to the point.

"Houston, we have a problem," he said. Bernie sighed. He had been feeling so happy and relaxed before.

"What is it?" he asked nervously.

"Nice fire," the vet said, abruptly changing the subject. "Pine logs?"

"We lost a big tree last summer," Bernie replied, trying to stifle his impatience.

"Lightning storm?" Winterflood asked, gazing into the fire. Why doesn't he just tell me what's wrong? Bernie thought anxiously.

"I've been checking the maiden mares…to see if they're ready…"

"Ready to breed, yes," Bernie said eagerly.

"I'm afraid I have some surprising news for you. Three of them are already in foal," Winterflood announced.

"In foal!" Bernie cried, his horrified gaze shifting to the calendar on the wall. A silhouette of a horse jauntily pulling a sleigh through crisp white snow and the single word *March* confirmed he hadn't suddenly taken a leap through time. "How could this be?" he demanded.

"Helter Skelter, Gold Digger and Heart of Darkness," the vet continued. "All three supposedly maiden mares. There may be others. As to how…" Winterflood smiled. "Your guess is probably better than mine!"

"It is not possible!" Bernie moaned.

"Someone slipped up…or slipped out!" Winterflood said, his smile widening. Bernie threw his arms to heaven.

73

"*Sacre bleu!*" he cursed.

"There may be others," Winterflood repeated. Bernie looked up at the ceiling and swore silently on his mother's memory that he would find whoever or whatever had done this to him. Then he would kill him with his own bare hands.

"I need to know how many," he stuttered realizing he sounded hysterical, like a woman. He made an effort to regain control, but failed. "Now!" he added hoarsely.

"No more time today," Winterflood replied flippantly. "Gotta get back." Bernie thought he might begin by strangling the vet, just for practice.

"Tomorrow, then." he said, trying to adopt a stern tone.

"How about tomorrow afternoon?" Winterflood proposed. "In the meantime, start looking for the guilty party."

"You mean the horse? How do I know who did it? Some pony down the road, who knows? What about termination?"

"Too risky," Winterflood replied immediately. "At this stage, it could compromise the mare's ability to breed in future. Better to let them have their foals, I think."

"At this stage?" Bernie echoed. "Just how far along are they? How many days?" An all too familiar burning sensation in his chest signalled an urgent need for antacid. But he did not intend to make a spectacle of himself by taking his pills in front of the vet.

"Days?" Winterflood replied, "we're not talking days here. We're talking weeks. They're pretty solidly in foal. Nice healthy embryos." Bernie finally blew his top.

"When I find that son of a bitch I am going to tear him to shreds!" he declared.

"See you tomorrow," Winterflood replied, beating a hasty retreat, leaving Bernie to face the prospect of twenty-four hours of torment until the next report.

"Marta!" he shouted. "Where is my antacid?" He found Marta in the kitchen washing the pots from lunch. "My pills!" he repeated.

"Probably in your pocket," she said soothingly. She sighed. "Bad news?"

"A mystery," Bernie replied, gulping down six pills, the maximum dose. "How could three mares be in foal already? Tell me Marta." The smell of grilled chicken and herbs hung in the air, mingled with the heavy smell of garlic.

"We went away," Marta said. "In January…remember?" The memory of calm turquoise waters and white sands brought a smile to her tired eyes. "It was wonderful."

"It was a disaster!" Bernie exclaimed. "My God! The dates fit. That's when it happened! I left Theo in charge. I did everything for that good for nothing and this is how he repays me. My own nephew!"

"Maybe it wasn't his fault," Marta pleaded.

"I'm calling him right now!" Bernie declared, striding back to the living room. A few minutes later, he was back. "The son of a bitch has shut off his phone! They're outside mares, Marta," he groaned. "If they give birth before January first, their foals will be worthless. They won't be eligible for any of the two year old stakes. Our reputation will be ruined. The owners will sue us. We'll be a laughing stock. People trusted us. What timing! Just as the article came out."

"The one on Night Raider? Let me see that!" Marta exclaimed delightedly.

"Wait till you see the next article you read about us," Bernie stated gloomily, "then you won't be so happy. They'll crucify us."

Theo Vettore's phone rang at 7 a.m. the next morning. He was still in bed.

Bernie began hurling insults down the line, without even wishing him a good morning.

"Calm down," Theo said, as soon as he was able to get a word in. "What makes you think it was me that let Night Raider out? It could have been Crawfish Brown."

"Who is Crawfish Brown?" Bernie demanded.

"A guy I hired. I needed help when you went away. But I threw him out after one day on the job. He was useless!"

"But why would he do such a thing?"

"Revenge?" Theo suggested, speaking a language he knew his uncle would understand. "I fired him."

To Theo's relief, Bernie believed his story.

"Just wait till I get my hands on that piece of filth!" he raged. "He'll wish he never heard of Bernie Vachon."

"What's going on?" Ginny, the Iroquois Downs outrider and Theo's current live in girlfriend, murmured.

"Go back to sleep," Theo told her. He needed time to think. Night Raider had got three mares in foal that night…maybe more. How in heaven had he managed it in the short time he'd been loose? Theo was filled with admiration for the horse. What a stud! But he'd landed Bernie in big trouble and if his uncle ever found out what really happened that night…Theo didn't even want to think about that. Still, he reasoned, things could be worse. It was Crawfish's word against his, after all and no one believed anything that low life said. It was lucky he hadn't had to talk to his uncle face to face, he realized. Bernie would have spotted the lie in a heartbeat. He had calmed down a bit after Theo had assured him that Night Raider had been the only stallion on the farm at the time. It was unfortunate that Helter Skelter was a trotter and Night Raider was a pacer, but you couldn't have everything. Luckily, the other two mares were pacing bred. As long as Bernie didn't run into Crawfish, Theo would be safe. The yearling sales were the only likely point of contact and they were eight months away. So, no worries!

"Put on the weather station," Ginny mumbled, "I gotta truck Smoky clear over to Doc Henry's today."

"Temperature at Pearson Airport is a chill minus seventeen degrees centigrade with a light north-westerly wind, so dress up warm, folks. It's gonna be a cold one! Clear sunny skies, chance of snow forty percent by nightfall. Storm warning in progress so stand by for updates, right here at FM97…"

"Oh boy!" Ginny exclaimed, rolling out of bed. "I better get outa here if I wanna beat that storm!"

"Why not let Winterflood take a look at him. Save you a trip," Theo suggested.

"No way! That guy gives me the creeps!" Theo didn't bother arguing with her.

"Hey, give me the sheet for today's qualifiers, will ya?" he asked lazily.

"Get it yourself," Ginny retorted, slamming the bathroom door. A few minutes later he heard the shower running. Since his "accident" as he liked to call it, Ginny hadn't acted the same. She used to look up to him. Not anymore. She'd told him that he didn't need sympathy, he needed to know that actions had consequences. What he needed, Theo decided, was to get his own apartment!

There were ten qualifying races due to take place that morning. On a freezing day like this, some of the drivers would stay away, giving him the chance to step in and take their place. It was time to get his driving uniform out of cold storage. He'd been away too long. He had once been the king of the track. He would find no peace until he'd taken back his crown.

LADIES IN WAITING

As winter melted into spring, Heart of Darkness and her friend Gold Digger were jolted out of their routine at Ferme Victoire. A truck ride to the Spring Sale, a short spell in the sale ring and a second truck ride landed them somewhere new: Harmony Farm. Unaware that the odds of the two of them being purchased by the same breeding farm were about a thousand to one, the mares settled down happily in their new field where they quickly discovered that the grass was top quality and the care was excellent.

As spring warmed into summer, Heart of Darkness was overwhelmed by a strange languor. Instead of running and playing, jumping at every sound, she put her head down and grazed quietly. Side by side, she and Gold Digger picked the paddock clean, accompanied by an orchestra of buzzing insects.

The days rolled by. Summer heat gave way to harvest moons, glowing in the night sky. The first snow fell. Heart of Darkness hadn't a mirror or a calendar. She had no way of knowing what was to come. Mere words could never tell her. But soon, her baby would be born.

There were no babies on the horizon for Scotty McCoy. He and his wife were still at war. However, during his spell in the wilderness working as a janitor at Erinsville General, he had snared a rich owner and had moved back into Rivers Training centre with a half dozen racehorses. He was looking forward to the New Year's Eve celebrations, especially Harry Harper's party.

Scotty never passed up on a chance for free beer.

A snow storm had hit Ontario, snarling traffic, delaying flights and cancelling the races at Iroquois Downs. As Theo Vettore parked his black Ferrari outside Evelyn Barreaux's house, it started snowing harder. Evelyn had his new winter driving suit set out on the sofa. He didn't bother to try it on. He never gained an ounce of weight and she had been making suits for him for five years now.

"I made it good and warm," she told him. "Gonna be a cold one this year. I can feel it in my bones. You need any gloves? I have a pair that'd fit you."

It was still snowing when he left, but Theo didn't feel like going back to the apartment. He'd had a flaming row with Ginny about New Year's Eve. Harry Harper's parents had gone on vacation and Harper was throwing a party at their house. It was somewhere out in the country, near Winterflood's farm and it sounded like fun. Everyone was going. Ginny had other ideas. If Theo was honest with himself, he had always felt a little bit scared of Ginny. At times, she reminded him too much of his Uncle Bernie. And if she wanted him to go somewhere romantic on New Year's Eve, she was going about it all the wrong way. He wasn't going to get all dressed up and go out dancing with a girl who pushed him around.

Without realizing it, he had ended up at Iroquois Downs Raceway. The racetrack was plunged in darkness, which after his experience in the parking lot made him uneasy. But slowly he simmered down. Here at least he was the king! Despite his late start, winning the drivers championship was in the bag, even without his cocaine fix. There was a full card of racing on New Year's Day. Maybe Ginny had a point, he thought, relenting a little. He couldn't exactly show up with a lousy hangover and expect to start the New Year with a string of wins. But if she was angling for a proposal, she was dead wrong. That was never going to happen! The mercury was dropping. Shivering, Theo turned the engine back on and jacked up the heat. He still didn't feel like going home. Instead, he decided to drop in on Ferme Victoire. The cross country route took him directly past Harmony Farm but he didn't stop, even though he wouldn't have minded seeing Heart of Darkness again. The breeders who'd bought her, Val and Joey Harris, were decent people. But, he guessed, no one connected to Ferme Victoire would be welcome at Harmony Farm for some time to come. He couldn't help wondering; had Heart of Darkness dropped her foal already? Or would she by some miracle hold off foaling until the New Year? For everyone's sake, he hoped the answer to that last question was a big fat yes! The lights in the farm house twinkled as Theo drove past Harmony Farm.

In the cozy farmhouse kitchen, Val and Joey Harris were sitting at the old wooden table, having a council of war.

"Look," Joey said. "You've fixed a lot of things, Val, but you can't fix this." Val, a willowy blond who looked fragile and was anything but, just shook her head. "It can't be fixed," Joey repeated. "Not even by you."

"I'm telling you, we'll be fine," Val replied serenely.

"Listen!" Joey exclaimed. "Those two mares have been bagged up for days. Now they're waxed up and...we're ruined," he concluded, burying his head in his hands.

"It isn't gonna happen," Val replied firmly.

"We only have...," he paused and squinted at the clock. "Thirty hours to go before the New Year. But what does that matter? They're gonna fuckin' foal tonight!"

"Nope," Val replied matter of factly. "Maiden mares. They'll run late. You'll see. It'll be okay. Listen," she offered, "I'll do the night shift. You look all in. Go get some rest."

Joey staggered upstairs, stripped down to his thermals and slumped down on the bed. He stared up at the ceiling, besieged by doubts. Ever since he'd failed to get into vet school, life hadn't been an easy ride. As a veterinarian, he could have afforded a picture perfect horse farm. Instead, he'd had to settle for an old dairy farm with barbed wire fencing and a milking parlour with concrete floors. Yet he had stubbornly refused to give up on the dream: to make his living by breeding and raising youngsters, preparing them for the annual standardbred yearling sales. Without Val, it would have been a lonely business. He still couldn't quite believe that a city girl like Val, who was both brilliant and beautiful, had chosen him, a country boy from Western Ontario. They had met at university. With her looks and brains, Val could have married anyone she wanted. There were plenty of high fliers at uni who could talk the talk even if, in Joey's opinion, they couldn't tell their asses from their elbows. Val could have been living in a big house in the heart of Toronto, working as a dentist in a successful city practice. Instead, she was stuck on a farm only ten minutes from Iroquois Downs Raceway but over half an hour from Erinsville, spending her spare time helping out as an unpaid farmhand. Thankfully, her fledgling dental practice in the nearby village of Indian Falls was prospering. It was currently their only reliable source of income.

When Joey had eventually qualified as an accountant, he decided he hated the whole idea, especially after he'd gone for a few interviews. With his solid build, thick wavy brown hair, ruddy complexion and trusting expression, he didn't exactly fit the mould. Besides, he was far too busy on the farm to entertain a full time job. It had taken him a full year of hard labour to transform the former dairy farm into a suitable place for top quality broodmares like Heart of Darkness and Gold Digger. All the century home had needed was a coat of paint. But the solid concrete floors in the cowsheds had posed a much thornier problem. Joey knew most of the horsemen in the area, having spent countless summers working as a groom to pay his tuition. They were all in agreement: the concrete had to go. After getting a couple of quotes for the job, Joey had decided he would have to dig it out himself by hand using a power drill. He had calculated that he could finish the job in six months by working twelve hours a day. He had accepted that he would be deaf afterwards from all the noise, but he figured the lung trouble from the dust probably wouldn't show up until much later.

If it hadn't been for Val, he might still have been chipping away at it. She took charge and made a call to their local farm co-op. The non slip, interlocking rubber mats that now covered the entire barn had made them the envy of the horse racing community. There was a great deal to be thankful for, Joey concluded. He said a prayer to the patron saint of broodmares, whoever that might be, and promptly passed out.

6 a.m. The bedside clock always clicked just before the alarm went off. Joey was awake instantly, silencing it before it woke Val, who was sprawled out on top of him, breathing deeply. After he'd disentangled himself, he reached for the light switch and was greeted by a scribbled note, propped up on the bedside table.

NO FOALS YET THANK GOD!

STAYED UP TILL 4:30AM

DON'T WAKE ME!

Joey jumped out of bed. He pulled on a pair of well worn coveralls, grabbed a fleece and ran downstairs. His boots were sitting by the kitchen door. He didn't bother to fasten them. Rushing out into the darkness, he made a beeline for the foaling barn using the light shining from the roof top to guide him. It had been Val's idea to buy a couple of broodmares in foal "to give them a head start," as she'd put it. The pedigrees of Heart of Darkness and Gold Digger had looked good on paper. The farm that had bred them, Ferme Victoire, had an impeccable reputation. That reputation was now in doubt.

"Stud fee paid," the sales catalogue had stated. "In foal to Night Raider." Joey prayed he could hold Bernie Vachon to that promise, at least.

It was dark outside and freezing cold. His boots crunched on the newly fallen snow as he walked over to the barn, willing the two broodmares inside *not* to have given birth. He didn't want to see a new foal struggling to its feet. Not yet.

Just one more day, he prayed. Wait one more day. Please God if you exist, help me now. Don't let them be born on December 31st and ruin me. Tomorrow would be fine. I'd love them to arrive healthy tomorrow. They'd be early, sure, but they'd be legal. I wouldn't have to lie. I'd be able to call the vet.

Please God, don't make me lie, you wouldn't want that would you, God?

He flung open the barn door and stepped into the brightly lit barn. The two big-bellied mamas munching hay looked back at him calmly. He checked each one over carefully. There were no foals yet, but their udders were dripping with milk. It wouldn't, couldn't be long now.

"I'll never buy a broodmare in foal at a sale again, ever!" Joey swore to the mares. "How did this happen? Did you get out and get bred by a quarter horse or an appaloosa? Did I give my last dollar for the two of you to produce a Shetland, or a Shire horse? Who knows? But give me a sporting chance eh? Hang in there, ladies, please!" They were drowning in hay (Val always overdid it), so he topped up their water buckets and turned off the lights, before thinking better of it. "Stay alert," he told them switching the lights back on "Whatever you do, don't relax!"

Outside, dawn was breaking. A light dusting of snow covered the barn roof, like icing on a cake. Snowflakes clung to the tall silhouettes of trees planted decades earlier for shelter in winter and shade in summer. Joey loved this place! Ever since he and Val had bought it at a knock down price, it had given him something to feel proud of. He couldn't bear to think of losing it, after all his hard work. But financially, they were on a knife edge. Any setback could spell disaster. And disaster could be looming today. Back at the house, Val was in the kitchen making toast. Her long blond hair was tied back loosely from her face.

"You woke me," she said reproachfully. "I knew you would. You should feel guilty."

"You look terrific!" Joey replied, kicking off his boots. "No one would ever guess you'd been up half the night. We'd better call the vet." Val choked on her toast. "No foals," Joey said quickly. "No need to panic."

"Then why?" Val protested, taking a gulp of coffee.

"I want him to take a look at Heart of Darkness and Gold Digger."

"Oh! Can we risk that?"

"If he comes today, he'll be a witness. They were still in foal on December 31st."

"Why not get a copy of today's Toronto Sun, hold it in front of their bellies and take a picture like they do with hostages?" Val suggested.

"Will you call?" Joey persisted.

"Give me the phone," Val said. She knew the number off by heart. She'd memorized it in case they had trouble with a foaling. This was a different kind of crisis. "Dr. Winterflood?" she asked. ". . .How are you? Could you come out to Harmony Farm this morning? There are a couple of mares we need you to see…well, not exactly. You'll understand when you get here." She put the phone down. "He's on his way here right now. I caught him just as he was leaving for the day," she said, sounding pleased with herself, as well she might. It wasn't easy to reach Winterflood. Since he had given up his job as track vet, he'd been kept busy day and night. Horsemen had been quick to discover him and exploit his talents. "Make some more toast for me, Joey. Mine's gone cold," Val yawned. "If I didn't have so many patients today, I'd cancel and go right back to bed."

"Jesus! I forgot to pick up the feed!" Joey exclaimed, spooning sugar into his coffee.

"So call Reggie Blair. He'll bring it," Val said. She had a solution for everything, Joey thought, except for their present problem. They were in too deep even for her. "Wouldn't it be something if we had a foal born right at the start of the New Year," Val was saying dreamily. "It'd be the earliest in the whole of Ontario. They'd write about us in *Horseman's World*. The first baby of the year. It'd be great advertising." A white truck flashed past the kitchen window.

"He's here!" Joey said. "I gotta go!" He jumped into his boots and ran outside. The vet sometimes drove right out again if he wasn't there waiting for him. And Joey knew that Winterflood didn't recognize niceties like doorbells. He was a restless spirit, driving through his territory like the wind. Nothing escaped his sharp eyes and ears. He must have treated half the horses on the Iroquois Downs circuit, done business with good trainers and bad, yet Joey had never heard him pass judgment on any of them. The vet stayed in his truck until he saw Joey, then he wound his window down.

"What's up?" he asked, his jet black hair sticking out from the baseball cap he wore, bearing the logo *Beaver Creek*. The grey snow clouds had rolled away and the sun was shining in a pale blue sky. The light reflecting off the snow was dazzling. Long icicles hanging off the barn's eaves were dripping in a steady rhythm, but there were no birds. Even the Canada Geese were gone. It was a frozen world, empty of life except for the broodmares, who were clustered around the big round hay bales in the home paddock.

"What's up?" Winterflood repeated, getting out of his truck.

"Not too sure, chief," Joey replied. The vet raised his eyebrows.

"Come," Joey beckoned, sliding open the barn door. Winterflood hesitated, then took his doctor's bag with him and followed Joey in.

The light was dim after the brilliant sunshine outside. It was a good deal warmer too. The sweet smell of hay was in the air, bringing to mind summer days. Winterflood hardly made a sound as he walked through the barn, making Joey conscious of his own boots landing heavily on the floor. When he opened Gold Digger's stall door, Winterflood went inside, moving softly like a cat, his light feet making little impression on the straw.

"Hold her for me, Joey," he said. He put his hand on the mare's neck and stroked her, speaking to her sweetly. Joey had never heard any other vet talk to a horse like that. Gold Digger's ears flicked back and forth for a moment, then pointed forward. Her eyes glazed over and she leant her head on Joey's shoulder. Winterflood moved quietly around her, checking her over thoroughly, but gently. Then placing his stethoscope on her stomach, he listened intently. The whole exam took about five minutes. "Nothing wrong here, so far as I can see," Winterflood said reverting to his normal, happy go lucky manner. "Nice, strong, healthy foal, due any time now. First time for her?" Joey nodded. "She should be fine…A little early isn't it?" he asked, looking at Joey quizzically. The mare snorted and pulled away. Joey felt like he was exploding inside, but he didn't say a word. Instead, he concentrated on the business of unbuckling Gold Digger's halter. The truth was, he hadn't dared risk talking to anyone he knew about his problem with the mares. If word got out, it would be all round the racetrack in no time. That would only make things a whole lot worse. As for his parents, how could he possibly tell them? They had raised a mortgage on their own farm to give him the down payment for his. Winterflood walked over to Heart of Darkness who was pacing restlessly round her stall.

"I know this mare," the vet said, after looking her over. "Last time I saw her, she was out at Bernie Vachon's place." He frowned. "She's gonna drop her foal real soon. Could be any time now," he warned Joey, glancing at his watch as if to confirm the date. "Cutting things pretty close, aren't you?" Joey busied himself with closing the stall door. "So what's the scoop? D'you make megabucks at the sales if they're foaled this time of year?"

"Megabucks?" Joey blurted out, unable to keep it to himself any longer, "I'll get next to nothing for a foal born in December! The worst of it is, I don't even know for sure who the sire is! It could be a riding horse for all I know. They'd never breed Night Raider in January. It's a big mess and I'm stuck right in the middle of it!" He stared at Winterflood defiantly. Bet you weren't expecting that, he thought. He'd even surprised himself with his emotional outburst. The secret was out now. But if anything, he felt worse than before. Winterflood acted like he hadn't spoken. Terrific, Joey thought, I spill my heart out to this guy and what does he do? He shuts up like a clam! The vet was gazing into the middle distance, his eyes focused on nothing in particular.

"Great barn, this," he said. Something's up, Joey realized. The vet wasn't known for compliments or polite conversation. Joey dug his hands deeply into the pockets of his coveralls and waited.

"There's a wild story going round the track…" Winterflood revealed, then he shrugged. "Don't know whether it's true or not…" Please, Joey thought, let it be something good, just this one time.

"Theo Vettore may be involved…and Night Raider."

"Vettore?" Joey exclaimed, his mind doing a series of somersaults and failing to come to any sensible conclusions.

"Talented driver, Mr. Vettore," Winterflood said. He seemed reluctant to condemn him.

"Go on," Joey urged.

"They're saying Vettore got high one night last winter out at Bernie's farm," Winterflood revealed. This didn't sound good, Joey thought.

"They're saying he put Night Raider in the broodmare barn and let him do his thing for half the night," the vet continued. He paused. "Sure you want to hear this? It's only a story…told by a groom who was probably drunk at the time."

"The date," Joey croaked, "What was the date?"

"Oh, the date. Yeah." Winterflood grinned. "I guess you'd kinda wanna know that." Joey's neck and shoulders were so tense he felt like he was encased in steel. "How does January 20th sound?" Winterflood asked.

Joey did some rapid calculations. "Jesus! The foals were due five days ago!"

"You can't always believe everything you hear, especially where Crawfish Brown is concerned," Winterflood said.

"Crawfish!" Joey exclaimed, feeling like he'd fallen off a cliff. "That guy's a drunk, a total low life and a liar!"

"Probably did it himself." Winterflood replied dismissively. He left the barn and got into his truck. Joey followed him. After the warmth of the barn, the cold air struck him like a knife.

"That creep's been fired from every job he ever had," he said vehemently. All his outrage about the situation he found himself in was focused on

Crawfish now. "I'll bet he did it out of spite!" Winterflood had his invoice book out. He didn't seem interested in the subject anymore.

"Heart of Darkness and . . . what's the name of the other one?" he asked.

"Gold Digger. Did you ever treat either of them at the racetrack?"

"Gold Digger...no...Heart of Darkness..." Winterflood's eyes had a distant look, as though he was peering inside his head at a memory tape. "Coffin bone fracture, right front I think. Mercer was sick about it!"

"Well he ought to be used to that sort of thing," Joey said. "The year I worked for Mercer he had so many horses break down he had to let half of us go. I ended up working on the steel that summer. Damn near killed myself up there!" Winterflood was scribbling in his invoice book. It seemed to take a long time. Joey felt a stab of anxiety. He couldn't afford a big vet's bill at present. He tried to find a silver lining in the clouds. "Looks like they might be in foal to Night Raider after all," he said hopefully.

Winterflood nodded.

"Could well be," he said, snapping his invoice book shut. The misery and worry must have showed in Joey's face for the vet gave him a searching look. "Listen up," he said. "I reckon you can count yourself lucky."

"Lucky?" Joey exclaimed incredulously. "What's lucky about it?"

"I heard two foals have been born already...last week. One of them was out of a trotting mare."

"Who's the sire?" Joey wanted to know.

"What d'you think I am . . . a psychic?" the vet asked. Maybe he was, Joey thought. The image of an Indian Shaman popped into his head. It was easy to imagine Winterflood in that role, the way he stood so tall and erect, the dark eyes that seemed to look off into the distance, the almost mystical connection he had with animals...the way he somehow held himself apart from other people.

"Fuckin' hell! Why'd this have to happen to me?" Joey muttered. Winterflood started up the engine.

"Don't call me out again 'til after midnight!" the vet warned. "And don't forget. You can always open up a riding stable!"

Joey heard him laughing to himself as he drove away. Joey didn't find the joke remotely funny. He needed a foal sired by a riding horse like he needed a hole in the head. He knew why Winterflood didn't want to get involved if the foals came before midnight. He didn't want trouble with the Canadian Pacing and Trotting Association. Joey realized he might have to foal them himself. He took a deep breath. So! He'd do it! They hadn't let him into vet school, but he'd show them! He wasn't about to let a little thing like foaling a mare for the first time send him crying into a corner.

It was 10:30 p.m., the start of the night shift. Val had fallen asleep in mid sentence sitting bolt upright in her armchair. Joey intended to wake her up to see the New Year in, not that they had a lot to celebrate. He was perched on a hay bale outside Gold Digger's stall. She was restless now, a sure sign that she was about to foal, according to Dr. D Thomas, DVM. Val had bought the heavy volume *The Broodmare and Foal: Modern Methods Explained* six months ago in the Iroquois Down's gift shop. Joey wished he'd made time to read it earlier. But he was studying hard now. Section 12A was entitled "The normal birth" and began on page 263. It had taken the revered Dr. Thomas a great many pages to work himself up to the actual foaling process and it looked like it would take him a great many more to cover it fully and completely. Every now and then, Joey stole a glance at Gold Digger. He took a swig of black coffee from his steaming thermos. It was going to be a long, cold night.

Scats the barn cat, a fluffy multi coloured female who craved affection, cat food and mice in that order, climbed onto his lap and settled herself down. Purring loudly, she dug her claws into his knees. It was painful, but Joey put up with it cheerfully. It was a small price to pay for a little company. The stable clock moved slowly forward. Gold Digger looked back at her flanks more and more frequently. Heart of Darkness was standing quietly in the corner of her stall, head down. Outside, the wind howled. Snow was drifting in under the big barn doors. A low grinding sound was followed by a blast of cold air. Startled, Joey dropped Dr. Thomas' tome and jumped up. Scats hot footed it to the nearest stall, meowing in outrage. One of the barn doors had blown wide open and was swaying back and forth in the wind. When he got up close, Joey saw to his dismay that some of the nails had come out of the hinges. The door was hanging by a thread. The barn was getting colder by the second. He threw out his arms to steady it, but a strong gust wrenched the door from his grasp. He lost his balance and the door came crashing down on top of him.

When Joey came to he could hardly breathe. The barn door weighed heavily on his chest. He was trapped. "Jesus Christ!" he wheezed, trying in vain to push the door off him. "Help!" But there was no answer, only the howl of the wind. He kept calling for a long time, hoping Val would hear him. Then slowly and painfully, he dragged himself out, inch by inch, ripping his jacket and tearing his coveralls. He lay on the barn floor for several minutes, exhausted from the effort. The snow drifting onto his face brought him back to his senses. He leapt to his feet and with a huge effort, lifted the big heavy door and propped it up, praying it would stay put. He was numb with cold. Suddenly he clapped his hand to his forehead. The mares! He'd forgotten all about them! He stumbled over to the stalls.

Gold Digger's foal was lying in the yellow straw, its long legs tucked under its body, its head a little wobbly, but alive and apparently healthy. Gold Digger herself was alternately licking the foal's belly and nipping its legs to encourage it to get up. Confronted by the miracle of birth, Joey forgot about the time and the controversy over the sire, and opened the stall door. It was a mistake. Abruptly the peaceful scene changed. Gold Digger charged at him, her ears pinned back and her teeth barred. He ducked out of the way just in time to avoid having his head bitten off.

"Jesus!" Joey muttered, shaken by the near miss.

The foal, a big bay filly, rose to her feet. When Joey looked at his watch, the numbers were a blur. The side door banged and Val burst in.

"Why didn't you wake me? It's one o'clock in the morning!" she cried. She stopped short. "Are you okay?" Then she saw the foal and hugged Joey, her eyes shining with excitement.

"Oh my God! We did it!" she said jumping up and down, hanging onto him.

"Ouch!" Joey shouted, "That hurts!"

"What happened?" Val asked, touching his forehead gently with her finger tips. Joey told her. "You need ice for that. Stay here, I'll be right back," she said.

Joey sat down on a hay bale and held his head in his hands. He found himself staring down at Dr. Thomas' textbook, which had fallen open at "Abnormal births". It was a sign! It was up to him to see that both mares foaled safely. When Val returned, he brushed aside her efforts at first aid.

"Heart of Darkness!" he said hoarsely. "Go and check. Now!" Val returned, white faced.

"She doesn't look good at all. She's drenched in sweat and breathing hard. That's not normal, right?"

"Call Winterflood. Quick!" Joey gasped. "In my pocket," he added, pointing to the cell phone he'd purchased for emergencies.

"There's no answer," Val reported a minute later. "I'll have to leave a message. . . This is Val Harris," she said. "We've got a mare in trouble. We need help right away." She rang off, looking scared. "What do we do now?" she asked.

"We better have a look at her," Joey said, forcing himself to his feet. Heart of Darkness came right up to Val. She even allowed Joey to check her over.

"Nothing showing yet," Joey said. "We'd best keep her moving." It was all he could think of doing. At least it might slow things down a bit. The mare was plainly in distress. Her trust in the two humans was touching. "Try Winterflood again," Joey suggested. There was still no answer but a few minutes later they heard the screech of tires outside the barn. It was the sweetest sound in the world! Val opened the side door and Winterflood came marching in.

"Where is she?" he asked immediately. Joey pointed wordlessly to Heart of Darkness' stall.

"What on earth happened to you?" Winterflood asked as he walked past Joey. But he didn't wait for an answer. He pulled on a long plastic glove and lubricated it. "Hold her head, Val," he said. "I'm going to try to see what the problem is. She won't like this." There was silence as Winterflood got to work. Heart of Darkness leaned hard on Val's shoulder, but otherwise did not react. "Good girl," Winterflood whispered to her. "Now let's see. Yes! I thought as much. This is it! Hold on tight, Val!" The mare groaned. She swayed back and forth. Winterflood was sweating from the effort, despite the cold.

"I can't hold her," Val cried "She's going down!"

"Let her go!" Winterflood called out. "Get out of the way!" Heart of Darkness sank down on the straw. Val looked terrified. Joey was watching, his head over the stall door.

"What's going on?" he demanded.

"Foal had one leg too far forward," Winterflood replied. "Think I've fixed it...had to push it back inside!"

"She's stopped panting," Val said anxiously. "Is she going to be okay?"

"Let's hope so," Winterflood replied earnestly. A tiny hoof appeared, followed immediately by a second one. A mucus covered muzzle came next, then a delicate head. Heart of Darkness looked back at Winterflood. The expression in her eyes said it all. Do something! she was pleading mutely. Winterflood took a hold of the foal, braced himself and waited. The next time Heart of Darkness pushed, he pulled. The shoulders emerged. At the next push, the foal slipped out onto the straw.

A cheer went up from the three onlookers, joined by a fourth. Scotty McCoy had appeared out of nowhere. He lurched over to Heart of Darkness' stall and tried to barrel his way in, hurling his stocky body through the door like a missile.

"Get him outa here!" Winterflood snapped.

"Let me at 'er," Scotty insisted. "I'm as good as any vet!" It was an idiotic comment, yet it resonated with Joey. If only I'd got into vet school, he thought, I would have been doing this. But regrets were a luxury he couldn't afford, he decided, counting his blessings.

After a while, Heart of Darkness got to her feet. She looked astonished when she saw her foal and backed away.

"Got any clean towels?" Winterflood asked.

"In that cardboard box," Val said, "by the first stall." Before Joey could stop him, Scotty had staggered over and grabbed a stack of them. Most of them ended up on the barn floor. "Where'd he come from?" Val whispered to the vet as they worked on the foal.

"McCoy? Dunno. I found him in my truck fast asleep. Couldn't budge him! Must've wandered over from the party I suppose. You got a nice little colt here, Joey..."

"He's got a star on his forehead! Just like his mother!" Val exclaimed.

"Let's hope he's a standardbred," Joey prayed. He felt so exhausted, he was having trouble staying upright. Scotty McCoy had already succumbed. He was lying on the floor, leaning up against a hay bale.

"What party?" Val asked.

"Yeah, the one across the road from my place. Helluva noise they were making!"

"They didn't invite you?"

"I don't go to parties," Winterflood replied. Silence fell while they all waited for the foal to get up. After a while, Joey realized the colt wasn't going to stand on his own so quick. His mother was no help at all. She had retreated to one corner of the stall, looking extremely nervous. "Got a baby bottle?" Winterflood asked of no one in particular. Scotty McCoy heard the word *bottle* and jerked back to life.

"Give it here! Gimme!" he called out. He was ignored by everyone. Joey limped over to the big box marked foaling supplies. There were several bottles sealed in clear plastic. "We've got iodine, too," he called out.

"I'll get to that later. Let's get him drinking first. I'll need someone to hold the mare. Just gonna go and wash up." A few minutes later Winterflood had filled a bottle with the mare's milk, which contained the all important colostrum. "This'll do the trick." he said. "C'mon little guy." He held up the delicate head and thrust the bottle into the foal's mouth. Though tentative at first, the colt quickly got the hang of it. Soon the bottle was empty. "Yeah, there you go little fella!" Winterflood said, his angular features softened by a broad smile. After a couple of false starts, the colt finally got on his feet and stood on shaky legs, his eyes unfocused. His mother uttered a low whicker, as though she finally understood what this was all about. She walked over and stood protectively beside him, nudging him with her nose. He promptly fell over but was soon on his feet again, trawling her body as the instinct to nurse took over. The bonding process had begun.

"Happy New Year!" Winterflood exclaimed.

"Happy New Year!" Scotty McCoy repeated, slurring the words. He promptly fell back on his hay bale and passed out again.

"I'll take that iodine now," Winterflood said, gesturing at the foal. He daubed the umbilical cord and was on his way out when he spotted Gold Digger, whose filly was suckling vigorously. "Did you get to this one yet?" he asked, gesturing with the iodine bottle.

"Nope!" Joey replied. "But the mare got to me, nearly took my face off!"

"She really did the job on you!" Winterflood declared, backing away from the mare's stall. Joey didn't feel like going into the saga of the broken door. He let Gold Digger take the rap.

"She'll be fine with me," Val assured him.

"Well I'm all done here," the vet said, no doubt wanting to go home and get some sleep.

"Thanks for everything, Doc," Joey mumbled. The night's events were catching up with him. He joined Scotty on the hay bale. He quickly realized that Winterflood hadn't left after all. Apparently, Val wanted him to stay.

"I just need you to check him over in case there's anything broken," she was pleading.

"I'm not a doctor," the vet replied crossly.

"The barn door fell on top of him. He's had a really rough night," she said. To his astonishment, Joey realized they were talking about him.

"Then take him to ER! He could have internal injuries, concussion or anything," the vet countered.

"He's not gonna go!" There was a note of desperation in Val's voice now. "He hates hospitals. It's you or nothing!"

Beside him on the hay bale, Scotty McCoy was singing in his sleep. It was hard for Joey to tell what exactly he was singing, because Scotty was snoring so loudly, but it sounded a lot like "O Canada!", the national anthem played before every major sporting event, including the races, though not generally after a foaling.

"Hey!" Joey exclaimed, giving Scotty a poke in the ribs. "Wake the fuck up!"

Scotty sat bolt upright and opened his eyes. "What'd you do that for?" he complained loudly. "And when's this friggin' hockey game gonna start?" Joey burst out laughing. Val cheered and even Winterflood cracked a smile.

"Better get some coffee brewing for him, Val," the vet said. "Make it good and strong! Okay Joey…your turn now." His hands were surprisingly gentle. "Looks like he'll live," he told Val. "Nothing broken at any rate. Keep him warm and keep him awake. Take him to the clinic in the morning."

"Forget it! I'm not going to any clinic!" Joey declared.

"Thank God I'm a horse doctor." the vet replied fervently. "Let's get you home McCoy." Scotty jumped to his feet. The barn door wobbled alarmingly as Winterflood passed by it on his way out.

"Look out!" Joey yelled. Scotty hurled himself at the door and stood spread eagled against it. As it rocked back and forth, he eyed the big hinges that were hanging loose.

"Could a killed someone!" Scotty exclaimed.

"Damn near killed me." Joey said.

"I'll fix that," Scotty offered. "Where's your hammer at?" Despite his dishevelled appearance, McCoy looked as fresh as a daisy, as though he'd had a perfect night's rest. It was 2:30 a.m.

"G'night folks!" Winterflood said, slipping through the side door. "Have a good one!"

"I can watch the horses after I finish this," Scotty called out, halfway up a ladder already. Heart of Darkness was standing guard over her foal, who was curled up fast asleep in the far corner of the stall. From the expression on Val's face, Joey guessed that Scotty's offer of help with the mares was an alarming prospect. "Or I c'n stay with Joey over at the house. Don't make a bit o' difference to me," Scotty added. He had a big screw sticking out of his mouth.

"It's a tough call for her," Joey said, cracking a smile. "Me or the horses!"

"I'm sober now, Mrs. Harris," McCoy protested getting down off the ladder. "Could I have fixed that door otherwise?"

"You can fix anything, drunk or sober," Joey declared, crushingly. "I can never tell the difference and I've known you...what? Seven, eight years?"

"If you can keep an eye on the horses, that'd be great," Val said, making her choice. "I'll bring you over some coffee later." She took Joey's arm and they walked over to the house. The stars were faint points of light in the dark sky. A pale moon bathed the scene in an eerie light. The silence was broken only by their feet slipping along the icy path. "That was the most beautiful thing I've ever seen in my whole life," she said. "Watching that colt being born! I'll never forget it...I'll never forget the whole thing."

"Neither will I!" Joey said. "It's not every night I get half killed! I didn't even get to help foal them."

"So what?" Val asked. "We have two live foals, born January first. Let's celebrate!"

The farmhouse kitchen was snug and warm. Sleep! That's what he needed, Joey thought longingly. He lay back on the chair and closed his eyes.

"Coffee!" Val shouted in his ear.

"Go away! Leave me alone," he muttered. When he opened them again, she was standing over him with two pills in one hand and a mug of steaming coffee in the other.

"Swallow these." she said, wrapping him up in a blanket, which made him feel like an invalid. But the coffee was strong and sweet.

"You're looking a lot better," Val commented a few minutes later.

"I'd feel a whole lot better if I knew for sure Night Raider was the sire."

"Trust me, he is!" Val said with certainty. Joey knew better than to question her intuition. She was invariably right. "You know what the best thing is," she said.

"No," Joey answered, hoping she was going to say something really nice about what he'd gone through tonight, something sympathetic.

"The best thing is Winterflood was there and his reputation is impeccable. They won't challenge the date of foaling now."

"Couldn't you stop being a business woman for one minute and..." he searched for the right words, "give me some attention for a change?"

"Oh...sorry! I forgot something...sir!" she replied sounding exasperated. "Let's see...er...coffee...pills...ice pack." She was counting them off on her fingers. "Not enough attention, huh? She never said "huh" unless she was truly outraged. Joey decided to stand his ground. No good could come of backing down now.

"I don't want a waitress and I certainly don't need a nurse!" he said getting up and kicking the blanket off him. There were shadows under her eyes and straw in her tousled hair. She smelled of coffee, lemon dishwashing liquid and horses. He put his arms around her. "You look beautiful," he said.

"I'm a mess," she replied, turning away.

"Let's go up to bed!" he coaxed. "I want to get close to you. . . hold you."

"I don't feel like it," she said sullenly.

"I swear I'll stay awake," Joey promised.

"No you won't."

"I will…come on."

"What about Scotty's coffee?" she asked, but he could tell her heart wasn't in it.

"To hell with McCoy. He can wait the whole night for all I care!" Joey replied.

Val laughed, a tinkling laugh that gradually filled the room. Her eyes regained a little of their sparkle and the colour returned to her face. Tension was escaping her like steam out of a kettle.

Half an hour later they were both sound asleep.

Jay Winterflood was speeding down the empty road. When he reached home, the house was dark. He let himself in and crept up the stairs. But Helena was not in the big bed. Their son was sleeping so soundly, he didn't even stir when Jay flicked on the light. There was no note, no sign of her. Helena was gone. He ran outside and called her, his breath freezing in the clear air. He took the path down to the pond, her footprints in the snow leading him on.

She was skating by the light of the moon, dancing and twirling, her long dark hair flowing this way and that as she moved. He walked out onto the frozen pond and waited until she was so close he could hear the rasp of her skates on the ice. Then he held out his arms. She came in and he felt her warm breath on his face. As she kissed him, he vowed to himself he'd turn off his phone, wear a disguise, disable the doorbell, post keep off signs on the house, anything to spend the next twenty-four hours with this woman, who he loved better than life itself.

Val woke with a start. It was 4 a.m. Will this night never end? she wondered. She shook Joey till his eyes opened, then she raced over to the barn. To her relief Scotty McCoy was still there, still wide awake.

"Everything's shipshape here," he said. "Both foals are okay. I fed the cat. Friendly little thing isn't it?"

"Thanks!" Val said. "I'll take a turn here. You get some sleep. Go over to the house...I'm sorry I never brought you the coffee."

"Oh I found the coffee alright," Scotty said cheerfully pointing to Joey's old flask.

"But it was stone cold, wasn't it?" Val asked.

"Was it? I never noticed," he replied with a grin. "Plenty of sugar. Just how I like it."

"Scotty," Val said. "You're terrific." His face clouded over.

"Tell that to my wife," he said. "She don't think so! You know what? That coffee did the trick. I don't feel a bit sleepy. I reckon I'll go over to the house and give Joey a hard time."

He left, slamming the door behind him.

Finally, Val was alone with the horses. She went back and forth from one stall to the other, trying to decide which foal she liked best, the strong filly or the fragile colt, both staring wide eyed at her. The mares had a new soft look in their eyes. Motherhood suited them. It was quiet in the barn. Only the rustling of hay and straw broke the silence. The minute she sat down, Scats jumped on her lap and began to purr. This was better, far better than filling cavities in people's teeth, Val decided. It was heaven on earth!

Crawfish Brown's idea of heaven was simple: a roof over his head and a steady job. He had found both on the backstretch of Iroquois Downs Raceway working for Andy Price. He was currently looking for a safe place to park his wheels until spring. Riding his bike on the ice wasn't part of Crawfish's plan. He'd bought an insulated jacket on sale at Z Mart, where the lowest price was the law. He intended making it through this winter without getting sick or wrecked up. He reckoned his chances were about fifty-fifty. Last year he'd ended up in Erinsville General with a case of pneumonia. The food there was even worse than the track canteen. They didn't allow beer or plug tobacco. No wonder people kicked the bucket in there! He was keeping himself in shape with shots of equipoise. It'd worked wonders for him. Of course, it was meant for horses, but Crawfish wasn't proud. If it was good enough for a racehorse worth millions, it was good enough for him!

Dr. Jay Winterflood DVM wedged the thick comforter he had bought from Sears into the narrow back seat of his truck. Once a year, he returned to the Quebec Reserve bringing gifts he hoped would please his Cree mother. The bed of the truck was groaning under the weight of the logs he had stacked there for the stove she kept burning day and night. She was a proud woman, secretive too, never revealing the truth about the man who was his father. He didn't have a picture of him or even a name. He only knew he was a white man. With so little to go on, he had resigned himself to the fact that the mystery was never going to be solved. His mother called him by his tribal name, Blue Jay. Outside the confines of the Reserve, Winterflood had discovered that Jay raised fewer eyebrows.

The weather bulletins on the radio were warning of dangerous driving conditions on the back of strong north westerly winds. Winterflood remembered he had meant to get the defroster checked before he left, but it seemed to be working again anyway. He had left Helena and their young son behind. This was a trip he always made alone.

THE WRITING ON THE WALL

Nearly eighteen months after TCO2 testing had been introduced at Iroquois Downs, Al McTavish was shaken out of his complacency by a series of horse deaths, several of which occurred within the space of a single week. The autopsy reports arrived at his office on the fourth floor of the Grandstand by special delivery, promptly at 9 a.m. (Necropsy not autopsy, Al amended mentally, anxious to use the correct term at the next management meeting.) He put off dealing with the small, dispiriting pile of post mortems sitting on his desk for as long as he could. But by mid morning he had run out of excuses.

The first two were heart rending. A three year old filly making her debut at Iroquois Downs had shattered her hock during the race and had had to be destroyed. An apparently healthy six year old stakes champion had collapsed and died in the Race Barn. The necropsy had revealed a ruptured aortic aneurysm, which Al understood to mean he had bled to death internally. However, he took some comfort from the fact that both tragedies appeared to be part and parcel of the risks of racing. Neither seemed to have been caused by illegal drugs or excess baking soda.

He approached the remaining two reports with less trepidation. An hour later having read them both thoroughly, he was baffled as to why the pair had died. Though they were of different ages and sexes (one was a seven year old mare, the other a four year old stud colt) the two reports appeared identical. Try as he might, Al couldn't make any sense of it. It was time to call in an expert. The only expert Al knew was Dr. Jay Winterflood. When Winterflood, picked up, Al could hear horses neighing in the background.

"I'll be over at Rivers Training centre in half an hour, Bob Summers' barn," Winterflood said abruptly, before ringing off. Al sighed. The last thing he needed now was a long drive on icebound roads. He was bleary eyed from lack of sleep because Sofia had taken to switching the bedside lamp on and off during the night. It drove him crazy but he knew complaining about it would get him nowhere.

To his relief, the mercury had risen since the early morning and the roads were now clearing. The fields were still covered in snow which was sparkling in the hazy sunlight, a sight to raise anyone's spirits. But as he drove, Al bemoaned the fact that after over eighteen months on the job, he still knew virtually nothing about what was going on behind the scenes, drugs wise, at Iroquois Downs. The idea of any trainer confiding in him was laughable. The only trainers he knew were the two horsemen's reps: Bob Summers, who wasn't a bad sort and Jim Mercer, who was a pain in the neck.

To Al's surprise, Bob Summers welcomed him like a long lost relative.

"Just the man I wanted to see," Bob grinned, barely recognizable in a thick winter driving suit and a black balaclava.

"Going to rob a bank?" Al joked.

"Come on in," Bob chuckled, peeling off the disguise. He ushered Al into the barn and shut the door tight.

"Mercer's got a nice filly for sale. Just turned three. He's not asking a lot for her. Know anyone with fifteen thousand dollars to spare?"

Al shook his head.

"He's running her into the ground," Bob confided. "Thin as a rail. Trains her a double-header every day."

"Oh," Al said.

"Well think about it, eh," Bob said, dropping the sales pitch. He took Al on a tour of the barn and introduced him to the horses, who were a friendly bunch.

Winterflood still hadn't shown up.

"I better get on," Bob said. "I'm on my own today. Wife had to go home early." Al made sympathetic noises and glanced nervously at the clock on the wall. He was going to be late for lunch. Sofia wouldn't be happy about it.

Bob had a horse harnessed and ready to go in five minutes flat.

"Tell Winterflood I'll catch him another time," Al said, deciding he couldn't wait any longer.

"Good enough," Bob replied cheerily, swinging himself onto the jog cart. Al stepped out of the barn but immediately leapt back inside. A white truck sped past, narrowly avoiding him. He heard a squeal of brakes and caught a glimpse of someone jumping out.

"What are you trying to do, kill me?" Al shouted. "Oh it's you," he added in a more conciliatory tone, hoping Winterflood would be able to shed some light on the medical speak that had so far defeated him.

"Beautiful day," Winterflood commented, pushing past Al and disappearing into Bob Summers' tack room. Al crossed the wet tarmac and retrieved the reports from the back seat of his car. When he got back inside the vet was examining a set of X-rays.

"What's up?" Winterflood asked, holding one of the negatives up to the light and squinting at it.

"Need your help deciphering these autopsy reports," Al replied earnestly, gesturing at the papers he'd brought in.

"What d'you wanna know?" Winterflood said distractedly.

"I can't figure out why these horses died," Al confessed.

"Why come to me?" the vet asked, still staring at the X-rays

"I could always call the clinic, I suppose," Al said unhappily.

"The clinic!" Winterflood exclaimed, showing some interest at last. "You think those clowns are gonna tell you why those horses died?"

"They got paid enough for the job!" Al replied.

"Oh they'll tell you *how* they died," Winterflood said contemptuously.

"I don't even know that yet," Al confessed.

"Gimme those reports," Winterflood said, an expression of resignation on his face. He sat down on a rickety chair and began to read. Al opted for a faded blue sofa, supported by concrete blocks instead of legs and waited. Bob's driving suits were swinging from a rack on the wall, looking like a set of invisible men. Above them half a dozen old helmets jostled together like drunks at a bar. Winterflood made short work of the job.

"Putting it in layman's terms," the vet said, "organ failure."

"What? Both of them?" Al asked, astonished. "But why?"

"The report doesn't list a specific reason. You have to read between the lines for that." Al frowned. Trawling through medical reports was tough enough without having to read between the lines. "I thought you wanted the truth." Winterflood said, misunderstanding Al's silence. "But if you're going to accept the sanitized version, you won't need me." He didn't sound annoyed. He simply wasn't interested anymore. Before Al could respond, the door flew open and Bob Summers waddled in, covered in mud.

"Track's breakin' up. It's like quicksand out there," he declared throwing his gloves on the table and peeling off his goggles. "You still here?" he shot at Al.

"You bet," Al replied. He realized the vet was eyeing the exit. "Doctor Winterflood has something to tell me..." he added meaningfully.

"I'll get out of your way," Bob offered.

"I want you to hear this!" Al insisted. "You're the horsemen's rep."

"Let me get outa these first," Bob replied, kicking the door shut and unzipping his suit. Winterflood sat down again, tapping his fingers impatiently on the table. Rain was drumming on the roof. All we need now is a piano and we'd have a three-piece band, Al thought, but he kept it to himself. The vet was clearly in no mood for jokes. Eventually, Bob emerged clad in jeans and a sweatshirt. The empty mud splattered suit had joined its fellows on the rack.

"Shoot." Bob said, settling himself down beside Al on the sofa. When Al put him in the picture, Bob jumped up. "I knew it!" he exclaimed, pulling a clump of mud out of his ear. "You tell 'im Doc. Tell 'im about the bleach those guys are using."

"Bleach!" Al echoed, turning to Winterflood. A spasm of pain crossed the vet's face.

"Bleach has a devastating effect on the system," Winterflood explained. "Beyond a certain point there's no possibility of recovery.

"Why bleach?" Al asked feeling horrified. He could tell Winterflood felt the same way. "Are you certain?" Al added.

"A little black filly come by here last week, white spots all over her," Bob said dolefully. "She must'a tried to pull away...while they were dosing her with bleach, see."

Winterflood looked like he wanted to fall through the floor.

"Don't blame yourself," Al said.

"No?" Winterflood replied. "Looks to me like that paper I wrote just made things a whole lot worse!"

"No!" Al said firmly. "You're certain, right?" he added, knowing it was futile, but wanting to be sure.

Winterflood picked up the reports and flicked through them. Suddenly he threw them down as if they were red hot. "It's all in there. But the real question is, what can you do about it?" he said.

"Kill 'em," Bob said, punching the air. "Force bleach down their own fuckin' throats, the cheatin' bastards!"

"It's not that simple, Bob," Al pointed out. "Those horses were claimers. They were passed around to so many different trainers, it's going to be pretty tough proving who was responsible!"

"It'll be impossible!" Winterflood agreed.

"I bet I know who did it," Bob said darkly.

"We can speculate all we want, Bob. But we have to have proof," Al replied kindly. The man's heart was in the right place. If he ever did own a horse, he'd have no qualms giving it to Bob to train, he decided.

"You still need me?" Winterflood asked, his eyes apparently focused on some distant planet.

"Just how do we put a stop to it?" Al wondered, wishing Winterflood had a slightly longer attention span.

"Put 'em all in jail!" Bob stated emphatically. "All o' them claiming guys."

Al understood where Bob was coming from, but he had some pretty wild ideas. To his surprise Winterflood got on board.

"Bob's got a point," he said. "Holding them in a retention barn for twenty-four hours before they raced…it could work."

"The horses, not the trainers, right?" Al asked, wanting to be clear about it.

"Even better," Winterflood replied into a bitter laugh.

"They're doin' it down in Jersey," Bob said sticking stubbornly to the point. "Why not here?"

"A retention barn," Al remarked thoughtfully. "What exactly would that accomplish?"

"Plenty!" Bob exclaimed. "Those claimin' guys give the horses all kinds of stuff on race day!"

"So you really think a twenty-four-hour retention could be the answer?" Al asked, catching on.

"You know," Bob said, scratching his head thoughtfully, "there wasn't a thing wrong with a bit o' baking soda. I wish we could go back to them days."

"Turn back the clock, you mean?" Al said gently. "No one can do that," he added a little mournfully. Silence fell, each man absorbed in his own private regrets about the baking soda question. Finally, Bob Summers spoke up.

"You guys all done here?" he asked "'Cos what I wanna know is if that ankle's healed on the filly yet. How about it, Doc?"

"I'll leave you to it!" Al said, making himself scarce. On his way out, he saw a man in orange coveralls making a bee line for Bob's tack room.

"You in there, Doc?" he heard the man shout. The door opened. "I need a new jug hose. You got one on you? Mine's busted. I could use a few needles too." Al sighed. Despite all his efforts, despite the rules and regulations forbidding it, horsemen were carelessly sticking needles into horses every day of the week and he was powerless to stop it. Unfortunately, because of the laws governing private property, training centres couldn't be searched without a warrant.

Perhaps a retention barn would turn out to be nothing more than window dressing, like sticking a band aid on a fatal wound, Al thought. It would also penalize innocent trainers along with the guilty. But look at it this way, he reasoned, if it saves even a few horses' lives it will be worth doing. Right there and then he decided, come what may, to make the retention barn happen. What alternative did he have? Cleaning up racing was turning out to be a nightmare. Did Phil have any idea what he had let him in for when he had urged him to take on the job as Director of Iroquois Downs? he wondered.

It was snowing again. Al had one aim now: to get home and put his feet up. If he hurried he could steal a quick nap after lunch, providing lunch was still on offer. With Sofia these days, he could never tell.

After a fitful night, filled with bad dreams, Al woke up before dawn. His wife was brandishing a snow shovel. It was only 5:30 a.m.

"Alastair! You must get up now!" Sofia insisted. "There is too much snow! The Canada postman, he will not be able to bring our mail!" As soon as he'd finished clearing the snow off the path to the front door, before he'd even had a chance to warm up, she thrust a load of garbage at him.

"As you are already outside," she explained.

"I wouldn't be out if it wasn't for you!" he snapped.

"I am too cold to argue with you about this, Alastair," she replied, slamming the door shut.

Since Al had handed over the management of McTavish Construction to his daughter Billie, his wife seemed to think of him as her personal slave, available at any time of the day or night for a whole range of humiliating household tasks. He was wearing thick gloves but even so, his hands were clumsy from the cold. He struggled with the garbage can lid, cursing Sofia's zeal. As he hurried back to the house, he slipped on the icy path and fell headlong into the snow. Good luck to the mail man, he thought grimly as he picked himself up and tried vainly to brush off the ice plastered to his coat. When he reached the front door, he discovered to his dismay that it was locked. He pounded on the window but Sofia was nowhere to be seen.

When he eventually got back inside he retreated to the bathroom, bolted the door and immediately came up against Walter, the Maine Coon cat, who had stationed himself on top of the bathroom cabinet, his tail twitching, his eyes smouldering. Trying his best to ignore the cat, Al picked up his razor and prepared to shave. After a while the warmth and the fragrance of the shaving foam began to ease the unpleasant start to his day, until that is, he picked up a towel to dry his face and got a mouthful of cat fur.

"Damn you, Walter!" he hissed, spitting the hairs into the sink, keeping his voice low in case Sofia was listening at the door. Getting ready in the morning was always a challenge when Walter was in the house. Today the cat's antics were a welcome relief, not only from his marital troubles, but from the thorny question of Iroquois Downs. Though he'd acted in good faith by introducing TCO2 testing, the fact that things were even worse now for the horses weighed heavily on his conscience. He sighed and began brushing his teeth, watched avidly by Walter, who was moving his head in time to the toothbrush, like a spectator at a tennis match. Suddenly the cat reached out a paw and swatted Al's nose.

"Quit it, Walter!" Al exclaimed. He grabbed a comb and raked it through his thinning hair, bending down and peering into the mirror. His height had given him an edge playing centre on the college basketball team, but that was long ago. What with the steam and Walter's tail hanging down over it swishing angrily back and forth, looking in the mirror was quite a challenge. Walter wanted to go out, more than anything in the world! But Al knew that if he opened the window even a crack, the cat would squeeze through it, climb down the drainpipe and be scampering along the snow covered street in five seconds flat. Al was on Walter's side. It was natural for a cat to want freedom. But Sofia had decided the cold would kill him. There was no sense arguing about it.

Al understood that the menopause was a difficult time for a woman, but it wasn't much fun for him, either. Lately, Sofia was acting like an entirely different person. Wearily he cleared a spot on the mirror with the back of his hand. The face that stared back at him was unremarkable except for his eyes, which this morning burned with intelligence and passion. Winterflood had given him a wakeup call. Now that he understood what he was up against, he was determined to use his position as Director to push for a retention barn at Iroquois Downs. And that was just for starters. He was done with pussyfooting around. He had less than a week to come up with a detailed plan to present at the next management meeting.

With so little time left, he would need help. There was only one person he could depend on for that: his daughter Billie. If he hurried, he could catch her at Tangoes Coffee Bar. She stopped for her breakfast there most weekday mornings. Thanks to Sofia he'd had an early start.

"I'm going out!" he called to his wife. There was no reply. The house was spotlessly clean. He slunk out of the side door like a thief, in an attempt to foil Walter's escape plan then coasted out of the garage, honking his horn forlornly in farewell. Walter was sitting on the windowsill staring out at him, his eyes as wide as saucers. Sofia joined the cat at the window. Al thought for a moment that she was waving at him. Then he realized she was only cleaning the glass. It was not a great sign.

Tangoes Coffee Bar was humming. Tantalizing aromas of cappuccino and hot chocolate wafted past Al as he threaded his way through the crowded tables. The place was a haven for office workers seeking a little early morning fun. Waiters bustled to and fro. Outside, an orange sun peeked out between the high rise buildings, playing on the early morning traffic and the snow piled high on the pavement.

Billie was in her usual spot by the window, deep in conversation with someone. She was leaning forward, her face half hidden by her hair which he was relieved to see was still long and curly. Apparently she hadn't carried out her threat of cutting and straightening it yet. Her companion, Jeff Lamare, appeared to be doing all the talking. Al was fearful that Jeff was trying to poach her, offering her some free wheeling opportunity in his dot com business, with a salary up in the stratosphere. With the current crisis at Iroquois Downs, he desperately needed Billie to stay right where she was for now, running McTavish Construction with her usual combination of efficiency and flair. By the time he reached their table, any worries he might have had were quickly dispelled. He hung back just long enough to catch Billie's response.

"I told you! Lazer's a chemist!" she admonished Jeff.

"He's successful!" Jeff retorted. "If I'm gonna buy a racehorse, I want it to win! I'm not interested in finishing last, Billie."

"Is that really all you can think of to do with your millions?" Billie snapped. "Join forces with a druggist, Jeffrey!" Her voice rang out, over the buzz and conversation. In the uneasy silence that followed, Al cleared his throat noisily. "Dad!" Billie exclaimed, switching gears and greeting her father with a warm smile.

"I don't want to interrupt anything," Al assured her hastily, while inwardly cheering her curt dismissal of Jeff's plan.

"Jeff was just leaving. Sit!" Billie commanded, patting the seat next to her. "I'll call you later," she told Jeff as he slunk off looking crestfallen. He reminded Al of Walter when Sofia had reprimanded the cat for jumping up on the kitchen counter. But Walter, he reminded himself, was an innocent. Al sat down heavily, rocking the table.

"I'll have a glazed doughnut and a cup of coffee, black, no sugar," he told the slim waiter with frizzy brown hair who rushed up enthusiastically in response to his summons. The incident with the garbage felt like it had taken place on another planet.

"This is so nice!" Billie said, leaning over and hugging him. "You haven't been in all week. I've missed you. What have you been up to?" Al didn't feel like answering. Mercifully his order arrived quickly. He demolished the doughnuts, feeling his strength returning. "Did you lose weight or something, Dad?" Billie enquired. "What's going on?"

"Your mother woke me at daybreak," Al replied bitterly. "To take out the garbage."

Billie laughed. "Sounds like Mom!"

"She's driving me crazy!"

"You've got to do something about it, Dad."

"Give it up! She won't go on HRT."

"I could ask Jeff about it," Billie suggested. "He's into all this health stuff." So now Jeff Lamare was going to get involved with his wife's troubles too, Al thought.

"Oh I don't want to bother him with something like this," he replied unhappily.

"It wouldn't be a bother. He'd be happy to do it."

"He didn't look so happy just now!" Al said, finally alluding to Billie's outburst. She laughed.

"He'll get over it," she replied confidently.

"Your mother thinks he'd be quite a catch," Al said, voicing his deepest fears. The thought of having Jeff Lamare as a son in law sent shudders through his soul. It didn't surprise him that Jeff was thinking of throwing in his lot with Keith Lazer, a trainer who was winning so many races he was bound to be giving his horses something illegal.

"Jeff?" Billie laughed. "Mom's crazy if she thinks that! Jeff is a friend, nothing more. Unfortunately, I'm not sure he feels the same way about me!" She frowned. "I'd need someone a lot less comfortable with the status quo than Jeff, someone who questions things, you know?" A rebel? Al thought nervously. Was he going to have a revolutionary in the family? Help! He didn't dare ask if she had anyone particular in mind. "Don't worry, Dad. I'm not going to stay single forever. It's just that I'm not willing to waste my time. Everything has to be right. You got a problem with that?"

"Can't argue with you there," he said wishing his own life wasn't so fraught.

It was an unfortunate fact of life he reflected, that relationships changed with the passing of time. He and Sofia had had that special something once.

"What's wrong, Dad?" Billie asked again, staring at him. Al realized he was holding his empty coffee cup in a vice-like grip, as though if he let go of it, his whole life would fall apart. "It's just that…you look pretty unhappy," she added uncertainly.

"You want to know what's bothering me? I'll tell you!" he said, pleased to see that Billie was giving him her full attention now. If she was going to be able to help, she had to understand how things were. "You know lately, I've been half wishing I'd stayed right away from Iroquois Downs Raceway," he confessed, choosing his words with care. The intensity of Billie's gaze was achingly familiar. How was it he wondered for the thousandth time, that she resembled him so much but was so beautiful? The idle chatter at the next door table wafted across: ordinary people starting an ordinary day. Sometimes he wished his own life could be more like that, but no one's life was perfect, he told himself. He looked down at his empty plate and dropped his voice. "Things are getting really ugly, Billie. They're using bleach on the horses now," he confessed, wishing he didn't have to involve his daughter in such a shameful business.

"You mean," Billie said, looking horrified, "The stuff Mom won't keep in the house in case Walter gets poisoned? But how? Why?"

"One theory is that trainers are using it to mask baking soda, so it doesn't show up on a test."

"Oh my God," Billie breathed. "Those guys are sick!"

"They may be sick, Billie, but that's not deterring the owners. They're falling all over themselves to give them horses."

"Like Jeff hooking up with Lazer!" Billie replied angrily.

"God only knows what else is going into those claimers," Al continued gloomily. "The horses are passed around from one trainer to the next. Those guys don't give a damn about the horses!"

"Why aren't the animal welfare people doing anything about this?" Billie demanded. Al stared out of the window at the rush hour traffic. The tailpipes were staining the snow grey.

"Animal welfare sees what it wants to see: horses that are well fed, stalls that are kept clean with plenty of fresh water. They only deal with cases of obvious neglect."

"Okay. Why don't you stop having claiming races? Or at least phase them out?" Billie suggested.

"Can't do that I'm afraid," he replied. "The track needs the income. The handle's forty percent higher on claiming races."

"How come?" Billie asked, waving at the waiter to get his attention.

"How should I know? Bettors like them. Maybe it's easier to assess past form. Or perhaps they believe trainers are racing honestly because the horses are in for a price."

"Honestly?" Billie queried, raising her eyebrows.

"It's quite an irony," he agreed. The frizzy haired server was back.

"Ah...I'll take a frappuccino," Billie said.

"Anything for you, sir?" the waiter asked, turning to Al. Must be a college kid. . . he's still got dreams, Al thought. He could see it in his eyes. Al's whole being was crying out for a fresh start, something that would clear away the debris and disappointments and set his soul on fire, the way he'd felt in his early twenties.

"Just a refill," he replied, holding up his cup.

"And some pancakes," Billie added with a smile. "We've got to feed you up, Dad!" As soon as the two of them were alone again, Al broached the subject of introducing a retention barn at Iroquois Downs.

"I'm going to need your help, Billie," he said. "I've got an important meeting later this week at the track and need to come up with estimates, graphics and anything else you can think of to sell my idea to the committee...and if it's going to do any good I need it by tomorrow."

"Tomorrow!" Billie exclaimed, looking up alarmed. Then, seeing the expression on Al's face, she added with an air of resignation, "You better tell me your ideas, Dad. I'd be happy to do whatever I can to help, if it's really going to make a difference."

Al inwardly thanked whatever lucky star had shone down on the day Billie had been born. There was nothing wrong with her brothers, but they lived their own lives, held themselves at a distance, even when they came to visit. Billie was different, always had been.

Sounding more confident than he felt, he laid out his plan.

"So you're putting the horses in jail? And you really think that'll work?" she queried somewhat skeptically, after he was done.

"I believe it will," Al replied. She let it drop.

"Okay Dad, tell me what you need," she said, rifling through her handbag and producing a notebook and a pen.

"Big stalls, plenty of light, a good ventilation system, tight security, of course: surveillance cameras, only one way in and out…" He was pleased to see that she was writing it all down.

"All that for nickels and dimes! You're not asking a lot, are you?" Billie commented with a wry smile. The pancakes arrived. They were good and hot. Al decided to give the waiter a big tip. With Billie on his side, he hoped to come out on the side of the angels after all.

THE LAZER FACTOR

Out in the cold, Jeff Lamare blew on his freezing fingers and marched along the pavement to his office, the hub of his dot com empire. No one had called him Jeffrey since fifth grade! Generally, any time spent with the beautiful Billie McTavish was time well spent. They were friends. You could even say best friends. They had met two years earlier at Business School when Billie was twenty-two and he was twenty-seven. Back then, mere friendship hadn't been what Jeff had in mind. However, that was all water under the bridge now, he told himself, whilst still harbouring the faintest of hopes that one day he would achieve his goal: making Billie his wife.

Despite her obvious disapproval of Keith Lazer, Jeff wasted no time putting in a call to the trainer. He was sure Billie would come around, given time. He was well aware that Lazer's reputation wasn't squeaky clean but the man won races. Success was something Jeff respected. What's more he'd seen Lazer in action at Iroquois Downs, literally. The guy didn't just have brains, he had pulled off an incredible stunt. The accident had happened so fast that Jeff had missed the details, but he had caught the second act: Lazer's dramatic leap from the outrider's pony onto the back of a runaway horse called, appropriately enough, Midnight Madness. From Jeff's vantage point it had looked like something out of a wild west rodeo. Hooking up with someone like that would, he hoped, make for an exciting ride. He had been hoping to involve Billie McTavish. That now didn't seem too likely, alas!

When Jeff made the call, Lazer picked up immediately.

"Is that Keith?" Jeff said, taken aback.

"Yeah! Who's askin'?"

"Jeff Lamare. I saw you pull that stunt with Midnight Madness, Saturday night. It was pretty impressive."

"If this is a crank call, you can forget it!" Lazer replied. There was an eerie silence.

"I've got a proposition for you," Jeff said uncertainly, hoping Lazer hadn't hung up on him.

"Okay. What's the deal?" Lazer asked, sounding like he could care less.

"I've got a spare quarter of a million lying around," Jeff revealed, laying his cards on the table.

"Just a little spare cash, eh?" Lazer said, with a flicker of interest. "Who are you, anyhow?"

"I'm the CEO of Lamare Holdings," Jeff said going into some detail about his business interests. Why did he feel he had to explain himself to this guy? he wondered.

"Why pick on me?"

"I told you, I saw you jump on that horse!" Jeff said. Lazer laughed, a deep throaty laugh that was infectious. Jeff found himself laughing right along with him.

"Come out to my farm Thursday morning around noon," Lazer suggested. "Right now, I gotta go train a horse!"

Jeff Lamare found Lazer's farm easily enough. The half mile track with its wide sweeping turns was clearly visible from the road. As he drove slowly down the tree lined laneway, his tires scrunching on packed snow, Jeff counted at least a dozen turn out paddocks. Evidently Lazer believed in giving his horses plenty of fresh air. He hoped Billie would approve of that, at least.

He parked his car and strolled over to a yellow Dutch barn which was standing well back from the racetrack, but Lazer wasn't in there. Jeff spotted him eventually leaning on a fence, smoking a cigarette, his eyes on a bay horse standing quietly in his paddock, ankle deep in snow. Jeff hung back until a groom appeared leading a bright bay who looked like a little prize fighter.

"Okay to turn them out together, Keith?" the groom asked. Lazer nodded.

The bay sprang to life at the newcomer's arrival. The two of them blew at one another, their noses almost touching, then squealed and struck out, missing each other by miles. Jeff and Lazer went through a similar process of sparring and sizing each other up. At length the preliminaries were over.

"I like owning a piece of all the horses in my barn," Lazer pronounced. "Good to have some skin in the game."

"Works in my business, too," Jeff said, relieved to hear that Lazer would be putting up his own money.

"And don't expect me to blow your horses' heads off!" Lazer continued, looking down at his boots and confusing Jeff, who had no idea what he meant by it. "I don't know what you've heard about me but I've got no time for illegal drugs," Lazer clarified. "So don't try to get me to use them! I can't afford a bad test. I'd be finished!"

Jeff nodded, unsure whether to believe him or not.

"About these claimers…You wanna get involved in picking 'em or what?" Lazer asked. Jeff shrugged.

"I don't care," he replied.

"I'd want to have complete discretion. That's the bottom line," Lazer said firmly. "I can't do a good job if you try to do it for me. I charge eighty a day by the way, plus stall rent."

"No problem," Jeff agreed. "But I'd give a lot to know how you improve horses so much."

"You don't give away trade secrets in your business, do you?"

"No," Jeff replied with a quick shake of his head.

"Then you just judge what I do by results Jeff, okay? And let's get one thing clear. When you claim a horse, soon as that starting gate leaves, the horse is yours, dead or alive!" Lazer's eyes were a steely grey now. The guy was a risk taker, obviously and he wasn't a fool. A good combination, Jeff decided.

"Wanna think it over?" Lazer asked. Jeff read contempt in his eyes now.

"No way," he smiled. "We got a deal. We split everything down the middle fifty-fifty."

They shook on it, Lazer's hand clasp was firm. Nothing wrong with that, Jeff thought, but his fingers were stained dark yellow with nicotine.

"You ought to stop smoking for Christ sakes," Jeff said without thinking. Why the hell had he said that? he wondered. He didn't give a damn about the guy.

"Who are you…my mother?" Lazer snapped back. Jeff stood his ground.

"Bad for business," he replied automatically. And just how was he going to explain that one, he asked himself. Lazer jabbed him in the chest.

"You and your clean fingernails," he said. "Just why d'you think I need to have hands like that for?"

"Women?" Jeff asked innocently, his pale blue eyes expressionless. He knew he was totally out of line but he was certain he'd hit home this time. Lazer stared into the middle distance, evidently torn between his dislike of Jeff's comment and his desire to keep a potential owner sweet. Jeff let a twinkle creep into his eye. He wanted Lazer to feel that he, Jeff Lamare, vegetarian, non smoker, could have any woman he chose. Unfortunately, it wasn't true, but Lazer didn't know that.

"The hell with you," Lazer said, trying to look outraged, until laughter got the better of him. Jeff winked. Lazer laughed louder but finished in a paroxysm of coughing.

"See what I mean?" Jeff asked.

"Hey Jimmy! Get these horses in out of the cold, right now!" Lazer rasped.

"You wouldn't let any of your horses smoke would you?" Jeff said, feeling that he'd scored a point.

"They don't friggin' gotta choice." Lazer replied. Jeff beat a hasty retreat. "See you in the winner's circle!" Lazer shouted out as Jeff drove off.

Jeff Lamare, head of Lamare Enterprise Inc., hadn't spent a dime on harness horses yet, but already he was caught, hook, line and sinker. The conversation with Lazer had sparked his interest. It would give him something to live for, he concluded, with or without Billie McTavish. In fact, an opportunity to get Billie involved came up only ten days later. Lazer had struck a deal with Bernie Vachon on a four year old mare called Ballet Dancer, who had never been in a claimer. Bernie rarely, if ever, sold his horses.

"Wait till you see her race! She'll run rings round those suckers." Lazer boasted. "She won't be going in any claimer. This one's a keeper," he added. Jeff called Billie immediately. She appeared to have forgiven him for hooking up with Lazer, or perhaps it had slipped her mind. He listened patiently as she laid out all the problems of running McTavish Construction single handed. It was both stressful and boring, she complained.

"Hire a second in command," Jeff suggested.

"Not sure how Dad would feel about that," she countered.

"Ask him! And Billie...come to the races with me on Thursday night, okay? It'll take your mind off things." He decided not to mention Ballet Dancer. If the horse won, it'd be a nice surprise for both of them.

Ballet Dancer won at odds of 7-1. Keith Lazer had been so sure of her, he had put $1,500 on her, on the nose. He liked betting his own horses to win. Being on the inside gave him an edge. Later that night, he emptied his pockets onto his bed. It was soon covered in money. His deft fingers rapidly sorted the cash into bundles. The total for the night came to ten grand, give or take, a good night at the windows. He did a rapid review of his current finances and figured he'd have more than enough to buy a share in the colt shipping up from Jersey. The money that came from horses went into horses. It was that simple. Building an empire was what Lazer called it.

He didn't mind Jeff Lamare riding piggyback, so long as he didn't try to interfere. He stripped off to his T-shirt. His tall frame, taut muscles, razor short blond hair and whiter than white skin (which looked like it had never seen the sun) would never pull in the crowds but the force of his personality showed in his strong facial features: the prominent nose, determined chin and steely grey eyes. He looked at his watch. Four hours of sleep, it'd be enough. He pulled up the bed covers and lay still, hoping for erotic dreams.

Two weeks later, at the Olympus Gym, Theo Vettore was pumping steel and thinking about Billie McTavish. He'd never met anyone like her. She was as warm as a summer's day and as elegant as a thoroughbred. She had him coming and going.

There was no racing at Merryvale Downs that afternoon, so most of the Iroquois Downs drivers had congregated at the gym to warm up for tonight's eleven race card. The west wall was one vast window. A pale sun filtered through the pine trees and shone on the carpet of snow outside. Theo could feel the cold penetrating the glass, even at ten feet away. The weights rose and fell in a steady rhythm.

He had met Billie in the winner's circle, after taking over driving duties from Moose Rankin, Lazer's regular driver. Billie had come along with Jeff Lamare, Ballet Dancer's owner. When Theo had reached over and kissed her on the cheek, a privilege he sometimes claimed as the winning driver, her response had astounded him. Fire and ice! He'd felt it then for the first time: the warmth of her smile, the intense expression in her eyes. He was attracted to her immediately. Compared to Billie McTavish, Ginny looked like a cart horse.

There was no buzz at the gym today. Ned Beazer was loping along on one of the treadmills. Harry Harper was lifting free weights under the close scrutiny of the gym coach. Across the hallway, Moose Rankin was sullenly occupying the rowing machine, his eyes half closed. Several days ago, the judges had spotted him whipping a horse under the shaft, a foul equivalent to hitting below the belt in boxing and had handed out a five-day suspension. Moose had missed out on driving in several big stakes already and was still doing time. The irony was that Moose would have won that race anyway. He'd barely touched the horse. Still rules were rules and now Moose wasn't speaking to anyone. Theo was currently driving all Lazer's horses, including Ballet Dancer, who was competing in the Snowflake Series tonight. If Theo won with her, Lazer would have a tough choice for the final: give the drive to Theo or stay loyal to the Moose, who by then would have done his time.

Loyalty! What did anyone at the racetrack know or care about that? Business relationships! Theo had had his fill of them. Owners that were fair weather friends, trainers that dumped him after one bad trip, on again off again girlfriends like Ginny, who shared his bed, but left him cold. Billie held out the promise of something different, something better he hoped.

He carried on pumping until he was drenched in sweat. He had to be strong to stay on top. After that disastrous night at Ferme Victoire, over a year ago, he'd managed to stay away from the white powder that had been his ruination in too many ways. It was a struggle but so far, he was winning the battle. He headed for the showers and set the water on maximum pressure. A challenging night's racing lay ahead.

He had been surprised when Billie had agreed to give him her phone number as they walked back to the Race Barn after Ballet Dancer's win. He had wasted no time calling her. However, because of Ginny, he was taking it slow. All they'd done so far was spend a couple of mornings hanging out at Lara's barn and getting to know one another. He'd have to find a way to extricate himself from his live in girlfriend at some point. Meanwhile, he didn't even know if Billie and Jeff Lamare were an item, but nothing ventured, nothing gained. He emerged from the shower refreshed and ready for the evening show.

It was a clear still night. Working out how to win was going to be a simple matter of tactics. As to luck, Theo believed in making his own luck, good or bad. He arrived at the drivers room early, giving him plenty of time to study the card and figure out the two races that mattered most: the Trotting Classic and the Snowflake Series. A stakes race was a serious business. A driver only got one shot at it. If Theo did something stupid, it would come back to haunt him, not that he usually did. He was well aware that he saved all his mistakes for his personal life.

The Snowflake Series was for four year old mares who hadn't made a lot of money for their owners yet. It was a chance for the racehorse equivalent of Cinderella to look like a princess, for one night at least. Theo was driving a horse in both eliminations. His cousin Lara's mare, Ma Cherie, would need a covered up trip if she was to make the final. As for Lazer's entry, Ballet Dancer, her first start for the leading trainer had been against a very weak field. However, the move from Lara's barn to Keith Lazer's stable was a significant one. He cast the programme aside and put on his driving gear. Time to go to work!

His first impression of Ballet Dancer was that she had gained a hundred pounds since leaving Lara's barn, every bit of it hard muscle. He resisted the urge to ask Lazer what he had done to the frail filly to make her look like a heavyweight boxer, but he did ask Lazer how he wanted him to drive her. It was a loaded question.

"Just go to the top and stay there!" Lazer said, exuding confidence in every pore as Theo picked up the lines. "I've trained her pretty good over at my place. She'll win for fun!"

As he headed out to the track, Theo weighed up the pros and cons of following Lazer's instructions. He didn't want to make a fool of himself. In the past, hiding at the back of the field until the homestretch with Ballet Dancer had been a smart thing to do. But not tonight, he guessed. Not with the Lazer factor.

Nevertheless, it took courage to put her nose on the gate, follow it out and open up three lengths on the rest of the field, reaching the quarter in 27 seconds flat. It took still more courage to clock up a half in 56, then kick on to the three-quarters in 1.24, repelling all challengers. He dreaded the moment, coming all too soon, he feared, when the other fillies would come flying past him, leaving him helplessly backpedalling. Halfway down the stretch when no one had appeared beside him, hope began to dawn. He stole a backwards glance and saw, to his great joy that the rest of the field was far behind him. The once timid Ballet Dancer had become an entirely different horse! As they swept past the finish line his whip still on his shoulder, he saw the clock stop at 153.1. It was a new stakes record. Somehow, Lazer had turned a quitter into a bearcat.

When Theo was interviewed, he gave the filly all the credit.

"I just sat on her," he said, deliberately low key. "She did it all by herself!" This time, there was no sign of Billie McTavish in the winner's circle. She and Jeff weren't an item after all, he thought optimistically.

After Ballet Dancer's high profile win, Theo wasn't looking forward to going over to Aisle 3, where his cousin Lara would be waiting with Ma Cherie. He'd always known Lara didn't believe in treating her horses like chemistry experiments. Unfortunately, now the whole world knew it too. Lara would be seen as a fool or a saint, depending on which side of the fence people were on. But for sure, Theo thought, his cousin's cover was blown. Lazer had made

Lara look like a loser. It wasn't fair. She was a good trainer. But, good trainer or not, Theo didn't rate his chances of getting Ma Cherie into the final of the Snowflake Series very high. Trainers went all out for stakes races and they'd load a horse up pretty good come race day. As a driver, Theo approved. There was just no sense in sending a horse to a gun fight with a knife. Besides, if the horse couldn't compete, it was far too easy for everyone to dump the blame on the driver.

"You zink she has a chance?" Lara asked him uncertainly, clearly demoralized by the way Ballet Dancer had jumped up and won two in a row after she'd left her barn for Lazer's.

"I'll give it my best shot!" Theo replied. But as he scored Ma Cherie past the tote board, his heart sank. Ballet Dancer had felt like a souped up sports car firing on all four cylinders. Ma Cherie reminded him of his dad's old Ford sedan, badly in need of a tune up.

When the two hole opened up behind the favourite, he dived into it and sat tight, biding his time. However, halfway down the homestretch he found himself hemmed in behind a fading favourite, while beside him a wall of horses came charging for the wire. Cursing Harper for driving the favourite off her feet, Theo yanked hard on Ma Cherie's right line, extracted her from the trap and steered her towards a tiny gap that had opened up between sulkies, betting that the drivers on each side of him would instinctively move away to save their skins. Everything went like clockwork. Heeding his screams, the startled drivers instinctively moved aside and he came hurtling through at top speed to finish a flying fourth. Just enough to get into the final.

"I could have won if I been able to get out a little sooner, Lara," he said, encouragingly. Then he hurried off.

He was driving his old friend, Southview Sabre, in the seventh. Lara had kept the horse around out of sentiment. He was a real character: eight years old and still acting like a baby, spending half the day playing with the big rubber ball in his stall. At his age, with the money he had won, Lara had no choice but to race him in claiming races, but as he hardly ever won, he had become virtually invisible. The bettors regularly sent him off at 30-1 or higher. Because he had bad feet, Southview Sabre was only a twelve-thousand-dollar claimer in the winter months when the track was like a concrete road. But come spring when the track was softer, he jumped up to the fifteen or twenty thousand class. You could set your watch by it.

As the night wore on, Theo grew more optimistic of Southview Sabre's chances in the seventh. The snow had stopped and the mercury had hoisted itself above zero. A freak thaw had set in. The surface of the track was now tacky, providing a bit of a cushion for the old timer's sore feet.

Theo found both Lara and Southview Sabre looking bright-eyed and excited in their spot on Aisle 4.

"He is the best when I take him out," Lara exclaimed. "Jus' like in the past when he was a good horse!" Southview Sabre didn't say anything but his eyes were popping out of his head, always an excellent sign. However, the memory of that disastrous night, when he'd lost his bet on Southview Sabre, reached out and touched Theo on the shoulder like an icy finger. He'd ended up in pieces on the parking lot that night. The very thought of it made him shudder.

"Don't bet any money on him," he said.

"But me, I do not ever bet," Lara protested. "You know that." But before Theo had a chance to explain, he heard the Paddock Judge rallying the troops.

"Seventh race! Ready with the One horse!" Then casually, as an after-thought, the judge dropped his bombshell.

"Southview Sabre has been claimed. New trainer, Mr. Keith Lazer. Lead 'em out, men!" Lara looked astonished, then her face crumpled as the cruel reality sunk in.

"Watch me!" Theo hissed in Lara's ear. "I'm gonna win for you tonight."

He was as good as his word. But there were no celebrations in the winner's circle. It felt like a wake. Lara was ashen faced and silent. In a few minutes' time, Theo knew, she would have to say goodbye to one of her best friends, a horse she'd known since the day he was foaled and had cared for this past eight years. She had been planning to retire him at the end of the year. As the funeral procession arrived back at the Race Barn, they were met by Scotty McCoy.

"Judges wanna talk to you," he said tilting his head toward the Paddock Judge's office and taking a big bite out of the hot dog he was eating. "Both of you," he added. Theo walked into the office and picked up the red phone, preparing to feed them the usual pablum. The judges seldom left their perch, high up in the grandstand. But he wished Mr. *fuckin'* Roberts would quit staring at him.

"Can you explain why your horse improved so much tonight?" the disem-bodied voice asked.

"There was a cushion on the track tonight. The horse has bad feet," Theo replied defensively. Then it was Lara's turn.

"Why?" Lara asked Theo a few minutes later. "He is eight years old! Why does Keith Lazer do zis to me?" Theo knew. Southview Sabre was the only horse his cousin had in a claimer. Keith Lazer hadn't wasted any time. After Ballet Dancer's stellar performance, he would take any horse Lara put in a claimer from now on.

It was his first thought when he woke up the next morning.

"Hey, where d'you think you're going?" Ginny complained when he left the bed.

"Gotta go see Lara," he replied hastily. A show of solidarity was all very well, but it wasn't the only reason he was driving all the way out to Rivers Training centre on a freezing morning like this. He had promised to meet Billie McTavish at Lara's barn. There had been a fresh fall of snow overnight and the snowplows hadn't got around to clearing the country roads yet, so Theo drove slowly and rehearsed his condolences.

When he arrived at the barn, Billie was already there. She was standing in the aisleway holding a horse by the bridle, who was harnessed up and ready to go. Despite the heat in the barn generated by the bodies of a dozen horses, she was wearing cold weather gear. It made her look even more desirable, like a parcel that he couldn't wait to unwrap.

Lara appeared, looking pale and tense as if she had hardly slept the night before. But before he had a chance to say anything, she picked up the lines and sat on the cart.

"Let go of him, Billie!" she called out, heading for the frozen world outside without so much as a glance in his direction. After she left, Theo put his shoulder to the barn door and rolled it shut. When he turned back around, Billie didn't seem pleased to see him, not a great start. However, the reason soon became clear.

"What just happened?" she asked. "I was going to jog Reddi Boy!" With that she took off her hat, shook her long brown hair loose and unzipped her coat, looking confused.

"Listen . . . Lara had a tough night," Theo hastened to explain. "She lost one of her horses."

"Lost?" Billie queried.

"Yeah. Keith Lazer claimed Southview Sabre from her."

"She never breathed a word about it!" Billie said in an astonished tone.

"Probably too cut up," Theo replied, in an attempt to mollify her. Billie was twisting and untwisting the bobble on her hat until, predictably, it fell off. "What's on your mind?" he asked, leaning down to pick it up.

"How come Ballet Dancer's so much better now?" Billie asked in a worried tone.

"Now she's in Lazer's barn?" he asked. Billie nodded emphatically. There were a dozen things he'd have been happy to talk to her about. This certainly wasn't one of them.

"Lazer may just be a very good horseman," he replied cautiously.

"Better than Lara?" she challenged.

"Not that I've noticed," Theo admitted. "Listen, if I knew for sure what Lazer did to Ballet Dancer, I'd advise Lara to do the same thing. You have to understand, Billie..."

"Understand what?" she demanded.

"You think Lara enjoyed seeing Lazer win last night with that mare? My uncle practically gave her away. A nice, sound four-year-old like that! Her only fault was she was a little on the weak side." He was getting through to her now. He could feel it. "Ballet Dancer always had blazing speed, but she kept getting beat up by bigger, stronger mares. It wasn't fun for her, or for me!"

"I can see that," Billie conceded.

"Last night," he said, jumping at the chance to relive the experience, "she was a different animal! I cut huge fractions with her but she paced right up to the wire. She was unbelievably strong. She was a machine! You can't imagine . . ." He stopped short, floored by the look of icy disapproval on Billie's face. What was her problem?

"I think I do understand," she said coldly. "It's called cheating."

"Cheating? What are you talking about? She won for fun...she won like a champion!"

"A champion created by chemicals!" Billie burst out angrily. "But why should you care? Anything to satisfy your ego!"

"What are you saying?" he frowned. Didn't she realize a driver's ego was the only thing that stood between him and oblivion? He needed to believe in himself. Having the chance to drive horses for a trainer like Lazer was a gift. It cancelled out all the bullshit that dragged him down. "You don't know what you're talking about," he replied dismissively, then immediately regretted it. "Listen, I'm just the driver. I don't know what goes on behind the scenes, really I don't," he added in a more conciliatory tone. Billie appeared to relax her guard. She took a step towards him, then froze at the sound of loud banging at the door.

"They're back!" she cried, running to let the horse in. Theo silently cursed his cousin's timing.

"Didn't you hear me?" Lara complained. "I lost a knee boot out on the track," she added crossly. Theo busied himself by peeling the harness off Reddi Boy. When he turned around, Billie was nowhere to be seen. It looked like he'd blown the relationship before it had even begun, he decided gloomily.

"Why you play zis game wis zis girl, Theo? In my barn?" Lara muttered, throwing a cooler over Reddi Boy's broad back. "I have things to do here, you know?" Theo considered going after Billie, but he and Lara had been close since their families had moved down to Ontario from Montreal eighteen years ago, neither of them knowing a word of English. Being only five at the time, Theo had found it easy to pick up the language and fit in. It had been much harder for Lara and she still didn't have a lot of friends.

"Look, I know what you're thinking. Fact is I was afraid to go first up with your filly. I was certan she'd quit." Theo confessed. "But maybe I got it all wrong." He followed Lara as she led Reddi Boy over to the wash stall.

"Ze guys, zey were talking about it zis morning," she said, turning the water on and aiming the hose at the horse's front legs. "Zey tell me you do not want to win."

"And you believed that bullshit!" he exclaimed. Lara shrugged.

"You have Lazer's horse for ze final. What is it you need my mare for?"

"Because you're my cousin," Theo said firmly. "And blood is thicker than water! Where'd Billie go?" he added suddenly anxious on his own account.

"Why you don't tell her zat you are crazy in love with her?" Lara asked.

"Crazy about her," Theo corrected automatically. "Not crazy in love."

"We are not at school now Theo," Lara replied reproachfully, towelling Reddi Boy down. Theo mulled over Billie's impassioned speech.

"She can't stand the sight of me," he said at last.

"Call her," Lara suggested.

"Not gonna do that," Theo replied firmly. He didn't intend to apologize for who he was or the way he made his living. Either she accepted him or she didn't.

"Always, you are too proud Theo," Lara said with a sigh, leading Reddi Boy over to his stall.

"Let her call me!" Theo exclaimed. "Listen, losing Southview Sabre was a bad break. I know how you feel about the old guy."

"What can I say?" Lara replied. "I was there ze night he was borned. Eight years I take care of him. It makes me sad to see his stall empty like zis. I look and he is not there. It is hard, you know? He was my friend…now he is gone."

"Maybe Bernie will claim him back," Theo suggested.

"Never!" She led Reddi Boy back to his stall and tossed him a bale of hay. "If I had ze money," she said. She shook her head. "I do not have enough! But one day per'aps I will buy him back, when zey are done wiz him."

"Just say the word eh? I'm not exactly broke right now," Theo offered. Thanks in part to Lazer, he realized. The guy was taking all the purse money, leaving little for anyone else. The Lazer factor was beginning to have far reaching consequences. It was several days before Theo realized he'd never given Billie his phone number. But by then, he reckoned it was too late.

The next day was a Sunday. Billie spent the morning at *The Haven*, working out and trying not to think about Theo Vettore. After a week spent sitting at a desk, it felt good to be using her body again. She had reached 30 kms an hour on the cycle machine, when she heard her cell phone ringing.

"Hi Mama," she said, free wheeling to 15 kms an hour.

"Good morning my darling," Sofia replied warmly. "You are coming over to see us today, Billie, yes?"

"I'll be there soon," Billie assured her, hoping she'd get a chance to talk to her mother alone. Half an hour later, she left the gym and drove off through quiet streets. Erinsville was looking as pretty as a Christmas card: snow on the rooftops, frost on the trees. She was about to turn into 210, Laurel Drive when she spotted her father's car on its way out. Braving the cold, she rolled down her window.

"What?" Al asked distractedly, struggling to relight a recalcitrant cigar.

"Where are you off to?" she asked brightly, though she was pretty sure she knew. The only real friend her father had was Phil Harman. Al didn't reply.

"Whatever happened with the retention barn?" she enquired, anxious to know the outcome after all her hard work on the project.

"Oh that," he said, waving the subject aside. "They're still costing it out."

"But I did that, weeks ago!" Billie exclaimed in dismay. "What makes them think they can just toss my figures aside like that?" she added fretfully.

"It's politics, Billie."

He sounded so weary that she didn't pursue it.

"Maybe Phil will have news," she suggested attempting to draw him out.

"I doubt it," Al replied unhappily. "Listen I've gotta go, I'm afraid. I'm late already."

"I'm sorry!" she called out belatedly, as he drove off. She was tempted to turn around and follow him, but Sofia was waving to her from the living room window. The front door opened before Billie had even touched the bell.

"Come in! Quickly!" Sofia said. "Walter! NO!" she admonished the cat, who was making a beeline for the door. "It is too cold for you today."

"How's the big boy?" Billie asked, running her hand over his broad back. Walter waved his long, feathery tail back and forth and emitted a long rumbling purr.

"He's looking wonderful," Billie smiled, wishing she could have said that about her mother. Though Sofia had obviously gone to a great deal of trouble over her appearance, there were dark shadows under her eyes and she looked completely exhausted. There was no point in expressing concern, Billie knew. Instead, she gave her mother a hug that lasted a full minute. Sofia sighed.

"I am so glad you are here, Billie," she said, leading the way to the kitchen. "I have some hot soup for you, sweetheart." The stove in the kitchen was giving out a warm glow, a welcome contrast to the snow and ice outdoors. It was so good to be home. I don't want this house to change, ever, Billie thought fondly. It was like a stage set frozen in time, a living reminder of her happy childhood, a comfort in times of trouble.

"Where did Dad go?" she asked.

"To see Phil Harman, naturally," her mother replied, making her disapproval obvious. Billie quickly changed the subject.

"Heard from Jasper lately?" she asked taking off her coat and sitting down at the kitchen table. Walter jumped up onto the chair next to hers, purring loudly.

"Your brother's in Miami doing a photo shoot," Sofia replied, bringing a steaming pot to the table. "Walter, you are not having any soup today. It is mushroom and you know you do not like mushroom."

"Remember when we all used to sit around this table after school?" Billie reminisced. "You were the queen of the house. We all looked up to you. We still do. You did quite a job, Mama."

Sofia let her hand rest on Walter's head for a moment. The expression in the cat's eyes, as he stared up at her, was pure adoration.

"Now only Walter needs me," Sofia said. "You are all so independent."

"Well adjusted," Billie corrected, smiling at her. Sofia did not return the smile.

"What are you going to do, Mama? You can't sit around this house feeling miserable for the rest of your life," Billie said gently.

"Wait till you have the menopause," Sofia replied. Then her expression softened. "I don't wish it on you, sweetheart, believe me. It has made me feel…I don't know, so different. Perhaps it is because I am not sleeping well. I am so tired…all of the time. And then. . . one minute I feel like I am on fire! Then all at once I am shivering, I am so cold!"

"Did Jeff ever call you?" Billie asked, filling their glasses with red wine. "About the health store?"

"Jeffrey. Such a nice boy. But he cannot help," Sofia replied evading the question. "I made ravioli and some zucchini. Take care, it will be hot. Use the oven gloves." When Billie lifted the lids off the saucepans, the smell of basil and tomato wafted upwards, the scent of home.

"I've met someone," she revealed, busying herself with the saucepans. "He's a driver at Iroquois Downs." Sofia looked startled.

"A driver? What is his name?"

"Theo Vettore." The secret was out. "Don't tell Dad," Billie warned.

"Vettore," Sofia said, rolling the name on her tongue. "So he is Italian," she added delightedly.

"Don't get too excited," Billie cautioned. "He's nothing like anyone on your side of the family."

"But you like him," Sofia said approvingly.

"What if I do?" Billie replied defensively.

"Then I will be happy for you my darling. Do you imagine I want you to spend the rest of your life alone?"

"Don't worry," Billie said. "I'll find a way to mess it up. In fact, I probably already have. He hasn't even asked me out yet." Walter could restrain himself no longer. He took a flying leap and landed on the table.

"Get down, Walter. You are such a bad boy!" Sofia said severely. "Well if he is driving every night, how can he ask you out?"

"That's not it!" Billie replied quickly. Sofia cut up some ravioli on a saucer and placed it on the floor.

"Wait until it cools down, Walter!" she told him. "You are beautiful," she told Billie. "Beautiful and clever. You can have anybody you want. You just have to show him how you feel. That is all. Then everything will be alright, you will see." At these words, Billie relaxed.

"Your cooking is amazing, as usual," she said. "What's Dad doing about lunch?" Sofia shrugged.

"Your father!" she said dismissively. "He will be gone for hours…him and that Phil Harman."

"You've never liked Phil, have you?" Billie stated, taking a sip of her wine.

"I am supposed to like him?" Sofia asked incredulously.

"He's Dad's best friend!" Billie pointed out. "Besides, Phil's got all these contacts at City Hall…and Dad has to get support for this new scheme of his from somewhere." Sofia looked at her blankly. "How much has Dad told you about all this?" Billie added uncertainly.

"Told me?" her mother frowned. "He has told me nothing!" So they weren't talking to each other, Billie realized worriedly.

"It's just an idea," she said attempting to gloss things over. "Claimers, horses in for a price, would have to spend twenty-four hours in a retention barn before they raced…"

"A retention barn? But why?"

"You wouldn't believe what some trainers are doing to horses now, Mama," Billie replied, the words tumbling out before she could stop them. "It makes me so angry! The claiming trainers don't care!" Billie added, warming to the theme. "They only have the horses for a few weeks. They don't think about the consequences. It's terrible! Horses are dying, Mama."

"That is terrible!" Sofia agreed. "But what can your father do about it, Billie? What can any of us do? It is always about politics, and politicians, they only know how to help themselves."

"At least Dad's trying," Billie replied loyally. Sofia brushed her comment aside.

"You think politicians care about the animals! Horses are not able to vote you know. If they did…" Sofia trailed off, looking thoughtful.

"They'd vote against claiming races for sure!" Billie agreed. "Imagine if Walter had to go off to a new home every week. He'd be totally confused. Imagine the stress! What kind of life would that be for him?"

"Well," Sofia declared, "I do not think this retention barn of your father's is going to change anything!"

"It'll put a stop to trainers giving the horses anything on a race day, at least!" Billie replied.

"Anything? What if the horse has a condition that requires daily medication?"

"Then they shouldn't be racing at all!" Billie cried. "Surely?" she added hesitantly. Sofia was shaking her head.

"Not every medication is bad, Billie. As a pharmacist, I should know…"

"Yes, but…" It had to be at least thirty years since her mother had practiced her profession. However, Billie didn't want to hurt her feelings.

"Why should a horse be any different from a person?" Sofia continued. "Would you tell a diabetic he can't take insulin if he is competing in a race?"

"I don't know the rules," Billie admitted. "But I know you have to draw a line somewhere."

"Of course," Sofia agreed. "But this idea of your father's to ban everything. . . it will not work! It never does, sweetheart. Look at prohibition! And what about abortion?"

"What about it?" Billie frowned.

"In the past, when it was illegal, a woman had to go to the back streets to the abortionists, with their dirty knitting needles. Thousands of women died. Perhaps that is why horses are dying now, Billie. Of course, your father would not agree with me." Billie's mind was racing. "I hear the car," Sofia said suddenly. "He is back already." She didn't sound pleased about it.

"Dad's worried to death about you," Billie said.

"Your father! He is away all the time. He notices nothing."

"He notices a lot more than you think!" Billie replied stubbornly.

"You know what?" Sofia smiled. "I feel happy now because you are here sweetheart. It is nice to be just the two of us sometimes, yes?"

"I love you, Mama," Billie replied warmly.

The front door slammed.

"Hi girls!" Billie heard her father call out breezily from the hall. "I've just let Walter out. Is that okay?"

In the days that followed, Billie immersed herself in work. She followed Jeff's advice and hired a competent second in command, promoting from within. Then she launched into projects old and new, with a desperate energy.

When Saturday morning dawned and she still hadn't heard from Theo, she decided to drive out to Rivers Training centre, hoping to catch up with him, even though she had no clear idea of what she was going to do or say when she got there. Grey clouds hung low over the snowy countryside, creating an atmosphere of gloom that echoed her own mood. Here goes my precarious performance, she thought, walking over to Lara's barn and sliding open the barn door. A dozen horses thrust their heads out of their stalls expectantly, but there was no one around except a young girl with a blond ponytail. She was standing in the aisleway, braiding a horse's forelock.

"If you're looking for Lara," the girl said, "she just went out on the track."

"And Theo?" Billie asked hesitantly.

"He won't be here today! Not after what happened."

"Oh," Billie replied, praying it wasn't something to do with her storming out of the barn the previous week. The girl looked up.

"You're Lazer's owner right?" she asked, somewhat frostily. "I saw you in the winner's circle with Ballet Dancer."

"Ballet Dancer? She's not my horse!" Billie exclaimed. "And anyway..."

"Yes?" the girl prompted.

"I don't approve of druggists."

"You have amazing hair," the girl replied in a much more friendly tone. "You're so lucky. Is it naturally curly? I'm Evie by the way and this is Reddi Boy..."

"Billie Mc..."

"Lara's letting me paddock him tonight," Evie cut in excitedly. "I got him Show Sheen and ribbons...He's going to look amazing!"

"He's a sweet horse." Billie smiled.

"He'll win the race for sure. Theo's driving," the girl said confidently.

"So, about Theo..."

"Lara's still mad about Southview Sabre getting claimed. She's blaming Theo," Evie explained. That made absolutely no sense to Billie.

"Really?" she said, losing interest in the conversation and glancing at her watch.

"If you're in a rush, Lara's cell number's on the board," Evie said, undoing the braid and starting over. Billie found it, written in red, along with the numbers of the blacksmith, the vet and the feed man. It was another world, a world she knew very little about yet. But perhaps that was about to change she thought hopefully, studying the overnight sheet. She eventually spotted Reddi Boy. Theo Vettore's name was plastered all over the page. Most of the trainers at Iroquois Downs wanted him to drive their horses. On the racetrack at least, he was quite a celebrity. She wasn't sure whether to laugh or cry, remembering how she'd laid into him a week ago. She had no intention of taking back a single word, but somehow she needed to put things right between them.

She said goodbye to Evie, then headed back to Erinsville. An idea for a new business venture had been floating around in her head for weeks now. If it worked out, it would make a refreshing change from running her father's construction company. She decided to spend some time down by the river, looking around an empty warehouse that she had been offered at a reasonable rent. After she had trained Steve up as second in command, she intended to hand over the reins of McTavish Construction to him and strike out on her own.

She reached home around 6 p.m. her head spinning with ideas as she climbed the staircase to her apartment, a Victorian mansion in Erinsville's historic centre. The windows rattled and the wind blew straight through the old place in a storm, but in Billie's opinion that was a small price to pay for high ceilings and elegant, spacious rooms. She had painted the walls in bold glowing yellows so that even on a cloudy day, the sun always seemed to shine. Glad to be home, Billie picked up the phone and filled Jeff in on her plan to start up a fencing business using materials and technology that had been pioneered stateside. With so many horses in Ontario, Billie was certain it would go down well in Canada, too. Jeff was so enthusiastic about the idea, he offered to bankroll it for a share in the profits. Billie was happy to go along with that, but she turned down his offer to take her out to dinner, comforting though it would have been. It wouldn't have been fair to either of them.

Afterwards she took a long lazy bath, fixed a steak and salad and poured herself a glass of wine. After her solitary supper, she tuned in to the racing channel. She was just in time to see Theo pull his horse at the three-quarter pole and sweep the field. Considering he had won, he looked pretty subdued. She waited for him to do his usual thing and toss his whip to the crowd, but he just patted the trainer on the shoulder and walked off without a word.

Soon it was time for Reddi Boy's race. Billie watched with mounting excitement as Theo played a waiting game, popping off cover at the end of the mile to score. This time, even Theo cracked a smile. As for Lara, she was jumping up and down with excitement. The camera stayed with Theo as Reddi Boy was led off for a well deserved bath.

"Pretty good night so far, Theo. Two winners already," the interviewer remarked in a bland monotone.

"Thanks, Doug," was Theo's modest response.

"I hear you're abandoning us next week, going to warmer climes."

"Yeah, I'm going down to the islands. But it's only for a week. I'll be back!" Theo replied with a smile to camera.

"Can we talk a little about Reddi Boy?"

"Sure…he's won his first lifetime start tonight handily…and he's only a three-year-old…Lara doesn't push her babies. She likes to take her time and that gives her an edge, percentage wise."

"Well that pretty much wraps it up," the interviewer was saying, when Theo leaned in on the mike. "I'd like to say hi to Billie," he said, looking straight at the camera with a big smile.

Billie leaned back on the sofa and raised her glass in silent salute. Then she picked up the phone and dialled Lara's number.

Lara answered on the second ring. "Is that you, Papa?" she asked.

"It's me, Billie! I just called to congratulate you."

"You see ze race, yes?" Lara sounded really happy, last week's disappointment forgotten.

"He looked terrific," Billie said.

"You can come and drive him, anytime you like," Lara offered. "Listen, *un moment*, I find Theo."

Billie's heart began beating fast. Get this right, she told herself.

Theo sounded surprised to hear from her.

"You drove Reddi Boy beautifully," she heard herself say in gushing tones. "Like a maestro playing a violin."

"That's quite a compliment, especially coming from you," he replied. "You interested in a week in the islands?"

"I'm really sorry," she blurted out. "About the way I talked to you last time. I wasn't being fair to you."

"So, you're coming along?" Theo asked, sounding amused. She hesitated. If she said no, that would be that.

"Count me in!" she said, hoping for the best.

"That's great! I'll pick you up Thursday morning about 10 a.m."

"What about tickets?" she exclaimed.

"All taken care of," Theo assured her.

After he hung up, she realized she had no idea where she was going. She was far too elated to care. Switching off the TV, she put Billie Holiday on the stereo. She played one of the songs, "You go to my head", over and over again. It expressed the way she was feeling right now perfectly.

Three days later, they were on their way.

"I generally sleep on planes," Theo stated as the plane took off. "Feel free to wake me if you get bored." It's not like we're an old married couple with nothing left to talk about, Billie thought, wondering if she'd done the right thing agreeing to go along. She hardly knew the guy after all. However, she cheered up as the plane broke through the clouds into brilliant sunshine.

The next time she looked down, the blue waters of the Caribbean were sparkling in the sun. The sun was still shining when they touched down but the minute they stepped off the plane the heat and humidity enveloped them like a blanket, despite a light breeze blowing. Theo rustled up a taxi and soon they were speeding past little shanty towns where dogs were rooting in the dirt and clusters of people were gathering at run down eateries. Palm trees swayed in the soft air. The harsh cries of parrots and the scent of lemon followed them as they travelled.

"Where are we going?" Billie asked.

"Half Moon Bay," Theo replied. "We'll have to take the ferry."

"A boat?" Billie asked feeling alarmed.

"Don't worry, it's a short trip," Theo assured her.

The ferry taxied sedately down the canal, and once they reached open water, Billie was so entranced by the frigate birds swooping overhead that she forgot to be scared. The sea was a translucent turquoise.

"It feels like we're on a different planet," she exclaimed.

"Wait 'til you get into that water," Theo told her. "It's like a warm bath!"

The house was smothered in bougainvillea and sat dead centre in a crescent of white sand. Billie slipped into a bathing suit and made a run for the water, over the red hot sand. After a while Theo joined her.

"No more snow and ice!" she shrieked jubilantly, splashing him with water.

After several minutes, Theo was ready to admit defeat.

"Where'd you learn to do that?" he asked, looking like a drowned rat.

"Two older brothers," Billie replied. "First time I won, ever!"

"Let's go inside," he suggested. The sun was setting as they walked up the beach, its light extinguished as swiftly as a candle blown out by the wind.

"There should be something to drink around here," Theo muttered, eventually unearthing a bottle of red wine. There were no chairs out on the deck, just a big hammock swinging from the rafters.

"*Santé,*" Theo said, holding up his glass.

"That's the first time I've heard you speak French," Billie smiled.

"My mother's French, father's Italian," Theo replied smoothly.

"My mother's Italian too," Billie said. "But all Dad's family are from Nova Scotia."

"Quite a combination. It explains a lot about you that I didn't understand before." What's that supposed to mean? Billie wondered, with a frown, as Theo sank down on the hammock.

"Care to join me?" he asked lazily. It felt like the most natural thing in the world to be lying in his arms. The scent of salt on his skin was intoxicating. "Fire and ice," she heard him say softly, stroking her hair gently. She drifted off into a dreamless sleep.

She woke alone in the pitch dark, to the sound of running water.

"You interested in dinner?" Theo asked, emerging from the shower wearing just a towel around his waist.

The Calypso Grill was a short walk away, sitting on the beach, with its toes in the sea. Beneath the shelter of a tall palm, a steel band was playing. There were lights everywhere, strung over trellises and hanging in the trees.

"Any drinks for you?" a man wearing a shirt adorned with parrots and pineapples asked brightly.

"Just water," Billie said.

"Perrier," Theo amended. "And bring us a couple of Stingrays."

"What on earth is that?" Billie laughed.

"Island beer. You either love it or hate it." The moon was rising over the sea, its reflection shimmering on the water.

"How d'you ever find this place?" Billie asked.

"The bar?"

"The island!"

"Long story," Theo said, "It's my uncle's place. Didn't I tell you?"

"Lara's father?"

Theo nodded. "It's only a timeshare, but Bernie could have bought anything he wanted. He owns Night Raider and that horse paid for his farm, all his broodmares, everything!"

"Wow," Billie breathed.

The drinks arrived.

"Ready to order?" the waiter asked. Up on the makeshift stage, a young man wearing a big hat over his afro was moving with the beat.

"Feelin' hot hot hot!" he sang, repeating the phrase until Billie felt unable to sit still a moment longer.

"You want to dance?" she asked eagerly.

"Okay," Theo shrugged. She jumped up and ran to the small dance floor. Theo followed at a more leisurely pace. The singer flashed her a smile. The tempo was so languid, the rhythm so unfamiliar. She stood and swayed to the music until Theo caught the beat and rested his fingers lightly on her hips, their movements perfectly synchronized. Billie was totally caught up in the moment...the music...the sky studded with stars, the shadows of the palm trees cast by the bright moon...she wanted this dance to last forever. Abruptly the music stopped. Their waiter was waving at them.

"Food's up," Theo said.

Billie drank half a bottle of Stingray without stopping.

"Thirsty?" Theo grinned.

"You know," she smiled. "This beer's not so bad!"

After dinner, she insisted on picking up the tab. "You haven't let me pay for anything yet," she said firmly, when Theo started to protest.

"Stay with me tonight," Theo whispered as they reached the house. Billie hesitated. Fleeting images of past experiences fumbling in the dark...the empty feeling afterwards, popped into her head.

"It's too soon," she said, "I'm not sure that I...I'm sorry."

"It's okay," Theo muttered, disappearing into a bedroom and slamming the door.

Billie made her way to her own room, relieved, yet disappointed with herself, too. She hadn't been willing to take the risk. She was right about it being too soon but would she get another chance, she wondered or would Theo be too proud? The moonlight kept her awake a long time. The music at the Calypso Grill kept replaying in her head, until eventually she drifted off.

By next morning, an awkwardness had sprung up between them. Theo immediately launched into a fitness campaign. Dawn runs on the beach, swimming, and evening sessions at the gym took up most of his time and all of his energy. The early camaraderie of the first day had evaporated into thin air. He's sulking, Billie concluded with a sigh. She spent her time reading trashy novels, working on her tan and watching the pelicans swoop down on schools of fish, like a troop of low flying planes.

Four days later, when Sunday morning dawned, she didn't bother to get out of bed. She could hear Theo moving around, but she didn't feel like having yet another pointless stilted conversation with him over breakfast. If she stayed in bed long enough, she reasoned, he would go out and leave her in peace. She dozed for a while, until she heard a phone ringing in the next room. Theo sounded at first anxious, then downright panicky. Without thinking, she jumped out of bed and ran into the living room, still in her nightdress, her long hair tousled.

"What's going on?" she exclaimed. Theo threw the phone across the room, muttering to himself. "What's happened?" she persisted.

"That was my uncle on the phone," Theo replied unhappily. "My brood-mare…," Billie braced herself. "She lost the foal," he said, slumping forward and gazing down unseeing at the white tiled floor. "It was a colt," he added. Billie sat down next to him and put her arms around him.

"I'm so sorry," she said. Oh God, she thought, why did this have to happen now?

"A colt by Night Raider," Theo continued. "I would have liked that."

"What about the mare?" Billie asked. Please don't let her be dead too, she prayed.

"They're hoping for the best. They won't know for sure for several days yet." Know what? Billie wondered anxiously. "Don't worry, she'll live," Theo added. "It's just a question of whether I'll be able to breed her again." He patted her hand. "Thanks," he said.

"For what?"

"For understanding. I'll get over this, don't worry. Things like this happen in the horse business. It goes with the territory."

"Tragedies," Billie said.

"I claimed her for twenty-five thousand dollars. Never made a penny with her and now this."

"Disappointments," Billie added.

"Yeah," Theo replied with a heavy sigh. But he looked like he was recovering. He leaned back on the sofa. Billie nestled close to him.

"D'you feel like doing anything today?" she asked after a while.

"Good thinking," Theo replied. "No sense in sitting around here moping."

"I've been reading the guide book," Billie began tentatively.

"There's a boat that goes around the island, the Sea Princess or something. Sounds pretty cool…or we could just stay here," he said, registering the expression on Billie's face.

"It's just…boats terrify me," she confessed.

"Okay so…"

"We could rent a jeep…there are a few places off the beaten track we could try," she said brightly.

"Sounds good to me!"

"I need to make a couple of calls before we go, okay?" Billie said.

By 10:30 a.m. they were on their way. Billie took the wheel and headed north along the coast road which circled the island. The shallow turquoise waters stretched out to the horizon and it was sometimes hard to tell where the sea ended and the sky began. Eventually, Billie parked the jeep beside a beach strewn with clam shells. They sat listening to the distant roar of the surf as waves hit the reef, far out to sea.

"That's the most beautiful sound in the world," Billie said breathlessly, feeling like she was floating on air.

"It's like the roar of the crowd," Theo replied, his eyes alight. "When you're coming down the stretch."

"Missing the races? How about a ride on the beach?" she suggested.

"A ride?" Theo asked curiously.

"You like horses don't you?" she said. He grinned. Sometimes Billie thought, sometimes life cuts you a break. This was going to be one of those rare days, when everything works out. She could feel it. A heavy set dark-skinned man wearing a cowboy hat waved at them, as they approached.

"You the lady that call this morning?" he asked. "We all ready to go."

He was riding a magnificent looking stallion.

"Conrad?" Billie queried.

"That's me. Hey, Basee!" he shouted. A groom appeared, leading two horses with long manes tumbling over their arched necks.

"Need any help?" the groom asked, Billie shook her head.

"I'm okay," she replied, swinging herself up onto the mare's back, an appaloosa with spots on her hind quarters.

"How fast can they go?" Theo asked vaulting onto his horse in one easy motion.

"They fast, man!" Conrad exclaimed, grinning broadly. "They ship all the way from Brazil!"

The wide strip of sand stretched out like a racetrack, chasing its way between the sea grapes on the shore and the shallow waters of the reef. The noonday sun was dazzling. Theo edged ahead of her as the horses walked off, high stepping. They quickly broke into a canter. Theo kicked his mount into a gallop and drew away. Billie hung on tight, feeling the strength of the mare beneath her, hearing the thud of the hooves on the sand, her face whipped by the wind. All too soon, Conrad waved them down. The horses were sweating.

"You crazy, man!" he told Theo, rolling his eyes approvingly as he rode his horse into the water. Theo and Billie rode in after him, until the sea was washing around their ankles. When it rose to their knees, Billie let the reins go slack, trusting her mare to swim back to shore. The return trip by land was much more sedate.

"Hey Conrad, you know a good place to eat lunch around here?" Theo asked, his face glowing when they got back to base.

"Down the beach aways," Conrad replied, jerking a thumb.

"Come eat with us!" Theo suggested.

Otto's Fish Fry was a tumbledown shack, with a million-dollar view of the ocean. Inside, an amply built black woman wrapped in a long white apron was serving out food in generous portions.

"You lookin' for Otto?" she asked. "He gone fishin' but you folks are welcome to stay. We got jerk chicken, yellow rice, black eye peas, yams…you wan' beer? We got cold beer! You wan' some o' my rum, Conrad?" she added teasingly. "You know you gonna like it!"

"Can't never say no to you, Maisie," Conrad replied with a twinkle in his eye. Maisie threw her head back and laughed, a generous, full throated laugh that included everyone in the kitchen.

"Oh Lord!" she exclaimed.

"You lived on the island all your life, Conrad?" Theo asked as they took their drinks and sat down at one of the rickety tables.

"I was born here," Conrad replied. "But when it come time for me to work I had to leave this place. It just one big mangrove swamp in them days, man. There weren't no jobs…nothin'. You couldn't go near the water…the black mosquitoes'd git you."

"So when did all these hotels get built?" Billie asked. Two young bloods, sporting dreadlocks sat down at the next table, plates piled high, radio at full blast. Conrad leaned forward conspiratorially.

"I tell you what I heard, Miss Billie, he said, downing his rum. "Course it maybe not true…'Bout twenty-five years ago, two guys flies in here wearin' fancy clothes and carryin' big suitcases. You take a guess! What you reckon was in them cases, Miss Billie?"

"Cash?" Billie asked catching Theo's eye.

"Could be!" Conrad chuckled, leaning back in his chair.

"Drug money," Theo murmured. The food arrived. Conrad dug in.

"What you folks do for money back home?" he asked. They told him. "So you in the buildin' trade, Miss Billie, my, my! An' you a jockey!" he said to Theo with a grin. "Same as me! I seen you today man. You a wild one!" Theo laughed along with him. As soon as the food was finished Conrad got up from the table. "I gotta be goin'," he said. "I got four Americans waitin' on me. Them folks is always in a rush!" He touched knuckles with Theo. "You come back now, Miss Billie," he added, with a broad grin. Then he was gone.

"You got any ideas for this afternoon?" Theo asked. Billie shook her head. "Those hammocks are looking pretty good to me right now," Theo said, pointing to a shady spot on the beach.

"To me too," Billie agreed.

A light breeze was blowing off the sea. Billie collapsed into one of the hammocks, the roar of the reef was so soporific, she had to force herself to stay awake.

"Listen," she said, "about the first night…"

"You sure you wanna talk about this?" Theo asked sleepily.

"I just want you to know it wasn't about you."

"I'm glad to hear it…" Theo said, opening his eyes.

"Guys I've been out with, you know, it's pretty much been a disaster…," she confessed.

Theo pondered this for a few minutes.

"These guys…they were what? French, Italian…Chinese?"

"No!" she laughed. "They were regular guys."

"Well," he said. "I'm thinking you need to discover your Italian side."

Billie thought about it for a moment.

"Okay…I guess," she replied softly.

"Okay!" Theo repeated, reaching out and giving her hammock a push. It began swinging wildly.

"Stop!" she shrieked, collapsing with laughter.

The afternoon passed in a heartbeat. Why, Billie wondered, was her perception of time so strangely altered on this island? She never lost touch with the march of time back home.

"Want me to drive?" Theo asked. Billie nodded and scooted over to the passenger side. Getting in touch with my Italian side, she thought dreamily, as the jeep roared into life. It wasn't that simple, but she knew exactly what Theo meant. It had been so long since she had felt free to be impulsive, since she had been willing to put her trust in someone outside her immediate circle of family and close friends. Back at college, things had been way less complicated.

"What are you thinking about?" Theo asked.

"Thinking? Who could think in this heat!" she replied. A pony tethered by the roadside lifted its head as if it was trying to catch her words. She gave it up, moved closer to Theo. It really was too hot!

He glanced across at her then looked ahead at the road again, a smile on his lips. Cottages and palm trees flew past…sunny pastures where bony cows lazily grazed, white birds perched on their backs, like a scene out of Africa, and everywhere the bright turquoise water flashing in and out of the mangrove trees that grew down to the shore.

Finally, Theo drew up outside the villa, and the roar of the jeep was replaced by birdsong.

"I'm going to take a shower," Billie announced. "Want to join me?" If Theo was surprised, he didn't show it.

"Yeah, I need to cool down," he said, then catching her eye he added. "How about you?"

"I'm on fire, feel me."

"Hey, you are warm. I know what to do about that, Miss Billie."

A few minutes later in the shower, Billie didn't feel the need for talking. The cool water streaming down her body. . .the scent of strawberry soap. . . Theo's hands on her.

"Don't stop," she said, putting her arms around him.

In the big bed, their love making was as leisurely as the soft tropical air, as comfortable as if this had happened a thousand times before, yet each time had been thrilling and new. Outside, the waves lapped the shore, the sun set and the sky grew bright with stars.

"Does this mean I've discovered my Italian side?" she murmured.

"If you step out of the house," he replied. "Does that mean you're a world traveller?"

"So…this is just the beginning."

"Yes," Theo affirmed.

"What's that scar?" she asked later, tracing the line on his chest with her finger.

"What? Oh that," Theo said, looking downcast.

"An accident?" she probed gently. He shook his head.

"I brought that one on myself," he replied.

"Didn't you crash your car or something?"

"Now that really wasn't my fault!" he exclaimed.

"You don't have to tell me," she said quickly.

"I'd probably rather you heard it from me than someone else," he responded immediately. "There's a lot of things you don't know about me, Billie."

There was a pregnant pause.

"I owed some guy a ton of money," Theo revealed finally. "Let's just say they reckoned they could beat it out of me."

"Oh my God," Billie breathed. "I can't believe it!"

"Well believe it, not everyone's like you in this world, Billie." She had more questions, but she decided this was neither the time nor the place for it.

"Feel like getting dressed up tonight?" Theo asked her later on.

"I feel like celebrating!" she replied with a broad smile.

"I know just the place," Theo said.

When they finally arrived at the Royal Tropicana, the Maître D was full of apologies.

"We'll have a table ready in 'alf an 'our, *Monsieur*. Would you like to take some drinks per'aps?" He indicated a room next to the dining area with a horseshoe shaped bar.

"You okay with that, Billie?" Theo asked.

"Oh course, this is great. It reminds me of a place in Toronto I used to go to." At the far end of the room, a man with carrot coloured hair was playing jazz at a grand piano. "Hey, I think I've just spotted someone I knew at college," she said in astonishment. "Tim! What are you doing here?" she laughed running up to the pianist.

"Billie!" he exclaimed, clasping her hand in both of his. "Wow, you're looking good!"

"I'll be at the bar," Theo said. Billie's eyes followed him. He looked like a dancer, light limbed and strong. The white linen suit he was wearing fitted him like a glove. That and the tan made him look incredibly glamorous. She couldn't believe how much had changed since that grey morning in Toronto airport less than a week ago.

As Theo took a seat at the bar, he heard raised voices. An argument had broken out between the couple next to him. The girl was young, barely fifteen, he reckoned. After a while he realized the man with her was her father. She wanted to leave, her friends were waiting for her, she said. But her father insisted she should stay. He was meeting someone…someone important to both of them.

"I'll take a Perrier," Theo told the hovering barman, who was casting nervous glances at the warring pair. Theo was listening to the pleasant fizz of sparkling water pouring into his glass, when he froze.

"Message from the boss," a voice growled from somewhere behind him. "He regrets that he cannot meet you here tonight, but he has sent a car."

Theo shuddered. The strong Quebec accent, that voice! The last time he'd heard it he'd been lying helplessly in the dark, on the parking lot of Iroquois Downs Raceway. What the hell was the man doing here? The thought of him standing no more than three feet away from him sent shivers down his spine. Instinctively he turned his head away, not wanting to be seen. When he looked back again, the man was heading for the exit, leaving Theo with a view of the back of his head only. He had a neck like a bull with shoulders to match. The father was following him, pushing his daughter along. The girl twisted her head around and looked back angrily. Theo read despair in the slump of her father's shoulders. Then the door banged shut and they were gone. Theo's hands were shaking. The barman, busily polishing glasses, gave no sign he'd noticed anything was amiss.

Fear, anger and painful memories swept through Theo's mind, like storm clouds flying across the face of the moon. Then, like waking from a nightmare, he heard a woman start to sing, her sweet voice filling the air. Slowly, the music calmed him and he began to feel steadier. It was only when the song ended and there was a little burst of applause that he realized to his astonishment that the singer was Billie. He jumped up and rushed over to the piano, making a supreme effort to act like everything was normal.

"You're a star!" he told her, flinching as a camera flashed. But it was only a photographer from the local paper. A dazzling smile from Billie was his reward.

But almost immediately, her expression switched to one of concern.

"What happened? You look like you saw a ghost or something!"

"If only," Theo muttered.

"What's going on?" she frowned.

"Not here," he replied tersely.

"How about the beach?" she suggested.

"Why not?" he agreed, feeling his spirits lift a little. A full moon was shining. The palm trees cast eerie shadows on the sand.

"It's such a beautiful night!" Billie declared, throwing her arms around him. She looked up at him inquiringly.

"Listen, about that," he said. "Back there at the bar…I got a little jumpy…I thought I saw one on the guys that..," he hesitated.

"One of the guys that attacked you?" Billie asked, looking aghast.

"It probably wasn't him at all," he lied in what he hoped was a convincing tone. "It just sounded a lot like him." A host of questions he wanted to ask his uncle when he got back to Canada were forming in his head. How had Bernie happened to buy a timeshare on this island? And why?

"You're certain it wasn't him?" Billie asked anxiously.

"Trust me!" he replied. Billie looked satisfied.

"This is the most beautiful place I've ever seen!" she said happily. "I'm so glad you asked me to come along!"

"If it wasn't for you," he said, between kisses. "I'd have gone home after two days, tops."

"You're crazy!" Billie laughed.

"Trust me," he replied with certainty. "There's nothing to do around here."

"Let's go skinning dipping!" Billie cried, breaking into a run. Reluctantly, Theo followed, dragging his feet as they got further away from the restaurant and the safety of the lights. "C'mon!" Billie urged, kicking off her shoes and running into the dark water. The hairs on the nape of his neck rose. The incident in the restaurant had put him on high alert. Anyone could be lurking in the undergrowth and he'd never know it, until it was far too late.

"Wait up!" he called out. Her answer was drowned by the waves washing up on the shore. He shivered. For Billie, the night held no threat, no hidden menace. But for him the dark would always be indelibly linked with danger. He heard a thud somewhere behind him and spun around. Just a coconut falling, he told himself. Then he saw something move. He froze. A dog appeared out of the shadows and ran towards him, snapping at his heels.

"Stop that!" he yelled, but it only made things worse. The mongrel barred his way, barking, whichever way Theo turned. He looked around for help. By the light of the moon he made out the outline of a broken down shack, half hidden in the palms. There were lanterns swinging from the eaves. A man with dreadlocks was shuffling his feet along the rickety porch, staring straight ahead, his eyes unfocused as though he was sleep walking. Theo took in the ghostly scene in an instant. "A crack house! Right next to a five-star restaurant. I don't believe it," he muttered.

The dog had stopped barking. But it was jumping up at him now, clawing him with its paws, not vicious but not friendly, either.

"Down boy," he said. The dog growled, revealing a set of yellow fangs. Through it, Theo could hear a tuneless dirge. The crack man was singing. Don't look it in the eye and whatever you do, don't run, Theo told himself. And don't even think about rabies. He noticed that a second man had come out on the deck. "Hey!" Theo shouted. "Call off your dog!"

"Satan!" the shackman called out. "Where you at?" The dog was sticking to Theo like a burr. A woman's high pitched scream rang out through the darkness. For the first time since the dog had appeared, Theo wondered where Billie had got to.

"Satan! You come home now, you hear!" a man shouted. The dog cringed. Then he ran off, his tail between his legs.

Billie reappeared, splashing through the shadows.

"You okay? That was a little scary," she said.

He clung to her.

Anything could have happened to him, to her.

"I'm okay," he said. "Really."

As they walked back to the restaurant, he decided that nothing could induce him to set foot on this island ever again. The sudden appearance of his former attacker had poisoned its beauty for him. The crack house was a sign that someone was selling the filth here, too. Theo figured he could make a good guess as to who the supplier was. He couldn't wait to get away.

Ten minutes' drive away, at the Hermitage, a fortress perched on the cliff top, André Fontainbleu was resting comfortably, after a long day out on the water in his new yacht, the Shere Kahn. He was lounging in his big bed, one eye on the TV, the other on the bedroom door. He was expecting a visitor. Judging by the amount of snow he could see on the news channel, Canada was in the throes of a major blizzard. Why any

sane person would enjoy living in that climate in the winter months was a mystery to him.

While he was pondering this, there was a loud rap at the bedroom door, the signature knock of his main man, who answered to the name of Boxer.

"*Entrez*," André Fontainbleu called out.

Boxer strode in. "Got 'im!" he announced, an expression of grim satisfaction on his ugly face. André Fontainbleu stepped over to the two-way mirror, which afforded a clear view of the grand entrance hall. A plump man was wringing his hands, looking the picture of misery. André smiled contemptuously.

"We'll proceed the usual way, Boxer," he said. "After that he'll be willing to do almost anything."

"There's a complication," Boxer replied promptly, indicating a slender girl of around fifteen, who had come into view. "His daughter. He wants to know if we are…," he sneered, "interested."

"*Mon dieu*! For what?" André queried with a twisted smile. Boxer chuckled and made a coarse hand gesture. Subtlety was not in Boxer's repertoire. "I wonder just how far this imbecile wishes to take this charade?" André asked softly, moving closer to the two way mirror, which was wired for sound.

"Sylvie, please," he heard the man pleading with his daughter. "You don't understand how much trouble I'm in."

"You expect me to save you by…." The girl fell silent, looking shocked to the core. "This is low, even for you, Dad."

"You think I don't know that?" he groaned. She stamped her foot.

"No way," she exclaimed.

"I'll buy you a Blackberry…," he begged.

"Enough!" André interjected. "Get rid of the girl. We don't want any witnesses!"

"Understood," Boxer said, with a curt nod.

If her father imagined he could buy time to pay off the $100,000 debt he had run up on the online gambling site André Fontainbleu owned by offering up his fifteen-year-old daughter, he had made a serious mistake. She was perhaps worth a few hundred dollars, a pittance! Besides, sex with a minor would open up a golden opportunity for blackmail, something he was somewhat of an expert at himself. Her father might not perhaps be quite as stupid as he appeared to be.

Once the girl was out of the way, Boxer went to work on the father. He was soon as limp as a rag doll. After gagging him, Boxer tied him roughly to a chair. Then he ripped off his pants, exposing his privates for all the world to see. André watched avidly, licking his lips as Boxer cupped the man's testicles almost lovingly in his huge left hand, while his right hand held a surgical knife aloft. The man's screams were clearly audible, even through the gag. Boxer stopped, his hand in mid air. The knife hung there, quivering. The man screamed louder.

"No?" Boxer grunted. "You're sure?" The man nodded vehemently. Boxer let him sweat for a while longer. "Okay. This is the deal," Boxer said flatly. "You'll stay here tonight. Tomorrow you're flying back to Canada to pay a visit to your bank. You will take out a loan for the hundred thousand you owe and wire it to an account here, on the island." The moron was struggling to speak. Boxer ignored him.

"Next time you'll get no second chance. Understood?" The man's head, André Fontainbleu was pleased to observe, was nodding like a marionette. "And one other thing. No more credit for your vile habit. Ever." The man was weeping now. Great blubbery tears were spilling down his fat pink cheeks. No backbone! André concluded contemptuously, as he watched Boxer hustle him away. But that was the reason the man had landed himself in trouble in the first place. He preferred the girl, even with her tiny breasts which were the size of unripe limes.

The evening was not over yet. The young Frenchman, Henri, was at the bedroom door, alerting him with a discreet tap.

"Mademoiselle Anya is 'ere, Monsieur André ," he announced quietly. He had made a good decision hiring Henri, André decided. It made a refreshing change to have someone civilized, who understood the importance of *la politesse*. Someone who spoke his language. He tried to see to it that Henri was never exposed to any unpleasantness. He didn't entirely trust him.

"Show Anya in," he said.

"Zer is someone wiz her, *Monsieur*."

"Another girl?" André Fontainbleu asked, raising his eyebrows delicately. This could have possibilities, he thought.

"*Main non, c'est un homme. Desolé, Monsieur*," Henri said, with a small private smile.

"A man? Take them into the study. Tell them to wait," he said trying to disguise his irritation.

"*D'accord*," Henri agreed, retreating.

"To what do I owe this pleasure?" André Fontainbleu enquired, strolling into the study twenty minutes later. A blond Adonis the size of a small tree was sitting beside Anya, he noted with a spasm of anger.

"This is Pete," Anya said. André ignored him, brushing Pete aside like a fly. "I've brought you the money," she continued. "Five thousand of it anyhow." André's eyebrows shot up. "I told you I was going to try and pay you back, right?"

"So," André replied softly. "You insult me by throwing my gift back into my face, yes?"

"I told you not to bother," Pete said.

"Who asked you?" André snapped, rage engulfing him like a rogue wave. Why, he asked himself furiously, did this penniless Australian girl elicit such strong emotions in him? He who prided himself on being untouchable? She would pay! He always found a way to make everyone pay in the end.

"I don't want to be beholden to you," she blundered on. "Even though I really appreciate what you did for me."

"You appreciate it," he parroted mockingly.

"C'mon Anya, let's go. I told you not to come!" the blond Adonis said, leaping to his feet. She hesitated.

"Yes, go!" André urged, picking up the bag of cash and thrusting it into her arms. "Next time, come alone or not at all," he whispered in her ear. She was trembling. That was pleasing at least. After they had left, Henri appeared, carrying a tray of drinks.

"What will it be for you, *Monsieur*?" he murmured tactfully.

"A brandy," André replied. "Have one yourself and sit next to me. Tell me, what do you think of this friend of Anya's?"

"Oh, I like him well enough," Henri said, a pink glow suffusing his sallow face. "An I zink 'e like me too," he added shyly.

So, I was right about him, André realized. He's gay. Interesting. The situation had definite possibilities.

"He'd be a pleasant companion for you, Henri," he suggested.

"*Vous pensez ça?*" Henri asked.

"I do indeed," André said encouragingly. Boxer was back.

"I'll help myself," Boxer said, grabbing a beer.

"Well?" André asked, knowing Boxer had something on his mind. He could read him like a book.

"Guess who I saw tonight?" Boxer said, a glint in his eye.

"I cannot imagine," André replied, sipping his drink.

"Our old friend. Mr. Theo Vettore."

"Vettore? *Sacre bleu*! Why is he here?"

"No idea," Boxer replied, taking a swig of his beer.

"Find out!" André Fontainbleu exclaimed irritably. "You know," he mused. "I believe Mr. Vettore could still be useful to us in some way, even though he is not presently a paying customer." An interesting idea had just occurred to him.

"You're the boss," Boxer replied.

"I am," André agreed, but it gave him very little satisfaction.

As he had discovered a long time ago, paying people generally made them pleasingly compliant. In Anya's case though, it had backfired badly. He had no idea how, or even why it had happened. He only knew he needed her back in his bed, with those breasts which were the size of melons at his disposal.

Kindness had not worked apparently. Perhaps, he thought, clenching and unclenching his right fist, it was time to try a little cruelty.

THE RETENTION BARN

Phil Harman brought Al McTavish up to speed on progress with regard to the retention barn, over the phone.

"The politicians I approached didn't like the sound of it much, I'm sorry to say," Phil reported. "Couldn't get any of them to sign up to put horses in jail. Anyway, I don't think we're going to have any luck raising money from that quarter for a while. Looks like we used up all our credits on the TCO2 testing, I'm afraid. Sorry, I wasn't able to help this time, pal."

Where the hell am I going to get the money from? Al thought, after he'd bade his friend a cordial farewell, assuring him he appreciated his efforts even if they hadn't yielded any results. He spent the next half hour closeted in his office at Iroquois Downs, reading his contract conditions and as much procedural guff as he could lay his hands on. Eventually, he discovered a solution to the conundrum: refurbishment. He didn't need anyone's permission for that, so long as expenditure was modest and funds were available. Now all he had to do was locate a suitable building. With this in mind, he drove across the vast parking lot to the stable gate, the entrance to the barn area.

"But the barns are all full, sir," the guard replied reproachfully, after Al had explained what he was looking for. "Most of the trainers have been here for years!" Al got the message. There would be an outcry if he tried to turf any of them out. "Of course," the guard added tentatively, "there is the old bank barn...No one uses it anymore."

"Hallelujah!" Al cried.

"Alley what?" the guard asked, looking confused.

"Just tell me where it is," Al replied.

From the outside, the bank barn looked perfectly sound. Inside, it was a different story. Al counted ninety cramped stalls, covered in dust and grime. It was dark and airless too. Al realized he would have to change things around drastically if his plan was to succeed. The way the place looked right now, trainers would have a perfectly legitimate reason for refusing to participate. But he believed it could be done. Track maintenance would be able to do the bulk of the work. All he needed was a man to oversee the job.

Call someone! Anyone! was Al's preferred method of dealing with thorny problems like this. The trail eventually led to Harmony Farm.

Joey Harris took the call at the kitchen table, a cup of coffee at his elbow, surrounded by shoe boxes crammed full of papers: the day to day records of K. L. Stables which, with hotshot trainer Keith Lazer at the helm, had taken the claiming ranks by storm. Joey had been hoping to snatch a free hour and get to grips with Lazer's tax return, due in to Revenue Canada in a few weeks' time. After Al's phone call, that plan was now blown. McTavish was on his way to the farm, an unstoppable force.

Outdoors, clouds were looming overhead. If he was quick, he could bring in the two broodmares and their foals before it started snowing again. He jumped up from his chair, grabbed a jacket and pulled on his boots. It was near feeding time and with any luck, he'd be able to talk to McTavish and get the chores done at the same time. He had just reached the shelter of the barn when McTavish's Mercedes pulled in.

"Hi there. Nice day!" McTavish commented with heavy sarcasm, indicating the sleet sweeping across the fields. He greeted Joey with a firm handshake. Whoa, but the guy was tall! Sharp dresser too, Joey thought, uncomfortably aware of the stains on his overalls.

"I want to pick your brains. Where can we talk?" McTavish asked.

"I've gotta feed. You're welcome to come along," Joey replied, sticking to the task in hand and leading the way resolutely to the run-in shed where eight ladies in waiting quickly crowded round him, welcoming the arrival of fresh supplies. Then with Al at his heels, Joey marched back to the main barn and switched on the lights.

Once inside, McTavish got a look on his face like an evangelist preacher addressing the faithful. As Joey measured out the feed, he imagined what his life would have been like had he stayed in the city and gone to work as an accountant. No more sleepless nights, no more getting up in the dark. He'd be clean and rested…like McTavish. He'd get to do civilized things like watch ball games with his friends or go for a walk on the waterfront with Val…

"This is perfect!" he heard McTavish exclaim. "This is exactly what I want."

Joey wheeled around, all thoughts of feed forgotten, to the disgust of the two broodmares, Gold Digger and Heart of Darkness, who started kicking the walls. McTavish wants to buy my place? Joey thought incredulously. His world had just turned upside down! Giddily, he began to figure out how much the farm was worth now. At least twice what he had in it, he decided, feeling quite light-headed. He went so far as to picture himself and Val sitting down to a candlelight dinner at an expensive eatery.

McTavish's next remark put paid to all that.

"This is exactly what the old bank barn could look like with a little money and a lot of hard work," McTavish declared. Just like that, Joey's world landed right side up again.

"So, what's so special 'bout my barn?" he asked proudly.

"Everything!" McTavish enthused. "The big stalls, the rubber mats, the skylights up in the roof..." He flung his arms out in an expansive gesture, startling Heart of Darkness's colt, who scooted over to his dam and hid under her belly. McTavish was in full flow now, preaching his version of the gospel: a retention barn for all claiming races.

"I want to get rid of the bad apples. Create a level playing field for everyone," Al said.

"Why come to me?" Joey asked doubtfully.

"Because you can help me make it happen!" Al replied, a fanatical gleam in his eyes.

"I'd like to help," he said, half persuaded by the guy's rhetoric. Then, remembering all the chores he hadn't done yet, together with the paperwork piled up on the kitchen table, he exclaimed. "But I don't have the time!" Hurriedly, he picked up a broom and began sweeping up. McTavish didn't say anything, just looked him over in an almost fatherly fashion.

"You take care of all these horses yourself?" he asked.

"That's not even the worst of it." Joey replied, ducking the issue. "I took on a whole bunch of book-keeping work, but lately I've been letting it slide," he confessed.

"You like accounting?" McTavish asked looking a little puzzled.

"Hate it!" Joey replied cheerfully. "But it keeps the money coming in and pays the feed bills. So I'm sorry, Mr. McTavish but I'm afraid I can't take anything else on just now."

"Makes sense, I suppose," McTavish said in a resigned tone.

"You ought to think about buying a yearling yourself," Joey suggested. "These two, the colt and the filly, they'll be in the sale next year." But McTavish didn't seem very taken by the idea. Well, that's that, Joey thought.

"Listen!" McTavish said suddenly. "I've got a proposition for you. I'll pay you to design and oversee the refurbishment of the bank barn at Iroquois Downs, pay you well. The only proviso is you'll have to stick to a low budget on materials costs. How does that sound?"

"Oh, I'm used to that," Joey laughed.

"You can hire someone else to do your paperwork," Al said in a tone that brooked no refusal.

"Who could I possibly get?"

"You leave that up to me. I've got someone in mind. She's…" but Joey didn't let him finish.

"A woman! I'm not sure how Val would feel about that," he frowned.

"You don't need to worry. She's old enough to be your mother. And trust me, she's terrific at her job."

"Alright, I'll do it!" Joey said gratefully, throwing caution to the wind.

"Listen," McTavish said. "You've done a great job with this place, you know that?"

A little appreciation went a long way, Joey reflected as McTavish drove off. The lights were on in the kitchen. Val was back. With a heavy heart, he pushed open the door. To his surprise, she greeted him with a big smile.

"Look what I've got," she said, waving a stack of twenty dollar bills in his face. "Eight hundred dollars I was paid for today. Cash money!"

"So the root canal went well, then," Joey replied, glancing at the kitchen clock. "D'you wanna go out to dinner?" he asked earnestly. "Somewhere classy?" Val's response was a peal of laughter. He was uncomfortably aware that he was the butt of the joke.

"You mean," she said, pausing dramatically. "You'd rather spend the evening with me than with a bunch of broodmares?" He nodded emphatically.

"Okay," she said. "This is the deal. I'll go book a table for us at the Old Mill for seven o'clock. That gives you exactly ten minutes to get rid of that smell and get into something suave and sophisticated. I'm betting you'll never make it." He noticed she was wearing a new dress, a low cut one.

"Just watch me!" he said, kicking off his boots and running up the stairs. He didn't need to give up on his dream to be a breeder of champions, he thought, stepping into the shower, to have a bit of fun, a little happiness.

"I've got some good news!" he shouted down the stairs as he towelled his hair dry.

"Four minutes!" Val shouted back. "And counting!"

Billie McTavish was sitting on the sofa in her second floor apartment, watching snow fall out of a black sky. After a while, she drew the curtains and turned on the racing channel. It was snowing at Iroquois Downs, too. Had the time in the island with Theo changed anything? she asked herself. It was Saturday night and here she was, alone in the house again, watching Theo on TV. If she had fallen for someone with a regular job, things would have been very different. They would have probably ordered a takeaway, shared a bottle of wine and watched a movie together, snuggled up on the sofa. But the realist in her knew that guys like that bored her to tears, sooner or later. She fixed herself a bowl of hot soup. Then she called home. Sofia had gone to bed early but Al was happy to hear from her. He hadn't bought anything for Sofia's birthday yet and he was desperate for ideas.

"Why not take her out to dinner at the racetrack?" Billie suggested. "You could get her birthday announced, even sponsor a race. It'd be fun for both of you."

"You know that could just work," Al replied happily.

"So! Problem solved," Billie said. "Goodnight, Dad."

"Wait!" Al exclaimed. "You haven't told me anything about your trip!"

"It's late and I'm tired," Billie said. "Call you tomorrow, okay?"

This wasn't the right time to tell her father that she wasn't going to be running McTavish Construction for very much longer. As for her relationship with Theo Vettore, she intended to keep that to herself until she had a clearer idea of where things were headed. She reached for the phone again, called Jeff Lamare and told him she'd decided to take him up on his offer to finance the start up costs of her new enterprise, in return for an interest in the company, which she'd named *Fence Sense*. To his credit, Jeff didn't mention her nemesis, Keith Lazer, or the incredible run of luck he was having with the horses. But before she rang off, she let it drop about her and Theo.

"It's such a beautiful island, Jeff," she hurriedly added. "You've gotta see it. Promise me you'll go."

"As long as you'll come with me," Jeff replied optimistically.

"Goodnight, Jeffrey," she said firmly. Would he ever give up? she wondered sleepily, sitting back on the sofa. On the TV screen, the snow was abating. She fell asleep in the middle of the sixth race.

She was roused by a noise at the window. Wondering if she'd imagined it, she opened her eyes. There it was again! Something had landed with a soft thud on the glass. She turned out the lights and drew back the curtain. A big snowball came flying up towards her, hitting the pane with a plop. Just kids having fun, she thought, opening the window and peering out. On the pavement below, Theo was standing under a street lamp, snowball in hand.

"Hey! Want to come up?" she laughed.

He tossed his snowball high in the air. It hung for an instant, caught by the light before disappearing into the night. Billie flew down the stairs and opened the front door. He was waiting on the pavement, sports bag in hand, holding a paper bag.

"Coffee and doughnuts," he explained. "I thought it'd be better than flowers. You can't eat flowers.

"Come on in," she smiled. Her normal Sunday routine was going to be disrupted. Happily, she tossed it out of the window. Things were going to be different now. For the first time it looked like she finally had someone to share her life with. She thanked her lucky stars for that.

A BIRTHDAY PRESENT

Thankfully, Billie's idea of celebrating Sofia's birthday at Iroquois Downs was a success. Encouraged, Al timidly broached the subject of buying a race-horse for Sofia as a present. To his surprise she told him that she quite liked the idea, so he called Bob Summers and told him to start asking around for something suitable. Professionally too, things were looking up for Al. The twenty-four-hour retention barn had been rubber stamped by the board. There had been no objections, no threatened strikes and no bad press. In fact, Al had been proclaimed a hero by the Provincial Racing Commission. In a month or so the retention barn would no longer be just an idea in his head. It would be up and running.

However, Al's life was still far from ideal. Billie seemed to have disap-peared into a black hole, seduced, he assumed, by the dual attractions of her first solo business venture and her first ever live in boyfriend, Theo Vettore. Al hadn't had a proper conversation with her in weeks. As for Sofia, he tried to avoid conversations with her altogether, laced as they were with complaints about her birthday present, a young filly named Millie D, which instead of bringing them closer together, was driving them even further apart.

Millie D was completely sound. She was good gaited and had a sweet nature. But Jim Mercer had known what he was doing when he offered her up for sale. Millie D was a tie-up mare. Mercer had apparently dealt with her problem by training her hard every day and half starving her, something Bob Summers wasn't prepared to do. Lately, Al had learned more about the effects of lactic acid build up than he ever cared to know. But, despite Bob's best efforts, Millie D's AST and CK scores were still in the stratosphere, as were Winterflood's bills, for a long list of approved medications. Al wouldn't have minded the expense so much if the treatments he was paying for had actu-ally worked. But, to date, Millie D had never finished better than seventh. He could tell failure was getting to Bob Summers. Ironically, Millie D was glowing with health, a far cry from the half starved creature that had moved from Jim Mercer's barn a month earlier.

Al had imagined that things couldn't get any worse. He was proved wrong. After her next effort, Millie D was relegated to the Judges List, for poor per-formance. Post race, Al retreated to his study and drowned his sorrows in a large glass of brandy. He could hear canned laughter coming from the living room. Sofia was watching a comedy on TV, to cheer herself up no doubt. He was about to call it a night when the phone rang.

"She's not on the Judges List anymore," Bob Summers reported happily. "Lucky enough she's broke a hobble, so they let 'er off, see."

"What now?" Al asked wearily, ready to put Millie D up for sale to the highest bidder, to any bidder in fact.

"I got a plan," Bob pronounced mysteriously. "I'm racin' her at Merryvale next week. Bring that wife of yours along. I'm puttin' Harry Harper down to drive. She's gonna win!"

"Harry Harper?" Al cried, dumbfounded. Clearly, this was an act of madness on Bob's part. Picking a driver with an accelerator but no brakes made no sense.

"Trust me!" Bob replied.

"What about Theo Vettore? He's a far better driver," Al countered.

"If you can get Vettore to slum it at Merryvale Downs, you're a better man than me," Bob chuckled. No driver was going to solve Millie D's problem, Al realized. Only baking soda could do that. It was a bitter irony that he himself had led the charge to ban it, he concluded sorrowfully.

Having a connection, via Billie, with the top driver in North America, proved useful. The very next Wednesday, on a freezing afternoon at Merryvale Raceway, Theo Vettore took Millie D to the lead and opened up five lengths on the field. Al held his breath and waited for her to fall apart. But instead of quitting, she won easily. The euphoria washing over him in the winner's circle was unlike anything he had experienced before. Even his wedding day paled before it. He hugged everybody concerned: Bob, Bob's wife, even Theo Vettore! The despair of recent months faded to a distant memory. Even Sofia's expression softened. As for Billie, she looked thrilled, though that probably had more to do with Theo's success than Millie D's, Al reflected soberly.

The next morning, he came to his senses and picked up the office phone.

"What did you give her, Bob?" he asked, dreading the answer. What if Bob had lost his head and used something illegal?

"Nothin'," Bob laughed. "Nothin' illegal, anyhow." Al waited him out. Eventually the silence got to Bob. "I asked Lazer," he confessed. Al continued to apply the pressure by keeping mum. "Nothin' to worry about. It's a kind of a jug, is all," Bob added finally.

Al gazed out of the big plate glass window onto the racetrack below. He had watched that scene so many times in the last eighteen months. It looked so innocent: scores of horses out for a bit of healthy early morning exercise. It was only recently that he had begun to understand that what lay under the surface was anything but innocent. As for healthy…

"Is it an amino acid jug?" he asked hopefully, dredging his memory. Winterflood had mentioned it once.

"It's a watcha-macall it…er…wobbly jug," Bob revealed. "It's not on the list of banned substances if that's what you're thinkin'."

Al breathed a sigh of relief. It sounded innocent enough, to his untrained ears at least.

"It ain't gonna make 'er go faster neither. Jus' helps a tie-up horse is all," Bob added reassuringly.

"And it won't hurt her?" Al asked anxiously.

"Never!" Bob replied vehemently. "Tyin' up is what was hurtin' her, see. Fuckin' painful it is."

Al felt like a heel. His next idea was to call his guru, Dr. Jay Winterflood, and ask him what a wobbly jug was.

"Guaifenesin," Winterflood replied promptly. "Horsemen call it a wobbly jug because some horses get a bit shaky for a few minutes after it's administered. It's what they give people before operations to relax their muscles." Al wondered briefly how the drug had migrated to the standardbred industry.

"Is it harmful?" he asked, hoping for reassurance.

"Only if used to excess. It's as good a way of dealing with lactic acid build up as anything else, sometimes better," the vet said. "Apparently."

"How come you never mentioned it?" Al asked in an outraged tone, thinking of the small fortune he'd shelled out so far on useless medications.

"It's not my job to recommend drugs that the Veterinary Establishment has not approved for use on racehorses," Winterflood replied testily. "You and I never had this conversation," he added, cutting Al off abruptly.

Al swivelled his office chair around in a circle and considered the alternatives. Option one: tell Bob Summers he couldn't use the only thing that had solved Millie D's tie-up problem. Two: sell the mare and wash his hands of her. Probable result, the new trainer would use illegal drugs or even bleach on her. She wasn't a claimer, so she wouldn't be racing out of the retention barn. Option three: carry on and hope for the best. He had no idea what the outcome of that would be and he wasn't generally a man who liked to take chances.

He rejected the first option. The businessman in him recoiled from that solution now she had won a race. Besides, Sofia would never understand it. Option two was cast aside on humanitarian grounds. That left only the third option. But at least something would be going right in his life then. To his bewilderment, despite Millie D's spectacular win, Sofia still wasn't happy. Why couldn't she just tell him what was wrong? It would make things a hell of a lot easier. Winter was almost over. Perhaps Al thought, when spring broke his wife would feel more cheerful. Failing that, he would just have to carry on and pray for a miracle. At least there had been no more horse deaths since the introduction of the retention barn, he thought, comforting himself.

COPS AND ROBBERS

After the heated conversation with Al McTavish, Dr. Jay Winterflood spent several minutes reflecting on the futility of trying to change things for the better. He sometimes wished he had never written the paper on the effects of baking soda on the equine athlete. However, he was quite sure he had done the right thing resigning as track veterinarian. Being a mobile veterinarian had its limitations but at least his time was his own, making it simpler for him to spend a week at the Reserve in Quebec visiting his mother.

Before he set off, he put in a call to Metabec Pharmaceuticals and ordered another case of Sarapin. Demand for this soared from December to March, when the frozen racetrack was like a concrete road. Injected into the heel, it deadened the sensation in a horse's front feet for a few weeks at least, unlike moth balling which only lasted a few hours. As he drove he pondered Al McTavish's latest wheeze to catch the crooks: the retention barn. He had a feeling that clever trainers would find a way over this hurdle too, just as they seemed to have done with TCO2 testing. He had been hearing rumours lately of a crossover, drugs wise, from athletics to horse racing. Unfortunately, it sounded all too likely to be true.

The retention barn, referred to by all horsemen as the detention barn, had made Dave Bodinski's life a whole lot more complicated. It had given him hours of extra work, shipping horses back and forth and he'd had to put up his owners bills to take account of it all. He lived in fear of getting a call from one of them complaining about it or worse, taking the horses away, so he had stopped answering the barn phone. It hadn't affected the top claiming trainers, though. Lazer, Price and Larson were still powering ahead. Only poor schmucks like him were suffering. However, as he walked his new trotting mare over to the blacksmith's shop, Dave was feeling pretty good about one thing: the injectables he'd bought from Doc Meecham. They were only out of date by a month or so but they had saved him a ton of money. Maybe he'd have a few winners this week, he thought hopefully. He reckoned he deserved some luck, even if he had quit school after sixth grade.

He spent the next hour putting his horses away, greasing their heels and packing their feet with a concoction he mixed up himself. Then he headed back to the blacksmith's shop to collect his trotter. Since the cold weather hit, he had been hanging out there most afternoons, keeping warm and catching up on the latest gossip. The heat from Jeremiah Hostetler's forge kept the place snug.

"She's all done," the Amishman announced, his bulky frame covered with an enormous leather apron, his forge glowing red. "I've done the best I could. Her feet were all wore down at the heel."

Andy Price could be found most winter mornings in the track kitchen at Iroquois Downs, warming his toes and thanking his lucky stars that he was done driving by 10:30 a.m. thanks to his number one groom, Crawfish Brown. Crawfish didn't bother with time wasting niceties like prettying horses up before they went out on the track. He just slung on a harness and they were ready to go. There were no holdups, no pointless questions and no neurotic observations. Crawfish carried on regardless, enabling Andy to get out of the weather in time for a well deserved second breakfast and a natter.

But the detention barn had put at end to Andy's carefree life. He ran a claiming stable, composed mostly of aged geldings. By the time these seasoned warriors reached his barn, they had had practically everything happen to them, yet had somehow survived, beating the odds, which Andy, prone to inflating figures, calculated to be about a million to one.

In the past, he and Doc Meecham had worked out a clever system for treating these battle-scarred veterans on race day for the usual ailments such as bleeding, allergies, ulcers, even tying up, without resulting in a positive test. The exact calculations involved hours, not days. Before McTavish had rumbled him, Andy's horses had been virtually unbeatable! Andy had boasted that his success was all down to his number one groom, Crawfish Brown. No one had believed him, but what did Andy care? Now everything had changed. Banning all medications, even perfectly legal ones on race day was, in Andy's view, sheer lunacy. How could a horse do his best if his treatment was forcibly stopped at the very moment it was most needed: during the race? Even Crawfish couldn't save him now!

Though he didn't dare to say so to Andy, Crawfish Brown was a big fan of the detention barn. It had saved him a ton of work. He walked the horses over there the evening before they were due to race. After that, the girl Andy had hired took over. Crawfish had been with Andy Price over a year now, a record for both of them. He'd had to lay off nicking the injectibles, though. Andy had cottoned on to the fact that stuff was going missing and had bawled him out for it. He was feeling pretty good anyhow. The stomach gismo most of the horses were on had helped him, big time! Crawfish's rule of thumb for horse powders was simple. He never took more than one scoop, in case there was something wrong with it. It had worked out okay so far.

As for winter, that hadn't fazed him! It had taken him less than ten minutes to double glaze his groom's quarters at Iroquois Downs. Some clear plastic he'd salvaged from the garbage and a roll of tape he'd "borrowed" from his employer had done the job on the small window that overlooked the horseman's parking lot. Life was good. The detention barn was ace! All the same, he was glad winter would soon be over and done.

SPRING

The Canada Geese had left their winter feeding grounds and looking like black dots in a washed out blue sky, they were flying north, helped along by a warm spring wind. In their wake, the horsemen who had also wintered in the south (the lucky few) were on their way back to Iroquois Downs, their horse trailers loaded up with promising two and three year olds prepped for the big money.

In Ontario, the earth was still cold but the ice had melted. Water flowing into lakes and ponds lured the geese in. They flew in a great arc, a v-shaped formation that formed and re-formed as they travelled. They ducked and dived, their hoarse cries waxing and waning in the ears of anyone below who cared to listen. Their return was a sign of spring, of better times to come after the long, hard Canadian winter. To those who loved wild things, the birds offered reassurance. The natural cycle of life was still in place. The geese had come home and the spring stakes season was about to begin.

As the geese passed over Harmony Farm, a dozen birds broke off from the main flock and dropped earthwards. Outside the barn, Joey Harris heard the beat of their wings as they made for the big pond in the centre of his hayfield. Shading his eyes against the rising sun, he watched them land, skidding to a stop in the icy water. From a distance, Joey looked like his usual self: khaki overalls stuffed into workman's boots, a healthy colour in his cheeks. But there were shadows under his eyes. He had overslept again. It was no wonder. He had been working late into the night at his job as a horseman's book-keeper. He couldn't afford to hire help at present, even though the accounts season was in full swing. Also, there were eight mares to breed and feed. Lately, he'd been feeling like he'd been juggling one too many balls in the air. Something was bound to give.

As Joey entered the dark barn, he tripped over Scats the cat, who'd thrown herself at his feet, as usual, desperate for attention. Heart of Darkness and her foal had finished their breakfast and were ready to go back out again. The wiry little colt, the image of his dam, was whirling round the stall in tight circles and his mother was tossing her head in classic "Let me out of here!" fashion. By contrast, the mare Gold Digger and her filly were a picture of over the top calm. They were standing motionless basking in a shaft of sunlight, eyes half closed, looking for all the world as though they were practicing meditation, Val's latest fad.

Joey led the mares and foals out of the barn into the April sunshine, up the gravel track to the two-acre paddock, figuring they would have more room there to let off steam. Tall trees surrounded it and a shallow stream ran through it, a natural playground for the foals. Heart of Darkness spent the first few minutes running for the sheer joy of it, chasing two Canada Geese that were trying to take a drink from the stream. No pushovers, the geese retaliated, hissing and beating their wings. It was hard to tell who was winning, the birds or the horses. Joey smiled and shook his head. She was still such a baby! Her son did his best to keep up with her as she sprinted back and forth, twisting and turning, her long mane flying and her tail flowing out behind her. Whenever she slowed down, the colt grabbed her halter with his teeth, egging her on, longing for the game to continue. Gold Digger and her filly followed at a more sedate pace.

Joey stood watching the four of them for a good ten minutes. Heart of Darkness was safely back in foal to Night Raider. With the mare's exciting record on the track and her colt's racy looks, next year's yearling sale could spell a big payday and hopefully provide Harmony Farm with some badly needed cash. Joey thanked God for that. But his personal favourite was the filly. He had already named her Harmony Gold, after her mother, Gold Digger who was solidly built with strong farmhouse legs. However, Harmony Gold had also inherited Night Raiders' speed and class, which combined with her dam's strength had produced a perfect example of a good pacing filly, in Joey's opinion at least. She was pacing now and as he watched her all of his everyday worries slipped away. Both were January foals, both were good-looking but the filly stole the show. When Joey looked at the colt, he saw dollars and cents. But she was the stuff dreams were made of. Joey Harris, happily married for four years and five months, true to Val during all of that time, was hopelessly in love! The toot of the feed man's horn brought him back to reality. There were stalls to clean, mares to breed, fences to mend. No time to dream. It was almost nine o'clock!

Reggie Blair delivered the feed along with a few choice pieces of gossip. Jim Mercer's wife, Pam had left him and was working as a cocktail waitress at the Hot Tamale. The former groom, "Trake" Jake was touting drugs on the backstretch. Al McTavish had rumbled the cocaine tongue tie dodge at Iroquois Downs. Talk soon turned to weightier matters.

"One of my best customers is getting out of the breeding business," Reggie clucked disapprovingly. "They'll have a half a dozen weanlings for sale, come fall. I reckon you could get yourself a deal."

"Me?" Joey asked in what he hoped was an astonished tone. "Why me?"

"You can't keep colts and fillies together forever. Sooner or later, there's bound to be trouble," Reggie warned. "You'll need something to keep 'em company."

"I haven't even weaned them yet," Joey protested.

"Early foals…Can't put it off forever…Got a name for the colt?" Reggie probed.

"No," Joey contested, wishing the feed man didn't have such a habit of sticking his nose into everyone's business.

"Went to church last Sunday. Had a bit of an inspiration," Reggie declared.

"Oh?" Joey replied, unaware that Reggie took his religion so seriously.

"Book of Genesis," Reggie said. "Out of darkness He created light. Get it?"

"Get what?" Joey frowned, fearful that he'd never get his chores done if Reggie carried on like this.

"Dam's name is Heart of Darkness," Reggie explained patiently. "Out of Darkness…"

"Light!" Joey exclaimed, clapping his hand to his head. "Of course, Harmony Light! I'll tell Val."

"Tell her about the weanlings, too," Reggie urged, obviously trying to regain some of his lost custom. "If you get in early, you can have your pick of them."

After a full morning's work, Joey fell into the worn old armchair in the farmhouse kitchen and gazed up at the rafters, trying not to think about the farm's dire finances. Where was he going to find the money to buy two more weanlings? Their first cash infusion wasn't due until the yearling sale, eighteen months away. They'd gambled everything on Heart of Darkness and her progeny.

Out in the paddock, her first foal, Harmony Light, trotted up to his mother, looking for milk and comfort. He found both. She stood patiently while he nursed, as if one movement on her part would have put her son's life at risk. When he'd finished, she nuzzled his neck with tender affection. She was his whole world. There was no thought in either of their minds that this blissful existence would ever end. After a while, she communicated to him, in the wordless way that mothers do, that it was safe for him to sleep. Lying out in the afternoon sun, stomach bulging with milk, head pillowed on a tuft of grass, Harmony Light slept the sleep of the angels. For a few hours, there was perfect harmony at Harmony Farm.

A DANGEROUS LIAISON

Anya's arrival at the Hermitage, moments before he was due to leave for Miami, came as a complete surprise to André Fontainbleu. She was wearing a short dress which showed off her large breasts and long sun-tanned legs and she was alone. The idea of cancelling the trip crossed his mind but he swiftly rejected it.

"Come with me, to Miami," he suggested to her, astounded by his own foolhardiness. "You will need just a passport," he persisted, seeing her hesitate.

"You know I can't leave the Sea Princess, André," she replied unhappily.

"Not for one day?" he asked, acutely aware that the invitation was breaking his own strict protocols. "Henri is waiting," he added, picking up his suitcase.

"Okay," she said, biting her lower lip. "I'll come."

So, he mused, the die was cast. Addiction was a marvellous and terrible thing, he reflected, feeling not the slightest hint of remorse. He would cancel his usual hotel, he decided and book the Oasis with its honeymoon suites and panoramic views of the ocean.

Once in Miami, he ordered champagne, which they drank greedily and supper which lay untouched. They were far too busy with one another. After a while he sank down on the bed, the cool white sheets on his bare back, caressing her breasts which hung down like ripe fruit, drowning in her long dark hair which flowed over him like a river. It felt like no time had passed since he was twenty, with his whole life ahead of him. No time at all.

He slept little, dozing after making love, waking and making love to her again, knowing only that his desire for her was overwhelming. Her sudden reappearance after so long had sent him into a swoon, sweeping away his normal disciplined self in a torrent of emotion and taking him to a place where caution, control and calculation were no long relevant.

With the dawn, came reality. He was old enough to be her father. She was merely a terrific fuck who reminded him of a wild past...a past he could never revisit in the flesh. Paradoxically, he hid his feelings from her, playing the part of the lover until she was safely on her way back to the island. Then he stood under the shower, berating himself for his risky behaviour and for his weakness. Addiction, his old friend! He knew her so well. He knew too, that there was only one cure: *laisse le seul*. Stay away! Never, but never, let down your defences. Vigilance! Abstinence! Fortitude! Three simple words. Was not the Revolution in *la belle France* driven by just three words? *Liberte, Egalite, Fraternite*! He would win this battle, he swore savagely, fighting off the memory of raven black hair swinging in the breeze. At all costs, he promised himself fiercely.

At last, plastering down his soaking wet hair and holding himself erect, he was ready. Ready for a morning's business, followed by an afternoon at the Kennedy Stadium, watching Ritchie Sanchez set a new Florida state record.

SEPARATION

At Harmony Farm, the early morning sun was streaming into the barn, swallows were darting in and out but the beauty of the scene could not console Harmony Light. His ever present mother, his source of comfort and food had walked away, leaving him alone for the very first time. Outside, the air was ringing with her desperate cries. He responded with a shrill whinny. As her cries grew fainter and fainter, he hurled himself against the door of the stall they had shared in vain. It was shut tight. Wheeling around in the deep straw he tried desperately to escape, his feet pounding the ground going nowhere fast. Eventually, he dozed from sheer exhaustion. When he woke, anguish struck him afresh. She was not there! He reared up pawing at the air, kicking the walls. There was no escape. Needing milk, he did not drink. Needing her, he did not eat. The filly Harmony Gold stood quietly in the stall next door and wondered what all the fuss was about. Out in the field, Heart of Darkness and Gold Digger stayed close to one another and spent most of their time hanging around the big round hay bale that Joey had set out for them. Though their attachment to their foals was strong, they quickly accepted the new situation and made the best of it. Sensing his despair, Scats the cat came to the little colt's rescue. By night, she slept curled up in a corner of the little colt's stall. By day, she crouched up on the rafters, staring down at him.

Harmony Light mourned his mother for four days and nights. On the fifth day, he woke up at dawn, feeling unbearably thirsty. He took a long drink of fresh water from the bucket that Joey had patiently refilled day and night. As soon as he had drunk, he felt desperately hungry. The feed smelled delicious. He wolfed it down.

Later that morning, Joey led him and the filly out to the small paddock near the barn. Harmony Light ran rings round Harmony Gold, kicking his heels up, running for the sheer joy of it. Up on the hill, the two broodmares broke off from eating hay. Heads up, ears pricked, the mothers stared at their foals intently, their bodies straining towards them. Heart of Darkness whickered, so softly it was almost inaudible. Harmony Light froze for a moment, scenting the air, then whinnied shrilly back. The filly took off, leaping like a deer, tossing her head. Harmony Light hesitated. Then he carried on playing as though he hadn't a care in the world. Only the dullness in his eyes bore testimony to his ordeal. Scats went mousing for the first time that week. Joey closed Dr. D. Thomas' *The Broodmare and Foal: Modern Methods Explained* and whistled as he cleaned the stalls. Harmony Farm was back to normal.

Best to make the most of the peace, Joey thought to himself. A horde of new arrivals come fall, would soon put paid to it. He and Val had heeded Reggie's advice. But instead of choosing one colt and one filly to keep their weanlings company, they'd taken all six of them. The deal (not a penny to pay until after the yearling sale) had been too good a chance to miss.

A few weeks later, the tropical sun had turned the sea to a startling shade of turquoise but Anya hardly noticed it. She hadn't heard a word from André Fontainbleu since Miami.

"You're pretty quiet today. Nothing much to say for yourself," Pete remarked after another idyllic day in the Sea Princess with a boat load of tourists. "You're not still brooding over that Fontainbleu guy, are you, Anya?" he added in an exasperated tone. "He's a creep and he's far too old for you anyhow. Do yourself a favour – let it go!" Anya didn't trust herself to speak. "Ever since you went to Miami with him, you've been brooding. It's been, what, four, five weeks now. What's going on?"

She tried to explain.

"Bullshit!" Pete exclaimed, startling a lone passenger who had lingered on the quayside to watch the sun set.

"I just don't get it," Anya confessed. "I'm so confused."

"Well, get this. You used him. Now he's used you," Pete stated brutally.

"No! You don't understand. It wasn't like that. Not that last time!" She couldn't cry, not in front of Pete.

"Want me to ask Henri?" Pete offered.

"Ask him what?" she replied a little belligerently.

"He's been on at me to go out with him forever."

"Since when?" she asked, wiping a tear away with the back of her hand.

"Ever since that night you tried to throw money in the guy's face." Pete grinned. "Lucky Fontainbleu didn't take it. New sails don't come cheap on this island." Anya nodded. She should have never gone to the Hermitage at all, she thought. She should have listened to Pete.

The next day, Pete came back to her with an answer of sorts to the puzzle. André Fontainbleu had apparently left the island for a while. Henri had no idea when he'd be back. It didn't satisfy Anya in the least.

As time passed and she had still heard nothing, she had a long, honest talk with herself. The fact that she'd ended up stranded in the Caribbean was her own fault. She couldn't keep blaming her parents. She could have stayed behind in Melbourne...if she hadn't been so taken by the idea of seeing the other side of the world. Well, now she'd seen it. Some of it, anyway. Her parents had filled her up with stories about Greece, about the old country, like it was some kind of Disney World. It wasn't like that at all. The place was still in the Dark Ages. Give her Australia any day. There at least, women had rights. André Fontainbleu had treated her like some kind of call girl. He was all crippled up emotionally. She should have seen him coming a mile off. Even if, like a bloody boomerang, he reappeared to ask her to play again, she didn't want any part of it.

She was done with him. But it still hurt. A lot!

The gossip Reggie Blair had passed on was all too true. Cocaine was once more freely available on the backstretch of Iroquois Downs. The introduction of new regulation tongue ties in the Race Barn had forced Keith Lazer to truck Midnight Madness to Merryvale Downs instead. The horse had a great deal in common with the driver Theo Vettore. Cocaine settled them down and enabled them to focus. The fact that Vettore snorted his and Midnight Madness ingested his via a cocaine laced tongue tie hardly mattered. Without his dose on race day, Midnight Madness was a nervous wreck and a danger to himself and everyone else.

Lastly, Pam Mercer had indeed moved out of the family home. Evie Mercer had been thankful, at first, not to have to listen to her parents arguing all the time. After a while, though, the silence in the house got her down. When the long summer vacation began, she started spending most of her time at Rivers Training centre. However, because Pam wasn't around anymore, Evie had to put up with a lot of hassling from some of the low life grooms who worked for her dad.

Will was different. Like her, he was going back to school in the fall, the so called "School for Dummies" that everyone at Evie's school cracked jokes about. Despite that, she and Will became friends. The stakes season was in full swing. Her dad's horses were competing all over the province of Ontario. Summer flew by with long trips to small tracks under a burning blue sky. Will rode in the truck with them. It was good to have someone her age to talk to. Often, one of their horses won and Evie would get to have her picture taken in the winner's circle with Theo Vettore, her favourite human being on the entire planet. On weekends, Theo's girlfriend came along. But it was obvious Billie McTavish didn't know a thing about racehorses. What in the world did the two of them find to talk about? Evie wondered. By the end of the summer, her bedroom walls were covered in win photos with Theo Vettore standing centre stage, in Evie's mind at least. In September, she went back to school. It was hard concentrating on lessons, especially when Sammy was named Two-year-old Trotting Colt of the Year.

The yearling sale came and went. Evie did her homework in the track kitchen on race nights and got the chance to eat a proper meal, which made a nice change from delivery pizza. She took to cooking supper at home a few times a week. It was a bit hit and miss at first, but her dad wolfed it down. At school, everyone was counting the days until the winter vacation. Evie had no idea what she and her dad were going to do in the holidays. But she knew that with her mom gone, Christmas was going to be weird.

SPECIAL DELIVERY

Jean Claude stopped his truck, turned on the dashboard lights and checked the delivery book. Yes! He'd come to the right place. Yet in twenty-five years in the horse trucking business, he had never heard of Harmony Farm, even though he knew every breeding farm from here to Quebec City. It looked like he had a brand new customer. The last time he had seen Joey Harris he had been working as a groom to pay his college tuition. Apparently Joey had come up in the world. Hearing banging in the back of the horse van, Jean Claude quickly started up the engine again. His small passengers were getting restless. It was no wonder! They had had a long journey. They were miles away from home and from their mothers. Jean Claude felt for them.

He and Joey unloaded the boys first. The flashy bay with a striking white blaze walked boldly, his head held high, looking like he owned the place. The slender grey took the ramp in a single flying leap. But the little black colt came down sideways, one step at a time. Then it was the fillies' turn. The tall rawboned chestnut trembled and her legs shook as she carefully made her way to the bottom. The pretty little filly, a bright bay, stepped out elegantly like a girl in high heels, her tiny hooves *click clacking* all the way down. His personal favourite was the strong filly with the white heart on her forehead. She followed him willingly, trusting him implicity. He hoped her trust would not be misplaced in the future. It was such an innocent age. Feeling relieved that all six weanlings had been safely delivered without a mark on them, Jean Claude climbed back up into his truck. He felt a snowflake touch his cheek. Winter was coming.

Joey's wife caught up with him as he was passing the farm house.

"What about the bill?" she asked, a little anxiously.

"I send it to you later," he replied, smiling down at her. So young, so earnest! They were all like that in the beginning. But after a while, the expression in the eyes would change. The people in the standardbred business, they had to live with many disasters and misfortunes. As for Jean Claude, he was content to move the horses around. It was not necessary for him to own them. He had not the stomach for it.

Past Toronto, he pulled into a truck station. After filling his tank, he picked up a pack of *Truckers Friend*, the caffeinated sweets which he hoped would keep him alert during the long drive back to Montreal. Ah, Quebec!

It would feel good to be home again. Ontario was a foreign land to him; a place where people put the dollar first and friendship last. It had no soul, no warmth. . .and also the worst food! Before he got back on the road, he took out his cell phone and punched in the number closest to his heart. It was answered immediately.

"Jean Claude? *Ou es tu maintenant?*"

"Sylvie, *cherie. J'arrive!* In five hours I come home to you."

"I wait for you, Jean Claude," she replied tenderly. He'd be home for twenty-four hours only, unfortunately. A rumour was spreading that the harness racetrack in Montreal might have to close. Already, a steady stream of horses was leaving Quebec for Ontario. As for the cheap ones, the slow ones, they were staying where they were for now. But if the rumour was true, these ones would end up in the abattoir. There would be nowhere else for them to go.

SNOW SEASON

Harmony Light's first winter coat grew in, a deep rich brown. He had never experienced winter before but resistance to cold was deep in his genes, as was his ability to adjust to change. First his mother, then his companion Harmony Gold had left him. These days Harmony Light spent his time with a band of brothers. The fragile grey and the little black colt quickly gave way when he challenged them. However, he had met his match in the bay colt with the striking white blaze. While the other two played, Harmony Light and the strong bay sparred, testing one another's strength and courage. In the fillies' paddock, the picture was very different. Harmony Gold had taken the newcomers under her wing. The three of them followed her lead on everything. When the trio lay down to rest, Harmony Gold stood guard over them, as protective as any mother.

It grew colder. Tiny icicles clung to the horses' whiskers. Snow clouds rolled in, obliterating the watery sun. Feed time came earlier, before darkness fell. When they heard Joey's voice calling them in, the colts scampered across the field, steering a zigzag course, snowflakes stinging their eyes, their warm breath freezing in the frigid air, their hoofbeats muffled by snow. Harmony Light pushed past the others easily. But at the front of the pack, the colt with the white face always blocked his way. The run in shed where they spent their nights, was a frustrating combination of warmth and confinement. Harmony Light slept fitfully.

The colt with the white face danced across his dreams.

Pam Mercer's preparations for winter were a little more devious than Harmony Light's. She had rented a nice two-bedroom apartment in a respectable building on Erinsville's east side. But she was tired of sleeping on the floor and eating off cardboard boxes. It was time to put her daring plan into action: to sneak into her old home via the side door, borrow her ex's credit cards for a few hours and go shopping at an outsize furniture outlet on the outskirts of Toronto, where anonymity was guaranteed. She had a long list of things she needed for her apartment and she wasn't leaving until she had it all. For her plan to work, she needed an accomplice. The part time groom, Trake Jake, fit the bill perfectly. Jake would do anything for easy money. He'd been selling drugs on the backstretch for years. She had offered Jake five hundred dollars in cash to impersonate her ex and forge his signature. By the time she was done, Mercer's credit cards would probably be maxed out, but what did she care? She was as excited as a child at Christmas at the thought of all the beautiful things she was going to buy. At last, she would have everything she needed to make a nice life for herself. And Evie of course.

Mercer would probably never let their daughter live with her but at least Evie would be able to visit, even stay over at weekends. The Hot Tamale, where Pam had wheedled the manager into giving her a job as a cocktail waitress, was only a few blocks away. Also at the Hot Tamale was a big hunk of a Newfie called Sid. Sid was looming large in Pam's life, but not in a romantic way. She was done with all that. Men were nothing but trouble.

Unknown to Pam, the hunk of a Newfie hailed from Prince Edward Island. Though he regularly acted as a barman cum bouncer, he was in reality a Mountie, assigned to the Hot Tamale after a tip off that the bar was a hot spot frequented by cocaine dealers. His real name wasn't Sid, either. Sergeant Campbell McClaren was merely a cog in a wheel, part of a nationwide crackdown by the RCMP. The US was taking a hard line on drugs and urging the rest of the world to do the same. North of the border, the Canadian government was under pressure to follow suit. It was a mammoth task. Canada had become a country under siege. Nevertheless, drugs continued to breach its borders every day.

The war was on! Campbell's fellow Mounties were carrying out covert operations in every major city, coast to coast, from Montreal to Vancouver. Patrols were scouring the highways of Ontario, targeting the long distance trucks which ferried vegetables and fruit into Canada from the United States. In the province of Alberta, even horse drawn carriages were being searched. Word had reached the RCMP that a few renegade Mennonites were also involved in the shipment of cocaine. In British Columbia, sniffer dogs swarmed over vehicles entering the country, some of which had begun their journey in far away Mexico, taking the direct coastal route through California. In Campbell's home province, divers were retrieving bags of cocaine from ships' hulls, hidden deep beneath the water line.

Campbell longed to be in the thick of the action, instead of playing a waiting game at the Hot Tamale, but orders were orders. He had joined the Mounties straight out of school. His eighteen-year old self had wanted to make a difference. Ten years on, he was honest enough to admit that it had been more about chasing glory. But there was precious little glory in his life these days and he was becoming increasingly disillusioned. As a low ranking sergeant, Campbell's ideas were not welcomed by his superiors. They had given him little choice either about his posting to the Hot Tamale, or in the name he had to go by: Sidney Herbert Kingshott. It was ironic, Campbell reflected as he dressed for work, that following orders to the letter seemed to be the approved method of climbing the ranks. An organization like the RCMP actually needed leaders: men who could think for themselves. If he had been put in charge of the fight against cocaine, he would have looked well beyond Canada's borders. He would have tracked the shipments back to their source, back to the criminals pulling the strings. But for that to happen, some sort of international co-operation was essential. Failing that in Campbell's view, the only way to get rid of the criminal element was to decriminalize hard drugs. He was well aware that this view was neither shared nor appreciated by fellow members of the RCMP. It was time he was at work, Campbell realized. He prided himself on being punctual, even if his assignment had so far been a waste of everyone's time.

On the island of Sainte Marie, André Fontainbleu was watching recent developments with interest. The Mounties had declared war – a war he did not intend to fight. He was much too intelligent for that.

WHISTLING IN THE DARK

Campbell was killing time by polishing highball glasses when Pam finally showed up for work, two hours late. It was no big deal. Wednesday was a slow night, a welcome relief from the wild weekends at the Hot Tamale. Pam was generally punctual, either hungry for money or just plain bored. Not tonight! When she did arrive, she was positively glowing. She looked fully ten years younger, affording Campbell a glimpse of what she might have been once. Luckily for him, she had accepted his story about management needing to know about their clientele for security reasons. Besides, Pam was a natural snoop.

The sound system was rolling out one hit song after another, in an attempt to hype up the atmosphere. On the tiny stage, a striking redhead was performing a solo dance, grinding her hips to the beat.

"Your pal Jake was in here earlier throwing his money around," Campbell stated, neutrally. He had noticed her making eyes at Jake for weeks. What she saw in a guy like that he couldn't begin to imagine. Pam didn't reply. She reached down and rubbed an imaginary spot off the toe of one of her teetering high heels. Then she straightened up abruptly.

"That's my table!" she exclaimed. "I should be serving, not that bitch Lisa!" She flounced off, leaving Campbell to reflect on the futility of his life at present. Eleven weeks spent hanging out with a crew of unsavoury characters had so far yielded nothing of value. All Pam had picked up so far was useless trivia about the Hot Tamale's customers.

She was back.

"Four cokes! Those guys are nothin' but cheapskates!" she said contemptuously. Campbell set about filling glasses with pop and ice. He topped them with lemon slices and threw in some rainbow coloured drinking straws for good measure. No one could say they didn't get their money's worth when he was filling the order. Pam picked up the tray of drinks and bustled off. Campbell had no idea how she managed to keep her balance wearing those sky high heels. Just so long as they don't ask me to go to work in drag, he thought, I won't complain! He watched her coax the cheapskates into a laughing, joking foursome. She was obviously angling for a good tip. He hoped he'd got it wrong about her and Jake, for Pam's sake. Given the man's sinister appearance, Campbell had assumed Jake had acquired the jagged scar on his throat in a knife fight. Pam had set him right on that. She'd been in the Race Barn the night Jake had been kicked in the throat by a stud colt. Campbell could hardly believe that Pam had worked as a groom for seven years. She certainly didn't come over as an animal lover. As he was thinking this, Pam, the cheapskates and the rest of the Hot Tamale disappeared and the entire scene went black. The raucous music died, replaced by a brief, ringing silence. Then the screaming began.

At Iroquois Downs an arctic wind was howling. It was twenty degrees below, but Theo Vettore didn't feel cold. The countdown to the seventh race had begun. Theo turned his mare and followed the starting gate which was rolling forward. As it gathered speed, he urged his mare on, her freezing breath sweeping towards him like white smoke, mingling with his own. The floodlights were shining down onto the track, the flagpoles casting pencil like shadows across it. The mare kept her nose pinned to the gate and when the starting car sped away, she followed it eagerly as though attached to it by an invisible string. Theo wanted shelter from the gale, so he allowed Harry Harper to grab the lead. True to form, Harper set a lightning fast pace. No one challenged him until the half mile point. Then, out of the corner of his eye, Theo spotted Moose Rankin coming up on the outside. As Moose drew level, despite the speed at which they were both travelling, Theo was able to take in every detail of Moose's mare as she went by: her pinned back ears, her head tilted away from him, her tail held high, filling Moose's arms. Slowly, Moose inched ahead until he had collared the leader. Then he urged his horse forward, anxious to take over the lead. As they rounded the turn and came into the stretch, Moose began to cross over, intending to duck down onto the rail. He was about to make a fatal error.

"Hey!" Theo yelled sharply, realizing that Moose's wheels were on a collision course with the leading mare's fragile front legs. "Look out!" he tried to shout. But the sound that came out of his throat was wordless, like a primal scream. If Harper's mare goes down, I'll go flying over the top, Theo thought. Before he had time to react, his own mare lurched sideways, fleeing impending disaster. The next instant the entire scene vanished, as swiftly as if someone had thrown a bag over his head and he was flying through the air, trying desperately to hold onto the lines which were snatched from his fingers as he crash landed onto the ground. The power cut had hit Iroquois Downs at the worst possible time.

When the Hot Tamale's emergency generators finally kicked in, the flickering lights revealed a badly shaken, alcohol fuelled young crowd. Campbell immediately took charge, vaulting onto the tiny stage in one easy stride. Big, burly and fully clothed, he made quite a contrast to the strippers, who were huddling together looking scared to death.

"Settle down, folks!" he began, using a reassuring but firm tone, beloved by generations of head teachers. "As you may have noticed, we're experiencing a bit of a power cut," he continued, stating the obvious. The titter of laughter that greeted his remarks had something to do with his PEI burr, he guessed, but it was a vast improvement on the screaming. "The emergency lighting will remain on until…" he broke off midstream, looking questioningly at the manager who was pushing his way through the crowd.

"The whole town's out!" the manager mouthed.

"Sorry folks! The Hot Tamale is closing," Campbell said decisively, leaving no room for doubt. "No more drinks will be served tonight. Please take your empty glasses to the bar and file out quietly." The noise level was rising again. Campbell ignored the moans and groans. "We'll look forward to seeing you all soon, folks," he shouted, trying to wrap up on a positive note, satisfied that the situation was under control.

At Iroquois Downs, there was chaos. Horses were streaming past Theo Vettore, their drivers cursing. Theo leapt to his feet and yelled, "Whoa!" into the blackness praying someone (anyone!) would hear him and the crazy merry go round would stop. It didn't happen. Seeing nothing, he groped around in the dark until he bumped into a horse, standing motionless. Slowly, he felt his way to her head. She was blowing hard.

"It's okay," Theo said, trying to reassure her but knowing he was telling her a bald faced lie. At any moment a horse could come careening into them and smash them to pieces. He couldn't believe the floodlights had gone out smack in the middle of the seventh race. How the hell could this have happened? The mare was trembling. Theo groped his way to back to the sulky which felt, by some miracle, to be in one piece. Hoping for the best, he climbed aboard. But when he urged the mare forward, she stayed rooted to the spot. He'd lost his whip somewhere, so he did the only possible thing he could think of to get her moving. The technique had taken him to the winner's circle countless times in the past. But now, he reflected ruefully, it was more likely to take him to the hospital. Here goes! he thought, grabbing her tail, lifting it up bodily and screaming as loud as he could. The trick worked all too well. The mare took off like a rocket. Theo clung on for dear life, feeling terrified, forced to trust in his horse to make her way, to guide them through the darkness. For the first time in his life, he got an inkling of how it must feel to be a racehorse, to give up control to someone else. Quite a turn-around, he thought, as his eyes finally adjusted and he could make out faint stars like pinpricks in a pitch black sky. He heard people calling out, their scattered voices like beacons in the dark. The shadowy figure of a horse with no driver loomed up next to him, banged into the wheel of his sulky, then disappeared again. After that, the mare lost momentum. Up ahead, he could make out faint flashes of light. He urged her on, still fearful of being run into from behind. Eventually, the starting car ventured out into the racetrack, its headlights illuminating the eerie scene. Trainers were running up to find their horses, some of which were wandering around the infield. The mare's trainer, Andy Price, sounded astonished to find that Theo and the mare, even the sulky, were still in one piece.

"It's a goddamn miracle!" he exclaimed as he led the mare away to the Race Barn. As Theo followed him, Moose came limping up, a sheepish grin on his face.

"Hey," he told Theo. "I owe you one!" He licked his index finger and wrote an imaginary "1" on the night sky. "How in hell did you know the goddamn lights were gonna go out? Huh?" he added, plainly puzzled.

"Give it up! You don't know what you're talking about," Theo replied shakily. "You got a smoke?"

"Sure," Moose said, lighting up a cigarette and tossing one over to Theo. "Hey! don't scream like that again, okay? You scared the shit out of me."

"You asshole!" Theo exclaimed. "You came close to bringing the whole field down. Your friggin' horse was on a friggin' line and you didn't even know it. You still don't know it. Fucking cowboy. You and Lazer deserve each other. Lazer should rot in hell letting a moron like you drive all his good horses!" He took a deep draw on his cigarette. If he just concentrated on the act of smoking, he'd feel okay, he thought. People and horses were making their way back to the Race Barn, trainers dragging broken sulkies, drivers nursing battered limbs.

"I got scared shitless out there, myself." Moose replied good naturedly, ignoring Theo's diatribe. At the entrance of the Race Barn, they were met by

Mr. Roberts the Paddock Judge, shining a flashlight in their faces. He was counting heads.

"Rankin, Vettore," he muttered as he checked their names against the seventh race programme. "Hundred dollar fine each," he added without even looking up. Theo kept his mouth shut. They'd been caught smoking red handed and he knew better than to argue with Mr. Roberts. Moose wasn't so reticent.

"Hundred dollar fine, for what?" he demanded, his famous hot temper ready to fire.

"Smoking," Mr Roberts replied dismissively. Moose rose to the bait.

"Listen to me, you son of a bitch!" he exclaimed, grabbing the Paddock Judge by the coat and glaring at him, his eyes wild. "You saw what happened out there. You have to get your fuckin' two cents in, do you? You think it's okay to torture us like this? Huh?"

"A hundred dollars for threatening behaviour and two hundred for abusive language," Mr. Roberts replied calmly, brushing Moose off as if he was a fly. "I'd watch yourself Mr. Rankin, if I were you. The way you're going you'll get yourself banned from Iroquois Downs. Permanently!" Shocked, Moose let go.

"Four hundred fucking dollars," he muttered. "I don't believe this."

"You young guys think it's so tough out there," Mr. Roberts said, condescendingly, "You've never driven on the county fair circuit, boys. You should try it sometime. This place is a picnic compared to it. I've seen some wrecks in my time you wouldn't believe." If he could only get on another horse and drive in a race now, he'd get over this, Theo thought. But there was little chance of that.

"You may as well go home. Rest of the card's cancelled," Mr. Roberts told them. He walked off, disappearing into the murk. The lights were still out.

The freezing air outside the Hot Tamale had sobered up the majority of the revellers in record time. Campbell stayed put for a while, organizing rides for those still too drunk to drive, and warning everyone to take it slow on the pitch black streets. Feeling he'd done all he could, he locked up and drove home, pleased that he'd be getting a rare early night. Back at his seedy apartment, a couple of blocks away, he dug out his old camping lamp which served well as emergency lighting and treated himself to a cup of hot chocolate, using a primitive camping stove, before finally calling it a night. Living in a cramped apartment filled with hockey memorabilia and cheap beer was all part of the job. He fell asleep instantly.

Somewhere out there in the dark, everything had changed, Theo thought. How could he go from being certain nothing could touch him, to feeling scared to death in a single instant of time? Lately, he'd been on a roll. Now he felt like he had fallen off a cliff. He wasn't sure he was going to snap back to normal so quickly, either. Unfortunately, he recognized all the signs. This wasn't the first time he had lost his nerve. So many fucking things could go wrong in a race, it was better not to think about it, better to shut it out and focus on the real agenda: winning. Something he'd been a master at before. But from now on, he would be driving scared, worrying that the starting car's engine could cut out at the critical moment, that the lines would break apart in his hands, that the horse in front of him would stumble and fall. It wasn't the way to win races. To win, he had to be fearless, free to make split second decisions, to put his life in the hands of his fellow drivers, day in day out, without a moment's thought for his own safety. Now, he couldn't even trust the damn lights to stay on!

On the west side of the town, George Aldright, the surgeon who had operated successfully on Theo Vettore at Erinsville General, ran his hands through his flyaway grey hair, cursing the day he'd left England and moved to Canada. The electricity was out. The heat was out. The internet was out. Even the phone was out! The only thing that worked was the lavatory and that wasn't going to last much longer. With this freeze on and no heat, the pipes would burst and he and his wife would be in real trouble. The worst of it was, he'd been in the middle of a long distance call with his brother's daughter. At the tender age of twenty-five, Caroline Aldright was engaged to a man who made his living training hunters and jumpers in the south of England. The fact that her fiancé, Kipling Radcliffe Lewis Powell, was fairly successful didn't comfort George much. Despite the man's preposterous sounding name, he wasn't even British. He'd been rescued from a slum in Brazil when he was six weeks old. And a slum was a slum, even if they did call it a *favela*. The one crumb of comfort was that at least Kip's adoptive parents had sent him to all the right schools. But if he was going to be good enough for Caroline, George's favourite niece, he had a lot to live up to. George had been on the point of inviting the pair of them over to stay when the electricity went out. At least it hadn't gone out in the operating theatre in mid cut, he thought gratefully. The hospital generator always took a few vital seconds to kick in.

He little guessed, as he trundled off to bed, at the events which were unfolding on the other side of the pond, events which were to bring Caroline over to Canada before the year was out.

Theo Vettore joined the procession of cars heading for the backstretch of Iroquois Downs intending to shine their headlights, still the only light source available, into the pitch black barns. How long could this go on before the hydro guys found the problem? Theo wondered angrily. He thought of Billie, alone in the apartment. He knew he ought to give her a call. His cell phone was still shut off and she'd probably been desperately trying to reach him, worried sick. But he didn't call. He didn't feel like talking and anyhow, she couldn't help. Instead, he shone his headlights on the first barn he found. Its doors were wide open and silhouetted in the light, blinking like an owl, was the last person on earth Theo wanted to see: the groom, Crawfish Brown. Standing next to Crawfish was a dripping wet horse.

"Stay with 'im now, while I get 'im a blanket. Don't go 'way," Crawfish begged. "I bin 'ere forever wiv 'im like this. Every time I leave, 'e tries to throw 'imself an' if 'e gets sick, Andy'll dock my pay." Theo almost felt sorry for Crawfish. Drenched through and shivering with cold, he made a pitiful figure. Crawfish hastily returned with the blanket and threw it over the horse's back. But while he was fastening the straps, he kept sneaking a peek at Theo.

"What are you staring at?" Theo snapped.

"You're not looking so good," Crawfish muttered.

"No? Well neither are you!" Theo replied irritably. Fucking retard! he thought, backing away and wishing he'd never tried to help. He got in his car and was about to drive off when Jake came up. Reluctantly, Theo rolled down his window, letting in the freezing air and the aroma of cigarettes and beer. "What do you want?" he asked, his foot poised above the accelerator.

"Jus' wanna help," Jake said silkily.

"Help? Don't make me laugh," Theo replied, bitter memories of his addiction to cocaine flooding back. Jake had fed him a steady supply, but what a price he'd paid!

"You need fixin' up," Jake said.

"Nothing doing," Theo replied shortly, preparing to drive off.

"I'll give you a real good deal. Won't cost you a cent. That's a promise."

"I'm not interested in your deals," Theo replied, but he didn't pull away. Jake edged closer.

"Jus' hear me out," Jake said. "You don't have to do nothing if you don't want to." He had nothing to lose by listening to what Jake had to say, Theo reasoned. It would be like an insurance policy, just in case he really had lost his nerve, something to fall back on if worst came to worst, that was all. He couldn't face making a fool of himself in front of his fellow drivers, despised by the bettors, written off as a has been. That was a risk he just couldn't take. He opened the passenger door and let Jake in.

MAXED OUT

Jim Mercer picked up the phone and called *Horseman's World*. Christmas was coming. It was time to remind horsemen and owners that he was still part of the standardbred scene. He ran the same ad every year, a sleigh pulled by standardbred horses bearing the message: "Wishing you and yours the best of racing luck in the coming year. Happy Holidays! From Jim Mercer and family." Even though Pam had left, he didn't see any reason to change it. All went well until he tried to pay using his credit card and it was declined by Visa. A familiar, sinking feeling gripped him. Something like this had happened once before. A phone call to Visa confirmed his suspicions. He had apparently run up over four thousand dollars at Leon's Furniture Store, going over his credit limit.

"Goddamn it," Mercer exclaimed, slamming down the phone and glaring out of the window at the falling snow. "That bitch!" he shouted to the lawn as he ran outside, slamming the front door behind him. "I can't believe she did it to me again," he muttered as he jumped into his truck, and revved the engine. "I'll have to change all the locks this time!" The snow fell faster as he headed over to Erinsville's East Side.

SOUTH FLORIDA: SPRING TRAINING

Ritchie Sanchez was poised on the starting blocks, waiting for the signal for the 800 meter dash to begin. To his inside, a little ahead of him, crouched the prompter. It was warm and still, perfect conditions for record breaking. Ritchie was the Florida State Champion. But this season, he was hell bent on competing at the national level. That's where the big bucks were at. One more push, he muttered, psyching himself up. The pistol shot rang out across the green field, reverberating inside Ritchie's skull as he leapt forward, sticking closely to the prompter who was wearing a red vest. Together, they tore around the 400 meter oval.

"Fifty-five seconds," Coach sang out as they reached the half-way point. "Keep it up, fellas!" Ritchie felt the familiar serge of adrenalin. Time to go! He flew past the prompter with wings on his feet, then lengthened his stride, cruising along to the home straight, his breath coming deep and slow, his heart pumping steady and strong. He was almost there! At the finish, he ducked his head and sailed past the finish line. But there was no jubilant shout from Coach Bailey. What was wrong? Had he blown it? He was certain he'd gone a lifetime best. He pulled up. Coach wasn't even looking in his direction! What the hell? He followed Coach's gaze. Two black dots at the edge of the field were scurrying towards them. Halfway across, the dots morphed into two men in dark suits. Ritchie's heart leapt. Were they spotters looking for talent for the next Olympics? He felt a stab of disappointment. If so, they'd missed his stellar performance. Before he realized what was happening, Coach Bailey, all two hundred pounds of him, barrelled into him and he toppled to the ground.

"Wh…what?" he stuttered.

"Shut the fuck up!" Coach mouthed, a wild expression on his long bony face, his big hands busy with Ritchie's left ankle.

"Aaaah!" Ritchie screamed as Coach grabbed the ankle and twisted it back on itself.

"Does that hurt, son?" Coach asked with mock concern.

"What the hell?" Ritchie moaned, thoroughly confused. Normally, he'd have figured it out, but he couldn't think straight. He felt like he was going to throw up. Two black shadows fell across his chest.

"Mr. Sanchez? Mr. Ritchie Sanchez?" one of the suits said. His faced contorted in agony, Ritchie forced himself to look up and face them.

"Yeah," he gasped.

"We're here to do a routine drug test. We're gonna need blood and urine samples from you…" the other suit said. "just spot checking . . .it's the new protocol." His voice faltered. "Is something wrong?" he asked. In the silence that followed, Ritchie's labored breathing sounded unnaturally loud. Between the pain and the panic, he didn't trust himself to speak. Coach Bailey jumped up, six foot five inches of sweaty athlete, towering over the two officials.

"Test!" he exclaimed. "Can't you see the lad's hurt? Hurt bad! I gotta get him to a medic!" He pulled Ritchie to his feet. "Lean on me, son," he gestured, as Ritchie grimaced in pain. "Take a look at that ankle, it's starting to swell," he told the suits.

"We see that," they said sounding awkward and embarrassed now. "We'll come back some other time. The scores'll be screwed up anyhow."

Back in the changing room, Coach dropped all pretense of sympathy. He slapped an icepack on the ankle and gave Ritchie a shot of morphine. Then he made the pronouncement Ritchie had been dreading his whole career.

"You're all washed up, son."

"I'll recover," Ritchie protested fiercely.

"The ankle, yes," Coach agreed matter of factly.

"So…I don't understand any of this," Ritchie mumbled, still in a fog.

"D'you have any idea how many illegal drugs you're carrying around inside your body, right now?" Coach asked. Reluctantly, Ritchie nodded. He knew. He just didn't want to face it. "You'd have failed that test on about ten counts, ruined my reputation into the bargain! I just saved your butt, kiddo!"

"You told me it was okay!" Ritchie shouted defiantly, trying to pass the buck, wanting desperately to hold onto the dream for just a little longer.

"Bullshit! I kept you in the picture every step of the way. You knew exactly what you were getting and what it was going to do for you."

"I trusted you," Ritchie said hotly.

"Ritchie. . . Ritchie," Coach Bailey replied wearily. "Use your goddamn head. You had to stop using all this shit before every competition, right?"

"Of course," Ritchie agreed. "So they couldn't pick up the traces."

"Yeah! So you passed their dumb tests but you still got most of the benefits. But they've wised up. They found a way round that, with those random spot checks." He slapped a fresh icepack on Ritchie's ankle. "I was hoping we'd get away with it," Coach added. "Nah, I was gamblin' on it, I guess," he admitted. "We just ran outa luck, kiddo!"

"I could have tried to go clean!" Ritchie maintained stubbornly.

"And fall flat on your face? That sure as hell would have set alarm bells ringing!" Coach replied, turning his back on him and marching towards the lockers. "Where's my damn towel?" he shouted.

He just wants to take a shower and go home, get shot of this whole business, Ritchie realized bitterly. But I'm not some fucking horse that's broke down. I'm a human being for God's sakes, he thought angrily. He remembered a dog he'd had as a kid. Even animals had feelings. "Why'd you have to break my ankle?" he demanded.

"It ain't broke! It's just a real bad sprain." Coach replied.

"Oh yeah. Tell that to the birds!"

"I just saved you from a scandal that would've turned your name to mud!" Coach snapped. Ritchie hung his head. "Listen," Coach added in a gentler tone. "You're a fucking hero. You've got nothing to prove. You've won every race in this goddamn state. You broke the state record for the eight hundred meters, broke it by two seconds, too! You're a fucking household name here in Florida. You're a star, kiddo!" He paused. "But you gotta move on. Believe me, it's for the best."

"What do I do now, Coach, huh?" Ritchie said despairingly. "I'm twenty-eight years old and all I know how to do is run fast."

"I'll make a few calls, see if I can't find you something," Coach offered. "Listen," his mentor added. "You gotta let things cool down a bit. Don't you go blabbing to the press. Let me handle it, okay? We've had us one hell of a ride, haven't we?"

"Too bad it had to end," Ritchie replied, a catch in his voice, disappointment washing over him. He knew it was over and the plain truth of it was, he couldn't find anyone to blame, not Coach, not even himself. Especially not himself.

"Think you can make it to the parking lot?" Coach asked. Ritchie shook his head. "Stretcher case," Coach agreed. "I'll call Doc." Finally, Ritchie understood. Once the news got out, it would be all over the papers. Somehow Coach had engineered precisely the kind of injury any runner could get from a stumble or a bad step. No one would suspect a thing. Coach was right. He should drop out of sight for a while.

The paramedics had the ankle strapped up in a matter of minutes.

"I'll see you," he told Coach as they carried him off, but he knew he wouldn't be seeing Coach again, not ever, except on TV. He was out of the loop, turned out to pasture at twenty-eight. He told himself that when one door closes another one opens. But he didn't believe it. Not then.

THE NAMING OF NAMES

After a relatively mild February, Southern Ontario was in the grip of a winter storm. Harmony Farm was rapidly disappearing under a thick blanket of snow. In the normally snug farmhouse kitchen, Val and Joey Harris were wrapped in coats and scarves, huddled beside the stove trying to stay warm.

"We can't put it off any longer," Val said plaintively, cradling a mug of steaming hot chocolate. Joey started guiltily. There were a thousand and one things that needed fixing on the farm. Val kept tabs on all of them. Which one was it this time? he wondered. But how could he do anything in this weather? It was still snowing hard. Val was laughing.

"What?" he demanded in an accusatory tone.

"You wouldn't believe how comical you look!" she said. "Relax. We need a new furnace and all the windows rattle, but what I was thinking of was coming up with some interesting names."

"Names," Joey repeated blankly.

"Yes," she said patiently as if speaking to a small child. "We need six of them. Any ideas?"

"Ah," Joey replied. "You mean the yearlings." He'd been so busy, he'd hardly taken a breath since the new youngsters had arrived in the fall. "Fire away."

"Okay," Val said picking up her notebook. "So the black filly with the white heart on her forehead."

"That's a no-brainer."

"Has to be Harmony Valentine," Val agreed. "I've already named the little filly. She's going to be Harmony Princess," she added in a tone which made it clear that matter was closed.

"Fine by me," Joey said, hoping this was going to be over soon. In his opinion, yearling buyers didn't set much store by names. Potential owners studied the pedigree page carefully and took a look at the horse in person and…"Videos," he muttered, making a mental note to set something up for August, half a year away.

"You're getting ahead of yourself," Val pointed out.

"How about Harmony Jet for the little black colt?" Joey said. "As in jet black."

"I like it!" Val exclaimed.

"What about the grey?" Silence fell. They were both stumped.

"Let's sit on that one. The chestnut filly?" Val asked. Joey tried, but inspiration did not come. "Nothing? What about my favourite? The beautiful boy with the white blaze."

"Why not call him Harmony Whiteface?" Joey suggested, sneaking a look at the clock on the wall. It was getting near feeding time. Val vetoed his suggestion.

"He's a special horse," she said. "He needs a special name. He's showy, too, like those quarter horses the cowboys ride out west.'

"Calgary, you mean?"

"Cowtown? No!" Val laughed. "Wait, you've just given me a great idea. How about Harmony Stampede? You know as in . . ."

"Calgary Stampede. Brilliant!" Joey agreed happily.

"So that just leaves the grey and the chestnut."

"Harmony grey and Harmony Red?" he suggested. That went down like a lead balloon. "See if you can do any better then," he said, jumping up. "I'm going out to feed."

"Not yet," Val pleaded. Reluctantly, Joey sat down again. "Talk to me," Val said. "You're with the babies every day. I'm out of touch now. Since the weather turned cold all I see is people's teeth. But not a word about colour!" she admonished, as Joey opened his mouth to speak.

"Hey, d'you want to hear what I have to say, or not?" he exclaimed.

"Go ahead," Val said in a conciliatory tone. "Please."

"Well…the grey colt's a nervous wreck. Lashes out at the slightest thing, the little son of a bitch," Joey said, venting his frustration on the horse. "Kicks up a storm if you do anything too sudden, like."

"That's it," Val cut in, her eyes alight. "Storm! Harmony Storm, it's perfect!"

"It works," Joey conceded, cracking a smile.

"And the chestnut?"

"She's not as bad as the grey colt. But she's high strung. She can get fired up pretty quick, I can tell you."

"We could call her Harmony Fire," Val remarked thoughtfully. "It sounds like it suits her."

"People'll sure know what they're getting into!" Joey agreed. "That's it then?" he asked, astonished that it had been so easy.

"All but…," Val confirmed. "You better pray none of the names are taken already or we'll have to start over."

"No worries," Joey said confidently. "I fixed it with CPTA. No one else is allowed to use Harmony as a prefix."

"Prefix," Val replied teasingly, staring at him wide eyed and waving her pen at him. "That's a big word for you isn't it, Mr. Harris?"

"Just because I'm covered in muck all day," Joey retorted grabbing a cushion and throwing it at her. "Doesn't mean I don't have a brain!" Val caught it and held it aloft.

"Not fair, I'll get you for that," she said, leaping to her feet and bopping him over the head repeatedly with the cushion.

"Happy now?" he asked, emerging red faced from the fray.

"I'll talk to you about the other thing later," she replied. He reached out for her and drew her in close.

"There's another thing?" he asked worriedly.

"There's always another thing. Go feed. It'll keep 'til you get back." If it wasn't for the horses, he'd have taken her up to bed right now, he thought.

"But you're okay, I mean…you're happy, right," he asked praying her mood wouldn't have changed by the time he got back.

"Very," she replied with a winning smile. Joey heaved a sigh of relief. Keeping eleven females happy appeared to be his mission in life these days and that included his wife. When he went outside, he had to shovel his way through the snow to the barn. Some of the drifts were knee deep. The fact that Val had something to tell him flew right out of his head.

RUM MARTIN

Caroline Aldright was speeding through the one-way system of a small town on the south coast of England like a racing driver, with one eye on the time, the other on the speedometer. Every second counted. She was late! She jammed on the brakes and reversed into a parking spot. Then she grabbed her keys, leapt out of the car and sprinted to Sharpe's on the corner.

When she entered the smoky atmosphere of the betting shop, her eyes sparkling with excitement, she created a minor sensation. Her fashionably cut, shoulder length hair and smart suit drew incredulous stares from the cigarette toting, unshaven male clientele huddled around the TV screen and the lone female, her platinum hair done up in rollers, drumming her nicotine stained fingers on the counter. Thankfully, the betting crowd had only a moment to take in Miss Caroline Aldright. Their eyes were drawn back inexorably to the screen, unwilling to miss more than an instant of the finale of the Cheltenham Gold Cup, the biggest race of the hurdle season.

Caroline had almost missed it. She strained to make out her fiancé's horse, Rum Martin, wishing she and Kip could have been at Cheltenham today. But Kip was in hospital. Clouds scudded across the sky above the race course, casting a changing pattern of sun and shadow on the rolling green hills. As the horses rounded the final turn and straightened out, one horse broke away from the pack. She heard the race caller's voice loud and clear.

"And they're coming to the last now. Only one more to jump…and Rum Martin has taken the lead! Sole Mio sets off in pursuit, but he's not going to catch him! Bob Sanders takes Rum Martin up and over the last…and he jumps it cleanly…ears pricked! There's a great roar from the crowd. Rum Martin is pulling further ahead with every stride. What a horse! He's coming to the finish. And he's done it! Rum Martin has won the Gold Cup in fine style! A great ride by Bob Saunders and a fairytale ending for his trainer, Kip Powell, who is watching this race from his hospital bed…injured in a fall from this same horse exactly one month ago.

"And so Rum Martin makes his way to the winner's enclosure and he's getting a standing ovation from this record crowd here today…this great racehorse has proved his ability beyond doubt this afternoon. He's been a good servant to his owner, Sir Adrian Dobson. Rum Martin's name will be added to the list of champions. . ."

"Trap 4. All in at Hove. All in." A harsh voice cut across the mellifluous tones of Cheltenham and the euphoria of the Gold Cup faded. Sharpe's had gone to the dogs. Several pairs of eyes followed wistfully as Caroline left the warm fug of the betting shop and stepped outside. As she did so, the heavens opened and rain began to pour down like a cold shower. No umbrella, her suit drenched, she splashed her way through the puddles until, soaked through, she dived into the safe haven of her soft top VW, the only pink car on the street. There was a parking ticket on the windscreen which was rapidly disintegrating in the rain. Caroline helped it along by turning on the wipers. Another fifteen pounds down the drain, she thought philosophically. But this time it had been worth every penny. Something good had happened at last. Rum Martin had won the Cheltenham Gold Cup!

This had been the worst month of her life, she decided, putting her car into gear. First, Kip's accident. Next, her favourite aunt had died, leaving everything to Caroline, which had sent the relatives into fits of rage, eventually culminating in icy disapproval. Lastly, her hugely enjoyable job was over. Funding for the popular, innovative educational scheme she had pioneered for the local council had been slashed. The after school workshops had failed to find a home within the existing framework of the County Council, so despite their success they were being axed. Two hours ago, she'd received the unwelcome news that she was being thrown out, hardly worth putting on a suit for.

The rain stopped as abruptly as it had started. The sun appeared. The heater breathed warm air and Caroline began to dry out. When she reached open countryside, she called Kip on her mobile and did a fair imitation of an Indian war party celebrating victory. Then she settled down for the long drive. Never one to stay down for long, Caroline told herself Rum Martin's win was a sign. Bad luck came in threes and it must all be behind her now. Good times were on the horizon. The blue sky was still studded with rain clouds but the blossom on the bare branches of the trees heralded the onset of spring. She arrived at the Royal Free Hospital in buoyant mood.

THE VOICE WITHOUT A NAME

For two weeks, Ritchie Sanchez didn't hear from anyone, not a single soul, except his step brother "Cat" Ciardi, currently a two-bit horse trainer in New Jersey, which didn't really count. Days went by with no one to talk to and nothing to do but knock himself out with pain killers every six hours. As soon as he was able to hobble around on crutches, Ritchie slunk up to Jersey and holed up in Cat's tiny apartment beside the highway, a stone's throw from Freehold Raceway. He had to sleep on the sofa which sucked, but it was better than spending his money on some cheap motel. He was standing up at the sink shaving, when his cell phone went off, its cheerful ringtone chosen by him when he was in a different place, another world. Startled, he cut himself, his bright red blood mingling with the water swirling down the sink. Let it be a sponsor, he prayed, asking him to advertise products. But it wasn't. The voice on the phone was unfamiliar. The guy had a French Canadian accent. At first, Ritchie didn't get his drift, but slowly, despite his reservations, he allowed himself to be drawn in. It wasn't like he had any other offers on the table. The guy treated him like he mattered, at least. He gave him full credit, not only for the records he'd set on the athletic field but for Ritchie's inside knowledge of what the guy referred to as "helpful medications". He said he had a proposal to put to him. If Ritchie accepted, he wouldn't ever have to worry about money. He suggested that Ritchie think about it for a few days and promised he would call back.

A week later, the phone rang again. This time, Ritchie picked up on the second ring. I'll hear him out, he decided. I'll lose nothing by doing that. Surprisingly, a critical part of the proposal was getting Ritchie's kid brother Cat, on board. The guy was calling on behalf of a new racing syndicate, the Lucky Seven Stable. Apparently, they wanted to hire a private trainer. If he played his cards right, Ritchie's little brother could find himself in the catbird seat, racing a stable of good quality horses at a premier harness racing track in North America with a guaranteed paycheck every week. The stable was planning to purchase a farm and spend over a million dollars on racehorses. The voice on the phone revealed that Coach Bailey had recommended Ritchie to advise them on leading edge performance enhancing drugs that could boost their horses' performances, on an ongoing basis. When Ritchie expressed his doubts, especially about spot checking, he learned that harness racing was way behind athletics testing wise, which put his worries to rest. Ritchie was pretty sure he could get his brother to agree to take on training duties for this Lucky Seven Stable. It was a great opportunity and the kid only had a few cheap horses. But before agreeing to anything, Richie wanted to know what was in it for him.

"How about running your own beach bar on a Caribbean island?" the mysterious voice suggested. "Would that appeal to you?"

"Sounds pretty good," Ritchie conceded.

"You'll need to invest around twenty thousand US dollars," the voice cautioned. That was precisely the amount he had in his bank account, Ritchie realized uneasily. What else did this guy know? he wondered anxiously. The thought unsettled him.

"We know a great deal about you, Mr. Sanchez," the voice said softly, as if reading Ritchie's mind, "and about Coach Bailey also…But I do not imagine either of you would enjoy reading about it in the *Miami Herald*." Ritchie gulped. It looked like he was caught between the carrot and the stick. "The syndicate wishes to pick your brains, Mr. Sanchez," the voice continued reassuringly. "That is all. A little cooperation is all that is necessary and things will work out perfectly for you." At times like this, a father would have come in pretty handy, Ritchie concluded. He had only hazy memories of his father. He'd left when he was two years old. Since then, Ritchie had had to find his own way through life. He decided he had nothing to lose by trying to make this deal happen.

When his baby brother got home later that day, tired, frozen, discouraged, Ritchie pitched him the line. Cat took the bait. But the kid held out for one thing; he wanted to pick out a yearling to train by a top sire, something he couldn't afford to buy himself.

"*No problemo*." Ritchie told him. The sale wasn't until fall. He'd worry about that later.

A FAIT ACCOMPLI

By the time Kip escaped the confines of the Royal Free, it was summer and the hurdle racing season was over. It was just as well. Unlike most trainers, Kip had always relished the chance to ride out with his string of horses every morning, rather than watching them from a Range Rover. The way he felt right now though, riding a horse was an impossibility. As the weeks went by with no improvement, Kip was forced to admit that he was not bouncing back as quickly as expected. His bones had set perfectly, but the big muscles in his back were taking longer to heal and he was in constant pain.

"You left the hospital too soon. Try a physiotherapist," the Royal Free advised him. But none of the highly qualified experts his mother lined up for him was able to help. He returned home after presiding over the daily ritual known as evening stables, to be greeted by Caroline and his mother at the garden gate.

"You're going to Canada," his mother announced, shepherding him into the drawing room. She poured him a large whiskey and soda and when he waved it away, she began drinking it herself. "It's all arranged," she added. Caroline shot him a warning glance. Don't argue with her, she communicated silently. Kip sighed.

"Why, Mother?" he enquired.

"I cannot imagine why Caroline didn't mention it before."

"Mention what?" Kip frowned.

"Her uncle...the one that emigrated," she replied, with obvious disapproval. "Apparently, he's a surgeon."

"I told you about him, remember," Caroline explained. "He lives in Erinsville."

"I don't want another operation!" Kip replied firmly.

"You won't have to!" Caroline cut in quickly. "Uncle George told me about this therapist who uses a brand new technique called A.R.T. Apparently it breaks down scar tissue. He's pretty sure that's what your problem is now."

"Why can't I get it done here?" Kip inquired.

"It's not available in the UK yet." Caroline explained.

"Extremely unprofessional of course, diagnosing you over the telephone," his mother remarked. "But honestly Kip, something simply has to be done. You can't go on like this." Kip opened his mouth to protest then closed it again. "I'm paying for the flights to Toronto," his mother continued. "Caroline's uncle has insisted on putting you both up. How soon can you leave?" Kip knew better than to argue with one of his mother's *faits accomplis*. He'd watched her boss his father around for years. Anyway, what did he have to lose? If it gave him any chance of riding out with the string again, he was willing to try it. Besides, he wouldn't have to go on his own. Caroline would be there.

A BIRTHDAY

In the clapboard farm house which she had lived in all her life, Izzy Brown was putting the final touches on her birthday cake when she heard a knock at the back door. Her son was standing outside.

"Crawford!" Izzy exclaimed. "You should've let me come 'n get you, son, instead of ridin' all the way. And in this heat, too!"

"It's a'right, Ma," her son replied. "We was racing a horse at Merryvale this afternoon. I didn't have to come far."

"That was lucky!" Izzy exclaimed.

"Where's that cookie jar at?" Crawford inquired.

"Cookie jar?" Izzy asked, smiling to herself as she reached into the back of the cupboard.

"That Midnight Madness of Lazer's won again today," Crawford said, holding up a wad of bills. "That's seven in a row now." he added, popping the money into the cookie jar. "We'll get you your kitchen, Ma...don't you worry none." Izzy held out her arms. But the hug that should have taken place didn't happen. She wasn't sure why.

"I'm gonna park my bike round the back," Crawford declared. "Pa home?"

"Your pa's in the barn. Some people came to look at the filly," Izzy replied. There was always a filly! Her husband, Craig, bought one every year. She watched Crawford as he limped off, pushing his bicycle. This was her son, she thought fondly. The only one of the five boys to have a regular job, well, regular employment anyhow. Where had she gone wrong? The girls had turned out well: one was a nurse, the other a secretary. What had she done right? She wished she knew. The boys had been headstrong, too much for her and Craig to handle really. At times, the only way to break up their fights had been to turn the cold hose on them. They'd all picked on Crawford. Heaven knows why! After the accident, things had calmed down for a bit. All five boys, drunk, in one car, out of control downhill on the ice at one o'clock in the morning. It was a miracle they'd all survived. A miracle! Izzy thanked God for that. She set the birthday cake down on the kitchen table. The 'I' on 'Izzy' was crooked. She'd been making her own birthday cakes ever since her mother died.

It was so hot! She switched on the ceiling fan. They couldn't afford air conditioning. Crawford had been asleep when the car had slammed into a truck.

193

His left hip had been broken and the left side of his face had been smashed in. The doctors had done their best, but he'd never looked the same as he did before. The other boys had got off lightly. Two broken legs, a broken arm and a concussion between them. They hadn't learned a thing from it, still drank themselves silly, still lived at home too, even though they were all in their twenties. If it hadn't been for the boys, she and Craig could have been happy now. He wasn't a bad husband. He wasn't a bad horseman neither. Folks laughed no doubt at the old farm house they'd lived in all their married lives, with its crooked walls and sloping floors and the higgledy piggledy rooms added on here and there as the family grew. But she had been born in this house. Apparently, everyone had fitted kitchens and microwave ovens these days. Well, she didn't need anything like that to bake a cake or rustle up a decent meal.

Craig and Crawford were back from the barn. Like a good boy, her son took off his shoes.

"They've offered twelve grand," Craig beamed. Twelve thousand! It was an awful lot of money for a horse. But she'd never see one penny of it. It would all go back into horses. She was thankful she had her job at the grocery store. At least it put food on the table. "Well what are you waiting for?" Craig said, gesturing at a small packet wrapped in foil that Crawford was holding. "Open it, Izzy!"

She hesitated. Crawford's presents were a bit hit and miss. One year he had given her a gerbil.

"Nora said you'd be sure to like it," her son said shyly. Reassured, she tore open the wrapping. Inside was a packet of hair dye: a blond rinse.

"Why it's lovely, Crawford," she said, smiling up at him. "What a wonderful idea."

Crawfish Brown was not the only one to benefit from Midnight Madness's winning streak. The horse had attracted a loyal band of followers who bet him every week. However, all good things were bound to come to an end sooner or later. The very next week, the hammer fell. Regulation tongue ties were issued at Merryvale Raceway too. At a stroke, Midnight Madness's time as a star performer was over. He was now a liability, a danger to himself and everyone else on the racetrack.

In the past, Keith Lazer had tried everything legal, equipment wise, training wise and drug wise, to calm the horse's nerves. Using a cocaine laced tongue had been a last resort and it had worked beautifully. However, there was no point in wasting time on regrets. Faced with the surprise new ruling, Lazer swiftly buried the evidence in a pile of manure. Then he took Midnight Madness out onto the track for his warm up mile and allowed him to ram his muzzle into the wings of the starting gate, the gelding's favourite ploy. While the blood was still flowing from Midnight's nose, Lazer returned to the Race Barn to be greeted by the track veterinarian.

"Lazer! I'm scratching your horse! He's bleeding!" the vet declared. Problem solved, Lazer thought happily. They would have to get up very early in the morning to beat him, he decided as he drove back to his farm with Midnight Madness in tow. Soon the horse was tucked up safely in his stall, none the worse for wear. As for Lazer, he was on the computer, looking up sale dates. Inevitably, the gelding would eventually end up with the Mennonites. But he pitied the poor family who tried to drive their buggy to church with Midnight Madness between the shafts!

MIAMI INTERNATIONAL AIRPORT

Ritchie Sanchez huddled into his light jacket and shivered. He wasn't cold, just nervous. He'd never been further south than Florida, never left the good old U.S. of A. Now he was on his way to the island of Sainte Marie, an hour and a half's flight away, in the Caribbean. He was excited about buying his own little piece of paradise: a slip of beachfront going for a knockdown price. All he would need was a liquor licence to turn the ailing food stall into a thriving beach bar. If the mysterious voice on the phone was on the level, that part of it was going to be easy. As for running a business down there, with the high prices he could charge and the low cost of local help, Ritchie reckoned it'd be like shootin' fish in a barrel!

Apparently, the sellers wanted hard currency. So, following the voice's instructions, he had purchased two suitcases with hidden compartments and filled them with hundred dollar bills. He tried not to think of those suitcases, which were out of his sight but were, pray God, on their way to the plane or already on it. Boarding for his flight had begun. Time to go, he thought anxiously. He'd gone too far to turn back now.

CULTURE CLASH

Holidays in southern europe where the languages were foreign but the culture was familiar, had not prepared Caroline Aldright for Canada. Trouble began right away in the baggage hall of Toronto International Airport. Leaving Kip to wait by the carousel, she went off in search of a luggage cart, expecting things to be simple. However, despite her best efforts to pull one away from its fellows, the trolleys remained locked together in an impenetrable embrace.

"Ya need a loonie!" a man called out.

"A what?" Caroline asked, thinking she must have heard wrong.

"A loonie!" he repeated.

"I need a lunatic?" she asked incredulously. "You have lunatics here to get the trolleys out?" The man looked at her like she was crazy.

"What are you talkin' about?" he asked, holding out his hand. "That's a loonie. It's a one-dollar coin." He put the coin in the slot. Magically, the trolley disengaged. "Here, take it," he said. "You're holding everyone up here, ma'am." Behind her a dozen people were waiting politely.

"Thank you so much," Caroline gushed.

"It's no big deal," the man replied, walking off.

Outside the baggage hall, a crowd was eagerly waiting.

"That's him! That's Uncle George!" Caroline squealed as a board with the name *ALDRIGHT* on it began moving rapidly towards them.

"Caroline!" Uncle George exclaimed. "How are you, my dear? Good flight? And you must be Kip!" He added, smiling and grasping Kip by the hand. Kip winced, still only half healed. "We've heard a great deal about you…all of it good I may say!" George chuckled.

"Where do I pick up the car?" Caroline asked. Kip was going to Erinsville with Uncle George, while she followed with the rental car. How she longed for things to be back to the way they were before the accident, with Kip his normal, happy self again.

"Are you sure you're okay to drive, Caroline?" Kip enquired anxiously.

"I'm fine, really," Caroline said, summoning a smile as she took the lift to Ground Transportation.

"Remember to drive on the right!" Kip called out as the lift doors closed.

Three thousand kilometers to the southeast, Ritchie Sanchez hit the dirt road with a sickening thud. The fall knocked the air out of his lungs and for what seemed like an eternity, he fought for breath. It was pitch black. The stink of dog shit was overpowering. He felt around for his bag and recoiled. It was covered in the stuff. As the noise of the car that had unceremoniously dumped him by the side of the road faded to a distant hum, Ritchie tuned in to the sound of a couple in the midst of a screaming argument, egged on by barking dogs. Where the fuck was he? Hell?

He'd landed on the island of Sainte Marie, two hours ago. Everything had gone to plan, until the taxi that picked him up at the airport had broken down. Next thing Ritchie knew, he was being bundled into a dodgy looking vehicle, driven by the taxi man's cousin. How could he have been so dumb? Truth was, the dazzling sun and the downright beauty of the place had lulled him into a false sense of security. He'd felt like he'd just arrived in paradise, where nothing bad could possibly happen. Some paradise! The cousin had stopped off at a neghborhood bar, where four huge black guys had elbowed their way into the taxi. Ritchie's alarm bells had gone off, but he was pinioned on the back seat between them by then. Halfway to nowhere, they'd picked him up and thrown him out into the dark street, taking off with his luggage and US$20,000 in cash. 'Now what?' he wondered miserably.

A red light was flashing on the dashboard of Caroline Aldright's rental car. Blinded by the sun shining in her eyes as she drove west, Caroline had missed the Erinsville exit and, eighteen kilometres further on, she was about to run out of petrol. She was saved by exit 183, the turn off for Iroquois Downs. There was no sign of a petrol station anywhere close by, so she headed for the racetrack, coasting into the parking lot just as the engine began to splutter. She then discovered to her dismay that her mobile phone didn't work in Canada, so she wasn't able to call for help or even let Kip know the fix she was in.

It was a warm, balmy evening, reminiscent of southern Spain, so she threw her jacket on the back seat and headed for the grandstand, a tall building rearing up from a sea of asphalt where she hoped, someone would be able to help her. As she approached the main entrance, a pint sized figure flew out, knocking her to the ground. Caroline was back on her feet in an instant, handbag at the ready, poised to go into a kickboxing manoeuvre that she had learned in self defence class.

"Sorry, lady…didn't see ya," the diminutive man stuttered, looking up at Caroline. "Gee you look scary. Don't hurt me! I'll make it up to you, I swear."

"How?" she asked, surprised by this turn of events and noticing that her elbow was bleeding.

"Bet Sleepless Nights in the second race," the man said. "She's a lock. You'll double your money."

"Not interested. I want a telephone," Caroline countered, sensing that she had the upper hand.

"Wait," the man replied, delving into his pockets and discharging scores of betting tickets, which fell to the ground like autumn leaves, before handing over his mobile phone. "Make it quick, lady," he added, diving for his tickets which were being scattered to the winds by passing cars. When she punched in Uncle George's home number, no one answered, so she left a message.

"Thanks," she said, turning to her attacker. "I'm Caroline, by the way."

"Better get that arm seen to…Car'line. See you in the winner's circle, baby!" He grinned at her and ran off, leaving Caroline a clear path to the grandstand.

When she pushed open the doors, to her surprise, she appeared to have arrived at an enormous betting shop, studded with TV screens and crowded with people snacking on pizza. It certainly wasn't anything like Ascot. No fashion hats or smart suits here! Caroline stood out a mile in her sundress. Everyone else was in jeans and T-shirts. But, pleasingly, there was no cigarette smoke, only the aroma of fast food. It made her realize how hungry she was. It felt like the longest day of her life.

After a series of misunderstandings at the food and drinks counters (no one had heard of lager, and chips were apparently only used by gamblers in casinos) Caroline went outside, clutching her hard won beer and the precious portion of "french fries". The warmth of the sun and the cries of the gulls were a welcome relief from the freezing temperatures inside. What were the birds doing here, so far from the sea? she wondered, watching them as they circled above her, wheeling across the cliff face of the grandstand, its huge glass windows reflecting a dazzling sun. There was so much light! She had left Heathrow on a cool, grey day. The contrast was startling.

A bugle rang out. Horses, harnessed to small, two-wheeled carts filed out onto the all weather track. Their drivers wore brightly coloured silks, like the jockeys back home and the horses were beautiful, with flowing manes and tails. As she watched them, an outrageous idea occurred to her. Sitting on a cart looked like a far safer option than balancing on a horse's back, perched high above the ground. Right then and there, she decided to persuade Kip to give it try, come what may, before they went back home to the UK. They had only just arrived, she reminded herself sharply. Kip was in no state to do anything strenuous, yet.

It was 7:30 p.m. on the tote board clock, half past midnight in the UK. No wonder her head was throbbing! It was time she tried Uncle George again. Kip would be worried to death about her. She went back inside. A young woman in a security guard's uniform gave her directions to the public telephone.

"What about the ladies' room?" Caroline asked, feeling the call of nature. A blank look appeared on the young woman's face.

"What did you say?" she frowned.

"I need to powder my nose," Caroline explained. There was still no response. "Loo?" Caroline said (this was discreet middle-class speech for ladies' room). The girl waited, as though giving Caroline a chance to complete the thought. It was after all, Caroline realized, the first syllable of the word loonie, as in one dollar coins. She wracked her brains. "Bathroom!" she said at last. She felt like she was playing a bizarre game of charades. But it wasn't fun. It wasn't Christmas and she wasn't tipsy. Well perhaps she was, just a little. The lager (beer, she reminded herself) had gone straight to her knees.

"You mean the washrooms?" the woman asked. She really should have taken language classes before coming here, Caroline decided.

"Well...um...where are they?" she asked.

"Right by the pay phones," the woman replied. "You should get that arm seen to," she added as her pager went off. "This is Becky," she said. "I'm on Level One...Everything's okay down here." Caroline left, hoping the washroom wasn't going to be place where people went to wash their clothes, though her's certainly needed laundering. She had been wearing them for eighteen hours. She found the telephones easily enough. But making a call was more problematic. She didn't have nearly enough change to make the call and no one understood what reverse charges meant. Again, she realized it had been a big mistake to assume that Canadians spoke the same English as people did in the UK. Eventually she was put on an automated system offering her a dozen options, none of which she wanted. She began giggling helplessly, not that the situation was remotely funny but it was one way to relieve the tension at least.

THE HERMITAGE

Ritchie Sanchez's left shoulder had taken the brunt of the fall. Cradling it with his good arm, he sat up. It hurt like hell! A pair of headlights heading his way fast panicked him into a standing position. He flattened himself against a nearby wall, listening to the whine of a siren. He'd heard horror stories about police in the Caribbean. He had no doubt they'd take advantage of his situation and soak him for everything they could. Thanks to the taxi man's cousin, all he had left in the world was his computer and a few twenty dollar bills.

The car stopped, Ritchie raised his hands.

"Don't shoot!" he begged. A man in a navy blue uniform climbed out of the car. He didn't look like a gangster, but who knew?

"What's up, man?" the officer asked, looking at Ritchie inquiringly. "Jus' tell me your name, son." Ritchie supplied it. "What? *The* Ritchie Sanchez! You gotta be kiddin' man. I seen you on TV. I'm a big fan!" Ritchie smiled with relief and told his sad story.

"I gotta get to the Hermitage," he said urgently.

"Let's get you back to the station first," the officer replied.

After he'd had a chance to clean up in the "Officers Only" men's room, Ritchie was handed over to an eager young Spanish speaker called Pepe, driving an ancient Citroen CV2.

"My wife's brother," the officer said, handing in Ritchie's computer through the car window. A volley of Spanish followed. It was too bad, Ritchie thought, that his Dad hadn't stayed around long enough to teach him the language. Pepe immediately set off at breakneck pace, straight up the mountain road which snaked back and forth like a switchback. The ride was a welcome distraction from Ritchie's troubles. Suddenly, Pepe slammed on the brakes.

"Hermitage!" he announced brightly. Praying he'd arrived at the right place, Ritchie took out one of his precious twenty dollar bills. Pepe waved it aside and handed him a small piece of paper. "This me," he confided, pointing at the handwritten card detailing services available, which included various odd jobs. "Other day," he added with a winning smile.

"Okay!" Ritchie agreed, putting the twenty-dollar bill back in his wallet and feeling a little more cheerful. Gloom descended however, when he caught sight of the castle like structure he was about to enter. Through the narrow slits in its high walls, he glimpsed glittered candelabras and a soaring ceiling. He'd pictured his arrival many times, imagining himself as an honored guest, a businessman with something to offer. Now, he'd lost his all to a crew of thugs. He felt like a total loser. When he pulled the bell rope, he heard chimes echoing all over the house. The door was eventually opened by a slender, elegant young man.

"Monsieur Sanchez?" he asked. "Monsieur Fontainbleu, 'e ees expecting you." Was everyone a fucking foreigner on this island? Ritchie wondered, feeling painfully homesick even though he'd only left Florida a few hours ago. The Frenchman led the way to a small room lined with books off the main hall. Two sofas faced each other across a glass table. Hoping he wasn't still stinking of dog shit, Ritchie sat down to wait, then immediately jumped up again, startled.

A man had entered the room.

"*Merci*, Henri," the man said. Ritchie recognized the soft, resonant voice instantly. It was the voice on the phone. He took in Fontainbleu's trim figure, the crop of brown curls, the dark eys appraising him…the cruel mouth. He was nothing like the picture Ritchie had been building in his head. This guy was as hard as nails. He would not look kindly on failure or excuses. And Ritchie had failed already, fallen at the very first hurdle. How was he going to explain it? Fontainbleu was watching him, a knowing expression on his face, as if reading his thoughts easily. "You desire to tell me something, perhaps," he said at last.

"No…yes," Ritchie replied, stumbling over the words. Under Fontainbleu's penetrating gaze, he told his wretched story for the second time that night.

"You lost everything?" Fontainbleu asked, looking astonished.

"I've still got my computer and my medals. But they took the rest of my gear and all my cash."

"How much?" Fontainbleu asked sharply.

"Twenty grand," Ritchie croaked. Fontainbleu was staring at him now as if he could see right through him.

"*Ah voila*," Fontainbleu said in a welcoming tone as Henri appeared carrying a tray of drinks. The tension in the air evaporated. Henri handed his master a glass of colourless liquid.

"And for you *Monsieur*?" he asked politely, turning to Ritchie.

"Just water," Ritchie mumbled.

"With a dash of brandy," Fontainbleu added firmly, taking a seat beside Ritchie on the sofa. "So," he said. "Some island boys had fun at your expense. That is no way to treat a guest of mine. They will be punished." Ritchie was glad about that, but it wasn't going to help him get his money back. "Tomorrow," Fontainbleu added smoothly, sipping his drink, "you will open a bank account." Ritchie's eyes widened.

"With what?" he asked, startled.

"I personally will deposit twenty-two thousand US dollars into your account. *Ce n'est rien*. It is nothing," he said, brushing aside Ritchie's protests. "The extra two thousand is for you to buy yourself some new clothes. Then, if you wish it, you can return to the US."

"You don't want me to stay?" Ritchie stuttered.

"You still wish to proceed with the purchase, then?"

"Of course!" Ritchie blurted out. "I can make a go of the bar, I know I can!" Fontainbleu looked satisfied.

"Tomorrow, we shall discuss the question of the Lucky Seven Stable, yes?" he said, taking another sip of his drink.

"Cat's dead keen," Ritchie told him, gulping down the brandy, which slipped down his dry throat like water in a desert.

"Cat...that is your brother, yes?"

Ritchie nodded.

"He'll do anything you want," he said. It wasn't entirely true but Ritchie was in no position to bargain. Fontainbleu looked back at him thoughtfully.

"What they wish for, my clients, is sole control, total privacy," he said. "Henri will show you your room now," he added abruptly, getting to his feet. Ritchie decided this was definitely not the right time to mention his brother's request: the purchase of one well bred yearling by the Lucky Seven Stable. "For now, I shall bid you a pleasant night," Fontainbleu murmured.

"Thank you, sir," Ritchie replied humbly.

Ritchie's room turned out to be a luxurious apartment on one of the lower floors. He stripped off and took a shower. When he looked in the mirror he noticed a bruise running up and down his left arm. It was badly swollen too. Though it was only 8 p.m. he fell into bed. The events of the day had finally caught up with him.

At Iroquois Downs, the horses were parading for the second race.

"Number one is Hustle Bustle," a voice announced over the loudspeaker. "with Harry Harper at the reins. Number two, Sleepless Nights, trained by Dave Bodinski, driven by Theo Vettore…" Sleepless Nights! Caroline thought excitedly, abandoning the phone. Right now, watching a horse race appealed to her much more than negotiating her way through the Canadian telephone system. She might as well have a flutter, she decided. The little man who'd given her the tip had looked somewhat disreputable, but what the heck?

"Where do I bet?" she asked a man with grizzled grey hair.

"Better hurry, lady. Over here!" the man replied, guiding her over to the tote board windows. "Who d'you like?" he asked.

"Sleepless Nights," she replied without hesitation. "Ten dollars on number two to win," she told the teller breathlessly.

"Next!"

"Same as her," the old man chimed in.

"It's post time!" the track announcer cried. Excitedly, Caroline pushed her way through the crowd, reaching the rail just in time to see the horses rounding the last turn. People were yelling out the numbers of the horses, not their names, urging them on.

"Six, c'mon six, c'mon baby!"

"One, one, one…you son of a bitch! You blew it again, Harper!" a man cried, throwing his ticket down, his face contorted with rage. The horses were coming down the stretch for the finish now. It was so different from hurdle racing in England. The speed, the sound of whips cracking, the thunder of hooves as the horses swept past…it was thrilling!

"Yes!" a man wearing an oversized T-shirt yelled. "I knew Vettore would do it for me!" Raising his arms above his head, he did a victory dance. A little more sedately, Caroline made her way to the winner's enclosure.

"The winner of the second race is number two, Sleepless Nights by Night Raider, out of Sleep Tight! Winning trainer Dave Bodinski. Winning driver Theo Vettore. Mile in 1.55. A new lifetime mark." Caroline joined the small crowd of people clustered around the winner's circle. The camera flashed. The horse threw his head, and the groom who was holding him, up and down. And there was the little man who'd knocked her down, the one who'd given her the tip. She waved at him, smiling. He didn't notice her, but the driver did. Their eyes met. He tossed his whip into the crowd. To her astonishment, it flew straight to her. Reaching out, she caught it easily. There was an expression of amusement on his handsome face. Before she had a chance to react, she heard her name being called.

"Caroline Aldright! This is a special announcement for Caroline Aldright! Please make your way to the main entrance…"

How on earth did they know her name here? Caroline asked herself. What was going on? Then she came up with the only possible explanation. Kip had come to the rescue! She sprinted towards the main entrance, dodging through the crowd, whip in hand. Most people jumped back in time, but she scored several direct hits unfortunately. On the whole, people were pretty good about it but she created quite a commotion.

"I'm most frightfully sorry!" she gasped, with a quick glance over her shoulder. She didn't dare stop, despite the fact her legs were starting to wobble. Jet lag was finally setting in. Kip wasn't there, but Uncle George was waiting outside. "Am I glad to see you!" Caroline shrieked.

"Thank goodness you're safe!" George said, enfolding her in an avuncular embrace. "We were really worried about you!" His mobile rang. "Bingo!" he exclaimed. "No, she's fine. It'll take us about half an hour. Is Kip there? Oh, alright, see you soon then. Jolly good!" he added, ending the call. "Kip's asleep! Frightfully sorry about the mix up…we didn't get your message 'til we got back to the house. I'm in trouble with the boss…er your Aunt Bee. Should've given you the mobile number apparently." He paused, as if looking at her properly for the first time. "Where on earth did you get that whip?" he asked. "What *have* you been up to?"

"One of the drivers gave it to me," Caroline replied, realizing she still had the win ticket in her pocket.

"Did he indeed?" Uncle George replied, smiling down at her. "C'mon old girl, let's get you home. You must have quite a story to tell. Where did you abandon the car? I've got a spare gas can in the van."

"Zone D," Caroline replied promptly.

"Any idea whereabouts?" Uncle George enquired a little while later, gazing at the sea of cars surrounding them. "It's a huge area. Must be at least a dozen D's here. Wonder why they didn't use all the other letters in the alphabet?" He shook his head. "Typical bureaucratic cock up, excuse my French. Oh well, you're probably not keen on driving anyway. We'll come back in the A.M. Pity about your luggage. It'll still be there tomorrow though. That's one thing we don't need to worry about over here. No crime." He started up the engine. "Home John and don't spare the horses!" he exclaimed, taking off at eighty kilometres an hour.

Caroline Aldright spent her first night in Canada wearing Aunt Bee's nightdress, using a borrowed toothbrush and with no makeup or clean clothes for the morning. She didn't care. She would have gladly gone through all of it again for the sight of Sleepless Nights in the winner's circle and the secret hope that, before too long, Kip could be back where he belonged, in a world where horses, not people, formed the main topic of conversation. It didn't matter that it was Canada, rather than England. Racehorse people were the same everywhere or so she hoped.

"I knew you'd be alright," Kip said sleepily. "You always come out of everything smelling like a rose."

"I'm exhausted!" Caroline replied.

"Good night, sleep tight," Kip yawned.

"She's the dam of Sleepless Nights," Caroline mumbled.

"What?" Kip exclaimed, jerking wide awake. There was no reply. When he switched on the bedside light, he noticed a long black whip, propped up against the wardrobe. He was certain it hadn't been there before. He stayed awake a long time, trying to puzzle it out.

Bondage wasn't Caroline's style.

THE HERMITAGE

André Fontainbleu took out his personal private cell phone, the one nobody knew about, not even Henri, especially not Henri! Boxer answered right away.

"I want the cash back tonight," André said coldly. "Is it all there?"

"Twenty grand, on the nose. All in hundreds," Boxer replied. "The boys want to keep the sports gear. Okay with you?"

"Anything interesting that I should know about?"

"Nothing of any consequence," Boxer replied shortly.

"Nothing at all?"

"Listen, I've been through everything, thoroughly. He's your all American blue-eyed boy. Not a kink in him."

"Where did they drop him?"

"Dog City," Boxer chuckled. Both men laughed. André Fontainbleu was the first to recover.

"Be here before midnight," he said. "I want to put that money in the bank, first thing tomorrow morning."

"Understood, boss," Boxer replied.

After the call, André Fontainbleu lay back on the bed, staring up at the ceiling. He had discovered all he needed to know about Ritchie Sanchez. He was gullible, he was honest and, thanks to André's little game, he now felt vulnerable. If his brother, Catalino Ciardi, was fashioned from the same cloth, everything would work out perfectly.

The idea of acquiring a string of horses racing and winning every week appealed to André. The expensive yacht he had purchased had won the Sainte Marie Island Race with Boxer as captain. But André had so much cash rolling in from his various activities, he hardly knew what to do with it. With one notable exception, he had always been able to buy people. Buying horses would be much simpler – more exciting too. He needed a new challenge: another mountain to climb, another hill to conquer. That was what gave meaning to life. He did not allow himself to think about Anya these days, even when he caught a glimpse of the Sea Princess on her daily rounds of the island beaches. She no longer interested him but her friend Pete who skippered the boat, was about to receive an unpleasant surprise. Henri had been an unwitting assistant in this regard.

The trap was set.

BACHELOR PARTY

Three thousand kilometres to the north, flashes of green and pink were swirling and dancing across the night sky, unnerving the horses at Harmony Farm. The northern lights were making a rare visit to Southern Ontario. The colts had never seen anything like it before. Long after the show was over, they were still restless. Storm, the grey, was trotting nervously back and forth, his tail flowing out behind him. Harmony Stampede was patrolling the perimeter fence, testing its strength with his muscular body. The little black colt, Harmony Jet, was hiding out in a clump of pines, his ears tipped forward listening intently. Nearby, a pack of coyotes was gathering.

The coyotes howled. Harmony Light pirouetted, his dark silhouette spinning round and round, his nostrils flaring. Out in the bush, the coyotes made a kill, their shrill yapping filling the air. Harmony Light took off like a rocket, galloping down the field. The others chased after him, moving like shadows beside him, leaping over the stream in unison.

At sunrise, Harmony Light took a run at the fence and jumped it cleanly, clearing it by several inches. Then he trotted back and touched noses with his brothers over the gate. For a few moments, chaos reigned. Storm kicked out at the little black colt, who pushed up against the barrier. In the scuffle, the colts' combined weight landed on the gate and it crashed to the ground. For the first time in their lives, they were free. They cantered to the barn and raced down the aisle, grabbing wisps of hay as they ran. Then they headed back into the open air to visit the fillies in the paddock nearby. But the fillies did not hold the colts' attention for long. The band of brothers had bigger fish to fry. A rosy glow shone over the fields in the early morning light as they sped past the house, down the laneway, through the gate and into the big world outside the confines of Harmony Farm. It was hard to say who was more surprised, the colts, or the farmer driving his tractor. Both stopped and stared, unable to believe what they were seeing. The colts broke rank first, wheeling around and heading back down the road which led to the village of Indian Falls, just a hop, skip and a jump away from Iroquois Downs Raceway and Highway 501.

As they trotted down the road, Harmony Light took over the lead. The colt with the white face stayed at the rear, driving the others along. It was a straight run but eventually their pace slackened as hunger got the better of them and they started snatching mouthfuls of grass and wildflowers from the side of the road. A pond caught their attention but as they approached it, a gaggle of geese appeared, flapping their wings and hissing at them. The colts moved on. Seeing an open gate, they raced through it and soon settled down to graze. But they were not the only animals in the hayfield that morning. An unwelcome visitor slipped out of the bush. Smaller than the geese, he had a humped back and walked with a curious gait. Busily grazing, most of the colts didn't notice him at first. But Harmony Light was intrigued by the newcomer. He stalked him until he was only inches away. The others soon joined in the fun. Stretching out their necks, they curled back their upper lips, scenting the strange new odor. Snorting, they pawed at the ground. It was too much for the porcupine. He let fly with his quills, scoring a direct hit on Harmony Light's muzzle which was quickly covered in a mass of quills. Harmony Light bolted. The others turned on a dime and followed him.

The church bells were ringing as they came into town.

Joey Harris woke up with a start, to the sound of thundering hooves. He made it up to the bedroom window just in time to see the colts' rear ends as they disappeared through the farm gate.

"What's going on?" Val asked sleepily, rolling over in bed and stifling a yawn.

"The horses got loose!" Joey exclaimed, throwing on some clothes. "Be at the back door in two minutes!" By the time he had collected lead shanks and hitched up his two horse trailer, there was no sign of the colts anywhere.

"Which way?" Val asked frantically as they reached the end of the lane-way. Joey decided to take a shot at it. He turned left. Pretty soon they came across a tractor going at a snail's pace. The farmer waved them past. "Wait," Val said, rolling down her window. "Did you see any loose horses?" she asked. "Some of ours broke out." The farmer pointed back down the road.

"You're going the wrong way!" he shouted. "I saw a whole bunch of 'em… one of them had a big gash on its leg!"

"Turn around," Val said, rigid with fear. All their hard work and most of their money was galloping to Indian Falls, on a mission to self-destruct. "I'm calling Winterflood!" she exclaimed.

"We gotta catch 'em first," Joey reminded her.

"Thank goodness it's Sunday," she remarked a little later. "Not so much traffic."

"Lucky thing," Joey agreed gravely, going as fast as he dared with a horse trailer in tow. Ten minutes later, there was still no sign of them.

Caroline Aldright was up bright and early on Sunday morning. She couldn't stay in bed any longer. It was 7 a.m. which was noon in England. She tiptoed out of the bedroom so as not to wake Kip, longing for some clean clothes. Uncle George was drinking a cup of tea in the kitchen and munching toast and marmalade.

"Would you…" Caroline began awkwardly. "That is, could you tell me who I should ring for a taxi? I really need to pick up the car."

"Nonsense," Uncle George replied briskly. "I'll take you. It's Sunday, so I don't have any rounds to make at the hospital today. But we'll have to take the camper van, I'm afraid. Bee's gone to church in Indian Falls."

A few minutes later, they were on their way. But instead of going directly to Iroquois Downs to collect Caroline's rental car, Uncle George took a detour.

"Thought I'd show you the village of Indian Falls," he said. "It's a pretty little place." They didn't get very far. Traffic on the high street had ground to a halt in both directions. "What the devil's going on?" Uncle George frowned. "Now that's something you don't see every day," he said, as a group of wild looking horses with tangled manes and tails and mud up to their knees picked their way across the road through the line of cars. One of them looked as though he had sprouted dark whiskers or taken up smoking long cigars.

"It's just like the New Forest!" Caroline exclaimed. After gaining the safety of the wide pavement, the horses decided to tuck in to some hanging baskets outside a shop. But when one of them caught sight of his reflection in the window, they were soon off again. They were heading towards the church, with its doors open wide.

"I do believe," Uncle George remarked gleefully, "they're going in there."

Inside the church, the pastor was winding up the service.

"May the Lord bless you and keep you. May He spread His love amongst you and give you peace. In the name of the Holy Spirit and His son Jesus Christ…*Oh my Lord!*" The parishioners looked up, startled. But the pastor had not had a divine vision. The clip clop of hooves echoed up and down the pews as four unkempt colts covered in quills, leaves and wildflowers trotted up the aisle to the nave. They made an unusual group of Sunday worshippers.

"Horshees," a little boy called out, delightedly. The congregation was in an uproar. The colts wheeled around and made a swift exit. They came thundering past Uncle George's camper van.

"Do let's follow them," Caroline begged.

"Your wish is my command!" George replied, executing a clumsy U-turn, no easy feat with a camper van. A few minutes later they were careening into Iroquois Downs' empty parking lot, twisting and turning as the horses changed course.

"Watch out!" Caroline screamed.

"Piece of cake," George replied, swerving violently and narrowly avoiding a tattered looking man riding an old bicycle. Ahead lay Racehorse City, where endless rows of barns stretched as far as the eye could see. As the gates swung open to let a white feed truck out, the horses, followed by the camper van, flew in, whizzing past an astonished guard at the gate.

"Hey! Where's your licences?" the guard shouted after them, clinging, even in these unusual circumstances, to the demands of protocol. Then he whipped out his pager. "Loose horses!" he cried. "Loose horses on the backstretch." In the rear view mirror, Caroline saw the feed truck swing around and join the convoy. The horses made for the only open spot in view: the racetrack. After a spirited start, they appeared to lose interest in the idea of a race and by the three quarter pole, they were ready to throw in the towel. The grassy infield beckoned. There, they ground to a halt, fighting for breath, their flanks heaving.

"Who the fuck let these horses loose?" the feed man demanded, descending from the truck and glaring at the two of them.

"Steady on, old boy," Uncle George remonstrated. "It wasn't us! We were just trying to help."

"Okay, what are we waiting for?" the feed man asked, without bothering to apologize. "Let's go get 'em." But, despite their best efforts, the horses eluded them. "It's no use," the man panted, mopping his brow. "We'll never catch 'em like this." Help arrived in the shape of four hefty security guards, crammed into a tiny golf cart. They only made matters worse.

Val and Joey Harris arrived on the scene to find the colts quietly grazing on the infield. Val slid down from the truck and walked up to Harmony Light, who allowed himself to be caught with a minimum of fuss. She led him away, porcupine quills and all, thanking her lucky stars that his halter had stayed on. When she looked around, seven people were staring at her, open mouthed. Realizing that four of them were security guards, Val made a hasty retreat. Out of the corner of her eye, she could see the porcupine quills bobbing up and down.

"Where to now?" she called out to Joey.

"Hang on!" Joey called back, rolling open a large barn door. "You can put 'im in here . . . looks like it's empty. Watch out!" he yelled, as Harmony Stampede pushed past her, nearly knocking her off her feet in his eagerness to get inside. The other colts followed. One by one, they dived, thankfully into the open stalls. They'd obviously had enough of freedom for one morning. Only Harmony Storm was still loose, racing up and down the aisle, one hind leg oozing blood.

"We're going to need Winterflood," Val said, reaching for her phone.

"Tell him to come to the ship-in barn. He'll know where it is," Joey replied.

A short while later, Ted Hawkins, Head of Track Security, came striding in.

"Who's the person responsible for this?" Ted demanded, the word outrage hanging in the air, unspoken.

"That would be me," Joey admitted.

"Come with me, I'll have a make a full report to management," Ted said severely. "Those animals could have done all kinds of damage. Who owns that camper van?" A man with grey hair put up his hand, looking shame-faced. "You'd better come along too. No one's allowed on the backstretch without a licence!"

"Golly!" the man said, looking like a deflated balloon. "You'd better move the camper, Caroline," he added nervously, handing over the keys to a girl in a crumpled sundress. The foursome collided with Dr. Winterflood who was on his way in. The weary expression on the vet's face made Val feel incredibly guilty. It was Sunday morning, after all. Storm chose that moment to make a dash for the open door. Val's heart sank. They were in trouble with everyone, it seemed. This was exactly the kind of publicity Harmony Farm didn't need. Reggie Blair saved the day by blocking the exit with an enormous bale of hay, which he picked up as if it was as light as a feather.

Winterflood looked concerned when he caught sight of the gash on Storm's leg, as the horse came flying past him.

"I'm going to have to tranquilize him," the vet warned. "But we'll have to catch him first." After a brief struggle and a few near misses with the syringe, Winterflood hit the target.

"Little bugger got me good," Reggie complained, cradling his split lip. Val felt worse than ever.

"Right," Winterflood said. "He'll need stitches."

"Reggie?" Val asked, looking alarmed.

"The colt!" Winterflood laughed.

"Anything I can do to help?" the girl in the sundress enquired earnestly, coming back inside. "I've got my own horse back in England, so just say the word."

What word? Val wondered distractedly holding onto Storm as Winterflood went to work.

"Looks like your husband will get off with a caution this time," the grey haired man told Val kindly, breezing back in. That accent! Val thought. She'd never heard anything like it.

"Thanks," she replied gratefully. She paused. "Hey, we're having an open day next month. You guys are welcome to come and see the horses." She was inviting everyone she could think of, including her dental patients. Hopefully, there would be quite a crowd. Joey had even asked Al McTavish.

"We'd love to," the girl said, flashing her a smile. "We'd better get back, Uncle George," she added reluctantly. George nodded.

"Yes, better go! Toodle pip!" he said, exiting with a flourish.

"Toodle what?" Reggie asked incredulously after they left.

"British," Winterflood replied succinctly, putting in the last stitch on Storm's leg.

Val pulled Harmony Light out of his stall. When the vet caught sight of the long porcupine quills, he burst out laughing, tears streaming down his cheeks. He held himself together just long enough to tranquilize him, before succumbing once more.

Ten minutes later, the quills were history and the colt was lying out on the floor like a dead thing. He looked like a drunk now, sleeping off a binge.

"Little troublemaker," Winterflood said, looking at him fondly. "You'll need to water them all out," he told Val. "No more than ten swallows at a time. They could use a few electrolytes...and a good bath!" he added with a smile.

"D'you catch that big stake last night?" Reggie asked as Winterflood deftly administered a tetanus shot before Storm registered it was happening. "Unbelievable!" Reggie added. "Two year olds going in 1.53. In July!"

"Get rid of those for me, please," the vet said pointing to pile of syringes on the floor. Reggie volunteered.

"Mercer wasn't even in the frame," Reggie continued. "Some guys I never heard of shipped in from the other side of Ontario. They took all the money!"

"Hey, check this out," Reggie called out a few minutes later. "This bin's chock full o' needles. Those guys were shooting up those two year old stakes colts last night. Right here in the ship-in barn!"

"I can't believe what I'm seeing," Val cried, joining Reggie and staring down into the bin.

"Makes you sick, don't it?" Reggie agreed. "Hey Doc! Sell any good drugs lately?"

"I'm a lameness vet," Winterflood replied primly.

"They give Scotty McCoy twelve months jus' for fuckin' soda. An' there's guys like this blowing horses' heads off, right under the judges' noses and gettin' away with it!" Reggie said bitterly.

"Well, I'm done here," Winterflood declared picking up his bag. Reggie followed him, leaving Val by herself in the dark dusty barn, so very different from the one at Harmony Farm, where sunlight shone down through the skylights and swallows flitted in and out through the wide open doors. The Iroquois Downs' retention barn, revamped by Joey, was a palace compared with this. Evidently, Al McTavish hadn't gotten around to making any more improvements on the backstretch. Leaving Harmony Light to regain consciousness, she turned her attention to the other three colts. Harmony Stampede had come out of his adventure virtually unscathed. The glamour boy had his head over the stall door, his ears pricked, his eyes alert as if he'd had a taste of something out there on the racetrack that he was anxious to revisit. When she tried to smarten up Harmony Storm using an old brush she found in the wash stall, the grey colt flattened his ears and pinned her into a corner. Harmony Jet was much more cooperative which was just as well. He looked like he'd waded through a sea of mud and had picked up half a forest on the way. Getting the burrs out of his mane and tail was going to take hours. She decided to leave it to Joey.

Harmony Light was struggling to his feet. Wishing he didn't look quite so bedraggled, Val set about brushing the worst of the mud off his legs. It was an uphill battle. But in exactly two months' time, at the Annual Yearling

Sale, Harmony Light would have to look glamorous and desirable. His long whiskers would be shaved, the hair growing out of his ears neatly clipped. His manners would have to be impeccable, his hooves trimmed, shod and polished. They had just eight weeks to accomplish a miraculous transformation. Val had been looking forward to the sale. After seeing the needles, however, she felt like a traitor, as if she was going to sell a beloved child into slavery. This time next year, Harmony Light could be in this barn, for real, Val realized, shot up with drugs. Drugs which would blow his mind and his body. Thinking about it brought tears to her eyes. But what could she do? This was Joey's dream.

Joey was back.

"Well that went well," he said. "I have to report to the judges and the Church Council. Apparently, Our Lady of the Sacred Heart called in and complained about horse droppings in the aisle. Some Sunday morning I'm having."

So little time left, so much to do. Val could hear a clock ticking in her head. Only sixty days to go before Sale Time. How could she tell Joey about the needles? How could she not? Suddenly, being a dentist didn't seem like such a terrible way of making a living after all.

Dr. Jay Winterflood was flying down a country road lined with wildflowers when his cell phone rang. He scooped it up from the passenger seat.

"Yeah," he said distractedly.

"Are you okay?" he heard Helena ask anxiously. "I thought you'd be back by now." She was trying not to sound reproachful, he realized.

"I got held up," he explained.

"You're working too hard. Please come home." The phone went dead. He was out of range or out of luck and too tired to care. He'd been called out at 3 a.m. for a foaling that had gone badly wrong. The team at the Equine Hospital had slung the mare upside down from the ceiling and got the foal out, saving her life and, crucially, her future breeding prospects. There weren't too many sentimentalists in this breeding business. It had been too late to save the foal. His Cree mother had been right, he reflected as he sped along, through dappled sunlight and shade. One step down the white man's road, she had warned him, and he would never find his way back. How true that was! Since he had resigned as track veterinarian, nothing much had changed except his income stream. Owners paid sporadically, if at all. His time still wasn't his own and he was driven by the twin demons, desire and fear.

How different his childhood had been. He had lived in the land of his mother's stories, walking on an earth that was alive, finding his way through the bush that covered the ground like hair on an animal's back, wading in streams that flowed like the blood in his own veins, feeling the sweet breath of the wind, acknowledging the wild creatures he came across as members of other tribes, deserving equal respect.

That view of the world seemed like an impossible dream, now that he was living in his father's world. The desires of white people: land, possessions, achievement, had ensnared him. The mortgage on his farm hung like a noose around his neck. It was the reason he laboured night and day. The fear of losing what he had gained drove him on. The image of the needles and syringes lying in the bin reproached him cruelly. The phrase "a man is your friend or your enemy, nothing else is possible" rang through his head. Not for the first time. Yet, ironically, he'd discovered his own tribe in the horses and through them the horse people. They called him chief. He didn't deserve it. The conversation with Reggie had unleashed doubts he kept firmly in check, during daylight hours. They resurfaced only after he was called out on some emergency in the middle of the night. Afterwards he would lie awake torturing himself.

He considered making a call to the Director of Racing, Al McTavish. Sunday morning or not, McTavish ought to know about the stakes colts being treated like living pin cushions. Better later, Jay decided, than sooner. Helena would be waiting for him. She was outside, standing in the shade of the sugar maple tree. Tomorrow, perhaps, he would call McTavish. He couldn't think about it now.

SAINTE MARIE

Ritchie Sanchez was sitting by himself on the beach listening to the waves and watching a fiery orange sun hanging low over the Caribbean Sea. In a few weeks' time, things wouldn't be so quiet. There was still a lot of work to do but opening night at the place he'd renamed the Sunset Bar was now in his sights. Soon no trace of the down at heel eatery he had bought would remain. In its place would be a circular bar stocked with Stingray beer and everything else besides, while on the sandy beach sun-loungers and umbrellas would jostle with artfully arranged tables and chairs, perfect for casual dining. He could see it all in his mind's eye.

It was time to call his brother and bring him up to date with events.

"Ontario?" Cat asked, sounding utterly astonished on the other end of the line. "Why Canada?"

"Many reasons," Ritchie replied, unwilling to go into all the details (the laws about private property, the cheaper dollar, the purse structure at Iroquois Downs). "Just go with it, okay."

"No!" Cat replied stubbornly. "It's not okay."

"You can stay with Mom's uncle until I've got things organized."

"Eddie Clearwater! He's still alive? He must be about ninety," Cat said disgustedly.

"Seventy-six," Ritchie corrected. "He'll give you a roof over your head and you can work for him until I've found a farm for you. . ."

"No way!" Cat exclaimed.

"Hey!" Ritchie replied, feeling a little panicky. He couldn't believe the kid was trying to unwind everything he'd worked for. "You can't back out. Not now."

"Eddie taught me how to juggle, that's all I remember," Cat stated unenthusiastically.

"Listen, you're about to have barn full of great horses, an entire house to live in, your own training track and a brand new truck to drive. Most guys would kill for that."

"It won't be mine," Cat pointed out. "I like having my own place."

"What? That shoebox!" Ritchie exploded. "You're not serious." There was an ominous silence on the other end of the line. The sun had disappeared beneath the horizon. With one eye on the darkening sky, Ritchie persisted. He used some of the techniques he'd picked up from Coach Bailey to persuade his brother to stay on board. When Cat finally said *yes*, it was pitch black on the beach. Ritchie rang off feeling he'd got off relatively lightly.

AUGUST

"August really sucks!" Reggie Blair grumbled to himself as he travelled down the dusty road after dropping off his last load of feed for the day. "It's hard on people. It's hard on horses and it's hard on my damn Ford engine," he muttered, pulling his truck over into the shade of a stand of oak trees. A flock of turkey vultures was holed up in the branches, waiting out the afternoon. Time was money, but Reggie wasn't going anywhere. He was afraid of blowing the engine. It wasn't the only thing that was overheating, Reggie thought. The humidity was brutal.

The Annual Yearling Sale catalogue was lying on the passenger seat beside him, daring him to pick it up. He resisted it for a while, fiddling with the dials on the radio, before giving in to temptation. Pretty soon, though, he tired of looking at mere words on a page. He needed to see a horse in the flesh to know what it was made of. Number 140, Harmony Stampede, was a stand-out. He remembered the first moment he'd clapped eyes on him, the day Joey Harris's colts got loose on the Iroquois Downs backstretch. He was going to have to buy a new feed van soon and that wouldn't leave a lot left over for a horse. But he couldn't stop thinking about the sturdy little colt with the white blaze. He was a stunner! His reverie was interrupted by a deafening thunderclap, followed by a flash of lightning that lit up a mass of dark clouds to the west. Flocks of small birds dived for cover as raindrops began tapping on his windscreen.

Hastily, Reggie started up the engine and pulled out. The last place he wanted to be, in a lightning storm, was stuck under a tree. He hadn't gone far when the heavens opened. The rain came pelting down like Niagara Falls. He slowed down to a crawl until the lights of the Happy Shopper appeared through the torrent. Then he turned hard right. The truck lurched, missing the gas pump by inches. He climbed down from the cab and made a run for the store. Nora McClean's bright orange hair was shining like a beacon behind the counter. Reggie grabbed a cold drink, tossing Nora a five-dollar bill. Nearby, a tall skinny kid was fooling around, juggling a set of miniature bottles.

"That's my last case of ginseng," Nora said crossly, handing Reggie his change. "He's bound to break them and he hasn't even paid for them yet." The juggler had a captive audience, folks trapped by the pouring rain outside.

He was showing off, tossing the bottle higher and higher, while Nora clucked her disapproval.

"He oughta join the circus," Reggie chuckled.

"You reckon?" Eddie Clearwater commented drily, taking his nose out of a copy of *Horseman's World*. He was kitted out, as usual, in the sky blue overalls he wore summer and winter, rain or shine.

"Wicked storm out there," Reggie remarked conversationally.

"Ain't it just!" Eddie agreed.

"Need any feed?" Reggie asked hopefully. Eddie shook his head.

"I've bin usin' the same feed mill for forty years. I ain't about to change now," he replied, retreating to his magazine.

"He'll switch if I tell him to," the juggler declared, a gleam in his eye.

"This here's my niece's boy," Eddie revealed. "Quit it now, Cat. That's enough juggling for one day. You'll give poor Nora a heart attack."

"Give me a few days to work on him, okay?" Cat said, handing back the ginseng. "I'll get him to switch."

"There's one missing," Nora complained, counting the bottles "That's a toonie you owe me."

"If you pull that off I'll eat my hat!" Reggie exclaimed.

"You're on!" Cat grinned. "Watch this!" He made a great show of checking his pockets, then reached up to the ceiling and produced the missing bottle out of thin air. "This isn't a library," he added, pointed at Ed's magazine. "You gotta pay before you read."

"I'm going home," Ed declared. "You can walk if you like."

"In this rain? No way!" Cat protested, hurrying after him. At the door, he paused. "Three days," he grinned. "You'll see. Bye Nora!" Nora waved at him brightly, her worries forgotten. A few minutes later, Cat was back, looking like a drowned rat.

"Need a ride?" Reggie offered.

"Ten bags," Cat said. "He wants ten bags of your best feed. Bring it tomorrow. He'll pay cash." Then he was gone. "Goddamn it," Reggie swore softly to himself. The kid was too much. Getting Eddie Clearwater's custom was about as likely as winning the lottery. He was a charmer, alright. He wasn't anything like Eddie. The old timer had isolated himself from the dog eat dog world by concentrating on young trotters. He'd been pretty good in his day too. But he was no match for Cat. The kid could walk on water.

Billie McTavish waited for a break in the downpour, before making a dash for her front door. Halfway up the narrow staircase that led to her apartment, she paused for breath. She was loaded up with groceries. The bags seemed a lot heavier since she'd had two people to shop for, even though Theo rarely ate a meal at home. The door to her apartment opened suddenly and Theo came bursting out. He didn't act pleased to see her. His "Hi Billie" was hardly enthusiastic, but at least he helped with the bags. In the kitchen there were dirty dishes on the counter top, the remains of Theo's lunch.

"You ate already?" she asked, unhappily.

"I had a sandwich. I'm going to the gym."

"On a Saturday? I thought we'd go out somewhere." Her plans for the afternoon (lunch at Tangoes, followed by a movie or a trip to the mall) were evaporating into thin air.

"Look," he said, glancing at his watch. "What d'you want me to do here, Billie?"

"I'd like a hug," she heard herself say. She hadn't felt this disappointed since she was three years old and her brother had refused to take her to the playground, even though he had promised her. Theo threw down his sports bag, kicked the front door shut in one easy motion. Then he took her in his arms for a long moment. But why, Billie wondered as he held her close, did affection always have to convert so rapidly into lust, where men were concerned? As Theo ushered her into the bedroom, random truisms popped into her head: you can't always get what you want. . .beggars can't be choosers . . .you gotta take what you can get. It was better to settle for what was on offer, she decided, thinking of the alternative: a long Saturday afternoon spent entirely on her own.

Later, stretching out in the empty bed with Theo's "You're incredible" ringing in her ears, she couldn't help feeling like a little kid who'd been coaxed out of a tantrum with the promise of ice-cream. A quickie with one participant's eye on the clock was no substitute for a meaningful relationship. But she didn't feel too unhappy about the way things had played out. Outside, the weather had taken another turn for the worse. She lay back on the pillow, listening to the rain tapping on the window pane. It suddenly felt good to be home. Despite Theo's absence from the bed, it was warm and cozy under the covers. It was good, too, to have the place to herself. She decided to have a long, lazy bath then fix herself lunch, maybe watch a movie on TV. But before she'd lifted a finger, her eyes closed and she began breathing deeply. An instant later she had drifted off into a dreamless sleep.

As Theo drove away from the apartment through the wide tree-lined streets of Erinsville's old quarter, his thoughts turned from Billie to the coming night's race card with a profound sense of relief. Horses! They were the first thing that popped into his head when he woke up in the morning and the last thing he thought of before he fell asleep at night. He lived, breathed and dreamt about winning races. You could call it an obsession…or you could know it for what it was: the reason for being alive. Nothing could ever take its place, not even a woman like Billie.

He decided to go over to his place later on and take some time to pin up his latest win pictures on the walls. There was nowhere at Billie's apartment for stuff like that, not even for his prized collection of Night Raiders old horse shoes, the ones the old timer wore when he swooped the Breeder's Championship parked every step of the mile! The courage the horse had displayed that night would never be forgotten, not by Theo at any rate.

It was raining again. The trees, standing like sentinels guarding the streets, were swaying now, their branches whipped by the wind. It would be a dirty night, Theo guessed. Bring it on! he grinned, anticipating the chase and the final rush to the wire to steal a win from right under the other drivers' noses. Lately, he'd found his rhythm. He was currently on the biggest win streak of his career. Of course, it helped that Jake was supplying him again. But it was his own skills that made the difference. He was sure of it! Call it arrogance, but he knew he was better than anyone else. He could feel the magic in his fingertips. Billie would never understand how it was for him. At first, her fancy apartment and the easy life that came with it had appealed to him. Lately though, he'd begun to feel suffocated by it. Luxury was a poor exchange for excitement, in his view. Living on the edge, as he did nightly, he needed to keep his body strong and his mind focused. He was a master of the split second decision, the difference between success and failure. He couldn't afford to waste time trawling the mall, sleepwalking his way through the afternoon. If Billie didn't like it, it was just too fucking bad.

The repartee in the drivers' room at Iroquois Downs that evening put Theo in a far better mood.

"Hey swinger," Harry Harper complained. "You keep this up, winning all the races and none of us is gonna have enough money to eat!" Theo reached into his pocket and tossed a toonie in Harper's direction.

"Here, buy yourself a burger and quit whining, for God's sakes," he said. Harper's wild driving style had landed him precisely nowhere in the drivers' standings. He was a loser who belonged on the B circuit, in Theo's opinion.

"Why don't you take another vacation, bud," Ned Beazer suggested coolly, his back to the wall, his whip tucked under his arm.

"Yeah, you look like you haven't slept in a week!" Moose Rankin teased, pulling on his driving suit. "Take the night off, eh? I could sure use the drives."

"Anyone wanna go Vegas with me for a couple of days?" Theo grinned. "I'm feeling lucky."

"Don't rub it in. We don't all have rich girlfriends like you," Harper said, the envy in his voice making Theo feel doubly fortunate. Maybe he shouldn't be so quick to give up on Billie. His winning streak had begun the day he'd met her. Maybe she was his lucky charm.

"Forget Vegas!" Moose said. "There's a party out at Lazer's farm tonight. After I'm through here, I'm heading out there."

"A party? I'm up for that," Theo said, feeling a buzz of excitement. "Hey, I'm in the market for a racehorse…know anyone who's got anything interesting for sale?" Beazer shrugged. Moose was hunched down, smoking a cigarette with one eye on the door, wary of the ever vigilant judges. "It's gotta be something special," Theo clarified. He was getting his cocaine fix for free, now that he was a courier. The cash was piling up in his account. "I'm willing to fork out sixty grand for the right one." A gasp went up from his fellow drivers, which gratified Theo no end. He was in a happy place and he wanted to stay in it for as long as possible.

"Ask Lazer. He'd know, eh?" Harper offered. "He's got a ton of horses. Some of them gotta be for sale."

"Yeah, the ones he doesn't want," Moose laughed.

"If you got that kind of money," Ned Beazer stated solemnly. "Don't waste it on a horse, bud. Get yourself a farm, something solid."

"There's a nice place over by Keith's," Moose dropped in casually, taking a final drag on his cigarette. "I'd buy it myself if I had the dough." His comment was drowned out by the loudspeaker system.

"First race goes out in one minute," the voice of the Paddock Judge boomed out. "Get 'em ready, men!" It was the signal they'd all been waiting for. The edginess was gone in a flash, replaced by the usual rituals. Moose hitched up his rain pants. Theo tightened the strap on his helmet. Beazer bent down and checked the fastenings on his boots, Harper grabbed his whip. Then they were off, Theo leaping down the steps three at a time, certain of victory, the rest following at a more sedate pace. They were in no hurry. The first act was about to begin and they were all keenly aware that only one of them could be a winner. With Theo's track record lately, it felt like a foregone conclusion.

TOGETHERNESS

On the morning of Harmony Farm's Open Day, Joey Harris showed up to feed as usual at 6 a.m. When he saw the damage inflicted on his beautiful new stalls, he felt like crying. Ever since the colts had run off en masse that Sunday morning, he had been taking no chances: separate paddocks, separate stalls, no contact with other horses. Everything had gone to plan until now. Today, it was the fillies' turn. Princess and Goldie had spent the whole night tearing down the wooden partition between them. Whatever had made him decide to become a breeder of standardbred racehorses? he asked himself. Breeder! he thought derisively. The term didn't come close to describing the real nature of the job. A breeder had to be an expert matchmaker, a midwife, a nurse, a nutritionist, a psychologist, a fucking kindergarten teacher and at times sadly, an undertaker. A breeder had to be a gambler too, he reflected ruefully, noticing that Princess' front leg was swollen.

"What are you trying to do, ruin me?" he asked Princess in an accusatory tone. "This isn't a good time to bang yourself up, Madam! Not with the Open Day!" The two fillies stared brazenly back at him, standing amidst the broken beams, evidently proud of their night's work. "Heck!" he exclaimed, relenting. "You two wanna be together that bad, I'm not gonna stop you." Before beginning the cleanup operation, he led them out to the paddock in tandem, a leadshank in either hand. Belatedly, as the paddock gate clanged shut behind them, he realized he'd forgotten to check out the damage to Princess' leg. But when he tried to catch her, she sprinted away from him.

A loud banging from inside the barn sent him scurrying back inside again. The bachelors had finished their breakfast. They wanted out. Now! First to make it into the sunshine was Harmony Light. Joey watched him as he stretched out his neck and leapt forward, circling his paddock at a wild gallop. The rest of the gang were soon celebrating the morning, whinnying over to the fences and eyeing the fillies with a brand new intensity. The bachelors had discovered girls!

After he'd finished his chores, Joey walked back to the house, took a shower and smartened himself up a bit, ready to showcase his yearlings to the crowds of visitors he was praying would show up today. At least the weather was cooperating. In a few short weeks, all eight of the youngsters he'd cared for and worried over would be gone, taken by the highest bidder. All he could do was hope they'd go to a good trainer, someone who'd give them a chance. Right now, none of them had a care in the world. All of that was about to change. They'd have to grow up fast.

Playtime was over.

THE GREAT DEBATE

Jim Mercer was dog tired. His barn felt like a fucking hospital and he didn't know how he could face another year of crushing disappointment. All his hard work, the thousands of hours he'd spent out on the track in the freezing cold…the countless days he'd leapt out of bed at the crack of dawn to beat the heat, had all been for nothing.

This year, only one of his two year olds had made the races. The others, all sixteen of them, were on stall rest: sick, lame or fresh from the surgeon's knife. But the thing that had really got to Mercer today was the son of a bitch that had been the only decent two year old in his barn until last night. The bum had cracked a knee and was done for the season…perhaps forever… leaving Mercer's racing tank empty.

After touring the stalls, treating the sick, seeing to the crippled and cursing the grooms, Mercer retreated to his office for the morning, with a mug of coffee and a copy of the Annual Yearling Sale catalogue. As he turned the page, his forehead puckered in concentration, his mood lifted and his craggy face weathered by sun and wind, lit up with a smile of pleasure and recognition. He wasn't sentimental. No one in their right minds would have called him that. But as he trawled through the yearling catalogue, the names of horses he remembered leapt off the page at him. Sires he'd watched win, week after week, fast mares he'd trained and raced (or raced against)…horse families he knew all the ins and outs of. . . their strengths and the things that let them down. His pen hovered above number 85, Harmony Light…the son of Heart of Darkness. What a filly she'd been! Her first foal wouldn't be cheap, but he had to have this colt! Had to! As he stared at the page, his eyes glazed over, his head sank down to his chest and, his hat slipping down over his eyes, he drifted off into a fitful sleep.

The next thing he knew, someone was banging on the door.

"Hey boss!" a voice called out. "Ain't nothin' lef' to do round here. The guys are gonna go grab a burger." Startled, Mercer jumped up to his feet, knocking over his cup of coffee, which spilled out in a stream, flowing towards the precious yearling book. He quickly tossed an old T-shirt onto the spillage and opened the door, to be greeted by the sound of running feet.

"I know who's put them up to this!" he muttered furiously. "Stinker the slacker!" It was only eleven o'clock. What in the hell were they thinking,

228

quittin' this early? Then he remembered. Ted Rivers was putting on a barbecue today. It was perfect weather for it and the guys couldn't wait to get dug in. He made his way to the only open space in the place, between the barns and the racetrack. A dozen or so people were already there, clustered around a big table. As Mercer approached, he spotted Ted Rivers himself, wearing a striped apron and a chef's hat, hard at work flipping burgers. Feeling a little sheepish, Mercer helped himself to a hot dog and a pop. He'd sent Evie to stay with his sister in Jersey, to be around a normal family for a change. It was better for her than hanging around the racetrack all summer. She was sixteen now. It was no place for her to be. There were far too many bad apples. He was standing next to some of them now: the crook Dave Bodinski, who'd gotten hold of something good at last, judging from the way his horses were doing. Then there was sourpuss Tony Hall, who couldn't win a race to save his life, Gerry Lake, who wasn't a bad guy for a total loser and Scotty McCoy, who had a beer in his hand already and it wasn't even noon. He'd heard Scotty's wife had moved back in with him. She'll be sorry! Mercer thought.

"Nice win with that filly last night," he told Lara Vachon, as she joined the throng. Lara acknowledged his comment with a smile.

"Jus' some onions for me, Ted," she said, declining the burger. "I find a blind splint on 'er," she revealed. "Dr. Jay 'e come and freeze it for me."

"So that's why she was makin' breaks," Mercer replied, filing the information away for the future. Like him, Lara was a babies' trainer and though her approach was very different, he had a lot of respect for her. Her reputation had hit rock bottom the day Lazer had taken Southview Sabre away from her. But she hadn't let it get her down. She had carried on with the business of turning the homebreds that arrived in her barn each fall, soft bellied and ignorant, into tough racehorses, clocking up an impressive win percentage, better than him this season. The only guy that hadn't shown up yet was the one Mercer called the Saint: Eddie Clearwater. He and Eddie had been trading insults for as long as he could remember. Well, he wouldn't have to put up with him much longer. Eddie was moving his horses to Meridian Acres, hoping his luck would change, no doubt, a pointless exercise in Mercer's view.

"Hey, Jim!" Scotty McCoy called out. "How's your colt doin' today?" Snoopin' son of a bitch, Mercer thought.

"'Bout the same," he muttered, taking a bite of the hot dog, which was dripping with onions. "Hey, this is pretty good!" he declared with an approving nod to Ted Rivers, thinking it wouldn't hurt him to be nice to the guy. He was at a safe enough distance now and Ted was hardly gonna yell out, "How 'bout that stall rent you owe me eh, Jim?" At least he hoped not. It was damn near impossible getting money out of owners at this time of year, when their horses weren't getting any purse cheques.

"I had a two year old colt break down this week too," Gerry Lake stated morosely, running his hands nervously through his mop of red hair.

"It's the speed they're goin' these days," Tony Hall declared, tossing a chunk of bread at one of the track dogs, who had sidled up, tail wagging.

Moron! Mercer thought. They're bred to go fast. "Speed's got nothing to do with it," he grunted.

"It's the winters," Dave Bodinski declared. Mercer ignored him. What did he know? "You take a two year old out on the ice and you're askin' for trouble."

"Yeah, look at Donny Grogan," Scotty agreed. "He trucks his babies down to Florida. He done good last year." There was general agreement on this.

"He ain't got a win this season," Eddie Clearwater commented drily, finally making an appearance. "Here's every last cent I owe you, Ted," he added, handing over a cheque and helping himself to a burger. "Hey! Watch yourself!" Eddie exclaimed as Stinker rammed into him. One or two of the grooms had decided to liven things up by spraying Stinker with ketchup. It was a welcome diversion for Mercer. The last thing he wanted to talk about now was two year olds. The very idea of them made him sick.

"Hey guys! Quit it!" Ted Rivers protested, waving his spatula at the grooms. The dogs thought it was some kind of a new game. One of them threw himself playfully at Ted Rivers. This set the rest of them off in a frenzy of barking.

"It's the fuckin' drivers' faults I reckon." Tony Hall said bitterly, when things had quieted down a bit. "I sent out a nice little two year old filly last season and that son of a bitch Vettore zinged her to the front. Took her to the quarter in twenty-six seconds and damn near crucified her...she wasn't ready for that."

"Drive 'em yourself then," Eddie suggested smugly.

"Don't listen to him!" Scotty exclaimed, licking his fingers. "He don't even race two year olds."

"No, I don't!" Eddie agreed, popping the top off his cola. "Wanna know why?"

"'Cos you're an asshole!" Mercer said cheerfully. "You smug son of a bitch," he added grinning. It was really too bad that Eddie was deserting them, going upmarket, he decided regretfully.

"'Cos it's the quickest way to ruin a horse I know," Eddie pronounced. "And some folks around here have wrecked up more colts that way than I've had hot dinners," he added, casting a knowing glance in Mercer's direction. Gerry Lake was staring at Eddie, open mouthed.

"You reckon?" he frowned.

"Don't encourage him," Mercer laughed. But it was too late. The old coot was on a roll.

"One of these days, I'm gonna give the Racing Commission a piece of my mind," Eddie declared. You couldn't ruin a good horse, Mercer thought. This season he'd run out of luck, is all. It happened to everyone.

"Hey, Jim! Got something for you!" Reggie Blair, the feed man, said, handing him a piece of paper. Not another bill, that's the last thing I need, Mercer thought, pocketing it automatically. "It's an invite to Harmony Farm," Reggie proclaimed. "They're havin' an open day today. You going? They got a bunch of yearlings over there. It ain't far."

"Sure!" Mercer said. Yearlings! Fresh, sound and ready to go! What better way to bury the past? Suddenly, he felt like a kid at Christmas time. Yet he remembered too, after the holidays, his mother gathering up the old, broken toys and disposing of them. How? Where? He never asked. The memory was deeply, disturbing, though he hardly knew why. He quickly brushed it aside. "Let's go together!" he told Reggie. "Seen anything you like yet?"

"Wouldn't tell you if I had." Reggie grumbled. "I got no chance against you, Jim! Hey Lara, there's a tub of that herbal stuff in the van, if you want it. You comin' out to Harmony Farm today?"

"I 'ave too much to do 'ere," Lara replied. "But I take ze 'erbs." Reggie was wasting his time with Lara Vachon. Mercer knew for a fact she was going out with a trainer who'd moved to Ontario from Montreal. The French kept to themselves.

"Stinker!" Mercer yelled. "I'm leavin'. Call me on the cell if there's anythin' alarmin' goin' on."

"Okay, boss," Stinker said, putting his hand to his forehead in salute. As he was covered in ketchup from head to toe, this ruined the effect somewhat.

"Hey!" Mercer said. "Clean yourself up before someone thinks you're a burger and eats you." This was greeted with roars of laughter from the other grooms.

"Don't worry," one of them said, grabbing Stinker by the collar. "We're gonna put him under the hose!"

"No way!" Stinker screamed, twisting away from him. He tried to make a run for it, but with half a dozen fellows chasing him, he was bound to get caught eventually. As Mercer hit the road and the big blue sky arched above him, he felt lucky

It was a perfect day to chase dreams.

AN IMPORTANT DECISION

Dr. Jay Winterflood was driving fast down the straight empty roads that crisscrossed the countryside. Far above him, puffy white clouds were scudding across the sky. It was decision time. A week ago, out of the blue, he'd been offered the chance to pursue his dream, running his own clinic, replete with all the latest techno wizardry by connections representing the owners of the Lucky Seven Stable. Of course tools like fluoroscopes, digital X-rays and MRI scanners usually confirmed what he had already diagnosed, using the tips of his sensitive fingers. But pictures were what trainers wanted: physical proof, showing the damage in black and white. Maybe then, he thought optimistically, they'd start listening to him more and give the horse enough time to heal. For once a bone had fractured, once a ligament had torn, no amount of blistering, freezing, shockwave or hydrotherapy was going to speed up the healing process in his experience. Trainers were always looking for a quick fix to keep their owners sweet. That kind of wrong thinking got him mad. It was the latest version of a very old story: the impatience of white people, their greed and arrogance, believing they could cheat nature and roll forward time.

He reached home, parked his truck under the big maple tree and made the call he'd been obsessing about all week.

"Dr. Jay?" the voice he remembered exclaimed eagerly. "What's happening man? You got an answer for me yet?"

"Yes," he replied. "The answer is yes."

Ritchie Sanchez lay back on his bed in the cramped room he'd rented at the Cherokee Inn, relief washing over him. Having a veterinarian on the premises to deal with everyday problems, was crucial to the smooth running of the Lucky Seven's operation. Winterflood wasn't just any vet. He was the best. One more obstacle had been removed, paving the way for the arrival of the expensive blood machine Ritchie had ordered. It was the latest in technology, far more sophisticated than the machines the labs used to test samples sent in from Iroquois Downs. Staying one step ahead was crucial. Coach Bailey had managed to do that brilliantly, until the authorities had fought back with the spot checks that had put an end to Ritchie's career. It was a safe bet that nothing like that would happen anytime soon in Ontario. He'd been assured there'd be no money for it. Apparently, there was no political will, either. However, he wasn't out of the woods yet. He'd kept Cat in the dark about something important. Important to Cat, anyway. It was preying on Ritchie's mind.

The yearling sale was only a week away.

HELP WANTED

Eddie Clearwater had filed his invite to Harmony Farm in the trash can. They only had one trotter to sell. The rest were pacers. Eddie was a trotting man through and through. Switching to pacers was a move he wasn't prepared to make anytime soon. All you had to do to get a pacer to stay on gait was slap on a pair of hobbles. Shoeing was simple too: steel swedges all around. Gaiting a trotter was an art. You needed time, a lot of knowhow and more patience than God. Pacing guys were always in a hurry. That wasn't Eddie's style. He had to admit, though, that switching feed mills hadn't turned out half so bad as he'd expected. Reggie's extruded feed, which he apparently cooked up in a gigantic oven, had got his filly eating again and she'd gained fifty pounds. He'd only done it to please Cat. But Cat had quit on a whim, leaving him in the lurch. It was really too bad. Cat had been a real help, both on and off the track.

It had been near on fifty years now since Eddie had shot to fame as the youngest owner/trainer/driver to win the richest trotting stake in North America. Since then, he'd been on a long run of bad luck. He'd missed out on buying a top colt, who had gone on to win a million, because he was short five thousand of the asking price. He'd had high hopes for countless young horses, only to see them turn into mediocre performers after he'd spent months, sometimes years, training them. He'd been dragged over fields and fences, half killed by a promising two year old who'd spooked when she saw a deer on the track. He'd bred top mares to top stallions only to see them lose their foals, or not get in foal at all. He'd had a great horse ruined by a careless groom and another one wrecked up by an incompetent veterinarian. He'd had perfectly sound horses who wouldn't try and cripples who went out every week and gave their all, nearly breaking his old heart in the process. He'd seen horses drop dead for no explicable reason and he'd saved horses that appeared beyond saving. He'd driven home seven hours through the pouring rain after a talented filly had broken stride in the mud, just before the wire, blowing a victory. And through all this, he'd maintained his sanity, somehow. He'd battened down the hatches and kept his mind focused on the one thing that mattered to him, the only thing he wanted now: another top trotter. It wasn't too late. He lived in hope that it could still happen again one day. Age was no barrier to success in this game and Eddie's head was up in the clouds today. The colt he'd stolen for six thousand dollars at the sale last fall had just trained brilliantly.

As he steered his horse back to the barn, he noticed a young woman standing by the door waiting for him. Was she looking for work? he wondered, hopefully. But as he got closer, he realized this girl was much too smartly dressed to be a groom. She was probably an owner, he thought. Ignoring her for the present, he led his trotter to the wash stall and began stripping the harness off him. The girl followed him.

"I'm Caroline Aldright," she said. "I came to see you because Joey Harris told me you're the best trainer in the business."

"Did he now?" Eddie replied a little defiantly. The colt shook his ears as the water bounced off his head. If he put a light toe weight on him, he'd be perfect, Eddie decided. "Just as long as it's a trotter," he added firmly."

"Do you take care of all these yourself?" she asked, looking up and down the barn.

"Yup!" Eddie replied. He wasn't going to tell this girl that the best help he'd ever had, his niece's boy, had quit and left him up the creek, all because some character had promised him a job as a private trainer. You couldn't find anyone to work for love nor money at this time of year. All the guys from the Maritimes had gone home for their annual holidays. He led the colt back to his stall and tossed him a flake of hay.

"You've got a good reason to get up every morning," the girl stated. And you don't? Eddie wondered.

"Is that why you want a yearling?" he asked.

"It's complicated."

I'll bet it is, Eddie thought. "How'd you end up in this neck of the woods?" he asked.

"It's a long story," she replied. She wasn't going to tell him. He didn't want to know anyhow. He had to get going. It was starting to heat up out on the track and he wasn't even halfway done. "Listen, couldn't I help out here...at least in the barn?" she added.

"You're askin' for a job?" He stared at her in disbelief. Her in her smart outfit, not a hair out of place with her natty little jacket and shiny shoes...

"I've got my own horse in the UK. My boyfriend trains hunters and jumpers there. I love horses and I'm not afraid to learn. You want me to clean stalls? I'll do that too." Eddie thought about it while he topped up the water buckets with the long hose.

"What'd you say your name was?" he asked.

"Caroline. Caroline Aldright." She didn't look like she was used to hard work, but he was willing to give her a try. Not for the first time, Eddie regretted the fact that he had never married. A wife to help him in the barn and later a son or a daughter, now that would have felt pretty good.

"Well, Caroline," he said, "I feed at 5 a.m., do a few stalls, then I start driving, at around six. You could start tomorrow if you want."

"Brilliant!" the girl exclaimed, proffering her hand. He realized she was trying to shake on it. He was suddenly conscious that he was covered in dirt from the track and water from the hose was dripping off his hands in muddy rivulets.

"Hope you know what you're getting yourself into!" he said with a little grimace. "Best get yourself a pair o' overalls…" he called after her as she left.

"See you tomorrow, Eddie!" she called back. She was crazy, he decided. But a girl with that amount of enthusiasm could stand a whole lot of disappointment.

And disappointment was what the horse business was all about.

Caroline created quite a stir later that day when she went back to Uncle George's house sporting farmer jones overalls, a pair of hefty work boots and a baseball cap, adorned with gaudy red maple leaves.

"It all sounds simply thrilling!" Aunt Bee exclaimed delightedly when Caroline broke the news about her new job. "This calls for a celebration. George! Open a bottle of booze!"

"What about Kip?" Uncle George asked quietly, as he ushered Caroline into the dining room. "What's he going to think about all this?"

"Right now, I couldn't care less what Kip thinks," Caroline replied. "I'm not going to let him risk his neck a second time."

"I see," George said thoughtfully.

"What are you two plotting?" Bee asked. "I hope you've got my whiskey ready, George."

"Coming right up!" George replied, snapping to attention. What a pair they made, Caroline thought. Is that how she and Kip would act in thirty years' time? She sincerely hoped not. But as she sipped her drink, she felt more optimistic than she had in weeks. She had made something happen at last. Anything was possible now, she decided, thinking of the yearling filly she had seen at Harmony Farm. They were raising their glasses for the third time when Kip walked in. Immediately, the party was over.

When Kip put his head round the dining room door, he knew something was wrong. Instinctively, he looked around, searching for the reason, but all he saw was his own tense, serious face staring back at him in from the hall mirror.

"Kip! You missed all the fun," Caroline said. Behind her, George and Bee were quietly exiting into the kitchen like a pair of naughty children, Bee stifling a giggle. Was that really the effect he was having on people nowadays? Kip asked himself. It was obvious he needed to get back to his old self, to the joy he'd felt every morning when he had jumped out of bed every morning. But how? He'd been through another hellish day at Erinsville General, enduring a multitude of gruesome tests and clocking up miles on the treadmill. To cap it all, just when he thought it was all over, they had dropped a bombshell, the implications of which he was still mulling over in his mind.

"Better news," he said, trying to sound cheerful. "I got the thumbs up today."

"That's good," Caroline replied. But she didn't exactly look thrilled. Somewhere in this whole mess, he had let Caroline slip through his fingers. That was unforgivable, he thought. He had been so preoccupied with getting better, he had neglected the one human being he really cared about.

"Look," he said, in as conciliatory a tone as he could muster. "The last four or five months have been hell for both of us."

"You're telling me!" she exclaimed. He pulled out one of the dining room chairs and straddled it back to front, jockey style.

"Would you like to know what the medics had to say?" he asked. After a long paused, she shrugged her shoulders.

"Alright," she said in a polite but uninterested tone. This wasn't going well, he thought wearily. And why was she dressed like a farm girl? Better not to go there, he decided. He ploughed on.

"Apparently, I came this close," he said, holding up his thumb and finger a hair's breadth apart. "To being paralysed from the neck down."

"Paralysed!" she repeated, staring at him in disbelief. He hastened to reassure her.

"But they said I'm making good progress. We should be able to go back to England soon and restart our lives." She considered this for a moment.

"Restart...as in you riding out on the gallops again?" she asked. He winced at the sharp edge in her voice.

"Actually," he admitted. "I never mentioned it."

"Of course," she replied in an exasperated tone. "I mean, why would you want to mention that? No need for them to know."

"Sarcasm doesn't suit you," he parried.

"Nor does having you in a wheelchair for the rest of your life, Kip!" she hit back, her eyes blazing. He got up, walked over to the French windows and stared at the garden which was glowing in the warm evening light. He was in unfamiliar territory. He and Caroline had always overcome their troubles by laughing their way out of them. That was no longer possible, it seemed.

"I always knew I'd have to give up riding out with the horses at some point," he said quietly. "Just not now. Not like this. I thought I'd have another ten years, at least." The truth was, he'd never felt anything but sympathy tinged with contempt, for trainers who drove up to the gallops in their Land Rovers, forced to peer at their horses through binoculars. Now the shoe was on the other foot.

"Poor Kip," he heard Caroline say softly. Something touched his hand, but it wasn't her. It was only the curtain swaying in the blast of cool air coming up from the vent. He remembered a young lad at his yard who had ended up in a wheelchair. Just one unlucky fall off the back of a galloping horse. That's all it had taken to change that boy's life forever. He glanced back at Caroline. She was nervously folding and unfolding a piece of paper.

"I'm not a coward," he said. "But I'm not a gambler either. Maybe it would be better for me to stay away from the horses altogether. Perhaps I should ask my father for a job in his law firm," he added gloomily. "I'm sure he could use a person who knows nothing whatsoever about the law."

"That's a brilliant idea," Caroline mocked, crumpling up the paper and tossing it onto the table. "You'd love commuting to London everyday in a pinstripe suit and a bowler hat. Plus, you'd get to spend your weekends doing something really pointless like waging war on the dandelions! Take the blinkers off, Kip," she continued in the same exasperated tone. "Think outside the box. We don't have to live in the UK forever. We could go to South America. You were born there, after all. Or we could stay here." His heart lurched at her use of the word "we". His heart lifted too at the thought of no more rain and fog, no more metaphorically doffing his cap to trilby clad owners, no more shipping horses to race halfway across the country down narrow winding lanes.

"I'd miss England," he said truthfully. With all its warts, the country would always feel like home, even though he was about as British as a Brazil nut. "And besides, what could I do here in Canada? I'm not Canadian."

"Oh, I don't think you'll find it's that big a hurdle," Caroline assured him. The word hurdle took him back to the last time he'd ridden Rum Martin. In his mind's eye, he saw it all, the sweep of the gallops, the way the horse met each jump perfectly…then the jarring sound of the fire engine's siren… the moment when he felt himself falling and the sky came crashing down on top of him. But, he reminded himself, he was still in one piece. It could have been far, far worse. He knew that now. "Eddie Clearwater's offered me a job," he heard Caroline say.

"Who on earth is Eddie Clearwater?" he exclaimed.

"Have a guess," she challenged. So that's what these ridiculous clothes were all about, he thought, looking her over. Even dressed like this, she still was the most beautiful woman he'd ever known.

"I've got it," he deadpanned. "Some utterly unhinged farmer has hired you to drive his hay wagon." To his relief, the insult seemed to please her.

"Close!" she exclaimed with a mischievous smile. "He's a harness horse trainer. According to Joey Harris, he's a really great guy."

"And according to you?" he asked, a hint of jealousy creeping in. The way he'd been acting the last few weeks, God knows what she had been thinking.

"He's ancient!" she laughed. "But he still drives and trains his own horses. I thought we could work for him, learn the business, maybe buy a couple of youngsters to get started. Remember that trotting filly we saw at Harmony Farm?"

"Oh my God!" Kip said, suddenly catching on. "You've got it all worked out haven't you?"

"Well," she shrugged. "You think it's a crazy idea?"

"Yes," Kip replied. "But that won't stop you, will it?"

"I've missed you," Caroline said, her eyes bright. "Don't go AWOL on me again, okay?"

DREAMS FOR SALE

With less than twenty-four hours to go until sale time, the parking lot at Merryvale Raceway was awash with horse trailers and vans delivering horses. The barns had been cleared out and spruced up in readiness for their new occupants: three hundred and fifty yearlings who would be going under the hammer over the coming weekend.

In Barn 10, Val Harris set down her brushes beneath the green and white Harmony Farm banner and surveyed her flock of yearlings, her heart swelling with pride. There wasn't a scratch or a bump among them. After weeks of practice, the youngsters now stood quietly while they were being brushed and pampered. All of them led perfectly too, following her wherever she went, except Harmony Jet who dragged his feet and Princess, who cast anxious glances behind her looking for her friend, Harmony Gold. Smiling, Val checked them over one last time. Every whisker was neatly shaved, every stray hair clipped and they were wearing tiny silver shoes on their front feet. However, Harmony Fire, the trotting filly, was going barefoot. Three blacksmiths and two veterinarians had failed to coax her into being shod. The hip numbers, she noted with relief, were still stuck securely onto their gleaming flanks, which she had sprayed liberally with show sheen. Harmony Storm's grey coat was a little dull, but that was the least of her worries. The colt could cow kick hard enough to break a man's ankle. Harmony Stampede looked as pretty as a picture with his four white socks and his white blaze. She'd braided Valentine's forelock to show off the perfect white heart beneath it. But Harmony Light stole the show. His coat had grown darker, throwing into relief the startling white star on his forehead. The only plain looking one was Harmony Gold, with her big donkey ears. Well this is it, Val thought, win or lose. Praying there wouldn't be any dental emergencies over the next three days, she squared her shoulders and hoped for the best.

Dawn broke bright and clear on the morning of the sale. It was a warm day without a breath of wind: Indian Summer. While the sun was still hidden behind the tree tops, Al McTavish was on his way. He didn't feel lonely, with the sleek Mercedes hugging the road for company. True, he'd asked Billie to come along and she had declined. That hurt, just a little. Theo apparently never went to yearling sales. Instead they were heading out to Mennonite

241

country to look at a horse Theo wanted to buy. Al could have ridden up with Bob Summers in his pickup truck, but it didn't appeal to him. As for Al's wife coming along, that was unthinkable. The atmosphere of disapproval she would have created would have made any purchase impossible.

"So much money! For only one horse!" Sofia had exclaimed, when he had informed her he was going to the sale. But he hadn't wavered. His plan was to find an exceptional colt and pay up for him if necessary. "Why?" Sofia had demanded, through pursed lips. To Al, the answer was obvious. Buying Millie D had given him a taste for the racing game. But she was in for price now, up for sale every time she raced.

Everyone had dreams. He needed one too. He wanted to own a horse that could be a champion. He couldn't afford to buy one ready made, but he could try to pick one out as a baby. . . a baby with a big future in front of him, that's what he wanted. . .something beautiful and simple, a relief from the headaches he faced at home and at work. Of course he didn't say anything like that to Sofia. Instead, he told her he'd made a heck of a lot of money in his life and he had a right to spend some of it before he got too old to enjoy it. Sofia had thrown up her hands and flounced out of the room. It was better not to think about that, just concentrate on the road, he told himself. He regretted not making time to visit Harmony Farm on their open day. But he was making up for it now.

Catalino Ciardi skidded to a stop outside Merryvale Raceway's stable gate and spun around, staring at his brother with a face like thunder.

"Now! You wait 'til now to tell me, Ritchie," he exclaimed in disbelief. "See this?" he asked, thrusting a battered yearling catalogue in Ritchie's face. "D'you have any idea how many farms I've gone to, how many videos I've watched, how much fuckin' time I've wasted on this? Why Ritchie, why?" Ritchie hung his head. "You're a total asshole. You know that? There's no point in staying here...it'd be like torture," Cat added, striking out in the direction of the parking lot.

"Wait!" Ritchie shouted, hurrying after him. "We can figure this out."

"Yeah? Your guy said no yearlings. I don't see what there is to figure out, brother. You totally messed up. You're so in his debt now. You got no leverage whatsoever. Admit it, you're a moron!"

"You're right," Ritchie agreed, red-faced.

"So?" Cat challenged, his hands on his hips.

"Listen, I got a little extra cash, it's not much but we could pick up something cheap, maybe," Ritchie offered, half heartedly.

"We?" Cat exclaimed. "There is no *we*, not after this."

"Okay," Ritchie agreed, backing off. "I'm gonna need every cent for the bar anyhow. But I'll make it up to you somehow."

"How?" Cat asked sullenly.

"Just wait 'til the bar opens," Ritchie replied. "We can have a few days of hell raising together. It'd be like old times."

"What old times?" Cat said plaintively. "If I don't have a yearling to train, this whole deal's off!" he added belligerently.

"So, buy one yourself," Ritchie suggested. "There'd be zero pressure. No owner breathing down your neck."

"Oh yeah? Where am I gonna get the money from?" Cat demanded.

"You've got credit cards, right?" Ritchie said. "You'll soon be making enough to pay it off, right?"

"You just ruined my entire year!" Cat replied angrily.

Side stepping a couple of guys who appeared to be in the midst of an argument, Al McTavish strode through the stable gate, his catalogue tucked under his arm. He rounded a corner and felt like he had stepped into another world. Everywhere he looked, there were yearlings, walking nervously up and down between the shed rows, guided by grooms holding long gold chains and surrounded by eager buyers who were watching their every move. The horses' coats were shining, their feet polished, their short manes braided and ribboned. However, the look in their eyes was wild and untamed. Millions of dollars were about to be poured into dreams over the next two days. Three hundred and fifty yearlings, all of them for sale! The sheer choice was overwhelming, but Al had a plan. He wanted a colt sired by Night Raider. As there were only twenty-five of them in the sale, that narrowed his options. He weaved his way through the throngs of people peering at horseflesh, dodging horses wheeling and kicking. He found Ferme Victoire easily enough. After viewing their consignment, he decided that all ten of their Night Raider colts were nice. But none struck him as special. He wandered aimlessly, sipping a pop, looking idly at the yearlings parading up and down.

Suddenly, he caught sight of a dark bay colt, whose feet appeared to hardly touch the ground. As Al watched, transfixed, the horse tossed his regal head and took off. Al left his drink on a nearby tack trunk and hurried after him, anxious not to lose sight of this striking looking animal. Just when he feared he had lost him, the horse reared, turned on a dime and appeared to make a beeline straight for him. He came to a halt just a few feet away. Al flipped through his catalogue. Number 85 was a colt by Night Raider, a first foal from the stakes winning dam Heart of Darkness. Al remembered the name, remembered too, her defeat by two rank outsiders on his first week at the job. Her defeat had led directly to Iroquois Downs banning baking soda. Al still wasn't sure he had done the right thing. However, the jury was still out, he thought hopefully. The familiar face of the breeder appeared.

"Would you like to take a look at him, Mr. McTavish?" Joey Harris asked. Al nodded, taking in the colt's bold eye, his arched neck and his powerful shoulder muscles. It was like being in the presence of royalty! With his dancing feet, the name Harmony Light suited him well. Al decided he'd do anything, spend any amount, overcome any opposition to secure this beautiful, arrogant creature as his. He had found his colt. The only problem was how he could contain himself until three o'clock that afternoon when, he estimated, the horse would be going through the ring.

It took Ritchie nearly an hour, but eventually Cat gave in.

"Okay, I guess," he reluctantly said, at last.

"Let's go see some yearlings!" Ritchie replied happily, leading the way through the stable gate.

"We can start at Barn 10," Cat said. "I want you to see number 85, so you can tell your guys what they missed out on. The colt's a stand out…Hey, she's cute," he added, catching sight of a girl in tight jeans, who was busy texting on her cell phone.

"Wait up, Dad!" the girl called out. A man with ruddy cheeks and a neck and shoulders like a prize bull pulled up short.

"C'mon, Evie!" he said in an irritated tone before immediately marching off again. The girl caught Cat's eye, then blushed furiously.

"Hey," Cat said. "Don't hurry on my account, Evie." The girl threw him a grateful glance before running off.

"That's Jim Mercer," Ritchie pointed out.

"So?" Cat asked.

"I heard he's got a really bad temper and his daughter's still in school, by the looks of things."

"So?" Cat repeated.

"Watch yourself," Ritchie warned.

Harmony Light was a stunner. Ritchie didn't know much about horses, but he recognized athleticism when he saw it. They looked at several more in Barn 10. A Night Raider filly caught Cat's eye, called Harmony Gold.

"She might go cheap," was all Cat said, but he looked a little happier. Ritchie suggested they trawl the barns and make a short list. "You better hope I find something I can afford," Cat warned. "Or I'm out of here."

Jim Mercer had seen it all. He'd been to scores of yearling sales. This one was no different. There was the usual clutch of small time guys from the furthest reaches of the province, who'd driven all night to get to the sale to save on the cost of a hotel room. There were top trainers from Iroquois Downs, buying for wealthy owners on ego trips. There were country people with a few acres hoping to pick up a horse to while away the time; and dreamers who wanted a chance at a champion at any price, forgetting that horses were made out of flesh and blood, not dollars and cents.

Every one of them, including him, was being courted by the breeders. The ones at the top of the tree like Ferme Victoire, had yearlings to suit all pockets and tastes. They were wooing customers with sandwiches piled high and coolers chock full of cold drinks, enticing potential buyers to stay and watch the show: colts and fillies parading back and forth, or trotting flawlessly in cleverly edited videos. Most breeders were fairly honest. But there were crooked breeders too, who covered up flaws with trick shoeing and cortisone injections. Mercer had learned to stay well clear of them. At the other end of the continuum were the small breeders with sad faces, hoping their horses would go to a good home, whatever that meant. Mercer was a realist. If you can't stand the heat, get out of the kitchen, he thought as he marched past them on his way to inspect his picks. Evie never got tired of looking at horses, but he wouldn't linger long. He just wanted to be sure none of them had been injured on the trip to the sale. He had done his homework already, touring the farms. He'd rustled up a new crew of owners, too.

The beer hall beckoned.

When Bob Summers arrived, he tried to talk Al into changing his mind about Harmony Light.

"You'll never get him," Bob warned. "Not at this sale. Not for your price.

Not that colt!" Al refused to be put off. Bob stationed himself beside the parade area, where horses were shown off, before entering the sales ring. Al stuck to Bob like glue, in case his trainer tried to sneak in a bid on something behind his back.

Finally, the moment arrived. Harmony Light entered the ring and the auction began. The price swiftly jumped to $20,000. Bob's bidding style was to discreetly tip his cap. As the price leapt to $40,000, Bob still hadn't bid. At $45,000 he tipped his cap.

"What am I bid?" the auctioneer shouted, waving his gavel. "Forty-five now fifty *liddle liddle liddle* who'll give me fifty?" After the flurry of bids, there was a long silence. Praying that the bidding had stalled, Al held his breath. But the auctioneer wasn't done yet. "Forty-five, I need fifty. First foal from the outstanding mare Heart of Darkness." Immediately, to Al's dismay, the bidding took off again. "Fifty, fifty-five, sixty, seventy. Seventy thousand." Bob looked at Al questioningly. Al shook his head, despair in his heart. That picture of perfection would never be his now. The bidding eventually stopped at $90,000. "SOLD!" the auctioneer cried, banging down his gavel and pointing at Jim Mercer, who was grinning like a Cheshire cat.

Blindly, Al pushed his way through the crowd, following the colt back to the barn. What he hoped to accomplish, he had no idea, but he couldn't help himself. He discovered the breeders, Val and Joey Harris, jumping with joy.

"Ninety thousand!" Val kept saying. "I can't believe it!"

"You got him?" Joey asked Al.

"Not me, Mercer," Al told him. The words stuck like a knife in his throat. The colt, now back in his stall, lay down to rest.

"It's been a long day for him," Joey said. "So many people wanted to see him."

"How've you done so far?" Al asked, wanting to spend a few more precious minutes beside the colt. The price was prohibitive. He couldn't possibly justify that kind of expense to Sofia.

"Not so bad, thanks to Mercer," Joey said. "He's already bought another one of ours." He pointed to a grey colt. "He didn't go for much, though. This ninety thousand has made our year."

"Yes," Al said heavily.

"Ready?" Joey asked Val, who was putting the finishing touches on a raw boned chestnut. "Our only trotter. A filly," he told Al. "Doesn't like loud noises," he added as he led her away.

"So what d'you have left?" Al asked, unable to tear himself away from this small haven of calm. He couldn't face returning to the mayhem of the sales ring and Bob Summers *I told you so*'s just yet. "Any colts?" Al added.

"Two. One by Night Raider, one by Mr President," Val replied. The little Night Raider colt, Harmony Jet, could barely get his head over the stall door. But Harmony Stampede was a different animal altogether. On paper, Al wouldn't have given him a second glance, but something about this colt pleased him. He was sturdy. His eyes were intelligent. Al felt a flicker of hope.

"You like 'im, eh?" he heard someone say. Sporting blue overalls, was the living legend Eddie Clearwater. Al had read about the old timer's former glories in *Horseman's World*. "He's a nice enough colt," Eddie continued. "For a pacer."

"Think I ought to go for him?" Al asked.

"I'm a trottin' man myself," Eddie replied.

"What's wrong with pacers?" Al frowned. Eddie didn't answer him directly.

"The chemists ain't found a way to make trotters go faster…yet," he said darkly. "But you being the Director of Racing…you'd know all about that I guess." The expression of disapproval on Eddie's face made Al feel distinctly uncomfortable.

"I'm doing everything I can," he declared.

Eddie snorted contemptuously and turned away. "You don't wanna know my opinion of the detention barn," he said dismissively.

"Yes, I do," Al assured him. But before Eddie had a chance to respond, a girl, wearing an identical pair of sky blue overalls, came racing up.

"We got her! We got her!" she screamed, sweeping Eddie up in a jubilant dance. Eddie, Al was amused to see, coloured up and quickly disentangled himself, plainly discomforted by this display of emotion. The girl collected herself. "Sorry about all this!" she said, noticing Al for the first time. "I'm just so thrilled. I'm Caroline Aldright," she said, taking Al's hand and shaking it effusively.

"Al McTavish," he replied kindly. "And don't be sorry. I'm glad you got lucky. I need some luck myself."

"Don't we all," Eddie agreed fervently. A young man appeared waving a sheaf of papers.

"It's official," he said. "Harmony Fire is ours. All expenses to be met by yours truly from here on in." He caught Eddie's eye, who grimaced.

"Don't be a spoilsport," Caroline said. "Kip I want you to meet Al. Al um…"

"McTavish," Al confirmed. The British clung to politeness like a security blanket, he'd observed. These two were no exception.

"Why did she go so cheap?" Kip queried. "We only had to give sixteen thousand Canadian dollars for her. That's nothing in English money."

"Her dam's never had one make the races," Eddie replied succinctly. Kip plainly wasn't convinced.

"The dam's full sister was a world champion," he pointed out. "She's a nice big filly too."

"You don't buy 'em by the pound, sonny boy," Eddie exclaimed, thrusting his hands deep in his pockets. "Besides, she'll never make a two year old. She's too big!"

"We overpaid, then," Kip concluded in a tone of mock despair. "What's the story on this one?" he continued, pointing at Harmony Stampede, who after a long primping session, had emerged from his stall.

"Too rich for your blood," Eddie replied curtly, pulling out a pipe. "An' he's a pacer."

"Shame," Kip said softly, looking at the colt over with eyes that appeared to miss nothing.

"You like him?" Al asked curiously.

"Like him?" Kip grinned. "I like every horse I've ever set eyes on. Can't get away from them, no matter hard I try." He glanced at Al, a knowing expression on his face. "You've got the bug," he said. "You might as well admit it." Al smiled despite himself.

"What else am I going to do with my money?" Al asked, throwing caution to the winds. A small annoying voice in his head suggested *take your wife on a cruise this winter*. He ignored it.

"This guy's got more money than God!" Eddie remarked, jerking a thumb at Al and puffing away at his pipe.

Al shook his head. "Only Mercer's got that kind of money," he concluded regretfully.

"Best of luck!" Caroline said, giving Al's arm a little pat. "Hope you get him. He's gorgeous!"

"Love's young dream," Eddie Clearwater commented, watching Caroline and Kip heading over to Harmony Fire's stall. "I remember my first horse, a plug called Buffalo Bill. I gotta go! Got a trotter I want to bid on." He hurried off. Al watched him. He was pretty fit for a guy his age. Al hoped he'd be in as good a shape when he was in his seventies. He came to a decision. He was going to bid on Harmony Stampede and he intended to take him home, no matter what it cost him. No more dithering. That was over. He and Sofia seemed to be over, these days as well, he reflected sadly. He stifled the ache in his heart. If he could just get this colt, he thought, he'd have something to hope for. There was no law against the Director of Racing owning a horse so far as he was aware.

HUMILIATION

Harmony Light's breeders were not the only people gratified by the high price the horse had brought. The tag of ninety thousand dollars had afforded Bernie Vachon some welcome relief. Two years and eight months had passed since his stallion, Night Raider, had gone on the rampage and impregnated five maiden mares in a single night. At each yearling sale since then, Bernie Vachon had had to endure countless jokes at his expense, not to mention the sly looks and the occasional insult. This year was no different. He was sitting on the top row of the Sales Pavilion with his daughter Lara, trying to stay out of sight, while keeping a close watch on proceedings. Whenever a yearling sired by Night Raider came into the ring, Bernie's stomach went into convulsions. He had used up his entire supply of antacids, yet there were still many more Night Raider yearlings to be sold.

If prices were good, breeders would return to Ferme Victoire, attracted by Night Raiders' popularity and hoping for a good return on their investment. However, the farm's reputation had been sullied by the good for nothing groom, Crawfish Brown. Despite the passage of time, the wound was still fresh in Bernie's mind. When the Night Raider filly, Harmony Princess, entered the ring, Bernie tried vainly to calm his fraught nerves. She was well bred. Her dam had been a New Zealand Champion. But he quickly realized the filly was far too small to bring a top price. In the end, she went for a mere $14,000.

"Who bought her?" he asked Lara. "Anybody you know?"

"That is Craig Brown, I think," Lara replied. "And next to him, his son, Crawfish," she added, as the man sitting next to the successful bidder lurched to his feet.

"Crawfish Brown?" Bernie queried, feeling light headed, a sure indication that his blood pressure was soaring again. Lara nodded. "Crawfish!" Bernie roared, in his distinctive carrying voice. Immediately, without even looking back, his nemesis began scrambling over the empty seats in front of him in his haste to get away. Guilty conscience, Bernie surmised grimly, leaping down the steps which he took two at a time, trying to ignore the heartburn gripping his chest like a vise. By the time Bernie had reached ground level, it was almost too late. The fiend was getting away. "You will pay for this!" Bernie cried, paying no attention to the exclamations of astonishment from the crowd. The man, Crawfish Brown, was scuttling along like a crab, covering the ground rapidly, in spite of his awkward, lopsided gait. Huffing and puffing, Bernie chased after him, thinking dark thoughts. I shall kill him with my own bare hands, he swore to himself.

Outside the Sales Pavilion, he saw his enemy hesitate. A long line of horses was waiting in the sunshine, ready for their turn to enter the parade area. Bernie stumbled to a stop, unable to take another step. For the first time since the chase began, the traitor, Crawfish Brown, turned around. When he caught sight of Bernie, panting and clutching his stomach, he fled. There was nothing Bernie could do. Nothing! But fate took a hand. A pair of security men in blue uniforms appeared. Impulsively, Bernie said the first thing that came into his head.

"Stop, thief!" he gasped, pointing at Crawfish. He was trapped, Bernie thought exultantly. But to his dismay, Crawfish quickly double backed and dived into the parade area, startling the yearlings who pulled on their lead shanks, wild eyed. "Go!" Bernie told the security men, gesturing wildly at the runaway. But instead of pursuing the miscreant, they began asking Bernie questions which were impossible for him to answer. How could he explain to them that Crawfish had stolen his reputation, his good name, even his peace of mind? They were not Quebecois. They were from Ontario. They would never understand. He was forced to invent a story, that he had imagined his wallet had been stolen but that he had been mistaken. The look on their faces, the humiliation he suffered at their hands was almost too much for him to bear.

Helplessly, he watched as Crawfish made his way to the tall double doors that led to the sales ring. A large solidly built filly was waiting to go through, lazily flicking her long ears. As Crawfish gyrated towards her, she swung her ample hind quarters around, pinning the wretched man leading her up against the wall. Bernie watched hopefully. Perhaps this filly would do the job for him. Perhaps she would break Crawfish's legs and send him to the hospital, a place that was far too good for him in Bernie's opinion. Regrettably, it did not happen. Crawfish squeezed past, sidling along the opposite wall, like some giant crustacean and Bernie lost sight of him. With a deep sigh, he made his way back to the sales ring.

Cat's heart was pounding. Hip number 125, Harmony Gold, had still not entered the ring.

"What's going on?" he frowned. He had bid on seven yearlings so far, with no result, eight if he counted Harmony Light, not that he'd been able to even raise a finger. He prayed Mercer wasn't interested in Harmony Gold. Mercer had been outbidding everyone all day. Behind closed doors, the shouting was getting louder. Bizarrely, the auctioneer had launched into his usual sales pitch. No one was listening.

"Where's the horse?" someone called out, amid scattered laughter.

"Maybe she's been withdrawn from the sale," Ritchie suggested.

"No! Wait!" Cat replied, peering at the big doors, wishing he had X-ray vision. "Something's coming." He was right, but instead of a horse, a man shot through the doors, like a cork out of a bottle. He was limping and his body was twisted to one side. "What's wrong with *him*?" Cat added.

"No idea," Ritchie shrugged. "But he looks scared."

"That's Crawfish Brown!" a man sitting behind them exclaimed, snapping his catalogue shut. Just then, Harmony Gold strolled out into the ring, looking like butter wouldn't melt in her mouth, a stark contrast to Crawfish, who was casting nervous glances behind him.

"We'll proceed with hip 125," the auctioneer pronounced firmly, eyeing the rows of horse people as if daring them to defy him. Crawfish began darting this way and that, plainly looking for an exit, defeated by the six foot drop beneath him. "What am I bid?" the auctioneer asked, foolishly attempting to carry on as normal. No one responded. Eventually, Jim Mercer held up two fingers. One of the scouts took the bid and passed it along. Two thousand dollars duly appeared on the screen.

"Hey!" Mercer yelled. "I said two dollars. . .Crawfish Brown ain't worth two grand!" One by one, the zeros came off, until only the number 2 was left on the screen. A ripple of laughter swept through the crowd. Crawfish began twirling around like a spinning top. He was finally rescued by two security guards, who vaulted onto the podium, picked him up and carried him off between them, despite Crawfish's loud, outraged protests.

"What was that all about?" Ritchie asked the man sitting behind them.

"Crawfish must've put someone's back up pretty good," the man replied. "He's made himself plenty of enemies." Cat was only half listening. The bidding for Harmony Gold had begun in earnest. The buzz of conversation had halted. Cat buried his head in his catalogue, acting like buying this filly was the last thing on his mind. After a shaky start, the auctioneer switched tactics, ratcheting up the price one thousand at a time. At $10,000, the bidding stalled. The crowd was growing restless.

"Ten now eleven," the auctioneer said. "Nice filly," he added, but Cat could tell his heart wasn't in it. It was time to make a move. He caught a spotter's eye. "Ten now eleven," the auctioneer repeated, picking up his gavel. Cat inclined his head. "Eleven now twelve," the auctioneer said. Everything went quiet. Cat's spotter was holding his hand, palm out. "Eleven, I have," the auctioneer warned. "SOLD!" he said, pointing his gavel at Cat, before bringing it down with a bang.

"You're getting a package, Monday," Ritchie hissed in Cat's ear.

"Oh yeah?" Cat murmured distractedly as he signed for his filly. Ritchie waited until the admin girl was out of the way before continuing.

"It'll be in cash on delivery," he warned.

"Cash? How much?" Cat exclaimed.

"A grand. But no worries," Ritchie smirked, patting his pocket. "The money's right here." Cat stared at him, taking it in. "Get ready for stardom, kid." Ritchie said. The smirk was still on his face. Cat grinned. He'd done it! He'd got his yearling and, lucky enough, he wasn't totally cleaned out. He still had a few thousand dollars left on his credit card.

Harmony Valentine's turn had come. The tall black filly with the heart shaped mark on her brow had followed Joey without hesitation. She was used to their little promenades by now. They were a welcome relief from the confines of her stall. But as Joey led her further and further away from the herd, she planted her feet, calling out to her stable mates. The other fillies responded, sounding as anxious as she felt. Joey tugged on her halter, urging her on. She responded by digging her toes in. Joey was making soothing sounds now, stroking her neck. She felt calmer, but she still wasn't leaving this spot. Then he reached into his pocket and put something in her mouth. When she crunched it, she felt astonished. It was so sweet! Sweeter than carrots or new grass or anything she had ever tasted. Without thinking, she followed Joey, arriving eventually at an enormous barn. Somewhere in there, a man was shouting his head off! Horses were hanging around outside. One of them, a handsome colt, showed an interest in her. But she strode right on by. He was such a baby!

When she went inside, she discovered she was in the strangest paddock she had ever seen. To her dismay, there was no grass. People were lining the fence, staring straight at her, openly hostile. She pinned her ears back and rolled her eyes. If they wanted a fight, she'd give them one! But she felt torn;

part of her was desperate to run back to the safety of her stall. Distracted, she marched through the paddock, then through a set of open doors. She had never seen so many people all in one place! The sounds they made were like the wind in the trees before a storm. Soon it would rain, she thought, looking up at the sky. But there was no sky. There was only a barn roof, as high as the clouds. Where had Joey gone? The shouting started again, up close. The noise filtered up through the soles of her feet, filling her whole body until she could hardly bear it. She wheeled around, but there was nowhere to go, no escape. Suddenly, there was a loud bang, right next to her head. Mercifully, everything went quiet after that. Her friend Joey appeared and everything was alright again. Humans were crazy. She didn't understand them but Joey spoke her language. She trusted him. Besides, she knew now what he kept in his pocket. She wanted more. She broke into a trot as they headed back to the herd. As long as she stayed with Joey she would be safe.

"Who got her?" Val asked urgently, as soon as they returned.

"Looked like Larson," Joey replied unhappily.

"And?" Val queried.

"He's a fucking cowboy," Joey said. "Keeps cattle on his farm. Doesn't know a thing about yearlings." Val's face fell. "He may send her off to someone else to break and train. A lot of claiming guys do," Joey said, without really believing it.

"We'll just have to hope for the best," Val said. Oblivious of her fate, Harmony Valentine was in the midst of an ecstatic reunion with the other fillies. During her short absence, fresh hay had appeared. Life was good again.

Al McTavish managed to track down Bob Summers eventually. He was drowning his sorrows in the cafeteria. When Al told him his plan, Bob jumped up, leaving behind a half eaten hot dog and an untouched chocolate doughnut.

"Finish your food," Al begged him.

"Be back in two ticks," Bob said, striding off and disappearing into the men's room. He reappeared instantly, like a ball bouncing off a wall. "Call security! There's a war going on in there," he told the woman serving at the counter. "What number's your horse?" he asked Al.

"140," Al replied.

"Well, what are we waiting for? Let's go see 'im!" Bob exclaimed. He was halfway to the viewing area before Al caught up with him. "He's from a decent enough family," Bob said approvingly, nodding at Harmony Stampede who was being led around in a wide circle. Obligingly, the colt stopped right beside them. "Lines up okay, too," Bob added. At these words, the colt took a great leap skywards. All four of his feet left the ground and for a split second he was airborne, before executing a perfect landing.

"Vertical take-off!" Al exclaimed.

"He's athletic alright," Bob agreed, looking pleased.

"Let's go buy a horse," Al said, turning on his heel and marching purposefully towards the sales arena. Gesturing to Bob to follow, Al climbed the stairs and chose a seat on the top row. "I want to keep my eye on the competition," he explained, feeling like a gunslinger at high noon.

"Seen Mercer's new owner?" Bob asked glumly. Sitting next to Mercer was a big man with a huge stomach and a petulant expression on his face like an overgrown toddler about to throw a tantrum. "That's the Porn Guy," Bob whispered in Al's ear. "Owns all the strip joints around here." Al prayed Harmony Stampede wasn't on Mercer's got to have at any price list. He wouldn't know that until the bidding was over.

"What was going on in the men's room?" he asked. Bob grinned.

"Bernie Vachon had his hands around Crawfish's neck!" he said.

"What?" Al gulped, feeling horrified. That kind of publicity was all Iroquois Downs needed.

"Don't worry. . .probably just empty threats." Bob reassured him. "I…" He fell silent, gesturing at the podium far below them. Harmony Stampede had entered the ring. He was standing, centre stage, staring out at the crowd, his steady gaze unmet by most of the people present. The auctioneer called for bids.

"Who'll give me twenty thousand? Ten thousand? Five thousand? Three thousand?" With his bright bay coat and four white socks, the colt was too showy for the mennonites, who often started off the bidding. Sensing an opportunity, bargain hunters crept out of the woodwork, appearing out of dark corners. Someone a few rows down started things off. "Three thousand, now five." the auctioneer shouted. A man with flaming red hair jumped in. As the price climbed to twenty thousand, Al steeled himself. He intended to wait this out. "Twenty now twenty-five! Handsome colt!" The pace was picking up. There was a great deal of hidden interest here, Al realized grimly. "Twenty-five now thirty. He's a steal at this price…thirty!" the auctioneer added, with an air of triumph.

"That was Reggie Blair!" Bob Summers hissed in his ear. "I never saw him go this high for anythin' before!"

"Go!" Al whispered back. Bob tipped his cap.

"Thirty-five now forty!" the auctioneer cried excitedly, waving his gavel. "Here we go!" After a minute or two, it was clear the bidding wasn't going anywhere and Al dared to hope the colt was his. Then the auctioneer's assistant, who had been sitting as still and silent as a store front dummy, startled Al by springing to life.

"Just look at the progeny of the second dam," the manikin said, adjusting his bow tie. "She's never missed!"

A little while ago they could hardly get a bid on him, Al thought furiously. Now thirty-five thousand's not enough? Why doesn't he keep his stupid mouth shut! Why pick on the only horse I want to buy? He didn't do that for the others! If I was a different kind of guy, he decided, clenching his fists, I'd walk up there and punch him in the mouth. That'd stop him!

Reggie Blair offered 37,000.

"Thirty-seven now forty!" the auctioneer cried. Al realized Bob was looking at him, wanting to know if he should counter the bid. They hadn't talked about how high they'd go. Tired of proxies, Al jumped to his feet, waving his arms. A hint of a smile played on the auctioneer's face as he confirmed Al's bid. "Forty, I have forty thousand," he confirmed. "Any advance on forty? C'mon help me get to forty-five here."

To hell with that! Al thought angrily. Reggie Blair came in at forty-two. Al immediately threw his arms up again.

"Thank you, sir, forty-five thousand. Let's get to fifty now folks." Al's heart was pumping hard, so hard it almost hurt. Staring at the screen, he willed it to stay at $45,000. "Any advance on forty-five? Bidding's still open, I need forty-six...any more bids?" Al gestured once more. "You're in at forty-five, sir!" the auctioneer said firmly. Al put his arms down, but only half way. Then he jumped as the gavel came down with a thump. "Sold for forty-five thousand!" the auctioneer cried. "At the back," he added, pointing at Al. "Next is hip number 141." Al metaphorically holstered his gun. He grinned at Bob, who threw his cap in the air.

"We got ourselves one hell of a colt!" Bob exclaimed happily. His cap had fallen on a man's head three rows down. "He'll be a two year old!" he predicted confidently. They made their way down the steps, retrieving Bob's cap and passing Reggie Blair, who looked crushed.

"Must be nice to have that kind of money," Reggie muttered.

"Plenty more fish in the sea, eh?" Bob replied kindly. Al felt little sympathy. The guy had cost him ten thousand dollars. Back at the Harmony Farm stand, he was surrounded by well wishers. The buzz of excitement was in stark contrast to the bleak look on Reggie's face.

"I'd like to watch the video again," Al told Val, who pressed a sandwich into his hand.

Reggie Blair studied Harmony Stampede's pedigree one last time before closing the book on him. A whole summer of hopes and dreams had vanished in a puff of smoke. Bob's well meant comment hadn't comforted him one bit. When he caught sight of Al McTavish tucking into a sandwich in the video room, Reggie had a good idea. The man had ruined his day, possibly his year. Why not return the favour? He took a seat beside him. Harmony Stampede was pacing flawlessly, flying past the prompter.

"Know why I didn't go any higher on that colt?" Reggie said, gesturing at the T.V. McTavish's eyes left the screen reluctantly.

"Well?" he queried.

"Dam's American bred," Reggie pronounced.

"What about it?" McTavish asked nervously.

"EPM," Reggie clarified. "It's rife down there. Most of 'em have it." McTavish frowned. "She coulda passed it on to the foal," Reggie added, making it up as he went along. "You'd better pray he's okay, 'cos otherwise," he gestured, both thumbs pointing at the floor, "he'll be good for nothin' I reckon."

"Really?" McTavish asked, looking worried to death. Reggie didn't reply. He got up off his chair and walked off, leaving McTavish gasping like a stranded fish. Revenge was sweet! But Reggie had no time to savour it. He ran slap bang into the middle of an argument. Joey Harris was in battle stance, glaring at Val, who was holding a small black colt by the halter.

"You did what?" Joey asked incredulously.

"I told you! I bid him in. I didn't want him going to the Amish," Val replied, standing her ground.

"What's wrong with that?" Joey exclaimed. "Some of them take very good care of their horses."

"He was going too cheap!" Val replied stubbornly.

"But we agreed…we'd never bid a horse in. Why'd you do it, Val? You wanna ruin our reputation?"

The run-in with McTavish had put Reggie in a good mood. "I might be in the market for a cheap colt," he offered. A few minutes later, Harmony Jet was his. The price was only six grand, not bad for a Night Raider colt. He was a bit on the small side, but he'd grow. Reggie reckoned he'd stolen him.

"Don't worry," he told Val. "I know the girl at the office, she'll fix it so it looks okay on the sheet."

"You're a real friend, Reggie," Joey said, looking relieved.

"Anythin' for a customer," Reggie smirked. He decided he'd give this colt to Tony Hall to train. The guy owed him three grand in feed bills. It'd be a way to get his money back. All in all, things had worked out pretty good.

When Al finally emerged from the video room, he found Jim Mercer rounding up his haul of yearlings, which included two from Harmony Farm.

"Hi folks," he boomed, to no one in particular. "The shipper'll be along in two shakes. I got ten to load, so let's get things rolling!" He was shouting out orders as if he owned the place and the people in it. "I'll take the grey colt. Jean Claude'll take the Night Raider. Make sure he gets the right one!" Mercer joked, playfully jabbing a fist in Val's direction. "Bye folks, see you in the winner's circle!" he called out as he left with Harmony Storm. He looked like a butcher, Al decided, insensitive and crass. Yet he had ended up with Harmony Light who was exquisite, like a piece of delicate china. There was no justice in this world!

"*Ma chere* Valerie!" he heard a voice sing out.

"Jean Claude!" Val cried greeting the shipper warmly.

"What eez zis I 'ear?" Jean Claude said. "You 'ave, er, 'ow do you say, ze sale topper?" Val's face lit up.

"Yes! Harmony Light. He went for ninety thousand dollars. Unbelievable!"

"*Incroyable*," Jean Claude agreed. "Eh *bien*…it goes well for you, yes? Joey, 'e 'ees 'appy *mais* Valerie…she is sad…she loses her children, *n'est pas?*" Val nodded, her eyes bright with unshed tears. You didn't often hear a man talking like that, Al realized. The French had a way with words…and women. He envied the guy. He was pretty sure even Sofia would succumb to his brand of French charm. "*Mais, il est magnifique!*" Jean Claude exclaimed as Val led Harmony Light out of his stall. "Do you not zink so *monsieur?*" Al nodded. There was so much he could have said. The anguish, the longing he felt for this beautiful animal. The British guy had put it perfectly. This business was like a drug: once you had a taste for it, you could never give it up. "*Magnifique*," Jean Claude repeated as he walked away, the colt dancing beside him.

After he'd left, Reggie's warning about EPM resounded in Al's head. Self doubt gnawed at his insides and a sense of anticlimax suddenly overwhelmed him. In picking out Stampede, he'd acted on pure instinct, trusting his gut as he always did in any new situation. It had worked out pretty well for him in the past, in his business deals. Did it apply to yearlings? How could he possibly know? Only time would tell.

Craig Brown was driving his purchase home, high as a kite.

"That filly's the best thing on four legs I ever did see," he said.

That's the third time he's said that, Crawfish thought, twisting around in his seat, worried about his most precious possession: his wheels. The bike was bouncing up and down in the truck bed but it'd stood far worse. He was glad to be getting away from the sale. He'd had a thorough drubbing there. Bernie Vachon was a crazy man, he decided, feeling his neck which was still sore as all hell. That lunatic had damn near killed him. He'd never been so pleased to see the police in his whole life. For once, they were on his side. His pa was still going on about the filly.

"They didn't like her 'cos she was small. Didn't stop her mother winning a ton o' races down under!" he said. It was all Vettore's fault, Crawfish reckoned. The bastard had stitched him up. Blamed him for that stud's shenanigans and got off scot-free himself! Crawfish knew things about Vettore that'd put the son of a bitch away for years. He'd get his comeuppance one day, he promised himself, gritting his teeth. But he didn't want to rock the boat just now, not while his own little bit o' business was goin' so good. Dimly, in the background, he heard his pa talking about how he was gonna give the filly time to grow, turn her out for a month or two and let 'er get 'er head down.

Crawfish had his own plans to think about. Tomorrow bein' Sunday and the sale bein' on and all, he reckoned the backstretch'd be nice and quiet. He'd get a chance to lift a bunch of injectables, easy like, taking his time, for resale. He knew the places trainers stashed their crap. They figured they was pretty clever, hidin' it all from security. But they couldn't fool him. What he took didn't hurt no one. Not like that creep Jake, who sold coke to folks. The stuff Crawfish took was for horses, not people. Long as he didn't overdo it, no one complained. Who were they gonna complain to anyhow? They shouldn't have had it on the backstretch in the first place. Too bad his boss was off limits. But Andy Price had been onto him like a flash. He had fourteen hundred in cash now, not enough for his ma's new kitchen yet, even though he'd been saving up for a year. But he and his ma would get there one day. Then she'd be happy, maybe. First thing he did when he got back to his room was check out the hole in the wall where he kept his precious dough. It was still there. He was glad to be back. It would be a long time 'til he dared stick his nose out of the racetrack again.

It was a fuckin' madhouse out there!

A NASTY SURPRISE

The phrase *irrational exuberance* fitted her boyfriend perfectly, Billie McTavish decided, glancing across at Theo. Behind them, the sun was low in the sky, but they were only halfway through the long drive back from mennonite country. There'd been no time for sightseeing. Instead, Theo had spent the entire day trying to track down the owner of a horse he was desperate to buy (an eight year old named Midnight Madness). Lunch had consisted of a sandwich, snatched from a gas station on the edge of town. Billie profoundly wished she had gone to the yearling sale with her father. It would have been a lot more fun. When they eventually found the horse, she took an instant dislike to him. He had ruined her day and he had evil eyes.

"Why him?" she asked. "He may be fast but you heard what the guy told you! He's a total maniac. He'll get you killed!"

"I need him. Besides, he didn't cost a lot," Theo maintained stubbornly.

"And what? You couldn't afford anything better?" she exclaimed, her temper rising.

"I know the horse," Theo snapped. "Leave it Billie, okay! What makes you think you have to get involved in every fuckin' detail of my life!" He was shouting now, jamming his foot down on the gas pedal. Stunned into silence, Billie watched helplessly as the speedometer climbed to a hundred and forty, the countryside flashing past, a green blur. Theo was gripping the steering wheel so hard, his knuckles were white, his face set. This wasn't the guy she'd fallen in love with on the island. Lately, he'd been staying over at his own apartment a lot. She hoped he'd do that tonight. After a while, he took his foot off the gas. "Look," he explained in a calmer tone. "I gotta lot of things on my mind right now, understand?"

"Okay," Billie replied shakily. She didn't understand, but she knew it was the only apology she was likely to get. She felt too intimidated to say anything more. Peace descended. But it felt more like a temporary truce, a ceasefire agreed by warring parties. It wouldn't be long, she guessed, before hostilities resumed.

André Fontainbleu was perusing the Sales Results on the CPTA site, a compelling pleasure. The internet was a perfect tool for a voyeur like him. *Mon Dieu*! Where did these rich men keep their brains? Did they not see? Purchasing one of these yearlings was like leaping blindfolded off a clifftop and falling into the abyss below. Diving *en masse* like this, would certainly produce the occasional survivor, a freak of nature, a miracle. This did not mean it was a sensible idea.

Even his own trainer, Catalino Ciardi, had succumbed to temptation. For someone in his financial position, his behaviour made absolutely no sense, *rien du tout*! Ritchie Sanchez, despite his speed on the athletics track, was a steady plodder. This brother of his was a gambler, selecting a filly with no real breeding. André could, he supposed, have wished him *bonne chance*. He did not! There was a very good reason for highly bred horses fetching high prices. Genetics mattered. It was a virtual certainty that Ciardi would lose his gamble. No matter.

Soon proven racehorses would be filling the Lucky Seven Stable's barn, their previous owners content to exchange their animals for crisp hundred dollar bills. André Fontainbleu was currently awash with cash from his bingo halls, his lucrative drugs trade and his online gambling operation. How willingly people ran to fill his pockets! In a few short weeks, Catalino Ciardi would be fully occupied winning races. He would have no time to think about a lost cause like Harmony Gold.

Perusing the results of the sale, though pleasurable, had been merely the *hors d'oeuvre*. It was time for the main course. He took out a tiny memory stick and inserted it into his computer. His face twisted with pleasure as he observed the antics of the lovers. Having these pictures reassured him *vis a vis* Henri. His loyalty was now guaranteed. As for Henri's boyfriend, Pete, Fontainbleu had some small plans for him, plans which would change his life.

But not for the better.

AN EDUCATION

It was three in the afternoon. Normally, Tony Hall would have been done for the day hours ago. Instead, he was out on the track, the sun beating down on his head, staring down in disbelief at Harmony Jet. The yearling was splayed out on the ground. But he hadn't tripped and fallen. He had thrown himself, just like Gerry's toddler did when he was having a tantrum.

Tony had tried everything to get him back on his feet. First, he had yelled at him. Then he had whipped the living daylights out of him. Finally, he had resorted to dangling hay in his face. Nothing had worked. In the end, Tony had had to admit defeat. The minute the harness was off him, Harmony Jet leapt to his feet and allowed himself to be led back to the barn. Grimly, Tony put the harness back on him, hooked up the bridle to the long lines and tried again.

"You're not going to beat me!" he told the horse. "You have to learn!" he added, tucking the long whip under his arm and heading back onto the racetrack.

Eddie Clearwater waited until the help had left for the day before setting about breaking Cat's yearling, Harmony Gold. She had spent the last two weeks running out with the trotting filly Harmony Fire. It was time!

He spent fifteen minutes looking in all the tack trunks, before he remembered that he had stowed the rope in an empty harness bag. The rope was Eddie's secret weapon. With it, breaking a yearling was a picnic in the park. He had learned the trick from an Aussie, forty years earlier. The guy was a trickster, a thief and a liar, but what Mick didn't know about horses wasn't worth the trouble of learning. Eddie took one end of the rope and tied it securely to a stout post. He attached the other end to Harmony Gold by way of her halter. Then he sat himself down to wait. Harmony Gold was about to find out that, no matter how hard she pulled back, the rope wouldn't yield. Eventually, the penny would drop and she would give up trying to break free. As to the how and when of it, Eddie didn't want to miss that. It would help him to understand her true nature and disposition.

As the minutes ticked by, Eddie couldn't believe the filly was acting so calm. She was pulling hay out of the haynet which he had hung beside her, seemingly without a care in the world. He decided to move things along a bit.

To his astonishment, she allowed him to harness and bridle her as casually as an aged racehorse. With a deep sense of unease, Eddie took away the haynet and closed the stall gate behind him. She would be sure to react now, he thought, picking up his blacksmithing tools. He tapped his hammer on the anvil. There was no response. He tapped louder. Nothing! He seized a body brush and banged it down on the nearest tack trunk. Then he picked up the lid and slammed it shut. Every horse in the barn jumped, except Harmony Gold. She merely flicked her long ears, sauntered over to the stall gate and stared down at him lazily. Was she deaf? The post he had attached her to was leaning over at a forty-five degree angle. Good God, but this filly was strong! He had never seen anything like it! Was she really a yearling, or had Cat gone and bought himself a two year old who had been tried and found wanting? No! he hastily reassured himself. Joey Harris would never try anything like that. The filly was a freak of nature. She had no nerves. She would either be a champion, or a wash out. Eddie reckoned the latter was far more likely. She probably wouldn't go at all on the racetrack. Well, the sooner he found out, the better for all concerned.

The following afternoon, he hooked her up to the cart and went out on the track. To his great joy, she acted like an aged racehorse, paced right along, hardly breaking a sweat. It made a nice change, Eddie reflected as he sponged her down, from the lunatic Kip and Caroline had bought. Harmony Fire was a nervous wreck. The first time he put the harness on her, she stepped out of it in two minutes flat. It would take a great deal of patience and cunning to get the better of her. But Eddie had no doubt he would get there in the end. As for Harmony Fire's owners, after the sale they had hightailed it back to England for the jump racing season, whatever that was.

Well, winter in Canada wasn't for the faint hearted!

The leaves turned to gold. They clung to the trees for a brief time, until strong winds swept them away, leaving bare branches silhouetted against a grey sky. It was a perfect fall afternoon: cool, clear and sunny. Evie Mercer had been looking forward to Saturday all week long. But now it had arrived, she couldn't enjoy it. There were too many things on her mind. School for one. She followed Will as he led the grey colt, Harmony Storm, out of the dark barn into the sunshine. She didn't mind that Will was kind of slow. At least he wasn't a creep like Stinker and the rest of the gang, coming on to her whenever her dad wasn't around. As if she'd ever be interested in any of them. No way!

She had found out about the guy who'd talked to her at the sale, though. Cat was pretty cool…he had a cool name too. But she couldn't think about that now. They were about to hitch Storm to the cart for the very first time. He was way behind the others. To date, he'd destroyed two sets of harness and broken Stinker's nose, so her dad was expecting trouble. Will came to a halt in an open area, halfway between the barns and the racetrack. Stinker, who was following with the cart, stopped too. When Evie glanced back at the barn, she had to pinch herself to stop from laughing. They had an audience! Every window had a horse's head poking out of it, ears pricked, totally focused on the show.

"Now remember, Will," Evie heard her dad say in a low voice. "Whatever happens, you don't let go!" Silently, Will nodded, afraid of spooking Storm. On Mercer's signal, Stinker picked up the cart and quietly lowered it over Storm's hind quarters. The colt didn't move a muscle. As he was blinkered, he had no clue about what was going on behind him. It was a bit like playing Grandmother's Footsteps, Evie thought, stifling a giggle. There was a loud click as Mercer connected the shaft with the quick hitch on Storm's harness. Immediately the colt went berserk, spinning like a top, jerking Will around like a rag doll, while the cart, half on and half off, whipped around behind him, a lethal weapon. Everyone ran for cover. All except Will, who was hanging on like grim death. Her dad, who'd been struck by the cart was lying on the ground, groaning. Meanwhile, Stinker was being totally useless, hovering at a safe distance.

"Go get some help!" Evie shouted. As Stinker sprinted to the barn, she saw horses' heads popping in and out of the windows as though they couldn't quite believe what they were seeing. Mercer was struggling to his feet when Stinker came running back with Rob and two other grooms. But there was nothing they could do. No one could get anywhere near Storm without getting wacked by the cart. The colt was totally out of control, dragging Will along like a dog on a lead. Something had to give. And soon!

"Will!" Mercer yelled, wincing from the pain, as he took a step towards him. "Let the horse go!" Quickly, Evie checked out the racetrack. It was empty. Storm might end up in the lake, but she guessed that was better than getting somebody killed. For the first time ever, Will disobeyed a direct order. A second later, Evie was thankful that he had. Ted Rivers started up his big tractor and headed for the track, dragging the long harrow behind him. If Storm got caught up in that…she didn't want to even think about it.

For an instant, she thought she was imagining it, but then she was certain she'd seen a splash of red…then she saw another.

"He's bleeding! Do something, Dad!" she screamed.

"Whoa!" Mercer roared. "Whoa boy!" Miraculously, the horse obeyed. Will's face was as white as a sheet, but his right hand was stuck like glue to Storm's bridle. The colt was trembling. Blood was gushing in a wide arc from his hind leg, like water from a hose. Without thinking, Evie moved in towards the horse's hind quarters.

"Get back!" Mercer snapped. "We gotta unhook him first. What the fuck's the matter with you all!" he shouted at the grooms. "Get the fuckin' cart off 'im! Move!" Precious seconds ticked by as they struggled to separate the cart from the harness. Eventually, Storm was free.

"We'd best take 'im back to the barn," one of the grooms mumbled.

"No! He'll have bled to death by then!" Evie screamed. "Gimme your shirt, Rob, quick!"

"Watch yourself girl! The bastard cowkicks!" Stinker warned as Rob obediently stripped off.

"It'll be okay," Evie said calmly. She crouched down under Storm's back legs and applied a makeshift tourniquet. The bleeding slowed to a trickle. The colt was shaking like a leaf now. It terrified her. "He's going into shock!" she cried. "We've got to get him inside before he goes down. He's lost a ton of blood!" She was dimly aware that her dad was talking rapidly on the cellphone.

"Vet'll be here directly," he told her.

Back at the barn, Evie hastily attached Storm to the cross ties and covered him with a cooler. He was so weak, he could hardly stand. A few minutes later, she heard the squeal of brakes and Dr. Winterflood appeared.

"Who put the tourniquet on?" he enquired gravely as he examined Storm's leg.

"It was me," Evie confessed nervously. Had she done something wrong? she wondered.

"He severed an artery. Luckily, not the main one, but if he had, you'd have saved his life," Winterflood said approvingly.

"No! That was Will!" Evie replied. "Will saved his life. He held on. He didn't let go!" Will's smile was as wide as the sky.

"I hung on!" he said proudly. "Jus' like Mister Mercer said!" As the vet stitched up the wound, Evie thought about school on Monday. She'd been branded as uncool by the group she used to hang out with. Suddenly, that didn't seem to matter so much anymore.

LUCKY SEVEN

By mid October, Catalino Ciardi had a house to live in, his own training track, a brand new truck and trailer, several jogcarts and sulkies, his own barn full of harness bags and tack trunks (all done up in the Lucky Seven Racing colours of black and gold), a score of horses and a half a dozen grooms. He'd patched things up with old Uncle Eddie by helping him break his trotting filly in the afternoons. It was only fair. Eddie had broken Harmony Gold for him, after all. But it was a punishing schedule. In his first week on the job, Cat raced ten horses and had eight winners and two seconds, making quite a splash at Iroquois Downs. The mysterious packages arrived almost daily. Each time, Cat handed over a thousand bucks to the courier for the dozen or so unlabeled glass bottles. Judging by the results on the racetrack, at least, the owners were certainly getting their money's worth, he decided as he followed the instructions in Ritchie's distinctive sloping handwriting. He had no idea who the Lucky Seven were. A group of wealthy businessmen, he guessed, out for a bit of excitement, but Ritchie wasn't telling.

A month in, Cat didn't much care. He was too drunk on success.

The first snow fell...Christmas was coming...Sparrows flitted in and out of the barns, searching for spilled grain. Cats slunk under horse trailers seeking shelter from the weather. All over the province, trainers were driving the latest crop of babies, their hearts flickering with hope. In December every yearling was perfect. Every yearling was sound. All they needed was a little gentling. There were lessons to be learned. Not to fear the tractor and the harrow, whirring past them like monsters...to pay no heed to the dark shadows that chased them on bright sunny days...not to rear in terror when the snowplow's engines roared. Sensible...that was the aim now. Speed...that, hopefully, would come in its own good time.

Harmony Stampede took to pacing like a duck to water. Each Saturday, Al McTavish drove over to Meridian Acres to watch his colt go. The roads turned white with frost and the puddles iced over. Snow lay on the fields. Stampede paced on, through fair weather and foul: black ice, fog, snowstorms, none of them mattered to Al or the colt. The track froze as hard as iron and the pond was a solid lump of ice. Al was buoyed up by impossible dreams. The colt was in his element.

Dave Bodinski and Scotty McCoy laid to rest an inglorious year by getting gloriously drunk together, ending up at the Hot Tamale, where Pam Mercer had her hands full with the Erinsville Raiders, the local ice hockey team.

The shenanigans at the Hot Tamale were quite a contrast to the rarified atmosphere of Claridge's New Year's Eve Ball in London's West End. Kip and Caroline spent the evening dancing cheek to cheek and making wedding plans. At the stroke of midnight, Greenwich Mean Time, they joined in with everyone else for a spirited rendition of *Auld Lang Syne*. Their filly, Harmony Fire, was half a world away.

THE SEA PRINCESS

Jeff Lamare lay on a hammock in the shade of a grove of coconut palms, listening to the waves lapping on the beach, a collection of magazines at his feet. He hadn't opened a single one since arriving on the island ten days earlier. The muffled roar of the waves breaking on the reef had drowned out every intelligent thought in his head. Who needed a brain when the sun was shining down on a dazzling, white sand beach and the sea was a seductive shade of turquoise? Eventually, Jeff rolled off his hammock and picked up his mask. A trim thirty three year old, he attracted a few appreciative stares as he ran down to the water and threw himself in. He waded through the warm sea, while above him, an ungainly pelican stretched its wings, hunting for fish. Jeff put his head down and swam out to sea. Minutes later, he entered a secret world, hidden beneath the waves. Coral clung to the rocks, waving in the water, green parrot fish were cruising up and down the reef and fish striped like bumblebees begged for food. The sound of a motorboat buzzing in his ears, Jeff dived deeper until he spotted a stingray, half hidden in the sand. A school of blue tang were grazing the coral, constantly on the move. He followed them for as long as he could then came up for air gasping for breath, the taste of salt on his tongue.

As he swam back to land, a trio of local boys on ponies splashed through the shallows, riding island style, bareback, with only a rope to guide them, hooting and hollering as they cantered along the beach. The sun was burning hot. Jeff waded to the shore, dazed but happy. The faint but insistent sound of his cell phone broke the spell. He sprinted back to his hammock. There was an echo on the line and the reception was terrible. But there was no mistaking that voice. It was Billie McTavish, he realized, his heart quickening.

"Having fun?" she asked.

"Listen, this place is great…even better than you said."

"I knew you'd like it. One of your horses won last night by the way. The new one."

"Great," he replied, wondering if that was why she had called.

"Wanna hear the latest?" she asked excitedly. "There's a rumour going around…they're putting slots in at Iroquois Downs."

"Wow," Jeff exclaimed. The purses would go through the roof if that happened, he thought, feeling pleased.

"Oh, and some guy called…Danny something or other, looking for you. He tried you at the hotel but you weren't there." The line went dead. Suddenly, Jeff felt like a shadow had come over the idyllic scene in front of him. He had only a few more days left on the island. But that wasn't his main problem. Billie's phone call had highlighted the fact that he was alone in this paradise. Being in a place like this by himself didn't feel so great all of a sudden. Business was a welcome distraction. He made a series of calls to the geeks who were working on the new software, ensuring that it would be on its way to clients on time. His internet company operated with a skeletal crew of brilliant nerds who, like himself, had a passion for computers. Setting them free to do their thing had brought rich rewards, cash wise. Some of that cash now fed Jeff's other passion, standardbred racehorses, which was also prospering, thanks to his trainer Keith Lazer. He didn't mind paying Lazer's sky high bills, so long as the horses were winning.

Business done, he drove his rental jeep over to the nearby harbour. He had discovered an excellent eating place there, perfect for a lazy lunch. After ordering a cold beer, he sat himself down at a table near the water and watched the boats bobbing up and down, enjoying the ambience of the place: the brilliant Caribbean colours, the huge shade umbrellas and the gentle, cooling trade winds wafting over him. The girl sitting at the next table was an olive skinned beauty wearing a skimpy top and short shorts. She had long dark hair which she wore braided. He was tempted to say "Hi" but just then the waitress arrived with the food menu and the girl was joined by a boyfriend, an outdoors type of guy, suntanned and strong.

Jeff drowned his sorrows in plantain chips and conch chowder. He was aware that conch wasn't vegetarian, but as it had come from the crystal clear waters that surrounded the island, he reckoned it had to be healthy. He was considering the idea of ordering a dessert called *sticky toffee pudding,* when he noticed the girl had got up from the table and was smiling at him. It looked like he would get to say "Hi" after all, not that there'd be a lot of point, given the boyfriend.

"Wanna come on the charter, today?" she asked. "We got room for one more on the boat." Like most Australians, she sounded friendly. But he recognized a sales pitch when he saw one. "I'm Anya. Pete's the captain," she added glancing at her companion. "We go all the way round the island. It's only thirty-five dollars. Why not give it a try? You'd have a good time!"

"When?" Jeff asked.

"We're leaving in half an hour," Pete said. Jeff paid his bill, wishing he hadn't eaten quite so much food. But at least he would have some company for the afternoon. The prospect cheered him.

An hour or so later, Jeff and a score of other passengers were sitting beneath the billowing white sails of the Sea Princess as she tacked back and forth with Pete at the helm. Anya was up on deck, coiling ropes, snugging up the sail, making everything shipshape, a pleasing sight to Jeff. Soon they left the shelter of the harbour far behind. There were white caps on the waves and a stiff breeze was blowing. As the boat heeled over, Anya had to grab the mast to stay upright. She frowned at Pete and shouted something Jeff couldn't make out, gesturing with her arm and nearly losing her footing in the process.

"Bearing away!" Pete sang out, evidently taking the hint. Perhaps the two of them were only business partners, Jeff though hopefully, relieved that the Sea Princess' deck was now horizontal again. After the lunch he had eaten, he was content to sit quietly, gazing out at the water, listening to the sound of the waves slapping at the hull and the whistle of wind on canvas. But Pete had other ideas for him.

"Wanna take over for a bit, mate?" he asked. Jeff stared at him, uncomprehending. "Just follow the coast," Pete added. Somewhat reluctantly, Jeff rose to his feet. It was a lot harder than it sounded. It wasn't anything like driving a car. The wheel seemed to have a life of its own. He did his best to steer a straight course, but it wasn't a lot of fun. When Pete came back up, Jeff handed over control immediately.

"Boats aren't really my thing," he admitted ruefully.

"Looked alright to me," Pete replied shortly.

After a while, they changed course again, heading back towards the shore, with the wind directly behind them. The rolling motion brought on a bout of sea sickness. Jeff could tell he wasn't the only one feeling queasy. The woman across from him was white around the gills. Suddenly the boat swung around and came to a stop, its sails flapping. Anya scrambled to pull them down. Then, thankfully, everything went quiet. The passengers exchanged grateful glances. They'd made it and not a moment too soon!

"Right! Swim ladder's at the back." Pete announced. "Snorkels and masks are here if you want 'em. The water's shallow, so no worries. But if you see a ray, better not grab it by the tail. They can sting, bad enough to kill you." Anya had stripped off her top and shorts and was wearing a black bikini. She didn't bother with the swim ladder. She dived off the side of the boat and then looked back at Jeff. He allowed himself to hope. He jumped in after her and tried to catch up with her, but she was too quick for him. She dived down deep, her long braids streaming out behind her. Jeff put on his mask and watched her. She was much better looking than the fish, he decided.

The trip back to the harbour was a lot more enjoyable than the journey out. The sea was calmer and as they headed for the shore, the Sea Princess surfed home, skimming the waves. Seabirds followed along, riding the slipstream while behind them a blazing sun, the colour of molten gold, edged its way to the horizon. Close to shore, the wind dropped and all too soon the ride was over. As the boat slowed to a crawl, dark shapes appeared in the water.

"Tarpon!" Anya called out, throwing a box of raw fish over the side. Jeff caught a glimpse of metallic blue as the fish snapped at the food. They looked huge. Every one of them was a perfect predator, he thought, staring down at them. No welfare system here! It was every man for himself. That was nature in the raw, he thought, feeling a healthy respect for these supreme survivors. They reminded him a little of Keith Lazer. In the dog eat dog world of harness racing, Lazer was the king.

Back at the harbour, the day trippers streamed off the Sea Princess. Jeff stayed put. Anya had offered to make them a couple of Rum Daiquiris. The drink, when it came, was sugary sweet. It washed away the salty taste of the sea. The setting sun cast a warm glow on Anya's face.

Pete went on home.

Anya put a CD on the ship's stereo. The lazy sound of slow jazz floated out on the evening breeze.

"Ooh look at that sunburn," she exclaimed, pointing at Jeff's shoulders. "I've got something for that." The lotion she smoothed onto his back was cool and soothing. Jeff felt anything but. He decided to risk kissing her. To his surprise, his kiss was returned with enthusiasm. Tentatively, he pulled up her skimpy top and felt her breasts. Her heart was beating fast. She put her arms around him and held him close, kissing him all the while. The big tropical sun plunged into the sea and was gone. The darkness didn't seem to bother Jeff and Anya too much.

The next few days passed in a blur of happiness for Jeff. But soon, far too soon, his time was up. As his plane took off, he looked down at the little island floating in the turquoise water, hoping to catch one last glimpse of the Sea Princess. He had learned a great deal about Anya in the short time they'd spent together. He knew that her parents were Greek, that they had emigrated to Australia when she was a baby only to leave it two years ago, retiring to their home island of Thassos, a place she couldn't even remember. He had learned too that she had been shipwrecked on Sainte Marie whilst trying to work her passage back to Melbourne, that her permit was about to run out, that she wasn't certain it would be renewed and that days off were a waste of time. There was nothing to do, plus she had no boyfriend.

"This island's just too small," she had said, a hint of desperation in her voice. "Too much gossip for that." She had told him stories about Melbourne, about Christmas barbecues on the beach and the friends she had left behind. He had told her about the internet company he had built up from scratch and his winning stable. She knew all about harness horses. She called them *the trots*. They were big in Australia, apparently. The drinks trolley knocked into Jeff's elbow, breaking his train of thought. He asked for a daiquiri. It tasted bitter sweet. Was Anya using him? Maybe. Did he care? Not so much. He wanted to bring her to Canada on any pretext. She'd driven all thoughts of Billie McTavish totally out of his head. That hadn't happened in a very long time.

ALONE AGAIN

Billie McTavish awoke with a jerk. She had fallen asleep with the light on again. The pillow next to her was empty. It was 1:30 a.m. If Theo had been a normal person, he'd have called, but she had learned by now not to expect him to keep in contact. She had been frantic with worry about him the night the lights had cut out at Iroquois Downs. He hadn't called then, either. Lately, things had been deteriorating between the two of them but Theo hadn't appeared to notice that anything was amiss. He was far too focused on winning the drivers' championship. She could have dyed her hair blue and sprouted horns, for all he cared. Even Sundays were work days for Theo. Every single weekend, he'd go off to Cree Horse Park, driving halfway across the province on icy roads covered with snow, through blizzards and storms. Nothing stopped him. He made it clear she was not welcome to come along. The romantic holiday they had shared on the island felt like it had happened half a century ago.

Perhaps it was time she faced up to reality, she thought. Theo was not the person she was going to spend the rest of her life with. Being married to him would certainly be a lonely affair. Theo was already married. To his career. She had tried to overcome the anti social hours he worked, spending Friday and Saturday nights at the racetrack cheering him on. But for what? For a fleeting glimpse of him in the winner's circle only to be told to drive herself home because he'd be along late? That was what had happened tonight. Did he think she hadn't noticed the look that had passed between him and the girl who rode the lead pony? Is that where he was now...with her? Was that why he'd been so short tempered with her recently? No! Not recently. For months! Her resolve hardened. She and Theo were done, over with. The sooner he was out of her life, the better.

She jumped out of bed, rummaged in the closet for some bags, then began packing up his things. There were surprisingly few of them. Apparently, he had never really moved in. She walked into the kitchen and switched on the coffee maker. While she was waiting for it to heat up, she went through the kitchen cupboards, looking for anything of Theo's. Spotting a six pack, she added it to the pile. The clear out was having a cathartic, energizing effect. She realized how passive she had become, always waiting around for him. Climbing up on a stool, she searched the top shelves...nothing. Then, above the microwave, she discovered half a dozen cartons of what appeared to be cake mixes. They certainly didn't belong to her! She considered tossing them in the bin, but instead she wrapped them up in a grocery bag and threw them on top of his stuff. Then she broke down and cried, tears streaming down her face. This wasn't just about Theo, she realized. She blamed herself...for being an idiot...for being so gullible...for wasting so much time...his as well as hers.

The sound of a key turning in the lock brought her to her senses. Hurriedly, she splashed her face with cold water from the sink, dabbing herself dry with kitchen paper. She didn't want him to see her like this, vulnerable and sad. Theo came bursting into the kitchen. It was 2:30 a.m.

"What's going on? What are you doing up?" he asked, flicking the switch on the overhead fluorescent lights, dazzling her. "Why've you packed up all my things? Are you out of your mind?"

Silently, Billie drew her robe tightly around her, as if he was a stranger, an intruder, not the man who had shared her bed for over a year. Theo backed away. Standing in the doorway, he frowned at her, reading the signals she was giving out. Without her saying a word, he knew. At least he wasn't a fool!

"Billie?" he asked. Was he giving her a chance to change her mind? She shook her head. It was an automatic gesture, one which he interpreted correctly. "You're right," he said. "I'll move back into my place. I can't keep waking you up at all hours of the night like this. It's not working out. I know that. I've known it for a while." An overwhelming sense of relief, that he was being so reasonable, swept over her...followed swiftly by an emptiness that hit her like a thunderclap. "I'll go tonight," Theo was saying. "I have to drive to Cree Horse Park tomorrow anyhow, have to make an early start." He glanced at his watch and laughed, a brief, bitter laugh. "Hardly worth going to bed is it?" he added, turning his back on her and reaching up into the empty slot above the microwave. Abruptly, his mood changed. "What did you do with it?" he shouted, turning on her, his face contorted with rage. "Tell me! Right now, Billie! Where's my stuff?" He wasn't just angry, she realized. He was hysterical.

"Over. . .th. . . there," she stuttered. "In th...the...hall...with the rest of your things. I didn't throw anything out..." What was going on? Taking a hold of herself, she added "why are you getting so uptight about it? You're not making any sense!"

"It's all here," he said, without so much as a glance at her. He picked up his belongings and opened the front door. He walked out and slammed the door behind him.

"Goodbye, Theo," she said softly.

KILLER ON THE LOOSE

The virus struck Iroquois Downs with no warning. This was no spring sickness, hitching a ride on the horses shipping up from Florida. It was a homegrown killer spawned in the cold. Erinsville Equine Clinic was full to bursting. Local veterinarians drove from track to track, working late into the night. With so many horses laid low, the race secretary could hardly fill the card. Short fields were made even shorter by late scratches, as horses who had been healthy when entered to race had to be called in sick. No one was ordering much feed these days. However, the pharmaceutical industry was raking in profits. With a barnful of two year olds, Mercer was reduced to taking temperatures and dispensing antibiotics. The grooms were done with their work by 9 a.m.

"Good horses don't get sick," Mercer kept repeating like a mantra as one horse after another succumbed. Only Harmony Light appeared to be unaffected. On his biweekly round, which was all he could manage these days, Winterflood spotted the little black colt, Harmony Jet, coughing after a workout.

"That horse is sick," the vet exclaimed. Somewhat reluctantly, Tony Hall allowed him to administer emergency treatment. "Don't take him out of the barn again 'til I give you the all clear," he admonished the scowling trainer. He had barely finished the lecture when one of Mercer's grooms came running up.

"Doc! You gotta come quick," he gasped. Winterflood grabbed his bag. "It's that grey colt," he panted as they hurried over to Mercer's barn. "He don't look good at all!" On the way there, they picked up Scotty McCoy, who was anxious to catch the vet before he left. Harmony Storm had his back to the stall door. His head was down, his coat dark with sweat.

"Pneumonia, I'd guess," Winterflood pronounced, after listening to the stethoscope he had placed on Storm's ribcage. "His lungs are full of fluid," he explained to the silent onlookers. "I can't treat him here. He's far too sick. He'll have to go to the clinic."

"They ain't got no more room in there, I heard," Scotty McCoy declared gloomily. Winterflood was undeterred.

"I'll see what I can do...maybe I can call in a few favours."

"Go ahead!" Mercer said. "You know," he added, a look of exasperation on his ruddy face. "That colt was jus' comin' around, jus' gettin' sensible. Last time I trained him he acted perfect. Perfect!"

Throughout the province, rumours of the virus fanned out like ripples in a pond. When Craig Brown tried to drive through the gates of Merryvale Raceway, he found them firmly closed.

"We're not letting any horses in or out," the security guard told him.

"But my mare's in the first race!" Craig protested, pointing back at the trailer. "And I've brought my two year old to train. They're not sick!"

"Judges have scratched all ship-ins!" the guard replied, running back to his box, as if Craig was carrying the plague. Bowing to the inevitable, Craig turned his truck around and took his horses back home. What now? he wondered, standing in his kitchen in his stockinged feet and staring out at the frozen fields. He owed the vet, the blacksmith and the feedman. But if they wouldn't let him race, he couldn't pay them. Izzy's job at the grocery store put food on the table but with four layabouts to feed, the money she made didn't stretch very far. The house was silent. No doubt his boys were still sleeping off last night's rabble rousing. Where had all that come from? he wondered wearily. He hardly touched the drink himself. He picked up the phone and cradled the receiver in his hand, weighing up the pros and cons of asking for his old job back at the tire plant.

The manager remembered him. "We could likely find a spot for you on the afternoon shift," he said. "But we're short two men on the night shift. Know anyone who could help out?"

"I reckon so!" Craig replied, his heart skipping a beat as he committed his sons to a spell of night work. He and Izzy had carried the four of them for long enough. If they refused to work for a living, he was going to tell them to move out. At least his horses were healthy, he reflected, looking on the bright side. Out here on the farm, away from everything, they had a chance to stay that way too.

Harmony Stampede was in good hands. Bob Summers was taking no chances with Al McTavish's good looking colt. His training had been put on the back burner for now. Eddie Clearwater, too, was playing it safe. He had trucked Harmony Fire to his farm and he intended to keep her there until spring. She had a nice snug run in shed for shelter on his farm and she had Cat's filly Harmony Gold for company. The virus hadn't reached Meridian

Acres yet, but it soon would. It was only a matter of time. The big black filly with the heartshaped white patch on her forehead, Harmony Valentine, was also staying well. Tom Cowboy Larson had moved her out of the main barn and into an outside stall, well away from his racehorses. So far the ploy had succeeded. Her temperature was a normal 100.4.

At Erinsville Equine clinic, the colt was discovered by staff just before dawn. They gently unhooked him from the IV drip hanging from the ceiling. He wouldn't be needing it anymore. After he'd been wrapped in plastic in an effort to contain the infection, one of the crew, a first year student, waited behind with the veterinarian in charge.

"He fought so hard!" she said, her eyes brimming with tears. "He was just a baby!"

"We can't save them all," the vet replied, a look of understanding on his haggard face. "Let's hope we get lucky with the next one, eh? How's that grey colt doing?" The girl dried her tears.

"Still alive," was all she said.

Scotty McCoy arrived at his barn that morning and discovered two of his horses lying dead in their stalls. Sighing deeply, he removed the blankets they'd been wearing and called the meat truck. Then he called the owners to give them the bad news. That afternoon, his wife packed her bags for the second time in a year and left.

"I can't handle it no more," she cried, after Scotty had begged her for an explanation.

"What? Me or the horses?" Scotty called after her as she ran down the stairs.

"Both!" she exclaimed, slamming the door behind her.

INTENSIVE CARE

Mercer cursed himself for his carelessness. He'd left the report on Harmony Storm lying on one of the tack trunks, available for anyone to read. He prayed no one had. He hadn't even told the owner yet. Retreating to his tack room, he made the call. He couldn't put it off any longer.

"They saved his life," he said. "But his lungs aren't too good, apparently. What d'you want me to do with him?"

"What are the choices?" the owner asked.

"Well, I could turn him out, start back in two, three months…," Mercer suggested half heartedly.

"Nah!" the owner replied. "Put 'im in the sale! Got any better news for me?" he asked.

"I trained Harmony Light in 2:30 today," Mercer reported happily. "The way he's going, he'll be ready pretty early, I'd say."

"Jus' like the mother!" the owner said, sounding pleased. "I'll come out and watch him go in couple of weeks," he promised.

"With all this sickness, a lot of 'em'll get held back. There won't be so much competition," Mercer said, wrapping it up. He heaved a sigh of relief. The Porn Guy had taken the bad news pretty well. But wait 'til he sees the bill from the clinic, Mercer thought. He'll bite my head off. Three weeks that horse was in there! He glanced up at the clock. In a few hours' time, his daughter would be home. He wasn't looking forward to telling her that her favourite horse, Harmony Storm, was going in the sale. To his surprise Evie called him. He swallowed hard, bracing himself for the tears, the histrionics and God only knew what else.

"Had some bad news today," he said, trying in his clumsy way to be gentle.

"If it's about Storm, I already know," she replied. "I called the clinic."

There was no sense in beating around the bush, he decided. "He's going to have to be sold, Evie," he said firmly.

"I guessed that," she replied. Her icy calm worried him far more than tears.

"I'll come home," he started to say.

"I won't be there. I just came back to pick up my stuff…Annie's driving me over to Mom's. I'm gonna stay with her for a few days. Bye Dad."

"Wait!" Mercer shouted down the phone, but it was too late. She had already hung up. He glared at the wall. He couldn't believe what he had just heard. A horse she'd doted on had almost died and she was running to her mother, a woman who had no idea what being a mother meant. And this girl Annie, he was certain it was the one with the nose ring. What was happening to his daughter?

Someone was rapping at the door. "Come on in," Mercer said automatically. The door swung open. Scotty McCoy was standing there, looking a little sheepish. Probably on the scrounge, Mercer guessed.

"Any news on the colt yet?" Scotty tried as an opener.

"He's okay," Mercer replied glibly. "But he's missed a lot of time. The owner wants to sell him."

"That's too bad. Still, you gotta lot o' other pay horses."

"These things happen," Mercer agreed.

"Tell me about it!" Scotty said with feeling.

"That wife of yours come to her senses yet?"

"I reckon so. She's left me again."

"Women!" Mercer said bitterly.

"Ah, you can't be too hard on them," Scotty replied tolerantly. Like hell! Mercer thought. "They're not like us," Scotty added. "They can't take it when things get ugly. I don't blame my wife. Not really. She's had a lot to put up with." Like you going out on a drunk once too often, Mercer thought.

"She'll be back!" he called out encouragingly, as Scotty left with a handful of "borrowed" sulfur pills. But it was Evie he was thinking about, not Scotty's long suffering wife.

It took a month for the virus to run its course, but finally, in March, the worst was over. The end result was thirty-seven horses turned out with suspected permanent lung damage, fourteen horses dead, two divorces and one trainer put out of business. Winter training had taken an even greater toll than usual but the illness had affected the youngsters, not the older horses whose immune systems were more mature. Trainers like Catalino Ciardi had got away scot-free.

THE SIX O'CLOCK FLASH

The clouds rolled in right on cue, wrecking the main event of the day: the sun's dramatic plunge into the Caribbean Sea. Luckily, the crowd at Ritchie Sanchez's beachside bar were far too wasted to care about another dud sunset.

"Hey, we could use a half a dozen Stingrays over here, mate!" an Australian called out cheerfully. Just then, the phone rang. Ritchie ran to answer it.

"Be right over!" he called out to the Aussies. Where's the help when you need it? he thought as he grabbed the old black handset on the seventh ring.

"What took you so long?" a voice boomed in his ear. It was the guy that was a stickler for punctuality, the one he called the Six O'clock Flash. Ritchie glanced at the bar clock.

"You're two minutes late!" he remarked, feeling like he'd scored a point.

"You got a problem, moron?" the man roared.

"No sir!" Ritchie blurted out, knocking over several glasses in his haste to find a pen.

"Then get this down!"

"Yes sir!" Ritchie said, one eye on the Aussies, the other on the rapidly darkening sky. It was a sizeable order. Six grand on big ticket win bets and a couple of thousand worth of exacta and tri combos. It was, so far, the only downside to the deal he'd made to buy the bar. He couldn't survive selling soft drinks and virgin pina coladas and it had been made abundantly clear that his liquor licence would be cancelled unless he cooperated. As usual, Cat's horses formed part of every bet. He was curious as to why the Six O'clock Flash placed bets through him. Ritchie concluded it had to be something to do with privacy issues.

The days when Cat's horses went off at 10-1 were long gone. His brother was a big shot now. He'd snared the leading driver Theo Vettore and his training average was up in the stratosphere. By the time Ritchie had everything down right, the Aussies were well into their third rendition of Why are We Waiting? Richie was certain that the song was laced with insults about his dismal performance as a bartender. Forget the tip, he thought miserably. As he popped the tops off the beers, he consoled himself. At least he wasn't having to put up with the freezing weather in Ontario like Cat.

"Apologies for the delay, fellas," he said.

"No worries," they replied good-naturedly, tossing their empties onto the sand. It was okay for them, he thought. They were on vacation. He lived here. Later, he'd have to get down on his hands and knees and clear up, dodging the broken glass in the semi-darkness. Help came cheap on this island but, aside from Pepe, it was hopelessly unreliable.

The memory of being able to run faster than anyone was kept fresh by the many visitors from Florida who recognized him. With them, he had a chance to relive the few short years when he'd been a phenomenon. Once in a while he'd ask himself: was I really that good, or was it Coach Bailey's drugs that won all those races? Since his ankle had healed, he'd taken to running on the beach in the early mornings. But try he might, he couldn't summon up the adrenalin to push himself faster and faster like he'd done in the past. Why?

Right now, he had a more urgent puzzle to solve. The phone lines to North America were down. His cell phone wasn't working either. Out here on the beach, there was no internet access. If he was unable to get through to his betting account before the races started at Iroquois Downs, he'd be in big trouble. The Six O'clock Flash invariably won. If that happened tonight Ritchie might have to end up paying him off from his own funds. That was the deal they'd made, to ensure he stayed honest. Nervously, he picked up the phone and pressed redial. After fifteen tries, he threw down the phone in disgust. If he didn't reach his betting account soon, he could well face ruin.

A BREAK IN THE PATTERN

Ritchie's brother, Cat Ciardi, was on his way to the races, his spirits high. The mercury had been rising all week. The snow had retreated from the fields, which were now a muddy brown. Cat's first winter in Ontario had been a blast and he had the win pictures to prove it. They were plastered all over the walls of the old farm house, his current home. He'd had so much success that most trainers were scared of claiming his horses from him, a good place to be. However, most of his horses weren't claimers. Instead, they were competing in high class conditioned races. But if anyone thought he had it easy, they were dead wrong. His day started at 5 a.m. and didn't end until well after midnight on race nights. After a couple of months on the job, with twenty-five racehorses to train and new ones arriving all the time, Cat had crashed and burned. He'd learned his lesson. These days he left the training to Brad (his second in command), shoeing to the blacksmith, and any lameness issues to Doc Winterflood. Meanwhile, he concentrated on stuff no one else could do: the blood work and the pre-race. This critical job took place in the afternoons when he had the barn to himself and he could needle the horses in peace. As for what to give and when, Ritchie had done the calculations for him. All he had to do was follow his handwritten instructions that came with each delivery.

Confident of yet another winning night at Iroquois Downs, Cat sauntered into the Race Barn, which was rapidly filling up with horses coming in from the track, their bodies steaming, their legs covered in mud. Heeding Ritchie's warning about Jim Mercer, he managed to dodge Evie Mercer who was usually hanging around. He had plenty of other fans, mostly girl grooms falling all over themselves trying to get a job at his star stable. At present, his barn was a totally male space but he wasn't planning to keep it that way. He barely recognized his second trainer when he came in from the track. Brad looked like he'd been dipped in batter, ready to be deep fried.

"It's a fuckin' quagmire out there," Brad moaned. "It's gonna be a nightmare warming them up."

"Wait 'til you're in the winner's circle," Cat grinned. With seven horses racing, he expected to scoop at least two or three wins.

The night did not go to plan. After the third horse had broken stride, galloped all the way home and finished last by twenty lengths, Cat's driver, Theo Vettore, laid into him.

"What the fuck are you playing at, Catalino?" Theo shouted savagely, throwing the lines at him. "For Christ sakes, pull the fuckin' hopples in! What do I have to do, train the fuckin' things for you, as well as drive 'em?" Speechless, Cat flushed crimson. As Vettore turned on his heel and marched off, the groom in the next door stall sniggered. Cat felt like falling through the floor. The whole Race Barn had heard the outburst. Vettore could have taken him aside, shown a bit of loyalty. The worst of it was, Vettore was right. The hopples were way too long. Cat always did let the hopples out a couple of inches when he got a new horse. It helped them stretch out and they were able to pace faster. That had worked brilliantly all winter, when the track had been rock hard. But in the mud, a pacer needed more support, not less. He'd been so caught up in needling horses that basic horsemanship had flown out of his head. Fixing the problem was as simple as tightening a belt a few holes.

I'll get my wins yet, he thought optimistically. A win was the only way to put a stop to the grinning faces that seemed to follow him everywhere now. He felt so low that he even tried to put in a call to Ritchie. The phone rang and rang, but no one picked up.

By the time Ritchie finally got through to his betting account in Jersey, the races at Iroquois Downs were over. It took an age for the girl to find the results, but when she did, Ritchie cried with relief. None of Cat's horses had won. He debated with himself what to do. In theory, The Six O'clock Flash was down eighteen thousand dollars. If he told the truth, he might be able to negotiate a less risky deal for himself. On the other hand, eighteen grand would come in pretty handy. He decided to keep his mouth shut. After his nerve-racking ordeal, groping around for bottles in the dark was a picnic in the park!

The next evening, The Six O'clock Flash called half an hour early.

"You double-crossing little cunt!" he shouted down the phone.

He thinks it was a setup, Ritchie realized, feeling panicky. He thinks Cat and I fixed it for him to lose.

"I never got to put the bets on," he protested.

"Oh yeah?" The Flash sneered.

"I couldn't get through! All the phone lines were down," Ritchie hastened to explain. "I tried all night. I'm telling you the truth. Check it out if you want."

"Already did," The Flash replied. He rang off, leaving Ritchie feeling dumbfounded. How had he known that the bets never went on? How had he accessed Ritchie's private betting account? It worried the hell out of him.

THE STUD

At Rivers Training centre, Harmony Light was climbing the walls, desperate to escape his pungent smelling stall. Every so often, he paused briefly, taking a peek at the white world outside, then banged his empty feed tub before beginning the whole routine all over again. He knew eventually someone would notice him and he would be let out. It worked. Every time! He wanted to be outdoors, away from the stale air, out in the cold where he belonged. No one came. He banged at his gate, the only thing that stood between him and freedom, then reared up and tried to jump over it.

"Someone get that sonofabitch out of there before he kills himself!" a man yelled. When Harmony Light felt the brush on his body, he relaxed. He knew the harness would soon land on his back. When it did, he eagerly lifted his tail, ready for the crupper. He made the usual fuss about the bridle going over his ears, as he did every morning. But, as soon as he felt the weight of the cart, he began dancing, impatient to be off.

Outside, he leapt into the air and landed pacing, racing down the laneway towards the racetrack. Then, he grabbed the bit between his teeth and took off, bellowing a challenge at a rival stallion, strutting as he caught the whiff of the mares running in the snow filled paddocks. The man driving him was bellowing too, joining in the fun. But all too soon it was over and he was back in the barn. After his bath, he ran into his stall and leapt up to touch noses with his neighbours. Then he settled down to his hay. All too soon, the hay was gone. He spent a while nosing the shavings, hunting for every last piece of it, then took to climbing the walls again.

"That son of a bitch needs gelding. Needs it bad!" Rob told Jim Mercer. "He damn near killed me out there today!"

"No manners," Stinker agreed fervently.

"Listen up, guys!" Mercer shouted. "Listen up good! The owner's paid ninety grand for this goddamn colt. An' he didn't pay all that to end up with a gelding. Get it?"

"You're the boss," Rob replied meekly.

"Quit loafin' and get on with your work," Mercer exclaimed irritably. Harmony Light chose that moment to aim a kick at the back wall of his stall. "Maybe Rob's got a point," Mercer muttered to himself. What if the animal broke a sesamoid? It would be the last straw for the Porn Guy. He could even lose him as an owner. Maybe keeping the horse a stud wasn't worth the risk. Five months had passed since the sale. Harmony Light had changed. Gone was the boyish charm, the slender, feminine body. In its place stood a rugged colt, muscular and strong. Even the look in his eyes was different. The boy had become a man.

Mercer made the call. The vet waited until after the full moon. Then the deed was done.

INSIDE INFORMATION

Billie McTavish was sitting in the coffee shop round the corner from her apartment, drinking a latte and enjoying the fact that it was Saturday morning. After the split with Theo Vettore, she had retreated into work, an effective antidote to her low mood. Right now she had a big fencing contract pending with an outfit in BC. Alberta, too, beckoned. All that wild country needed taming. Yet paradoxically, the more she learned about horses, the more she understood that what most of them really wanted was companionship with their own kind and freedom to roam. Unfortunately, in today's world that wasn't on offer. Fence Sense's customers were only too happy to spend their money on grand barns and smart looking paddocks. But to most horses, that must have felt like solitary confinement. Was her business really any different than McTavish Construction? she asked herself. People in Erinsville shuttled back and forth between high rise office buildings and high density housing. No wonder so many of them lived for the weekends when they could escape to a cottage on the lake. It was too bad that horses didn't have that option. She had to stop dreaming and get moving, Billie realized. For the first time in a long while, she and her father were getting together. If she didn't hurry, she would be late.

Harmony Stampede was harnessed up and ready to go by the time she reached Bob Summers' barn at the prestigious Meridian Acres Training centre, ten minutes west of Erinsville.

"You just made it!" her father called out cheerfully when he saw her.

"Gotta get 'im out before the track breaks up," Bob explained. "What d'you think of 'im, then?" Billie ran her eyes over Stampede's chunky body, his striking white blaze and the four perfectly matched white socks. Immediately, she was smitten.

"He'd make an amazing riding horse!" she said.

"Now we don't need any of that talk around here," Bob clucked disapprovingly. "He's gonna make a stakes colt. Riding horse!" he added crossly, jumping onto the cart. Glamour didn't count for much on the racetrack, Billie realized, resolving to persuade her father to keep Stampede as a pet after his racing days were done.

"C'mon, Billie," Al urged. "I want to watch him go." Together they hurried over to the viewing stage, a wooden structure overlooking the track.

"This is new!" she said, looking around approvingly.

"You haven't been here in quite a while," Al reminded her. "Neither has your mother." All winter long, Billie realized guiltily, there had been no one to keep her father company on his weekly visits to Meridian Acres. She tried to imagine Al's solitary vigil beside the racetrack as he followed the colt's progress. Where had she been all this time? Not in the real world, certainly. Hooking up with Theo Vettore had been exciting and thrilling, like travelling to a brand new planet. But she was back on earth now, back to a familiar country, a shared set of assumptions. It was a relief, she thought, glancing at her father. He was fussing with his stopwatch, watching the colt as Bob guided him around the track, readying him for the mile. It was the dreariest time of the year. Winter had ground to a halt but there was no sign of spring yet, not a green leaf or a blade of new grass to be seen.

"Here we go!" Al called out excitedly. Harmony Stampede was pacing flawlessly, stretching out his neck and flinging out his front feet, as if he couldn't wait to get to his destination.

"Poetry in motion," Billie murmured, bewitched by his beauty. He had that rare quality in a male: perfection!

"2:50!" Al cried happily, checking his stopwatch. "He'll be ready to drop three seconds a week now, Bob says!"

"Next stop 1:50!" Billie smiled.

"I wish!" Al replied fervently. They walked back to the barns in companionable silence. A girl gave them a cheery wave as they passed by.

"How'd your colt go today?" she called out.

"Perfect," Al replied happily. The girl smiled warmly, before darting back inside.

"Who's your friend?" Billie asked curiously.

"She works for Eddie Clearwater," Al replied.

"Who's Eddie?" Billie asked.

"He's a trotting man, best in the business."

"And Bob Summers?"

"The only choice for pacers," Al said firmly. "Doesn't do drugs, honest, hard working. Happily married too!" He sounds almost too good to be true, Billie thought privately. But she didn't want to burst her father's bubble. After a tour of Bob's barn, she was glad she hadn't said anything. Bob struck her as a down to earth type, with a wealth of experience. His wife Connie worked alongside him and she and Billie chatted while the men disappeared into the tack room. But when Al finally emerged, he was looking grave.

"What's wrong?" Billie asked anxiously, the instant they were out of ear-shot. Al gestured at the barns, the fencing, the horse walkers…all painted the same shade of pale grey, creating the effect of order and class.

"Doesn't look too much like a war zone, does it?" he said. "But it is!" He pulled up short and began patting his pockets. "We're not winning the battle, Billie," he declared, pulling out a cigar and lighting up.

"It's not bleach again, is it?" she frowned.

"Oh no, the claiming guys have moved on from there," Al replied bitterly, reading from a tattered piece of paper. "They're using Winstrol, HGH and something called Elephant Juice, Bob says, whatever that is."

"Mom would know," she said, then immediately regretted it. The expression on Al's face was bleaker than ever.

"Your mother's in Toronto," he replied.

"She's only gone for a week," Billie pointed out. "She'll be back."

"Will she?" he asked gravely. "I've failed, Billie." What was he talking about? His marriage or Iroquois Downs? "Know what the biggest seller in the tack shops is now? Liver flush!!"

"You can't let them get away with it," she said, deciding to skirt the marriage issue. Al plodded off to his car. She hurried after him. "Listen, I know we haven't spent a lot of time together lately but…"

"You've got your own life to lead," Al replied gruffly.

"Oh, and this isn't anything to do with me?" she retorted. "You think I don't care about what happens to the horses, Dad?"

"It's nice of you, Billie, but…"

"No buts!" she said. "We've got to up our game, that's all. Leave it with me, I'll call you later on, okay?" Al nodded wearily, then clambered into his car. "The colt's great!" she said, trying to coax a smile from him.

"Glad you think so," he replied wistfully. He took a halfhearted puff at his cigar, then drove off.

Al McTavish dawdled on the drive home. There wasn't much to go back to. With Sofia gone, only Walter the cat cared whether he lived or died. At first, being by himself hadn't been so bad. Sofia's absence had given him a chance to catch up on some much needed sleep. But after a while, he began to feel lonely. Today being Saturday, a long afternoon on his own lay ahead. He managed to while away twenty minutes at a gas station, picking up a sandwich and the Saturday papers. When he finally got home, Walter was nowhere to be seen. He ate the sandwich standing up in the kitchen, then retired to the living room sofa and tried to relax: an exercise in futility.

Bob Summers had lit the fuse on a time bomb and Al could hear it ticking away inside his head. Horsemen often invented wild stories to account for another trainer's success, but Bob had been right before. Besides, he had mentioned specific drugs, none of which Al had ever heard of. The inescapable fact was that since arriving at Iroquois Downs, Catalino Ciardi's training average had gone from mediocre to meteoric. The guy raced mostly conditioned horses but even the claimers he raced were apparently immune from the retention barn. That was a bitter blow. Al spent a fruitless hour wracking his brain for solutions. Just as he was dropping off, the phone rang. Hoping it was Sofia, he eagerly jumped up to answer it. But it was only Billie.

"I've got an idea," she said.

"An idea," Al echoed, still half asleep.

"Horse racing is way behind other sports events, like athletics," she said forcefully.

"I'm sure it is," Al agreed, waking up a bit. "People actually want to watch it," he added gloomily.

"You're right. But that's not what I meant. Jeff's met someone by the way. I think it's serious this time," she added. Was that a good or bad thing? Al wondered, thinking about his daughter's situation. "You need to introduce spot checking," Billie continued. "It's what they did in athletics…and it worked. Plus, I discovered something called a mass spectrometer…it can pick up anything in the blood that shouldn't be there, even in minute quantities."

"I don't imagine it comes cheap," Al said.

"No," Billie agreed. "But with those two strategies you'd have the whole situation under control."

"You've certainly done your homework," Al acknowledged, feeling a lot less optimistic than Billie sounded.

"You okay, Dad?" she asked anxiously.

"I'm fine," he replied heartily. "I'll talk to Phil about your idea today, if I can get hold of him."

"Why Phil?" she asked uncertainly.

"With all his contacts at City Hall, he'll know the best way to go with it," Al explained.

"I'm sending you some links on your email," she said. Al sighed.

"Your mother's better at that than I am," he confessed.

"I could send it direct to Phil," Billie offered.

"That's not necessary," he said quickly.

"You got a pen and paper though, right?" Billie laughed.

"Of course," he said, reaching for his diary.

"Then write this down. It's dynamite!"

After she got off the phone, Billie felt better than she had felt in quite a while. She really missed being part and parcel of her father's daily life. That had come to an abrupt end when she had left McTavish Construction to start up her fencing business. But it was only part of the story. The disastrous relationship with Theo Vettore had sapped her of energy. She had found it almost impossible to focus on anything else. Since the breakup, she had deliberately avoided anything that triggered her emotions. Until now. She recognized the signs. She was starting to heal. One day, she promised herself, she would be able to play her Billie Holiday CD all the way through without bursting into tears.

She hadn't wanted to give her father the really bad news. Of the drugs Bob had told Al about, one caused liver damage, another carried a risk of cancer; and that was if they were administered to humans. Goodness knows what effect they had on racehorses.

As for Elephant Juice, she wasn't even going to try to go there!

THE RINKS

Constable Campbell McClaren had stayed well clear of romantic entanglements for over a year. Not by choice. But no decent girl was going to be interested in his undercover persona: a bouncer at the Hot Tamale, a seedy club in an even seedier neighbourhood. Today he had a few hours free but his idea of time off wouldn't have suited most people. Unfortunately, the ski season was over, so after a brisk run along the Speed River to warm up, he headed over to the local rink to kit up for a game of ice hockey. It was something his alias, Sidney H. Kingshott, was keen on. His cramped apartment was littered with hockey memorabilia. It was too bad, Campbell thought, that his superiors had decreed that Sid would be a mediocre player (presumably so as to not draw attention to himself). After a suitably dismal performance as goalie, he headed for the snack bar. Pam Mercer, the Hot Tamale's star waitress, was sitting on her own beside the tall glass windows that afforded a bird's eye view of the rink where another game was now in progress.

"You lost!" Pam said disgustedly. "An' I had ten bucks on you!" She pointed to the occupants of the next table who raised their beer bottles, grinning.

"Here's to you, loser!" one of them jeered. They had apparently wasted no time converting Pam's ten dollars into alcohol. Campbell tried to appear appropriately downcast.

"Want a sandwich? I'm buying!" he offered. "Two BLTs and a couple of bottles of water," he told the woman at the counter, ignoring the sullen expression on Pam's face.

"That guy's playin' worse than you. He's let in two goals already!" Pam declared cheering up a bit and lighting a cigarette. Campbell was soon wreathed in smoke. A staunch non smoker, he endured it, waiting for the right moment to bring up the subject of the crew of thugs known as the Undertakers who had been frequenting the Hot Tamale lately, parking their sinister looking limousines in full view, scaring away regular customers. It was no wonder! Their methods of violence and intimidation, and their links with the town's darker forces, were well known. Campbell was hoping their presence would throw up an opportunity. Twelve months of sustained effort on his part had turned up precisely nothing at the Hot Tamale; not a whisper of the drug distribution network that he had been told to unearth. It was common knowledge that unscrupulous businessmen employed the

Undertakers to collect overdue debts. No doubt drug dealers used them too. With their reputation as a close mouthed brotherhood, it wouldn't be easy to get one of the gang to grass on their paymasters, but Pam had a way of winkling out information from the unlikeliest of characters.

"Food's up," the bar woman called out. The sandwiches didn't go down very well. Pam picked over her bacon with a knife.

"They haven't cooked it right," she complained.

"Send it back," Campbell suggested.

"I'm not really hungry," she replied, with a little shake of her head. "This ain't a date, right?" she added nervously. "Because if it was, I'd have dressed different." That's all I need, Campbell thought.

"You're right," he confirmed hastily. Pam looked so unhappy, he tried to think of something to say to cheer her up. "What'd you do to your hair?" he asked. "It looks different." Pam patted her gleaming platinum locks.

"I went to the beauty salon," she revealed. "I had it done special."

"It looks nice. . . it suits you."

"You reckon?"

"Those heavies," he began tentatively.

"Which heavies?"

"The ones hanging around the Hot Tamale."

"What about them? They tip okay," Pam remarked. "One of them kinda likes me." This sounded promising, but Campbell had learned to his cost it was better not to act too interested.

"What did you do today?" he asked, deliberately changing the subject.

"Nothin'!" she replied moodily, lighting up another cigarette. "Evie took a day off school and I thought she was gonna spend it with me but she went down to Jersey with Mercer for some goddamn stupid race. She's just like her father. Horses is all she cares about."

"You make it sound like some kind of disease," he chuckled.

"It is!" Pam said, throwing her head back and blowing smoke in his face. "I should know. I worked my butt off for Jim and his damn horses for years! Up at 5 a.m., covered in shit all day. I can't believe I put up with it for so long. I should'a come back to the Hot Tamale a lot quicker."

"Come back?" he echoed.

"It's where I met my ex," Pam explained. "I was a dancer, see. Up on the stage." So she'd been a stripper, he realized. That made a lot of sense.

"See if you can find out what those heavies are up to," he suggested, opening his wallet and taking out a couple of twenty dollar bills. "I don't want any trouble at the club," he explained. "But don't you go taking any risks, okay?" Pam eyed the money, then glanced at the guys at the next table. One of them winked at her. "I gotta go. You need a ride?" Campbell asked.

"I may as well stay," Pam replied, tucking the bills away in her purse. On his way out, Campbell looked back at Pam. She was rifling through her bag. Then her hand went to her mouth and she took a gulp of water, swallowing hard. He'd seen enough. It could have been aspirin, but he doubted it. She was probably on some kind of uppers…and he was pretty certain she hadn't got them from a doctor. He felt bad about not even trying to help her, but he had learned from experience that he would be wasting his time. He couldn't believe he was dependent on a woman like Pam for information. If she failed, he would be back where he started: at a total dead end. He was desperate to break cover, call a halt to the charade. But he needed a good reason. So far, none had appeared.

BACK TO SCHOOL

The big trotting filly Harmony Fire returned to Meridian Acres at the beginning of April. The frost was out of the ground but there was still no hint of green on the bare branches of the trees, a far cry from England, Kip thought regretfully, where spring was in full swing and the flat season was about to start.

"She's massive!" Caroline said, reaching up to brush the mud off the filly's shaggy coat, grown as a defence against the harsh Canadian winter. "Just how big is she going to be?" she asked anxiously.

"I'll soon tell you," Eddie Clearwater replied, pulling a string off a nearby hay bale and walking over to the horse with a sprightly step. He measured the distance from her ankle to the top of her foreleg, then swung the string upwards. "She's got a good four inches to go yet," he pronounced. "Now you folks get a harness on her, while I see if I've got a bridle that'll fit her."

The atmosphere in the barn reminded Kip of something but he couldn't think what for a moment. Suddenly he was transported back to his childhood. His mother was buying his uniform for a new school, a boarding school miles from his home. The shop smelled of starch, wool and Harris tweed. Kip had felt scared but excited about what lay ahead, trusting his parents that everything would somehow come out alright. The earnest expression on Harmony Fire's eyes, as she stood quietly waiting for something to happen, seemed to echo his own feelings that day. He patted her neck reassuringly. As she pricked up her ears, Eddie slipped the bridle over her head.

"It's a perfect fit!" the old timer declared happily. "Now, see if she remembers her lessons," he added, pointing at Kip who hastily picked up the lines, pleased to be the one to take her out. Sobered by his brush with potential paralysis, he was content to go along with Caroline's love affair with Canada and harness racing for a little while longer. Rum Martin had won the Cheltenham Gold Cup for the second year in a row, a satisfying ending to the season and he had left his horses in the capable hands of his head lad, a man with a wealth of experience.

Out on the track, Harmony Fire was foot perfect, but Kip braced himself when a flock of geese flew in, landing in a nearby pond, with much squawking and beating of wings. Sure enough, the filly took off. Kip hung on tight, glorying in the sudden burst of speed.

All of a sudden, being in Canada didn't feel so bad after all.

MUD

It was a wet spring. Horsemen came in from the track splashed with mud and cursing the rain. There was water everywhere. The grass grew long and lush. The Canada Geese revelled in the overflowing lakes and streams. Jim Mercer carried on, regardless. He had a schedule to keep to and he wasn't going to let a little thing like the weather stand in his way. He stuck to his plan: his best two year olds would be pacing in 2:10 by the end of May.

Tony Hall was jogging the little black colt, Jetson, when Mercer's top string of two year olds powered past him going the other direction. The horse Mercer was driving finished five lengths ahead of the rest.

"Who the heck was that?" Tony called out as Stinker went by, driving a high stepping trotter. Stinker pulled his horse back, so Jetson could catch up.

"That's the Harmony colt," he replied gleefully. "He's going to beat all them two year olds to a pulp."

"Whatever happened to the grey colt?" Tony asked, hoping to put a dampener on things.

"Storm? He's gone. Crazy as a coot he was!" Stinker grinned. It was plainly a compliment. "Some old geezer from Alberta bought him. Too bad Storm ain't around no more. He sure as hell livened things up!"

"Don't be such an old softie!" Tony called out after him as Stinker drove off. Jetson was light years behind Mercer's colts, Tony realized gloomily. He needed to drop him down, timewise, but he had no idea how to do it. The lazy son of a bitch didn't want to go at all!

The first stakes were only two months away.

MAY

The cool rainy spring had thrown a monkey's wrench into the broodmare business. At Harmony Farm, pregnant mares were stubbornly hanging onto the foals in their big bellies, apparently reluctant to bring them into a cold, unfriendly world. It wasn't good news for Joey Harris. It meant an extra month of sleepless nights waiting up with the mares, an increased risk of problems during foaling and youngsters who would be several months behind their peers born south of the border. The one bright spot was his wife's dentistry practice. The damp weather had brought in a whole slew of new clients, complaining of toothache!

In mid-May, the sun appeared, the rain let up and eight mares foaled in a single week. One little filly never made it out of the mare alive. Another, after trying his hardest for twenty-four heartbreaking hours, couldn't stand and had to be put to sleep. The other six were born without a hitch and were strong and healthy. Joey thanked God for small mercies.

THE OLD MILL

Al McTavish and Phil Harman were flush with expensive wine and good food. Lunch at The Old Mill had been highly enjoyable as usual. The pair of them had swapped stories and jokes, tossing the ball back and forth as they generally did on these occasions. With Sofia away on yet another trip to Toronto, spending time with Phil had cheered Al greatly. He didn't want to spoil the mood. Nevertheless, he had a job to do.

"Need to talk to you about something serious," he said, hoping the strong coffee he had drunk would kick in soon and nullify the effects of the wine.

"Fire away," Phil replied nonchalantly. Al proceeded to share his concerns about the drugs some trainers were reportedly using now.

"Who did you hear this from?" Phil asked sharply, his expansive demeanor vanishing in a flash.

"Bob Summers told me," Al revealed. Phil's expression hardened. "Bob's a straight shooter…he's not given to passing on wild rumours and he's a horseman's rep…" Al added, coming to Bob's defence. Phil nodded as if acknowledging this as a fact that could not be got around easily.

"And what exactly do you propose to do about it?" Phil asked, looking across the table, his blue eyes searching Al's face inquiringly. Under that searching gaze, Al faltered.

"Billie had some ideas but they're not cheap, I'm afraid," he confessed.

"Your daughter," Phil said pensively. "Right?"

"Yes," Al replied, only too happy to give Billie the credit.

"So?" Phil prompted. Encouraged, Al put forward his proposal, explaining his principles of spot checking and supertesting, citing athletics and cycling as successful pioneers of the practice. Phil listened attentively.

"So, you see, it gets results," Al ended confidently.

"I'm sure it does," Phil was quick to agree. "The problem, as I see it, is the expense. How are you going to persuade the politicians to spend that kind of money on an ongoing basis?"

"I was hoping…," Al began.

"You remember their reaction to the idea of building a retention barn, Al. What makes you think this'll be any different?"

"To be fair, that would have required a pretty hefty sum," Al replied. "And in the end I didn't need it."

"You found a way through," Phil agreed. "But this is going to be a little tougher. The money will have to come from somewhere."

"Why not take it out of purse money?" Al suggested. Phil looked dubious.

"That's not going to go down well with the horsemen. If you're not careful, you'll have a strike on your hands," he warned.

"I still want to give it a try," Al replied, refusing to be put off.

"Well," Phil said after a long silence. "You've given me a lot to think about. I'll do my best for you but frankly, my old friend, I'm not too optimistic." Al maintained a stubborn silence. "Are you quite sure you want me to do the rounds on this?" Phil continued. "It's going to put a lot of people's backs up. It's a sensitive time you know, with the Slots proposal on the table. You don't want to do anything to rock the boat. The extra revenue could increase purses by forty or fifty percent, maybe more."

"I'm fully aware of that," Al replied. "But all it would take is a small percentage of that revenue to carry out my plan." He sighed. "You know how I feel about slot machines, Phil," he added soberly.

"It's just a bit of fun for people," Phil laughed. "No one takes it too seriously."

"Well, I do!" Al said. "But if it's inevitable, let's at least earmark some of that money for schemes that would benefit horses," he argued, warming to his theme. "They put on the show after all and we should be giving something back. A good place to start would be keeping them safe while they're racing, in my view. And, what about afterwards? Horses who've made thousands of dollars are entirely dependent on people's charity once their careers are over. Does that seem fair to you?"

"What are you saying here, Al?" Phil asked uncertainly. "Are you against the idea of a casino at Iroquois Downs?"

"I believe I've made my position pretty clear," Al replied, feeling Phil had completely missed the point. "Look, just have a look at this," he added, eagerly passing over the list of websites Billie had given him. "It'll tell you everything you need to know."

"About what?" Phil enquired, raising his eyebrows at him.

"About the latest technology. They can pick up virtually anything illegal these days…in humans at any rate."

"Who's the internet buff?" Phil asked drily. "Not you, surely?"

"Not me," Al conceded, feeling uncomfortable about dragging Billie into it again now, though he had no clear idea why. "Just give it a try, okay?"

"Fair enough," Phil said. But he didn't sound pleased.

ALBERTA

It was a rainy morning in Alberta. Old Dan Mills was whistling through his teeth as he rubbed Storm's body with a soft cloth. Brushing and curry combing the colt until his coat shone had become part of Dan's daily routine. It took his mind off his troubles for a while, but soon enough they came back to haunt him: the painful loss of his pedigree herd, the crippling loan he'd taken out on his land and the combine harvester sitting idle in the drive shed. A few weeks ago, he'd gone and made things a whole lot worse. He'd done something which didn't make any sense, whichever which way he figured it. He believed they had a name for it these days. They called it buying on impulse. Dan had done it. Yes, sir! He'd driven all the way from Alberta to the sale in Ontario, on a mission to purchase three or four broodmares, cheap, for a new scheme his wife had set her heart on. Instead, he'd blown the entire three thousand on a pacing colt named Harmony Storm. What he was going to do with him, he couldn't begin to imagine. But he'd always had a liking for greys, ever since he'd ridden with his grandfather behind the team of plow horses, as they plodded along, patiently tilling the earth. Those were happier times, simpler times too. Why did everything have to be so damn complicated nowadays?

Five years ago, he'd had a nice herd of milk cows and owned his farm free and clear. When the bottom fell out of the milk market, he'd taken out a loan to buy machinery and set about growing soybeans. It hadn't taken him long to find out he couldn't make a profit there either. Then he'd got to talking to a fellow down at the feed mill and found out about a new scheme to save his farm from bankruptcy: collecting urine from pregnant mares. The way the fellow had described it, it had sounded a lot like milking cows. But his cows hadn't had to spend half the year in standing stalls, wearing some contraption to catch their piss, all to make Premarin for menopausal women. If those women knew what was in the pills the doctors gave them and how much suffering it caused the horses, they might think twice before going on HRT, he thought. There was money in it. He couldn't deny that. At eleven dollars a gallon, he'd have made fifty bucks a day off a big Clydesdale mare. But he couldn't do it. No sir! He knew that by now. Knew he was a stubborn old fool, too.

He hadn't sold his prize bulls, despite Abigail's pleas, despite the fact that he had no real use for them now that the cows were gone. "You can't allow a woman to tell you what to do all the time," Dan had confided to the feed store manager. "Even if she is your wife." The manager had quietly agreed with him but that wasn't going to do him any good, not when he'd have to 'fess up to Abigail. He was worried, sure but a little defiant too, certain that he'd done the right thing. Of course, his wife wouldn't see it that way at all. Well, he reflected gloomily, maybe he'd keel over and die one of these days and solve the whole darn problem. She would collect the insurance money, pay the bank what they owed and move into town. It's what she'd always wanted. As for him, so long as she buried him out on the back forty, (his treasured field which had never been under the plow) mebbe it wouldn't be so bad.

After he'd finished rubbing Storm, he stood back and looked him over. No doubt about it, his purchase was beginning to show improvement. The dapples were appearing and in this farmer's opinion, there was nothing in this world to beat a dappled grey. This happy state of affairs was rudely interrupted by the appearance of Abigail who burst into the barn, plainly distressed, waving a letter. It looked powerfully like a statement from the Credit Union.

"What is it, Abbie?" he asked, feigning ignorance. But he knew. Yessir!

"Three thousand, three hundred and sixty dollars!" she cried. "That's what you gave for this useless horse. Have you lost your mind?" The rain was lashing the barn roof like some vengeful god. "Whatever possessed you?" his wife demanded. "You took good money and what did you do? You threw it away!" He hated seeing her like this, her plump face blotched red with anger. But, like the leak in the bedroom window he'd never been able to fix, some things you just had to live with.

"He's a stud," he replied doggedly.

"He's two years old! He's never going to get any mares in foal! He could barely reach up to their armpits!" She was right, there. Dan took off his cap and smoothed his silver hair, an automatic gesture repeated many times over the years. He stood there quietly, waiting patiently for the storm to pass. He had spent his life outdoors in all kinds of weather. He treated his wife's outbursts in the same way, safe in the knowledge that soon enough the sun would come out again and things would be back to normal. "You told me you was going to that sale to buy mares. You could've brought home three or four of them for that money!" The colt was standing by the window, staring out at the empty fields which stretched to the horizon. "Listen to me, Dan!"

"I am listening," he said gently.

"Do you want us to lose the farm? Is that what you want?"

"Not sure I care much anymore," Dan muttered.

"We've got no choice and you know it. We've got to pay the bank what we owe. What else can we do?"

"I'll think of something."

"You bin saying that these past five years, Dan. I reckon I oughta go out and buy those mares myself!" The minute she said it, she got a look on her face, like she always did when she knew she'd gone too far.

"Now listen here, Abigail," Dan said firmly. "We ain't gonna start no PMU programmes on this farm. I made up my mind. We ain't gonna take no foals to the market when they're barely three months old and listen to 'em bleating for their mothers. It ain't right! Besides, you know what happens to most of them in the end." He gestured with his old hands crisscrossed with blue veins, the finger nails embedded with dirt, and pointed a thumb at the barn floor. There was a bleak look on Abigail's face now. He'd made her face up to the truth.

"You were okay about the calves," she said weakly.

"Horses ain't the same thing," the farmer explained. "Our cows were happy enough. I saw to that. They never wanted for nothing."

"Well, you can't make money from cows no more," Abigail said with a note of triumph.

"I know that," he replied gruffly. Silence fell.

"You gotta do something!" She was pleading with him now.

"I'd like to shove this loan of our's up the bank's ass," Dan said. "Now maybe I done a dumb thing with this here colt. I give you that."

"I reckon you did," Abigail replied, not unkindly.

"If I had a mind to, I could sell the colt easy enough," he said calmly. "There's a track not twenty minutes ride from here. I could train him up and find a buyer. We might even make a bit o' money on him!"

"More expense if you ask me!" Abigail complained, unmoved by this rosy picture.

"Tell you what," Dan proposed. "I'll go down there and see what I can find out. Soon as this rain lets up. But this here thing with the mares. It has to stop right here!"

"I guess there's no way I can get you to see sense," Abbie replied. But she sounded resigned, not angry any more.

After she left, Dan started up his battered old Dodge and headed south. The racetrack was easy enough to spot. He parked outside the barn, which was wedged between the road and the track. There were two turnout paddocks. Both of them needed tearing down. The fence posts were leaning at odd angles and someone had strung an electric wire along the top in an attempt to stop the horses breaking out. Inside the barn though, everything was neat and clean. There were about a dozen horses, not a human soul to be seen, but Dan could hear voices down the far end. When he pushed open the tack room door, he found six or seven men, all farmers like himself, huddled around a stove drinking coffee. He recognized most of them from the cattle auctions.

"I'm looking to hire one of your stalls," Dan declared, directing his remarks to Carl Prentiss, a big man with a bald head.

"Fifty dollars a month it'll cost you," Prentiss replied. "Straw's a buck a bale." Follow the money and generally you could find a Prentiss at the end of it. Abigail was right, he decided ruefully. That horse was just going to be more expense he didn't need. He turned to go. He'd found out what he wanted to know. But little Tommy Perkins thrust a mug of coffee in his hand.

"Why don't you pull up a chair, Dan," he suggested in a friendly tone. "This here might be your lucky day, I reckon. Ain't that right, Carl?" Carl Prentiss stood up and stuck his thumbs into the straps on his overalls.

"Well, don't you look like the cat who got the cream," Dan exclaimed. "What you want me to do fellas, fix the barn or the fencing? C'mon, out with it!" Everyone laughed.

"Better'n that!" Tommy said with a wink.

"How many acres you got up there, Dan?" Carl asked, screwing up his eyes and frowning mightily.

"Two hundred and eighty-seven," Dan replied proudly, though the truth was his land was more of a liability than an asset these days.

"Whatcha growin' in them fields of yours nowadays?"

"Nothin', I guess." Dan wasn't telling Carl anything he didn't know already, but there was no sense in hurrying a Prentiss.

"Kep' all ya' machinery, did ya?"

"I did so."

"How'd ya like," Carl said, pausing theatrically, "to plant up them fields this year?"

"What d'ya got in mind?" Dan asked patiently.

"Mint," Carl declared

"Spearmint," Tommy cut in excitedly. "Spearmint, peppermint...all kinds."

"Mint! Whatever for?"

"Murrays have told me," Carl said with an air of self importance, "to find two and a half thousand acres around these parts."

"Chewing gum, Dan," Tommy supplied eagerly.

"We're about two, three hundred acres short," Carl stated. "It's the last slot, but it's yours if you want it."

"What'll it pay?" Dan asked warily.

"You'd clear around a hundred dollars an acre by my reckoning," Carl assured him.

"I'm in," Dan said, shaking on it. "And I'll take the stall from you while I'm at it. I'll move my horse in tomorrow, if that's alright with you."

"Need a feed tub or a water bucket?" Tommy asked hopefully. "I gotta bunch of 'em for sale."

"I'm fixed up in that department," Dan told him. "But I'll need a harness and I ain't got a whole lot to spend."

"I'll see what I can find," Tommy promised. "But you gotta come see my trotting horse. He's a beauty!"

Dan stopped off at the gas station on the way home.

"Fill her up, Steve," he told the station attendant in a rare show of extravagance. Out of curiosity, he bought a packet of chewing gum, spearmint flavor. A load had been lifted from his bony shoulders. When he got home, he went straight to the horse barn. The colt was standing right where he'd left him, staring out of the window.

"Let's you and me celebrate," he told the colt. He walked over to the pile of square cut hay at the back of the barn. He took his time searching for the right bale, with the air of a maitre d' picking out a vintage wine for a favoured customer. And when he eventually cut the pale blue string, he did so with a flourish, like a waiter uncorking a bottle of champagne. The hay was his cherished third cut from the back forty. He'd been saving it for a special occasion. As he broke open the bale, fragrant with clover and alfalfa, it took him right back to Indian Summer the year before. He was perched up on the big tractor, the sparrowhawks hovering in the big blue sky above him, the tractor blades slicing through the grass and the rabbits' white tails bobbing as they broke cover, making a quick break for the bush, panicked by those sharp watchful eyes. He threw Harmony Storm four large flakes and felt happier than he'd felt in a long time. The rain had stopped. A wind had sprung up and swept away the dark clouds to someplace else. "I'll make a racehorse out of you yet!" he told Storm. "You'll see if I don't!"

SUMMERTIME

Al McTavish was mystified and confused. Sitting out on the deck on a sunny afternoon, he pondered his two unknowns, trying to ignore the state of the lawn. The grass was five inches high. Without Sofia to prompt him, he had let things go at 210, Laurel Drive. The pool heater had died, but he hadn't replaced it, so despite the spell of hot weather they had been having, the water was still ice cold. Swimming would have been a welcome distraction and might also have cleared his head but Al didn't want to risk catching pneumonia. His wife and his best friend had both gone missing. Hopefully not together, Al thought morosely. Of course he knew perfectly well that was not the case. Sofia was staying with her sister in Toronto "recharging her batteries", as she put it. She had made it abundantly clear that Al was not welcome to join her.

But Al's friend Phil Harman had completely disappeared. Ever since he had floated Billie's idea to him, Phil had maintained a stony silence. Al was no super sleuth, but even he had no trouble figuring out the reason. He recognized the technique only too well. He had just never been on the receiving end of it before. It wasn't personal, he was certain of that. Phil just didn't have any good news to impart, so he was lying low. No doubt he had floated the concept of supertesting and spot checking to his contacts at City Hall and had met with fierce opposition. What had worked for athletics was unlikely to happen in harness racing any time soon. But why not just level with him? Admit the money wasn't there or the political will was nonexistent? Being rebuffed at City Hall had never had this effect on Phil before. Anything, Al reflected miserably, would be better than the silent treatment. In his present situation, it felt like yet another door closing, increasing his sense of isolation, confirming his theory that he was alone in the universe.

CAFFEINE FIX

Jake reckoned it'd been an A-1 performance, but he wasn't gonna win any prizes. He'd made such a good job of cutting his hair (well, he'd borrowed Andy Price's clippers, anyhow) that the guard at the detention barn hadn't even registered it was him. Now that he'd lost his long locks, he looked like any other groom. A hundred bucks wasn't bad pay for a few minutes' work. Course he'd timed it perfect, coming in right after Crawfish Brown, who was limping along, leading his horse and taking it nice and slow just like he'd been told to do. Jake just flashed his badge and slipped in. If the guard wanted to check him on the way out, that was no problem.

Keeping a watchful eye on the guard, he took out a roll of *Trucker's Friend* from his jacket pocket. The mare next to him scoffed the lot. She made such a racket though, crunching them up, that he got nervous, certain that someone was going to cotton on. But lucky enough, the guard was still stuck with good ol' Crawfish, who was pretending he couldn't find his licence. Jake had had to shell out twenty-five bucks for his little bit of help. Nothing came cheap these days. But *Trucker's Friend*, which was loaded with caffeine, came cheap enough. It kept truck drivers awake, stopped accidents. The mare wouldn't be getting a lot of sleep tonight either. Too bad she wasn't a truck driver! he thought, grinning to himself as he slipped back out.

Five hours later, Al McTavish was at Iroquois Downs waiting for the third race to start. It was a warm, June evening. After weeks of drawing outside posts, Millie D had the 2 hole. Al was optimistic. Theo Vettore was driving her for the first time. Taking advantage of the fine weather, Al was standing down by the rail, fortified by hot pizza and cold beer, hoping to catch a close view of the action. There was, he was pleased to see, a pretty good crowd attending the Friday Night card. Millie D looked skittish in the post parade. Theo's magic hands, Al surmised, had woken her up. His theory was confirmed when the race began. Vettore went for the lead and stayed there, rebuffing all challengers. She won easily. Elated, Al ran to the winner's circle, pleased that something good had happened for a change, giving him a much needed boost. To his relief, there was no awkwardness between him and the driver. Vettore gave no sign of harbouring any hard feelings about the breakup with Billie. Al ordered several win pictures. Millie D had only won a relatively cheap claimer. But a win was a win. It was just too bad no one from the family had been there to share it. Sofia was still absent and Billie was much too busy with her new business.

After the races, Al drove slowly home, reluctant to go back to an empty house and a phone that hardly ever rang. He still hadn't heard from Phil. As usual, he stopped off at the gas station and bought a sandwich and a black coffee. He picked up a paper too. By the time he pulled into 210, Laurel Drive, it was raining. He discovered Walter waiting for him at the front door, dripping wet. Grateful for any kind of companionship, Al got a towel and rubbed the cat down. However, when he tried to pick him up and carry him into the living room, Walter struggled, clawing at him wildly. He leapt from his arms and ran up the stairs at top speed, pausing at the top to gaze down at him, a reproachful expression in his green eyes, before disappearing into one of the bedrooms.

"Was it something I said?" Al asked out loud, examining his wrist, which was bleeding profusely, staining the cuff of his last clean shirt, the only one he had been able to find despite the fact that he estimated he owned at least twenty of them. There was no sense in asking Billie for help. She had found it amusing when he had told her he had run out of clean socks. "D'you even know where the washing machine is, Dad?" she had laughed. By the time he got around to drinking the coffee, it was cold. He put the sandwich in the refrigerator, so he would have something to eat for breakfast the next day. Then he headed for the sofa and tried to catch a nap.

Sleeping was an excellent way of passing the time, he had discovered. People had been commenting lately on how wonderful he was looking. But he was sick at heart. In spite of the way Sofia had been acting for months now (the long silences, the frantic cleaning sessions) he missed his wife. With so much time on his hands lately, he had been thinking about the past, about his student days, about how beautiful Sofia had looked when she was young: her delicate face, her long dark hair. He remembered too his frequent visits to the family's restaurant where she had worked on weekends. "They help me...I help them," she had explained in her exotically accented Italian English. "Soon, I shall finish my studies. I shall be a pharmacist!" Thanks to him, she had only practiced for two years. She had given up work when the boys came along and just as she was starting to be free of them, a longed for girl, Billie, had been born. Now that all three children had moved out of the house, the years spent growing them up seemed like a dream to Al. Apart from one Maine Coon cat, the house was empty of life. No wonder

Sofia was so attached to Walter. To him, and him alone, she was able to act like a mother again, a job she had done supremely well. I could use a little mothering myself, right now, Al thought wistfully, looking at the scratches on his wrist. Walter's claws had dug deep. Sofia would have taken care of it for him. But she wasn't there. Neither was Phil.

Exactly one week later, Al took a day off from Iroquois Downs to go over things with Steve, Billie's replacement at McTavish Construction. The two of them had been closeted up in the office all day. Al had to admit that Billie had chosen a worthy successor in Steve. But as they went over cost estimates and plans, Al's mind kept wandering. It wasn't the same without her. He missed Billie's unique take on things, the way he knew she was a hundred per cent on his side even when she was bawling him out. He didn't exactly know whose side Steve was on; probably his own, he concluded. That was generally the case with young guys who had climbed the company ladder as Steve had done.

Late Friday afternoon was a time in most offices when the need to meet deadlines conflicted with the urge to escape and start the weekend early. Steve was no exception. Al noticed him glancing discreetly at his watch from time to time. Al himself though, was in no hurry. Going home held no particular allure these days. Sofia had still not returned. Dust was gathering on shelves and tables at 210, Laurel Drive and smudges of dirt obscured the view through the living room window. But the worst thing was the all pervading silence that filled the house these days. Would he end up all alone, like Phil? Rationally, Al knew Sofia would never leave him. But his heart told a different story.

At two minutes to five, he heard the phone ring in the outer office.

"Call from a Mr. Harman," the receptionist informed him over the intercom.

"Phil!" he exclaimed happily, putting the phone to his ear. "I'm glad you called!"

"You won't be when you hear what I have to say," Phil warned.

"What is it?" Al asked anxiously.

"I've got some good news and some bad," Phil replied evasively. This didn't sound so terrible.

"Tell me the worst," Al replied carelessly, relieved that Phil had finally surfaced. Later, he would remember how carefree he had felt then.

"It's an awkward situation," Phil began. Al stared out of the window at the blue sky.

"Go ahead," he said. "Fill me in."

"There've been two positive tests on horses at Iroquois Downs," Phil replied, catching him completely wrong footed. Al practically jumped out of his chair!

"Why on earth wasn't I informed?" he exclaimed, aware that Steve was hovering in the background, uncertain whether to leave or stay.

"They've been trying to reach you all day," Phil explained. "You weren't at your office and there was no answer at home. Finally, someone had the bright idea of looking up who you'd said to contact, in case of an emergency. I was the second name on the list." Al struggled to take it all in. "There were two trainers with bad tests," Phil continued smoothly. "One of them was Tom Larson...his horse tested positive for penicillin."

"Ah well," Al said, feeling relieved. "He won't get hung for that."

"And the other is Bob Summers. Brace yourself!" Phil warned. "They got him for a Class One drug."

"Bob...surely not," Al frowned.

"The name of the horse is Millie D."

"My mare?" Al exclaimed. He was having trouble taking it in.

"Your mare," Phil confirmed. "Her blood and urine both showed excessively high levels of caffeine."

"Caffeine!" Al exploded.

"Of course you're aware that she'd been in retention for twenty-four hours before she raced," Phil pointed out. Al's hands were shaking. He heard a door close. Steve had left the room. How on earth could this have happened? he thought desperately. Could it have been an accident? But how on earth would a horse accidentally drink several cups of strong coffee?

"Could there have been some kind of mix up, er...an error at the lab?" he asked, wanting to find some way, any way, out of this nightmare.

"Not a chance!" Phil replied tersely. "I've already checked that out thoroughly on your behalf." How could he have got it so wrong about Bob Summers? Al thought miserably. The trainer had an impeccable reputation, talked a good game too. Admittedly, he had raced Mille D on guaifenesin, which probably hadn't been administered by a veterinarian. But caffeine? The credibility of the retention barn had been dealt a mortal blow, he realized. It was quite an irony that Bob Summers had been one of its staunchest supporters. Probably, he'd had a way of getting around it. But how? "There's obviously a huge breach in security, here," Phil was saying. "Whoever's been put in charge of your retention barn plainly isn't up to the job." The Head of Security at Iroquois Downs was a bluff, no nonsense type in his late fifties.

"Burrows is no kid," Al admitted. "But he's hard working and conscientious. This will come as a big shock to him."

"A little early retirement never hurt anyone," Phil replied drily. Steve reappeared with a glass of water and a bottle of aspirins. Al tried to take a drink, but his hands were shaking so badly, he quickly gave it up.

"What's the good news?" he asked hoarsely.

"It looks like the government is finally giving the green light on Slot machines at Iroquois Downs," Phil said. Al pondered the implications, glad to take his mind off the thorny question of Bob Summers for a minute.

"What will that mean in practice?" he enquired, watching Steve slip out again.

"The track will be given a low interest loan by the government, to build the casino," Phil revealed. "On top of that, they'll be a great many changes, reorganization of the corporate structure and so forth." As Phil talked, Al's brain slowly clicked into gear. He helped himself to an aspirin and gulped down some water. "I'm assuming you'll be staying on through the transition. They'll need your expertise, old friend," Phil added. Al's hands stopped shaking. The phrase *old friend* had a sour note to it, all of a sudden. He chose his next words with care.

"What about the backstretch?" he asked, trying to sound neutral.

"The backstretch?"

"Yes, what do they intend to do with it?" he asked.

Phil laughed. "No idea," he replied.

Liar! Al thought furiously. Phil had had his eye on Iroquois Downs' backstretch for years. It was a prime piece of real estate. With all his contacts at City Hall, Phil's property development company stood to benefit hugely if the barns were knocked down and replaced by hotels and housing developments.

"There'll still be a racetrack, don't worry, pal." Phil assured him.

"What about the proposal that's on the table right now?" Al asked.

"Which proposal is that?" Phil replied, after a silence which went on a little too long.

"The idea of spot checking and supertesting," Al reminded him.

"Oh that," Phil said. "Well, I couldn't tell you for sure, but I do know the government will want to stay away from anything controversial, at least until the new casino is up and running." Phil must have known this was coming weeks ago, yet he never breathed a word about it! Al realized. All this time, he had been beavering away trying to clean up racing, forgetting that Phil had an entirely different agenda. He should have seen it coming a mile off.

"I'm not sure I'll want to stay on as Director," he told Phil. "I'm a lame duck now. Tainted too, what with the positive test on Millie D."

"Alastair," Phil remonstrated, somewhat feebly, Al thought. "Everyone knows you didn't give that horse anything. Your trainer's on trial here, not you!"

"It happened on my watch," Al said truthfully.

"Even so..."

"I'll have to give it some thought...talk it over with Sofia. I'll let you know in a few days, after the weekend, maybe."

"You have a good one, pal," Phil said heartily, ringing off. He hadn't tried very hard to dissuade him, Al realized. There hadn't been much sympathy in Phil's voice, either. Whatever forces were operating here, they apparently mattered more to Phil than twenty years of friendship. And who was he fooling? He couldn't talk anything over with Sofia. He hadn't had a real conversation with her in months. He heard a discreet knock at the door, followed by a respectful cough. Steve was back.

"Message for you, McTavish. Your wife called while you were on the phone. She said she'd try you again later. The receptionist asked if it's alright for her to leave now." Al nodded, acknowledging Steve's presence with a vague wave in his direction. It was all he could manage. The implications of the news Phil had given him were hitting him with the force of a tidal wave. He, who had always been on the side of the angels, campaigning for clean racing, had now been shamed and disgraced. The reputation of his flagship, his twenty-four-hour retention barn, had been irrevocably damaged. He had been proud of his achievements at Iroquois Downs. Now, he'd never be able to hold his head up there again. Dimly, Al registered the distant honking of horns outside the office window. Traffic was starting to to build and drivers were becoming impatient with the slow flow. It made him realize that soon, he too would have to be going home.

"You okay, sir?" he heard Steve ask. "You don't look like you're feeling too good. D'you need me to call someone?" Al shook his head.

"No. I'm alright," he said firmly, getting up from his chair. "Listen, can these figures keep 'til Monday? I hate to rat out on you like this…"

"That's okay. I'm going to be driving into Toronto tonight," Steve replied. "It'd be a big help if I got away a little early." He followed Al out to the car park, chatting about his plans for the coming weekend. Al wasn't fooled by this attempt at normality. Steve's body language spoke volumes. The man was obviously genuinely concerned about him. He had been wrong about Steve. He had written him off as unimaginative and boring. But he seemed like a decent human being and a perfect second in command. He would never replace Billie. But who could? Al had never given him a chance, never even let him in the door.

"Listen," he said. "If you're free someday next week, let's have lunch together." Steve looked pleased.

Al drove off. He'd been wrong about a lot of things apparently. After two decades of friendship, Phil had turned his back on him at the first hint of trouble. He remembered that Sofia had never liked him. As for Bob Summers, he intended to keep an open mind. His head was buzzing with questions, which urgently required answers. Despite what he had said to Phil, he intended to have the Head of Security at Iroquois Downs on the mat first thing Monday morning. Unfortunately, he would need to find a new trainer too.

It was a bleak homecoming. The light on the hall phone was flashing, but he ignored it. He didn't feel like talking to anyone right now. Even Walter's ecstatic welcome did little to cheer him. There was nothing to eat in the house, only catfood.

"No sense in both of us going hungry," Al mumbled, opening a can of tuna fish. He was about to lay a sheet of newspaper on the kitchen floor, Walter was a messy eater, when a headline caught his eye. Walter, who had been supervising the opening of the can, gently batted him on the arm. "Okay," Al said. "You can do without the tablecloth tonight." He set down the dish on the grimy kitchen floor. "Live it up," he told the cat, giving him the whole can. He couldn't face another tuna fish sandwich himself.

Feeling like a wounded animal, he picked up the paper and sank down on the sofa. The article entitled Saturday Night Racing turned out to be about stock car racing. The *Erinsville Herald* never covered the races at Iroquois Downs, despite the fact that the racetrack was practically next door. When he turned on the TV, hoping to watch Millie D, he found out that the judges had scratched her from the sixth race. He knew rationally he should have expected it, but it still came as a shock. Soon everyone would know the truth. Millie D, her trainer and her owner would be pariahs and there was nothing he, or anyone else, could do about it.

STITCHED UP

"You can't bring that horse in here," a surly security guard told Bob Summers, when he proffered his licence at the entrance to the Race Barn. Bob realized the guy was talking about Millie D. What on earth was going on? "Your mare's been scratched," the guard added. "Mr. Roberts wants to see you, right away."

"What am I supposed to do with her, then?" Bob asked indignantly, looking back at Millie D, whose reaction to the delay seemed to echo his own feeling of astonishment.

"No idea," the guard replied unhelpfully.

"Well, I'm not putting her back in the trailer," Bob declared. Taking the guard's silence as consent, he stuck her in a lasix stall. What the hell is this all about? he wondered, as he pushed open the door to the judge's office. Mr. Roberts, the Race Barn King, wasted no time on niceties.

"Summers! You've had a positive test," he snapped. "Judges want to see you first thing Monday. Now, get out of here and take that mare with you. She can't race again 'til she's clean." Dumbfounded, Bob left.

After he'd dropped Millie D off at Meridian Acres, Bob unhitched his trailer and headed back to Erinsville. But home was the last place he wanted to go right now. He needed time to recover. His wife Connie would be sure to ask him a thousand questions. For now, Bob had no answers. When he reached the highway, he put his foot down hard on the accelerator, anxious to put distance between him and the night's events, his mind anywhere but on the road. Too late, he realized he was in the wrong lane. He was being routed off the highway, to a place known by locals as "Sinsville". When he tried to change lanes, a car came speeding up behind him, its horn blaring. Bob ended up on the hard shoulder. He heard a sickening crunch as he ran over a pile of junk someone had dumped there. It had looked harmless enough but, seconds later, his steering went haywire. He had a flat! There was no avoiding Sinsville now.

The first chance to pull over was at a place with flashing lights and two huge plastic cactuses flanking the entrance. When he got out of his truck to inspect the damage, he saw his front tire had been ripped to shreds. It was the second tire he'd destroyed this week. Two days ago, he'd run over a harrow someone had left lying around at the training centre. He wasn't carrying a spare. This *was* the spare. To Bob's astonishment, he heard his name being called. A slim, peroxide blond, wearing a very short skirt and an artificial flower in her hair, came running up to him, tottering on high heels.

"It is you!" she exclaimed. "I was sure it was!" Bob wracked his brains. He had no idea who this woman was. "Remember me?" she asked brightly. "Pam! Jim Mercer's wife. You bought a horse off us. Let me think now, Millie D. That was the one!" she added, looking pleased with herself.

"Yes, it was," Bob replied unhappily. The mare had got him into the worst kind of trouble, but that wasn't her fault. "I do remember," he added.

"I work at the Hot Tamale now. Me and Jim split up." Pam revealed. There were dark shadows under her eyes, which the heavy makeup couldn't quite conceal.

"I heard about that," Bob replied, trying to sound sympathetic, but wanting to get away and find a place where they sold tires.

"I don't mind, not so much," Pam said cheerfully. "But I miss my little girl. She lives with her dad, see."

"Know anyone who could give me a hand here, Pam?" Bob asked. "I've got a flat tire. No spare either." To his surprise, Pam smiled warmly.

"I'll go find Sid. He'll help," she said. "You go and have a drink at the bar. No worries, eh?" With that, she tottered off. Pam Mercer, he decided, was an ace. Still, she didn't exactly fit his picture of a perfect mother. He couldn't see Mercer as a perfect father, either. His sympathies were with the daughter.

Inside, the barman was pouring cocktails. He tilted his head in Bob's direction midstream.

"Sir?"

"I'll take a coffee," Bob told him.

"We only have Irish coffee," the barman said. "Would that do?"

"Okay," Bob replied. "But make it strong." When he tried the coffee, he quickly put it down. It was loaded with Irish whiskey. Bob had wanted strong coffee, not strong liquor! He took a peek at the tab, tucked under a saucer. Eighteen bucks! He couldn't believe the price! Reluctantly, he took out a twenty-dollar bill and waited for help to arrive, hoping Sid would be worth it.

"Someone here with a flat tire?" A man called out. He was from the Maritimes, Bob realized, recognizing the east coast accent.

"That'd be me," Bob replied. "You must be Sid." Sid acknowledged this with a firm nod of his head as if to say *I'm in charge here, buster, so don't try anything stupid*. Bob heaved a sigh of relief. He was in safe hands.

"Let's go find your car," Sid said, walking towards the exit. He moves quickly for a man of his size, Bob thought irrelevantly. Who was he? Pam's boyfriend? Unlikely! Still, he couldn't be sure. Maybe Sid was the protective type.

Sid took the wheel off in two minutes flat. "I'll take you to Tire Central," he offered. "They'll still be open."

"I hope I'm not wrecking your night," Bob said, as they set off in Sid's car. The wheel was occupying the back seat, its chrome disc glinting in the moonlight.

"I'll tell you what'd wreck my night," Sid confided. "Some drunk coming out of the club at two in the morning and thinking it'd be a bit of fun to wreck up your truck."

"You work at the club then," Bob said. "Security?"

"Affirmative," Sid replied.

"Thanks for helping me out, eh. I've had one hell of a night," Bob said.

"Let's hope it improves," Sid replied reassuringly.

Tire Central wasn't cheap, but they got the job done. On the way back, traffic slowed to a standstill. Sid tapped his fingers on the steering wheel.

"Ten o'clock!" he exclaimed. "Tim'll be wetting himself about now."

"Who's Tim?" Bob enquired.

"The manager," Sid laughed. "Friend of the owner's. Needs to have his hand held at all times."

"What's it like, working there?" Bob asked, partly to take his mind off his problems and thinking that if the judges took away his training licence, he'd have to find some other way of making a living.

"You should've seen the place when I started. Some of the things that went on you wouldn't believe," Sid replied. "We only sell drinks with a lid and a straw nowadays. Makes it harder for a guy to slip something into a girl's drink. You've heard of date rape, right?"

"Brother!" Bob said, shaking his head. "What a world!" How on earth could he have had a bad test? he wondered. He hadn't done anything different than usual. Connie would be frantic with worry by now. The Irish whiskey had taken its toll. It was a warm evening, but he had the chills. He let Sid put the wheel back on.

"Take it slow 'til you get the tires balanced," Sid advised him.

"I will. And thanks, eh."

"Don't send me any flowers!" Sid joked. A girl who looked fifteen dressed up as twenty-five was waiting by the entrance. "Let's see your ID," he heard Sid ask her.

Bob didn't envy Sid his job. He knew he'd have to find work somewhere, but it certainly wouldn't be at the Hot Tamale.

THE HOT SEAT

Al McTavish awoke in the early hours of the morning drenched in sweat. The air conditioning was out. It figures, he thought drowsily, remembering the bombshell Phil had dropped the day before. He threw off the covers and took a long, cold shower. Then he put on his only set of clean clothes: a black tracksuit with lurid yellow stripes that he'd found on the sale rail at Sears. The doorbell rang. By the time he got to the front door, the ringing had turned to banging. Outside, he was surprised to see an army of women wielding mops and brooms congregating on his front porch.

"Mr. McTavish!" exclaimed a heavy set female, who appeared to be the ringleader. "Your wife. . .she have told us to clean her house. Can we come in, please?" Al nodded speechlessly. The cleaning ladies trooped past him, talking away. He had no idea what they were saying, but it sounded like Spanish. "Mr. McTavish!" the heavy set one repeated. "It is very hot in your house! Mucho calor!" The other ladies seemed to agree, nodding their heads emphatically.

"The air con's out," Al confessed.

"*Vamos!* Clean everything. *Todos*!" the squadron leader exclaimed, gladdening Al's heart. The ladies dispersed. "I call my husband now," she added, getting out her cell phone. "He will come in one hour…and he will fix it! I, Maria Rodriguez Garcia, promise that to you."

At 11 a.m., after the women had departed, Al settled down on the living room sofa, nursing a cup of hot coffee and surveyed the scene. The mirrors sparkled, the wood shone and best of all, cool, clean air was blasting out of the vents. After a while, he sat back and fell into a deep sleep.

He awoke abruptly. Something had disturbed him. He heard rustling in the hall. Was there an intruder in the house? he wondered anxiously, still half asleep. At the sound of a footstep, he leapt to his feet.

"Alastair?" a familiar voice called out. "Is that you?" Sofia was standing in the hall, wearing an unfamiliar outfit and an inviting smile. A small suitcase sat on the floor beside her.

"I thought you were a burglar," Al replied sheepishly. "Why didn't you tell me you were coming?"

"There is a message from me, I think," she said, pointing to the phone, which was still flashing red. "Alastair?" But he wasn't really listening. He was gazing at his wife. There was a different expression on her face. He hadn't seen her look that relaxed and happy in months.

"You got a new outfit," he said, but it wasn't just the clothes, though he liked them well enough. "I've missed you, Sofie," he added, called her by the name he hadn't used in decades, not since the children were born.

"Where's Walter?" was her answer.

"Around," Al replied vaguely. A terrible thought had struck him. She had come back to collect Walter and then she would be on her way again. "They cleaned the house," is all he could think of to say. She nodded, seemingly disinterested. Walter came bounding down the stairs.

"How's my boy?" she asked fondly, ruffling up his fur. I wish she'd act like that with me, Al thought, feeling pretty sorry for himself. One hand still on Walter, who was purring loudly, Sofia looked Al up and down. "Whatever are you wearing Alastair?" she asked.

"A tracksuit. What's wrong with it?" Al shrugged. "There's no food in the house, I'm afraid," he added. Sofia didn't reply.

"We should go to Tangoes," she suggested. "It will be a good place for us to talk, yes?" Al's heart sank. Talks always turned into complaint sessions or worse, where Sofia was concerned.

"Great idea," he said heartily. "I'll get the car. Meet you out front." His oldest friend had turned against him. He had been discredited as Director of Iroquois Downs. Now his wife was probably going to leave him. How much worse could it get?

Tangoes was, as usual, a hub of activity. The chatter was a welcome contrast to the somewhat chilly silence that had fallen between the two of them in the car on the way over. Al hadn't had a hot meal in weeks. He ordered an extra large pizza. Sofia chose the house salad.

"You can have some of my pizza," he offered.

"I am not hungry," Sofia replied, unfolding her napkin and eyeing the crowded tables. "You know, Alastair," she added. "During these past few weeks, I have had time to think. Nothing stays the same forever. Do you agree with that?"

"I don't like change," Al replied doggedly. Sofia frowned.

"But you are always wanting to change things!"

"Not in my personal life," he clarified. She nodded. Al tried to read the expression on her face. Was it hopeful or wistful? It was hard to tell.

"You see, Alastair," she began nervously. "I believe it is time to…" she hesitated. "Move along."

Move on, Al amended silently, feeling panicky. Perhaps if he just didn't say anything, this would all go away. The food arrived.

"You are making this very difficult for me," Sofia said reproachfully, after the waitress had left. Al stared down at his food. The red peppers stared back at him. "I think we should sell the house," Sofia pronounced after they had sat through another long silence. She was going to leave him, he realized with chilling certainty. Pictures of the past flitted through his head: games of catch in the backyard with the boys. . . teaching Billie to swim in the pool. . . Sofia calling them all in for supper. "I knew you wouldn't agree," Sofia said coldly. Maybe, he thought, somehow he could persuade her to take a little more time before making such a drastic decision and give him another chance. "You see, Alastair, it is no good for me anymore," Sofia continued. "It is such a very large house...and it is so lonely now...I thought we could..." She fell silent.

"We could what?" Al asked, a tiny bubble of hope forming in his head. "Please tell me what you want." She took a deep breath. She hadn't touched her salad. The waitress breezed up.

"Everything okay here?" she asked.

"Fine! Everything's fine!" Al insisted much too heartily, waving her away impatiently. "Go on," he urged Sofia.

"I would like for us to...find a nice townhouse...in the historic quarter perhaps." He'd got it all wrong! She didn't hate him at all. Winter and summer he'd dutifully cut the grass, swept leaves and snow, vacuumed the pool which no one ever swam in anymore. They'd be much better off without a big house!

"No problem!" he exclaimed happily.

"I have not finished yet, Alastair," Sofia said, sending his spirits plummeting to rock bottom again.

"Go on," he said.

"It does not matter!" she replied looking away.

"It does matter!" he said loudly, banging his fist on the table so hard that all the plates rattled. He noticed a middle aged couple at the next table were staring at him and lowered his voice to a whisper. "It matters very much."

"Calm down, Alastair," Sofia said, taking a forkful of salad.

Al picked up a slice of pizza and waved it at the couple next door as if to say, *See, everything is normal here, no reason to get excited!*

"You are always so busy," Sofia complained. "And I...I have nothing really to do...except..."

"Cleaning?" Al supplied, instantly regretting it. "But what about your evening classes...all the things you made for the house," he added hastily in an effort to make amends.

"Evening classes!" Sofia said contemptuously. "Do you think that is what I want, Alastair?"

"No! Of course not! You qualified as a pharmacist. You're a trained professional. You need something a lot more challenging than that."

"Exactly!" she agreed, a look of determination on her face.

"So, what are you proposing?" he frowned, polishing off the last slice of pizza.

"You were going to share that with me," she said plaintively.

"Oh God!" he exclaimed. "I'll order another one. It was cold anyway."

"You do not change, Alastair," she remarked with an unreadable smile.

"Wait 'til you hear the latest," he stated grimly. "You'll think I've changed, then." To her credit, Sofia looked horror struck.

"Why? What has happened, Alastair?"

He immediately spilled the beans, thankful to get the whole sordid caffeine scandal off his chest. Fresh pizza arrived.

"None of this is your fault," Sofia declared loyally.

"That's hardly the point," he replied testily. Sofia gazed at him steadily as if gauging his fortitude.

"Philip Harman," she said at last. "He is not your friend, I think."

"You're right!" he agreed. Sofia's face cleared.

"You know, the false positives on blood and urine tests. . .it can happen," she said thoughtfully.

"They do?" he exclaimed.

"But I do not believe this is what occurred here," she continued, removing the tiny seed of hope that had sprung up deep inside him. "It is curious!" The restaurant was emptying fast. No wonder, it was nearly four o'clock. Al couldn't believe the time had gone by so quickly. "I am boring you," Sofia said, folding her napkin and pushing away her plate.

"Are you crazy?" Al cried. "You're right! None of this makes any sense."

"Perhaps it is not too late to make a call," Sofia suggested tentatively.

"A call?" Al frowned

"To the laboratory," Sofia explained. "They will close soon I think."

"The lab that did the tests. Okay!" Al said, wracking his brains for the name. He searched through his notebook, where he kept everything important but in no particular order.

"Got it!" he declared triumphantly, a few minutes later. Sofia proffered him her cell phone. To his surprise, someone picked up.

"Beacon Lab. This is Greg."

"I need to speak to one of the technicians, right away," Al said.

"I'm the only one here," the man replied.

"It's about a blood and urine test," Al said, praying he wasn't talking to the cleaner.

"We only test animal samples here, I'm afraid."

"This is Al McTavish, Director of Racing at Iroquois Downs," he cut in quickly before the man could ring off. "We had a horse test positive for caffeine."

"Oh that," the man said. "I heard about that."

"What can you tell me about that?"

"All I know is the levels were off the board. Everyone was talking about it. No one could figure out how you'd get that much caffeine into a horse. Look, it's late. I gotta go. Call back on Monday, okay? We open at nine."

When Al relayed the news to Sofia, her eyebrows shot up.

"That is very curious indeed," she remarked.

"Curious? I'd call it downright suspicious," Al exclaimed.

"You and I...we shall make it our business to find out, yes?" Sofia said, a hint of a smile on her lips. Al nodded. He wasn't sure about Sofia's detective skills, but having her back on his side again was a tremendous comfort.

That evening, with his wife beside him on the sofa, a spot she hadn't occupied in about a year, Al found it easy to convince himself that every cloud had a silver lining

"I've been so worried about you," he confessed, praying that this happy state of affairs wasn't going evaporate into thin air.

"I am sure that you were. But all that worrying, it did not help," she remonstrated gently.

"What did?" he asked eagerly.

"Many things," she replied, reaching into her purse and handing him a little bottle of pills.

"Menoherbs?" he asked hesitantly. The phone rang. Billie was on the line. But, unusually, Sofia didn't want to talk to her for long.

"I am going to get ready for bed," she announced.

"But it's only nine thirty!"

"Good! Then we shall have plenty of time," she said with a smile. "Come on, Alastair. I want you to brush my hair." Hardly daring to believe his luck, Al followed her up the stairs. It looked like another break in the pattern of his life lay ahead. Bring it on! he thought, with a bravado he hadn't felt in years. Events at Iroquois Downs had turned his world upside down. But, on the home front, things were looking up. It suited him just fine!

THE HOT TAMALE

Constable Campbell McClaren soon forgot about Bob Summers. A rash of stag parties at the Hot Tamale made for a weekend filled with incident. He spent Monday, his day off, training for a triathlon to raise money for the town's Children's Hospital. It was Campbell's idea of time well spent.

A week ago, the Undertakers had taken their sinister looking black limousines and relocated to a club down the street, complaining that the Hot Tamale was far too tame these days. It was regrettable. Campbell had been hoping to trace their paymasters, with a little help from Pam. In the end though, that had all come to nothing. The guy who liked Pam had half a dozen tongue piercings, apparently. That had put her right off, she'd said. When the Hot Tamale reopened on Tuesday night, Pam was all charged up. Campbell had known her long enough to read the signs: the toe tapping, the head tossing. He guessed she had some news she was bursting to share, for a small fee, of course.

"What's up?" he asked casually.

"Wouldn't you like to know?" she responded coyly. Campbell retreated. He eventually found an opportunity to slip her a twenty-dollar bill. He loathed all this cloak and dagger stuff but in his line of work, it was unavoidable. Pam glanced back at the tables, anxious not to miss out on any business coming her way.

"That fella you helped out last week," she began conversationally, leaning back on the bar.

"Which one?" he asked. He'd helped out a fair number, most of them too drunk to drive themselves home.

"The one with the flat tire…coming right over, sir!" she called out, rushing off to collect an order.

Five minutes later, she was back.

"Bob Summers is an idiot!" she pronounced with glee. "He got caught using caffeine on a horse!"

"Caffeine?" Campbell frowned. "How'd you find out about it?"

"It was on the CPTA site," Pam replied eagerly. "Everyone's talking about it…you know…in the chat rooms. You wouldn't believe some of the things they're saying." Then her face fell. "Bob didn't even remember me," she said, clearly upset.

"That's because you were all glammed up," he assured her. "He just didn't recognize you, that's all."

"Prob'ly so," she agreed, looking mollified.

Though it had nothing whatsoever to do with his remit at the Hot Tamale, Campbell followed up on the story. He felt personally involved. Bob Summers hadn't struck him as a sleazy character, far from it. It intrigued him that the owner of the horse who'd tested positive to caffeine was the Director of Racing, a Mr. McTavish. As far as he could see from studying past history on the CPTA site, this Al McTavish was a bit of a reformer, leading the charge for clean racing. He was hardly likely, Campbell reasoned, to give his horse to a trainer with a reputation for drugging his horses. Now, it seemed, Bob Summers was facing a year's ban and as a consequence, Al McTavish's effectiveness as a campaigner for drug free racing had been compromised. Something smelled bad here. Exactly what, Campbell couldn't say. He was just following his gut. It rarely let him down.

THE COFFEE SHAKES

Bob Summers, known around the track these days as "the caffeine kid", gave Scotty McCoy quite a jolt when he showed up at his barn, looking like he hadn't bothered to shave or change his clothes in quite a while. The name the guys at Rivers Training centre had slapped on him didn't seem so funny to Scotty all of a sudden. The man was really suffering. Scotty had been looking forward to drinking a carton of hot soup he'd bought from the *Gut Rotter*, the mobile canteen that made the rounds of the local tracks. However, as soon as he clapped eyes on Bob, Scotty handed over his lunch without a second's hesitation. Bob tore off the top and wolfed it down while Scotty busied himself sweeping the barn floor. Eventually, Bob began to talk.

"Those fuckin' sons of bitches won't listen to reason," he said.

"The judges are total bastards," Scotty agreed.

"I told 'em I never gave that mare caffeine. They're going to give me a year's ban, anyhow! How am I supposed to support my family? Connie's so damn mad, I'm afraid she'll go out and kill someone."

"Jesus," Scotty breathed.

"Who on earth would do that to me and why?" Bob pleaded. At this, Scotty stopped his sweeping and rested his broom against a stall door. Instantly, one of the horses picked it up with his teeth and began swinging the broom around wildly.

"Look what you've gone and done!" he told the horse in an accusatory tone. "Brand new broom and it's all chewed up already. Son of a bitch . . . what you gonna do now, Bob?"

"I gotta get myself a job," Bob said. "You know anyone who'll let me work around here? I can't go anywhere near a racetrack."

"Mercer might have something for you," Scotty suggested. "Will quit last week, so they could be looking for someone. I'd give you a job myself but I don't have enough stock. I'll ask around, eh."

"You're a real pal," Bob replied gratefully. "I'll come back in a day or two."

"I been there...where you're at," Scotty said kindly. "You'll be alright, just keep your head down and do your time. Things'll work out...you'll see."

"McTavish is talking about giving his horses to Tony Hall," Bob remarked bitterly.

"Tony's not so bad," Scotty replied without much conviction.

"That colt'll never make it now," Bob said, a look of despair on his gaunt face.

SUPERMAN

"I can't afford to hire no help!" Tony Hall cried when Scotty came around to ask about a job for Bob Summers on Saturday morning. It was raining. After jogging five horses in the wet, Tony Hall felt like a drowned rat, even though he was wearing mud gear. His old rain pants had held up for eight good years, thanks to a stout piece of binder twine that served as a belt. Tony had saved the little black colt for last in case his owner, Reggie Blair, showed up to drive him.

At eleven o'clock, Tony gave it up and went out onto the track. The rain had been falling in a steady drizzle all morning, topping up the pools of water that lay at every low point. After two or three rounds of the track, Tony decided he might as well train Jetson a slow mile. He'd named the horse after a cartoon he'd watched as a kid. What kind of dumb name was Harmony Jet anyhow? It didn't suit him. Jets were supposed to go fast, weren't they? Jetson took forever to go anywhere and it wasn't like he was going to join the New York Jets anytime soon, even though he did spend a lot of his time head butting the big ball Tony had rigged up for him in his stall. The colt balked, as he generally did when Tony turned him to go his mile but eventually Tony got him moving again, albeit at a snail's pace.

Tony hadn't had a winner in months. He lived by himself, didn't have any close friends, but at least he had his own stable. True, his horses hadn't exactly set the world on fire yet. But he had a secret hope, a dream he hadn't told anyone. One day, his name was going to be up in lights. All he needed was one good horse. Then everyone would know he was the greatest trainer ever. Owners would flock to him, drivers would court him, hoping for a chance to drive a winner. In Tony's dream life, the weather was always perfect, plus he had a smart looking truck, a nice place to live and an attractive girlfriend who loved barn work.

Just when he'd decided on a black truck with orange lettering, Jetson veered left, plowed into the infield and tipped Tony out, unceremoniously. Tony lay on the ground feeling dazed for a long moment, then jumped to his feet. He spotted Jetson immediately, standing quietly under a tree. Better catch 'im before he does himself a mischief, he decided. Along the way, the mud sucked off Tony's shoes. He soon understood why the horse was standing so still. Jetson was stuck fast, up to his knees in mud.

When Tony looked around for help, he saw the track was deserted. Feeling God only knew what was squelching between his bare toes, he waded on. He grabbed Jetson's bridle and urged him forward, but the colt put up a fight. In the struggle, the binder twine gave way and Tony and his rain pants parted company. There was no saving them, he decided regretfully, looking down at them laying in the mud around his ankles. As he bid them a fond farewell, the hood of his rain jacket fell over his face. There was a loud rumble of thunder.

"Help!" Tony yelled, panicking. "Someone come and fuckin' help, d'you hear?" After a while, Tony realized there was no sense in yelling. No one would hear him. Rain was coming down in buckets now.

I could drown out here! he thought miserably, one eye on Jetson. No one'd know 'til Monday morning. I could've starved to death by then. He felt around in the pockets of his rain jacket but all he found was a screw eye and a double snap. He thought longingly of the lasagne he'd bought from the Gut Rotter, imagining he'd be back at the barn in twenty minutes.

"I'll probably die of pneumonia and it'll be all your fault," he muttered, eyeing the horse.

A few minutes later, Jetson pricked up his ears. The roar of an engine was followed by the squeal of brakes. Mercer's red truck was sitting there. One of Mercer's grooms was leaning out of the window, a foolish grin on his face.

"Is'at you Tony?" Wha'cha playin' at?"

"Stinker!" Tony screamed, thankful that someone had finally showed, but exasperated that of all people it had to be a moron like Stinker. "Get outa that fuckin' truck and help me outa here, you son of a bitch."

"Sure thing," Stinker replied, jumping down from the truck. After he was freed from the jog cart, Jetson made it out of the mud easily. But to Tony's surprise, Stinker let out a loud guffaw.

"What's so damn funny?" Tony snapped.

"I never knew you was *him*," Stinker replied, giggling like a schoolgirl and pointing at Tony's rear end.

"What the fuck are you blatherin' on about?" The guy was a total retard, Tony thought angrily.

"Superman!" Stinker exclaimed. Tony frowned. An awful thought struck him. He'd been in a tearing hurry that morning and he'd grabbed anything that was halfway clean to wear. "McTavish is lookin' for you," Stinker announced. "Wants to give you a horse or somethin'. Guess he don't know about you being Superman in your spare time, Tone!" The giggles started again. Furtively, Tony glanced across the track. Sure enough, right beside the barn, he could just make out what had to be McTavish's car.

"Oh my gawd," he moaned to himself. His one big chance to get a good owner and he was wearing his Superman boxer shorts, the ones with the big S on the back that he'd scoffed from Scotty's stag party years ago. Plus, he was up to his knees in mud and barefoot, to boot. "Listen," he hissed at Stinker. "I'll give you twenty bucks if you can find me some pants and another twenty if you can keep your fuckin' mouth shut."

"This is gonna cost you," Stinker replied, jumping back into Mercer's truck. Silence fell. What's takin' so long? Tony wondered nervously. Finally, Stinker emerged.

"How 'bout this?" he asked, holding aloft a white sports bag. "This worth anythin', then?"

"I'll take it!" Tony snapped, rifling through the bag and holding Jetson at the same time, no easy task. "Jus' my luck," he cursed, spying a pair of pink sweatpants and a matching pair of trainers with silver hearts on the laces.

"Hey! Them's Evie's things," Stinker exclaimed, trying to snatch them back. "I shouldn't be givin' 'em to you!"

"They're mine now!" Tony replied fiercely, swinging the bag out of Stinker's reach.

"Gimme!" Stinker shouted, making a lunge for it.

"I'll give you a hundred bucks," Tony promised desperately, watching Al McTavish's car roll out onto the racetrack.

"I don't want no hundred bucks," Stinker replied maddeningly. "Gimme fifty and one o' them thingummies they give you when you're in one o' them big races."

"A stakes jacket?" Tony asked in disbelief. Stinker nodded. "Where am I gonna get one of them from?" Tony asked. Stinker shrugged and walked off. "Okay!" Tony gasped, eyeing McTavish's car and squeezing himself into Evie's pink sweatpants. "But you gotta give me your trainers." Stinker didn't hesitate.

"Fine," he said, tossing them over. They were filthy and there were holes in the toes, but at least they weren't pink. "Here comes the big guy now," Stinker added, lashing the jogger to Mercer's truck.

"Get outa here," Tony hissed at him. "Be right with you!" he called out cheerfully, waving at McTavish. He urged Jetson along, until the colt broke into a stumbling trot. McTavish's car did a U-turn and headed back to the barn area. Tony followed, dragging Jetson behind him. But when he got back to the barn, McTavish was nowhere to be seen. Just ain't my lucky day, Tony thought unhappily. Ain't never is!

Stinker was hanging around outside the barn in his socks, which had collected a fair bit of mud along the way.

"Wait there," Tony said. He bathed Jetson, then sneaked into his tack room and barricaded himself in. Pretty soon Stinker was hammering on the door. Tony sure as hell didn't feel like paying him. McTavish was never going to give him a horse now, he decided miserably, his mouth full of cold lasagne.

"Hey Tone!" he heard Stinker yell. "You in there or what?" Tony decided to lay low, hoping that Stinker would get fed up and leave. Losing out on the chance of getting an owner like McTavish was quite a blow. The guy could afford to buy decent horses and he paid his bills. That's what a trainer needed. How could Tony make a name for himself with a good for nothing like Jetson? The stupid animal pulled himself up if Tony took him around the racetrack too many times, but it wasn't like horses could count! His cell phone was ringing. It was Reggie Blair wanting to know how Jetson had trained today.

"He was good," Tony lied, extricating himself from the skin tight sweatpants. Reggie sounded pleased. That's the way, Tony thought, congratulating himself. Feed 'em stories and keep 'em happy. That's what owners wanted. No sense in passing on bad news. It only made for awkwardness.

"I've got 'im in the General Custer. Think he'll be ready by then?"

"Sure to be!" Tony replied emphatically. He stopped short when he noticed Stinker leering at him through the tack room window.

"I knew you was in there, Tone!" Stinker shouted, banging on the glass. He was wobbling from side to side, probably standing on a garbage can, Tony guessed. He watched fascinated as Stinker swayed back and forth, his arms flailing until he lost the battle and disappeared.

"See you next week," Tony told Reggie. He decided to go home. The rain had started again, pouring down like a waterfall. "It's a wonder 'e ain't drowned," Tony sniggered, peering through the downpour at Stinker, who was covered in mud but alive and kicking. Leaving him to fend for himself, he headed out to where he'd parked his truck. To his astonishment, McTavish was there waiting for him. Thanking his lucky stars, Tony sloshed his way through the puddles.

McTavish rolled down his window. "You're Tony Hall, right?" he said. "I've got a couple of horses I'd like you to train for me." It's an ill wind that don't bring nobody no good, Tony thought, as he drove home. Fate had finally given him a leg up. It was the break he'd been waiting for. He'd be a star yet!

After concluding his business with Tony, Al was pulling out of Rivers Training centre when Doctor Winterflood came flying in. Al flagged him down. The rain had declared a temporary truce, but the heavy cloud cover spoke of more rain to come so both men stayed in their vehicles.

"What are you doing here?" Winterflood asked curiously, rolling down his window. Al told him. "So you've hooked up with Tony Hall," the vet remarked with a wry smile.

"Reggie Blair gave him a yearling to train," Al replied defensively. "That's a good enough recommendation for me. What d'you know about caffeine?" he added abruptly, moving onto a subject closer to his heart.

"Apart from the fact that it's a banned substance?" the vet asked, cutting the engine. "I'm sorry you got caught up in that," he added, looking genuinely concerned. "You of all people. It's not fair." He leant out of the truck window, an intent expression on his face. Al waited him out. "I'm not sure I should tell you this," the vet said at last. "But I'm sure you've noticed the number of horses on the lasix list has increased quite dramatically over the last year or two."

"It's the winter racing, isn't it?" Al asked. Winterflood shook his head. Al got a sinking feeling in the pit of his stomach. He wasn't in the mood for yet another sordid story.

"It's all about baking soda," Winterflood revealed. "They allow higher TCO2 scores for a horse on lasix." Al connected the dots. Banning baking soda had resulted in more trainers putting their horse on lasix, which took a heavy toll on a horse's system. The rain had started again…spitting from an iron grey sky. "Lasix is a diuretic," the vet added. "Diuretics mask drugs."

"The road to hell is paved with good intentions, I guess," Al concluded, sadly. Winterflood nodded. He started up the engine, raising his hand in farewell. Al followed him out. He had made up his mind. He was going to resign as Director at Iroquois Downs. He would have to allow a decent interval, of say, a couple of months or so, so that his departure wouldn't be directly linked to the caffeine scandal. But it was time to admit failure and throw in the towel.

A MYSTERY

Evie Mercer was in a thoroughly bad mood. Will had quit; the other grooms had called him a retard once too often. She was never going to see her little champion Harmony Storm again; he'd been bought up by some guy in Alberta. Plus Cat, her secret crush, was ignoring her. She'd tried everything, appearance wise. She'd even done her nails, a first. It hadn't helped. Eventually she had given up. The one bright spot in her life at present was the mysterious disappearance of her pink sweatpants, a gift from her mom. They'd have been great if she was still six years old. Pam just didn't get it! She wasn't a little kid anymore.

However, Harmony Light was due to race in the biggest stake of the year so far, the General Custer at Cree Horse Park. The elimination was in two weeks' time. If he made the final, she'd earn her first stakes jacket. Of all the grooms in the barn that her dad could have picked to go along for the big race, he had chosen her! The only downside was the constant carping from Stinker and the rest. She eventually figured out that they were jealous of her.

That actually felt pretty good.

HARMONY STAMPEDE

The first time Tony took his new colt a training mile, he felt like he had died and gone to heaven. Unfortunately, there was just no way Harmony Stampede was going to make the General Custer. Tony blamed Bob Summers and his snooping ways. Stampede had good manners, a perfect gait and a ton of speed. But Bob Summers, still known in the racing circles as "the caffeine kid", had spoiled it all. He was working as a groom in Mercer's barn, which faced the track at Rivers Training centre. Every time Tony went a mile, there was Bob, watch at the ready, lurking like the proverbial Provincial Police in a speed trap. Bob had cornered Tony weeks ago, on the very first day he'd taken possession of the colt.

"You go too much with him before he's ready, I'll strangle you!" he'd threatened. "You can start at 2:20, but come down three seconds a week, no more, or I'll go straight to McTavish!" It wasn't fair or right. But as Tony feared losing out on McTavish as an owner, he only cheated a little. He went faster on the last sixteenth of a mile than he should have. Otherwise, he kept to the times Bob had set, though he knew Stampede was ready for much, much more. Eventually, Bob disappeared. Rumour had it, he was working off the rest of his year's ban at Keith Lazer's farm. Summer arrived. The warm weather didn't bother Harmony Stampede. Like most studs, he thrived on it. Tony grinned whenever the colt's name came up. His luck had changed at last.

At the beginning of July, Harmony Stampede was still pacing flawlessly, thrilling Al McTavish; he had paid him up to all the major stakes two year old stakes in Ontario. When he was three, Al planned to send him down to the US, too. Every time Tony Hall asked the colt for speed, Stampede eagerly responded. Despite his modest stature, he had a big stride and he never looked like he was going fast. But Tony's watch told a different story. Watching him train was a merciful distraction from the caffeine scandal, which was still very much on Al's mind. In mid July, Stampede made a little skip at the three-quarter pole. He recovered immediately but Al was rigid with anxiety. It was the first mistake he had seen his perfect colt make. Tony brushed his worries aside.

"I'll tighten the hopples up a bit," he said, referring to the light plastic loops all pacers wore to keep them on gait.

The next week, to Al's untutored eye, Stampede appeared to be struggling. Back at the barn, Tony conceded that the colt had changed. That night, Al lay awake, wondering where things had gone wrong. The next week, Tony confessed that his vet hadn't been able to identify a problem.

"Probably colt sore," Tony said glibly.

"Meaning?"

"Oh…little aches and pains…from growing too fast." Al wasn't convinced. The colt was only a couple of inches taller than he had been the previous fall and his eyes, which had always been clear, looked cloudy now. He seemed moody too, not at all like his normal perky self.

"Needs gelding!" Tony declared.

"No way!" was Al's instinctive response. It would be the end of a dream. A great racehorse could retire and have a second career breeding mares. A gelding had no long term future. Al felt responsible for this colt. He had picked him out. He didn't want to let him down. Doing the right thing was an uphill battle with Tony looking over his shoulder all the time. Somehow he needed to take back control. But how? Joey Harris had helped him out once. Maybe he could do so again. "Let's turn him out for thirty days. At Harmony Farm," he ventured. Tony muttered that young stud colts should be kept well away from broodmares, but Al stood his ground. Eventually, Tony agreed.

Al called the only vetinarian he felt he could trust: Dr. Jay Winterflood.

"What's the problem?" Winterflood asked.

"I was hoping you could to tell me," Al replied. They agreed to meet over at Harmony Farm the very next afternoon.

There was a fresh breeze blowing when Al arrived at Harmony Farm. The fields were full of broodmares and foals. The rainy spring had delivered a lush crop of grass and the leaves on the shade trees dotted around the paddock were a brilliant green. But Harmony Stampede wasn't grazing. He was standing with his back to Al, kicking at the fence.

A few minutes later, Winterflood appeared. He drove his pickup truck right up to Stampede's paddock and jumped out. The colt didn't move a muscle. The vet reached in through the open window and held down the horn. The horse galloped off. But he settled into a steady trot, once he understood the sound wasn't going to hurt him.

"Look at the left hind," Winterflood said. He leapt over the fence. "I'll get him to run again. Watch closely!" Al tried to keep an eye on Stampede's hind legs, but the front legs kept getting in his line of vision, confusing him. The vet chased the horse along, moving with an easy grace. "Did you see how uncoordinated he was?" Winterflood asked at length.

"Kinda hard for me to tell," Al admitted.

"Looked like the left hock to me," Winterflood said. "We can't discount EPM." That doesn't sound good, Al thought, remembering Reggie's warning at the yearling sale. "My best guess though is he's got an OCD in that hock," Winterflood concluded dismissing Stampede with a wave of his hand. Al had heard things about bone chips, none of them wonderful. "I'll take an X-ray," the vet offered. "Most times you can operate. Bring him to the clinic on Monday."

"Great!" Al said, gazing at the vet like a drowning man spying a life raft. The two of them, the horse and the man, turned and looked at him, standing motionless, poised for flight. There was a wildness about them both, an untamed quality that had somehow remained intact. Stampede tossed his head, a picture of perfection. But the colt was no longer perfect, Al reminded himself. The disappointment he felt was like a knife in his heart.

As Jay Winterflood drove home, the breeze picked up a notchnotch bending the branches of the trees and sweeping through the wildflowers lining the roadway. He parked his truck, as always, under the big maple tree. One day it would come crashing down but he hoped, not today. The farm house had been built in the old way, nestled among the trees that gave shelter from sun in summer and wind in winter. Down by the pond, the willows were swaying wildly, whipped by the wind. Above them, a kite was flying, its long tail feathers flapping as it soared skywards, before diving back to earth. Hanging onto the strings, his small body tense with concentration was Jay's son, Josh. The sound of Helena's laughter reached Jay sporadically, snatched by the breeze. Suddenly the boy's arms flipped upwards, his feet almost leaving the ground.

"Hey!" Jay yelled. The boy jerked his head around. The string broke and the kite was free, swept by the uplift higher and higher.

"Daddy!" the boy cried, stumbling over to him like a tiny boat on choppy waters, buffeted by the wind. He threw his arms around Jay's legs and clung to him. "Make it come back, Daddy!" his son implored him, looking anguished, tears welling up in his brown eyes so like his own. There was so much Jay wanted to teach him: never to hold anything or anyone captive, to love his brothers and sisters, including the deer people and his cousin the horse, to treat even the coyote tribe with respect. All of them had a right to enjoy their lives in peace and freedom. The boy's lower lip was trembling now, his expression so like his mother's. Helena was staring up at the sky, a look of wonder on her beautiful face.

"Make it come back, Daddy!" the boy cried again, shaking a fist at him.

"The kite has gone on an adventure," he began.

"No!" the boy cried.

"We shall build a new kite together," Jay replied hastily, forgetting all his good intentions in his need to comfort his son. "And this time," The boy's lip had stopped trembling, he observed with relief. "This time the string will not break." He picked up his son and carried him back to the house. Helena did not speak, apparently absorbed in her own thoughts.

"Bath time for you, Josh," she told the boy.

"Don't want one!" the child complained.

"No bath, no story," she replied promptly. "A woman called while you were gone, Jay…" A tiny frown had appeared on her brow. "Something about a paternity suit. They need a DNA sample. What is this about? I don't understand."

"Not now," he warned, looking down at the child. It had happened so long ago. But, he mused, still waters ran deep. He spent the rest of the evening trying not to think about it. There was a horse Cat Ciardi was racing in the seventh that he wanted to watch. He had given the horse Bacox, the latest treatment for EPM. The virus, which attacked a horse's nervous system, was rife south of the border. It was supposedly carried by possums. Wild animals generally got the rap for things like that, he thought unhappily, especially the ones which weren't cuddly or pretty, which possums decidedly weren't. If someone's puppy went missing, the coyotes got the blame. But they were just trying to make a living, the only way they knew. It wasn't like all human beings were blameless vegetarians! Helena hadn't sat down once the entire evening. She could never sit still when she was upset. Tonight he would have to tell her about the paternity suit.

It was time.

CRAWFISH BROWN

It was past midnight. A moonless night. Traffic was speeding along Highway 501, blind to the drama taking place overhead: Crawfish Brown dangling upside down from the Iroquois Downs flyover. The Undertakers had the man's ankles in a firm grip, for now. If they loosened their hold…but Crawfish didn't want to think about that!

"Let's drop 'im," one of the men snarled. Shitface! Crawfish raged silently.

"Nah, we'll have some fun with 'im first. Give 'im a good scare." An' you're a pervert, Crawfish thought savagely.

"Don't kill me! I ain't done nothin'," he whimpered knowing full well it was a whopping lie.

"Ain't done nothin', eh? That's not what we was told. We've got our orders."

"What orders?" Crawfish spluttered.

"Shut the fuck up!" Shitface snapped. "You talk too damn much. You're a fuckin' blackmailer! Plenty of folks'd be glad to see you dead and that's the truth." Crawfish got the message. He didn't feel much like talking anyhow. He'd been hanging upside down for far too long. The roaring in his ears and the drumming in his head was driving him crazy. But he reckoned it was better than being dead.

"So you can keep your mouth shut. Good!" Shitface said. "Here's the deal. You're gonna pick up and leave the province tonight. If we catch so much as a whisper of you, you're toast. Got it?"

"Nah, that's too good for 'im," Pervert replied. "He's a thief and a liar." The menace in his voice made Crawfish's flesh crawl. "Drop 'im, I say!" He let go of Crawfish's ankle, sending him swinging over the precipice, dangling by one leg.

"Oh my gawd, I'm a goner," Crawfish gasped, as the lone hand that held him began to slip. A car horn blared. It would be the last sound he ever heard! he thought, wallowing in self pity. Then someone grabbed his arm and wrenched it backwards. Next thing he knew, he was flying through the air. He landed in a crumpled heap beside the road. A pair of headlights blazed, half blinding him. He heard running feet, then the roar of an engine which quickly faded into the night. He sat up and tried to figure out what had just happened. But none of that mattered now. He was alive!

"Hey, you!" a man's voice called out. Instinctively, Crawfish hunched back down feeling like a whipped dog. "Are you okay?" The voice sounded friendly, Crawfish decided. He dragged himself to his feet and immediately felt strong arms supporting him.

"What the hell was going on here?" the man asked.

"Those fuckin' guys were trying to murder me," Crawfish blubbered. Even in his muddled state, he knew that for certain sure. But he'd got lucky! He'd been saved!

"Can you make it to my car?" the man asked. Crawfish took a step forward. Everything seemed to be working okay, he concluded as he hobbled along. "You're hurt," the man added sympathetically. "You're lucky I came along. I just finished my shift at the tire plant." Crawfish didn't reply. He just crawled gratefully into the passenger seat. "You oughta call the police," the man declared. "Those men looked dangerous. D'you want me to take you to ER?"

"I gotta get som'it first," Crawfish replied. "I gotta go to the racetrack... down the road aways."

"Iroquois Downs, right?" his rescuer said. "My boy works for one of the trainers."

On the way to the track, Crawfish came to a decision. He needed to lay low for a while, until he figured out what to do. His ma and pa's farm would be perfect, but he'd never make it on his bike. He'd have to catch a bus in the morning. If he could cadge a ride to Erinsville from this guy, he could go to the Hot Tamale, where Pam Mercer worked. Maybe she'd let him doss down for the night at her place. Pam wasn't a bad sort. She'd stuck up for him once when Mercer was on the rampage. The sign for Iroquois Downs Raceway came up a lot faster than he expected. But then he was used to travelling everywhere by bike. The guard at the gate just waved the car past when Crawfish showed his groom's licence. Lucky enough, he didn't ask no questions even though it was the middle of the freakin' night. His rescuer drove slowly through the barn area, which was wrapped in shadow and silent now, a far cry from its bustling daytime self.

"Stop here!" Crawfish cried when they reached the grooms' quarters. What times he'd had here, he thought, blinking away a tear. What larks! It'd been his home for this past seven years. But if he didn't leave tonight, Shitface and Pervert would come and finish the job on him for certain sure. He pulled his cash out of the hole in the wall, then he packed up his possessions. A few minutes later, he was on his way to an unknown future.

Two hours later, a taxi deposited an ancient bicycle, a lumpy looking package done up with string, a rolled up blanket and Crawfish himself, clutching a plastic shopping bag to his chest. He'd had to part with the best part of twenty bucks for a ride from ER to the Hot Tamale. He reckoned his life was worth that much. Besides, he couldn't stay at ER forever. Skirting the two giant cactuses, he walked boldly up to the door man, casting an anxious glance behind him at his worldly goods, which lay in a heap on the ground. The doorman didn't act very friendly. It was 3 a.m.

"I come to see Pam," Crawfish announced, ignoring the posh folk pushing past him.

"I can't let you in," the doorman declared. Crawfish popped a plug of tobacco in his mouth. The ice pack they'd slapped on him at ER had worked a treat. He was almost back to his old self.

"Get Pam to come out here then," he said chewing with gusto. "I can't leave my stuff, see." He fished in his pocket and took out his groom's licence. "This'll fetch her," he added, his mouth full of tobacco juice.

"There's no spitting allowed here," the doorman replied sourly.

"I don't see no notice about it," Crawfish complained.

"Listen, d'you want me to help you or not?" the doorman demanded as a woman in a tiny little dress came out of the club. She glared at Crawfish like he was vermin, before lighting up a cigarette.

"Hey," he declared boldly. "I've got as much right to be here as you!"

"You try anything, I'll call the police," the doorman threatened.

"Keep your hair on," Crawfish replied jauntily. "I ain't gonna do nothing, honest." While he waited for the doorman to return, Crawfish tried to figure out who had turned the dogs on him. If I ever find out, I'll fix 'em good! he vowed silently.

A few minutes later, the doorman returned with a big, burly man Crawfish had never seen before.

"This ain't Pam!" he cried indignantly.

"I'll take it from here, Bill," the man replied.

"You ain't her," Crawfish asserted.

"You're welcome to him, Sid," the doorman replied, setting his cap straight. "Here's your ID back…Mister Brown."

"I won't be needin' it anymore," Crawfish muttered, but he stuck it in his back pocket, anyhow. You never know, he thought hopefully.

"Come round the back," Sid told him calmly, helping Crawfish pick up his belongings. Once they were out of the doorman's hearing, though, his tone changed abruptly. "What d'you think you're doing coming round here, looking for Pam Mercer at this time of night?"

"It ain't so late," Crawfish said blithely. "She's got a good coupla hours work yet ain't she?"

"You'd better come in here," Sid replied, unlocking the door of a room at the back. Crawfish hesitated, reluctant to part from his precious set of wheels. "Leave that bicycle outside," Sid exclaimed. "No one's going to steal that old thing!"

"It'll be on your head if she does go missin'," Crawfish cried, leaving his prized possession to take its chances.

"Find yourself a seat," Sid suggested, settling himself down at a big old desk.

"You Pam's boyfriend or som'it?" Crawfish enquired, in an effort to figure out what was going on here.

"No!" Sid replied vehemently. "You still haven't told me why you're here. So tell me...and make it quick. I've got better things to do than babysit you and your old bicycle."

"Babysit?" Crawfish spluttered. "Me? I've been damn near killed tonight by the Undertakers, but I escaped didn't I? I don' need no fuckin' babysitter. Not me. Not Crawfish." Sid grabbed a pen and a notebook.

"Okay. What's your name?" he asked, in a businesslike manner.

"Crawford, Crawford Brown."

"Not Crawfish?"

"That's jus' what they call me, see," he explained. He could see he wasn't getting the better of Sid so easily. An' no bed for the night, neither, he guessed.

"Where d'you live?"

"The racetrack," he replied automatically, before he remembered. "Nowhere...I don't live nowhere no more," he quavered.

"Why'd you come here tonight?"

"Pam an' me, we're friends, I used to work for her old man. Anyways, I don't have nowhere else to go."

"Okay," Sid said, in a kinder tone. "Tell me what happened to you tonight. But don't give me any bullshit. Just stick to the facts."

"Right, boss," Crawfish replied meekly. He proceeded to relate his narrow escape from death, embellishing things a bit and avoiding anything that made him look bad. "When can I see Pam?" he demanded.

"Wait here. I'll be back," Sid told him. Left alone with his thoughts, Crawfish remembered something important that he'd heard whilst hanging upside down. "A lot o' folks'd be glad to see you dead. You're a fuckin' blackmailer...you know too much." So that's why they'd come after him, he thought, feeling outraged. Hadn't he kept his mouth shut, like Jake wanted? Him and that big shot, Vettore? They were running some scam or other, but he'd never breathed a word about it, even though they'd given him peanuts for his silence, while they were getting filthy rich. He'd stashed a little bit of cash in the shoe he wore on his left foot, the one with the built up heel. Lucky for him, Pervert and Shitface hadn't cottoned on. He'd been too clever by half he thought, grinning to himself.

Sid returned without Pam, but carrying two beers.

"Pam's gone home," he said, handing one over. Crawfish downed it in a trice. Getting half killed was thirsty work. The big man hadn't touched his.

"Gimme the other one then," Crawfish said.

"Uh-uh-uh!" Sid replied, picking the glass off the table and holding it aloft. "Have you figured out why you're in trouble with the Undertakers yet?" he asked.

"Why d'you wanna know?" Crawfish asked sullenly, still eyeing the beer.

"I'm interested in stuff like that."

"What's it worf to you?" Crawfish enquired. "You gonna pay?"

"Maybe," Sid shrugged. Crawfish's left eye began twitching uncontrollably, like it always did whenever he got excited.

"I gotta have som'it up front. Cash money, that's what I need. No maybe's. Maybe's ain't worth nothin' to me. An' I'm gonna need a ride to my folks' place after."

"You'll just have to trust me," Sid declared.

"Trust you?" Crawfish replied incredulously, his mouth twisted in pain. What did this guy take him for? An idiot? The silence was deafening. Crawfish broke first. Truth was he had had it in for Vettore ever since the son of a bitch had forced him out of Bernie Vachon's farm. It had been a long hard ride back from there on his bike, in the freezing cold, too. The memory of it still rankled. "What if I tell you about some guys I know...how they move stuff...you know, like coke...and such?"

"Go on," Sid said.

"What if I was to tell you where one of these guys lives, the car wot he's gonna drive, what day he's gonna do it...where he keeps the stuff...the whole fuckin' caboodle. What's it worth, eh?"

"I'll give you five hundred in cash if I like your story. Tonight. That's the best I can do. But that's got to be the end of it," Sid replied. Crawfish couldn't believe his luck.

"Put this in your book," he said, perking up.

After he was done talking, Sid handed over four one hundred dollar bills.

"Wot's this? You said five hundred!"

"I'm deducting a hundred for your taxi."

"Taxi? Wot taxi?" Crawfish demanded, looking around. "I don't see no taxi!"

"The one that's taking you to your folks' place," Sid replied.

"It's fuckin' 4 a.m. I ain't leavin' now! I gotta sleep." With that, Crawfish rolled out his old grey horse blanket and spread it out on the floor. I ain't gonna let this guy push me around no more, he decided fretfully. Using his cap as a makeshift pillow, he lay down, closed his eyes and immediately fell into a deep and dreamless sleep.

Sidney H. Kingshott a.k.a. Constable Campbell McClaren weighed up the pros and cons of acting on Crawfish's tip-off. The idea of the leading driver at Iroquois Downs transporting cocaine across the province sounded pretty unlikely. As for his source, even choirboys told lies on occasion, as he knew to his cost and Crawfish was certainly no choirboy. But if this lowlife curled up on the floor like a dog was telling the truth, Theo Vettore could soon be spilling the beans in order to avoid a spell of jail time. Campbell decided it was worth a shot. Four in the morning wasn't the best time to call his detachment commander. But time was marching on.

In the event, Commander Davies was skeptical. Campbell didn't blame him. He felt the same way himself. While he waited for a callback, he googled Cree Horse Park on his computer, which he kept in a locked drawer away from any light fingered clientele. Cree Horse Park, he discovered, was located in the town of St. Helens about three hundred kilometres west of Erinsville, deep in Mennonite country. The racetrack was the venue for the General Custer stake, the highlight of the season for two year old standard-breds. When he looked up the date of the event, he felt thoroughly vindicated. It was due to take place that very afternoon. The town, he read, put on a huge parade which wound through the streets arriving at the racetrack just before the races began. All that razzmatazz would provide excellent cover for all manner of criminal acts. It made Crawfish's story much more credible.

His cell phone rang, loud and shrill in the quiet of the night. Down on the floor, Crawfish's legs twitched, but the snitch carried on snoring gently.

"You took the basic Encryption 101 course, right?" Commander Davies asked brusquely.

"What if I didn't?" Campbell parried.

"You might have a little trouble getting into the subject's car. I've checked and it's keyless."

"What about backup, sir?" Campbell asked, trying not to sound as uncertain as he felt.

"It's a no go! All other members in the area have been deployed elsewhere." No surprises there, Campbell thought. "Do you want the suspect's details or not?" Davies enquired somewhat irritably.

"I'll take them, yes. Thank you, sir."

"There's an OPP station just down the road from Vettore's place, so you lucked out there," Davies said.

Some luck! Campbell thought rebelliously. He almost wished Crawfish hadn't shown up, or that he'd thrown him out on his ear. But regrets were pointless. He had after all, chosen a career nowhere near the ordinary. Chances had to be taken. Sacrifices had to be made (as per he'd get no sleep tonight). He rose to his feet. Time to get going! He threaded his way through the inebriated couples clinging to each other for support as they swayed together to soporific music on the Hot Tamale dance floor. He was taking a chance blowing his cover, but he didn't hesitate. He spotted Tim, the manager, happily sipping tequila and gazing up at the tiny stage.

"Tim!" he said urgently, pulling him bodily to one side where they wouldn't be overheard. "Remember I told you when I took this job on that I might have to leave without giving you notice?" Tim nodded distractedly, his eye on the singer who was performing a soulful version of *Summer Time*. "That time has come. As of now, you're on your own." Tim's mouth opened but no sound came out. "I'm leaving. Now!" Campbell added, driving the point home.

"You can't do this to me!" Tim protested, coming back to life.

"You'll be fine," Campbell reassured him, turning to go. "Oh. Almost forgot. There's a guy sleeping in your office. Throw him out whenever you feel like it. Here's a hundred dollars for his taxi fare. That's all he's getting. . .don't let him tell you any different." With that, he hurried off before Tim began to howl. He had completed step one: exiting the Hot Tamale. Steps two and three weren't going to be so simple.

Back at his apartment, he moved his bed away from the wall and levered up the floorboards. Underneath, wrapped neatly in brown paper was his RCMP uniform, complete with pistol and handcuffs. It had lain there for the past fifteen months, unwanted and unloved. Now it was required. There was nothing like the sight of a Mountie's red coat, Campbell reflected as he pulled on his uniform. It had an instant effect on doubters, impressing them far more than a badge, even if it did have his picture and serial number on it. Once he was dressed, he grabbed his laptop and dashed down the stairs. Then he jumped into his car, setting a course clear across town.

Vettore's apartment building was west of the town centre, where most decent folks lived. Or was he confusing decent with prosperous? Campbell wondered. Probably so. He'd always thought of himself as a decent human being, yet for the past fifteen months he'd been shacked up in Sinsville. As for Vettore's morals, who knew? Hoping he'd soon find out, he drove through the deserted downtown business district, trying to dredge up what he knew about decrypting a 40-bit code system. Finding the car, he decided, was going to be the easy bit. Sure enough, a black Ferrari was parked right outside Vettore's front door at 38, Park Street. Here goes nothing, he thought, setting up his laptop and beginning the labourious process of hacking into the car's computer. He was close to cracking it when, predictably, the car's protection system kicked in, bringing progress to a halt. The minutes ticked by. A faint light appeared in the eastern sky. Losing his cover of darkness would be a serious setback. For the first time that night, Campbell seriously doubted himself. Who's crazy? Crawfish, or me for believing him? he asked himself. Suddenly, he was in! Seconds later, he was sitting in the driver's seat of Vettore's car. With one touch of a button, the engine purred and he was on his way to the OPP station, where hopefully a forensics expert would be waiting for him.

At the station, the officer in charge snapped to attention when he caught sight of Campbell, resplendent in his scarlet tunic with gold buttons. Campbell quickly stated his business. There was no time to lose. But here, too, officers were thin on the ground.

"Where is everyone?" Campbell frowned.

"St. Helens. Same as you guys," the officer told him. "You're putting on a show out there too, at the Horse Park right?" The Musical Ride, of course!

Campbell realized. "Beer country," the officer was saying dreamily. "Best beer in the province." Curious how there was always money and manpower for the Rides, Campbell thought, trying not to feel too cynical. "We've sent sixteen of our officers to that precision motorbike gismo," the officer added pleasantly. "But don't worry, I've got you Burgess from forensics. He's not on the team this year and he's okay. Anything else you need?"

"How about a sniffer dog?" Campbell suggested. "Oh, and I'll need a ride to pick up my car."

"You got it!"

When Campbell returned, Burgess was hard at work on Vettore's Ferrari. They had taken the car round to the warehouse, which doubled as an inspection facility. Watching him, Campbell realized Burgess was a lot better than okay. Someone thrust a scalding cup of coffee into his hand. He sipped it gratefully, peering up at the sky through the windows in the roof. It was getting brighter by the minute. Soon, Vettore would be awake. Sometime after that, he would discover that his car was missing.

"Is this what you were looking for?" Burgess enquired holding up a large wicker picnic basket.

"Maybe," Campbell replied guardedly.

"Better put these on," Burgess suggested, proffering a pair of plastic gloves. After Campbell had dutifully pulled them on, he opened the basket. At first glance, the contents looked innocent enough: a dozen or so packets of cake mixes, reminiscent of an east coast bake sale. The sight brought on a bout of homesickness for his native PEI.

"Is that it?" Campbell asked. "Nothing else?"

"Not a thing," Burgess replied. Campbell stared at a picture of an apple-cheeked mother serving up cake to three tousle haired children and had bitter thoughts about Crawfish Brown and his unlikely story. People like Crawfish never missed a chance to cash in whatever bankrupt currency they happened to be holding at the time. However, the average driver of a souped up sports car, who raced horses for a living, wasn't usually a cookery buff. Vettore wasn't even married. For a moment, Campbell pictured himself with a wife and kids, but quickly let it go. Marriage wasn't a good fit with his chosen career. "Well, what d'you think?" Burgess asked, an expectant look in his face.

"I'm wondering what a man like Vettore is doing with a trunk full of cake mixes," Campbell replied. "You took samples of all of it, right?" he added, imagining the jokes that would be made at his expense if he had got it all wrong. He picked up a box at random and read the ingredients: white flour, cornstarch, white sugar…unhealthy…just like cocaine.

The car was still in pieces and it was broad daylight. Campbell told Burgess to put it all back together again, but he had made up his mind. The Ferrari wasn't going anywhere.

"Okay, but could you let me have one of the lemon sponges. It's always been my favourite," Burgess said, the smirk on his face a tad too broad for Campbell's liking. But he took the ribbing in good part, even though the man was out of line. "You'll get the results tomorrow, eh," Burgess added, reverting to his professional tone.

"I'll need a match on those prints," Campbell told him.

"Unless this guy's a felon, I'm going to come up empty," Burgess replied.

"He's a race driver," Campbell explained. "He'll have been fingerprinted and police checked when he got his licence." That seemed to do the trick.

"I'll get on it right away," Burgess promised, packing up his things. "You can lose those gloves."

"Hey," Campbell asked. "What happened with the sniffer dogs?"

"Search me," Burgess shrugged.

Campbell poked a finger into one of the cake packets and tasted it. He smiled. He knew exactly what it was now. His RCMP uniform was surplus to requirements. He changed back into civvies, headed for the nearest grocery store and picked up a bunch of cake and cookie mixes. He saved the receipt.

The RCMP would be picking up the tab.

THEO VETTORE

Theo Vettore's first thought of the day was, as always, Billie McTavish. But as always, a few minutes later, he had convinced himself he was better off without her, even though she had the best body by far of any woman he had ever fucked. Ginny, the outrider at Iroquois Downs, was back in his life. It felt right. She worked the same hours and knew all the same people. She didn't take any bullshit either, a quality which he had never fully appreciated until now. Hiding his drug problem from Billie had been child's play. Ginny was on to it in a flash.

"I'm not moving back in 'til you're off whatever it is you're using," she had declared, after he'd told her he and Billie were history. "Go cold turkey, check into rehab, whatever. Just stay away from me 'til you're clean!" He'd done it. He had finally rid himself of his crutch.

Today was Sunday, but it wasn't a rest day for him. He had a plan, one that didn't include Ginny. Surreptitiously, so as not to wake her, he packed his driving colours and his helmet into his sports bag. His destination, Cree Horse Park, was three hundred kilometres away. It was high time he got on the road. Driving inexperienced two year olds in the first major stake of their young lives would be far more of a challenge than cruising home on one of Cat Ciardi's top conditioned horses, but Theo was up for it. Despite his recent drug free status (he relied on those old standbys, nicotine and caffeine, these days) he was on top of his game. What was making him antsy wasn't the races. He had a delivery to make. The package was currently resting in the trunk of his car, well away from Ginny's prying eyes. It was the last time he was going to have to make a drop off. After today, with all the skeletons cleared out of the closet, he would be a free man. He closed the bedroom door softly behind him and went outside.

It was a warm summer morning, not a hint of a breeze. Ideal conditions for two year olds to break track records, hopefully with him at the helm. Car keys at the ready, he blinked, froze and did a double take. There was a gap in the line of parked cars, right where his Ferrari should have been. It was 8:07. The rendezvous was at noon. He was in deep shit. Losing his car and its cargo, especially its cargo, was a disaster. After five minutes of fruitless searching, he called the OPP. The officer on the other end of the line didn't sound surprised when he reported the disappearance of his Ferrari.

"We get a lot of that on a Saturday night," he stated in a disinterested tone. "You'll have to come down to the station." At least Ginny's face hadn't appeared at the window, he thought with relief, glancing up at the blinds on the second floor bedroom, which were still firmly closed. Fortunately, there was an OPP station not too far off, on College Avenue.

Theo set off purposefully down the empty street, striding past a cat sunning itself on a garden wall, the only visible sign of life. It was so quiet, the sound of his footsteps seemed to echo off the pavement as he walked along, his eyes darting here and there, hoping to see the sleek outline of his Ferrari. It didn't happen. There are thousands of vehicles in this town. Why couldn't the bastards have picked on someone else? he thought angrily. But what if the thieves had discovered the package? What if they had cottoned on to the fact it was worth a small fortune on the street? He broke into a cold sweat just thinking about that possibility. He started to run, fighting a rising tide of fear. As he hurried along, his sports bag, weighted with the heavy driving helmet, whipped his thigh. Cursing, he hoisted the bag up onto his shoulders. At the station, the officer on duty, who seemed to have only half his mind on the job, entered the information on his computer painfully slowly.

"You need Room 115," he told Theo at last, pointing down the hall. "Looks like they may have found your car already. Must be your lucky day."

"Great!" Theo replied happily. At the time all he felt was relief. Later, he recalled the quizzical expression on the officer's face. The door to Room 115 was wide open. It was sparsely furnished, containing only a computer, the table it was sitting on and two hard chairs. At the threshold, Theo halted. He had caught sight of the man standing inside. He was wearing an OPP jacket thrown over a white shirt and blue jeans. But Theo grasped immediately that this was no ordinary cop. The look in his eye, the combination of strength and alertness, the calm confidence, call it class, breeding, whatever; every top racehorse had it. Coming across someone of this calibre in this setting was like spotting a champion in a cheap claimer. The man stood out a mile.

Get out! Theo's instincts screamed. Can't do that. It'll seem like I'm guilty...or crazy, his rational mind replied.

"What do you need?" the cop asked, as if noticing him for the first time. Nothing you can give me, Theo thought, making a supreme effort to appear calm.

"They told me at the front desk...er, my car's gone missing," he explained, hovering in the doorway, reluctant to put his foot in the trap.

"C'mon in. Take a seat. Shut the door, will you?" the man suggested in a friendly, no-nonsense fashion. "I'll see if I can help you out. What's your plate number?" Feeling he had no choice, Theo complied. But he left the door ajar. He was getting a really bad feeling now, the way he did in a horse race just before an accident. The feeling escalated when he heard a click and realized his escape route had been closed by an unseen hand. He had always depended on his quick reflexes to get him out of trouble. They were of no use here. "I need to confirm you're the owner of the vehicle," the man said, interrupting Theo's train of thought. "Just check that the details are correct and sign at the bottom of the page, please." Theo did as he was told. With his heightened sense of awareness, the scratch of the pen and the rustle of the paper sounded unnaturally loud. "Theo Vettore," the cop stated, looking across the table at him for confirmation. "What d'you do for a living, Mr. Vettore?"

"I'm a harness horse driver...at Iroquois Downs," Theo replied edgily, shifting in his seat. The stern expression on the cop's face reminded him of the way the judges looked when they were about to hand out a fine. Trouble! His innards clenched. The clock ticking loudly on the wall sounded like a countdown to hell. Stay cool, he told himself. "My car.." he said.

"I'm Constable McClaren," the man cut in. He's from the Maritimes, Theo registered belatedly. The name was a dead giveaway. But he should have realized it from the accent. "Your car wasn't stolen, Mr. Vettore," McClaren stated, deadpan.

"Wasn't stolen?" Theo echoed, trying to sound puzzled, not panicked.

"It's been impounded. We were acting on some information. The RCMP is involved. That's why I'm here. Drugs, Mr. Vettore, in case you were wondering."

"Drugs," Theo repeated, playing dumb. This was the worst kind of news!

McClaren leaned across the table at him. "Anything you'd like to tell me?" he asked meaningfully. Should he try to deny everything? Theo wondered anxiously. It probably wasn't a great idea to flat out lie to this man, he decided. He wasn't dealing with an amateur. He delved into his pants' pocket and pulled out his lighter and a pack of smokes, his mind racing. When he looked up, McClaren was watching him intently.

"So what d'you want to know, exactly?" Theo asked, taking out a cigarette.

"Let's start with why you're carrying five kilos of high quality cocaine disguised as home baking mixes. With your fingerprints all over them,"

McClaren replied, sounding like a prosecuting attorney. He had barely let this sink in before adding, "Enough incriminating evidence to put you behind bars for an extremely long time." Shit! Theo thought, nervously tapping the end of his cigarette on the bare table.

"I need a smoke," he said, flicking his lighter, acutely aware that where he was heading he'd no longer be free to light up whenever he felt like it. He took a long drag on his cigarette and tried to lean back on the hard wooden chair, an impossibility as it turned out. "What do I get out of it, if I do tell you what I know?" he asked. McClaren was searching for something, patting the pockets of his jacket. "If I'm going to prison anyway, why should I tell you anything?" Theo added.

"That all depends," McClaren replied enigmatically. He was holding something. Theo hoped it wasn't a taser.

"On what?"

"You're in no position to negotiate, Mr. Vettore." Hell! Theo thought, staring at the patch of blue sky he could see through the single small window in Room 115. It was a beautiful summer morning out there. A narrow shaft of sunlight cut a swathe through the swirling cloud of smoke from his cigarette. Someone had talked. Someone had turned him in. "I can't give you any guarantees," McClaren added.

"You pick up my car, you trick me into coming here!" Theo snapped. McClaren shrugged.

"Suit yourself," he replied calmly.

Who was it? Jake? Well it hardly mattered now. Think! he urged himself, glancing up at the ceiling. A spider was descending, hanging from a long fragile thread. It echoed his own sticky predicament. He'd have to concoct some sort of story, a half truth that'd maybe get the cop's sympathy, he decided. But how? Perhaps if he went back to the very beginning, to the city of Montreal, where, as a child, he had first heard about the Scorpion. Under pressure, memories of conversations which had taken place literally above his head, came flooding back, along with the whispers and the rumours. With a little editing, he might be able to spin a story that hung together, or so he hoped. His cigarette had burned down to the filter. He looked around vaguely for a place to dump it. McClaren slid a recording device across the table towards him.

"Start talking," he said. Theo tossed the butt over his shoulder.

"We left Montreal when I was still a child," he began quietly. "But I remember hearing stories about the man they called the Scorpion…the many ways he destroyed people's lives. My parents believed we would be safe from him in Ontario. They were wrong. His tentacles stretch all the way from Quebec to B.C. and everywhere in between. All his wealth, every last cent of it has come from exploiting people's weaknesses, their addiction to gambling or drugs."

"Gambling?" McClaren frowned.

"It's where he put his first profits from cocaine," Theo explained. "Into the First Nations' casinos outside Montreal." His brain was working overtime, filling in the gaps of what he knew with inspired guesswork. "The Cree took his money, but they got more than they bargained for, apparently."

"Meaning?" McClaren asked, looking puzzled.

"I don't know! No one told me. I was five years old at the time for God's sakes," he said. To his relief, McClaren appeared satisfied. The tension in the room lessened somewhat.

"Go on."

"You don't ever beat the Scorpion," Theo continued thoughtfully, looking at a spot just over the cop's head. "If you owe him, he sends his own special crew of debt collectors."

"Debt collectors?" Campbell asked sharply.

"People call them the Undertakers," Theo asserted. "I was under a lot of pressure," he said, making a bid for the cop's sympathy. "Driving horses isn't an easy way to make a living. I needed something to steady my nerves. I was snorting it once or twice a week. For the big races." He hesitated. The town was starting to wake up. He could hear the rumble of traffic outside.

"Go on," McClaren said.

"In the end, I owed thirty-five grand…and no way to pay it back. They offered me a deal," he lied, splicing the two ends of the story together. "If I made a dozen or so deliveries, they'd let me off the hook."

"You became a courier," McClaren confirmed.

"I had no choice," Theo said. "They half killed me, left me for dead." The story was sounding plausible, even to him. But he quickly realized McClaren wasn't buying it.

"This Scorpion fellow, does he have a name?" he asked doubtfully.

"Uh uh," Theo replied with a rapid shake of his head. "No one knows that. No one who's alive, anyhow."

"How do I know he's not just a figment of your imagination, then?" McClaren asked, looking skeptical. Theo had guessed it would come to this.

He was between the proverbial rock and a hard place. He had two lousy choices: keep his mouth shut and take the rap, bringing shame on his family and a hefty jail sentence, or talk and spend the rest of his life looking over his shoulder, living in freedom whilst flirting with death. It wasn't a choice he wanted to make.

"I'm pretty sure I know where the Scorpion hangs out," he said, feeling sick to his stomach, thinking about what he was about to do. "But if I tell you." He stopped short. A look of understanding passed between the two men. "If I tell you," Theo repeated. "My life will be in your hands...and if you let me down, I'm a dead man."

"You're going to have to trust me, I'm afraid," McClaren replied wearily. Theo motioned for him to turn off the recorder.

"He's down south...living it up in the Caribbean," he said bitterly. McClaren whistled softly.

"The islands," he exclaimed. "No wonder he's been giving us the slip." Silence fell. McClaren was staring off into the middle distance. Theo was having second thoughts about the whole idea. To his relief, McClaren didn't press him. "Here's the deal," McClaren said, coming out of his reverie. "I'll need a lot more details, names, places, everyone you've ever dealt with in Ontario and, critically, everything you know about the Scorpion's activities down in the islands."

"I have to be in St. Helens at noon to make my delivery," Theo replied firmly. "If I don't show, it'll set off alarm bells." The atmosphere in the room had subtly changed. He knew he had something McClaren wanted...badly enough to bargain with him. However, McClaren wasn't offering any guarantees.

"From this moment on, you'll be followed...for everyone's peace of mind, including mine," McClaren told him. "But, if your story checks out and you don't try to double cross me..."

"Yes?" Theo exclaimed, jumping at the chance of a reprieve.

"First you got to make your delivery as scheduled," McClaren continued gravely. "After that, we'll see."

"I walk out of here, no shit?"

"All I need is your cell number," McClaren replied. Then he got up and opened the door. "Get going," he said.

Half an hour later, Theo was on his way to Mennonite country. It was 9:30 a.m. He reckoned he could still make St. Helens on time if he stepped on the gas. He was banking on the Provincial Police having better things to do on a Sunday morning than patrol an empty road, giving out speeding tickets. Freedom was sweet. He had never really appreciated just how sweet until this moment. The sun shone brighter and the countryside looked more beautiful than he had ever known it. The two year old stakes races beckoned.

McClaren was tailing him, but the blue Escort McClaren was driving was no match for his Ferrari. It bothered him, though, that he had no idea who had given him away. Could it have been Crawfish? he wondered briefly. No way! He would never go to the police, not in a million years. Had Jake been told to dump him? That didn't make any sense either. But what did he care? Laughing out loud, he raced down the highway, flying past a convoy of Beco Banana trucks until there was no more traffic, just open countryside and the straight, empty road until McClaren was a mere dot on the horizon. A hundred kilometres later, the road plunged through a dark forest, forcing him to ease off the gas. But finally he was out in the open again, speeding through a wide, fertile valley, his foot to the floor, past green corn and yellow sunflower fields.

Up ahead, traffic was starting to build again. He began switching lanes, weaving between cars…anxious to get to the rendezvous with time to spare. Glancing in his rear view mirror, he caught sight of a blue Ford Escort. It was McClaren. Theo's exhilaration faded. He'd bought his freedom, but at a terrible price. Betraying the Scorpion to the RCMP had been a huge gamble and he was already regretting it. However, he'd had plenty of experience with danger. It was how he made his living, after all. If he had wanted a soft life, he could have remained on his uncle's farm. No, this was something he'd just have to live with, like the ache in his jaw, an unpleasant reminder of the Scorpion's vindictiveness when crossed. With a blast of his horn, he swerved off the highway and took exit 312, hoping to catch McClaren off guard. A set of stop lights foiled his plan. It gave McClaren a chance to catch up. Accepting the inevitable, Theo set off at a more leisurely pace through mennonite country.

The clock was striking noon as he coasted into the little town of St. Helens. Morning worship was over in the old grey church that towered over the high street. The congregation was pouring out of the building, the women in blue, the men dressed in sober black, their short beards framing their ageless faces. Briefly, Theo envied their innocence, the simplicity of their lives. He parked his Ferrari next to a shop selling souvenirs. Across the street was an expanse of green, shaded by oak trees, a perfect spot for a picnic, but not today, not for him. He got out of his car and stood for a moment, absorbing the sights and sounds of St. Helens: the warm bright air, the joyful ringing of church bells, the cloudless blue sky and the distant hoot of a goods train. It was a world away from his own predicament. Three cars back, the Mountie was watching him. Braving it, Theo opened up his trunk and carried the basket over to the park, dodging the onslaught of buggies bearing the churchgoers home to their farms. If they only knew what was inside his basket, Theo thought ruefully, they'd believe he was the devil himself. The park, the rallying point for the General Custer Parade, was full of people who looked like they had stepped out of a history book. Hopefully, it would provide perfect cover for an unobtrusive handover of the goods. To whom, as yet, he had no idea. That information would, as usual, reach him at the last minute, via a text message.

The beating of a drum, followed swiftly by the ragged chorus of a brass band, signalled the start of the parade, its destination Cree Horse Park, half a kilometre away. Following the brass band was the OPP precision motorbike team, their gold helmets glinting in the sun. Theo tried to melt into a crowd of tourists who had gathered to watch. After the motorbikes, the parade took a dive into the past: the blue coats of the US army, a posse of cowboys, even the feathered headdress of an Indian Chief. The RCMP Musical Rides team came next, their horses prancing past Theo. That's all I need, he thought nervously, Mounties hunting in a pack! Anxiously, he waited, mind and body on high alert. A team of Clydesdales, their feet as big as frying pans, trotted past, followed by a motley crew of homesteaders' wagons. Still nothing.

At the tail end of the procession a two wheeler appeared, powered by a racy black horse, all legs and muscle. Theo recognized the horse immediately. It was Midnight Madness! The driver was tall and gaunt, sporting a long black beard, looking like a modern day Abe Lincoln. His eyes flitted this way and that until they settled on the picnic basket Theo was holding. This was it, Theo realized, getting ready to hand over the goods. To his surprise, "Abe" yanked on the lines, forcing the horse to a halt.

"Get in!" he said gruffly, moving over to give Theo room. Theo didn't waste any time. Abe immediately wheeled around and shot off back through the park, steering a course down a wide avenue shaded with trees, a relief from the baking sun. "We got company," Abe stated grimly, urging Midnight Madness onwards. Theo glanced back. Sure enough, the blue Escort was following them. White foam flew from the horse's muzzle and landed on Theo's face. He brushed it aside, one hand still on the picnic basket. Tennis courts and a bowling green flashed past.

"Gotta shake 'im off!" Abe muttered, heading for a frail looking footbridge that spanned the choppy waters of the river. It was going to be a tight fit, Theo thought anxiously. Before he had time to worry about it, Midnight Madness' hooves were clattering on the wooden bridge, startling a flock of ducks, who took to the air, flying so low that Theo could feel the beat of their wings. Over on the other side of the river, Abe followed a path which led eventually to a baseball field. He drove Midnight Madness across the grass, then turned sharp right onto a road crowded with parked cars. Thankfully, the blue Escort was nowhere to be seen. Theo breathed a sigh of relief. To his surprise, Abe pulled the horse to a stop beside a fancy silver sedan with chrome wheel discs.

"Stash the stuff in the trunk," Abe said, gesturing at Theo's basket. "Then let's get the hell outa here." The trunk, Theo discovered, was unlocked. Despite McClaren, everything had gone like clockwork, he thought. As they flew down the road, he sent the usual text, confirming safe delivery of the goods, without mentioning the small problem they had had along the way.

Mission accomplished!

Constable Campbell McClaren had to drive another five kilometres until he found a bridge over the river suitable for motor vehicles. By the time he drew level with the footbridge, predictably, the two-wheeler had disappeared. Doggedly, he drove slowly on, following the road beside the river, searching for clues that a horse and buggy had passed by. Eventually, he found what he was looking for: a clear set of hoofprints and the imprint of wheels on grass. Congratulating himself on his tracking skills, he followed the road, the sound of children's laughter wafting through his open window. Automatically, he slowed down. An instant later, he slammed on the brakes.

There had been no mistaking the note of terror in that hoarse voice, the desperate, fearful cry. Out of the corner of his eye, Campbell saw someone or something streak across the road, inches in front of him. He leapt out of the car and saw a towheaded toddler standing stock still on the tarmac. As

Campbell bent down and scooped the child up, a tall gangly man appeared at a run, sweat pouring from his brow.

"Is he okay?" he gasped. "Oh my lord," the man exclaimed. "Tommy, you scared me half to death. How can I ever thank you?" he asked, as Campbell handed the boy over.

"I heard you shouting back there," Campbell replied. "That's why I stopped. I guessed some kid had got loose." The father laughed with relief. "You didn't see a horse and buggy go by I suppose?" Campbell added hopefully.

"Sure did," the man replied. "Came flying down the road, just as I was parking my car. One of them dropped off a package. I'm pretty sure it was that one. . .the car that's just pulling out. Yes!" he confirmed, gesturing at a silver sedan.

"Thanks," Campbell replied, jumping back into his car. "You could just have made my day!"

He followed the silver sedan at a safe distance, afraid of alarming the woman at the wheel. He could see two little girls in the back seat, eating an ice cream. The sight of a woman and two innocent children being used as pawns in the drug game enraged him. It wasn't long before the sedan reached its destination: the garage of a modest house in the middle of a trim, suburban street. Campbell waited until he had confirmation by phone that the vehicle hadn't been stolen and that the plates were registered to 42, Elm Avenue. Then he left for the nearest OPP station. How long would it be, he wondered, until his substitution of cocaine, with a street value of a million dollars, for cake mixes, which cost pennies, was discovered?

At that point, for sure, Vettore's life would be in jeopardy.

CREE HORSE PARK

The irrepressible Billie McTavish was standing as close to the racetrack as she could get, hugging the railing, the sweetest spot, in her experience, from which to view the greatest show on earth: the General Custer Stake Parade. And she should know. She'd been coming here every year on Industry Day since she was six: for twenty years in fact, a scary thought which she quickly dismissed, along with her worries about the haggard expression on her father's face these days and the empty place in her heart since the ugly break up with Theo Vettore. It was difficult to put Theo out of her mind on a day like this. His name was on everyone's lips. According to the tipsters, Vettore was a golden boy who simply couldn't lose. She knew better! It still got her mad, just thinking about it.

In her early twenties she had felt she had plenty of time to meet her ideal man. Now, she wasn't so sure. Her exacting criteria just didn't seem likely to exist in a single human being. She didn't care so much about having kids. It was companionship with a true kindred spirit that she craved. But, she told herself firmly, she had much to be thankful for. She was far too busy running Fence Sense, the business she'd started with Jeff Lamare's help, to have any time for self pity! Disappointingly though, Jeff hadn't shown up yet, though he had promised to meet her here.

The parade was in full swing now, the big blue sky soaring above her. Banishing dark thoughts, she gave herself up to the magic. The sun was glinting on the trumpets and horns, on the golden helmets of the motorcycle teams, their engines purring like cats, on the draft horses' harnesses festooned with brass, on Sitting Bull's feathers, on the cowboys' lassoes as they tossed them high in the air...and through it all she heard the boom boom of the big drum. The spectacle never failed to excite her. Like fireworks on Canada Day, she found comfort in the repetition of much loved rituals.

After the parade was over, she returned to the VIP lounge where a crowd of her parents' friends and acquaintances had gathered, including Phil Harman whose company was sponsoring one of the races. Situated on the top floor of the grandstand, the VIP lounge afforded a spectacular view of the finish line. But being the only person under fifty there, Billie felt quite out of place. To her chagrin, she found herself almost envying her parents. They weren't kids anymore, but at least they had each other. Unlike her, they were obviously enjoying the party. She picked up a race program and flipped through it in an effort to distract herself.

"Hey Dad," she exclaimed. "There's a horse called Harmony Light in the big race. Isn't that the one you bid on at the sale last year?" The unhappy expression on Al's face made her wish she had kept her mouth shut. She turned to the first race, an event for two year old pacing fillies. After eliminating several no hopers, and watching the post parade, she decided Southview Sue had the best chance. Vettore was driving her for the first time. Maybe I should become a professional gambler, she thought as she stood in line at the windows. It would fill my evenings and weekends and I'd be sure to have more luck at the races than I've had with relationships to date. She put ten dollars on the filly at 10-1. She was disappointed when Vettore took Southview Sue to the back of the pack. In fact, to Billie's utter frustration, at the half mile point he was still sitting last.

"He's not even trying!" she exclaimed to nobody in particular. Across the room, she noticed Phil Harman talking to someone on the phone. He didn't look happy. Billie ducked her head down and concentrated hard on the state of her nails. At the three quarter pole, she heard Southview Sue's name being called. She got to her feet and cheered as Theo nursed the little filly past tired horses and won the race.

Betting is the answer! Billie thought exultantly. As a driver, Theo had given her a moment of sheer unadulterated pleasure, something that had rarely happened in the eighteen months they'd spent together. By the fourth race, she had turned twenty dollars into two hundred, a small compensation for Jeff Lamare leaving her stranded with a bunch of people approaching retirement age.

At the OPP station in downtown St. Helens, Campbell McClaren took the proffered cup of strong coffee and gratefully gulped it down. A night with no sleep was finally catching up with him. Then he called his commander and did his best to give him an accurate version of events. Commander Davis took the news in his stride, responding not with enthusiasm or praise, but with a reminder that Campbell was to be sure to submit a full written report within the next twenty-four hours. The thought of having to file a report wasn't enticing. Campbell despised paperwork.

"We need to continue tailing Vettore," he replied mutinously, failing to tone down the rebellious streak that reliably surfaced when talking to his superior officer. "He could easily give us the slip and we'll probably need to take him into protective custody."

"Aren't you forgetting something?" Davis asked dourly.

"Sir," Campbell hastened to add. Davis laughed, something he did so rarely it sounded like two rusty chains clanking together. He recovered himself quickly and got back to business.

"What I meant," he explained patiently, "is that we can easily trace him via his cell phone."

"Where is Vettore now?" Campbell enquired.

"At Cree Horse Park," Davis replied.

"In my humble opinion, sir," Campbell said, feeling anything but, "that's not good enough. We need some back up here. He needs to be followed. There's a great deal at stake here...if Vettore slips out of our hands...we've got a lot to lose," he ended lamely. There was silence on the other end of the line.

"I'll see what I can do, Constable," Davis said at last. "I'll keep you informed." He rang off leaving Campbell little choice but to wait by the phone, though his entire body was aching for sleep. After a long cold shower, he had recovered somewhat. A helpful OPP officer had retrieved a set of fresh clothes from his car, so he wasn't a disgrace to the Force but now that the immediate crisis was over, Campbell felt shattered. By the time Davis rang back, Campbell's eyelids were drooping. "The only member available is the sub for the Musical Ride," Davis revealed. "He's fairly inexperienced, but he's all we've got. Unless you feel able to volunteer yourself, Constable."

"I'd probably fall asleep at the wheel," Campbell admitted. "But if Vettore sticks around until the last race, that'll give me a shot at catching up with him. I've got to get some sleep first. Sir," he remembered to add, before putting down the phone. "Loan me a cell for a few hours?" he asked the officer on duty. "I haven't slept since the day before yesterday."

"Can't do that. Cells are for criminals," the man replied firmly. Spotting a fire extinguisher, Campbell ripped it off the wall, setting off the alarm system.

"Criminal damage," Campbell stated, deadpan. "Arrest me. I'm giving myself up." The officer reached over and switched off the alarm.

"Okay," he said in a tone of resignation. "But if we need the cell..."

"Understood..." Campbell replied.

Back at Cree Horse Park, Billie's ability to pick winners was paying off. There were long lines at the windows after the sixth race, but when she finally got to cash in her ticket, she walked away with almost four hundred dollars. Vettore had won again! As she tucked away the last twenty-dollar bill, she spotted Phil Harman watching. She longed to run a mile. But he was her father's oldest friend so despite her misgivings, she stayed put.

"Well, if it isn't Miss Billie McTavish," Phil drawled in a voice that made her flesh creep. Weirdo! she thought, looking around nervously. Where on earth was Jeff? she wondered, retrieving her phone from her bag; there were no new messages. "I see you hit the jackpot, you naughty girl," Phil declared, wagging his finger at her like she was a small child. "Got any more hot tips from Vettore for the rest of us poor suckers?" he added, gesturing at the line of bettors, some of whom were now looking at her curiously. Shocked that he was practically accusing her and Theo of fixing races, Billie felt the blood rush to her cheeks. It would only make things worse if she tried to defend herself, she decided, so she kept her feelings to herself. Phil must be drunk! she realized, as he swayed gently, before regaining his equilibrium with a jerk.

"Oh, I'm sure you don't need any advice from me, Mr. Harman," she said with a show of friendliness she certainly didn't feel.

"That's not what I've been told," Phil replied nastily. "I hear you're a great success, my girl. You have all those farmers wrapped around your little finger. Coast to coast and everywhere in between."

"Oh you mean my fencing business?" she asked, relieved that he'd moved on to a safer subject.

"Of course! What else would I mean?" Phil asked, his body language at odds with his words. He sidled up to her, and spoke so quietly she could barely make out the words. "I'm sure that once you get on that telephone, no one can say *no* to you, young lady." he said.

'I can't believe he's coming on to me,' she thought angrily. 'What a jerk!' The next thing she knew, his hand had grasped her shoulder. Before she could stop him, his lips were brushing against her ear. "I won't tell if you don't, sweetheart," he whispered huskily. Nauseated by the stink of alcohol on his breath, she longed to lash out at him, to humiliate him. But, for her father's sake, she held her tongue. However, she instinctively shrank from his grasp, her rigid body giving out a silent message that spoke volumes. It appeared to have a salutary effect on Phil. His blue eyes snapped back into focus. Dimly, as if through a fog, she heard the announcer calling the post parade for the seventh race. "Act the innocent by all means, Billie McTavish," Phil said calmly. "It's a good ploy and it suits you."

"What are you talking about?" she asked angrily.

"Yes," Phil continued, ignoring her question. "Leaving McTavish Construction when you did. A clever move. I have to congratulate you. Excellent timing, very prudent, to be safely out of your father's company when. . . how shall I put it. . . the shit hits the fan. A vulgar American expression but one which fits the situation perfectly, I fear."

"Just where d'you think you're going with this?" Billie asked, feeling panicky. Was Al's business in trouble? Surely, her father would have told her, but he had stopped confiding in her lately. Ever since the caffeine fiasco, he had clammed right up. She had only found out about Stampede's operation from her mother, of all people.

"Tell me," Phil put in smoothly. "How do you imagine your father made all his money?"

"In construction of course!" she replied hotly.

"By bidding for construction contracts," Phil corrected. "Now Miss McTavish, you're aware of all the arguments your father made for the twenty-four-hour retention barn two years ago, right?" Billie nodded uncertainly. Why the abrupt change of subject? She didn't like the way the conversation was going at all. But she felt powerless to stop it. "Just how difficult do you imagine it would be to create a secure environment at Iroquois Downs?" Phil asked in a hostile tone. He began counting on his fingers. "One retention barn, thirty or forty horses, a security staff of say twenty-five or thirty men?"

"Oh, I really couldn't say," Billie hedged trying to figure out what was coming next. It was like hearing the sound of a rattlesnake but having no idea where the creature was coming from, or where it would strike next.

"Couldn't you? Let me ask you another question. Do you believe the average horse trainer is capable of masterminding an operation akin to breaking into Fort Knox?" The venom in his words did not escape her.

"I shouldn't imagine so," she replied uneasily.

"I thought not. So you'd agree with me that your father's retention barn must have had holes in it the size of Lake Ontario!"

"I didn't say that!"

"Then, how do you explain that your father's own horse tested positive to caffeine after racing from the retention barn? Incredible isn't it?"

"That was Mom's horse and besides, it wasn't Dad's fault!" she replied fiercely.

"Not his fault?" Phil mocked. Billie's mind was racing. Avoiding his gaze, she focused on the bright blue tie, the silk handkerchief folded, just so, into the pocket of his suit. They matched his eyes perfectly. He was always so immaculately dressed. Most people didn't bother, she thought irrelevantly. "I see I have your attention. Good! Next time you want to defend your father, get your facts straight," Phil added.

The bettors had all filed out. The call for the seventh race was coming over the loudspeaker. The time had come to ask the difficult question.

"So," she said hesitantly. "What is it you're saying here?"

"Just how do you imagine Al made his millions?" Phil asked softly, ignoring her question.

"What has that got to do with anything?" Billie exclaimed.

"Ah, the loyal daughter. But you know, Billie, it pays dividends to know your history." She stared at him, uncomprehending. "You see," Phil continued. "Your father's company only began bidding for commercial contracts in the private sector relatively recently…Oh yes," he nodded, acknowledging the look of surprise on Billie's face. "Big…local…government projects, the type they issue municipal bonds for, that's how McTavish Construction got started. Profit margins are, let us say, generous,'" he clarified, emphasizing the word. "Easy money, Miss Billie, like taking candy from a baby, as they say south of the border, provided of course that you have the right connections, if you get my drift. If the press were to get hold of the story, it might even make the front page of the local paper." Billie opened her mouth to speak but Phil silenced her with a look that was pure poison. "Inside information certainly comes in handy," he continued with a sneer. "But then, you'd know all about that…I don't have to explain to you what bid rigging means do I?" Billie stared at him, her eyes blazing.

"That's enough!" she shouted, furious that she had allowed him to go so far, to strike at the very heart of everything her father stood for: honesty, integrity…a sense of honour and justice, a determination to do the right thing. For a long moment, she struggled to find the words to express the fury she felt. People were returning to the windows, like moths to a flame. For them it was payoff time. And for her? "You're supposed to be his friend!" was the best she could come up with in the end.

"You're a smart girl," Phil replied calmly. "You'll figure it out." He walked off, leaving her rooted to the spot. She stood there, watching him disappear into the crowd, fighting back the tears of frustration, thinking of what she could and should have said to him. Then she fled like a wounded animal.

Diving into the washroom, she splashed her burning cheeks with cold water and dragged a comb through her hair. The familiar rituals soothed her. Gradually the tide of anger receded and she was able to think. Despite her total trust, the absolute loyalty she still felt for her father, Phil had sown a painful seed of doubt in her mind. How could she be a hundred per cent certain about what Al would or wouldn't have done years before she was born? He was a businessman, after all, like her friend Jeff; and she knew very well what Jeff was capable of, from personal experience. Setting up an online gambling site, breaking Canadian law, was just one of the whacky ideas that thankfully, she had talked him out of. Al and Phil Harman went way back and if Phil now decided to break that friendship, there might be a good reason for it. The problem was that if Phil carried out his veiled threat, to go to the press with a story of corruption that had taken place in the dim distant past, her father's reputation would be in shreds, whether or not the story was true. In a town like Erinsville, reputation was all. Any hint of corruption and people would take their business elsewhere. The truth was, Phil had always played the role of fixer in the relationship. Her father had made no secret of that fact. Phil's contacts at City Hall had been invaluable, Al's own admission. But why bring it up now? You're a smart girl. You'll figure it out, Phil had told her. She had to find her father!

Al was sitting in the VIP lounge nursing a drink, his eyes closed, his skin an unhealthy muddy grey. But for his tight hold on the glass, Billie would have sworn he was asleep. Sofia was nowhere to be seen.

"I need to talk to you," Billie said urgently. Al opened his eyes.

"It'll have to wait," he replied. "It's been a long day. Your mother's tired. I'm taking her home. She's gone to get the car."

"But. . ." Billie stuttered. As far back as she remembered, her parents had never left before the big race.

"You can come back with us if you want," Al said. "But I asked Phil and he's happy to give you a ride later if you want to stay."

"Phil?" Billie exclaimed, feeling horrified. "I wouldn't get in a car with him if he was the last man on earth!" Al rose to his feet.

"Are you coming or not? Make up your mind, Billie," he said with a swift enigmatic glance in her direction as he headed for the elevator. Billie was torn. Should she gamble, hoping Jeff finally showed, or what? She hesitated. By then, Al had disappeared. She considered running after him, but she couldn't face spending the next three hours in the back seat being blasted with Italian opera. It had been bad enough on the way up. A second later, she regretted her decision.

"Young lady!" she heard a horribly familiar voice call out. "I understand I am to have the pleasure of driving you home!"

"That won't be necessary, Mr. Harman. I already have a ride," she replied coldly. She fled down the stairs and saw, to her relief, Jeff Lamare standing at the bottom, looking up. "So! You finally showed!" she exclaimed.

"Good to see you too," Jeff said drily. "Hey! This isn't like you!" he added. "What's going on?"

"Phil Harman is a total creep," she said through clenched teeth, grabbing Jeff's arm. "Let's get out of here."

"I've only just arrived," Jeff complained. "The traffic was terrible...I was stuck on the highway for two hours. A big truck had rolled over and spilled its load. Bananas all over the place! Couldn't even get a signal on my phone."

"So that's why I didn't hear from you," Billie said, relenting a little.

"Come on, I've booked us a table, right by the finish line," Jeff said.

"Okay," she agreed. "But I want to bet on the General Custer. It's going off in five minutes!"

"Woah!" Jeff exclaimed when she opened her wallet, which was stuffed full of fifty dollar bills. "You've been doing well, I see. Who d'you like in here, Billie? Count me in!" He handed her a $100 bill.

"I need to see the horses first," she replied, forging her way through the crowd.

"There's no time," Jeff protested, following her out.

"I'm going for Harmony Light," she pronounced a couple of minutes later, after seeing the horses post parade. "You want in?"

Jeff nodded. "But you'll never make it," he warned.

In the end, there was plenty of time. When Billie returned with her tickets, a battle of wills had broken out between a small black colt and his driver. Despite whip urging from Moose Rankin and encouragement from the outrider and her pony, Harmony Jet was refusing to line up behind the starting gate.

"Looks like the horse is on strike!" Jeff laughed, as they made their way to the dining room.

"He doesn't belong in the General Custer," Billie replied, consulting her race program. "Look at the odds, he's a hundred to one!"

"Smart little fellow," Jeff commented in an amused tone as they watched Harmony Jet, now divested of his sulky and harness, walking jauntily back to the Race Barn. His trainer, Tony Hall, was staring down at the ground as if hoping it would swallow him up. Moose Rankin, following with the sulky, was taking the disappointment badly, whipping the air and talking to himself.

"Fasten your seat belts, folks. The final of the General Custer for the top two year old colts in Canada is about to start. Seven horses now behind the gate, racing for three hundred and fifty thousand dollars!"

"How much did you bet?" Jeff asked, as he and Billie sat down at their table which, Billie had to concede, afforded them the best view in the house.

"Not telling," she replied, handing Jeff his ticket. She had gambled everything she had won today on Vettore. If he won with Harmony Light, at least she would make money. If he lost…it proved he was a loser. It was win, win. But that was the least of her worries. The interchange with Phil was weighing on her mind. She considered confiding in Jeff but decided against it. She needed to talk to her father first. "Heard from Anya lately?" she asked, as the starting gate sped down the stretch, followed eagerly by seven colts at the peak of fitness.

"Yeah, I was talking to her this morning," Jeff revealed. "That's why I was late setting out."

The race had begun.

"They're off!" the announcer cried. "Harmony Light got away well, but Get Real and Big Brown Bear have beaten him to the punch. He's had to settle for the third spot."

"They're flying!" Billie breathed.

"Twenty-seven seconds to the quarter!" Jeff confirmed as the number flashed up on the teletimer.

"Too fast!" Billie frowned, fearing that her pick was getting the worst of it. However, Harmony Light appeared to be floating effortlessly along on the leader's slipstream, his feet barely touching the ground.

"The half was a lightning fast fifty-six seconds!" the announcer said excitedly. "Vettore is taking Harmony Light to challenge." After an agonizing ten seconds or so, it was obvious that the challenge had failed. Yet Vettore continued to chase the colt along.

"Give him a break!" was Billie's heartfelt comment. If he did no good, at least her father would feel better about missing out on him, she decided, finding consolation in the thought.

"Tough trip," Jeff agreed.

As they rounded the turn for the last time, Harmony Light finally made it to the lead.

"They're coming into the stretch! This is it folks. Looks like a three horse race! Harmony Light, Get Real and Big Brown Bear. They're slugging it out!"

"Think he's got anything left in the tank?" Jeff wondered anxiously. Billie didn't reply. She was watching Harmony Light intently. Just how long, she asked herself, could a two year old colt run on empty? She eyeballed the two horses chasing him, willing them to hit the wall, to run out of gas. She could barely hear the announcer over the noise of the crowd.

"Harmony Light is still a neck in front, only fifty yards to the wire!" the race caller yelled. Jeff's eyes were flicking back and forth, between the three colts. Billie's hands were clasped in prayer, her worries about her father forgotten for the moment, all her thoughts on winning. It's only a horse race, she reminded herself.

"Here comes Big Brown Bear!" the announcer suddenly shouted. "Has he left it too late?" His voice was drowned out by a roar from the crowd as the three horses flashed past the finish line in unison. There was a taut silence. The crowd held its breath. When the numbers went up on the tote board, to Billie's astonishment, Harmony Light had held on. She had won her bet. Down in the winner's circle, Jim Mercer and Theo Vettore were grinning at each other. The owner was slapping Theo on the back, his stomach protruding like a pregnant woman's.

"There's Evie!" Billie exclaimed, watching a girl jumping up and down, her blond pony tail flying. The crowd's reaction to the win was more muted. Harmony Light had been the third choice.

"Here come the breeders, Joey and Val Harris," the announcer declared. "The colt is a credit to Harmony Farm, a very courageous winner..." Theo was looking the happiest Billie had ever seen him. For once he wasn't posing, just enjoying the moment. If only, she thought wistfully, he could have been more like that with me.

"What a horse!" Theo exclaimed when his turn came to be interviewed. "I can't believe he kept going for me like that!"

"Typical Theo!" Billie remarked. "Grabbing all the attention! Giving himself all the credit!"

"Vettore's a total scumbag," Jeff agreed, giving her a comforting thump on the back.

"No," she said. "It's not true. He could be…" But she had to leave whatever Theo could be unsaid, overwhelmed by emotion.

In the Race Barn, Evie's elation at Harmony Light's win swiftly evaporated. Six entire minutes after the race, the colt was still blowing hard, his body drenched in sweat, his ribs heaving. After the track vet diagnosed heat exhaustion, Mercer took charge. Soon after, a line of horsemen stretched from Harmony Light to the nearest tap and brimming full water buckets were being passed from hand to hand, like fire fighters putting out a blaze. The horse, doused repeatedly with cold water, soon looked like a drowned rat. Eventually, his core temperature went back to normal. The crowd of horsemen dispersed. Though thankful for her father's prompt intervention, Evie had no illusions. He was merely protecting a valuable commodity, one which would bring new owners flocking to the stable in the fall. The thought of it sickened her. But at least Harmony Light was safe, for now.

While she and Jeff were waiting in line to cash in their win tickets, Billie heard an announcement over the loudspeaker.

"Attention folks! In the eighth race, Pete Summers will be taking over the driving on number three, Chevy Chase."

"Vettore was down to drive Chevy Chase," Jeff said. "What's going on?"

"Search me," Billie shrugged. The prima donna was letting people down as usual, she thought contemptuously. It looked like his drug habit wasn't just affecting his personal life now; it was impacting on him professionally, too. Not that I give a damn, she thought, suppressing the small, totally uncalled for sob that surfaced occasionally, taking her completely by surprise.

Two minutes later, she had recovered. There were far better men in this world than Theo Vettore, she knew.

The sun was still shining brightly as Theo Vettore exited the Race Barn and walked quickly into the horsemen's parking lot. There was no sign of McClaren, or anyone else for that matter. He heard someone running up behind him and whirled around. But it was only the Moose begging a smoke off him. A small part of Theo felt insulted. Was he really that unimportant? Did nobody give a damn? The Mounties must be playing cat and mouse with him, he decided. He had no doubt that the bastards would haul him in for questioning soon enough. He was hoping by skipping the last few races he would elude them for a little longer. He dived into his Ferrari and started up the engine. Late afternoon and not a hint of nightfall in the air. But it was coming, just like his arrest. He didn't trust McClaren, didn't believe in his promise of immunity. The Mounties would haul him in and charge him and he'd get five, maybe ten years for trafficking in cocaine. When he eventually got out, he'd be a marked man. As for his career, that would be down the toilet.

He pulled out of Cree Horse Park, watching out for a tail. There was none! It made no sense. What the hell! He might as well get the most out of his last taste of freedom, he thought. When he got to the highway, he stepped down hard on the gas pedal. The engine roared like a beast. Soon, he and his Ferrari were destroying the speed limit, making a mockery of rules and regulations. Dicing with death always gave him a rush. Today was no exception. Somewhere up ahead, he knew the highway would fork in two, divided by a bottomless ravine. It came up surprisingly soon. But at 150 klicks an hour, that made sense. He waited until the last possible moment to switch lanes, right up to the point where the road ended, teetering on the edge of a precipice. It was all good fun! The gas light lit up a lot quicker than he'd expected. Must be the speed he was going, he concluded carelessly, not a thought in his head of foul play. His cell phone rang. He ignored it. There was no one he wanted to hear from right now. Spotting a service exit, he jammed on the brakes and pulled off the highway, coasting into the gas station with a defiant expression on his face. He had succeeded in adding dangerous driving to his crimes, he realized, with grim satisfaction. Well, they could take away his licence, even his freedom, but they weren't going to take away today's victory in the General Custer!

Constable Campbell McClaren woke up with a start. He was in a police cell and a man was rattling a heavy set of keys in his face. He blinked. He could tell by the change in the light that he'd been asleep for a long time. Too long!

"We need the cell, eh," the man with the keys explained apologetically. Campbell jumped up and consulted his watch. He was getting an uncomfortable feeling in the pit of his stomach. He prayed that, on this occasion, his gut instinct was wrong. Leaving a young, inexperienced officer to follow Vettore's Ferrari was asking for trouble.

THE GAS STATION

Winning the big race had felt good, better than good, Theo decided. Harmony Light was a plucky little colt. He didn't have his dam's quick speed but he had her courage in spades. Theo cut off the engine and felt his mood of recklessness begin to fade, like the high after a win. Another hour and he'd be home safe. Somehow, he'd come out of this okay, he told himself. He'd get a lawyer. But you can't unsay what you've said and on the record too, a nagging voice in his head reminded him. Dismissing this inconvenient truth, he pulled out the gas gun and plunged it into the tank, distracting himself by watching a tall redhead wearing a pair of miniscule white shorts. She was making quite a business of unscrewing the cap and fumbling with the nozzle, stamping her foot when she broke one of her long red fingernails. Then the gas gun kicked back hard into his hand, interrupting his reverie. He decided to leave the redhead to her fate. Being a nice guy and helping her out wasn't on the agenda today, he concluded somewhat reluctantly, the sour taste of gasoline in his throat.

Inside, he grabbed a sandwich and a drink and waited in line, passing the time by speculating on how bad prison food could be and whether they'd let him watch the races on TV. Then he headed back outside to a sky that was still bright, despite the late hour. He didn't feel in the least bit hungry, he was too keyed up. But he knew Ginny wouldn't be cooking supper for him. She cared more about her horse's food than what he ate, he concluded moodily. Back in his car, he switched on the radio and headed for the slip lane, catching the end of a mournful French ballad that resonated with his predicament. He was so absorbed by it that he almost rammed into a tow truck which was barring the way ahead. He braked hard, glancing automatically in the rear view mirror and nearly jumped out of his skin! A pair of icy, menacing eyes were staring back at him. He felt the cold barrel of a gun jam into the back of his neck. A second man wrenched open the door and jumped into the passenger seat. Theo heard a tell tale click as the interior locks shut tight. Even with his quick reflexes, there had been no time to react. He was trapped. A wild drumming broke out on the radio!

"Shut that fucking thing off," a voice barked from the back seat, moving the gun higher so it was resting on Theo's skull. Theo froze. He knew that voice!

"Get rid of his cell phone, Ernie," the nightmare in the back directed. Ernie tossed it out of the window. Next, Theo's hands were pushed roughly together, secured with rope. It dug into his wrists. He heard the whine of a winch. His head tipped back and the car's front end lifted off the ground. Seconds later, he and his faithful Ferrari were the tow truck's prisoners. Someone must have told the Scorpion about the brush with the police, he realized, furious with himself. He'd been so careless, made it so easy for them, a huge error of judgment on his part. The redhead, he realized, cursing his stupidity, had been a decoy. And, like an asshole, he'd fallen for it. He hadn't even thought about locking his car when he went to pay for gas. How foolhardy that seemed now!

"Message from the boss," the horror in the back seat announced in a tone that sent shivers down Theo's spine. "You are going to learn a lesson." The tow truck took off, heading west on the highway, back towards St. Helens. Where were they taking him? Theo wondered vainly. "But this is not a lesson you personally are going to benefit from very much, Mister Vettore!" He dug his gun harder into Theo's skull. "Toss me that soda, Ernie."

"Yeah, 'cos you'll be a dead duck!" Ernie pointed out helpfully, handing over the can and ripping open the sandwich that Theo had bought only minutes earlier. A silent scream of denial rang through Theo's head. Watching Ernie scavenging his food brought it home to him like nothing else could. They weren't bluffing. Not this time. Random pictures of the past popped into his head as his brain shuffled through his memory bank, frantically searching for the wild card that could save him. He was five years old, sitting with his uncle on the jog cart, taking the lines for the very first time. He was ten...a big black mare was running away with him, spooked by a bonfire. He was in church taking his first communion...he was flying through the air, catapulted from the sulky...he was lying on the tarmac beaten to a pulp... Billie McTavish was slamming the door in his face...he was running along a rooftop in the moonlight as free as a bird...it seemed to go on forever. With a huge effort he turned away from this comforting fantasy and forced himself to return to the nightmare present. Time appeared to have slowed down. His vision had changed. He could see every last detail on the cars as they rolled past him at a snail's pace.

He flinched violently as something sharp pierced his neck: a needle big enough for a horse by the feel of it.

"That'll teach 'im not to fuck with Fontainbleu!" someone laughed, the voice sounding unreal, like it was echoing off the walls of a deep well. As Theo lost consciousness, he heard the whine of an ambulance. But he knew it wasn't coming for him. He'd been handed a one way ticket to purgatory.

There was no going back.

Ever.

By the time Campbell reached the horsemen's parking lot, there was no sign of Vettore or his black Ferrari. The horses for the ninth race were out on the track. Anxiously, Campbell called HQ. It turned out that the sub for the Musical Ride had never set out. His horse had a bad case of colic and he hadn't dared leave him. Vettore's cell phone was heading east on Highway 501 at 150 kph. Hoping for the best, Campbell followed. Cars were thin on the ground, so he made good time. Unfortunately, the lack of traffic had given Vettore an even greater advantage, speedwise.

An hour later, Campbell stopped and checked with HQ again. The cell phone had been traced at a service station, only 10 km back. Feeling more cheerful, Campbell proceeded east. A rapid check of the service station where Vettore should have been, revealed nothing. There was no sign of him or his Ferrari. Campbell called HQ again. The cell phone hadn't moved. He eventually came across Vettore's phone, buried in the dirt beside the exit. When a cooperative manager let him study the CCTV records, Campbell pieced together what had happened. A fuzzy picture of a man's back as he dived into Vettore's car wasn't a lot of help, though. The trail had gone cold. As he had feared, they had lost their star witness.

Vettore had disappeared.

IROQUOIS DOWNS, 8 P.M.

The first race was over at Iroquois Downs but there was no sign of Theo Vettore. They had hosed down the floor of the Race Barn. Ginny the outrider was standing beside her track pony, staring blank eyed at the puddles, watching the ceiling fans reflected in them whirling around and around like the questions in her head. Try as she might, she couldn't for the life of her remember a time when the son of a bitch Vettore had failed to show up to drive a horse. He'd let her down often enough of course: whenever she'd had a trip to the movies planned, or they needed to go grocery shopping. But he'd always found a way to make the races, even when he was running a hundred and three fever. Until tonight.

She had checked her cell phone over and over, shaken it and even put more money on it. Nothing. Not a peep. Everyone was talking about Theo's big win at Cree Horse Park. That only made her feel worse. He hadn't even bothered to call her about it. Must be some girl, she decided angrily. He'd been acting kind of weird lately. It reminded her of the time he had started up with Billie McTavish. He'd been acting preoccupied then too. Damn him! She had wasted far too much time on Mister Smooth talking, Lying, Cheating Vettore!

Taking a deep breath, she mounted her horse.

"Where the hell's Vettore? I'm gonna kill that SOB!" she heard Mercer curse as she rode out onto the track. She dug her heels in. The horse broke into a canter. Maybe she'd give that security guard a chance, she thought. He'd been pestering her to go out with him all summer and he seemed like a nice guy. Dull, but nice. She had put up with Vettore's addictions, his on the side girlfriends and his crazy moods. But tonight, he had crossed a line. After the second race, Ginny noticed Lara Vachon making the rounds, asking drivers, trainers and grooms alike the same question.

"Have you seen Theo?"

"What's the matter, Lara? Your cousin let you down?" Andy Price asked. "Plenty of other drivers. . . any one of them'll be glad to drive for you."

"I do not care if Theo does not drive my horse!" Lara exclaimed in an exasperated tone. "I am worried that something has happened…something bad."

"He's on four of my horses tonight," Cat said. "But if he doesn't show," he shrugged. "Nothing I can do about it."

"So you are not concerned, no?" Lara frowned. Cat shook his head.

"Nuh uh."

"Well, I am," Lara replied. "The police, they need to hear about this, I think."

"You sure Theo would want you to do that?"

"Yeah, maybe he's just having a beer some place," Cat said. "Takin' it easy…celebrating…he's made plenty of money today, winning the General Custer."

The seeds of doubt had been sown. "I pray that you are correct," Lara replied earnestly.

"First Crawfish goes missing…now Vettore," Andy Price muttered, as Lara walked away. "What d'you reckon, eh? Should I tell someone?"

"He'll show up," Cat reassured him. "Soon as he sobers up and runs out of cash."

"I don't know," Andy replied unhappily. "Crawfish has never done anything like this before…honest to God."

"There's always a first time," Cat said reasonably. "Look at Vettore…he's not here either. Hey," he added brightening up. "Maybe the two of them are out on a date."

Andy guffawed. "Who you gonna put down on your horses if Vettore doesn't show?" he asked.

"No problemo," Cat replied coolly. "I'll get Beazer or, better yet, the Moose. They've both been falling all over themselves for a chance to drive my horses."

The horses came in from the track drenched in sweat. The humidity was killing everyone. It was just another summer race night at Iroquois Downs. One of the principal players was missing, but no one was too worried yet.

A phone was ringing shrilly through the house, echoing off the high ceilings in the vast empty rooms. The man who answered it was in a hurry, it seemed.

"Yes!" he said impatiently. His expression changed from irritation to concentration. He listened intently, his eyes roaming over the paintings in their heavy, gilt frames, coming to rest at last on his own expensively clad feet. "Silence him!" he said abruptly, his voice harsh.

He poured himself a glass of wine, sat back on the sofa and tried to relax. But peace was not to be found so easily. The voices in his head

chattered until he could ignore them no longer. Nodding to himself, he picked up the phone.

"Dismantle the entire cocaine operation in Ontario," he said quietly. "Immediately." There was a shocked silence on the other end of the line. Then the words came, so many of them, each more futile than the last. "Don't waste my time!" he snapped. "You heard me. This call is over." He put down the phone. "Be still!" he told the restless voices in his head. "I am and always will be the Master of my Domain!"

Outside, stars twinkled in the dark.

2 a.m.

The black Ferrari left the highway, crashing through the safety barrier as effortlessly as a runner breaking the tape at the finish line. It sailed in a graceful arc through the moonless night sky, its headlights illuminating the rocky gorge beneath. It defied gravity for a fleeting moment, suspended in mid air before plunging into the abyss which yawned menacingly like the jaws of some great beast, readying itself to devour its prey. The noise of the explosion reverberated along the highway, startling a lone long distance truck driver two kilometres away. But no one was there to witness the Ferrari's spectacular destruction, to watch the flames burst into life or hear the dull roar as the car burned, fed by a full tank of gas, as brightly as a dying star. Eventually, the last echo faded. The night was silent and dark once more. Only the gap in the barrier gave any indication that the charred remains of a black Ferrari lay in pieces far, far below.

Harmony Light woke up with a start. He had been dreaming. A quick glance around the stall reassured him. He was back on solid ground. There was no need to splay his legs out, fighting to stay upright as the floor swayed from side to side. But though he was back in his own barn, nothing was the same. This was not his own stall! His neighbours had always greeted him enthusiastically whenever he returned home. These new ones had kicked the walls when he arrived and were now pointedly ignoring him. And where was the hole in the corner that the mouse popped in and out of? Where had that loose board gone? He had spent many happy hours playing with it. He felt its loss keenly. He picked up his head and whickered, listening intently to the answering calls ringing out in the dark barn. But his old playmate, the grey colt, was still missing. One minute Storm had been there, the next he was gone. There had been no chance to call him back …no chance to say goodbye. For the first time in his young life, Harmony Light felt truly alone. There was only this: the emptiness he felt…his heavy heart. Eventually, exhaustion pulled him earthwards.

But sleep did not come.

Crawfish Brown was restless. A tap was digging into his ear. Sleeping in a bath was okay but as Pam Mercer had refused to give him any covers, he'd had to make do with a couple of towels. Using the bath mat as a pillow hadn't really worked out either. But the good thing was he was still alive! He'd outwitted the monsters who had tried to throw him off the bridge. Quietly, he unlocked the bathroom door and crept towards the kitchen, figuring he'd get himself something to eat in peace, before Pam woke up and chased him out of the house. He was rifling through Pam's refrigerator when, to his dismay, he heard a noise coming from the direction of the front door. He froze. There it was again: the sound of a key turning in the lock! It could only mean one thing. Shitface and Pervert had come after him! They were gonna finish him off for good this time! Panicking, he grabbed a sharp knife, ran back to the bathroom and locked himself in. He'd climb out the window, that's what he'd do! Give 'em the slip again! But some bastard had painted the window shut. He just couldn't shift it. The sound of footsteps was getting louder and louder. It sent him into frenzy. He circled the room frantically. There was nowhere to hide! He banged at the window. But it was no use! He'd been caught with only a knife to defend himself, like a rat in a trap!

Billie McTavish awoke to a glorious, clear morning. Overnight, the humidity index had dropped precipitously. The painful conversation with Phil Harman felt like a bad dream. She immediately put it out of her mind. Today was a holiday in Ontario, Industry Day. She had arranged to meet up with Jeff Lamare later that morning. They were planning to take a walk along the Speed River, followed by a long, lazy lunch at one of the riverside cafes. In the meantime, Billie intended to make the most of the day by taking an early morning bike ride around the neighbourhood, ending up at 210, Laurel Drive for breakfast with her parents. The weather was much too good to spend any time indoors.

Campbell was awake long before the phone rang with the news about Vettore. He'd been half expecting it. Today should have been a red letter day, a day to celebrate a major breakthrough in the cocaine trafficking racket in Ontario. True, he'd have owed it all to luck and a character who went by the name of Crawfish Brown. But that's the way things went in his line of work. That was the reason he befriended the lowlifes, the no hopers caught up in the underworld. That and the fact he felt sorry for them. Grateful too. People at the high end of society, pillars of the so called establishment, were never any help that way. To be fair, their taxes paid his salary, he acknowledged as he ran his fingers through his thatch of brown hair in place of a comb, which he had failed to find in the cramped apartment of his undercover persona, Sidney H. Kingshott. At least that sham was now over.

Of course, he reflected, guys like Crawfish didn't generally turn informant for any noble reason. Far from it! It was usually because of a grudge, or some other unsavoury motive, a desire to see a particular enemy of theirs behind bars. What grudge did Crawfish Brown have against Vettore? He had absolutely no idea. Not that it really mattered now. He had a job to do and despite his reluctance, it was best to get on with it. As this was to be an official visit, he donned his uniform before setting out.

As today was a holiday, he was hoping to catch Al McTavish at home. Sure enough, when he rang the bell at 210, Laurel Drive, McTavish came to the door. Campbell took in the decent clothes hanging loose on McTavish's bony frame and the general aura of anxiety, before zeroing in on his receding hairline and his tense facial muscles. Plainly, the man had quite enough on his plate already without Campbell adding to it. In an ideal world, he wouldn't have been here at all. In the circumstances, the RCMP would have to shoulder most of the blame for Vettore's disappearance. But the truth was, Vettore had engineered his own demise by taking one too many chances, not having enough sense to know when to play it safe.

"Mr. McTavish, could I have a word with you, sir?" Campbell asked politely.

"What the devil's going on?" McTavish exclaimed, gesturing at Campbell's full dress uniform, gold buttons and all. "Last time one of you fellows crept up on me like this, the backstretch was on fire!"

"That would have been the OPP, sir," Campbell pointed out respectfully. "I'm not bringing you news of a fire, sir. You can rest easy on that."

"You'd better come in," McTavish replied wearily, the slump of his shoulders indicating that he was readying himself to receive yet more bad news. Added to all the rest, his body language seemed to say, it hardly mattered. He led the way to a small room dominated by a heavy, old fashioned desk. "Take a seat," McTavish said shortly, pointing to the only other chair in the room.

"I'll come straight to the point, sir," Campbell stated. "One of the drivers at Iroquois Downs, where you are the Director, I understand, has disappeared." McTavish frowned deeply. "His car has been found in pieces at the bottom of a crevasse." McTavish's eyebrows shot up. "They haven't found the body yet, but the reason I'm here is that Mr. Vettore stands accused of trafficking in cocaine."

"Cocaine!" McTavish groaned, cradling his head in his hands. "You think he went on the run?" he asked in a horrified tone, staring at Campbell. Campbell shook his head.

"That is pure speculation at this point," he replied. A spasm of pain swept over McTavish's long face. "Are you alright?" Campbell asked, feeling alarmed.

"Billie will be pretty cut up about this," McTavish replied grimly. "She and Theo…" He broke off and clutched at his chest. His face had turned a deathly grey.

"You're not well, sir," Campbell stated urgently, jumping to his feet.

"It's nothing," Al croaked, waving him aside irritably. "Just my indigestion."

Campbell wasn't buying it. He recognized a heart attack when he saw one. "I'm calling 911," he said, picking up the phone on the desk. "Now!"

After an exhilarating bicycle ride, Billie McTavish turned into 210, Laurel Drive, to be greeted by the sight of an ambulance parked in the driveway. She was stunned. A split second later, the ambulance crew emerged from the house, carrying a stretcher.

"Dad!" Billie exclaimed as she caught sight of her father's face, white as paper under the oxygen mask, his eyelids shut tight. "Mom!" she added a second later as Sofia came flying out after the stretcher clutching her handbag, before climbing into the ambulance, oblivious to Billie's cries. Sick with fear, Billie jumped off her bike. She felt the hedge dig into her back as the ambulance took off, missing her by inches, its siren wailing. What's happened? she wondered, feeling horror struck. Had there been a break in? Had her father played the hero and paid the price? Worse, had Phil threatened to slander him in the press? People had strokes, didn't they, if they got a shock like that? Dimly, out of the corner of her eye, she caught sight of a Mountie in full dress uniform walking towards her. She could still hear the wail of the siren. Please, she thought desperately. Let Dad be alright.

"Miss McTavish?" the Mountie asked, squinting into the sun which was directly behind her. "I'm Constable McClaren," he added, showing her his badge.

"What's going on?" she asked haltingly.

"I'll explain on the way," McClaren replied, picking up her bike which was blocking the driveway. "We need to get you to the hospital." She felt his hand on her elbow guiding her to the car. It was curiously comforting.

"I believe your father's had a mild heart attack," McClaren told her soberly as he accelerated down Laurel Drive, past trim front lawns and neat houses where other lucky people were having an ordinary day.

"Mild!" Billie declared in an outraged tone. "Nothing about it looked mild to me!" McClaren did not reply, but he drove at the same breakneck pace, eventually pulling up right outside the entrance to ER.

"Go on in, I'll try to join you in a minute," he told her. Billie stood on the sidewalk, watching the car vanish around the corner and into the parking lot. Away from the Mountie's comforting presence, the full horror of what she had just witnessed came crashing down on her and she felt panic stricken. Taking her courage in both hands, she strode up to the big doors and pushed them open. There wasn't a doctor in sight, just a crowded waiting room and a desk manned by a uniformed nurse, who was as bulky as a prizefighter and who appeared to have everyone cowed. The nurse looked up sharply as Billie walked in but she carried on grilling some poor man about his lack of a health card, regardless. Every part of Billie was desperate to burst through the barrier yet she obediently got in line, feeling angry and confused, unable to summon enough strength for a confrontation. As the minutes ticked by and she made no forward progress, her imagination went into overdrive, replaying the image of her father's face as he lay immobile on the stretcher over and over again.

The situation improved when McClaren reappeared. He cut through the red tape with a wave of his badge. The sight of a Mountie in full dress uniform seemed to neutralize the power freak at reception. She allowed them to go through the doors to the treatment rooms. To Billie's dismay, however, she remained in a semi-frozen state. It's the shock, she told herself. In the end, it was McClaren who tracked down the doctor in charge of her father's care,

McClaren who brought her the news that Al was slated to jump the queue for a multitude of tests including an MRI.

"He must be pretty bad then," she said stifling a sob.

"He's conscious," McClaren replied firmly, handing her a wallet. "You want to do something to help? Find his health card." Her fingers didn't seem to be working properly, but she did her best. As she searched among the dozen or so cards stacked there, she came across a photo of herself as a child sitting on a swing with her father standing proudly behind her. She couldn't believe how young he had looked back then. "Wait here," McClaren said, taking the health card from her and disappearing again. He returned, mercifully, a short while later.

"Let's go to the canteen," he suggested cheerfully.

"Now?" she protested. "What about Mom?"

"She's with your father," McClaren replied. "I've asked them to page you the instant there are any developments." Billie was glad to have some company but she had no idea why the Mountie was still hanging around. "Your father is not in any immediate danger," he assured her.

"Oh and you're guaranteeing that are you?" Billie replied angrily. Then she considered the alternative: sitting in the waiting room for hours with no news. "Okay," she agreed.

"Good girl," McClaren replied in a satisfied tone.

The hospital cafeteria was on the second floor. The sight of trees and grass, of cars trundling along the street was therapeutic. Her life might be in crisis but outside it was a sunny day and the rest of the world was carrying on as normal. She found an empty table. The clock on the wall showed 11 a.m. She couldn't believe so much time had gone by. It felt like thirty minutes, not three hours, since she'd first seen the ambulance in the driveway of 210, Laurel Drive. It increased her sense of disorientation. Where was McClaren? He returned a few minutes later with two bowls of soup, a glass of water and a cup of black coffee.

"Get some of this into you," he advised. "You'll feel better, trust me."

"I don't feel at all hungry," she replied, pushing the food away.

"You have to eat," McClaren insisted, picking up a spoonful. "Mmm…it's good," he added, smacking his lips.

"I'm not five years old!" she exclaimed. But he had made her smile. That eased the tension. The soup helped too. It was part of the normal everyday world. It grounded her.

"You've had a shock," McClaren said a kindly manner. It struck her that in his line of work, he came across hysterical females fairly often and knew exactly how to deal with them. She didn't intend to be filed in that slot.

"Look," she said, in what she hoped was a normal voice. "It's not going to change anything, but I need to understand exactly what happened, back at the house. And why you….why the RCMP…"

"I'll tell you," McClaren assured her, looking her in the eye. Was her father on his way to jail for bid rigging? she wondered, with a feeling of dread. "I was calling on your father in his capacity as Director of Racing at Iroquois Downs," McClaren began formally. "The leading driver's car was discovered early this morning thirty kilometres west of Erinsville." He paused. "At the bottom of a ravine."

"Theo Vettore!" she gasped, her hand flying to her mouth, before she could stop herself. "Oh my God, is he…?" She couldn't bring herself to say the word *dead*. It was much too final. Campbell shook his head.

"They haven't found a body yet. He could have been thrown clear or… er…it's best to keep an open mind," he ended enigmatically.

"You mean," she asked hesitantly, "it might not have been an accident?" A hundred regrets, a thousand if only's about Theo were buzzing around in her brain. Nothing like this had ever happened to any of her contemporaries, let alone to someone who she had known well. On top of her father's heart attack, it was suddenly far too much. She could hear McClaren speaking but his voice was muffled. She couldn't make out any of the words. Her brain went into denial, blanking out the news about Theo and revisiting the image of her father's face, ghostly pale. Without really knowing what she was doing, she picked up the glass of water and took a big gulp. Some of it made its way into her lungs. She spluttered, feeling like she was drowning, her eyes watering uncontrollably, her breath harsh and rasping. Eventually, she regained control. The room came back into focus and her brain clicked back into gear. Theo was a drug addict, she reminded herself sternly. Perversely, now her own small crisis was over, she felt better able to deal with two bombshells that had landed at her door. She took a spoonful of the soup. McClaren was watching her anxiously.

"You've got some colour back in your face," he remarked, looking relieved, after she had finished eating. "You and Theo Vettore. . ." he added tentatively, still with that watchful, concerned expression on his face.

"Look, Theo and I are history," she replied firmly. "I went out with him for about eighteen months," she added, feeling that it was a poor description of the ups and downs, the hatred and the passion, the utter contempt she had felt for Theo at the end. She felt unable to say more. "I'm much more concerned about Dad now," she ended. The loudspeaker rang out.

"Will a Miss McTavish report to reception at ER. Miss Billie McTavish!"

"I have to go," she said, grabbing Al's wallet and stuffing it in her bag. Then she dashed out and sprinted to the elevators.

Sofia was waiting for her. She looked like she had aged twenty years.

"Mom!" Billie cried, running to her and folding her in her arms. I have to stay strong, Billie thought, for my mother's sake. All these years, she'd depended on Sofia's support. That relationship had now changed irrevocably. It felt weird, like the world had turned upside down. She still had no idea whether her father was going to make it. Or even if he was still alive. Tears flowed down Sofia's face, the smudges of mascara around her eyes reminding Billie of a giant panda. But it wasn't in the least bit funny.

"They have tried to restart his heart, but each time it is no good," Sofia sobbed.

"Where is he?" Billie asked urgently, her heart heavy as lead, picturing her father's body lying in a coffin...the church was full...Phil Harman was giving the eulogy.

"Intensive..." Sofia replied falteringly.

"Wait here!" Billie exclaimed, pouncing on it. "I'll be back!"

At Intensive Care medical staff were clustered around a single patient who appeared to be clinging to life by a thread. A team of doctors and nurses were working on him, their faces grave. It took some time for Billie to realize that this corpse-like creature with sweaty pale skin and a face white as candle wax, was her father. She turned away, knowing that the image would stay with her forever.

"You shouldn't be here," a young man wearing a white coat said, taking her arm and attempting to lead her away.

"Who's the top heart specialist here?" she demanded.

"Dr. Aldright...they've paged him. But it's Industry Day. We're not sure he's in the building." Billie waited. The minutes crawled by.

"Oh dear. Things not looking too good here, are they?" she heard someone mutter. She wheeled around and saw a trim, middle aged man with grey flyaway hair. He walked briskly over and scanned the data displayed on half a dozen monitors that loomed over Al's body. Bill heard the sickening sound of the shock machine as the team fought to bring Al back from the brink.

"Aldright!" she heard one of them cry out. "Think you can help us out here?" After a brief, intense consultation with the team, Aldright shepherded her off to a corner and patiently explained what he was proposing, without using a single medical term. It was, she assumed, the British way.

"It's a risky procedure," Aldright conceded. "But in my opinion installing a heart pump will give your father a sporting chance. Anything else you'd like to ask, my dear?" Wordlessly, Billie shook her head. "We do need permission from the next of kin to proceed, I'm afraid," Aldright continued. "No need to rush," he added politely enough. But Billie was well aware that they were now almost out of time.

"Go ahead," she said decisively. "I'll sign anything you want."

"Right! I'll go and scrub up!" Aldright replied, rubbing his hands together with such a wild light in his eyes that she almost took it back.

"You're really very lucky to have him on the case," a sympathetic nurse confided reassuringly as Billie signed the consent forms. "Today being a holiday, we weren't even sure he'd be here."

"Thanks," Billie replied gratefully. "How long will it be before...you know..."

"If the operation's been a success?" the nurse asked brightly. "It'll be several hours. But we'll let you know as soon as there's any news."

On her way back to ER, Billie rehearsed what she was going to say to her mother. She was afraid of raising her hopes too high. What if the unthinkable happened and her father died on the operating table? With a pang, Billie realized she had probably missed her last chance to say goodbye to him.

Campbell McClaren stepped outside Erinsville General and took a deep breath of fresh air. Behind him, day and night, a hundred human dramas were playing out, witnessed by staff who had learned to treat everything, however horrific, as routine. It went with the job, he imagined, but it was something he had never acquired the knack of. He tallied the damage of the last twenty-four hours: Vettore missing, possibly dead, Al McTavish fighting for his life, Billie McTavish in shock...the three of them inextricably intertwined. Unfortunately, none of them would be much help piecing together the puzzle for quite a while, if ever. There was someone, however, who might be persuaded to talk: Crawfish Brown.

Once again, Campbell traded in his uniform for a white shirt and jeans and drove over to Iroquois Downs. There he discovered that no one had seen hair or hide of Crawfish since late Friday night. His room in the grooms' quarters, which was little better than a cell, was completely empty. Ominously, when Campbell put in a call to the family farm, he drew blank again. His parents sounded genuinely concerned but were unable to help. Eventually, he ended up at the Hot Tamale staring at Crawfish's banged up bicycle, which was propped up against the back wall exactly where he had left it two nights before. Crawfish would hardly leave his precious possession lying around for anyone to steal unless he was on the run afraid for his life, or worse, dead. Grudgingly, Campbell realized he actually cared about Crawfish. Vettore was just your regular fallen angel, slippery as an eel and beyond redemption, but Crawfish, for all his foul personal habits, was vulnerable as all hell. He unlocked the back office and made the call he should have made in the first place, to Pam Mercer. She gave him a hard time over skipping out on the Hot Tamale at the weekend, blaming him for a scene of drunken brawls that had broken out at 2 a.m.

"A man called Crawfish Brown came by the club on Saturday night. He was asking for you," he said, as soon as he could get a word in edgeways. This only made matters worse.

"Crawfish! Don't talk to me about Crawfish!" she raged. "I let him sleep in my washroom and he's only cost me two hundred bucks for a locksmith. That's besides fixing the paintwork on my window. Two hundred, imagine! To get into my own bathroom. That moron!" she continued in an outraged tone. "He locked my bathroom door and then jumped right out of my bathroom window. Why? What ever was he thinking? There wasn't nobody here but me and Evie! He's nothin' but a crazy man!"

"Don't touch anything! I'll be right over," Campbell said, pleased that finally he seemed to be getting somewhere.

Crawfish's personal possessions were scattered across Pam's bathroom floor. He'd certainly taken off in a hurry. The thought of Crawfish setting off alone in an unhinged state brought on a fresh wave of guilt. At length Campbell pocketed one of Crawfish's old caps and, after slipping Pam a few twenty dollar bills to console her, he went down to the station to unearth a tracker dog.

Alas, all the best animals and their handlers were presently halfway down a gorge searching for signs of Vettore's remains at the site of his crashed Ferrari, seventy-five kilometres due west. Campbell had to make do with an alsatian known as Awesome Albert. Apparently *Awesome* referred to his appetite which was prodigious, rather than to any tracking skills. He shared a late lunch with the dog and then got back to work. Hoping to avoid running into Pam Mercer again (once in a day was quite enough), Campbell fetched up on the pavement below the bathroom window which was on the second floor. Happily, one sniff of Crawfish's filthy old cap sent Albert into an ecstasy of excitement. The dog took off, straining at the leash, leading the way past nightclubs and bars, quiet at this time of day, through Maple Tree Park where, rumour had it, a flasher lurked in the bushes after dark. Albert nosed his way along, his muzzle skimming the pavement until he reached the town centre, oblivious to the ninety-degree heat. There wasn't a cloud in the sky. It was so hot that the asphalt underfoot felt as springy as a safety mat and the acrid smell of tar filled the air. Campbell tried to act like a resident out for an afternoon stroll. But he was certain no one was fooled. What a place, he thought as he was dragged along by the dog. He recalled with a pang the summers of his childhood in Prince Edward Island, the cool sand in between his toes and the fresh breezes coming from the Atlantic Ocean.

They ended up outside the main bus terminal, which to Campbell's relief cast a deep shadow like a vast black cloak over the street, giving them some much needed respite from the burning sun. Albert dived inside and made a beeline for a hot dog stand stationed near the back wall.

"Get that dog outa here!" the hot dog man yelled, without taking his eye off the onions. "This here's an eatery. No dogs allowed!" Albert took off again, his tail wagging, weaving his way past the departure stations, until he came out onto a two-lane highway, where traffic flowed ceaselessly. There, he pulled up short, lifted his head and uttered a single bark at the buses rolling past. Then, he looked up at Campbell plaintively as if to say: I give up. What do we do now?

"We go back to the bus terminal and ask around," Campbell said, hoping someone would remember seeing a man with a gammy leg. Albert followed along obediently enough, but Campbell could tell the dog felt like a loser from the way he carried his tail, tucked right down between his hind legs. "Don't worry, son," Campbell comforted him. "You did good today. No sense beating yourself up." He wondered if his tendency to talk to so called dumb animals was the real reason he had never made Watch Commander. Could be, he concluded, but there were so many other strikes against him it hardly counted.

He set about questioning every bus driver, ticket seller and food vendor he could find. None of them remembered seeing anyone who fitted Crawfish's description.

"I'm far too busy to notice anything like that," the hot dog man grumbled when Campbell questioned him. Campbell ordered two hot dogs from him anyway, one without onions for Albert, and wished the vendor a nice day. Waste of good irony, he decided, as he watched Albert tuck in.

Campbell walked back to the OPP station, deep in thought. Crawfish had apparently climbed out of a second floor window, negotiating a ten-foot drop like Spiderman, despite his crippled leg. Then he had set off to the main bus terminal, where he had apparently become invisible. He had spent some time beside the hot dog stand before heading out to the highway, where he had leapt onto a passing vehicle. But Crawfish did not have superhuman powers, Campbell reminded himself sharply. A less likely action hero would be difficult to find. Obviously, there had to be a better explanation but for now, he was baffled. He had to admit that being baffled by Crawfish was a humbling experience. He returned Awesome Albert to the station and did his paperwork, giving the alsatian top marks in his report. By the time he was done, the sun was a giant orange ball hovering above the horizon. If he hurried, he would have just enough time to go down to the river and watch the sunset. It wasn't anything like watching the sun slip behind the dunes on the beach back in PEI. But it was a link with home, practically the only tangible one he had.

The western sky was on fire as he put in a call to Erinsville General. When he got the news about Al McTavish, he stood quietly, gazing out over the water. It had been an eventful day, raising more questions than answers. As for Vettore, it bothered him greatly that he had slipped out of his grasp without revealing specifics about the man he had called the Scorpion. Despite the official view that it was only a matter of time before they found the body, Campbell was praying that Vettore was still out there somewhere, still alive. He had failed in his mission to find Crawfish Brown. That left only one other person who might be able to provide the missing pieces of the jigsaw puzzle: Miss Billie McTavish. But, for the next week or two, at least, he would have to stay well away from the McTavish family. Al McTavish was still alive, but how much longer could he hang on?

SAINTE MARIE

The servants have fled, his faithful Natalie gone. The busy airport, silent. The planes, grounded. The birds, hunkered down.

Unafraid, André Fontainbleu stands erect on the pool deck of the Hermitage, set into the mountainside like a buttress of some great medieval castle. He watches the storm, hears the sea roaring hundreds of feet below him, sees the trees swaying violently in the wind, shedding their branches carelessly as autumn leaves.

His mind is far away. South America beckons: Brazil with its promise of deep water oil wells. . . Suriname with its priceless anonymity. . .Canada, that milksop of a country where his bingo halls are prospering. The opportunity to squeeze its feckless citizens dry, perfectly legally with the blessing of the provincial government, is really too delicious! He smiles at the thought.

He pulls back to the here and now, where a blood red sun is losing the struggle against a mass of dark thunder clouds rising up from the west like a giant's fist, full of anger and menace, turning the turquoise water slate grey. He lingers for a while in the half light, defying the wind and weather, feeling like the captain of a majestic ship that is thrusting its way through the Caribbean Sea.

Inside, silence and fetid air greet him at the door. The hurricane shutters have obscured what little daylight remains, increasing the feeling of claustrophobia. The power is out. His links to the outside world have been cut like an umbilical cord. The lack of communication is inconvenient but being solitary is fundamental to his character. Self reliance is his by word. He flips the switch on his private generator.

He trusts no one. Even when he is surrounded by people, André Fontainbleu is always alone.

On the other side of the mountain, a hurricane party was in full swing, fuelled by an endless supply of rum daiquiris and a powerful generator. The snuggery was built into the rock, its back to the sea. Judging by the number of cars parked outside, half the island was there. The noise was deafening. One couple though, tucked away in the alcove, didn't seem to be enjoying themselves too much.

"We've done all we can, Pete," the girl said, her long dark hair pulled back from her face, her expression intense and serious. Her companion, a big blond Australian, swallowed hard and reached out for one of the daiquiris which jostled for room on the tiny table. Quick as a flash, the girl moved the glass away. "No more!" she declared. "You've had plenty!"

"Hey! I'm just getting started," he protested.

"She'll be fine," the girl replied reassuringly.

"The Sea Princess?" Pete cut in, looking astonished. "You think this is about the boat, Anya?" She stared at him, uncomprehending.

"What's going on?" she frowned. Pete picked up a drink. This time she let him go right ahead. "Man trouble?" she asked hesitantly.

"Nothing I can talk about," Pete replied abruptly.

"Is that why you've been taking the Sea Princess out at weird hours?" she probed.

"You could say that," Pete replied with a short bitter laugh. "Listen, I don't want to talk about it, okay?"

"Okay," Anya agreed reluctantly, after a long silence.

THE MOUNTAINS OF ALBERTA

So close to a sheer drop that one careless move would send him flying over the edge, impaling him on the razor sharp rocks hundreds of feet below, lies a man. It is a strange place to be sleeping, yet that is exactly what he appears to be doing…if it is a man and not a smudge of black in the shadows. Up here in the mountains, appearances can be deceptive.

Dawn.

His eyes flick open. He stares unseeing at the high blue ceiling topping the ring of mountains, then his eyes snap shut, loath to face reality perhaps or still deep in a dream. Meanwhile the sun just keeps on rising, flooding the mountain peaks with its golden light, touching the man's face, warming his fingers and bare toes. Casually, he stretches out his long legs, almost as if he imagines he's tucked up in his own bed on some sunny Sunday morning, instead of perched precariously on a mountain ledge, inches from certain death. He grows restless. Something, a bad dream perhaps, has disturbed his slumber. Thrashing about, he flings out his left arm, which goes swinging over the abyss, threatening to take the rest of him with it. A struggle follows, agonizing to watch as catapulted from a deep sleep into a waking nightmare, he fights desperately to wrestle back control from that implacable, invisible enemy that lurks in high places: Gravity. The only witnesses to the struggle are the bald eagles, wheeling high above him, their bright eyes intent on their first meal of the day. All seems lost. But then, making a herculean effort, he leaps to his feet like a gymnast. For a moment, he stands teetering on the edge of the mountain, arms outstretched, swaying this way and that, like a giant bird, fearful of its first flight from the nest.

But this bird has no wings.

It seems certain that soon he will reach the tipping point. But still, he hangs on, his bare toes clenched, clinging to the rock. Like a miracle, a wind comes up from the valley, blowing steadily into his face. It is enough. Slowly, painfully, he regains his equilibrium. He takes one tentative step back from the brink, then another, until he knows he is safe. He falls back to his knees, hands gripping the solid ground, breathing hard as if he has just run the race of his life. When he eventually lifts his head, his reaction is curious. He frowns and rubs his eyes, as if unable to make sense of his surroundings. He rifles through the pockets of his mottled brown track suit. When they reveal nothing, his frown deepens. He begins muttering to himself, softly at first, then louder until finally he rises to his feet and shouts to the morning sky.

"What is this place? What am I doing here?" The speech seems to expend what little energy he has left. He shivers, hunches over and goes down on his knees again. Someone standing close to him might just catch his whispered words.

"I don't remember...anything." Then, all at once he cries out, "Who am I?"

The sun climbs higher. The man slowly rises to his feet. He appears calmer now. Quietly, he takes in his situation, glancing up at the rock face above him, peering down at the sheer drop below. To his right, the ledge gradually narrows until it disappears completely. To his left, a path leads downhill, as far as the eye can see. He sets off but then pulls up short. He sees now that the ledge he is standing on, the one that saved his life, is a trap. Ahead lies a gap, a break in the rock. He strides towards it and measures it with his intelligent eyes. The gap is two metres wide, maybe more.

The decision is made.

Nervously, he licks his swollen lips with a tongue like sandpaper. Gritting his teeth, he backs away from the chasm. He readies himself for the challenge, running on the spot, breathing rapidly and pumping his arms. This is a gamble he must win, or die in the attempt. Either away the outcome will be swift, he hopes. He leaps forward, his scream echoing off the rocky walls. He is airborne now, his arms stretched out, his eyes fixed on the prize, as if mere willpower will get him to the far side. His upper body crash lands but his legs dangle helplessly in space. Gravity is merciless. Blinded by tears, he makes rapid sweeping movements with his arms as he slides back inexorably towards the abyss. Suddenly, his fingers lock on to a crevice on the rock. He hangs on. He moves his legs like a swimmer until he gets one knee over, then another. His hands are raw, and bleeding. He does not care! He feels no pain, only euphoria. He shouts out to the mountain, shaking a fist in defiance.

"I am alive!"

ONTARIO

Campbell McClaren was hard at work dismantling the stage set that had helped create the phoney character of Sidney H. Kingshott. He had gathered up the beer cans, the baseball caps, the hockey memorabilia and taken the saucy calendar down from the wall. All of it was destined for the garbage can. He kept the hockey gear. It had been the only enjoyable thing about the whole experience. Everything else had made him feel cheap.

The one quality he'd always prided himself on was integrity. But he had given up counting how many lies he'd had to tell to stay in character. It wasn't like he'd been working with hardened criminals. These were ordinary people: people who had trusted him to be who he appeared to be. He wasn't cut out for it. The only thing that could tempt him to go undercover again would be the chance to track down the Scorpion on his home ground.

That wasn't likely to happen any time soon.

NOWHERE MAN

The sun was high in the sky when the man with no memory of his past life stumbled into the pine forest. He threw himself on the ground, his chest heaving, thankful for the shade and dizzy with weariness. His bare feet, sticking out from his torn sweatpants, were bruised and swollen. Picking his way down the rocky mountain path had taken a huge effort. For a while, he lay spread eagled on the forest floor, breathing hard, feeling like the earth was moving beneath him. Yet the moment he caught his breath, he forced himself to sit up.

He had to find water. He listened intently, but heard nothing moving: not a squirrel…not a bird. As far as he could see, in every direction, stand upon stand of pine trees marched, crowded together shutting out the sun and providing a haven for creepy crawlies. He wasn't desperate enough to try eating those yet. Besides, without water, he would die. But which way to go? It would be so easy to get lost in here and wander around in circles for days. When a colony of ants discovered him, he jumped up. Trying to ignore the pine cones digging into the soles of his feet, he walked gingerly through the forest searching for a path leading downhill. There was none, but eventually the trees began to thin out. Encouraged, he redoubled his efforts and was rewarded by a view of a grey, cloudy sky.

Soon he was standing on the edge of a slope, gazing down at a steep, narrow valley. It wasn't encouraging. There was no sign of civilization, but the sun emerged briefly and he thought he saw a glint of water somewhere far below. It was enough. Before he had a chance to change his mind, he got down on his belly and swung his legs over the edge, feeling for a foothold. At first, he made good progress, using the occasional bush or stunted tree which clung to life at a sixty-degree angle, to break his fall. Then out of the blue, a mountain goat came leaping down the slope, passing so close to him it almost touched him. Instinctively he jerked sideways, lost his hold on the bush he'd been hanging on to and began sliding inexorably downwards, accompanied by an avalanche of earth and stones. They beat on his head and body like a troop of malignant demons. As he gathered speed, helpless to save himself, he had a moment of fearful clarity, certain he would be smashed to pieces.

The ordeal seemed to last forever.

All at once, everything stopped. Cautiously, he opened one eye. Terrified of starting another avalanche, he rose to his feet and shook off the dirt. There wasn't a single part of him that didn't hurt. But in the silence, to his great joy, he heard the sound of rushing water. Following the sound, he stumbled through the long grass, feeling like an old man. When he reached the river he dropped down on all fours and drank like an animal, experiencing an intense elemental pleasure as he slaked his thirst. He glanced up at the sky. Dark grey clouds were massing on the ragged peaks, shutting out the sun. He needed to find shelter, urgently. It was an instinct too powerful to ignore. However, the only trees were on the other side of the river. He didn't stop to think about it. As the first raindrops fell, he stripped off, tying his tattered tracksuit clumsily around his waist. Then he jumped into the water and struck out for the far bank. The icy water left him gasping for breath but he forgot about the cold when an invisible school of fish attacked him, nibbling ferociously at his legs as if they hadn't eaten in weeks and he was the only thing on the menu. Screaming at the top of his lungs, he kicked out at them, powering through the water in his haste to escape them. Sooner than he could have believed possible, he was bumping up against the far shore. He leapt out onto the mud, expecting to find his legs a mass of bleeding flesh. Instead, he discovered they were plastered with black leeches, hanging on like suction cups. He screamed again. Frantically, he picked them off one by one. It wasn't until he had managed to rid himself of every last one that he realized he had lost his only possession, his tracksuit, to the river. He now had nothing. Shaking from the cold, he headed for the trees. The rain began falling in earnest. It was getting darker by the second.

He was stranded in the middle of nowhere, the only human in a hostile world.

HARMONY LIGHT

Evie Mercer was praying that her eyes were playing tricks on her. The sun was low in the sky and the trees cast weird shadows, their branches tossed about by the wind. But no! Harmony Light was definitely walking down the ramp on three legs. The winner of the General Custer just two weeks ago, now looked like a cripple.

"Stop!" she shrieked at Stinker, who was heading for the barn like nothing unusual was going on. The sight of the frail looking colt struggling to keep up nearly broke her heart. "Stop!" she repeated. This time Stinker paid attention. But he still didn't get it. "He's dead lame," she added in a rasping voice she hardly recognized as her own.

"What?" Stinker asked, acting bewildered. "Oh that!" he added. "That's just him, he always does that." Stinker was a total retard, Evie thought furiously. Her father appeared.

"Hey, what's going on," he yelled. "Get a move on Stinker...you gonna spend all night on this?"

Stinker looked dumbfounded. "Make up your minds guys," he complained.

"Harmony can hardly walk, Dad," Evie declared.

"What? He raced great today!" Mercer sounding dismayed.

"Well, he's not great now," Evie replied.

"Let's get him inside first," Mercer said, waving Stinker on. As the colt limped painfully into the barn, Evie could hardly bear to watch. "I'll give him a shot of banamine. He'll be okay. He's been like this before." Mercer added. Evie glared at him. I hate you, she railed silently. You never tell me anything.

"Please! Call the vet," she eventually said, afraid to say more, worried she would set him off, fearful of his rages.

"I'll call Meecham. Don't go getting crazy on me, Evie," Mercer warned. They waited some time for Meecham to answer. "He's not picking up," Mercer said matter of factly. "We're gonna have to try again later. Calm down, Evie, it's not an emergency."

"I'm calling Dr. Winterflood," Evie replied firmly, reaching for her cell phone.

"Where d'you get that from?" Mercer asked in an astonished tone. "You don't have a phone!"

"I do now, Mom got me one," Evie replied, hoping he wouldn't start yelling at her again.

"I don't have his number anyhow," Mercer said, rallying.

"Well, I do!" Evie replied bravely, going to the pitifully small contact list she had stored on her phone. I may not have any friends, she thought defiantly, but I know the best veterinarian in the entire universe! Winterflood answered right away. If he was surprised to hear from her, he didn't sound it.

"Be with you in ten minutes," he promised. Evie walked over to Harmony Light's stall. The black and white cat she had rescued years before came up to her meowing for food. She picked it up and buried her head in its soft fur, listening to the silence. It felt like someone had died. The colt was standing stock still, his tail rammed up against the stall gate. She reached over and touched his hind quarters lightly with the tips of her fingers.

"It's okay," she said softly. He eased off the gate and she stepped inside the stall. But when she hugged his neck, he just stood there, droopy eared, barely acknowledging her. "Come on," she whispered, tickling his shoulder in the special place he liked, running her hands over the muscles in his back, rock hard from tension. He let out a big sigh. "Feeling a little better?" she asked, smiling up at him.

"What's up?" she heard someone ask cheerfully. Dr. Winterflood had arrived.

"Get that colt out, Evie," Mercer boomed. But by the time she had opened the stall door, the vet was there beside her.

"Leave him where he is," he said kindly. "I don't want to stress him. Just hold his head for me."

No one spoke for a long time after that.

ALBERTA

Rain was pouring down on the man with no memory, chilling him to the bone. Perversely, after a while, the water began to feel pleasantly warm. Darkness fell. After the rain let up, his teeth began chattering uncontrollably. Had he come all this way, pushed himself to the limit, only to end up dying of hypothermia? It certainly felt like it. But he couldn't give up now. The steely light of the moon, emerging from the ragged clouds racing across the sky, gave him a brief view of his surroundings. He headed into the woods. It was warmer and drier underfoot, but he couldn't eat pine needles! He stumbled around in the semi-darkness, then froze. An animal was padding along the forest floor, getting closer by the second, until suddenly it bumped against his bare legs. Terrified, he looked down. A pair of yellow eyes stared steadily back up at him, without an ounce of hostility. Was he delusional? Chancing it, he stretched a hand downwards. The creature responded by licking his fingers, making a sound somewhere between a whine and a bark. What was a dog doing here? Could there be people nearby? he wondered, feeling a surge of hope. The very idea thrilled him. But, after a few minutes, the animal ran off, leaving him more alone than ever.

"Wait up!" he called out to the ghostly shape of the dog, its blond tail waving like a banner. Desperate not to lose sight of it, he followed along as best as he could, tripping on tree roots, scraping himself on low-hanging branches. As he fought his way through the forest, he came very close to giving up.

At last, looming up through the trees, he saw the unmistakable outline of a log cabin. He was far too weary to feel anything but a vague sense of relief. The dog was waiting for him by the door. When he opened it, the dog pushed past him impatiently, eager to get indoors. It was even darker inside. It took the man quite a while to get his bearings. He stumbled around, bumping into various hard objects until by a lucky chance, he came across a torch. Its feeble light revealed a large room with a beamed ceiling, bunk beds and a fireplace in one corner. Quickly, before the battery gave out, he rifled through the cupboards and pulled open every drawer in the place. What he found was a can of soup, but no can opener, and a matchbox with only three matches left.

Stopping only to wrap himself in a rough blanket from one of the beds, he hurried over to the fireplace where he discovered a large pile of logs and a stack of newspapers. He soon had a blaze going. The dog joined him beside the fire and lay down, his chin on his paws, gazing at the flames. Rain was lashing at the windows. But indoors, warm and dry, the dog and the man lay their heads down on the rough wooden floor and fell into a deep and dreamless sleep.

Safe at last!

The man awoke in the dead of night to the pungent smell of woodsmoke. Hunger gnawed at his empty belly. He had a raging thirst. The logs had burned down to a pile of glowing embers. Feeling as stiff as a board, he crouched down and set about coaxing the fire back to life, using balled up newspaper. A photo of a horse caught his eye. He studied it by the light of the fire. It seemed curiously familiar, but he had no idea why. He tried to punch a hole in the can of soup but quickly gave it up. Weak with hunger, he flopped back down onto the hard floor, listening to the dog's steady breathing and watching for signs that the night was coming to an end.

Though he was the only human being for miles around, he was not alone, it seemed. He heard countless rustlings of small nocturnal animals, interspersed with the chilling sounds of a pack on the hunt. Slowly, the darkness faded. A chilly light appeared on the eastern horizon. Wincing with pain, he dragged himself to his feet and hobbled around the cabin, wondering how he was ever going to find the strength to leave this place. His body was covered in welts and bruises. He couldn't just wait around to be rescued. He could starve to death before then.

The dog jumped up and padded after him, plainly as hungry as he was. Together, they unearthed a pair of blue jeans with a broken zipper and a grey sweatshirt lying forgotten under a pillow. The dog discovered a pair of ripped sneakers hidden at the back of a closet. The man put it all on. The sweatshirt was several sizes too big and the pants were six inches too short. But it felt good to be wearing clothes. His spirits lifted. Until he caught sight of a stranger's face, gaunt and pale, unshaven, his black hair standing straight up from his head, staring back at him through the window glass. Fear gave way to disbelief as he slowly understood that this ragged apparition was his own reflection. He had no idea how long he spent gazing at the haunted eyes and the deep shadows beneath them, but he came back to earth with a jolt when he heard the dog's low growl. Its muzzle was curled back in a snarl, exposing a set of sharp fangs. Outside, something or someone was crashing through the undergrowth. He heard a shot ring out. Frantically, he looked around for a hiding place. But before he could make a move, the cabin door burst open. The dog flung himself on the intruder, barking wildly.

"Bacardi!" a deep voice sang out jubilantly. "You came back!" The dog leapt up over and over again, his high pitched barks making conversation impossible. "Down boy…that's enough now," the newcomer said firmly, tearing himself away from the dog's exuberant welcome. He bent down and picked up his cowboy hat, which had fallen on the floor. He was wearing a brown plaid shirt which matched his eyes, but a stout pair of hiking boots revealed that this cowboy was not all about show. The man with no memory stood there and drank it all in.

"Hey you!" the cowboy said, an irrepressible grin on his face. "Where in hell'd you find my dog? He slipped his collar las' week jus' as we was pullin' outa here. Me and my buddies were out here on a huntin' trip. I swore I'd come back for 'im an' I did, as soon as I could…But he's been out here so long." He shook his head. "Thank the Lord he ain't been eaten by coyotes… it's wild country out here! I scared off an elk. . .a big male. . . jus' now…" That explained the gunshot and the shouting, the man realized, relieved that he could make sense of some things. It was wonderful to hear another human voice, but he couldn't muster the strength to reply. His legs were trembling so badly that he had to lean against the wall to stay on his feet. "Hey! You ain't lookin' so good," the cowboy exclaimed, his rugged face full of concern. "You better sit down 'fore you fall down." As he slid to the floor, he realized the cowboy was watching him curiously. Then he made for the door. He was leaving! The man with no memory felt far too weak to stop him. He collapsed, resigned to his fate, not an ounce of fight left in him.

"Now, you stay with him Bacardi, d'you hear?" he heard the cowboy call out. "I'll be right back," he added cheerfully, walking out and closing the door behind him. He'd got it all wrong, the man realized thankfully. Bacardi lay down next to him and rested his head on his shoulder. The two of them, the man and the dog, listened intently as the sound of the cowboy's footsteps grew fainter and fainter, until there was only silence.

After what felt like an eternity, their rescuer returned carrying a bulging backpack.

"Lucky for you, I brought groceries," the cowboy announced happily. "An' I got dog biscuits for you, Bacardi. You ain't forgotten." With that, the cowboy got busy. A short while later, he handed over a bowl of hot soup, a bar of chocolate and a cup of milky coffee. "Now, get that all down you!" he said. For the next little time, the man was absorbed by the food: the feel of it in his mouth, the simple pleasure of filling his belly. There was no room for talk. He had come back! That had changed everything. To someone with a memory that went back a mere twenty-four hours, this rough outdoorsman was beginning to feel like an old friend. "Feelin' better, eh?" the cowboy enquired in a matter of fact tone, like this sort of thing happened every day. The man nodded weakly. "Now, see here," the cowboy declared, taking a seat on the floor beside him. "I wanna hear the whole story."

Hesitantly the man began to relate the events of the past twenty-four hours, beginning with his ordeal up on the mountain ledge and ending with Bacardi leading him to the cabin in the woods.

"Son of a gun!" the cowboy exclaimed, jumping to his feet. "Show me!" he insisted, gesturing towards the open door, through which the jagged peaks could plainly be seen, highlighted by the morning sun. With a shaking hand and dread in his heart, the man obediently pointed out the spot where just yesterday his troubles had all begun. "Why, that's Dead Man's Leap!" the cowboy said in a tone of astonishment. "You musta fell twenty feet, no lie. You're lucky to be alive! That road's been closed for what, five years now! Didn't you see the signs? That's a no go area. How in hell d'you get down from there, anyhow?" He gazed at the man with genuine admiration. "You're one tough hombre," he declared, extending his hand. "Put it there! Name's Wayne, Wayne Stevens, from Lost Valley Ranch. What do they call you, son?" The man shrugged his shoulders.

"I don't know," he confessed.

"Don't remember, eh? That'll be the concussion," Wayne replied reassuringly. "You must'a hit your head. You'll remember soon enough. What are you doing round these parts?" The man shrugged again. "Never mind! You found my dog. That counts with me. Can you ride a horse?"

"Maybe," the man replied.

"I could use a man like you out on the ranch. We're short of help right now. You look like a scarecrow now, but I reckon you'll be okay once we clean you up a bit!" Wayne shook his head, wonderingly. "Imagine Bacardi here savin' your skin an' all! He ain't nothin' special. Part mutt, part lab!" he chuckled. "I never figured him for a hero. C'mon," he added, slapping the man on the back so hard he almost fell over. "We can't stick around here all day. We gotta get you fixed up with some clothes, get you a haircut! I can take you into town. It ain't far!"

"Thank you," the man replied, grasping the lifeline he had been offered.

"Wait up while I get this harness on Bacardi here. He ain't gettin' away a second time," Wayne said. But the dog showed no signs of wanting to get away. He followed along meekly to the truck. The days of living rough had apparently left their mark.

By nightfall, the man with no past had a future and a brand new start. He was wearing jeans, a checked shirt, a cowboy hat and a pair of sturdy boots. He had a name: "Scarecrow". Also, he had a place in the bunkhouse at Lost Valley Ranch, where Wayne was the head man. As he lay in bed that first night, he wondered a lot about who he was and where he had come from. But during the days that followed, he was kept so busy from dawn to dusk that somehow his past, whatever it was, didn't seem to matter so much as the here and now. He liked everything about his life: the breathtaking scenery, the camaraderie with the ranch hands, the horses, especially the horses. Every day was a gift. He felt lucky to be alive. It would have been perfect, if it hadn't have been for the dreams.

THE STORM

Jay Winterflood was living the dream. Every morning, on his way to the Lucky Seven Stables farm, he felt like some of that luck had rubbed off on him. It wasn't just the clinic, where he had the latest technology at his disposal and the freedom to do as he pleased. Everything on the farm had been designed with the welfare of the racehorse in mind. The training track had wide sweeping turns, the barn was light and airy and the paddocks, each with its own shade tree, had automatic waterers and safe fencing. No expense had been spared and Jay felt proud to be a part of it. He was injecting a colt's ankle with the best hyaluronic acid money could buy, when Mike, Mercer's second trainer, walked into the clinic.

"Be with you in a couple of shakes!" Jay called out cheerily.

"D'you hear the latest about Vettore?" Mike asked eagerly.

"Not a thing," Jay replied. "He's done," he told the groom who was holding the colt with the bad ankle. "Those for me?" he enquired pointing at two vials of blood, poking out of the kid's pocket.

"Oh! Yes!" the kid exclaimed, looking flustered. It had obviously slipped his mind. "Cat's dead worried. It's Goldie. She's off her feed."

"Tell Cat I'll have the results later on today," Jay said. Harmony Light had arrived, led in by one of Mercer's grooms. Jay was saddened by the sight. The horse looked like a faded photograph of himself but Mercer's second trainer appeared to be oblivious of his plight. "Where's Evie today?" Jay enquired.

"School," Mike replied dismissively, clearly unimpressed by the whole idea of education. Yet for Jay, it had been a lifeline; a way out of the Reserve to the kind of career that few of his contemporaries could have aspired to.

"X-ray wasn't it?" he said.

"Stifle," Mike nodded. "Not sure which one," he confessed.

"We'll soon see," Jay assured him, wheeling out the X-ray machine.

"Looks like they've given up on Vettore," Mike remarked. "Not much chance they'll find him alive. Not after all this time, eh Stinker?"

"Nah, there won't be much left of 'im to find. He'll be all bits and pieces won't 'e?" Stinker agreed, with relish. Jay ignored them, and carried on taking pictures. After he had all the shots he needed, he headed for the back room.

"Not a bite to eat! No windows neither," Stinker muttered. "I don't like it 'ere no more 'n you do, 'armony," he added, evidently commiserating with Harmony Light, who was pawing at the floor impatient to be off.

"Be right with you!" Jay called out. To his relief, the X-rays were clean. There was absolutely no sign of anything out of the ordinary going on. "Looks like a locked stifle, plain and simple," he told Mike. "Keep him on anti-inflammatories until the end of the week. Then you can start back with him. But," Jay added sternly, "he shouldn't be shipped long distances."

"He's got races all over Ontario!" Mike exclaimed in dismay. "He's a top stakes colt!"

"It's bound to recur," Jay warned.

"I'll tell Mercer," Mike replied grudgingly. "But he won't be happy about it."

Dave Bodinski was next, bringing a trotter who had finished last in his previous start. A flurry of appointments followed. Several hours later, Jay printed off the last blood profile and prepared to close up for the day. What he saw on the print out put any thought of leaving right out of his head. Cat's two year old filly, Harmony Gold, was in serious trouble. Her kidneys had shut down; her immune system was malfunctioning; in fact, every one of her scores was out of whack. Swiftly, Jay threw together a five liter bag of fluid and an IV tube. Then he grabbed his bag and set off for Cat's barn. It was hot and humid outside, a stark contrast to his air conditioned clinic. Grey clouds were gathering on the southeastern horizon and there was a dull rumble of thunder. Racehorses were so sensitive, he mused, glancing over at the training track, a perfect replica of the Iroquois Downs oval. The slightest thing could have set the filly off: a change of feed or even the unsettled weather.

When he reached the barn, Cat was nowhere to be seen, but a lone horse was standing patiently on the cross ties. Someone was obviously still around. However, Cat wasn't answering his phone. Not surprising. It was two o'clock in the afternoon, a time when most horsemen tried to catch a nap. Jay paced up and down the barn, looking for the filly. There were no names on the stall doors. That was a problem. He glanced into the tack room. The door was wide open and inside lay a package, ripped open, its contents spilled out onto the bare table. It was probably some kind of vitamin and mineral supplement commonly given by trainers to horses in their care, Jay guessed. Officially, horsemen weren't supposed to inject vitamins. Unofficially, most people turned a blind eye, with good reason. It saved a great deal of time for the hard pressed veterinarians and a great deal of money for the long suffering owners. It wasn't like tubing which, done by an amateur, could be lethal to a horse. Injectables didn't usually cause any problems, in his experience. However, it was possible that something in the mix had triggered a reaction in Cat's filly. He went inside and picked up one of the bottles at random, looking for the list of contents. But, instead of the usual printed matter, there was only a white label with the neat handwritten instruction: 20 CC's, 5 hours out.

Hastily, Jay put the bottle down. He stood quietly, his eyes closed, his mind racing. Then he walked out. What on earth was an illegal pre-race doing in Catalino's barn? he asked himself. He thought about all the care he'd taken diagnosing and treating lameness, the hours he had spent on the horses' blood work. He had fondly imagined that his efforts were a crucial part of the stable's success to date. He should have realized that Cat raced a great many high class conditioned horses who, unlike claimers, were not subject to the twenty-four-hour retention rule. How could he have been so naive?

Footsteps were coming closer, padding on the barn floor, which was covered in wall to wall rubber mats. Nothing but the best, Jay thought cynically, his illusions shattered.

"Hey Doc, you get those bloods?" a voice rang out. It was Cat.

"There's one horse I need to see right away," Jay said, making a supreme effort to sound normal. "It's your two year old. She's in bad shape."

"Goldie?" Cat asked, looking alarmed. "I knew she was off her feed but... what's wrong with her?"

"I'll tell you...just as soon as I know myself," Jay replied curtly. After what he'd just seen, he wasn't in the mood for chit chat.

"She's down here," Cat said, leading the way. He hovered by the stall door as Jay stuck a needle in the filly's bulging jugular vein. "She gonna be okay?" he asked anxiously.

"What d'you give this horse?" Jay challenged, holding a bag of fluids aloft.

"Just a hot shot," Cat said. "She was horsing so bad..."

"What about that crap in your tack room?" Jay cut in angrily. Cat gulped. Then he seemed to recover.

"That! It's all natural, that stuff. They mix it up specially at some herbal place...," he said. "Goldie's not even racing," he added as Jay slotted in a second bag of fluids.

"Show me what you gave her," Jay demanded. Cat ran off and returned with an empty vial. "Chorionic," Jay said thoughtfully. "It shouldn't provoke a reaction like this. Are you sure this is all you gave her?"

"I swear it, Doc," Cat replied vehemently. This time, Jay was sure he was telling the truth.

"She's had a severe allergic reaction to something," he said. "Her kidneys have shut down. Let's hope the fluids do the trick, otherwise..."

"Otherwise what?" Cat asked, sounding panicky.

"Her chances aren't good," Jay replied gravely. Not trusting himself to say more, he beat a hasty retreat.

"Hey, what's up with you, Doc?" he heard Cat call out as he left. Jay ignored him.

On his way home, he tried to find the weather station, his truck lurching from side to side as he flipped the dials on the radio.

"Storm warning in effect later today throughout Ontario as Hurricane Edna, which hit the islands a week ago, makes its way north."

Jay wondered if they would cancel the races at Iroquois Downs. Probably not, he decided. The horses raced in all kinds of weather: bitter cold, drenching rain, searing heat. It would take more than a storm to shut the place down for a night. By the time he reached home, it was close on four o'clock. As he flew down the driveway, he nearly collided with Helena who was on her way out.

"Where are you off to?" he asked, rolling down his window.

"To pick up Josh!" she replied.

"Josh?" he asked stupidly, unable to make sense of it.

"Our son. Remember him?" she said sweetly.

"Day Camp! Of course!" he exclaimed. "I was hoping..."

"What?" she asked impatiently, revving the Ford's engine. "I have to go, Jay. He gets all upset if I'm late."

After she left, he sat on the sofa and thought about his son. So far, Josh had acted bored whenever he brought up the subject of his Cree heritage. As for horses, he seemed to positively dislike them. He would be starting school in the fall. If Jay did nothing about it, the boy would be swept up by the mainstream culture before he'd had a chance to learn about who he was. Probably he'd already left it too late, Jay thought despondently. Hopefully, though, it wasn't too late to save the filly. He put in a call to a colleague of his at Erinsville Equine Clinic, a man in his fifties with a wealth of experience.

"Certainly sounds like a reaction to something," the veterinarian agreed. "Never heard of a reaction to Chorionic though!" Jay was tempted to tell him what he'd seen in Cat's tack room, but he decided to hold his tongue. "You've gotta get 'em to eat," his colleague continued. "That's the key in a case like this. Grass is the best thing, but turning a sick horse out in a field in this heat isn't really an option."

"You're right," Jay agreed.

"Well, good luck with her," the veterinarian said heartily.

"Thanks," Jay replied unhappily. People in his profession never used that phrase unless they considered the chances of success were slim to nonexistent. The back door slammed. Helena had returned. When he walked into the kitchen, his son didn't even look up.

"Want some ice tea?" Helena asked, her hand on the refrigerator door.

"What kind is it?" the boy asked suspiciously. "We had Nestea at camp today."

"This is way better than Nestea," Helena said firmly, producing a large jug of iced tea. "It's homemade!"

"The other boys are making fun of my name," Josh complained. "They call me Wintergreen. Why can't I have a regular name, like everyone else?" Jay knew this was his cue, but he couldn't think what to say.

"Finish your drink," Helena said. "Then Daddy and I need to talk."

"What are you going to talk about? Is it about my birthday?" the boy asked eagerly. "I want a party...can I have a party?" Suddenly, Jay found his voice.

"We need to talk about a horse first," he replied. The boy's face fell.

"You always do that," he said, scowling. Jay held his ground.

"This horse is sick. Very sick."

"I don't care about the stupid horse!"

"Josh!" Helena said disapprovingly. The boy hung his head, but he looked sullen, not repentant. Things weren't going the way Jay had hoped, but he knew if he stopped now, he was lost.

"The horse's name is Harmony Gold," he began.

"That's a wonderful name!" Helena exclaimed. The boy looked up. "What does this horse look like, Jay?" Helena prompted.

"She's a light bay with big ears."

"What's wrong with her?" the boy asked curiously, a glint of interest in his brown eyes now.

"She's not eating. She hasn't touched her feed or her hay."

"That's 'cos she doesn't like it," Josh declared.

"It's because she's sick," Jay corrected gently.

"Horses like grass," Josh persisted. "Why doesn't she eat grass?"

"She's too sick to go outside," Jay explained.

"Maybe Josh could pick her some grass?" Helena suggested brightly. "I'll go and get an old pillowcase. He can fill it up."

"Let's go out back," Jay suggested, taking Josh's hand and leading the way out to the big field at the back of the house. He showed his son how to pick the tender grass and the clover, getting right down on his knees with him, surprising himself.

"I'll be right here, watching you," Helena called out, easing herself into a hammock slung between two maple trees. "So make sure you do a good job!"

After a while, Jay joined her. He gazed at the small, earnest figure of his only child, feeling slightly more hopeful.

"What happened today?" Helena frowned, picking up on his somber mood, reading the cues correctly as always.

"I saw something in Catalino's barn this afternoon." He paused. "I may be wrong but it looks like Cat could be using an illegal pre-race, one which doesn't test positive."

"And that's a surprise?" she asked, in disbelief. "Ever since baking soda was banned, trainers have been desperate to find a substitute. You told me so yourself!"

"It's true, yes," Jay admitted.

"Bleach, steroids, human growth hormone and heaven knows what else," she continued in the same accusatory tone.

"And that's my fault?" he responded hotly.

"Of course I don't blame you, Jay. But Al McTavish used your research for his own purposes. He wanted to put a stop to race fixing. He had his own agenda."

"Al's a decent guy," Jay replied loyally. "He was rushed to hospital a couple of weeks back with multiple heart attacks, apparently. They're still not sure he's going to recover."

"I'm sorry. I had no idea," she said, reaching over and taking his hand, squeezing it gently. Thunderclouds were filling the sky. The storm was coming closer. "They've offered me a job at Josh's school," she added quietly. "Teaching second grade. I'm thinking I should take it. I'll go crazy here all by myself. Besides, the way things are going, we may need the money." A woodpecker landed on the tree beside them and began tapping for insects.

"I'm making enough at the clinic for both of us," Jay pointed out. Helena gave him a look as old as time.

"You won't be at that clinic forever," she said. "I'll give you 'til the end of

411

the year." Jay longed to contradict her, but he let it go. "It's like a marriage," Helena continued wisely. "Once you have reason to suspect someone, you're always on the lookout for evidence to support your theory. Seek and ye shall find, as the scriptures say."

"What scriptures? You don't go to church!"

"Why didn't you say anything to Cat, by the way?" she asked, ignoring his jibe.

"I did, but he double talked me. In any case, I needed some time to think about it."

"Because you've got a lot to lose," Helena replied, a look of understanding in her face. "What d'you want to do about Josh's birthday, by the way?"

"Does he have to have a party?" he asked, glancing over at the small figure in the field below them. The pillowcase was getting alarmingly full. The peace wouldn't last much longer.

"I was thinking," Helena replied, swinging her hammock back and forth, startling two chipmunks who scampered off, chattering shrilly, "you could take him to the Indian Village maybe."

"The one by the lake? The people there weren't Cree," Jay said.

"Does that matter to a boy turning five?" Helena replied a little plaintively.

"Probably not," Jay admitted. "Okay, I'll do it. You want to come too?" She shook her head.

"You and Josh should go alone, I think. A guy thing, you know?" There was a clap of thunder. The first raindrops fell. The boy stood up, threw the pillowcase over his shoulder and started running towards them. "You never told me what happened with the DNA test?" The time for conversation had almost come to an end.

"All they've discovered so far is there were seven of us at the Reserve fathered by the same man."

"Unreal!" she frowned. "Will they ever track him down, d'you think?"

"It's so long ago," Jay said, bracing himself as Josh leapt on top of him.

"Let's go feed the horsey now!" the boy said gleefully. "I got loads of grass, look!" he added, holding out the bulging pillowcase which was almost as big as him.

"It's about to pour!" Helena warned, glancing up at the sky. They raced to the shelter of the barn. The rain came thundering down on the roof as the clouds dropped their load, like a fleet of fire fighting helicopters.

Further north, at Craig and Izzy Brown's farm, the wind was picking up, lashing the trees into a frenzy and driving away the humid air. The mercury dropped precipitously. Out in the paddock, Harmony Princess was hunkered down under a stand of fir trees, her back to the wind, head down, listening to the pitter patter of rain. All around her, trees were dipping and bowing, their trunks groaning from the strain, their rain drenched branches whipped by the wind. For one old pine that had seen out countless storms, it was suddenly too much. It fell with a deafening crash, missing Princess by inches. She galloped in terror, circling her paddock at top speed, until fatigue hit her like a wall. Rain came bucketing down, chilling her to the bone. Eventually, she made it to the gate and stood there trembling, her legs shaking.

Izzy watched the curtain of rain cascading down her kitchen window. Craig was out there somewhere, bringing in the filly. She could finally give way to all of the feelings that she tried to hold off when her hubby was around. Crawford was still missing. That wasn't Craig's fault of course. But sometimes, it felt like it was. She decided to wash the kitchen floor. At least she'd be doing something useful.

Half an hour later, Craig came back inside, sopping wet from head to toe, leaving pools of muddy water everywhere.

"Whatever have you been doing in this weather?" she asked crossly, wielding her mop. "I've just washed this floor!"

"Need to call the vet," Craig muttered, turning his face away.

"Not again!" Izzy groaned.

"I thought she'd never make it back to the barn," Craig replied, still unwilling to look her in the eye. "She's tied up so bad you wouldn't believe."

"Who's tied up?" Izzy asked, halting the mopping operation.

"Princess. Just toss me the phone, love," he said. Izzy bowed to the inevitable. There were a great many things she wanted to say to Craig but she couldn't now, not with the vet coming. That filly had been nothing but trouble ever since he'd brought her home a year ago. Fourteen thousand dollars he'd paid for her! He must've lost his mind that day! Izzy didn't earn that much in a whole year, not even with all the hours she worked at the food mart. "I've given her a shot of banamine, but it hasn't helped," she heard Craig tell the vet.

Sighing deeply, Izzy went upstairs and dug out a change of clothes for Craig. Then she threw on her rain jacket, the old one with the ripped pocket, and splashed her way over to the barn. She found Princess tied to a ring on the wall, just inside the door. She was a sight to behold, drenched to the skin and covered in mud. But when Izzy tried to lead her to the wash stall, she discovered the filly could hardly put one foot in front of the other. She quickly abandoned the idea.

"A nice rub down my girl, that's what you need," Izzy told her. The dryer was on. Evidently, Craig had had the same idea. She was still towelling Princess down when the vet arrived. Craig, she was relieved to see, had taken the hint and changed into dry clothes. "I'll leave you to it," she said, making herself scarce. Back at the house, she made herself a cup of tea. The first she'd heard about Crawford going missing was when some man from the RCMP had called, asking questions. At first, every time the phone rang she'd jumped up to answer it, hoping for news. But it had been five weeks now and there had been no sign of him. Crawfish usually popped in every couple of weeks. It didn't make any sense.

Craig was back.

"I know what you're going to say," he declared, before she'd said a word, before she'd even opened her mouth to speak. "You don't need to worry, I'm going out first thing tomorrow morning to get myself a job. I know we can't go on like this." It was a little late in the day for Craig to come to his senses but better late than never, she supposed. Surprisingly, she didn't feel relieved. Nothing seemed to matter much to her anymore. She walked into the lounge and turned on the TV. *Wind at My Back* would be on in a minute. "Doc's put her on Dantrium. She'll be alright in a day or two," Craig called out from the kitchen. Dantrium wasn't cheap but it was best not to say anything. She'd only get her head bitten off. "You're looking tired, Izzy," Craig said, following her into the lounge, a mug of tea in his hand. "Soon as I get a job, you oughta cut back on your hours at the food mart, take it easy for a bit."

"I don't mind working," she replied stiffly. Besides, what would I do all day? she asked herself. The boys had moved out, all four of them at once! They were making a fortune in the oil fields, apparently. She had hoped things would get better after they'd left. But the sight of all those empty bedrooms got her down.

"You know what I'm gonna do for you?" Craig pronounced cheerfully. "Soon as I get a job, I'm going to buy you a brand new kitchen."

"But Crawford was going to build it for me," she protested. "We had it all planned out."

"Don't you worry about a thing," Craig continued, as if she hadn't spoken.

"They've got them on sale at Kut Price. Doc told me. Nothin' to pay for two years. What d'you have to say about that, eh Izzy?" Dully, she noticed he'd slopped his tea all over the rug. A kitchen from Kut Price wasn't what she'd had in mind at all. Still, there wasn't any point in hankering over something she couldn't have, she decided, staring at the spreading stain. Craig liked his tea good and strong. She was going to have a terrible time getting that out. "While I'm at it I'll get the kitchen floor levelled out for you 'n' all," Craig said heartily. "You deserve it!" It looked like her dream kitchen was up in smoke. With Crawford going missing, there was nothing much she could do about it. "Mind if I turn this junk off?" Craig asked, switching over to the baseball. Izzy went into the bathroom and cried until no more tears came. She was in there a good twenty minutes before Craig realized anything was amiss.

"He'll turn up one of these days," he said comfortingly, when she reappeared red eyed. "He always comes out to the farm on your birthday. Wait 'til then. You'll see!"

But when her birthday came and went and there was still no sign of Crawford, she could tell even Craig was getting worried. That worried her all the more.

Andy Price had stopped worrying about Crawfish Brown. He was convinced he'd show up again sometime, like a bad penny. But he still missed him. Running a claiming stable was like being in a warzone in Andy's experience. His barn was full of battle scarred veterans. His job was to get them back on their feet after they raced, fix them up and send them out to do battle again, exactly one week later. There was no room for sentiment in the claiming game. In that regard, Crawfish had been a real asset. He'd never wasted time with pointless observations, never offered an opinion. He'd just buttoned his lip and got on with the job. As for Crawfish's odd looks and habits, his occasional drinking bouts and his pilfering, that didn't bother Andy at all. Looks weren't the most important thing in this business and he had known before he'd taken him on: Crawfish was no angel.

The scent of clover and wild onion filled the cab as Jay Winterflood drove slowly along the rain soaked country roads, with his son beside him. At Cat's barn, there wasn't a human in sight. They had all left for the races. This time the tack room door was securely locked. Harmony Gold greeted her visitors with a grace that was sadly lacking in most humans, in Jay's opinion. Despite her illness, the filly was holding herself erect, every inch a lady.

"Promise she won't bite me," Josh asked fearfully, backing away.

"Hold your hand out flat like a plate," Jay told him but the boy wasn't listening. He reached into his sack and threw great handfuls of grass over the stall gate, startling the filly who retreated to a far corner.

"She doesn't like it," Josh said, his small shoulders drooping.

"Wait," Jay whispered. Eventually the filly swung around, her nostrils flaring. His hands resting on his son's shoulders, Jay held his breath as Harmony Gold lowered her head. Several agonizing minutes later, the sound of her powerful jaws munching away reverberated around the stall. Jay heaved a sigh of relief, for both youngsters.

"I did it!" the boy cried, his eyes shining.

On their way home, Jay switched on the radio. A popular melody got underway, one he knew well.

"Listen, Dad!" his son suddenly exclaimed. "It's about Goldie!"

"Heart of Gold," Jay replied smiling to himself. "It's about finding true love, son, like I found your mother." That went right over the child's head.

"Tomorrow," Josh announced jubilantly. "Soon as I wake up, I'm getting more grass. I'm gonna get..." Jay could hear him counting earnestly. "This much!" he declared at last holding out both hands, fingers played out.

"What about Day Camp?" Jay asked, keeping his tone light. "It's your birthday tomorrow, remember?"

"For my birthday," Josh said dreamily. "Can I get whatever I want?"

"Maybe," Jay hedged, his eyes on the trees crowding the road ahead, their overhanging branches still shedding water from the rainstorm that had passed by.

"I don't want to go to Day Camp with all the other kids tomorrow, I want to stay and help Goldie," the boy declared. Jay hadn't seen that coming!

"Okay," he agreed. "If you're sure."

"You see, Dad," Josh explained. "Goldie is better than.." he stopped, apparently stuck for the right word.

"Better than camp?" Jay suggested.

"Better than everything," Josh breathed. Jay's heart swelled with pride. "Except ice cream," his son added. "Can I have my birthday cake tonight? Please?" They were back in the real world. But as he drove, Jay could not remember feeling happier than this. He gazed at the fields, refreshed after the rain, like Helena's face after tears. She was more precious to him now than ever, the mother of his son. How could his own father have abandoned him and his mother, walking away, never to return? he asked himself for the thousandth time. Now he had a son of his own, he would never understand it.

What kind of a man was he?

THE TRAVELLING CIRCUS

"Hey, Horse Boy!" the clown shouted in his deep carrying voice. "Boss wants to see you. Right away!" Crawfish peered out from behind the dappled grey he'd been grooming. "Yeah you!" the clown said, poking a finger in his direction.

"I ain't done nothin'," Crawfish muttered.

"Ain't you just," the clown replied nastily. Then he left, stomping off in his oversized shoes. Best spruce myself up a bit, Crawfish thought anxiously, legging it over to the water trough and wondering what was in store. Circus folk were a weird bunch. He couldn't figure 'em out. They liked grey horses for a start. But greys were always bad actors. Everyone knew that, so why use 'em in a circus act? Give him a nice bay gelding any day of the week. On the plus side, they were a tight bunch. They didn't trust strangers. If Shitface and Pervert ever showed their faces, they'd send 'em packing! Nabbing that circus poster at the Bus Station had been the smartest thing he'd ever done... no one'd ever find him here. So long as he hung on to his job, he was safe enough for now. He hadn't copped it like Vettore, poor sod. Still, he wasn't counting his chickens. Anything could happen.

A few minutes later, his hands washed and his hair slicked down, Crawfish knocked on the door of the circus boss's silver horse trailer, gleaming in the afternoon sun. The door opened.

"I'm moving you to the elephants," the Big Man announced, buttoning up his red waistcoat, readying himself for the early show. "Joel's a man short."

"Elephants!" Crawfish exclaimed, feeling horrified. "I don't know nothin' 'bout elephants," he stuttered.

"Easy! They're the same as horses, only bigger," the Big Man replied. Crawfish stood there, open mouthed. "It's that or nothin'. You want the job?" Crawfish craned his neck, trying to get a look see inside the boss's trailer. It was like a palace in there: flat screen TVs and comfy sofas, nothing like his own humble quarters. "Take it or leave it," the Big Man snapped, making to go back inside. Crawfish gulped.

"A' right, boss," he said.

"Joel will show you what to do. Now git!" The trailer door slammed shut. Crawfish swallowed hard and made his way over to the elephant tent. He couldn't go back home. Not yet. Fear had brought him here. But love had its hold on him now. A beautiful acrobat named Mirabella had laid claim to his heart. She was everything he was not. She moved with an easy grace that made him colour up with a confusing mix of pride and shame whenever she passed by. He had never missed a single one of her performances. But so far he had only worshipped from a distance. Night after night, he dreamed that she lost her balance and fell from the high wire, only to land safe in his arms to thunderous applause. When he awoke to reality, he lay alone in the dark in an agony of regret. Ever since the car crash, ten years ago now, he hadn't been able to recognize himself in the mirror, he was so changed. It hadn't seemed to matter very much before. His despair had been buried so deep by his teenage self he hadn't even known it was there.

Until now.

ERINSVILLE, ONTARIO

The evening sun glinted on the spokes of Billie McTavish's mountain bike as she free wheeled down Laurel Drive and coasted into number 210. She could have taken the car, but cycling was an easy way to stay in shape. She had let her gym membership lapse. In good weather, she preferred the great outdoors. Sofia was there to greet her at the front door.

"He's awake! I'll be in the kitchen. Just go on in, sweetheart," Sofia said, bustling off.

Al's study was flooded with light. Dust particles were dancing in the bright air. Tucked up in a makeshift bed, blinking at her, was Al himself. He had taken another leap forward, Billie observed. The deep lines had faded from his face which was now back to its normal, healthy colour. By operating when he did and installing a heart pump, Dr. Aldright had not only saved her father's life, he had given Al's damaged heart a chance to heal. The heart pump was no longer necessary. Al was out of danger and in full recovery mode.

"It's so good to see you looking better," Billie said happily, parking herself on the swivel chair beside Al's desk. At the bottom of the bed, Walter lay purring, basking in a shaft of sunlight.

"We're both of us getting on a bit," Al replied, looking at the cat fondly. "I see more of him than anyone else these days…I was hoping I'd be up and about by now. But your mother. . . she won't let me do anything! She's like a tigress with her young. Now I know how you children must have felt."

"That's Mom!" Billie agreed with a smile.

"The truth is, I'm lucky to be alive," Al said thoughtfully. "I've had a lot of time to think lately…I intend to make some big changes…I know it's a cliché but…"

"A good one," Billie put in quickly, her conscience stabbing her. She still hadn't told him about Phil's accusations of bid rigging. But how could she? This certainly wasn't the time. "So what are you going to do, Dad?" she asked hesitantly.

"It's more what I'm not going to do," Al said. "I need to take a break from Iroquois Downs…take some sick leave. At least three, maybe six months."

"Great idea," Billie replied enthusiastically.

"And I'm putting McTavish Construction on the market."

"What?" Billie exclaimed in disbelief. McTavish Construction had always been part of her father's life. It defined him.

"It's time," Al said.

"But…" If only she hadn't left her father's company to start Fence Sense, she thought guiltily. He wouldn't be talking like this now.

"No buts," Al replied kindly, but firmly. "It'll mean I'll have time for things I really care about."

"Such as?" she enquired. Was he going to go all sentimental and talk about spending more time with the family? That would be a first.

"Not sure yet…I failed, Billie."

"No!" she cried.

"Yes! I put a stop to cheating, but I made things far worse for the horses. Don't try to tell me otherwise."

"What about the retention barn…surely…," she trailed off.

"Mixed reviews I'd say," Al replied candidly. "If I do go back to Iroquois Downs, I intend to do something for the ones who put on the show, night after night."

"The horsemen?" she frowned.

"The horses, Billie. Get that right and the rest will follow."

"Okay! When do we start?" she exclaimed eagerly. "Just say the word, Dad!" Al lay back on the pillows.

"Not we…you," he replied faintly, looking exhausted all of a sudden.

"Walter, supper!" Sofia called shrilly. The cat was up and out of the room in two seconds flat.

"He hasn't lost his speed," Billie remarked admiringly.

"Not where food is concerned," Al agreed with a small smile.

"I'll leave you to rest," Billie said quietly. "Count me in, Dad," she added, tiptoeing out of the room.

Sofia was in the kitchen, washing up pots and pans.

"D'you have anything for me to eat?" Billie asked hungrily, opening the refrigerator door. "Dad's asleep, by the way," she added.

"Thanks God for Dr. Aldright," Sofia replied fervently. "He and the Mountie. Together they save his life. One day, I shall thank them both."

"Maybe I should order in a pizza," Billie wondered out loud.

"Delivery you mean?" Sofia asked in an astonished tone. "You want a piece of burnt bread with no cheese! Then yes. But a panini is quick…how would that be for you?"

"Terrific!" Billie replied enthusiastically. Her mother got busy, leaving Billie to her own thoughts. It had been well over a month, but Campbell McClaren still hadn't contacted her. Perhaps he never would.

The panini was amazing. She washed it down with a glass of Italian red and wondered why she was even thinking about Campbell McClaren. The answer came back to her in a flash.

The heart has reasons, that reason cannot know.

WESTWARD BOUND

Campbell McClaren hadn't had to resort to takeaway food for supper. Not quite. However, fish served up by room service wasn't a patch on the seafood in PEI, where shrimp, crab and lobster were always on the menu, even in the humblest of households. But there was no sense in indulging in nostalgia. He was on his way to the opposite coast, as far away from PEI as it was possible to go and still be in Canada. For six straight weeks, he had hardly drawn breath. He had hoped, once his spell working at the Hot Tamale had come to an end, that he would be able to close the door on working undercover and walk away. Things were never simple, apparently. Instead, he'd been subjected to a series of debriefing sessions, followed by a score of post mortems on the fiasco of Theo Vettore's disappearance. The loss of a potential star witness for the prosecution had made everyone jumpy. The only information they had to go on, the interview with Vettore dutifully recorded by Campbell, was sadly lacking in crucial details. So far, the finger of blame was not pointing directly at him. But he had no doubt they would get around to it in time.

After all the second guessing was over and done, he had joined his fellow officers in the fun task of rounding up the remainder of the small fry in Ontario. However, following the time honoured method of using the little guys to work their way up the ladder had produced surprisingly few results. Nevertheless, the RCMP were declaring the operation a success. Certainly the drug scene had quieted down, yet the little Campbell knew about the Scorpion left him deeply skeptical of easy victories.

Meanwhile, the search for Vettore had ground to a halt. Officially, the Provincial Police continued to treat the car's plunge into the abyss as an accident, making excuses for their inability to find a body, citing the charred remains of the car, blinding the public with pseudo science. Unofficially, it was a different story. But when Campbell suggested widening the search beyond Ontario, he was met with blank stares. He quickly dropped the idea, reckoning he was in enough trouble already. One problem was his lowly ranking. But that, he freely acknowledged, was his own fault. As a young recruit, he'd had a lot of foolish ideas which hadn't worked out in practice. He was older now and wiser. Unfortunately, like the boy who cried wolf, his ideas were no longer welcome. Perhaps it was time to give up on his boyhood ambition. For what, he had no idea. Life as a security guard didn't tempt him, nor did moving around obscene amounts of cash in armoured vehicles. He longed for a chance to use his brain, instead of being forced to let others do the thinking for him.

However, he would soon be leaving Ontario, with all its problems and unanswered questions, far behind. He had been given twenty-four hours notice, a night in a cheap hotel and a plane ticket west. According to his superiors, the cocaine trail led directly to Vancouver. In his opinion, it was a red herring. However, he kept his doubts to himself. Hurricane season or no, he would have much preferred to be travelling south. But there was little point in that at present. If only Vettore had revealed the name of the island where the Scorpion had his lair, he thought regretfully.

Next morning, he was up at dawn. It took him no time at all to pack up his small suitcase and check out of the hotel. His flight to Vancouver left at 7 p.m. That gave him about ten hours to track down Miss Billie McTavish. Now Crawfish had been added to the list of missing persons, she was his last hope. Had Vettore confided in her? He had no idea. There was only one way to find out.

McTavish Construction was his first point of call. She wasn't there, of course, but the switchboard gave him the number of Fence Sense without question. Erinsville was that kind of town. He drove over to the warehouse down by the river and parked his hired car in full view of the front entrance. Her line was busy for over half an hour. He persisted. Eventually, she picked up.

"Hi stranger," she said coolly. It wasn't a wonderful start.

"I haven't had a chance to get in touch until today," he explained apologetically. "I've been working twenty-four seven."

"Fighting crime?" she enquired in a tone that made it clear she wasn't buying it.

"Being grilled by my superior officers, mostly," he replied in a bid to get a more sympathetic response.

"Yes, well, it hasn't been an easy time for me either," she replied wistfully.

"I can imagine."

"Can you?"

"I've been getting regular updates on your father's progress," he ventured.

"Really?" she asked, sounding slightly mollified.

"I'd really like to talk to you," he said.

"Officially or unofficially?"

"Both."

"I'm not a criminal," she pointed out.

"I need to ask you some questions," he persisted. "It's important."

"Well, I haven't got time now,' she said matter of factly. "Maybe in a couple of hours or so. Where are you?"

"I'm parked right by the front entrance," he confessed.

"Stalker!" she replied in an accusatory tone. For the life of him, Campbell couldn't think of a suitable response. "Okay," she sighed. "But only because I don't want to make a scene in front of my staff. Come back at twelve thirty. I'll meet you outside."

That gave Campbell time to find a place for their meeting. It should be somewhere quiet, he decided. He bought a map and spotted an area of farmland which looked promising. He set out to explore and eventually came across *The Country Store and Restaurant* at a place called Four Corners. It felt like it was in the middle of nowhere, but in fact it was a mere fifteen minutes' drive from Billie's office. Outside the diner, picnic tables were sitting in the shade. A cool breeze blew in from the river. There was no menu, just plenty of home cooked food. It would do nicely, he thought.

He drove back and settled down to wait. When Billie eventually made an appearance, he was taken aback by the change in her. The past six weeks had taken a big toll on Miss Billie McTavish. He noticed it immediately: the telltale bony shoulders, the way she folded up into nothing when she got into the passenger seat. She was far too thin.

"Where are you taking me?" she asked a little defiantly.

"Somewhere with great food," he replied. A warm smile was his reward.

At 6:45 p.m., Campbell reluctantly boarded the plane to Vancouver. Outside, the sun was still shining as it had done all day. After takeoff, he looked down, searching the Ontario countryside for a glimpse of Four Corners, far below. Lunch with Billie had been an unsettling experience. The food, corn cobs, back bacon and fries followed by pancakes and maple syrup (typical Ontario fare), wasn't the problem. Neither was Billie herself. After eating a hearty meal, she'd answered all his questions with a disarming frankness. Thanks to her, he had one of the missing pieces to the jigsaw: the name of the island. There were no guarantees, but from what she'd told him, he was fairly sure he had hit the jackpot in that regard. He also had the names of two other people who had been close to Vettore: his uncle and his cousin,

Lara. But after spending an hour or two with Billie, he couldn't even begin to fathom what she had seen in a drug addict like Vettore.

As a couple, she and Vettore made absolutely no sense.

SAINTE MARIE

A phone was ringing shrilly through the Hermitage, echoing off the white walls and towering ceilings. A maid in black uniform ran to answer it, her heels click clacking on the marble floors.

"I am so sorry to disturb you, sir," she apologized, proffering the phone to the man sitting out on the deck, his lounge chair positioned perfectly to catch the last rays of sun as it took its nightly dip into the Caribbean Sea. André Fontainbleu held out his hand for the phone.

"*Oui, c'est moi*," he said. "*Fontainbleu ici.*" After that, nothing. Only the rustle of a bird's wing as it went to roost and the man's steady breathing as he listened intently, his eyes roaming over the pool, up the soaring marble columns, then out to the horizon. Dusk was falling. He laughed. Silently at first, then out loud in full throated delight. "Vancouver!" he exclaimed. "*Quelle surprise!*" A bat appeared, swooping over his head. He shivered, then swiftly recovered his *sangfroid*. "Natalie, my drink!" he called out, his voice echoing in the cavernous rooms. He settled himself down on a white sofa in the vast living room and prepared to wait.

The maid was back…with a very pretty young girl in tow. She looked twenty, but he knew for a fact she was much, much younger.

"My daughter, sir," the maid said, placing the silver tray she was carrying on the glass table.

"Leave us!" he said, dismissing the maid with a flick of his fingers. The girl was dark skinned like the mother, but she was nothing like her. Her looks, her manner, were entirely different. "What do they call you, child?" he asked, knowing the word would be an insult to her.

"Colette. And I'm not a child," she pouted. No, indeed!

"You like school?"

"School! What use is school to me? They teach me nothing," she replied, her hands on her hips. She was a firecracker, this one. But she was not his type. She was no innocent. Besides, the mother would be listening at the door. She was a good maid. He did not wish to lose her.

"I could use you," he said, looking the girl up and down in a deliberately suggestive manner. "To help entertain my clients. You understand what I am saying to you?"

"Perfectly, *monsieur*." He sent her away with a wave of his hand. He sighed. A long evening alone with his thoughts stretched out ahead of him. He picked up the phone and punched in the usual number.

"Yes, boss!" a voice answered.

"Tell me, my friend, what are the odds on the favourite in the fifth at Iroquois Downs?"

"To win?"

"To lose."

"Evens, boss."

"That's fair."

"The usual amount?"

"Yes. And Boxer."

"Yes, boss."

"No mistakes this time." He rang off. Easy money. Money he did not need. But it afforded him a *frisson* of excitement, like the girl, Colette. But pleasure was not everything. Lately, unaccountably, his brother had been occupying his thoughts. *Domage! Domage! Domage!* It was true what the English said: blood was thicker than water. But what was the use? Philippe had been dead for thirty years!

SASKATCHEWAN

In the crystal clear air, the distant mountains appeared close enough to touch, thrusting themselves forward like a girl with big breasts, tempting the man known as Scarecrow to roll down the window and reach out for them. He resisted the temptation. His fellow passengers were a good natured, tolerant bunch, but he didn't want to push his luck. He had found a safe enough refuge at Lost Valley Ranch. However, he still felt vulnerable, fearful of the harsh world outside its gates. The memory of his past life remained a mystery.

The truck was bouncing along the country roads, its suspension shot. None of them cared. It added to the fun, an excuse for hoots and hollas as they hurtled through a landscape of waving grass bleached blond by endless sunny days. A day without chores was something to celebrate! At long last their destination, North Wood County Fair, hove into view, tucked into the land as if it had always been there. As they passed under a red, white and blue banner, advertising the hundredth year of the fair, Scarecrow caught a glimpse of a Ferris wheel turning and below it, dust dancing and swirling on an oval track. Out of the blue, he felt a ripple of excitement so intense that, for a split second, he could hardly breathe. Then it was gone, forgotten as the truck careered around a corner, speeding past dozens of horse trailers parked chaotically, like a scene from a disaster movie he had watched recently. The place was alive with horses: tied unceremoniously to the backs of trucks, or tethered to trees, their harnesses hanging from branches or draped over car doors. And everywhere, small carts with shafts curved like wishbones stood upended, jostling for room in the mayhem.

The man called Scarecrow longed to stop and stare. His companions had other ideas. Abandoning the truck, they struck out for the bar, elbowing their way through the forest of Stetsons and cowboy boots, dodging the line ups at the hot dog and hamburger stands, ignoring the sizzle of frying onions and the fierce smell of mustard; Scarecrow followed in their wake. At last, drawn by the tangy smell of beer, like bees to honey, amid sounds as joyful as a children's playground, they reached their goal. Scarecrow stood on the sidelines while his workmates crowded around. Beer was anathema to him. It made him feel even more confused than he was already. He had had plenty of time to speculate about his situation. He knew in his heart that his problem wasn't just simple concussion, not after all this time. He was afraid to go to the police. The risk of being banged up in a cell terrified him. He could be a killer for all he knew. If so, he had found the perfect hiding place. But it puzzled him that so far no one had recognized him. It was both a blessing and a curse.

He took a token sip of his beer and was looking around for a discreet place to ditch the rest of it, when a bugle rang out, its harsh notes reverberating in his head like his morning alarm. For a sickening moment, he wasn't certain whether he was asleep or awake. A wave of nausea washed over him. Needing some air, he stumbled out of the bar, his head reeling. For one tantalizing moment, the fog that had obscured the view to his past had lifted, leaving in its wake a shred of memory which was already slipping through his fingers, like the remnants of a dream. Abandoning his companions, he followed the crowd streaming into the small grandstand. It was already packed with ranching families: the men standing shoulder to shoulder, scanning the racetrack with eyes more accustomed to spotting stray cattle, their wives, buxom women in jeans, taking advantage of a rare chance to gossip while their children played tag around the rough wooden benches.

Above them, the omnipresent mountains loomed like thunderclouds in a big empty sky.

"Here's your field for the first, folks," the announcer was saying. "Purse of eight hundred dollars for horses who haven't won a race yet, led off by Calgary Boy. Next up is Harmony Storm, owned by Dan Mills who trains and drives. Nice colt there, Dan, and he's only a two year old." Dan, whose driving colours looked as ancient as he did, responded with a curt nod, then immediately took his horse off to the farthest corner of the racetrack, away from the other horses. 'Must be high strung,' Scarecrow concluded. In the confusing world which he inhabited, horses at least were easy enough for him to read. "Now folks, we got us a celebrity here today," the announcer was saying proudly. "Moose Rankin, top driver at World Famous Iroquois Downs Raceway is in the box with me this afternoon. Grew up right down the road in Moose Jaw! Drove the first race of his life right here! Who'd you fancy in the first then, Moose?"

"Pal o' mine's driving the 3 horse," Moose confided. "But I gotta say, I kinda like the looks o' that Harmony horse."

"The grey?"

"Yup," Moose bellowed into the loudspeaker. "Jus' last week I won a big stake with a colt from the same farm, Harmony Light."

"You heard it here, folks!" the announcer declared enthusiastically. "Hot tip from the hottest driver in North America today. Number Two, Harmony Storm. Better hurry though, only four minutes to post! Get your bets in!" The odds on Storm came crashing down from 12-1 to even money, as over two hundred dollars went into the win pool, then crept back up to 3-1. Meanwhile, Storm launched a challenge at the 4 horse, striking out at him like a full grown stallion.

'I sure figured him out!' Scarecrow thought happily. Sure enough, when the wings of the gate opened, Storm stopped dead. Uh oh. Trouble! Scarecrow thought, wondering briefly where that phrase had come from as the horse wheeled around and took off in the opposite direction. Several minutes later the starting car was rolling and Dan Mills was back in control. He was hanging back, keeping Storm well away from the gate, allowing the horses on the outside to catch up as they swung around the turn. As they entered the straight, the car picked up speed. Dan tried to urge his horse on. But instead of going forward, Storm went skywards, rearing up, teetering precariously on his hind legs, his front feet pawing the air. A roar of despair went up from the stands. The race was starting without the favourite! The other horses were streaming past, but no one in the crowd cared. They were too busy watching the grey colt, who looked certain now to fall over backwards right into the driver's lap. Scarecrow watched too, fearing the worst.

"He's going ass over tip!" the announcer cried, losing his head in the heat of the moment. But they had all reckoned without old Dan Mills. He let up on the lines and gave Storm a resounding crack on the rump with his whip. A heart stopping second later, Storm came down from his perch and landed pacing. A ragged cheer went up as Dan steered him towards the inside rail. Astonishingly, by the quarter pole, Storm had almost caught up with the last horse. Scarecrow was on his feet, breathing hard, his palms sweating. It had nothing to do with the two-dollar ticket clenched in his hand. For a moment there, he'd been so involved he'd felt as though he had been the one in the sulky. Nothing like this had ever happened to him before. It had to mean something! Shakily, he sat down again, his eyes still riveted on the grey colt. Dan Mills was sitting quietly at the back of the pack now, his hands steady. He's trying to get the colt to relax Scarecrow realized. He didn't know how he knew that. It puzzled him. By the half-mile point, most of the drivers had got itchy fingers and had pulled their horses out, enabling Dan to slip through on the inside rail. He's taking the short way home, Scarecrow thought appreciatively. But as the pace slowed, Storm began high stepping, like he was going to climb clear over the horse in front of him.

"He's trapped!" Scarecrow exclaimed, gritting his teeth as he watched Storm's head plunging wildly up and down. At the top of the stretch, the horse sitting outside Storm began to fall back. "Pull!" Scarecrow screamed. "Pull, damn you!" A split second later, Dan yanked on the right line. But even though he was out and clear, Storm wasn't going anywhere. He's scared, Scarecrow thought. He's just a baby after all. But Dan Mills didn't give up. He gave Storm a little tap with his whip to encourage him to pass the 4 horse. As he drew level, the other colt broke stride. And no wonder! Scarecrow realized, remembering Storm's attack on the 4 horse before the race had begun. Buoyed up by success, the grey colt grabbed the bit and flew past the next three horses like they were standing still. There was only one left to beat now, but he was several lengths ahead. He'll never make it, Scarecrow thought, screwing up his win ticket and preparing to ditch it. But Storm was on fire now, gobbling up the ground. As he entered the stretch, he started hauling in the leader like a fish. All around him, people were jumping to their feet, chanting Storm's name. Scarecrow couldn't remember feeling this excited before, ever! The two horses went past the finish post so fast he couldn't tell who had won.

After a long delay, the judges declared Harmony Storm had finished first by a nose. The celebrity guy was suddenly everyone's new best friend. There were so many people crowding around the winner's circle. Scarecrow didn't even try to go there. Ramming his black Stetson down hard on his head, he sprinted for the exit, catching up with Storm as he left the track, still surrounded by wellwishers. "Great drive, Dan!" he called out. Dan Mills acknowledged the compliment with a broad smile, but there was no hint of recognition in the old man's face. After all Scarecrow's hopes that he'd finally found a place he belonged, this was a bitter blow. He didn't know what he had expected, exactly. He was just tired of being treated like an outsider everywhere he went. But he couldn't bring himself to walk away. Instead, he stood motionless, lost in thought long after Dan and his dappled grey had disappeared. He had come so close but the sliver of memory that had appeared out of nowhere had gone, never to return.

"Hey, what's up, Scarecrow?" he heard someone call out. One of the ranch hands, wearing leather chaps, came lumbering up alongside him, a foolish grin on his face.

"This whole place…feels weird! The crowds…the horses. I feel like I've seen it all before…," Scarecrow replied. He gave his head a little shake, in a vain attempt to dredge up the fleeting memory. "It's no good. I can't figure it out," he added sorrowfully.

"Yeah, that kinda thing can happen when you've had too many beers. It can really mess with your head," his friend laughed. "Only one cure for it! We gotta get us back to the bar. But this time you're buying. I only got five bucks left."

"Later. I want to catch the next race," Scarecrow replied decisively.

"Now you really gone an' wrecked my day," his friend grumbled good naturedly, trundling along behind him.

Four races later, Scarecrow was still no closer to solving the mystery, but he had picked out three winners at long odds.

"Hey! You're pretty good at this, Scarecrow," his friend exclaimed happily as he totaled up his winnings. "I'm coming back next year with some serious money. Make me a killing."

"Next year?" Scarecrow frowned, startled.

"Yup, this kind thing don't happen too often round these parts…'course there's always the rodeo but that ain't 'til next month. Anyhow, it's a helluva long way…took us the best part o' five hours to get here." But Scarecrow wasn't paying attention. Something that happened only once a year wasn't likely to hold the key to his past after all, he realized. In fact, he had probably imagined the whole thing. Maybe his friend was right. Maybe it was just his mind playing tricks on him.

"C'mon, I'll buy you a beer," he offered. Before, he'd been desperate to remember. But he was through torturing himself. All he wanted now was to forget.

Old Dan Mills steered a steady course back to the grove of birch trees which had been pressed into service as a Race Barn. It was slow going, what with all the folks crowding about him, waving win tickets, telling him what a nice colt he had there. Everyone loves a winner, he thought smiling to himself. Should've had the sense to back him myself, he thought. Well! Guess it's too late now. As for Storm being a nice colt, he didn't agree with that. Not anymore. Not after he'd attacked the 4 horse after the post parade, not after he'd reared up and almost gone over backwards before the race had even started. Back home, he'd always acted so quiet, but he'd changed!

"Keep this up and you'll be a gelding, my son," he muttered under his breath. "Mebbe I should let that hotshot driver from the big time take you home with him," he added. Moose Rankin had popped the question in the winner's circle. But that was just talk. He wasn't likely to offer much, not with a win time in 2:02. Truth was though, the thirty thousand dollars Dan owed on the combine harvester was a weight on his mind. It'd sure be nice if he could pay down the loan some, he thought. The four-hundred dollar purse he had won today had hardly covered his expenses. What with harvesting coming up, he wasn't going to have the time to go to the track every day anymore. "I reckon you're safe," he told Storm. "That celebrity guy'll come to his senses soon enough. I jus' gave you the drive of your life, is all." That tall, serious lookin' boy with the black Stetson had really made Dan's day. Any old fool could luck out with a good colt, but someone complimenting his driving skills: that was something special. Just the memory of it had Dan grinning like an idiot. Nothing could shake that warm, fuzzy feeling. Not when Storm knocked over his bath bucket before he'd finished bathing him, not even when the colt refused to drink a drop of the water Dan had carried a long way from the only tap in the place. He held onto that feeling every step of the long drive back home. After he'd put Storm away, he walked to the shed, climbed up on his old tractor and rumbled over to the back forty. Then he cut out the engine and let the quiet of the place wash over him.

"We won!" he cried, his old voice cracking, startling a deer, who bounded away, her white tail bobbing up and down among the wildflowers and tall grasses. The right thing to do would be to geld Storm and turn him out for a bit, he decided. He could start him back when the weather turned cold. He could picture it all now. The frosty mornings, the snug tack room where he and his fellow horsemen would gather after they were done driving, huddling round the single stove, warming their frozen feet and hands, sipping coffee laced with a slug of whiskey, and swapping stories…he'd get to relive Storm's win many times before spring came again.

A car door slammed. It was Abigail.

"I reckoned I'd find you here," she cried, a look of triumph on her face. "You're not gonna believe this. We've had an offer for the colt! Twenty-five thousand dollars! What d'you think of that then Dan?" Dan's rosy vision of the future went up in flames, as surely as if some hoodlum had doused the barn with gasoline and set a match to it. "That's close to what we owe on the combine," she added. "Isn't it?" There was no shirking that ugly truth. There was no sense denying either that the loan on the combine had plagued him night and day these five years. Selling Storm would mean he wouldn't have to put the back forty under the plow. And once lost, his prairie meadow would be gone forever. It would never be the way it was now: a perfect mix of grasses and wildflowers that made for the best hay in the county. No point in making hay if there's no livestock to feed it to, his logical mind replied. Abigail was still there waiting for an answer.

"I won't take a cent less than thirty thousand," Dan finally declared. The pull of the land was strong. He belonged to this place. The dirt beneath his fingernails bore witness to that. One day, he'd be buried out here. "An' I'll be taking out five thousand to buy me another horse," he added in a tone that brooked no refusal. He started up the tractor and headed back to the barn. "Gonna have to leave it in God's hands," he told Storm quietly as he led him into the top paddock, lined with trees. He glanced up at the sky. It wouldn't rain tonight. The air smelled of newly mown grass and honeysuckle. Tomorrow, he'd begin harvesting the mint. Then the whole cycle would start all over again. There was comfort in that. He lingered at the paddock gate, watching the setting sun cast its glow over the fields, feeling a tremor of excitement at the recollection of his win: their win, him and Storm. They'd set the world alight today. Whatever was to come, no one was going to take that away from him.

No, sir!

Elephants, Crawfish discovered, ate mountains of hay and had whoppin' great turds. Bathing the creatures was like washing a fuckin' house. As for groomin', the beasts were so tall he had to use a brush stuck on the end of a pole! Even so, he often had to stand on his tiptoes, no easy task with his gammy leg. But the day Joel handed him a whoppin' great rasp and told him to give a female a pedicure, really took the biscuit. Crawfish threatened to quit there and then.

"Suit yourself," Joel said. "But I haven't got time for this. The elephants need dressing up. It's show time!" Crawfish swallowed his pride and got back to work. Joel wasn't a bad sort, really. He let him take his break when the acrobats came on and he wasn't nosy neither, not like some folks.

Two months had passed since Crawfish had left home. Summer was nearly over. The circus moved to another town every week. He had no idea where they were now but he didn't care. What mattered was that he'd shaken off

Pervert and Shitface. That was enough for him to be getting on with. Besides, Mirabella was here. Hadn't he given up chewing tobacco just for her? Course, Joel had told him he'd throw him out if he didn't quit the habit on account of the elephants not liking it. But still…

Every evening at around 8 p.m. Crawfish hobbled over to the Big Top and slipped under the canvas. Tonight was no exception. Lotta empty seats! he observed with gloomy satisfaction, as he stationed himself in his usual spot beside the exit, safe from prying eyes. He was so intent on becoming invisible, melting into the darkest corner he could find, his eyes downcast, that he didn't see the clown until he was right on top of him.

"Hey, Elephant Boy! You gotta get outa here. Right now!"

"Why's that then?" Crawfish hissed, unwilling to leave his post.

"Candyfloss Kid wants you!" the clown snarled, pointing a menacing finger at him. "Git!" Sighing, Crawfish scuttled off. The clown did a good job making the audiences laugh. If only they knew what he's really like! he thought resentfully. And what on earth did Candyfloss Kid want with him? he wondered as he sidled up to the stand.

"About time!" the Kid exclaimed. Crawfish licked his lips nervously. An' no chance of a free piece o' the pink stuff neither, he realized as the Kid grabbed him by the elbow. "Do as she says okay? Don't make me thump you one!" he warned.

"What the…?" Crawfish stuttered as he was hustled along. He ended up outside a beat up trailer.

"Get in there!" the Kid said roughly, giving him a shove up the backside. Crawfish clambered up the steps and opened the flimsy door. Peeking inside, he did a double take. Sitting on a chair, wearing a sparkly costume that clung to her body so close it brought a flush to his cheeks, was his one and only love: Mirabella the acrobat! Could it really be her? he thought, rubbing his eyes. But she was there alright, looking like a princess in a fairy tale.

"Come in and sit down," she said. His heart leapt. She wanted to see him! His left eye began to twitch, as it always did when he was seized by some powerful emotion. "It's a' right Zack, I can handle him," she added. Crawfish gulped. This didn't sound like love talk! "What's your name?" she asked curiously.

"Crawford," he replied. Anyone who called him Crawfish better watch it or they'd get their face smashed in, he thought, clenching and unclenching his fists. Even Elephant Boy was better than that!

"Okay, Crawford, don't lie to me, a'right? Did the boss put you up to this?"

"Put me up to what?" he asked, mystified.

"Watchin' me all the time…you're always doin' it…you better tell me the truth. I'll find out for myself otherwise."

"That's crazy!" he replied stubbornly.

"So what are you doin' here every night? Don't try to bullshit me!" Sheepishly, he reached into his back pocket and took out the circus poster he carried everywhere with him, the one with her picture on it. Mutely, he unfolded it and handed it to her. She bit her lip. "You want me to sign this for you. Is that really it?" she asked, staring at him in disbelief. He nodded vehemently. If only he could tell her how he felt. But what was the use? He would never have a chance with someone like her. Not the way he was, all crippled up. "Listen," she said in a softer tone. "The thing is…it puts me off when you stare at me like that. I've got a new act…an' I can't make a mistake…not in front of all those people, see?" She handed the photo back. Right beside her picture, she'd written the lovely message: *To my friend Crawford, from Tammy.* His heart beat faster. "Tammy's my real name," she explained. "Mirabella's just a stage name. It was the boss's idea…I don't much like it myself."

"I'd do anything for you, Tammy," he blurted out.

"Really?" she asked, her voice trembling a little. "I need you to promise me something."

"A…a…anything!" he repeated, stumbling over the word in his eagerness to please her. Someone rapped on the trailer door.

"You're on in five!" a man shouted.

"Listen, if you wanna watch…jus' go up to the stands…okay?" she said. Realizing he was being dismissed, he rose to his feet and limped over to the door. Sitting always made him stiffen up something terrible. "What's wrong?" he heard her ask sharply.

"Wrong? Ain't nothin' wrong. It's the way I am. Since the accident, see," he shrugged. "'Course I wasn't always like this," he added, trying to straighten himself up. He didn't want her pity.

"You're on in two!"

"Gimme that paper back," she said urgently, taking his precious poster and scribbling something on the back. "Now listen to me! When you get to the winter quarters, you go and see this doctor. Tell 'im I sent you. He's a fuckin' miracle worker!"

"Dr. Sher-pan-ski," Crawford said, slowly sounding out the name. It sounded foreign. When he looked up, he was alone in the trailer. He hurried over to the stands and sat himself down, all of a twitter. It had happened so damn quick, it didn't feel real. Would she ever want to see him again? He had to face facts. The way she'd acted, it didn't seem too likely. That hurt.

It flew right out of his head when the acrobats came on. Tammy's new act was daring. The crowd couldn't get enough of it. But as he watched her swooping like a bird over the arena, trusting her partner to be there to catch her over and over again, he was sick with fear. When they took away the safety nets, the audience went wild. But he couldn't bear to look. She was crazy, risking her life like that.

That night, he hardly slept, worrying about it.

Next morning, he was in for a shock. Mirabella's trailer was empty. Candyfloss Kid was gone too. The story of their flight went buzzing from tent to tent. It explained why Tammy had acted the way she did, but not why she'd quit. Was it because she was scared? Well, there was no sense in hanging around anymore, waiting to be balled out by the clown. Except for one thing: the doc she'd called the fuckin' miracle worker. He hadn't expected her to swear like that. But it was okay. More than okay. No one cared about Candyfloss Kid. He got replaced right away. But the star act had to be cancelled. The circus boss wanted to kill the world. Crawfish hid out in the elephant tent and kept his head down. After a month of constant drizzle and full houses in Vancouver, the circus loaded up for the last time. The season was over. As they set off for the circus's winter quarters in Alberta, Crawfish's spirits lifted. He deserved a good break. Come summer, they'd be in Ontario. Back home again.

He was counting on it.

A SAD FAREWELL

Left to his own devices, Harmony Storm soon established a regular routine: grazing every morning, dozing under a tree in the afternoon, racing around like a mad thing at dusk when the bugs came out in their swarms and moving quietly through the dewy nights under a waning moon. He felt the absence of his own kind keenly but his lonely days were punctuated by the old man's visits. Though the grain was most welcome, it was company he craved. As the days went by, he grew more and more attached to him.

He was surprised but pleased, when the old man fetched him in from the field one morning. After so long out in the open, he was happy to be in the barn, away from the bugs. He enjoyed being brushed too, soothed by the sounds the old man made, whistling through his teeth all the while. In fact, Storm got so comfortable, he closed his eyes and dozed. Suddenly, he was wide awake. He'd picked up the vibration of a powerful engine, pulsing through the soles of his feet. Closer and closer it came, until he could hear it throbbing outside the barn. Sighing deeply, the old man snapped a lead shank on him and walked out into the sunshine. Storm followed, his senses on high alert. At the sight of the truck and a man he didn't know standing beside it, he reared in terror. The snap on the lead shank shattered and all at once he was free! Dodging past the old man, whose arms were swaying back and forth like a tree in a high wind, he ran past the barn, racing along with nothing on his mind but flight, until a rank smell reached his nostrils. Before him stood a monster: a strange creature, bulky and strong with hostile eyes and sharp horns. When it bellowed at him, Storm turned and ran. Stumbling through the long grass he made it back to the barn and stood there trembling, waiting to be caught. To his relief, the old man took hold of him. The stranger was nowhere to be seen, so Storm happily followed the old man up the ramp. He felt a pat on his neck, and heard a whisper in his ear like the evening breeze. The next thing he knew, the door behind him slammed shut. The truck was moving. His old friend had been left behind! Wild eyed, he called out. But when he looked back, he saw the old man walking slowly away, his head bowed. Frantically, he aimed a vicious kick at the door. It did not open. He braced himself. They were travelling faster now...further and further away from his home paddock. By the time they reached the highway, acceptance had set it. As the road rolled beneath him, he understood deep down what his old friend had tried to tell him.

Goodbye was a cruel word in any language.

HOME SWEET HOME

Under a clear September sky, Joey Harris was scrubbing out the water troughs with a big grin on his face. Rumours about slot machines coming to Iroquois Downs had been circulating all summer. A month ago, the racetrack had made an announcement. A government loan had been approved for the construction of a casino on the grounds. The track was currently negotiating profit sharing with the Horsemen's Union and the municipality of Erinsville. Hopes were running high. So was inflation. The cost of doing business had risen sharply as trainers, feed men, blacksmiths, veterinarians, even Harvey's Hot Foods, had jacked up their prices. Every owner was looking for a horse, a chance to be part of the action. Prices at the yearling sale were set to soar. Joey was hoping to hit the jackpot.

Until then though, he needed every penny he could get, so boarders at Harmony Farm had become a regular feature. One of them, Harmony Storm, was due in from Alberta that very afternoon. When Joey heard Jean Claude's truck, bumping its way down the laneway, he threw down his scrub brush and hurried towards to the barn, arriving just in time to see a flash of grey as Storm flew down the ramp. Once on solid ground, the colt halted, his ears up, gazing out at the fields. Then, he ducked his head and raced into the barn, dragging the shipper, Jean Claude along with him. By the time Joey had caught up with them, Storm was running around his stall, squealing with delight. He leapt up and touched noses with his neighbour Harmony Stampede, who was on stall rest after an operation to remove OCD chips from his hock.

"Zey are friends, I see," Jean Claude remarked with an indulgent smile.

"Grew up together," Joey confirmed, beaming at the sight of the two colts getting reacquainted. "Can't stop, I've got the vet coming…blacksmith's here too…busy day, eh." The blast of a horn cut him short. "Jesus! That'll be Mercer. I clean forgot." Who had the trainer brought this time? he wondered, praying the horse wasn't sick like the last one. He didn't need any of his yearlings catching a virus just before the sale.

As usual, Mercer didn't bother getting out of his truck. He was leaving the job of unloading to someone else. Feeling annoyed, Joey opened up the trailer. His annoyance turned to concern when he caught sight of the horse inside. He was a sorry sight, with a dull coat and a weary expression in his eyes. Who could it be? Joey wondered. He looked like some old claimer, but Mercer only raced youngsters. He must have been beautiful once, Joey thought, glancing at the long forelock and tumbling mane. The horse stumbled awkwardly as he came down the ramp. Realization dawned. It was Harmony Light!

"Been raced hard. Needs a bit o' time off," Mercer said irritably. Joey felt like crying.

"What've you done to him? He's only two years old for God sakes!" Joey replied in a voice like thunder. He heard a low whistle from somewhere behind him.

"Oh la la," Jean Claude said softly. Turning his back on Mercer, Joey tried to lead Harmony Light over to the barn, but he quickly abandoned the idea.

"He's lame!" Joey roared, his blood boiling, staring down at the horse's front legs. The vast bulk of Jeremiah Hostetler emerged from the broodmare barn, where he'd been trimming horses' feet.

"Shut the door will ya?" Mercer grunted.

"Gladly, sir," Jeremiah replied. He picked up the ramp with one enormous hand and shot the bolts home. Mercer started up his engine. But before he could make a move, Doctor Jay arrived in his white truck, cutting off Mercer's escape route. Joey had called him earlier that day to look at one of the yearlings. Winterflood spotted Harmony Light right away. Nothing got past the vet's sharp eyes, it seemed.

"Walk that horse for me, will you Joey?" he called out, leaping out of his truck. Harmony Light took a few halting steps. "That's enough," he said gently. He walked over to Mercer's truck and gestured for him to roll down his window. "I warned you!" he told Mercer sternly. "I told you if you kept pushing that colt, he'd break down." Mercer averted his eyes. "Look at him!" There was contempt in the vet's voice now. Mercer didn't say a word. "That leg needs to be X-rayed," Winterflood added.

"Do whatever you damn please," Mercer replied, gunning the engine. "Jus' don't come lookin' for me when you wanna get paid. The owner doesn't want to wait on him. He's going in the sale."

"If he's got a fracture, he's not going anywhere," Winterflood replied coldly.

"Get your fucking vehicle outa my way," Mercer growled.

"No problem," Winterflood replied, jumping back into his truck.

"I want to throttle that son of a bitch for doing this to you," Joey told the colt. How's Val going to take this? he wondered anxiously. She was six months pregnant. He didn't want her to get all upset. She would be coming back from work any minute now. Winterflood was back. He knelt down and ran his hands over the colt's legs.

"I'm hoping it's a simple cannon bone fracture," the vet said. "If so, it'll heal…it'll just take time. But, whatever happens, this horse won't be going in a sale any time soon. I'll see to that!"

"Take an X-ray. I'll pay for it myself!" Joey replied hotly.

"Might help him if I took his shoes off," Jeremiah suggested in his deep, resonant voice.

"Good thinking," Joey agreed.

"So, where's the filly you wanted me to see?" Winterflood asked after they had finally got Harmony Light settled.

Joey led the way to the yearling barn. Inside, half a dozen youngsters were standing awkwardly in their stalls looking unnaturally clean, like tomboys forced into party dresses. They'd have far rather been playing outside. But business was business. Apart from the one filly with the big leg, they were all perfect. Joey had been looking forward to the sale, what with everyone getting so excited about high purses because of the Slots coming to Iroquois Downs. But after seeing the state Harmony Light was in just one year on, Joey found himself dreading it. How could he justify raising and selling babies, only to see them ruined by trainers like Mercer? To his relief, Winterflood wasn't too worried about the filly.

"I'm pretty sure it's just a bang. Should come down in a day or two," he said reassuringly. "Poultice it and we'll see, okay?"

"Thanks Doc," Joey replied happily.

"Anything else you need?"

"Not really. I took Stampede to the clinic and got his stitches taken out. That hock's healing nicely."

"Then I'll be off." As they left the yearling barn, a flock of geese wheeled overhead, their wild voices calling. "They'll be heading south soon," Winterflood remarked, gazing up at the sky.

"This warm weather won't last much longer," Joey agreed. Fall was a glorious time of year in Ontario. But after that, came the long winter.

After he'd seen the veterinarian off, he went back to check on Harmony Light. He was lying down. Sunlight was streaming in through the skylights. It would have made a beautiful picture, Joey thought, if it weren't for the fact that he could count every single rib sticking out from his dusty colt. But not all the trainers were like Mercer, he reminded himself. There were plenty of decent guys out there.

Val appeared, her big belly leading the way.

"Moose is here," she said. "Oh my God, who's that?" she gasped, pointing at Harmony Light.

"Go get the camera," Joey replied, hustling her out of the barn. "I want a record of this."

"Where's my horse?" Moose called out.

"Over here," Joey said jumping to it. As leading driver at Iroquois Downs, the guy was practically royalty.

"Still in one piece?" Moose asked suspiciously.

"Take a look yourself," Joey suggested. "Has he ever grown, eh? I hardly recognized him."

"He looks alright," Moose acknowledged. Joey nodded distractedly. He had heard the feed truck. A moment later, Reggie Blair came marching in, a feed sack balanced on his shoulder.

"Races have been cancelled," he announced dramatically, throwing down his burden. "There's a horsemen's strike at Iroquois Downs and from what I've heard, it's not going to be over so quick."

"Great!" Moose exclaimed. "Just when I buy myself a horse…there's nowhere to race him."

Joey's dreams of high prices for yearlings went up in smoke. A strike would be disastrous for yearling prices. It was a huge disappointment and with the sale only a week away, it was the worst possible timing.

STRIKE!

The Iroquois drivers took off like a flock of wild birds spooked by a shotgun. Some fled to the furthest corners of the province, scrounging a living by ousting the locals. Others went south of the border. However, most of the trainers were not so mobile. Lazer was the only one to flee, chasing the money to be had in Jersey. The rest stayed put.

As the weeks passed, owners fell behind on their bills, grooms waited to be paid and trainers' lines of credit were stretched to the limit. Tom Cowboy Larson fired most of his help and spent his evenings watching the rodeo on TV. Evie Mercer lost her Saturday job at The Happy Shopper. She had given up going to the barn. There was nothing for her there. First Will had left and now Harmony Light was up for sale. Horsemen were short on cash these days, so Harvey's Hot Food had stopped touring the training centres. As Joey had feared, prices were flat at the yearling sale. Top trainer Cat Ciardi spent hours on the road, shipping horses to every small track in Ontario where he carried on his winning ways. Moose had stayed loyal to the Lucky Seven Stable, deserting Keith Lazer after decades of friendship.

OUT WEST

Campbell McClaren read about the strike on the CPTA website, his laptop perched precariously on the arm of a scruffy chair rammed into a corner of the shabby apartment he had inhabited since his arrival in BC. Outside a soft rain was falling, Vancouver's answer to Ontario's fall colours and frosty mornings. He hated this city, where on every main street the homeless begged for spare change and the mountains hid behind a curtain of drizzle.

Infiltrating the cocaine network had been no easy task. So far, they had only managed to bring in a few people at the low end of the totem pole. Campbell was being recalled to Ontario before they were even halfway done, not that he was complaining. He was only too anxious to start the search for Theo Vettore and Crawfish Brown. There was still no news about either of them. He felt responsible, foolishly no doubt. But there were plenty of opportunities for misplaced loyalty in his line of work. Billie McTavish was a different kettle of fish altogether. But her name was inextricably linked with the man who had gone missing in mysterious circumstances: Theo Vettore.

ONTARIO

By November the trees were bare, their leaves swept away by autumn gales. The horsemen's strike continued. At night, Iroquois Downs Raceway looked like a ghost town, its grandstand empty and silent. Meanwhile the walls of the new casino rose higher and higher, casting eerie shadows as dark clouds raced across the moon. The holiday season arrived, bringing snow flurries swirling in the clear air and wild rumours that Theo Vettore had been spotted on the Rodeo Channel. On December 20th there was a sudden announcement that the horsemen's strike had been settled to the satisfaction of all parties. Racing would resume in the New Year. There was a universal sigh of relief.

The day after the strike ended, at first light, a red truck rolled out of Harvey's garage, full of cartons of hot soup and other hearty fare. Sitting at the wheel was Harvey himself, thankful to be back in business and happy to be out on the road despite the ice and snow. His kids were driving him nuts!

Not everyone was happy about the Slots, though. Dr. Jay Winterflood had experienced the knock on effects of gambling growing up in the reserve, where the Cree had exercised their right to build the first casinos in Quebec. The fact that Jay owed his very existence to their presence did not make him look on them any more kindly. He had seen them ruin many lives including his own mother's, even though she had never gambled a single penny. The risk she had taken had not been financial; it had been personal.

Harmony Light knew nothing about strikes or casinos. He inhabited a simple world, one where pleasures like filling his belly or slaking his thirst did no harm to him or to anyone else. Long ago, his ancestors had roamed the grasslands, living in tight bands dominated by a single stallion and one lead mare. His psyche reflected those off days. During the breaking process, he had learned to accept man as the leader, trusting him to keep him safe and well fed. The urge to run with the herd, to test himself against his companions, was strong. The thrill of flying around the racetrack with wings on his feet, his body at peak fitness, was irresistible. The rush of adrenalin as he swooped past his rivals, the warm glow he felt afterwards surrounded by his caretakers, was addictive. Though grounded by injury Harmony Light was still a racehorse, heart and soul. It was in his blood. He was holding himself in readiness for the day he would return.

Courage was his middle name.

Two days before Christmas, Phil Harman boarded a jet to Miami. He was travelling first class, a reward for a job well done. He took a sip of the highball at his elbow and stared down at the frozen eastern seaboard snaking thousands of feet below him. Then he loosened his tie. Smiling to himself, he closed his eyes. These last months he had watched from the sidelines as the three warring parties: the racetrack, the horsemen and the Municipality of Erinsville disputed their percentage of the take. The strike had brought Iroquois Downs to its knees. Eventually one of his buddies at City Hall had come to him for advice. Phil's solution was simple: fifth generation slot machines with superior software that increased the number of apparent near misses. It enticed gamblers to play for longer, guaranteeing a higher gross take for the house. As if by magic, the gridlock was broken. All the principals involved got what they wanted. The politicians were now in his debt. That would no doubt smooth the way forward at some point in the future.

Phil Harman always played the long game.

HOME FOR THE HOLIDAYS

Constable Campbell McClaren was also airborne. Toronto was hardly an exotic destination. Nevertheless, when they touched down he felt a surge of excitement. He had an appointment with Commander Davis the next day. He was hoping that meant the plan they had been working on, to track down the Scorpion on his home turf had been given the green light. Toronto's clear, frigid air was a relief after Vancouver's drizzle. But the idyllic summer day when Billie McTavish had allowed him to take her to lunch by the river felt like an impossible dream.

The meeting with his commander the following morning did not go well. Standing in the glare of a bare bulb hanging from the ceiling in Commander Davis' spartan office, Campbell perused the confidential memo he'd been handed with a sense of impending doom.

"It's a bit of a hiccup," his superior officer admitted, staring at the papers on his desk, which were arranged in military precision.

"What are the implications exactly?" Campbell asked anxiously.

"Look," Davis replied briskly. "As you know, Vettore's body was never found. The prevailing view now is that he's on the run. So far, he's eluded us. The truth is, he could be anywhere."

"What about Sainte Marie?" Campbell asked. "Could he be there?"

"Forget it, Constable. The RCMP can do nothing in a sovereign country without that country's consent. Sainte Marie has made it abundantly clear that they won't tolerate any outside interference from Canada in any of their internal affairs."

"So what do we do now?" Campbell asked.

"We drop it!" Davis barked. "That's an order, Constable," he clarified, pre-empting any further response. "There's more. Take a seat." Wondering what was coming, Campbell sat down. "The Vettore family, notably the cousin, Lara Vachon, has been pressing us for answers," Davis announced. This sounded encouraging. "We're reopening the investigation into Vettore's disappearance," Davis continued. "I'm told it may lead to disciplinary action against you."

"Disciplinary action!" Campbell exclaimed, leaping to his feet. "Why, sir?" he tacked on belatedly, catching sight of the pained expression on Davis' face.

"Calm down, Constable," Davis replied, tugging nervously at his moustache. Campbell tried to comply. This must be coming from much further up the ladder, he realized. It wasn't Davis' fault. Still, it was a bitter blow.

"When's the hearing?" he asked.

"Date's not yet set."

This could drag on for months, Campbell thought. Even after the hearing, he would have to wait for the Committee's verdict. If he was eventually cleared of any wrongdoing (and, with his record, that was by no means certain) he would end up sidelined, discredited, a member who was no longer considered safe. No one in the force would ever really trust him. He had seen it happen to other men.

"You see," Davis was explaining, "someone has to take the blame for the botched up surveillance job on Mr. Vettore. He was a crucial link in the chain. The panel could argue that you, with your fifteen plus years of experience, should not have left a young officer without proper supervision on the ground."

"But why didn't he tell someone?" Campbell demanded. "I realize his horse had colic, but even so?"

"It was a grave error of judgement," Davis admitted. "But it could be put down to youth and inexperience, perhaps." Campbell got the message. Someone had to take the rap. It looked like he was to be sacrificed, rather than a young man at the start of his career. He should have seen it coming. The irony was that, deep down, he did feel responsible for Vettore's disappearance. Fatigue, no doubt, had clouded his judgement. Be that as it may, he didn't want his fate resting in the hands of a panel of anonymous officers who didn't even know him. He seized the initiative.

"I believe the right thing for me to do is resign my commission," he said quietly. It crossed his mind that he didn't have nearly enough years in for a pension, but he was strong and healthy. He could make a living somehow. It wasn't fair but life was often unfair. To his surprise, the atmosphere in the room changed for the better.

"Your offer of resignation is duly noted, McClaren but I'm not accepting it. You'll be suspended on full pay," Davis replied firmly. What was going on? Campbell wondered.

"So, searching for Vettore anywhere outside Canada is strictly off limits," Campbell ventured, seeking clarification. Davis nodded. "And that includes the island of Sainte Marie?" he added, wanting closure. Commander Davis rested his elbows on his desk, pressed his finger tips together and gazed off into space for a long moment.

"For the RCMP, certainly," he agreed. But not for him? Campbell wondered. Perhaps as an officer under investigation what he did was his own affair. If he succeeded, he could be resurrected. If he failed, he'd be disowned by the RCMP. Am I reading this right? he asked himself. There were certainly no clues coming from his commander. The expression on Davis' face gave nothing away. "Well, Constable," Davis said glancing at the clock. "I've another appointment. I believe we're all done here."

"All done," Campbell affirmed solemnly, leaving off the sir. He was free! Instead of having to wait for orders, he would be making his own decisions from now on. He marched down the hall, with the giddy sensation that anything was possible. Probably he was crazy. If so it was a good sort of craziness. True, he faced an uncertain future. But he had a chance now to redeem himself, to salvage his reputation. It increased his determination to find Vettore, bring in the Scorpion and see justice done through the Canadian courts. But with freedom came responsibility. He would have no one to blame but himself if things didn't work out. Telling his parents that he had been suspended from the force wasn't going to be fun. But it never occurred to him not to tell them. Honesty was his byword. Snow was falling as he boarded a plane bound for Halifax, Nova Scotia. There was no better place to spend the holidays than Prince Edward Island.

Nevertheless, Ontario and its inhabitants were still very much on his mind.

The horsemen's strike had decimated Iroquois Downs' emergency fund. With the added burden of a loan to pay for its new casino, the track was now teetering on the edge of bankruptcy. Expenses had to be cut to the bone. With Al McTavish still on sick leave, a proposal to close down the backstretch was passed unanimously by the Management Committee. Horsemen were given three months to move out of the barn area. But the Iroquois Downs grooms were hit hardest. Cheap living quarters and canteen food were history. One or two of the older men had to move into shelters. Stinker found a temporary berth on the floor of Mercer's tack room.

Jay Winterflood was in mourning. His Cree mother had succumbed to pneumonia suddenly, just before Christmas. He had intended to drive out with his son to see her over the holidays. Instead, they had gone to her wake. As she lay in her casket, the new moccasins on her feet, the sweet grass in her right hand and her tobacco pipe beside her, he explained to Josh that her body was going back to Mother Earth, and her spirit would soon be joining the ancestors. He tried very hard to sound like he believed it. But the truth was since he had left the Reserve, he had come across so many theories of the afterlife that in the end, he felt they had only one function: providing comfort to the bereaved and hope to everyone. Whether there was anything more to it than that he had no idea.

His mother had gone to her grave without revealing the secret she'd kept hidden for three decades: the identity of his begetter. Blood tests had confirmed what everyone at the Reserve had suspected all along. The seven of them shared the same stranger as a father. But tracking down that man was proving to be an insurmountable task. The trail had been obliterated by the passage of time. Personally, Jay didn't feel much like a victim. Thanks to the funds made available by the tribal council and his mother's good sense, he had been given opportunities that his peers with real flesh and blood fathers could only dream of.

In the rural idyll of Harmony Farm, the holidays brought no relief from the usual routine. There were sleepless nights ahead as Val and Joey Harris welcomed a new baby into the world. But this one wasn't going in any sale. She looked like Joey and had Val's eyes.

Reggie Blair was anything but starry eyed as he trawled through his records, tagging trainers who'd fallen far behind on paying their feed bills. Though it was the season of goodwill, those who made Reggie's list would shortly be receiving visits, not from Santa, but from some very persuasive individuals who thoroughly enjoyed their work. Reggie was not feeling in a generous mood. His colt, Harmony Jet, was now a gelding but the operation hadn't made a dent in his dismal performance on the racetrack. He was too small for the Amish. The next sale was six long months away.

Jim Mercer tossed Reggie's invoice onto the growing pile of bills. Paying the grooms came first. He was willing to take his chances against Reggie's infamous collectors. He could still throw a punch when pushed. Thanks to Harmony Light's owner being a short sighted son of a bitch, however, Mercer had lost his star two year old. Some man who couldn't wait to part with his money had bought Harmony Light privately. Rumour had it he'd given the horse to Craig Brown to train, heaven knows why. The man was completely useless.

Tom Cowboy Larson unwound the cool cast from Harmony Valentine's left front leg and ran his hand down the tendon. Not a trace of the bow remained.

"Harness 'er up, Will!" he called out. Will was the only groom Larson had kept on during the strike. The boy was slow, but reliable: exactly what was needed on a farm. After three laps around the jog track, Larson felt pretty pleased with himself. The big black filly was sound. As for the bow tendon, the owner need never know!

PRINCE EDWARD ISLAND

Campbell's parents were waiting for him at Arrivals. On the drive home, he broke the bad news about his suspension from the Mounties, giving them the official version. They didn't say much, but they managed to make it clear that they were a hundred per cent on his side. Charlottetown looked exactly the way he remembered it. There was a sprinkling of snow on the rooftops and holiday decorations in every front yard. It was easy for him to forget about his troubles during the countless family gatherings and festive meals in the week that followed.

On New Year's Eve he got together with his old friend Herbie, who ran a low cost, no frills training stable, even shoeing the horses himself. With the modest purses on offer, it was all local owners could afford. By 11 p.m., the two of them were at Herbie's house, sitting in front of a roaring fire with a seemingly inexhaustible supply of dry logs on hand.

"What's the best thing that's happened to you this year?" his pal asked, raising his glass of Moose Milk, which despite its innocent sounding name was a potent brew.

"Getting out of Vancouver, I suppose," Campbell replied.

"You can do better than that!"

"How about yourself?" Campbell countered.

"Racing in the Cup and Saucer!" Herbie grinned. "My horse made a break but it still felt pretty good to be in it!" After his pronouncement, Herbie sank into an alcohol fuelled doze. Campbell threw a stack of logs on the fire and sat back, enjoying the blessed familiarity of the place. The fire was crackling merrily and beside him his friend was snoring gently. There was nowhere like PEI. Campbell started to drift off himself, his mind floating free. Suddenly, he knew the answer to Herbie's question. Before he could think about its implications he heard a rocket explode, followed by the crackle of jitterbugs. Midnight. He wandered over to the window and pulled back the curtain. Stars were bursting out of the dark sky: red, blue and red again. Then with a gentle putt putt, showers of gold fell like rain.

A New Year had begun. With the disaster of Vettore's disappearance behind him, Campbell felt he could finally move forward. To what, he had no clear idea. But he knew the best thing that had happened to him all year was meeting Billie McTavish. What he had felt for her at first was sympathy.

Given Al's heart attack, that was understandable. Later on, his interest had been purely professional. However, what had started out as a chance to pick her brains on Vettore had led him down a very different path. The few hours he had spent with Billie over lunch beside the river had been a revelation. He'd been spellbound by her sensual beauty, her intellect and her warmth. She was unlike any other woman he had ever met. Up to now, his allegiance had always been to the Force. As a loyal Mountie, he had avoided making commitments, relationship wise. But loyalty cut both ways.

He spent the next morning helping Herbie out at the barn. That afternoon, he took a long walk along the beach, intending to watch the sun set behind the dunes, something he'd often dreamed of doing in Ontario. Then, before he could change his mind, he called Billie McTavish. Wishing her a Happy New Year wasn't much of a conversation opener, but it was the best he could come up with in the circumstances. He had been out of touch for months.

"Campbell McClaren...I seem to remember that name from somewhere," she replied in an off-putting manner. "Where are you? Don't tell me you're outside my front door!"

"No, I'm on the beach." She pounced on it.

"You're down in the islands!"

"There's a lot of white stuff about, but it's not sand," he assured her. "And I'm not in the Caribbean, not when I last checked anyway."

"Prince Edward Island? Wow!"

"Yes, well I thought it best to tell my family in person that I'd been suspended from the force," he revealed.

"Suspended? I don't believe it! What'd you do? Kill someone?" she asked worriedly.

"More like lose someone," he confessed.

"This is about Theo Vettore, isn't it?" she said, her voice dropping.

"Let's not go into it," he suggested, fishing for his gloves. It was so cold the phone felt like a block of ice.

"What happens now?" she enquired.

"I stay here, watch a lot of sunsets, sleep in late," he replied, in an attempt to lighten the tone.

"Goofing off doesn't sound like your thing," she cut in quickly.

"Take a trip down to Sainte Marie, maybe," he continued. Despite the gloves, his hands were freezing.

"Sainte Marie?" she exclaimed. "Why?"

"For a recce." This was met with baffled silence. "A scouting expedition…an information gathering exercise," he explained. "It's a military term," he added.

"I'm not in the military," she pointed out.

"I'd be looking for a man Vettore told me about," he replied steadily.

"Oh?"

"Code name: the Scorpion."

"Sounds nasty. Scorpions sting, don't they?"

"Find him and I might have a chance of finding Vettore," Campbell went on. "My reputation and possibly my career depend on it. Besides, I feel responsible."

"Don't!" Billie said sharply. "Vettore's not worth it!"

"Failing isn't really an option," he replied soberly.

"This trip is official, right?"

"You'd be wrong there," he admitted, stamping his feet and wishing he had done the sensible thing and called from the house.

"You know what? I might be able to throw you a lifeline," she said hesitantly.

"That'd be good," he replied eagerly.

"A good friend of mine goes down to Sainte Marie all the time. His girlfriend lives there…and she knows everyone."

"Wonderful!" he exclaimed. The sun was sinking. Behind him, he could hear waves breaking on the shore.

"Listen, you've got to promise me, if I do help you, don't do anything stupid down there, okay?"

"Can't promise that, I'm afraid. I'm not too smart," he replied. Billie responded with a peel of laughter, ironic yet warm. She was still laughing when she rang off. He reckoned he'd quit while he was ahead. Besides, it was so cold his ears were freezing off.

In the old quarter of Erinsville, it was still light. Snow had been falling steadily all day, covering the street in an icy blanket and marooning every house on its own private island. Billie McTavish couldn't decide what she was more astonished by: the fact that Campbell had kept her number all this time, or that he had waited so long to call. She was fairly sure that playing games with people wasn't in Campbell's repertoire. He ticked the honesty box, big time. Compared to him, Theo Vettore was as shallow as the waters of Half Moon Bay. She still felt angry, not with Theo anymore, but with herself, for imagining there could be a happy ever after with a player like Mr. Vettore. The trouble was, since that disastrous relationship, she had stopped trusting people. She was too afraid of getting hurt again.

New Year's Eve had been an anticlimax. Most of her friends were married and had small children, so that put paid to late parties. As for her best friend, Jeff Lamare, to hear him talk he was practically married to Anya. Nevertheless, she'd dragged him out to brunch at Tangoes before the snow got too bad. Since then, she'd been stuck in the house with nothing on TV but old movies. The only exciting thing that had happened the whole day was Campbell's surprise phone call. Now what? she wondered. It was New Year's Day, she dearly wanted to rid herself of the past and make a fresh start. Catching sight of her closet, choking with clothes, its doors swinging open, she got inspired. Putting a salsa CD on the stereo, she began pulling out hangers, ditching fashion disasters with gusto. Soon, there was a pile of clothes on her four poster, obliterating the bed she had once shared with her ex boyfriend. If only I could rid myself of Theo's memory so easily! she thought. Pretty soon the room looked like it had been hit by a tornado. But eventually her out of season things were safely stowed, the rejects were ready for recycling and her current favourites were dangling from the clothes rail. The transformation from crowded closet to seriously upmarket boutique was complete.

She closed the wardrobe door with a triumphant Yes! then celebrated by dancing around the apartment to the salsa beat pulsating from the stereo, until the elderly couple who lived downstairs put an end to her enthusiasm by banging on the ceiling. The events of the past year came crashing back: her father's heart attack, Vettore's dramatic disappearance and Millie D testing positive for caffeine, which had destroyed Al's credibility and put Bob Summers out of business. There was one other thing preying on her mind as well: the conversation she had had with Phil Harman at Cree Horse Park. Impulsively, she reached for the phone, then put it down again. Though her father was on the mend, she didn't want to risk telling him about Phil's vicious accusations. It could bring on another heart attack. But she couldn't keep it to herself any longer. She had to tell someone! There was only one thing to do: call the answerman!

Jeff Lamare picked up immediately.

"You again," he said, trying not to sound pleased. So, he was lonely, she realized. It wasn't surprising with his girlfriend thousands of miles away. At least he had one!

"Don't push your luck," she replied heartlessly. "I need your input and I'm assuming you're not busy right now."

"You'd be wrong there. I'm deep in enemy territory and my men are in grave danger…if I don't figure out a strategy…"

"Playing at *Heroes* again?" she interrupted. "This is way more important!"

"Okay, I'm listening," Jeff said. But she could tell he still had half his mind on the supposed invasion.

"First, tell me when you're going down to Sainte Marie again."

"I only came back last week," Jeff protested.

"I know, but…"

"I was planning to surprise Anya on Valentine's Day and…"

"Yes," Billie said eagerly.

"Nothing." She filed that date away and moved on to the main agenda: Phil Harman.

"I need some advice," she said.

"Okay, fill me in," he replied distractedly.

"I'm not telling you anything until I can see you. I want to be sure you're not cheating," she replied.

"As if," she heard him mutter. She booted up her computer and opened Skype. His image came up on her screen framed by twinkling lights and a Christmas tree.

"I've been thinking," she said.

"Another business idea?" Jeff asked eagerly. She ignored it. There was more to life than business, though she wasn't a hunded per cent sure Jeff felt that way.

"What if that whole caffeine thing was a set up to get rid of Dad as Director of Iroquois Downs?"

"You're still on that? I think you'd need a motive," Jeff said.

"Don't patronize me. Plenty of people didn't like what he was doing to clean up racing."

"Okay, but who?" Jeff asked reasonably.

"Could have been a disgruntled trainer," Billie suggested. "Problem is, I have no idea where to start looking."

"Yeah, I don't imagine your dad was too popular at the track," Jeff agreed. "It could have been almost anyone."

"What about Phil Harman?" Billie asked.

"Phil? Now I know you're crazy. That makes absolutely no sense."

"Why not? I can't stand the guy. He's a total perv."

"Because..." Jeff began patiently.

"Don't treat me like a five year old," she warned.

"Okay, listen. Phil Harman hired your father specifically to clean up harness racing. That's what TCO2 testing was all about, for God's sake."

"I'd forgotten about that. Yeah, you're right," Billie conceded, reluctantly dismissing Phil as a suspect. "But he's no angel," she persisted.

"Your father put a stop to the betting scandals that had plagued Iroquois Downs for decades, with Phil's help and encouragement. What's your problem?"

"If I tell you something," Billie began, then she stopped short. "You can't repeat this."

"Go ahead," Jeff replied decisively. She repeated Phil's attack on her father, word for word. The entire conversation was emblazoned in her brain. Jeff listened carefully with only one lapse of concentration.

"So you see Phil practically accused Dad of bid rigging," she ended, a catch in her voice. "I haven't dared tell Dad about it."

"Interesting," Jeff said.

"No!" she contradicted angrily. "Stabbing your best friend in the back when he's vulnerable is not interesting. It's..."

"A major put down," Jeff supplied.

"Worse. Much worse," she replied in heartfelt tones.

"Phil's a businessman," Jeff pointed out. "Men like him don't have friends. They have contacts, people who are useful to them. After the caffeine scandal broke, Al had outlived his usefulness. No doubt Phil assumed he'd do the right thing and step down. Why didn't he, by the way?"

"Because he hadn't done anything wrong, stupid!"

"Your father is a stubborn old fool," Jeff said. Reluctantly, Billie decided to let that go. "The way I see it," Jeff continued in a trust me I know best tone, "Phil was just pulling an old trick, distancing himself from the victim. It wasn't personal. He dredged up something from the past as a way of forcing the issue. The last thing Al needed then was a whiff of another scandal."

"So Phil was hoping I would tell him?" Billie asked, her voice trembling a little. "And you think it's true?"

"In the end you didn't have to tell him," Jeff pointed out. "And no, I don't for one moment believe those allegations are true. Your father is one of the most decent people I've ever met."

"Thanks Jeff."

"Happy now?"

Billie sighed. "I guess," she said.

"Good. Now can I get back to my men?"

"This is just a game, right?" Billie asked, letting just the right amount of skepticism creep into her voice.

"Goodnight!" Jeff exclaimed. The screen went blank. She felt immensely comforted, yet strangely bereft. Jeff wasn't just her best friend, he was like the brother she had always wanted. For even though she had two perfectly good brothers of her own, she'd had very little to do with either of them for a long time now. Since they had left home, they had stayed right away. Deciding to call it a night, she fell into bed. As her head touched the pillow, she heard the roar of the snowplows sweeping away the magical frozen wilderness outside her door. Soon there'd be nothing left of it, only the humdrum workaday world.

The holidays were over.

Theo Vettore's cousin, Lara had spent the holidays with Theo's parents, taking a trip down memory lane, looking at photos of her and Theo as children, tobogganing on the hills above Montreal, devouring beaver tails on the frozen Rideau River and diving for Coke bottles at Indian Lake on long gone summer days. Unfortunately, the RCMP appeared to have given up searching for Theo. As for the Provincial Police, they weren't even returning her calls. Nevertheless, she kept plugging away. Her cousin had so much to live for, still did. She refused to believe he was dead.

At the Browns' Farm too, the New Year marked yet another milestone with an empty chair at the table. The holidays felt more like a funeral than a celebration, despite the fact that Craig had been given the top two year old in North America to train, Harmony Light. There was still no word from Crawford. Ever since he had failed to show up on her birthday, Izzy hadn't smiled. Not once.

Ginny, Theo's on-again, off-again girlfriend, had spent the holidays schooling her horse in the indoor arena. Before she went back to work, she sent Theo an email, officially breaking up with him. She had no idea whether he would ever receive it, but she needed to move on. Besides, it wasn't like they'd ever made any long term plans or anything.

STARTING FRESH

January 1st was a significant date for standardbreds throughout North America. It was the official birthday of every racehorse, regardless of the actual day when they were foaled. In line with most systems, there were winners and losers. Surprisingly, many top performers were born, not in January, but in May, when their dams had access to new grass, producing the best milk and giving their offspring a head start. As the new year got underway, horsemen all over Ontario began hauling in their three year olds from the fields, returning them to training in the hope that any problems they had experienced as two year olds: the splints and curbs, the sesamoiditis, the tying up, the cartilage damage, the stress lines, the colic, the ulcers, the muscle damage and flipped palates, the track rash, sore heels, bruised feet and quarter cracks, the knee knocking and cross firing, the stumbling and breaking stride, the bowed tendons and pulled suspensions, the allergies, the reversed differentials, the bleeding, the bacterial infections, the bad acting, sulking and raging hormones (to name just a few) had been resolved by a few months out on grass and, like the ugly ducking in the nursery rhyme, there would be a fairytale ending: the troubled youngster would become a three year old champion. It was this fervent belief that kept the monthly cheques rolling in from the owners, because once in a blue moon, miracles did happen!

Al McTavish was no exception. For health reasons, he'd given up cigars, booze, fast sports cars, restaurant food and practically every other thing that gave him pleasure: except the colt Harmony Stampede. The two of them had spent the fall cooped up, the colt pacing his dark stall like a prisoner in solitary, while Al was confined to the house. In November, as Al began to recover, Stampede had been given a chance to stretch his legs before winter set in. Watching him circle his paddock covered in autumn leaves, had brightened the monotony of Al's week. He rejoiced in the fact that this well mannered colt had not yet been gelded. Better still, he was getting a brand new start, something Al himself badly needed. Al wasn't having dreams about holding up golden cups in the winner's circle anymore. Instead, he had a recurring nightmare about a horse stumbling and falling. He prayed it wasn't a harbinger of the future. He told himself his fears were irrational, merely reflecting his own state of mind.

When Stampede returned to Tony Hall's barn to resume training, Al's life took on a new sense of purpose. He spent his mornings at Rivers Training centre, pacing back and forth inside Tony's barn, or standing like a sentinel beside the track bundled up warm, his eyes glued on Stampede's hind legs. The colt paced through the cold, skimming across the rock hard surface, a sharp silhouette when the sun shone bright or lost in grey shadows thrown by giant ice clouds. Fair weather or foul, black ice, wet roads, snow storms! None of them mattered to Al or the colt.

Al was buoyed up by his dreams of success. The colt was in his element.

ALBERTA

Crawfish Brown was riding a bus into town, staring at the snowy Alberta landscape, gawping at the craggy mountain peaks sporadically visible through the fogged up windows. He had an entire afternoon free and he intended to make the most of his few hours away from the dratted elephants. He had assumed once the circus had reached its winter quarters that the job would get easier. It hadn't happened. To Crawfish's disgust, the whole bathing, brushing, nail filing, feeding, bedding down and watering business had carried on as usual. He'd done nothing but slave since they had arrived! Today, he was looking forward to watching a movie and eating a decent meal for a change. Circus fare couldn't hold a candle to the track kitchen. His eyes misted over at the memory of the hot dinners he'd enjoyed at Iroquois Downs, never guessing his days there were numbered. Still, at least he wasn't dead like Theo Vettore. But that was small comfort. He was too scared to go back to his old life yet, afraid that the monsters that had tried to kill him were still out there somewhere, watching and waiting to finish the job.

When he reached town he went exploring, feeling pleased that he'd stowed his hard earned cash in his boots, lest some good for nothing made off with it. In Crawfish's view, you couldn't be too careful. The store windows were brightly lit and for a while he was content to drift along with the crowd, checking out the countless baked goods on display, trying to spot a real bargain. Eventually, he got waylaid by a saddle and tack store. The sight of all those brushes and bridles quickly had him wallowing in nostalgia. When he finally tore himself away, he nearly jumped out of his socks. The ghost of Theo Vettore, wearing a black cowboy hat and leather chaps, was heading straight for him. The hair on Crawfish's neck stood up on end. Vettore's spirit was moving like a robot, his eyes blank, his face expressionless. Crawfish had heard that you could walk right through a ghost and it wouldn't even notice. He waited until the last second, then lost his nerve and lurched sideways, ending up in the gutter.

"Hey, Vettore!" he shouted out, mustering his courage after the phantom had passed by. But he might as well have been talking to the wall. The ghost kept on going. But something about him just wasn't right. While he was alive, Vettore had been a cocky son of a gun, swaggering around the Race Barn like he owned the place. Not anymore though. Still, Crawfish reasoned, death'd do that to a guy, wouldn't it? Knowing he'd narrowly escaped the same fate himself, Crawfish felt pretty shook up. The apparition had ruined his afternoon. Cars were whizzing past him, coming much too close for comfort, but Crawfish was oblivious to the danger. He had other things on his mind.

"Hey, what are you doin'? Tryin' to get yourself killed?" a man's voice boomed from directly behind him. Crawfish whipped his head around and was confronted by a cowboy wearing a ten-gallon hat, his hands on his hips. He had a yellow dog beside him, straining at the leash.

"What's your problem, mister?" Crawfish whimpered.

"Who were you shoutin' to just now?" the cowboy demanded. Crawfish went into a blue funk. Why had he blurted out Vettore's name like that? he wondered, as he struggled to his feet. The guy would think he was crazy. Maybe he was! The yellow dog was barking now, leaping up and down, twisting its head around. To Crawfish's horror, it slipped its collar and lunged at him. "Hey, Bacardi! Quit it!" the cowboy yelled. The dog took no notice. It didn't look vicious but Crawfish took off anyhow, ricocheting across the high street. His hip was killing him, but he didn't dare stop in case the dog jumped him.

"Where d'you think you're going?" a woman's voice rang out. Scared that he'd been caught by the traffic police, Crawfish skidded to a halt, narrowly avoiding an old gal with long grey hair and a basket over her arm who was a dead ringer for his long dead grandmother. He stood there mesmerized, breathing hard. "What's the hurry young man?" she enquired in the same ringing tones. Her take charge attitude steadied him. Slowly, his terror at seeing a dead man walking faded. The world went back to normal, where stuff like that just didn't happen. The dog had calmed down too. It was sitting on the pavement, good as gold, wagging its tail. Crawfish tried to bend down to pat it, but his neck had locked solid. It was that cowboy's fault, sneaking up behind him, he thought angrily. He wondered if he could sue the guy for whiplash. He'd heard of folks claiming for it and getting a ton of money. "Are you in some kind of trouble?" the old gal asked, looking at him shrewdly. "Don't lie to me!"

"I ain't done nothin'," he replied stubbornly. What was wrong with folks in this town? What made 'em think it was okay to stick their noses into other people's business?

"Tell me, young man," she said in a kinder tone, "when was the last time you had a decent meal?" Crawfish gulped. The situation was getting out of hand. He had to get away from this woman before she pried the truth out of him and had him locked up in the loony bin with all the other nutters that saw things that weren't there. Suddenly, he had a bright idea.

"I have to see the doc," he mumbled, taking off one of his boots and retrieving the precious circus poster that Mirabella had given him months before. Mutely, he held it out for the woman to see, whilst keeping a tight hold on his most treasured possession.

"Dr. Sherpanski," she exclaimed. "Why, that's just around the corner from here." She pointed down the road. "He's at College Street Medical centre. Just follow the signs! And son," she added as he prepared to leave, her eyes bright. "Call your mother!" Crawfish nodded, brushing away a tear he couldn't quite explain. Then, he set off, the dog at his heels. He was glad of its company now. It was almost like having a friend.

The doc's office was warm and cozy compared to the cold street outside and it looked like there was coffee on the go too. Crawfish made a mental note to nick some when he got the chance. The waiting room was empty except for a blonde behind the counter, wearing horn rimmed glasses.

"Can I help?" she asked. Crawfish opened his mouth to speak, but he was struck dumb.

"Not sure," he said at last.

"Do you have an appointment?"

He inclined his head. What did he have to lose?

"Name?" the blonde asked pleasantly.

"Craw...ford Brown," he muttered, remembering just in time to use his given name, not his handle.

"I don't have a record of it," she said, looking genuinely puzzled.

"Well that ain't right," he complained, eyeing the coffee machine and deciding to brazen it out. Luckily the phone rang and while no one was looking, he scooted over and poured himself two cups, spooning in as much cream and sugar as he dared and quickly gulping it all down. When he turned around, the blonde was staring at him.

"You one of them circus folk?" she asked curiously. "Where d'you get that dog from? He'll have to wait outside. Doctor Sherpanksi..." But before she could finish, a man in a white coat put his head round the door.

"I'm on my last patient, Cathy. You'll be able to go home soon," he said.

"Hold it, Doc!" Crawfish exclaimed, emboldened by two shots of caffeine.

"Ah!" the doctor said, popping back out again. "Didn't notice you there."

"I come all this way to see you," Crawfish declared, determined not to go home empty handed.

"Anytime," the doc replied amiably, taking a step backward.

"How 'bout right now?" Crawfish persisted. "That suit you?"

The doctor sighed. "You better come through," he said in a resigned tone. "How'd that dog get in here, Cathy?"

"Don't worry I'll deal with him," the blond promised.

"Don't let him run off," Crawfish warned her, suddenly concerned for his newfound friend.

Doctor Sherpanski led the way to a room with spotlessly clean white walls and proceeded to hog the only decent chair in the place, a stuffed leather recliner behind an enormous desk.

"Now, young man, let's have your name first."

"Brown," Crawfish replied, his left eye blinking like crazy.

"What seems to be the problem, son?"

By the time the doc was done with him, it was dark, but Crawford's prospects were bright. He was going to be spending a bit of time at the hospital, getting tests and X-rays before having an operation to fix up his hip. He was getting his teeth fixed too. Come summer, he'd be a new man. He'd be able to go anywhere without everyone staring at him, or so he hoped. When he reached the outer office, the blonde was still there, but she had her hat and coat on, ready to make a quick getaway. The dog was nowhere to be seen.

"What'd you do with him?" Crawfish demanded.

"That wasn't your dog," the blond said calmly. She picked up her handbag and slung it over her shoulder. "Don't you worry," she continued. "He's safe enough. Wayne came and picked him up. You just missed him."

"So...he's gone," Crawfish said forlornly.

"That was one of Corrie's pups. I know 'em all. She's Mom's dog," the blonde explained. "Tell you what," she continued cheerfully. "How'd you like to buy a puppy? Corrie has a litter every year. There's still one or two nice pups left. You interested?"

"Nah. I reckon it'd be too much," he said hastily, getting cold feet.

"Suit yourself," the blonde said, walking off, her car keys jingling. Crawfish stood rooted to the spot, in an agony of indecision, his mind twisting and turning until he remembered what the old woman had said about following the signs.

"Hey!" he shouted into the night. "Wait up!"

Two hours later, he was riding on the bus on his way back to the circus, with a warm puppy in his arms and a bag of dog kibble beside him. Crawfish was broke but happy, as proud as any new father. The ride into town had been a lonely affair, but the return trip was a different story altogether. Everyone on the bus wanted to meet the friendly little guy with soulful brown eyes and floppy paws. Crawfish was enjoying it all so much that when he got back to the circus, instead of going back to his bunk, he took a tour of the tents visiting all the animal sections and ending up at the stables. His old boss was there, feeding the horses, all by himself.

"How'd you like your old job back?" he asked Crawfish. "Larry went off on a drunk again. I'm not giving him another chance." Crawfish nodded his head enthusiastically. "You can start right now. Put the pup in Molly's stall. She don't mind dogs. What's his name?"

"I ain't exactly decided," Crawfish admitted. So far, whenever he'd tried to think of a name, he'd come up empty. The only thing on his mind now was food. He was starving.

"Look a here," his old boss exclaimed, picking up a case of empty beer bottles. "A dozen Bud Lights and Larry's drunk the lot in a night! He's gotta have a name," he added, jerking a thumb in the pup's direction. Suddenly, Crawfish got inspired.

"Bud," he said quietly at first, trying it out to see how it sounded. "Yup! I'm gonna call him Bud!" he declared loudly, happy with his choice.

"You sure?" his boss asked, making a face.

"Yes, siree," Crawfish replied. He carried the pup over to the mare's stall. "Ain't no one gonna talk me out of it neither," he added, mumbling it to himself so his old boss never heard him, which was good because he didn't want to cross him. Little Bud wouldn't have stood a chance against those blasted elephants.

VALENTINE'S DAY

Anya Papandreos stood at the bow of the Sea Princess, her long hair flying as fierce gusts of wind came hurtling through the gaps between the mountains. Out to sea, there were white caps on the dark blue water, making for exciting conditions in the Sainte Marie Ocean Challenge. The Sea Princess was in a perfect spot for its two dozen fee paying passengers to catch the start, cameras at the ready. Her boyfriend Jeff Lamare who had flown down from Toronto to see her, didn't seem to be enjoying himself though. Owning a dot com business gave Jeff loads of spare time and plenty of money to splash around but unfortunately, he was no sailor.

Across the water, a horn sounded: the signal for the race to begin. Scores of ocean going yachts surged across the starting line, hulls rocking gently in the swell, spinnakers unfurling in a blaze of colour, a freshening southerly breeze propelling them up the coast. Leading the charge was the mega yacht, the Sheer Khan, its towering mast dwarfing the crew. Rumour had it that the Shere Khan belonged to her former lover, André Fontainbleu. Anya didn't doubt it. The gaudy design on its billowing white sail: a pair of eyes, black as coal and scarlet lips open in a silent scream, was typical of André's extravagant and tasteless gestures. Besides, the yacht must have cost millions. Who else on this island had that kind of money? It brought home to her how paltry André's gifts to her had been: a shipwrecked boat, washed up by the storm and thirty-five thousand dollars in cash, a small fortune in her eyes but to him, just small change.

However, she'd take the sturdy Sea Princess any day over a racing machine like the Shere Kahn. With her wooden decks, wide beam and old fashioned gaff rigging, the Sea Princess had character and comfort in one endearing package. All that was lost on Jeff though. He was looking green around the gills. Weirdly, he'd brought a Mountie along with him on his trip. Was Jeff intending to check out her history or what? She sincerely hoped not! The Mountie seemed like a nice enough fellow, though. He'd made himself useful in the boat today, handing out life jackets and making sure that the passengers actually wore them.

After a full day out on the water, they headed back to port. The wind dropped and the Sea Princess was quickly becalmed in a path of pure gold as the sun dipped to the horizon. The dark silhouettes of frigate birds wheeled overhead, making one last pass over the water before night set in. But the beauty and tranquility of the scene were wasted on most of the passengers. They were too busy guzzling pina coladas and rum coke. As for Jeff, he kept checking the time on his watch.

"No worries," Pete told him. "We'll get back sometime tonight."

"I've got a dinner reservation," Jeff replied testily. "Can't you start the engine?"

"Hey, this isn't a water taxi you know!" Pete exclaimed. Anya could sense the hostility between the two men. It bothered her.

"Better start up the motor, Pete," she suggested, quitting her waitressing duties. "I'm gonna get the sails down…it'll save time later."

"Listen," the Mountie offered, "soon as we land, you guys go ahead. I'll stick around and help Pete finish up."

"I owe you," Jeff replied gratefully.

Half an hour later, Anya and Jeff were all dressed up and ready for the Royal Tropicana, the classiest restaurant on the island. As she drove her open top jeep along the busy main road with Jeff beside her, Anya spotted the Mountie trudging along, looking like a shipwrecked sailor. She pulled over and honked the horn.

"Hey!" she called out. "What's going on?"

"I need to clean up," he replied with a sheepish grin.

"Jeff and I are going to Paradise later," she said.

"It's a nightclub on Palm Island," Jeff quickly cut in.

"You should come," Anya added.

"Sounds too romantic," the Mountie replied, glancing at Jeff. "Besides I've got nothing to wear," he added ruefully. Anya felt a bit sorry for him.

"That's my line!" she teased. "Meet you at the harbour front at 11 p.m. You don't want to be all on your own on Valentine's Day! Besides, Pete'll be there."

Before Constable Campbell McClaren had a chance to explain that Pete might not be there, Anya drove off. Campbell decided he might as well give Paradise Nightclub a try, anyway. When he looked through the contents of his suitcase however, he almost gave up on the idea but he was desperate for some inside information. If it gave him a chance to talk to Anya alone, it was well worth a try. So far, his trip to Sainte Marie had been a dismal failure. There was absolutely no sign of the man Vettore had dubbed the Scorpion.

Half Moon Bay was idyllic, but Campbell hadn't come to the island for its scenery.

Since Billie's visit two years earlier, Sainte Marie had changed a great deal. It wasn't just the brand new air conditioned airport. Gleaming white condominiums had replaced the crack shack Billie had described so memorably. When he had checked out the riding stable on the far side of the island, he had discovered a clean cut young man, a recent arrival from Dominica, in charge. He had quickly realized that quizzing him about men arriving with suitcases full of cash decades earlier would be futile, so he'd shown him Vettore's picture and gone away empty handed. It was entirely possible, he supposed, that Vettore had conjured up the Scorpion as a way of exonerating himself. However, in his view, Billie McTavish was a straight arrow. She had told him the truth as she knew it. The problem was she didn't know very much. But he was counting on the old adage: where there's smoke, there's fire.

Promptly at 11 p.m. Campbell arrived at the waterfront, sporting a pair of white pants and a paper thin jacket over a T-shirt, all purchased from a shop in the hotel lobby. Style, Campbell discovered, didn't come cheap on the island of Sainte Marie. However, it was a necessary evil.

At 11:30 p.m, the lovebirds finally arrived.

"Meet the future Mrs. Lamare," Jeff said, proud as a peacock, while Anya glowed and showed off her diamond. Apparently, love had blossomed, even between two such unlikely people with an age gap of at least a decade. There was hope for him yet, Campbell decided.

"Where's Pete?" Anya asked, in a surprised tone. When Campbell described how Pete had been summoned via his cell phone and had set off immediately with the Sea Princess to points unknown, Anya didn't look pleased. Campbell decided not to mention that after the call, Pete had been jumpy as hell, hustling the passengers off the boat as if it was going to sink at any second.

"How are you getting to the nightclub?" he enquired, deciding a change of subject was in order.

"Water taxi," Anya replied promptly. "No worries, Jeff," she added. "Wind's dropped! It'll be a smooth ride."

Paradise Nightclub sat on a narrow promontory, surrounded by water. Anya led the way past tables laden with flowers and bottles of champagne, while music blasted out of a first class sound system. People of every colour and creed, speaking a dozen different languages were gathered here, exuding wealth, youth and glamour. Above the crowded dance floor was a star studded night sky. The sight took Campbell's breath away. Anya appeared to have recovered her good humour.

"Cool outfit, Cam," she remarked, glancing up at him. He'd never been called Cam before, let alone cool. She was tapping her feet to the beat.

"If you don't ask her to dance, I will," he warned Jeff, who promptly swept her onto the dance floor. Leaving them to it, Campbell strolled over to the jetty enjoying the cool breeze coming off the water. Spending important holidays like Valentine's Day on his own was becoming a habit he badly wanted to break. Before he had a chance to feel too lonely, he saw a boat approaching. The Sea Princess had returned. "You made it!" Campbell exclaimed happily, as Pete jumped off , rope in hand.

"I've been all over the shop!" Pete complained, bending down and tying the Sea Princess to the jetty. Then he turned around and caught sight of Campbell. "Strewth!" he exclaimed. "Look at you!" Unaccountably, his comment made Campbell feel quite self conscious. "Hey, where's your Sheila?" Pete asked.

"My what?"

"Your girl!"

"Back in Canada," Campbell replied, making it up as he went along.

"Get us a half dozen beers, mate," Pete suggested. "I'm not going in there... not my kind of place, but I could use some of the amber fluid!"

The first raindrops fell while Campbell was ordering a beer from the bar. A few minutes later, the skies opened. Judging from the shrieks of laughter coming his way, dancing under a waterfall was fun for some lucky people, just not for a lone male like him. Armed with a six pack, he made a dash for the Sea Princess and dived into the cabin. He joined Pete at the table, which was wedged between the galley and the sail lockers. After a while, Campbell broached the subject that had been on his mind all evening: the phone call which had apparently ruined Pete's night.

"Ask me no questions and I'll tell you no lies," Pete replied unhelpfully, before shutting his mouth like a trap. The atmosphere in the cabin became oppressive, intensified by the deafening sound of rain thundering down on the roof. Campbell decided to keep the news about Anya's engagement to himself for now. Pete would find out about it soon enough. A few minutes later there was a rap on the ceiling. Campbell jumped up, slid open the hatch and heaved a sigh of relief at the sight of Anya's smiling face.

"Someone throw me a towel. Better make it two," she said. Jeff appeared behind her, drenched to the skin but beaming.

"So you're getting hitched!" Pete declared flatly, gesturing at the ring on Anya's finger and wiping the happiness off her face.

"Yes! Anya's coming to Canada," Jeff agreed blithely, joining them at the table.

"Anyone got a gun?" Pete muttered. A stunned silence greeted his remark.

"Whatever for?" Campbell asked, frowning.

"So I can shoot myself," Pete replied. You could have cut the air with a knife; Anya looked mortified, Jeff merely puzzled.

"What's going on?" Jeff finally asked.

"Wouldn't you like to know!" Pete replied, his voice sounding unnaturally loud in the small cabin.

"You oughta tell them, Pete," Anya said quietly.

"I bloody well won't" Pete replied. "I've done nothing wrong. Except come to this stinking hole!" The despair in his voice shocked Campbell to the core.

"Anya?" Jeff prompted, looking worried to death. She looked down at the floor. "Is there something you haven't told me?" Jeff asked. "Are you and Pete..."

"No!" she replied immediately. "No. . . it's nothing like that," she reassured Jeff, placing her hand on his. "Everyone does things they regret, Pete," she added, an unreadable expression on her face.

"I've done nothing wrong!" he repeated. "Not in my book anyhow."

"If you won't tell them, I will. . . Pete's being blackmailed!" she announced abruptly.

"Blackmailed!" Jeff cried. "You should go to the police!"

"Haven't you been listening to anything I've been telling you about this island, Jeff?" Anya snapped.

"Will someone please explain?" Jeff said weakly. "I'm not enjoying this." Anya looked at Pete, who swallowed hard, but said nothing. Campbell couldn't stay silent any longer.

"My guess is that Pete doesn't want to go to the police because they're in the blackmailer's pocket," he suggested, eliciting a muffled exclamation from Anya.

"How come you know so much?" she demanded in an accusatory tone. "You're not from here!"

"Canada's not immune," Campbell replied, pulling out Vettore's photo.

"Take a look at this," he said. "Theo Vettore used to be the top driver at Iroquois Downs. He went missing last summer. No one knows for sure whether he's alive or dead." There was a stunned silence during which Campbell registered that it had stopped raining.

"Theo Vettore?" Jeff blurted out. "There's no mystery about that, surely? His car crashed into a ravine, right?"

"The day Vettore disappeared, he told me about a man he called the Scorpion," Campbell said.

"So it wasn't an accident?" Jeff exclaimed.

"We have reason to believe that the Scorpion's home base is somewhere on this island," he continued, glancing at Anya. "Sure there's nothing you want to tell me, Pete?" he added.

"Nope! I guess I'll go start up the motor," Pete replied stiffly. "It's getting pretty late."

Campbell took the hint and backed off. He joined the others up on the deck and stationed himself at the stern, listening to the gentle chug of the engine as they pulled away from the shore. Jeff and Anya had retreated to the bow. They were sitting close together, their heads touching. He could hear the soft murmur of their voices but he couldn't catch what they were saying. The sea was as smooth as glass, mirroring the clear night sky and reflecting a brilliant moon. Silent with wonder, Campbell surrendered to the magic, his only regret that he had no one special to share it with. After a while, a breeze sprung up, stirring the water. Campbell came back to earth with a bump.

"Blackmail is a crime we take very seriously at the RCMP," he told Pete. Pete's response, a short bitter laugh, was not encouraging. Campbell persisted. "Just how much does Anya know?" he asked carefully.

"Everything!" Pete replied. "But she's not like most people back home. She doesn't think any the less of me." Campbell wracked his brains for all the clichés he'd heard about Australia: the Micks and the Sheilas, the rough, male only bars where beer came out of hoses like gasoline, the barbecues and the beach parties...sharks...

"Where are you from in Australia?"

"Melbourne. It's a pretty good place to live."

"And the people?"

"Some of them are okay."

"What about the others?"

"Take over!" Pete said abruptly, abandoning the wheel and disappearing below deck. Up at the sharp end, the jib was flapping.

"Take her upwind, Cam," Anya sang out, standing ready to hoist the main sail, just as Pete emerged from the cabin with a flashlight. The two of them seemed perfectly attuned, kindred spirits. What was he missing here? Campbell wondered. The sails filled. The drumming of the engine was replaced by the sound of the sea. Pete took over the wheel.

"Shine the light on the sail," Pete said, handing over the flashlight. "That's so ships don't run into us," he explained. Surfer dudes...skin cancer...tarantulas, giant spiders, snakes, boxing kangaroos, deadly stone fish...Ayers rock, aborigines...homophobia. Pete didn't tick all the boxes, but Campbell was pretty sure he'd hit on the answer.

"What does he have on you? Photos...video...audio?"

"Yes to all that," Pete said, sticking out his chin defiantly. Pete . . .Theo Vettore . . how many others? Campbell wondered angrily. The situation Pete was in had the Scorpion's trademark stamped all over it. He was a cut above your average drug lord. The man was a sadist who apparently got a macabre pleasure from watching other people squirm. Campbell tried again.

"Tell me about him," he said. "What's he look like?"

"Typical French Canadian," Pete replied shortly. Campbell waited for more. "You know the type...dark hair, brown eyes..." Pete added.

"And his name?"

"No idea," Pete replied emphatically. It wasn't much to go on. But at least it didn't contradict what Vettore had told him. They were getting close to land. The lights marking the entrance to the harbour appeared.

"Where does he live?"

"Wouldn't you like to know!"

"If I'm going to be able to help, I'll need information," Campbell said.

"Nothing doing," Pete replied dismissively. Great! Campbell thought. I get this close and the door slams in my face.

"Want to chance it and sail her in?" Anya called out.

"Nope!" Pete said, starting up the engine. He was much too fond of that word, Campbell decided.

"Docking in sixty seconds," Pete announced suddenly. For the next few minutes, he and Anya were busy securing the Sea Princess for the night.

"So...are you any closer to finding the Scorpion? That's what you came for, right?" Jeff said.

"It's not that simple," Campbell replied. "Let's just say I've made a start."

"Anya never breathed a word about all this...until tonight," Jeff said, a little plaintively.

"Probably didn't want to worry you," Campbell reassured him.

"In a couple of months, she'll be away from here," Jeff confided. "She's going to fly out from one of the larger islands. She's not keen on leaving from the local airport...too visible."

"Sensible plan," Campbell agreed. It confirmed his suspicions that Anya was running away from something. Was it merely to do with Pete's situation, or was there more to it? If so, a price might have to be paid for her freedom.

Unless, of course, she had paid up front already.

The next day, Campbell woke up early. As soon as it was light he walked down to the harbour, arriving at the Sea Princess as Pete showed up with a box of provisions.

"Gonna be a scorcher," Pete remarked cheerfully. It was like the conversation they'd had the previous night had never happened. "Take a look at the front page," he added, tossing a copy of the local paper at Campbell. He read the headline: SHERE KHAN WINS ISLAND CHALLENGE. Beneath it was a picture of the mega yacht and a short piece about her owners: Tamarind Enterprises. He asked Pete what he knew about the company. "Tamarind," Pete said. "Not a whole lot."

When Anya showed up half an hour later, Campbell asked her the same question.

"Tamarind built this island," she replied immediately. "Before, it was nothing but mangrove swamp. The whole place was full of mossies."

"Mossies?" Campbell repeated curiously, wondering if they were some kind of native tribe.

"Mosquitoes to you," Pete clarified.

"I heard people came here with suitcases of cash twenty years ago," Campbell ventured.

"Not anymore!" Anya said sharply, shooting Pete a warning glance. So the story about the suitcases full of cash was probably true, Campbell decided. Sainte Marie had been built with dirty money. "Things are different around here now. They're cleaning the place up," Anya added firmly.

"Getting rid of the undesirables," Pete mumbled. "Like me."

"Hey," Anya said. "They're just sending them home, Pete."

"Home?" Campbell queried. "Where would that be?"

"Could be anywhere…the Caribbean, India, South America…this island's a great place to start a business," she replied.

"If you know the right people," Pete added pointedly.

"Need any help today?" Campbell enquired.

"No worries," Anya said. "We're gonna have to use the motor today. No wind. Jeff'll be happy."

"Hey, help yourself to a mask and flippers," Pete offered. "You'll see a lot of fish on a day like this."

"Thanks," Campbell replied appreciatively. He made his farewells and left. He hadn't gone far when he realized he'd forgotten to take Pete up on his offer. He turned back, then stopped in his tracks. An argument had broken out on the deck of the Sea Princess.

"You oughta tell him," he heard Pete say, his voice carrying across the water, clear as a bell.

"Hey," Anya cried. "You want everyone to hear you?"

"About you and that creep," Pete continued, undeterred.

"I don't have to!" Anya said vehemently.

"What about Jeff? He oughta know."

"Jeff? No way!"

"Someone in that house took those pictures," Pete persisted. "Henri's sworn it wasn't him and I believe him."

"More fool you!" she replied contemptuously.

"Are you blind?" Pete asked savagely. Campbell kept listening, but the argument petered out. In his view, secrets always sabotaged relationships in the end, so they were best out in the open. Pete had given Anya sound advice. If she knew what was good for her, she'd take it.

Ninety degrees Fahrenheit, thirty percent humidity. A hammock rocking gently in the blessed shade…a bottle of the finest champagne, ice cold. The island, desert dry, not a cloud, not a breeze…the murmur of doves…a caged parrot's rasping cry…an old man, his skin dark as night, sheltering beneath a wide brimmed hat as he perfects the pool, his slow rhythmic movements choreographed by a relentless sun.

André Fontainbleu is quietly celebrating. The Shere Khan has captured the crown. . . victory is sweet.

Campbell found the offices of the *Island News* tucked away at the end of a long sunny street. Its store front window was packed with pictures of partygoers from the night before. Valentine's Day was a big deal on this island, apparently. Surprisingly, the front office was deserted. Campbell went up to the counter.

"D'you keep archives of the paper here?" he asked a graceful girl with almond eyes and coffee coloured skin.

"Archives, you say?" she replied in a soft, lilting voice. "I would have to say no to that. You could maybe try the website."

"There's a website? Wonderful!" Campbell exclaimed gratefully.

"You Americans," she said. "Always in such a rush. You need to slow down. Get on island time." Campbell was struck dumb. He'd never been taken for an American before. Plainly, it wasn't a compliment. Determined to prove the girl wrong, he bought a mask and flippers and made his way back to the hotel, taking time to appreciate the beauty all around him: the tall green palms, the brilliant colours, the flash of a bird's wing. In the lobby, he logged on to one of the hotel's computers without his usual enthusiasm. The girl had a point. Why did he feel he had to be busy and productive at all times? Where did that idea come from? Not from his childhood in PEI, for sure. People there always had plenty of time.

As he read about events on the island calendar, the Annual Regatta, Carnival, Pirates Week, the construction of the new airport, one name cropped up, time and time again: Tamarind Enterprises. As for the mega yacht, the Shere Khan, Campbell knew his Kipling. Shere Khan was the tiger, the lord of the jungle. He took heart, convinced he was onto something. Then he came across the headline: SINGING SENSATION IN ROYAL TROPICANA and spotted a picture of Billie McTavish, carefree and suntanned. Theo was standing beside her. Something deep within him did a backflip. Jealousy? He was astonished. It had never happened before. He wasn't remotely acquainted with the green monster. But to feel jealous of a man like Vettore? He was far too involved, he decided. It was time to take a step back.

A concierge in a spotless white uniform appeared.

"A Miss McTavish is on the telephone, sir," he announced politely.

"I'll take it in the room," Campbell replied.

"Don't tell me you were in the pool," Billie said, "or I'll never speak to you again!" Incredibly, he could hear her as well as if she was in the room next door. If only she was! he thought wistfully.

"No," he replied truthfully. "I wasn't."

"Having fun?"

"Not really."

"How come?"

"Various reasons."

"I wonder why I don't feel sorry for you?" Billie replied acidly. "We're in the middle of a snowstorm here."

"You should have come along."

"Way too many memories," she said. The ceiling fan was circling languidly, fascinating a number of yellow butterflies which had fluttered in through the open window. Campbell jumped up and turned it off, releasing the fragile creatures from certain death, his good deed for the day. "So," Billie wanted to know. "How's it going so far?"

"Fair to middling," he replied, unwilling to reveal too much on an open line. Anyone could be listening in.

"You don't want to tell me," she said, clearly put out. "Why?"

"Nothing to tell. I'm too busy looking for answers," he replied hastily.

"Answers? I don't even know the questions! You know, perhaps you should take that swim. It might clear your head." Before he could think of a suitable reply, she rang off, leaving him as confused as hell. Putting his state of mind down to the heat, he decided to take a swim to cool off. The view beneath the waves was even more colourful than the one above.

The afternoon went by in a heartbeat.

The next morning, he tried to track down the offices of Tamarind Enterprises. But when he eventually located it, it proved to be a plaque on the wall of an accountant's office, along with many others. The man Theo had called the Scorpion was nowhere to be found either. The bald headed man collecting the prize for the Shere Khan's win looked nothing like Pete's description. With less than two days to go before the flight back to Canada, Campbell was at a bit of an impasse. At least he wouldn't have to report back to Commander Davis, he realized, trying to snatch some crumbs of comfort. But that brought to mind his disciplinary hearing, which could not be far off now.

Campbell spent his last full day in Sainte Marie on the Sea Princess, with a boat load of tourists. Not a breath of wind disturbed the surface of the turquoise water. It was perfect snorkelling weather. Anya was nowhere to be seen. He assumed she was with Jeff. Her name didn't come up until the end of the day, when they were back in port.

"Wanna come to the Sunset Bar tonight?" Pete asked in a friendly fashion. "Me and Anya generally go there on a Friday. If Ritchie's there, he gives us free drinks." Campbell slung his bag over his shoulder and they were on their way. The Sunset Bar was jammed between the airport and the shore. Incredibly, it bumped right up against the runway itself. It would have never been allowed in Canada, for safety reasons. Campbell couldn't understand how they had managed to obtain planning consent. Pete had the answer.

"Politics! Ritchie Sanchez knows all the right people," Pete said. With that, he grabbed some beers from the makeshift bar, which looked like it had been a passenger bus in a former life. Every spare inch of it was plastered with newspaper clippings of Ritchie Sanchez breaking records on the athletics track in Florida.

"The great man himself will be along soon," Pete remarked, glancing over his shoulder as they took their seats at a wobbly table, its legs in the sand. Campbell was already regretting the promise he'd made to Jeff that he wouldn't dig any deeper until Anya was safely away from the island. Well, he thought, he'd just have to carry on and make the best of it, like any good foot soldier.

The bar was popular. Tables were filling up fast. The only thing on the menu was something called tapas. Campbell decided to give it a try. The band was playing Careless Whispers, a song that had put George Michael on the map. Whoever wrote it knew a thing or two about pain and remorse. It brought Theo Vettore to mind. Judging from past history though, Theo Vettore wore an invisible shield that protected him from all that. It hadn't done him any favours so far: no pain, no gain. He wondered if Vettore was really dead or if he'd get yet another chance to screw up his life.

The food arrived.

"There he is!" Pete exclaimed, as a man with the darkest suntan Campbell had ever seen came swaggering in. "Gained a few pounds since his running days," Pete added with a grin. Ritchie Sanchez was quickly swallowed up by a swarm of people wanting his autograph. After a while, a brace of women with hard bitten faces peeled off from the crowd and began prowling nearby. American tourists looking for action, Campbell surmised, judging from their accents. After he'd made it pretty clear he wasn't interested, they fastened onto Pete. Good luck with that! Campbell thought, smiling to himself as the

Americans chatted away in animated tones. They ended up taking Pete onto the dance floor. There was still no sign of Jeff and Anya. Campbell waved at the waiter, intending to pay the bill and go back to the hotel. To his astonishment, Ritchie Sanchez came up to the table, pen in hand.

"Got something you want me to sign?" he asked genially, sitting himself down on Pete's empty chair. "What's your name?" Sanchez enquired lazily, picking up one of the menus and signing it with a flourish. When Campbell told him, Sanchez scrawled something illegible above the signature and handed it back. "So, what brings you to the island?" he asked, putting two fingers to his thick lips and whistling, as if he was calling a dog. "Pepe! Two Stingrays!" he called out. Judging from the former athlete's beer belly, the former athlete would be able to drink him under the table handily, Campbell surmised. But where had staying stone cold sober got him on this trip? Maybe he needed to loosen up a bit. He pulled out Vettore's picture, dog eared from carrying it around in his pocket for days on end, and proffered it to Sanchez. "What's this? And why show it to me?" Ritchie asked, looking genuinely puzzled. Campbell launched into the story of Vettore's disappearance, leaving out nothing, throwing caution to the wind. "But why look for him here? This happened in Canada, right?" Sanchez added.

"His uncle owns a timeshare on the island," Campbell explained. He had already checked out the villa. It was currently being occupied by a young family.

"Who are you anyway? A detective, a cop?" Sanchez demanded, looking nervous.

"A friend of the family," Campbell said. He had sound reasons for not telling him the truth, he thought, squaring it with his conscience. "I heard you're pretty well connected, I figured you'd know if anything unusual was going on."

"You really think Theo Vettore could be somewhere on the island?" Sanchez asked incredulously. Did he have a phenomenal memory or had he heard that name before? Campbell wondered. Most people didn't pick up on a stranger's name on a single mention. "Listen, the guy couldn't have arrived without the authorities knowing about it. Even small boats need to go through passport control..." Sanchez added. "Hang on, I've got to take this call," he declared, pulling out a small black cell phone.

What with the band and people talking all around them, Campbell hadn't actually heard the phone ring. He was getting an uneasy feeling in his gut, which had nothing to do with the food he had just eaten. He went off to find Pete, glancing back at Sanchez, who was talking a mile a minute to someone on the other end of the line. He needed to leave urgently, before Sanchez cornered him and bombarded him with questions. Plainly the man was no fool. Pete was only too thankful to be rescued from the Americans. Campbell strode up to the bar and paid the bill in cash. He did not wish to leave an imprint of his bank card for anyone to find. When he glanced back at him, Sanchez was staring at him, a deep frown etched on his swarthy face. But it was his eyes that gave him away. Campbell had seen that look once before: the mix of dawning comprehension mingled with fear. It reminded him of Theo Vettore the day he'd been caught with cocaine in his car.

What was Ritchie Sanchez afraid of?

André Fontainbleu cut off Ritchie Sanchez in mid sentence. He had another call to make.

"Boxer," he said coolly. "The small problem we have already discussed, it is becoming more serious."

"What would you like me to do about it?" Boxer asked eagerly. Lately, Fontainbleu had been feeling that his oldest friend was becoming a liability. The signs were there for anyone to read. However, he could never forget that Boxer had stepped in as his protector after Philippe had been shot down and killed. He owed him his life. There was, of course, nothing wrong with violence, especially the threat of it when necessary. However, the amount of pleasure Boxer appeared to derive from it was beginning to be a concern.

"Make sure McClaren gets on that plane tomorrow," he said. "He is no longer welcome on this island."

The next day, at the airport, Campbell was certain he was being watched. The burly bald headed guy who'd picked up the Ocean Challenge Trophy appeared to be stalking him. So! Someone had become aware of his presence on the island and was anxious to confirm his departure. Food for thought. Evidently, his search for Theo Vettore on Sainte Marie had set alarm bells ringing. It would be difficult for him to return a second time. It was disappointing. He had come so close.

After a four-hour flight, Campbell exchanged the balmy temperatures of

Half Moon Bay for the frigid air of Ontario. He put in a call to Billie McTavish from the airport.

"What'd you find out?" she asked eagerly.

"Good question," he replied thoughtfully. "I'd rather tell you in person. Listen, I'd really like to see you…d'you know a place called The Green Room?"

"I've heard of it," she said a little dubiously. It wasn't on her regular route then. So much the better.

"I could be with you in about an hour," he said.

"Tonight?" she exclaimed in an astonished tone. He braced himself for disappointment. "So I'll see you around nine then," she said, confounding him.

By the time he had picked up the rental car and got on the road, it was snowing. Skiers were sashaying down the floodlit slopes beside the highway. For once, Campbell didn't feel tempted to join them. The car heater was blasting out hot air, but he just couldn't seem to get warm. He was early but Billie must have been watching out for him. She appeared outside her front door almost immediately.

"It's like a sauna in here!" she declared, unzipping her coat, revealing a tight sweater that sent his pulses racing.

"A week on the island can make a man soft," he confessed.

"Don't complain, you got a good tan." Billie said.

He was silent, overcome by the sight of her pale features, framed by a cloud of brown hair. He had forgotten just how beautiful she was. Fortunately, she seemed unfazed by his reticence. As for him, he was content just to listen to her talk. Her voice was lyrical: a singer's voice. He sensed a different aura about her tonight. The spectre of Theo Vettore no longer hung in the air between them.

The Green Room was his kind of place: classy but not flashy. The pictures lining its dark walls were by local artists and the music was a mix of indie and retro, with its own unique style, one where it paid to listen to the words. He ordered minestrone and roast beef sandwiches for both of them, and some red wine for Billie. He, as usual, was sticking to water. By the time the coffee arrived, Richie Havens had launched into a rendition of The Great Mandala. Taking that as his cue, Campbell pushed a small box across the table.

"Open it," he said. He tried not to watch as she took the lid off and discovered the heart covered in red foil he'd bought on impulse in the hotel foyer.

"Chocolate!" she said, smiling at him. "It's perfect...so perfect." She hesitated, frowning. "I don't want to break it."

"Then don't," he advised.

"It'll just go stale."

"True...so what's the solution?" he asked, smiling across the table at her. He wasn't a hundred percent sure they were talking about chocolate anymore.

"Catch," she cried, breaking it in two and lobbing a piece towards him. It went wide but he reached out and snared it anyway. "Hey!" she exclaimed delightedly. "You'd make a good shortstop."

"Yeah. I was thinking of trying out for the Red Sox...Go down for spring training," he replied. "Least I'd be warm."

"And desert the home team?" she asked in mock dismay. "Where's your loyalty?"

"I'm loyal to Canada," he asserted.

"You're aware it's Boston Red Sox, as in Boston US, right?"

"That could be a problem," he acknowledged. As they finished off the chocolate in companionable silence, he noticed she'd taken the wrapper and carefully folded it before slipping it into her purse. He took that as a positive sign. Then again, she could be really, really into recycling.

"Tell me about Sainte Marie," she said simply. He told her how much the island had changed, about the Paradise Club and the Sea Princess, about the night sky studded with stars. "It's a magical place," she said, her eyes misty. He ended with the news of Jeff and Anya's engagement which came as no great surprise to her. "What d'you think of her?" she asked curiously.

"Anya? She's nothing like you," he said. Apparently that had been the wrong thing to say.

"Meaning you won't tell me," she replied, a hurt expression in her eyes.

"Meaning it's complicated," he said.

"It's getting late. I should go," she declared. He didn't try to dissuade her. What would be the point? The evening had turned sour for no good reason, but that didn't mean he didn't want to see her safely home.

Outside her front door, she halted, snowflakes festooning her hair like Christmas lights.

"D'you want a drink or something?" she asked, sounding a little nervous.

"I'm freezing," he confessed. "I could kill for a mug of hot cocoa."

"Come on up," she replied, sounding a good deal more relaxed. He was relieved but then hot cocoa wasn't exactly sexy...cozy, maybe...the thought depressed him.

"You don't drink do you?" she commented as he followed her up the stairs.

"Alcohol just sends me to sleep," he explained.

"Oh I see," she replied, apparently happy with his answer. In the small kitchen, they compared notes on the best way of making hot chocolate, then took the results into the living room. Billie made a beeline for the couch, while he built a fire from pine logs and kindling. "So when are you going to tell me the important stuff?" Billie asked, kicking off her shoes. He stayed on his knees by the fire, debating with himself how much to tell her. On the one hand, there was Billie, a sensitive, intelligent woman who wouldn't be satisfied with pablum. On the other hand, there was his job. The RCMP would frown on his giving away confidential information. To cap it all, there was Billie's friend Jeff, who had no idea that Anya had been involved with a man Pete clearly disapproved of, as lovers or business partners, it wasn't clear which. But, he reasoned, this trip to the island had been on his own initiative and any loyalty he ought to have felt to the organization had been compromised by his suspension. He proceeded to fill Billie in on everyone and everything that had happened on Sainte Marie, leaving out the argument he had overheard between Pete and Anya. As Jeff's friend, Billie would be stuck on the horns of a dilemma: to tell, or not to tell Jeff about it. There was no good way out of that one.

"It seems to me," Billie said, patting the sofa next to her, an invitation that he accepted with alacrity, "that you left the island just when things were getting interesting."

"I agree," he said.

"So what happens now?"

"I wish I knew." A blazing log fell off the fire. He leapt up, an instinctive reaction which wasn't necessary. The log had landed harmlessly on the hearth. It was one in the morning. Time had flown by. "I'd better get going," he said reluctantly, thinking of the frozen world outside.

"I have a guest room," Billie offered. "You're welcome to stay."

"A guest room sounds wonderful," he said, grateful that she wasn't throwing him out. Driving around looking for a hotel wouldn't have been fun on a night like this.

It was still snowing when he went outside to retrieve his case from the car. When he returned, Billie had her arms full of towels.

"One night or two?" she asked pertly.

"Er, two I think. If you can spare the room."

"Perfect. I have a plan," she said, leading the way to the guest bedroom. "You skate, right?"

"I play ice hockey," he confirmed. So, she didn't want to kiss him, he thought wistfully

"How about we go skate on the river tomorrow? It's a lot of fun. And the beaver tails are to die for."

"Count me in. But what do I use for skates?"

"I have an old pair of my brother's that I'm fairly sure would fit you."

"Then, 'til tomorrow," he said, setting down his case inside the room. He longed to take her in his arms but he felt instinctively this was not the time or place for it. He was after all, a guest in her house. In his rule book, it was up to her to make the first move. "Goodnight," he added warmly. At this rate, I won't just be wearing her brother's skates…I might just as well be her brother, he thought miserably. The next thing he knew, he felt her arms about him. Her lips brushed his for an instant. Then she pulled away. He reeled her back in. "D'you have any idea how beautiful you are?" he asked, holding her close and gently stroking her hair. "And smart and funny and…"

"Compliments!" she glowed. "I love compliments."

"You'll get plenty from me if you stick around."

"That's rich, Mr. World Traveller. Where are you off to next?"

"Nowhere," he replied. He meant it. She relaxed, leaning in close.

"I hope it's somewhere warm," she said, her voice muffled. "This jacket's paper thin."

"I dress to impress," was his comeback.

"Now that I really don't believe!" she laughed. This time the kiss lasted a good deal longer, before she quietly disentangled herself. "'Till tomorrow," she whispered, her eyes soft. Then she walked away, leaving him floating on cloud nine.

Meeting with Commander Davis two days later brought Campbell back down to reality. Apparently, his disciplinary hearing was due to take place in three weeks' time. Going back to PEI wasn't really an option. He needed a place to stay while he prepared his defence. But where? When he asked Billie to help, she came up with the answer: a bachelor pad on the western edge of town, with a sweeping view of the river.

"It's five floors up and there's no elevator," she explained. "That's what's been putting people off. Shouldn't bother you, though." He moved in immediately.

The hearing went better than he had feared. But, his commander warned, he might not get the judgement for weeks. Campbell didn't care anymore. Whichever way it went he had decided to call it quits with the RCMP. It was time to try life on his own, career wise. On the personal front, he was betting everything on Miss Billie McTavish.

THE MAD MARCH HARE

A month later, Campbell had learned a great deal more about Billie McTavish. Beneath that friendly, flirtatious exterior lay an intensity that frequently surfaced, often unnerving him. She was full of surprises and contradictions. Life with her was never going to be boring. All he had to offer was a steady hand on the tiller, something she appeared to appreciate. He wasn't sleeping in the guest room anymore. Unfortunately, progress on other fronts had not kept pace with his personal life. There was still no word from the committee deciding his fate and not a peep from Theo Vettore or Crawfish Brown. As for his trip to Sainte Marie, it had produced more questions than answers. Until Anya arrived safely in Canada, his hands were tied. Feeling a little like a ne'er do well, he tried to make the best of things. The ski season was winding down, but ice hockey was still on offer.

On a bitterly cold Saturday in late March, he was up early, waiting around to give Billie a call at a more civilized hour than 6 am in the morning when, to his surprise, she called him.

"Want to meet my ideal man?" she giggled.

"How could I turn down an offer like that?" he replied, wondering what was in store. Billie kept him guessing all the way to Rivers Training centre. The cheerful red barns and snow covered paddocks reminded him of the racetrack at Charlottetown in PEI. He made a mental note to call his parents. They would be anxious for news. The fact there was none was no excuse. The training track was empty, except for a lone horse circling slowly around it. A single figure was stationed alongside it, braving the bitter wind: Al McTavish.

After giving Billie a hug, Al grasped Campbell's hand warmly, saying, "I remember you! You just about saved my life!"

"Oh I think the doctors did that, sir," Campbell replied modestly.

"What are you up to these days?" Al queried.

"Not too much," Campbell confessed.

"Ever considered quitting the force and doing something else?"

"They'd probably love that, sir," Campbell replied candidly. "You see, lately, they don't seem to know what to do with me."

"Woah! This is it!" Al cried excitedly, gesturing at the colt. "Gotta get the time!" he added anxiously. "Tony's watch always stops at the critical moment."

"So you're in love with Tony," Campbell teased, smiling at Billie as Stampede came flying past, the wizened figure of the trainer hunched up against the wind.

"You guessed it. Can't help myself," she replied deadpan. "Harmony Stampede's still my ideal man, though."

"He's a pretty horse," Campbell agreed as the colt travelled down the backstretch, flashing his four white socks. But unless his eyes were deceiving him, something was wrong with the way he was pacing. When he came down the stretch for the last time, it was obvious. The horse was struggling.

"Last quarter was thirty-seven seconds!" Al pronounced in a tone of despair. "Something's wrong!" he added, staring down at his watch as if willing it to tell a different story.

Back at Tony's barn, the colt was drenched in sweat and gasping for breath, despite a harsh north wind.

"He's changed!" Tony Hall declared. "Pinned his ears when I asked him to go. Told you we shoulda gelded him!"

"With his breeding?" Al exclaimed, his words echoing off the rafters. After Tony took his harness off, Stampede stood motionless, his head hanging low, his flanks heaving. It was painful to watch. When Tony led him over to the wash stall, the horse whipped his hind leg up as if he was standing on hot coals. Tony gave no signs of having noticed anything amiss.

"What's with the left hind?" Al asked anxiously. Tony picked up the colt's opposite leg, forcing Stampede to put the other leg down, if only for a moment.

"That's nothin'. Jus' the way he's standin'," Tony declared.

"I want Winterflood to take a look at him," Al stated bluntly.

"Suit yerself," Tony replied.

"Better leave him in until then," Al advised.

"No sense in beatin' a dead horse!" Tony agreed brutally. The three of them trooped out.

"Well done, Dad," Billie said. "That was the right thing to do. We should go," she added quietly, glancing at Campbell.

"Let us know what happens with the colt, Mr. McTavish," Campbell said.

"Yes, ah…yes alright," Al replied distractedly. "You go ahead," he added impatiently. Obviously, he didn't want to talk about it. So reluctantly, Campbell left him to it, dicky heart and all.

Never again! Al swore to himself as he drove away from Rivers Training centre. No more yearlings for me! I've learned my lesson! Ruefully, he totted up the thousands of dollars he had spent paying Stampede up to every stake on the map. He'd been so preoccupied in getting the cheques in on time that he had completely forgotten about Valentine's Day, a poor reward for Sofia, who had waited on him hand and foot while he'd been convalescing. He could tell Sofia still held it against him.

"Is this light permanently on red?" he muttered, his frustration rising as he sat at a junction, his foot hovering over the accelerator. Then he saw the hare. It was standing on the pavement, staring intently at the stream of traffic. Al watched in disbelief as the animal made repeated attempts to cross the highway, hurling itself onto the road as if pulled by an invisible string, dodging back at the last second, inches from death as truck after truck roared blindly past. By the time the lights changed, the hare had retreated a hundred meters down a side road. But Al could tell it was going to try again, just as soon as it got the chance. Some instincts were just too powerful to ignore, Al concluded, rooting for the hare. Perhaps that was the real appeal of the yearling game. Perhaps, he thought, deep down he was a wild gambler and not the sober responsible citizen he had always imagined himself to be.

Meanwhile, back at the barn, Tony Hall was measuring out the noonday feed when Evie Mercer arrived, bringing treats. She knew Tony disapproved, but she didn't care. Tony's horses didn't get fussed over. Ever! After making the rounds, she realized one of the horses was missing.

"Where's Jetson?" she demanded. Tony carried on making the horses' lunch. "The little black colt," she added forcefully. Tony shrugged.

"Him? He's over at Gerry's."

"Gerry Lake? Why?"

"He was no good. Gerry's gonna use 'im as a riding horse for his kids. Reg didn't want to pay the bills no more."

Outside, the wind had piled up the snow in drifts, burying the frozen lake in the infield. Undeterred, Evie set off to find Jetson. There was no sign of the trainer with the flaming red hair in Barn 5. Gerry had fed lunch early and gone home. But Jetson was sitting in a pile of manure, his head tucked down, his eyes half closed. A bucket of dirty water hung from the wall. For a moment, Evie felt so enraged, she could hardly breathe. But then she set about putting things right. Half an hour later, with a clean stall, fresh water and plenty of hay, Jetson was looking a good deal happier. But, Evie vowed, Gerry was going to pay for this!

Two days later, Winterflood called Al with news about Harmony Stampede.

"Those clowns at the clinic left a stitch in him, buried deep inside his hock. The pain must've been unbearable!" the veterinarian said. "They'll have to take the stitch out of him. Looks like they did a good job on the operation though. No sign of any scar tissue. 'Course he'll lose some time now."

"I just spent seven thousand dollars paying him up to the stakes!" Al groaned. "I ought to sue those idiots for negligence. Thanks, anyhow," he added hastily.

"Hey, anytime," Winterflood replied breezily. "Listen, good luck with him. He's a nice looking colt, worth waiting on."

Al wasn't sure anymore. Stampede wouldn't be ready for weeks now. March! That old wives' tale was true, he reflected bitterly. It had come in like a lamb with warmer temperatures and a hint of spring in the air. Stampede had been pacing like a dream back then. Now, he was penned up in a stall and the countryside was buried under a foot of snow. He'd got it all wrong, Al thought. He should have stuck to racehorses. They made money every week. Yet the colt tugged at his heartstrings like a favourite child. He hadn't got attached to Millie D like this. This colt, however imperfect, was his own. For better or worse, for richer or poorer, in sickness and in health, Al thought. He already had one marriage in shreds. He vowed he would see this through to the end. Yet when he sat down and figured out how much the colt had cost him this year alone, he wished he'd spent the money on a luxury cruise for himself and Sofia. At least one of them might have been happy then. With the colt sidelined, there was little on Al's horizon but the much heralded opening of Iroquois Downs Casino.

OPENING NIGHT

On April 7th, Al set out for Iroquois Downs. In the passenger seat beside him, Sofia was chattering away, excited to be going out for the evening, which hadn't happened in quite a while. Thankfully, the roads were clear but now that the snow had melted, the devastation dealt out by five months of winter was only too apparent.

The sun was setting as Al and Sofia joined the crowds flocking to the casino, streaming in through the doors. The walls were studded with fake jewels like an Aladdin's cave and the floors were sparkling with gold dust. It was an auspicious start. However, once inside, the noise and the flashing lights got to Al. There were no clocks and no windows either, giving him the feeling that the outside world had ceased to exist. Perhaps that was the point of it all, Al thought, looking around. Everywhere, people were eagerly feeding quarters into the fruit machines and one arm bandits, seemingly without a care in the world.

"Al! Welcome!" his old comrade in arms Phil Harman exclaimed, strolling towards him, oozing charm and sporting what had to be a fake tan. There'd been no sun for weeks. Al looked around for Sofia but she had disappeared.

"Oh hi, Phil," he replied unenthusiastically. This time last year he'd been a gullible fool. No longer! The scales had fallen from his eyes. The reason he was getting a royal welcome from Phil was anybody's guess, Al thought cynically. Phil smiled, revealing a set of perfect white teeth, too perfect to be the genuine article.

"You're looking good, pal. When are you taking up the reins again?" Phil asked.

"Iroquois Downs, you mean? Bad ticker," Al replied, patting his chest. "Can't take the risk."

"Nonsense!" Phil said. "Best thing for you. The place needs you and you need the occupation!" So he knew about the sale of McTavish Construction, Al realized. He had to admit, it had left a yawning gap in his life. "Promise me you'll think about it," Phil added encouragingly, before moving on. Al nodded distractedly. Casting about for his wife, he spotted Tony Hall wolfing down a burger. The very thought of sending Stampede back to a man like Tony made Al feel sick. He walked in the other direction and ran into his old trainer, Bob Summers, drinking a pop.

"Just the man I wanted to see," Al said heartily, intending to give the colt back to the infamous caffeine kid. Despite Bob's positive test, Al couldn't think of a better man for the job.

"Before you go any further Mr. McTavish," Bob said earnestly. "Keith Lazer's offered me a job as his second trainer." Al couldn't contain his astonishment.

"Lazer?" he exclaimed. "He's got quite a reputation."

"It was either that or go back to plumbing," Bob replied soberly.

"Plumbing? But why? You're a horse trainer...a damn good one too."

"This past year's been pretty tough," Bob confided quietly. "I worked for a bunch of different guys behind the scenes like...didn't want to outstay my welcome you know...until Keith took me in."

Hiring a man who'd been suspended could cost a trainer his own licence, Al realized.

"Go on," he prompted.

"Keith's not such a bad guy. You'll never catch him racing a lame horse." Bob said. Al tucked that information away. After his experience with Tony Hall, it sounded pretty good to him. Perhaps he had been too quick to judge Keith Lazer, he thought. "Anyways, I learned something, Mr. McTavish," Bob continued. "Racing horses is much too complicated these days for a guy like me. With the Slots, the stakes are gonna be even higher. No way I can compete with those guys. I always thought I'd end up working for the Racing Commission, as a judge or something," Bob added sadly. "But that's out of the question now, of course."

"I understand. Good luck eh," Al replied, doing his best to recover from the blow. It looked like he might have to send Stampede back to Tony Hall, after all.

"I'll need it," Bob said in heartfelt tones. "Keith's a hard man to work for... doesn't believe in cutting corners. Still, it's a living. Oh . . . almost forgot, Andy Price was looking for you. Oi, Andy!" In a dark corner, a man sprang to life and began a headlong rush in Al's direction. There was no avoiding Mr. Price, Al realized, wondering what a claiming trainer like Andy could possibly want with him. There were beads of sweat on Andy's brow and he was sporting a paunch. Probably suffering from high blood pressure, Al decided. Since his own illness, he had become acutely aware of other people's state of health.

"They've thrown us all off the backstretch, Mr. McTavish, saying they can't afford to run it no more. I've been there for years. Years!" Andy cried.

"I heard about it. Wish I could help," Al replied, putting as much sympathy into his tone as he could muster, given that Andy's cause was probably hopeless. "I'm not really in a position to do anything…I'm still on sick leave," Al explained, deciding to leave his options open for now. A look of resignation replaced the eagerness on Andy's face.

"Meridian's got stalls," Eddie Clearwater piped up. Al couldn't believe the man was still in business at his age. But there he was, large as life, his thumbs stuck into his overalls. It made Al feel hopeful on his own account. "Good track with big wide turns, nice paddocks. Barns are decent too. What more could a man want?" Eddie asked. What indeed? Al thought, smiling at the simplicity of the old timer's world.

"Things just ain't the same no more," Andy pronounced gloomily. "Not with the backstretch closed and Crawfish gone."

"Still no word eh?" Eddie asked. Andy shook his head.

"Just plum disappeared. Him and Vettore the same day. Imagine? That's his ma over there," Andy said nodding at a gaggle of women clustered around a machine that was vomiting quarters. "They do say," he intoned, "she ain't the same woman." Conversation flagged. Andy Price didn't seem a bad sort, Al decided. He was about to feel him out about taking Stampede when Sofia reappeared.

"Come, Alastair," she said, taking his arm and marching him off. Swallowing his objections, Al allowed himself to be led away, hoping that if he co-operated she would let him off the hook for the Valentine's Day fiasco. A few minutes later, he came face to face with Jeff Lamare's fiancée. Superficially, she looked a little like his daughter: she was roughly the same height and had long hair. But there the resemblance ended. After the pleasantries and congratulations were out of the way and everyone had agreed about how well he was looking, Al was collared by Sofia again. "You are looking tired, Alastair," she pronounced.

"Where's Billie? She said she'd meet us here," he asked plaintively.

"Alastair," she replied sternly. "You need to go home." The idea of taking up the reins again as Director of Iroquois Downs was suddenly appealing. He was growing tired of being nurse maided constantly. They ran into Billie on their way out.

"Is Jeff there? Did you meet Anya? What's she like?" she asked excitedly.

"She looks a little like you," Al replied truthfully.

"Mom?"

"I only saw her for a moment," Sofia said. Her disappointment about Billie's chances of ending up married to Jeff was obvious, to Al at any rate.

"It would be nice to see Billie settled," he remarked mildly as they walked out into the dark cold world outside the casino.

"Our daughter is going to do very well for herself. You will see!" his wife exclaimed. There were some mysteries a man could not solve, Al decided. One of them was the inner workings of a woman's mind. But he had to admit that during the past year he had been every bit as baffled by Phil Harman's behaviour. What did it say about him, he wondered a little sorrowfully, that he was unable to read the two chief players in his personal life: his wife and his onetime best friend?

"Did you have a good time?" he asked Sofia anxiously.

Surprisingly, she had.

Unlike Sofia, Anya Papandreos was not having a good time. The casino, along with everything else in Canada so far, had been a huge let down. Jeff had filled her up with stories about swimming in the lake and barbecues in people's backyards. He didn't even have a backyard! After the first couple of days, he'd gone back to work, leaving her alone in his vast apartment with its bleak views of something he called the Escarpment: a looming cliff without an ocean in sight. Though it was April, there wasn't a leaf to be seen. The fields were empty and silent. Even when the sun shone, the air was cold and the harsh northern light got her down. Back in Sainte Marie, she and Jeff had spent their days outdoors. But in Canada, Jeff seemed to spend all his free time inside, watching TV and playing on computer games. She wished he would stop asking her how she liked her new home. It's different, was the only response she'd been able to come up with that didn't sound like a total put down. As for the Casino, it too was nothing like she'd expected. There were no gaming tables and not an ounce of glamour, just a maze of slot machines surrounded by sad people. It hadn't helped that Jeff's trainer had nabbed him as soon as they'd got in. The two of them were still locked in conversation, half an hour later. Anya was only half listening. A part of her felt like she was sleepwalking, like none of this was real. Why had she ever left Sainte Marie? she asked herself. She'd had so much going for her on the island: the climate, the Sea Princess…Pete…

"Well?" she heard Jeff ask sharply.

"Sorry, I was miles away," she confessed.

"Ask her again," Jeff said.

"What d'you think of Canada?" Lazer repeated, his blue eyes meeting hers, as sharp as a tack.

"Too soon to tell," she hedged. Lazer laughed.

"Come and work for me. I'll cheer you up," he said. The guy could charm the pants off a kangaroo. Jeff obviously wasn't appreciating Lazer's brand of charm, though. Anya decided to decline the invitation.

"Thanks but sailing is more my thing," she replied quickly.

"Sailing eh," Lazer said. "Catalino's got a big lake on his farm." He pointed at a young guy standing alone, his hands in his pockets, staring at the slot machines. "Stole my driver off me," Lazer added bitterly in an aside to Jeff.

"Moose?" Jeff asked.

"Yeah, arrogant, stuck up bum, not a shred of loyalty, just like all the other drivers around here. Hey Sunshine!" Lazer called out. The guy looked up. "Yeah you! Come over here! Cat's winning more races than God, but rumour has it he's getting a little extra help," Lazer said, lowering his voice, "from his owner...his brother," he added, his eyebrows shooting up almost to his hairline, as Cat walked towards them.

"Help?" Anya frowned.

"From Ritchie Sanchez," Lazer replied, as if that was enough of an explanation.

"Ritchie Sanchez!" she exclaimed. "There's a Ritchie Sanchez on Sainte Marie. He owns the Sunset Bar." Close up, Cat looked nothing like Ritchie. He was a lot younger, good looking too, in a blond Italian way.

"You know Ritchie?" Cat asked in an astonished tone.

"He owns horses?" Anya replied, feeling equally astonished. Ritchie had never breathed a word about it.

"He's not my owner, he's my brother," Cat said. "Well, half brother," he amended. "My owners have put a cool three million into the horse operation. Ritchie doesn't have that kind of money." She noticed that Jeff had lost interest. He was talking shop with Lazer again.

"I see Ritchie at the Sunset Bar every Friday," Anya said. It struck her that it was no longer true but she couldn't bring herself to use the past tense. Not yet.

"Yeah, the athletics superstar," Cat remarked sounding unimpressed. "Must love all the attention." Was he jealous? Anya wondered.

"Hey, why haven't I seen you down there?" she asked.

"Still waiting for an invitation from the son of a bitch," Cat laughed. He wasn't like his brother at all, she thought. Ritchie was a showman, plain and simple but Cat struck her as much more genuine. He seemed like an unlikely candidate for the top trainer slot at Iroquois Downs.

"D'you know anywhere I can sail around here?" she asked hopefully. "Lazer said you had a lake…"

"Lazer's full of bullshit." Another let down. She should have been used to it by now, but she still felt disappointed. "So when are you going back?" Cat asked her.

"Back?"

"To Sainte Marie…You're not…" A ripple of laughter drowned out the rest. Instinctively, she looked for the source of it and saw a swarm of people clustered around a man, his head turned away from her, his fingers pulling at his earlobe in a characteristic gesture that was painfully familiar. Her heart leapt, then began thumping against her ribs. For a moment, she was too shocked to react. André Fontainbleu? Here in Canada? She realized Cat was speaking, but she couldn't concentrate on anything other than the back of the man's head.

"Phil, you old rogue. You're looking disgustingly healthy!" a male voice boomed out. The man turned around. It wasn't him! She looked away quickly, a wave of relief washing over her. It wasn't him! He was a good two inches taller than André, she realized thankfully. His hair was straight, not curly. His eyes were a different colour and he wasn't even wearing an earring! Still, she felt shaken.

"Are you okay?" Cat frowned.

"I thought I saw someone I knew," she explained. Cat gave her a swift, appraising glance.

"Listen," he said. "It's not easy being in a foreign country. I'm from New Jersey myself. Totally different. Where's home?"

"Melbourne," she replied awkwardly. "But it's complicated."

"It's always complicated," Cat grinned, handing her a business card. "That's my cell number. If you felt like coming out to the farm to help out or just hang out…come over any time. I make a wicked bolognese!" She nodded distractedly, her mind racing. What if it had been André? Jeff still had no idea she'd lived with the guy on and off for over a year. Maybe Pete was right. Perhaps she ought to tell Jeff the truth. But even if he forgave her, Jeff would insist on her going to the police. She wasn't about to do that. For many, many reasons. But *not* telling Jeff carried its own risks. She didn't want to end up like Pete, afraid of her own shadow. Someone in the Hermitage had taken those pictures of Pete and Henri. Whoever it was could have a ton of incriminating videos of her and André going at it. She still didn't understand why André had disappeared from her life without a word, but that didn't make him a blackmailer. . . necessarily.

Staring out at the sea of people, she noticed a hand moving high in the air, moving rapidly towards her.

"Billie!" Jeff exclaimed, finally abandoning Lazer. "You'll finally get to meet my best friend," he added happily. Billie McTavish emerged from the crowd, breathless and smiling. She wrapped Anya in a warm embrace that challenged her view of Canadians as cool and distant.

"This is so great!" Billie said delightedly. "I've been waiting to meet you for...oh I don't know how long. Welcome to Canada!" Anya smiled for the first time that day. "Campbell's parking the car," Billie explained. "It's chock-a-block out there."

"Campbell's here?" Things were definitely looking up, Anya decided.

"Want to get something to eat?" Billie asked.

"Not really," Anya replied. So far, she'd found Canadian food bland at best.

"Come with me anyway," Billie urged. "I needed an excuse to get away," she confided, as soon as they were out of earshot. "Keith Lazer and Phil Harman. Two of my least favourite people."

"What's wrong with Lazer?"

"Dad says he's a druggist." Another strike against Jeff, Anya thought grimly.

"How about the other guy?"

"Phil? He's a creep. D'you want a beer?"

"I'd take a Corona," Anya replied.

"Two Coors Lights," Billie told the barman. "That's as close as you'll get to Corona," she explained.

"So you and Campbell...," Anya began hesitantly. She didn't want to put her foot in it.

"We've been seeing a lot of each other lately, yes!" Billie smiled, raising her bottle. "But Campbell doesn't drink!"

"Hey, Jeff doesn't eat meat!" Anya said, feeling they had a bit of a bond there.

"So, how d'you like the Slots?" Billie asked brightly. Anya decided to keep her feelings about the casino to herself. She didn't want to antagonize a possible friend, the only one she'd found so far. She needn't have worried. "No, me neither!" Billie declared.

"I just don't get it," Anya confessed. "Slot machines at the racetrack. How come?"

"Not enough people betting on the races," Billie said. "They had to do something to keep purses up."

"How much more money do these guys need?" Anya asked. "The purses are much higher than Sydney already and it's the top trot track in Australia!"

"Harness racing's not such a big thing over there then?"

"It's huge! It's on all the major networks! Everyone goes to the trots!"

"Really," Billie replied thoughtfully. "You know the worst of it? With all this money, there's been nothing put aside for the horses…not one penny to take care of them in their old age. They have to depend on charity! It's a scandal!"

"I haven't been on a horse since I was ten," Anya revealed. "But…" She felt a hand on her shoulder.

"We have to go," Jeff said. "Dinner reservation." She hated that he didn't give her a choice.

"It was great meeting you," she told Billie before she was hustled away.

It turned out dinner wasn't the only thing on the agenda. Jeff drove over to a huge car lot on the edge of town.

"Pick out something you like," he suggested. "Money's no object." A car would change things for the better. But it would come with strings attached.

Big presents always did.

Izzy Brown was tossing and turning in the bed she and Craig shared. It was 3 a.m., but she couldn't sleep.

"I never should've stopped playing," she moaned softly to herself, rocking back and forth. "I should've won the jackpot, not Eileen!"

"Go back to sleep, Izzy," Craig mumbled.

A night out with the girls from the food mart where they all worked should have been fun. It had been Eileen's idea, the deputy manager, to try out the new casino at Iroquois Downs, instead of going to the bingo hall or watching a weepy at the local cinema, like they usually did. Izzy dabbed her eyes. First, Crawford had gone missing, then she'd let Craig buy her that horrible kitchen from Kut Price and now this! Well, there was nothing she could do about Crawford and the kitchen, but there was a way for her to get back tonight's losses. A tremor of excitement ran through her.

Next time she wasn't leaving the casino until she'd won. Won big!

SPRING

It was a cool rainy April. The Casino attracted crowds every night, filling to capacity Iroquois Downs' parking lot. Horses raced in the slop, night after night, showering drivers with mud, confounding punters and landing grooms with twice their normal workloads. Foals slipped into the world, landing in straw to the sound of rain falling on the barn roof.

On a damp, grey morning in early May, Al McTavish returned to his post at Iroquois Downs. To his astonishment, the staff came out in force and applauded him. As soon as he decently could, Al retreated to his office on the fifth floor. Their enthusiasm made him distinctly uncomfortable. He didn't feel he deserved it, or the forty percent pay rise. During his absence, every last barn had been cleared of horses and horsemen and it was only a matter of time until a demolition crew moved in and bulldozed the backstretch out of existence. Aside from the Race Barn, the only buildings left standing would be a ship-in facility and Al's pet project: the retention barn. Change wasn't always a good thing, Al reflected, looking down at the dreary, rain washed racetrack which was bare and lifeless now, stripped of its parade of horses and jog carts. The sight had been a daily reminder of what his real job was: to protect a rural pursuit with its roots in the past. The Slots money was providing a desperately needed respite financially but, if Iroquois Downs was going to survive in the long run, Al knew he would have to drag the place, kicking and screaming if need be, into the twenty-first century.

How, he had no idea.

The modernisation of the racetrack wasn't the only thing on his mind. The plight of the racehorse was on his conscience. Despite his best efforts, trainers who treated the animals in their care like living pincushions were still all too common. Ontario's private property laws made catching them at it well nigh impossible. In fact, the closure of the backstretch had released scores more trainers to do as they pleased with impunity. The thought depressed him, as did the fact that he had failed in his mission to create a level playing field. He remembered how excited he had felt about TCO2 testing, certain it was the ultimate solution.

How wrong he had been!

One by one, his old allies had fallen away: Jay Winterflood, Bob Summers, Phil Harman, his mentor for decades and even his own daughter. Billie was ever more remote these days, preoccupied with expanding her business. Her new boyfriend was taking up the rest of her time, not that Al was complaining. He approved of her choice. In fact, ever since Campbell had let it slip that career wise, his future was uncertain, Al had been working on a plan: to fill the post of Head of Security at Iroquois Downs with a member of the RCMP on a secondment basis. Not just any member! With a man like Campbell McClaren in charge of security, Al hoped to gain an effective ally, one with a fresh perspective on the task of cleaning up illegal drug use at the racetrack. He knew one thing for sure. He needed help. He wasn't going to accomplish what he wanted on his own.

At the end of Al's first week back at work, Sofia was standing in the hall of 210, Laurel Drive, trying to summon the courage to pick up the phone. During Al's convalescence, the house had come alive again, so she had agreed to put the sale on hold. But she was not willing to spend her days alone any more with no clear purpose. Eventually, hardly daring to believe what she was about to do, she made the call.

It kept on raining.

Anya Papandreos was sitting in Jeff's apartment trying to summon up the energy to go work out at the gym. She'd shopped the mall to death. Lately, her only relief from boredom was meeting up with Billie on weekends. With the weather so dreary, they usually ended up going to lunch at Tangoes or catching a movie. Jeff always insisted on tagging along which was a drag. He acted so switched on whenever he was around Billie, pretty much taking over the conversation. That didn't work for her at all. It was better when Campbell joined them, though Anya was wary of being left alone with him. She was fearful he'd question her about Pete and Saint Marie. She'd left the island far behind and she intended to keep it that way.

The downpour continued. Horsemen everywhere huddled in blacksmith shops, exchanging gossip, accompanied by showers of sparks and the clink of hammer on metal, or sheltered in The Happy Shopper, commiserating about the weather.

The results of Campbell's hearing came in. He'd been let off with a caution, a blot on his record. No one in the force was talking about Theo Vettore anymore. Off his own bat, Campbell had interviewed Bernie and Lara Vachon, Theo's uncle and cousin. But he'd found out nothing that he didn't already know.

There was still no sign of Crawfish Brown.

Towards the end of May, farmers began to worry that they wouldn't be able to cut the hay before it went to seed because there had been so much rain. Only ducks and geese were happy. Harmony Valentine's front legs looked like two half moons. She had bowed both tendons in the heavy going.

On Victoria Day, which marked the beginning of summer, Bosun's Boat Hire opened its doors and Anya Papandreos got herself a job there for the season. Hiking boots, cottages on the lake, sail boats and swimsuits came out of storage. The Happy Shopper sold hanging baskets like hot cakes. Fly sheets and fly spray flew off tack shop shelves. Sofia McTavish started her Pharmacy Refresher Course with an emphasis on natural remedies. She knew she would have to tell Al about it someday. But not yet.

Overnight, the rain stopped and the sun came out. By the end of June, farmers were predicting bumper crops. Swallows fledged their young. School was out. Evie Mercer landed a job with the leading trainer at Iroquois Downs, Catalino Ciardi. The stakes season was in full swing. Harmony Light's two year old sister, purchased for a hundred thousand dollars as a yearling, was unbeatable. Campbell McClaren accepted the post of Head of Security at Iroquois Downs gratefully. It felt like he was being put out to pasture. But for Billie's sake, he didn't complain. A month of near perfect weather followed. He and Billie spent their weekends out of doors, cycling and hiking. Winter was a distant memory. Then the mercury soared, along with the humidity index, sending everyone with air conditioning scurrying indoors again.

Harmony Light wasn't a top stakes horse any more, but he was back racing, thanks to Craig Brown's undemanding training schedule. The trotter, Harmony Fire, finished third in a schooler, nursed along by Eddie Clearwater. Eddie's gruff "She'll do I guess" was drowned out by Caroline's screams of joy. She and Kip were planning to fly back to the UK at the end of August for the beginning of the jump season. Kip had agreed that riding out into the string, after his accident, would be far too risky. He and Caroline had hit on a comprise: a bombproof gelding named Sandy. They were banking on the old boy to keep Kip safe.

Dan Mills still kept tabs on Harmony Storm, the colt he had sold to the Moose. The grey colt was racing in conditioned claimers at Merryvale Downs now, picking up the odd cheque. Dan hadn't bought another horse. He was too busy on the farm, growing mint. Still had his bulls though!

THE CIRCUS CAME BACK TO TOWN

After the last afternoon performance, before the applause had properly died down, Crawfish Brown wheeled out the motorbike he'd bought from the clown after weeks of haggling. With the overgrown pup he'd named Bud riding in the sidecar, he set sail for the family farm, his head full of dreams. Bud needed a proper home. Besides, the travelling was getting them both down.

As Crawfish coasted down the laneway, it was hard for him to believe that a whole year had passed since he'd left. Everything looked so familiar: same pile of old tires, same bunch of rusty junk out the back and the usual couple of horses nosing around the paddock. It made him realize how much he himself had changed. Not that he could put it into words exactly. It was more of a feeling, like stuff was possible now that hadn't been before. When he caught sight of a Welcome Home banner done up in red and gold and his ma standing underneath it, his heart lurched. He opened up the throttle and ignoring Bud's frantic barking, covered the last fifty yards at top speed. His ma looked a lot older than he remembered, considering only a year had passed. But she seemed so happy to see him that he decided to keep his thoughts to himself.

"And who's this?" she suddenly exclaimed, catching sight of Bud, who was waiting politely at his heels. Bud was a good dog. He didn't jump on people or sniff up women's skirts. Crawfish had knocked that shit out of him right away.

"This here's…," he began. But before he could get to finish a heavy hand thumped him on his left shoulder. Crawfish knew that hand well. It had whopped him often enough.

"Hey! Look who's here! Lookin' good son!" Craig said, his face crinkled up in a rare smile.

"Hey yourself," Crawfish replied. He couldn't for the life of him think of anything to add to that. An awkward silence fell.

"Well, they sure fed you well at that circus," Craig pronounced looking him over. "Where'd you get this here dog from anyhow?"

"Long story, Pa."

"Does he play ball or fetch?"

"Course he does!" Crawfish replied, with a furtive glance at Izzy.

"Well, what are we waiting for?" Craig said happily, rubbing his hands. "Let's give him a try!"

"How 'bout you Ma?" Crawfish asked. "You comin' or what?"

"She's got supper to see to. Come on son," Craig said.

"What's up with Ma?" he enquired anxiously as Bud chased sticks in the hay meadow. High above in the still evening air, barn swallows were snapping at mosquitoes, swooping like acrobats, reminding him of his beloved Mirabella. His heart lurched.

"Nothin'. . . she's just tired. She's been working too hard. Worrying about you too, I reckon." Crawfish wasn't convinced. "I got that good colt, Harmony Light, to train now," Craig declared proudly. "Your Pa's come up in the world, son."

"How 'bout the filly?" Crawfish enquired. There was always a filly and she was always about to win up a storm. Hadn't happened yet though.

"Princess? She's doing great! Won a couple o' little races in the spring." He frowned. "Course the vet bills ain't cheap… not with her tyin' up'n all. Gerry gave me some pumpkin seed to try on 'er, but it was worse 'n useless…I spent all afternoon grinding it up. Burned out your Ma's machine, too. She wasn't too pleased about that."

When they got back to the house, supper was on the table. Izzy was bustling around, wearing the pinny he'd given her out of his first week's earnings, donkeys' years ago. She'd opened all the windows but the kitchen was still scorching hot. The big old fan was making such a racket he couldn't hardly hear her, not that she was saying a lot. She didn't eat much neither, just a couple of mouthfuls before she put her fork down.

"If you're not having that, give it here," he said hungrily.

"Leave your mother alone," Craig mumbled, shovelling food down his gullet. She switched plates with him right under Craig's nose. The food was capital, but he was relieved when the meal was over and he and Ma were clearing up together. Craig stayed put at the kitchen table, picking his teeth and studying sheets from the race office.

"Did you find a race for Princess?" Izzy asked.

"Not yet," Craig replied. "I better check on the horses," he added, jumping up. At last, he and Ma were alone.

"Let's have a cup of tea," she suggested.

"I see you went ahead and got yourself a new kitchen," Crawfish remarked as they waited for the kettle to boil.

"It's not as good as you could've done, son," she said. Bud came and rested his chin on his Crawfish's knee, staring up at him wanting more kibble no doubt, but the pup would have to wait.

"Is that what's bothering you, Ma? The kitchen?" he asked.

"I wish," she replied so quietly he had to strain to hear it. "I got worse trouble than that."

"You sick or som'it?" he asked, thoroughly alarmed now. She shook her head and patted Bud's head.

"I like his eyes," she said. "He's a sweet dog." Crawfish didn't speak. Best thing was to lay low and keep quiet, he reckoned. She'd tell him if she wanted to. "You sure you want to hear this?" she asked eventually. He nodded rapidly. "Ain't nothin' you can do about it," she said.

"Don't matter."

"How much you make at that circus lark?"

"Enough to buy me that motorbike," he replied proudly.

"I need sixteen thousand dollars," she said abruptly. "And how I'm going to get it I just don't know but I've gotta pay off what I've run up on the cards somehow."

"Sixteen grand!" he explained, feeling stunned. "Whatever for, Ma?"

"I knew I shouldn't have told you," she said, burying her face in her hands.

"Told me! You ain't told me nothin' yet," he said, getting up and patting her awkwardly on the shoulder. Craig would be back soon, and then she'd shut up like a clam. "You on something…coke…crack?"

"I ain't no drug addict, Crawford," she declared, looking him in the eye. "Your ma ain't sunk that low." Then her face fell. "Your pa'd kill me if he knew. He thinks I'm out working all these hours. But I'm not, see. I'm at that new casino."

"Casino?"

"The one at the racetrack," she explained.

"They give you free food there, Ma?" Crawfish enquired, wondering if it was worth a visit.

"They do not!" she replied vehemently. "Nothing's free at that place. Still can't believe I lost that much…sixteen grand!"

"You gotta tell Pa!"

"Can't do that!" she mumbled.

"Why ever not?"

"Too ashamed, I guess," she said, burying her face in her hands again.

"How 'bout all the thousands Pa's blown on them yearling fillies?" Crawfish demanded. "It'd come to a lot more 'n sixteen grand all told, I reckon."

"It's not the same," she wailed. The back door swung open. Craig had returned.

"What's going on?" he demanded. "Trouble already and you not even back one day yet?" No one spoke. "I leave you alone for ten minutes. . ." he added harshly. Poor Bud started whining, picking up on the sorry atmosphere.

"The boy's done nothing wrong," Izzy said firmly, wiping her eyes and sitting up straight in her chair. "There's something you need to know, is all." Craig's eyes darted back and forth, resting at last on Crawfish.

"What is it?" he asked anxiously.

"Time for bed," Crawfish said, beating a hasty retreat. "C'mon Bud."

"Take him out for a walk first," Craig shouted after him. "Your Ma don't want him messin' up the house."

"Leave the boy alone," Izzy pleaded.

Then he was outdoors with the clear air in his face and the smell of horse shit in his nostrils. He took a peek at the night sky. But there wasn't much to see, just faint stars like pin pricks in the blackness.

"This ain't a place we can stay," he explained to Bud as the dog did his business, good as gold. "So don't go gettin' too comfortable, you hear? We'll hole up here for a bit, then we're gonna get us a place of our own."

Back inside, he heard voices coming from the kitchen.

"Now, don't you take on, Izzy," he heard Craig say. "Only one thing can save us now and that's Princess. I've took out too many loans on the farm as it is. She's gotta start making some real money." Crawfish put his head round the door. There she was, his ma, her apron over her face, sobbing her heart out. "Whadda you want?" Craig asked, turning on him.

"Me? Nothing," Crawfish replied, making himself scarce. So no chance of a nightcap then, he thought gloomily. If he wanted a place of his own, he needed to get a job. His old boss, Andy Price, had to be around here someplace. He'd heard they'd closed the backstretch at the track, so Andy'd be renting stalls at one of the farms. Bound to be. Lucky thing, really. He didn't dare show his face at Iroquois Downs again.

Shitface and Pervert could still be out there, laying for him.

THREE VISITORS

The sun was peeking over the horizon as Andy Price parked his pride and joy: a black 4x4 Dodge truck with oversize wheels and special order hubcaps. It made him feel like a winner even when, thanks to Cat Ciardi, he wasn't. It was Monday morning and as usual on the first day of the week, Andy was bracing himself for bad news. Mark or Chuck could have quit on a whim, or gone on a drunk. No doubt he'd have to deal with at least one animal that had colicked, tied up or cast itself overnight because Sunday was a day of rest, a break from the usual routine.

"Gonna be a hot one," he mumbled as he trudged his way to the stables, cursing for the 'nth time Meridian's idiot policy of no vehicles in the barn area. Being in the horse business was no picnic. Anyone who told you any different was either a lunatic or a liar. It was a hard life for horse and man, one made even harder for Andy after his main man, Crawfish Brown, had done a bunk. Since that day, paid help had come and gone like ships in the night, making Andy's mornings a living hell. Crawfish hadn't been perfect, Andy freely acknowledged that. But he liked the fact that Crawfish had always showed up, never once missed a day. He hadn't talked much, either. He'd rarely ventured beyond How's it going? a question that didn't really require an answer.

Andy liked to get the horses out with military precision in the mornings. He needed to get a rhythm going: bring one in, take one out. No delays. Delays were fatal. They made him realize how tired, hot, frozen or just plain bored he was. Crawfish had kept the assembly line rolling. After all that fresh air, Andy had wanted nothing better than to grab a hearty lunch at the canteen, against the advice of his doctor, who had given him some pills and told him to lose fifty pounds. He was aware that, unsupervised, Crawfish had cut corners when he'd put the horses away. But in a few days, or weeks, Andy reasoned, most of the horses would be gone anyhow. Then any little oversights on Crawfish's part would be some other sucker's problem. That was the claiming game for you.

But where was the sense in looking back at happy times? Onward and upward, Andy told himself firmly. His resolve weakened somewhat when he spotted a man standing outside the barn, arms akimbo, obviously waiting to see him. Andy's pace slowed as he tried to figure out who it was. It wasn't the vet, and owners didn't generally show at sun up. Could it be a reporter from *Horseman's World*, come to do a piece on him perhaps? His heart leapt! Then, just as quickly, it sank to his boots. It was far more likely that the judges had caught him out on some petty infringement of the rules and one of them had volunteered to deliver the message personally. Bastards! Or maybe he'd got a bad test, he thought, feeling panicky. Chuck or whoever could have put baking soda in the horses' feed, out of spite. As Andy got closer, he realized the guy waiting for him looked more like a heavy than a judge. He was pretty far behind on his feed bills, Andy realized guiltily. Not surprising really. Owners generally dragged their feet when it came to paying their debts. Had Reggie Blair finally carried out his threat and sent out the dreaded Undertakers to collect what he owed? Or, he wondered nervously, had someone rumbled him on his billing scam? He should have never taken on the Porn Guy as an owner. What was he thinking? By the time he got close enough to see who it was, he was a nervous wreck.

"Andrew Price?" the man asked. He was from security, Andy realized with a pang.

"That'd be me," he admitted, glancing furtively down the shed row, where Mark stood rooted to the spot, all ears, beside a barrow load of shavings. "Everything okay?" he asked Mark, who immediately picked up the wheelbarrow and pointed it in the direction of the manure pile. Taking that as a yes, Andy returned to face the music. "How can I help?" he asked, gazing up at the stranger and trying to look innocent.

"I'm the new Head of Security, Campbell McClaren," the man announced, extending a hand which Andy pointedly ignored. This didn't sound like good news. Not at all! "Sorry to bust in on you like this but I'm looking for Crawford Brown and…"

"Crawfish!" Andy exclaimed in astonishment. "Haven't heard a peep from him in a year. It's a damn shame. Best groom I ever had."

"Really?" McClaren said, looking gobsmacked.

"What's he done?" Andy asked suspiciously, feeling a sudden surge of loyalty to his former employee.

"Nothing! I got a call from Izzy Brown. She said I'd find him at your barn."

"Well he ain't here!" Andy replied, gesturing at the empty air.

"That's too bad," McClaren said. "He did me a favour, you see."

"Well, I'll be…" Andy declared. The Crawfish he knew didn't do favours!

"Sure you got the right…" The roar of a motorbike drowned out the rest of it. Instantly, scores of horses' heads appeared out of barn windows, looking startled, then just as quickly popped back in again. Heading straight for them, flouting the rules, was an old Harley Davidson with, of all things, a sidecar attached at a drunken angle. The rider's face was hidden by a helmet and goggles but Andy got this weird feeling in the pit of his stomach. The man shut down the engine and peeled off his goggles.

"I come back," he said. Andy stood there, open mouthed. It was Crawfish alright! "Ain't you gone up in the world," his former groom clucked approvingly, giving the place the once over. McClaren, Andy noticed, had moved off and appeared to be scrutinizing the jog carts stacked up against the wall.

"S'pose y'll be wantin' your old job back, eh?" Andy offered, weighing up the possibilities. He'd keep Mark on, but the new guy would have to go.

"Got any place for us to bed down?" Crawfish asked hopefully, opening up the sidecar, startling Andy, who imagined for a moment that Crawfish had a small girlfriend or maybe a child stashed in there. But it was only a dog.

"There's an apartment up in the hayloft," Andy suggested. "It's yours if you want it."

"Perfick!" Crawfish declared. He grinned sheepishly, revealing a set of gleaming white teeth. Andy couldn't remember him so much as cracking a smile before. In fact, Crawfish reminded him powerfully of a racehorse that had been out on pasture rest. He'd put on a good bit of weight, he looked relaxed and whatever had been wrong with him before, wasn't anymore.

"Where you been, at freakin' holiday camp?" Andy demanded, his sense of outrage at being abandoned intensifying all of a sudden.

"Long story," Crawfish replied shortly. "What's he doing here?" he queried, jerking a thumb in McClaren's direction.

"Dunno. Said he owed you a favour or something."

"Hey, you!" Crawfish shouted. In the barn, Mark jumped guiltily. McClaren turned and walked towards them. With his physique, you'd kinda want him on your side, Andy decided.

"Welcome back!" McClaren said. "Well," he added, looking Crawfish over. "Wherever you've been, it's done you nothing but good."

"I ain't been in the slammer if that's what you're thinking," Crawfish retorted. The mutt whined, gazing up at his master.

"You takin' this one out or d'you want me to?" Mark yelled, indicating the horse standing on the cross ties, harnessed up and ready to go. Reluctantly, Andy headed into the barn. He didn't hear any more of the conversation after that. But he did see money change hands…so McClaren had been telling the truth. Satisfied that his main man wasn't in any trouble, Andy clambered onto the jog cart.

"We won't need the new guy after today," he told Mark. "I'm giving Crawfish his old job back." Mark scowled, but as he steered the brown gelding with the gimpy knee towards the jog track, Andy was whistling.

The arrival of a third visitor to his barn put a dent in Andy's carefree mood. He was never gonna get done in time to beat the heat at this rate, he thought, especially since the new guy was in a sulk because he'd been let go. Telling Mark to carry on, Andy wracked his brains, trying to figure out what the Director of Racing could possibly want with him. McTavish saved him the trouble by coming straight to the point.

"I'd like to give you a horse to train," he revealed. "He hasn't been racing great lately, but he's got a lot of talent." If he'd heard that once, he'd heard it a thousand times. It was seldom if ever true. Excuses were terrific but they didn't get you any money. Plus, if the horse was no good, there'd be a great big sign hanging over his head, saying: Don't give your horse to Andy Price, he ain't worth shit. Owners were hopeful buggers. Andy knew better. "His name's Harmony Stampede," McTavish continued. "He's a three year old."

"I'm full up at present," Andy countered. "But if one or two get claimed…"

"He's not a claimer!" McTavish insisted.

So why give him to me? Andy wondered. "I'll know more in a few days," he replied guardedly.

"He's in tonight," McTavish said. "Watch him, see what you think."

After McTavish left, Andy did his best to forget about the whole conversation. The prospect of training a horse for a man known in racing circles as Mr. Clean worried the hell out of him. Andy prided himself on draining every last cent of a horse's earnings from his owners, using a dozen clever ruses he'd picked up over the years. Envious trainers claimed he'd turned several multi millionaires into millionaires. It wasn't fair. Andy never thought that big! But hell, the truth was, a racehorse's real purpose was to massage some fat businessman's inflated ego. Armed with this simple fact, Andy treated an owner rather like a bank about to go bust, extracting as much cash as possible before disaster struck. Eventually, even owners with deep pockets had had their fill of disappointment and were ready to throw in the towel. Make hay while the sun shines was Andy's motto, 'cos pretty soon it's gonna pour down with rain!

He toddled over to the canteen and loaded up his plate with shepherd's pie. Then he begged a race program off Eddie Clearwater and looked over the lines on Harmony Stampede. The horse had reeled off a couple of wins back in June, but since then he'd sunk like a stone, quitting at the end of every mile. He had speed. No question about it. The current trainer, Tony Hall, was an amateur, so turning the horse around wouldn't be too much of a problem. It was tempting. However, the Director of Iroquois Downs was no fool. McTavish would look over the monthly bills with a watchful eye. For a start, markups would have to go. This was where bottles of liniment purchased for twenty dollars, acquired an extra zero on the invoice. Then, there was the pre-race, always popular with owners, a licence to steal at ninety percent pure profit, not to mention the rent he charged for the use of his old jog cart and sulky. With no solution to the problem in sight, Andy drowned his sorrows in dessert: a slice of apple pie and a scoop of ice cream. At least the apple was healthy.

That evening in the Race Barn, the word was out that McTavish had come calling to a trainer with one of the dodgiest reputations at the track. There was general disbelief. As for Andy Price, he could hardly credit it himself. He'd never pretended to be an honest Joe. But so far as he knew, he wasn't using anything illegal on the horses and out on the racetrack, where it counted, he got results. McTavish must have got tired of finishing last, was all. That left Andy with two choices: turn the man down and risk making an enemy, or suspend the habits of a lifetime. He couldn't decide what to do, but he was sure that whatever he did, things would turn out badly.

He woke up in the middle of the night with a brainwave. Breaking with tradition, he would offer McTavish an all in price of a hundred a day, excluding vet work and win tips.

It took McTavish all of three seconds to say yes. "But I haven't spoken to Tony yet," he confessed. "He's going to take this pretty hard."

"If the horse races like a dog again, he'll be on the judge's list," Andy pointed out, referring to the horse's dismal performance of late.

"I'll be in touch," McTavish promised. Being kindhearted was all very well Andy thought, but there was no place for that in the horse business.

He picked up Harmony Stampede a week later. The horse's coat was shining, he was a perfect weight and he was in great shape. He was friendly, too, a lot different from the usual fare of battle scarred veterans that landed in Andy's lap. He drew blood, then he led Stampede out to the paddock and let him loose. The colt arched his neck and broke into a high stepping trot flashing his white socks, before settling down to graze. There were at least a dozen things that'd make a horse stop at the three-quarter pole, Andy thought, hoping it was one of the simple ones. He awaited the results of the blood test with an open mind.

To say Crawfish was happy would have been a massive understatement.

"We're set for life," he told Bud repeatedly. "Set for life!" He had never even had a room of his own before. Now he had one end of a vast hay loft all to himself. Never mind that his "bedroom" was a windowless alcove, or that he had as yet no real furniture, he was thrilled to have a proper bathroom with its own shower stall and wonder of wonders, a narrow corridor he referred to proudly as "my kitchen". On his free nights when there was no racing, he experimented with cooking. Some things were beyond him, since the only oven he had was a microwave. But the frozen dinners he picked up at The Happy Shopper were ace. As for baking, he was working on making cookies, using the microwave and the toaster, while Bud stood at attention, waving his tail. Shitface and Pervert'd never dare come looking for him here. Meridian was far too classy. There was a lot to live up to in a place like this, Crawfish decided, so after his first payday, he went off to Z Mart, his favourite store where the lowest price was the law and picked up a bunch of T-shirts on sale. The pants weren't half bad neither. At five dollars each, he could afford to buy several pairs. But he didn't have money to burn, even with the tips from Sid or whatever he called himself these days. All his spare cash was going to help his ma. To his dismay, the debt kept on rising. It was all down to something she called "interest". Daylight robbery, more like! If he'd had a bunch of cash to spare, he'd have gone into the loan business himself. It sounded almost too good to be true! But he reckoned there'd be problems collecting, bound to be, really. He'd skipped out on a few loan sharks himself in the past. He'd been feeling pretty good since sampling the drenches Andy made up for the horses' pre-race. But the best thing in Andy's medicine cupboard, by far, was something called Equipoise. Getting the dose right was a challenge. But Crawfish had cracked it! This carefree state of affairs came to a screeching halt four weeks in.

"I'm docking fifty dollars from your wages," Andy Price announced, stunning Crawfish.

"Whatever for?" he enquired in an outraged tone.

"Pilfering from my medicine cupboard don't come free, d'you hear? Equipoise is for geldings, you idiot!" Andy said. Crawfish hung his head. "You'll be paddocking McTavish's horse next week, so make sure you behave yourself!"

"Yes boss," Crawfish replied eagerly, hoping for a win. If so, he stood to make an extra hundred, then he'd be way ahead. In any case, he decided, helping himself to stuff that didn't really belong to him might give Bud the wrong idea. It was up to him to set the dog a good example. Later that day, he passed on a rumour to Sid about what the guys were using now. To his delight, Sid tipped him an extra twenty bucks. He was on a roll!

THE WAR AGAINST DRUGS, CONTINUED

Campbell McClaren's new job as Head of Security was turning out to be a great deal more of a challenge than he had anticipated, even though Al McTavish had warned him about it. As the weeks went by, he had become painfully aware that the war against drugs was not restricted to major cities in Canada. There was one going on right under his nose at Iroquois Downs. Identifying suspects wasn't difficult. Catalino Ciardi, who trained horses for the Lucky Seven Syndicate, was an obvious candidate. Illegal drugs were the only reasonable explanation for the new records his horses were setting every single week. The problem was proving he was guilty. The current *drug du jour* according to Crawfish Brown, was something horsemen called elephant juice. Campbell discovered that the chemical name for it was etorphine. It was an analgesic which in small doses acted as a tranquilizer, presumably calming elephants down. Used on horses however, it was a powerful stimulant. There was as yet no test for it and that was the tip of the iceberg, he thought unhappily.

Campbell's options were limited. He couldn't search Catalino's farm without a warrant and that was unlikely to be granted. Catalino Ciardi was currently the golden boy of harness racing and as such, untouchable. Punters loved him (it made picking horses a breeze), tipsters fawned over him and the industry was handing out awards to him like confetti. Campbell had a hard time picturing a drug lord on the mean streets of Toronto or Vancouver being lauded by the government in this way. And to think, when he took on this job, he had fondly imagined he was being put out to pasture! He and Billie had talked about the problem at length but the only real solution, testing via mass spectrometry, was not something Iroquois Downs could afford in the current financial climate. That left Campbell with nothing to do but brace himself for more horse deaths. It was frustrating. Al McTavish had given him a unique chance to change things around at Iroquois Downs. He didn't want to let Al down, but it looked like his hands were tied.

In early August, the humidity index fell precipitously and Erinsville was treated to a long spell of dry weather known as Indian Summer. The vet bills for the steamiest July in years arrived on owners' doorsteps and were greeted with general consternation and disbelief. The Browns' farm was no exception.

"What's all this for?" Izzy Brown asked. "Fifteen hundred dollars! It can't be all for one horse, surely?"

"Give it here," Craig said, hoping that the vet had made a mistake. "Electrolytes, Dantrium, Robaxin, ESE, Azotorex…," he muttered to himself. All of it was for Princess.

"However are we going to pay for it?" Izzy asked, looking worried to death. Her desperation echoed his own. Something had to be done and soon. They could lose the farm otherwise. Keeping Princess in conditioned events at Merryvale Downs racing for peanuts was no longer an option, not with the credit card debts from the casino hanging over their heads. Damn McTavish and his fucking tests! Craig thought angrily. In the good old days, he'd have been able to solve Princess's tie-up problem the old fashioned way: a box of baking soda, some cake sugar and bob's your uncle! It cost pennies too, not a small fortune!

Andy Price never studied the vet bills too closely. He just passed them on to the hapless owner, along with his training fees, which, by comparison, looked like a terrific bargain. When Al McTavish opened the bill from Andy's veterinarian, he was in for a pleasant surprise. Sixty dollars for blood work and two hundred and fifty dollars for something called Bacox, whatever that was, seemed modest enough. Two weeks later Al was standing in the afternoon sunshine at Merryvale Downs, waiting for the start of the third race.

"If Pete Summers drives him the way I want, your colt'll win for fun," Andy Price assured him. Al was skeptical. Given Harmony Stampede's abysmal performance for Tony Hall, how could any trainer be so confident of success, even in the minor leagues? As the horses left the gate, Al prepared himself for a letdown. The first time around, it was the same old story. His colt was sitting at the back, going nowhere. But as the horses paced down the backstretch for the second time, Pete shook the lines and incredibly, Harmony Stampede responded, sweeping past everyone and powering ahead, his ears up, his eyes eager and his legs pumping like pistons. Al had no idea how he got to the winner's circle but suddenly there he was, listening to the track photographer tell him it was the best win picture he had ever taken, hearing the groom, Crawfish, boast it was his caretaking that had turned the horse around. As for Al, he was in a state of complete euphoria. Harmony Stampede had finally lived up to the promise he'd shown as a two year old. Next time, Al vowed, he wouldn't come alone. He would invite everyone he knew. A celebration in the winner's circle with family and friends was just what the doctor ordered.

Suddenly, the disparity between the big four: Price, Lazer, Larson and Mercer and those out of the loop like Tony Hall didn't feel like a problem. It felt more like a miracle!

"How did you do it, Andy?" Al asked, smiling at him.

"Your colt had EPM," the trainer replied promptly, looking him in the eye. "I Bacoxed him. No knowing how far he'll go up the ladder now!" There was more to a successful trainer than illegal drugs, a chastened Al acknowledged to himself. However, he had to concede that Catalino Ciardi was in a league of his own.

THE END OF SUMMER

By late August, a hint of fall was in the air.

Anya Papandreos didn't generally work weekends. Jeff expected her to be around. But as it was the last one of the summer, she had persuaded Jeff that she had to be at Bosuns Boat Hire to help out. Predictably, it was a hectic day. Families were lining up for the chance to go out on the river one more time before school started. She didn't get back to the apartment until late. Jeff was nowhere to be seen, which was highly unusual. Anya was thankful. Funny, she'd never felt that way with André. She'd always hoped he'd be at the Hermitage. It was something she hadn't generally been able to count on though.

She took a quick shower and changed her clothes knowing Jeff'd freak out if she went into the living room wearing her sodden, muddy trainers and ripped jeans. Afterwards, she grabbed a bottle of water and sank down onto the couch. The only thing that Jeff hadn't tidied away was today's edition of the *Erinsville Echo*. Idly, Anya picked it up, skimming through *Style*, giving *Autos* and *Sport* a cursory glance before turning to the main news section.

A headline immediately caught her eye: LUCKY SEVEN ? What on earth was an article about the Lucky Seven Stable doing in the *Erinsville Echo*? The paper never ran stories on harness racing! Intrigued, she looked closer. Beside the headline was a group photo. It wasn't about Catalino Ciardi after all. There wasn't a horse in sight. She was about to turn the page when she noticed a second photo: the blurred image of a young man with curly hair, wearing an earring. Her heart lurched. André had worn one exactly like it, shaped like a horseshoe. After all this time, she realized she still had feelings for him. This guy even looked a little like André. It could have been his son, or a much younger brother. When she read the caption, her heart lurched again. She threw the *Echo* aside and sat staring into space for a long, long time. Finally, she forced herself to pick it up again and read on:

"The elders of the Cree Nation, located north of Montreal, Quebec, got more than they bargained for when they decided to establish gambling casinos on their reserve, some 35 years ago. Twelve months after the grand opening, the tribe discovered that a number of their womenfolk, some of them underage teens, were in various stages of pregnancy. By then, the man thought responsible for the outrage, a white man from the city of Montreal known simply as Curly, had vanished into thin air. He left behind seven babies who were born without a father to provide for them. Dr. Jay Winterflood, 34, was among them (see group photo, top row, centre) although judging from his successful veterinary practice based in the Erinsville area, he has not suffered unduly, financially at least. Others were not so fortunate. In those faraway days, DNA testing had not yet been developed, but new modern technology may play a part in bringing the perpetrator to justice. Recent developments include the unearthing of a photograph, believed to be that of the biological father as a young man..."

Anya leapt up from the couch and began pacing the apartment, her mind in a whirl. What if? . . . One of the sons was living right here, in Erinsville. He was thirty-four. His father (the perpetrator, she reminded herself) would be in his mid fifties now, André's age. Coincidence? The very idea sent shivers down her spine. Restlessly, she googled Dr. Jay Winterflood, discovering his clinic was right on the grounds of the Lucky Seven Stable's farm. Another coincidence? No chance! What kind of sickie would choose the stable name *Lucky Seven* after pulling a number like that? Pete's words came echoing back to her: "He's a creep, Anya! Stop trying to protect him." Pete had been certain that André was the blackmailer, that Henri had not betrayed him. Why hadn't she believed him? She ran into the bedroom. As she stared at her reflection in the mirror, at her long dark hair and olive skin, the scales fell from her eyes.

She fled the bedroom, rushed through the living room and with trembling fingers slid open the big glass doors. Then she walked out onto the balcony and closed her eyes, feeling the warmth of the sun on her face . . .listening to the silence. Finally, she understood. It explained everything! Jeff's voice startled her.

"Anya? Guess what I've bought for you," he called out. She opened her eyes. "Hey! What are you doing out there?" he added falteringly. For once, she was thrilled to see him.

The article in the Saturday edition of the *Erinsville Echo* had come to Campbell's attention too. However, today was Sunday and Campbell had a more immediate problem to solve: getting the hired canoe back to the jetty without tipping Billie McTavish into the drink. They weren't exactly in the middle of a raging torrent. Erinsville's main waterway, meandering through the town's parks and gardens, was a tame river beloved by folk who liked to think of the natural world as benign. It was easy to believe that on a tranquil

Sunday afternoon like this, with the smooth green water slipping down-stream and ducklings bobbing along, mere bundles of fluff, their parents unperturbed. Billie though, was plainly terrified. Each time he had suggested a trip on the river, she'd come up with a better idea. Now he knew why.

Back on shore, she went along with his idea of tea at the Riverside Cafe, which was next door to Bosun's Boat Hire. There was no sign of Anya though, despite the crowds. After her second cup of tea, Billie perked up and ordered scones and cream.

"No more trips on the river," he assured her.

"Listen," she replied fervently. "I enjoyed the cycling. The hiking was great. Even the rock climbing was okay except for that time I got stuck in a crevasse. But boats!"

"Why didn't you tell me?" he asked, feeling baffled.

"When those geese ran into us, I was sure we were done for!" she said.

"We did come pretty close to capsizing," he conceded. "But only because you were rocking about so much." That would have spiced things up he thought, unable to suppress a smile.

"You know," Billie remarked, looking at him speculatively. "Most of the drivers at the track are total adrenalin junkies. I'm thinking you're not so different, maybe." He frowned, not liking the direction the conversation was taking at all. He and Vettore had absolutely nothing in common. "How'd you learn to swim?" she asked suddenly.

"What do you mean?"

"Did your parents just throw you in the water and trust you'd come up again?"

"What on earth would they do that for?"

"I just thought it might explain some things about you. You really like taking risks, don't you?"

"And you don't?" he exclaimed in disbelief. "Going into business is a huge risk, in my book anyhow."

"It's only money," she replied dismissively. "If Fence Sense folded tomorrow, I'd still be in one piece."

"Physically, maybe," he acknowledged. "But financially you'd be pretty messed up."

She waved that aside. "You can generally protect yourself against total disaster."

"I was always taught to be careful with money," he asserted.

"Money's replaceable. Your body isn't. Didn't your parents teach you any-thing?" He opened his mouth to protest but, before he could say a word, his cell phone rang. The security guard on the other end of the line sounded scared.

"I'll be there as soon as I can," Campbell promised.

"What's going on?" Billie asked.

"There's a problem at the track," he replied, tossing a ten-dollar bill on the table. "I'll explain on the way. Hurry!" he urged.

Exactly twelve minutes later, they arrived at Iroquois Downs Raceway. The place was in turmoil. An angry crowd had gathered outside the entrance to the new casino, holding up placards and chanting, "Out! Out! Out!" Camp-bell pulled out his pager and told everyone in range to drop what they were doing and come in. A pair of security guards spotted him and hailed him.

"It's gonna be on TV," one of them gulped, pointing at a bulky white van with the letters ETV splashed across its side. Billie grabbed Campbell's arm.

"Have you seen what's on those placards?" she asked, looking horrified.

"No, but I take it you have," he replied, turning his attention to the home-made signs: *SLOTS WRECK LIVES!. . . HELP! MY DAD'S A SLOT-A-HOLIC!. . . LIQUOR! CRACK! SLOTS!* They didn't make pretty reading. For the moment, though, Campbell was far more worried about something else. Gamblers were pouring out of the casino. Finding the way blocked by the demonstrators, they were trying to push and shove their way through the protestors. What had started as a relatively peaceful demonstration was rap-idly turning into a potentially explosive situation. Crowd control had been part and parcel of Campbell's basic training but as a Mountie, it had been on horseback not on foot. A group of flustered security guards was now looking to him for direction, clearly at a loss.

"Get into pairs, stay well back and don't do anything stupid," was the best advice Campbell could come up with for the moment. Meanwhile, a skeleton TV crew had emerged from the van and were busy setting up.

"Any of you guys got a megaphone?" Campbell called out. Thankfully the answer was a resounding "Yes!"

A few minutes later, Campbell clambered up into a makeshift podium and tried the time honored method of talking the crowd down. After a while it seemed to work. Those who wanted to leave were allowed to do so. Some people though decided to stay, once they understood they were going to get a chance to air their grievances on Erinsville's local TV station. Asking Billie to wait in the car, he worked his way back to the exit, where the reason for the mass exodus became clear. The power was out. Half a dozen people in wheelchairs were slowly emerging from the casino, shepherded by staff.

"It's pitch black in there," a man attached to an oxygen tank gasped.

"What happened to the emergency lighting?" Campbell asked.

"This is it!" a woman replied, handing him a flashlight. He went inside and did a thorough search in case anyone was stranded, but the casino was deserted. After clawing his way back to the fuse box, he discovered the main power had been thrown to the off position. The reason for the failure of the emergency lighting was harder to fathom though. By the time he got back outside, the TV crew was hard at work filming the demonstration. One of them was interviewing the protestors. As far as Campbell could tell, there was no sign of trouble so he and his men stayed on the sidelines, listening in to accusations about the Slots. Some of the things people were saying horrified him. But to Campbell's relief, when the show was finally over, the crowd broke up peacefully. There was a hopeful feeling in the air, an assumption that now people's grievances had been heard, there would be a positive outcome. Campbell didn't share their optimism. In his experience, highlighting problems was only half the battle. Change, if it happened at all, usually came about for reasons that no one could have anticipated.

He made his way back to the car, to find a new crisis brewing.

"Get in!" Billie cried, gunning the engine. "Jeff just called. I have to go home and record the six o'clock news."

"Why?" he queried, jumping in. "How come he can't do that himself?" he added as an afterthought.

"He doesn't have a VCR," she explained. "It's way too low tech."

"Okay, but we need to swing by 210, Laurel Drive and let your father know what happened here today."

"No time!" Billie replied, careening through the parking lot at sixty kilometres per hour. "Call him on the way," she suggested. He tried, but there was no answer from the house.

Ten minutes later, they were racing up the stairs to Billie's apartment. She fumbled briefly with the key before throwing open the door with a flourish.

"Plug in the VCR!" she said. "I'll turn on the TV. It's coming on now!" Campbell checked the leads, pressed record and hoped for the best, still wondering what this was all about.

"This is WETN, bringing you the latest news from Erinsville County," a man in a grey suit with hair to match announced brightly. "Business was halted briefly at the casino in Indian Falls today. Sam Walton was there." Sam skipped over the power outage and went straight to the human interest stories.

"The casino at Iroquois Downs has been open less than six months, yet it's already wreaking havoc with people's lives," he declared. "This afternoon, protesters blocked the entrance to the casino. You can see them behind me, waving signs and shouting out their grievances. One woman told me her husband had collapsed at the machines and had to be rushed to hospital. A man said his wife had taken out over fifteen thousand dollars on credit cards to feed her habit and they couldn't afford to pay it back. There are other stories too – a daughter who's about to lose her house, a son who's lost his job, all because they couldn't stop gambling at the casino. Most of these people are ordinary law abiding citizens who've never been in trouble before. One problem, apparently, is that the establishment never closes. Also, there are no clocks and no windows, nothing to let people know that time is passing. But that's not the only reason…"

"That's all we have time for," the anchor man cut in cheerfully. "Remember folks, if you gamble, do it in moderation and call your local helpline if the fun turns into serious addiction. Coming up next, the crop reports…"

"Wow!" Billie exclaimed. "When Dad hears about this he'll tear his hair out." Campbell tried Al again, but he still wasn't picking up. The doorbell rang. Voices wafted up the stairs. Jeff appeared. Then Anya came bursting in, looking distraught.

"You got it on tape, right?" she asked.

"Give me two minutes to rewind it and I'll run it for you," Campbell assured her. As he watched the casino story for the second time, Campbell kept his eyes peeled for a familiar face he thought he had glimpsed the first time around.

"See, I told you, there wasn't a problem," Jeff assured Anya. "We were nowhere near the cameras!"

"You were there?" Billie and Campbell exclaimed in unison.

"Just happened to be driving past," Jeff explained. "I thought I'd see what the fuss was all about. Then Anya saw the TV crew and went ballistic. She still hasn't told me why."

"I have my reasons," Anya snapped.

"Paranoia?" Jeff suggested in a tone of exasperation. Anya retreated into angry silence.

"Heard from Pete lately?" Campbell asked, hoping to draw her out, not that he had much hope of that.

"I caught up with him on Facebook," she replied enigmatically. That told him less than nothing about the fate of the skipper of the Sea Princess.

"Iced tea anyone?" Billie asked brightly.

"I'll give you a hand," Anya offered.

"What d'you think will happen now?" Campbell asked. "Any chance they'll close the casino?"

"Why would they do that? Purses are up forty percent with the extra revenue from the Slots!" Jeff replied.

"It'd be no bad thing maybe if the casino closed down, judging from what I saw today," Campbell said soberly.

"What do you mean?" Jeff asked.

"Some of the protesters that were interviewed claimed the slot machines have so many near misses, it can't be down to chance. That's why they're so addictive. I was there. I heard them. They didn't show that on TV!"

"Surely," Jeff argued, "the government wouldn't have allowed that here?"

"Well, it looks like they might have done. It could explain why people are so angry," Campbell replied.

"Actually," Jeff acknowledged, "there's a class action suit going through the US courts on that very point."

"I heard that!" Billie declared, coming in with a trayful of glasses. "Could that really happen here? A suit against Iroquois Downs?"

"Unlikely," Jeff stated. "People would think twice before taking on the Provincial Government."

"The government?" Anya frowned. "I don't get it."

"The casino isn't owned by a private company," Jeff explained. "It's run by the public sector."

"That makes no sense to me," Anya said.

"Gambling used to be illegal in Canada years ago," Campbell told her. "Until they changed the law."

"I never knew that," Billie said in an astonished tone.

"Some bright spark at the City Hall must've figured out it'd be a great way to raise some extra revenue," Jeff put in.

"Probably so," Campbell acknowledged reluctantly. Anya looked stunned.

"What's wrong with that?" Jeff challenged. "The track gets a modest share of the profits but most of it goes to the township of Erinsville."

"Profits?" Anya said contemptuously. "Is that what you call it? Didn't you see those people protesting, Jeff? They were in big trouble! I can't believe the government is fleecing its own citizens! What's the difference between that and a drug pusher I'd like to know!"

"No one forces people to gamble," Jeff replied stiffly.

"No," Anya agreed. "But if that casino hadn't ever opened…"

"Then Iroquois Downs would be history," Jeff replied promptly.

"Big deal!" Anya exclaimed.

"Horse people have a right to make a living too," Jeff replied defiantly.

"Saving harness racing by ruining people's lives?" Billie cut in angrily. "Doesn't make a lot of sense to me, Jeffrey!"

"Think you're not involved?" Jeff replied, looking daggers at her. "I know for a fact that the top brass at the track are paying themselves big fat salaries now the casino money's coming on stream. Your father included! Don't believe me? Ask him!" Two bright pink spots appeared on Billie's cheeks, a sure sign of strong emotion. Campbell held his breath and waited for the storm to break. It never happened.

"That's a low blow, even for you, Jeff," Billie replied quietly. "But why should you care about ordinary people trying to live their lives?" You could have cut the air with a knife. Jeff turned his back on her and switched on the TV. Outside, the shadows were lengthening but the sky was still a clear blue. Jeff had found the sports channel and appeared to be immersed in a baseball game. The sound of bat on ball was a beautiful thing, Campbell mused, though he preferred playing to watching, himself.

"Shit, is that the time?" Anya suddenly exclaimed. "I gotta call Mum!"

"At this hour?" Jeff asked looking bemused. "She'll be asleep! It's one in the morning over there."

"I said I'd call her Sunday," Anya replied doggedly. "Dad'll be in bed but Mum'll be waiting up, on tenterhooks."

Jeff sighed audibly and went back to his game. Not for long! Anya's phone call was soon over.

"We've gotta go, Jeff. I need to talk to you. Now!" she told him, turning off the TV.

"Hey, the bases were loaded!" Jeff protested, making a vain bid for the remote. But he followed along meekly enough. It was easy to tell who was the boss in that relationship. Campbell liked to think that he and Billie were on a more equal footing. Still, each to his own.

"What's going on with the two of them?" Billie wondered after they'd left. "Jeff's no angel. Even so, she was pretty hard on him."

"She was," Campbell agreed soberly.

"What if it's true?" Billie asked, close to tears. "About Dad…about everything!"

"Only one way to find out," he replied evenly. "Start asking the awkward questions. I want to show you something," he added, anxious to lighten the mood. He rewound the tape until he found what he was looking for. Lurking in the left-hand corner of the screen was the fuzzy yet unmistakable image of Crawfish Brown, brandishing what looked suspiciously like a pair of heavy duty wire cutters. "Recognize anyone?"

"Crawfish! No way!" Billie exclaimed.

"I think I just solved the mystery of the emergency power outage," Campbell said.

"Crawfish Brown, *saboteur*," Billie smiled. "Who'd have thought it?"

"Hope he doesn't go and get himself arrested," Campbell replied gloomily. The idea of Crawfish languishing in a prison cell was repugnant to him, though he couldn't have said why. He still got a lump in his throat every time he thought about Crawfish's old bicycle, which was stowed away in the evidence department, not that Crawfish needed it anymore. He had moved on to bigger and better things.

"You actually care about him," Billie stated in disbelief.

"Oh you know me, always rooting for the underdog," Campbell replied sheepishly. He decided this wasn't the right time to pass on the latest news from the battlefront.

There was a clap of thunder. Rain came pelting down. The heatwave was over.

MONDAY MORNING

As Monday morning dawned, gale force winds were swirling beneath threatening clouds: tornado weather. Up in the fourth floor apartment, Anya Papandreos was getting dressed. Jeff was eating toast, staring out of the vast windows stretching from floor to ceiling which afforded a spectacular view of the rising storm.

"Wanna head over to Lazer's later this morning?" he asked lazily. "He'll be done early on a day like this. I don't have anything planned."

"Too much stuff to do," Anya called out from the bedroom. "Like telling Bosun's I'm quitting."

"Call them, for God's sakes!" Jeff shouted back. Stubbornly, Anya slung her bag over her shoulder and walked into the living room. When she saw the superior expression on Jeff's face, she felt like punching him. What made him think he always knew what was best for her? "Be reasonable, Anya. Please! I know your mother's not well, but that doesn't mean you have to go off the rails!" he added.

"Dad's hopeless when Mum's sick. I need to book my flight," she replied, forcing herself to stay calm.

"Why does it have to be today? Why not wait a day or two? Maybe you won't need to leave after all."

"Stop micro managing me, Jeff," she snapped, finally losing patience with him.

"But we're engaged!" she heard him cry as she stormed out. Shaking with anger, she rode the elevator down to the basement car park. She took a moment to collect herself, then drove off. So! She'd overreacted. That didn't change a thing. She wasn't happy, hadn't been for quite a while. Canada wasn't the problem. The problem was Jeff. But this wasn't even about Jeff. Since Saturday night, when she'd read the ironically titled *Lucky Seven* piece in the paper, it'd been all she could do to stop herself from screaming out loud. Telling Jeff about it wasn't an option. She couldn't risk the whole Fontainbleu thing erupting. Besides, in his present mood, Jeff would probably tell her she was being paranoid. There was only one way to find out. After a lengthy session at the gym, she felt steadier. She got back in the car and headed west until the houses petered out and the roads were almost empty. She knew exactly where she was. She'd studied the local map at least a dozen times the previous day, sneaking a peek at it whenever Jeff left the room until she had it down pat.

Halfway down 29th Side Road, she spotted the sign for the Lucky Seven Farm, rocking wildly in the wind. As she turned into the driveway, it keeled over, landing face down in the long grass. Rattled, she continued down the laneway, past the old stone house, past the signs for the *Horse Spa* and the *Veterinary Clinic*, past paddocks and horse walkers until she reached the barn, which looked brand spanking new like everything else at the Lucky Seven Farm. This was a top drawer operation she realized, taking in the training track with its big wide turns, a dead ringer for Iroquois Downs. It put Lazer's place to shame! Someone had spent a bomb here. But who? She had an idea about that, but she was praying she was wrong. Discovering there was network coverage on her cell, she made two calls: one to Bosun's, the other to Erinsville Travel, repeating the lie about her mother being sick. Then she settled down to wait.

Around noon, the grooms began to file out of the barn. The last to leave was a girl with blond hair, wearing faded jeans and a hooded sweatshirt. By then, the wind was so strong that when Anya got out of the car, the door was practically wrenched off its hinges. She forced it shut and went into the barn, which smelled sweet, like breakfast cereal. Cat Ciardi was standing in the aisleway, his hands in his pockets, gazing into one of the stalls.

"Hey," she ventured. He swung around.

"You!" he exclaimed. "What happened? Wind blow you in?" It had been half a year but he recognized her instantly. That was a surprise. "So what can I do for you, Anya? It is Anya, isn't it?"

"How about lunch? You invited me, remember?"

"Yeah, like a century ago. What took you so long?"

"Better late than never," she countered awkwardly.

"Found anywhere to sail yet?" he enquired. She shook her head.

"Just canoeing on the river," she replied a little forlornly. Cat did not reply. "So, do I get a tour?" she inquired after a while. She glanced up and down the aisleway where a score of harness bags were hanging from the rafters, branded with the Lucky Seven logo: seven gold horseshoes on a sinister looking pitch black background. It gave her the shivers.

"This one you've gotta see," Cat said suddenly, beckoning her over. "Isn't she a beauty?"

"What d'you call her?" Anya asked, taking in the gleaming coat, which shone like burnished gold and the kind, calm brown eyes, like a milk cow.

"Goldie," Cat replied. "Go on! Stroke her. She won't bite!" Anya drew back, remembering the mare she'd befriended at Lazer's barn. The next week she was gone, claimed by Larson.

"It's too bad you'll have to lose her one day," she said.

"Lose Harmony Gold? No way! This one's all mine. Bought her as a yearling so I get to call the shots. She's making her first start on Thursday. She'll win."

The filly was so tall Anya had to stand on tiptoes to reach her head.

"What about the rest of them? Are they in for a price?" she asked.

"That's where most of them are headed eventually, I guess," Cat acknowledged, a hint of regret in his voice.

"It can't be easy for you, seeing them come and go."

"I just do what I'm told," Cat replied, slamming the gate shut. Goldie didn't move a muscle. "Bomb proof," he added proudly. "Aren't you girl?" The barn lights flickered. He was nothing like Lazer, she decided. With Lazer, it was all about cold, hard cash. The wind was whipping itself into a frenzy. The lights flickered again, then went out completely. "Another tree down," Cat said resignedly. "You'd think they'd bury the electric cable but it's not how things are done in Canada."

"Is lunch scuppered? I'm starving," Anya asked, anxious to bid for more time so she could ask all the important questions: the ones that would test out her theories about the owner of the Lucky Seven syndicate. As the stable's private trainer, Cat was bound to know.

"Relax," Cat said. "The stove uses gas." Outside the barn, the force of the wind almost swept her off her feet. Memories of the Sea Princess came flooding back: the good times with Pete, before the hammer fell. She landed on the front porch of Cat's house, clinging to one of the posts to stay upright.

"That was fun!" she laughed.

"Fun?" Cat replied in disbelief, "Where've you been lately?" he added as he opened up the front door.

"I must look a fright," she said, as a flash of lightning lit up the sky. There was a crash of thunder. Rain came pelting down.

"Come on in," Cat urged. "Before you drown out there!" He led the way to the kitchen, which was as snug as a ship's cabin. The floor, the cabinets, even the countertops were all fashioned from wood. There was only one small window. Outside, the storm was roaring like the sea. "We won't have water for much longer," Cat said, turning on the cold tap.

"When the rain lets up, I'll go start up the generator. But we'll manage okay for now." He lit the stove. It was an eerie sight: blue flames glowing in the gloom.

"Got any candles?" she asked.

"Somewhere," Cat said vaguely. After a search, she unearthed a bag of tea lights.

"Where are your matches?"

"No idea," he replied, sounding preoccupied. She found a lighter, then settled into one of the bar chairs. "Now all we have to do is wait for things to heat up," he announced, pouring wine into two chipped mugs. "Glasses all got broken," he explained. All around the kitchen were twinkling tea lights, set in a collection of odd plates and saucers. It was a far cry from Jeff's cold, spotless kitchen, all gleaming chrome.

"This is nice," she remarked, taking a swallow of the wine. It was a rough red, a stark contrast to the expensive stuff Jeff always chose.

"*Salut!*" Cat replied, raising his mug to her.

"You're pretty young to be running a big outfit like this," Anya remarked, trying to get a conversation going. He acknowledged that with a nod. "When d'you last go on holidays?"

"You mean a vacation? Forget it! I can't leave."

"Why ever not?"

"You think I'm gonna let a moron like Brad loose on my horses? They're racing for a million bucks a week for God's sakes! There's no way I'd trust any one else to do the job."

"A million dollars a week! That's huge!"

"It's nothing compared to what they sunk into this place!"

"Just how much is that?" Anya asked, feeling she was getting somewhere finally.

"Zillions," Cat replied. "Pasta's done!"

"Who's your owner? Must have pretty deep pockets," she ventured.

"No idea," Cat replied dismissively, slapping down a couple of plates on the counter top.

"Truly?" she asked, feeling like she'd been thrown for a loop. It was a major setback.

"Salad's in the refrigerator," he said. Then again, Anya thought, Fontainbleu always had been a secretive bastard. She had no clue about what he got up to when he left the island. "Let's eat," Cat announced.

"Hey, this is pretty good!" she exclaimed, taking a forkful. "You should open a restaurant!"

"Don't get carried away. It's the only thing I know how to cook." He was twirling the spaghetti on his fork like a pro. Not her. She just didn't have the knack.

"So, you don't have a big menu, people come just for the Spag Bol, right?" Anya said.

"Where have you been eating lately? Jail?" he laughed. The truth was Jeff had been trying to convert her to his camp. She'd been eating nothing but vegetarian burgers for weeks. She had to stop letting Jeff control her every move. Take a stand! She took a big gulp of wine, to give her Dutch courage and went on another tack.

"You know what's weird?" she said. "How come Ritchie never breathed a word about you or the horses? He had plenty of chances too. Pete and I used to go there every Friday."

"Who's Pete?" Cat wanted to know. She ignored the question.

"What I'd like to know is how you'd run an operation like this without ever talking to the owners."

"What's this? The inquisition?" Cat asked, sounding annoyed now.

"I've known Pete since primary," she said in an effort to appease him.

"Ritchie's the agent, everything goes through him," Cat explained with a shrug. It sounded like that was the only answer she was going to get.

"Your brother?" she enquired.

"Half brother," Cat corrected. The antagonism was unmistakable.

"So what was it like having a brother? I'm an only child myself."

"Scary," Cat replied soberly, reaching for the wine. "He was always bigger and stronger than me. Still is. Papa left when I was eleven. I had to grow up fast."

"I know what you mean."

"Do you?" Cat asked sharply.

"Yes! I've had to do a lot of that lately." Suddenly Anya felt an urge to tell him everything: losing her childhood home at eighteen, following her parents to Greece because she had thought it'd be an adventure, falling into Fontainbleu's clutches, landing Pete in the drink, running away from Sainte Marie, because she was frightened…Jeff had made that part of it all too easy. "I've made a lot of mistakes," she began haltingly. Before Cat could respond, the power went back on. The hum of the refrigerator and the glare of the fluorescents put paid to any exchange of confidences. Cat was staring at her left hand.

"Still with Lamare, I see," he said quietly. She snatched her hand off the table. Under his gaze, her engagement ring felt as cold as ice. "Lazer and Lamare: the dream team." Cat continued mockingly. "Wonder how it feels being knocked off the top spot."

"I wouldn't know. Racing horses isn't something I care about much," she replied.

"It's the only thing I care about!" Cat declared. "Why did you come here today, Anya?"

"Because I wanted to ask you something."

"Ask me then. I've got nothing to hide."

"Already did. You have no idea who owns the Lucky Seven Stable, right? It could be anyone. A gangster! A murderer! A drug dealer! Why are you doing this, Cat?" He stared at her defiantly for a moment. Then he looked down at the table.

"Maybe I was sick and tired of losing all the time," he said, his voice low. "Maybe that's why it was pretty easy for Ritchie to talk me into it." Anya delved into her bag.

"Read this," she told him, thrusting the clipping from the *Echo* at him. "You're not a bad guy, Cat! You deserve to know the truth. Read it!" He took it from her, but reluctantly. "Go ask your brother about a man called Fontainbleu. If I'm right, you're working for a monster."

"Ritchie?" Cat replied dismissively. "He'll never give me a straight answer! Climb a tree to tell a lie, that's Ritchie." Her phone went off.

"That'll be Jeff," she said tersely. "I gotta go or he'll kill me. Promise me you'll read it, okay? I'm flying out to Greece day after tomorrow."

"You're leaving?" Cat frowned.

"I can't stay here, not now. I'm scared. I know too much."

"Why drag me into this?" he asked unhappily.

"If I'm right, you're in it up to your eyeballs already. Wake up Cat!" she said. Then she walked out. Getting back to the car was a struggle. The wind was dead against her now. Cat didn't even come to the front door. She drove away before Jeff could call her yet again. Jeff knew nothing and Cat didn't want to know.

It felt like she was alone in the universe.

NOON

The mood in Mr. McTavish's office was as stormy as the weather outside. Campbell hadn't spared Al any of the uncomfortable truths about the fallout from the casino. He actually felt sorry for the guy. At his age, Al should have been putting his feet up, resting on his laurels a bit. Instead, he'd been landed in a mess that he'd had no part in creating. The only nugget of information Campbell had held back was that fleeting glimpse he'd had of Crawfish Brown. After their meeting, he intended to delete the tape. Withholding information and interfering with the course of justice were serious offences. Campbell was well aware of that. He was going to delete it anyway. If he was honest with himself, his motives for keeping Crawfish out of trouble weren't entirely disinterested. He was anxious to protect his only reliable source of information on the racetrack. He wasn't a poster boy for moral virtue after all, he realized. He was no better and no worse than anyone else.

It was a sobering thought.

BEST FRIENDS

By Thursday, the storm had died down. At 5:30 p.m a plane bound for Athens, Greece taxied down the runway at Toronto Airport with Anya Papandreos on board. Conditions were perfect for take off: cool and clear, without a breath of wind. That same evening, Craig Brown shipped Harmony Princess to Iroquois Downs. He'd entered her in a claiming race for three year old fillies. The protest against the Casino had come to nothing, unfortunately. Nevertheless, Craig was feeling pretty pleased with himself. With her allowances, Princess was in for the lofty price of twenty-six thousand dollars. No one'd take her, not at that price, but she stood to get a good piece of the purse, which was a hefty fifteen grand.

Craig was early. It wasn't every day that a trainer like him got a chance to race at the top track in North America. After unloading his equipment, which was spotless for a change, he hustled Princess into the Race Barn. After he'd got her settled, he scooted over to the nearest TV screen in case she got a mention on the pre-game show, which was just starting. After some inspiring music, the camera zeroed in on two men wearing identical white sports shirts.

"Welcome to Iroquois Downs," the skinny one said. "We've got a great program here this Thursday night! Let's begin with the Daily Double. Who d'you fancy in here, Ted?" Pudgy faced Ted seemed to be having a hard time looking at the camera. The odd furtive glance was all he could manage. It made him look a bit shifty.

"I kinda like Harmony Gold's chances to win the maiden, Ron. It's her first start, but she was strong in her qualifier. Catalino Ciardi's been winning up a storm lately and he owns this one himself."

"Looks like he's got the Trainer of the Year Award all locked up," Ron agreed heartily.

"Lotta stakes coming up this fall. My guess is Moose'll be pressing the button on this filly tonight, find out what they've got!"

"Sounds good. Let's move onto the claiming race for three year old fillies, Ted."

"Yeah, not much in here. Surprising really. Barefoot Babe, the rail horse, is the one to beat. But Harmony Princess isn't a bad sort." Craig's ears went out on stalks. "She won a couple of little races at Merryvale Downs earlier in the year," Ted continued. "She's been drawing outside lately, hasn't had the best of trips either. The big track ought to suit her. My money's on her, Ron."

As Craig hitched Princess to the jog cart, he was trembling with excitement. He was thankful he had gone to the trouble of sprucing it up a bit. People would be checking them out, now that she'd been picked to win. He didn't want to come over as some know nothing hick from the B-tracks. She trotted off, as loose as a goose. Good news! He'd double dosed her with everything the vet had given him. She wouldn't tie up tonight. He'd stake his reputation on it. It was early, so no one else was out on the track. He'd beaten the water trucks too, which was merciful. She went wild whenever she saw one. So far, so good!

Feeling relieved, he steered her back inside the Race Barn, which was starting to fill up. That's when the trouble started. Generally, after her warm up mile Princess stood quietly enough on the cross ties, so long as he was somewhere close by. Not tonight! She wasn't just fidgeting; she was calling out over and over again. At first, only one or two horses responded. But before long, the whole barn was in uproar.

"Shut the fuck up," he muttered, ashamed that she was the cause of all the fuss. "A good talking to, that's what you need my girl," he said, taking her by the halter. But she wasn't listening. At last, in desperation, he took her outside and walked her up and down. It quickly felt like a terrible idea, what with all the big rigs pulling into the parking lot. When one of the security guards yelled at him, Craig hurried back inside. Where to now? he wondered, looking around anxiously. Eventually he spotted the friendly face of Dave Bodinski.

"Pop her in one of the lasix stalls," Dave suggested. "Right at the back," he added helpfully. Craig hopped to it, leading Princess past blaring TV screens and cast iron horses heads that adorned every stall, recognizing drivers and trainers whose names were known to millions. No wonder his filly was upset! He felt pretty nervous himself. To his relief, a spell in the quiet, dark stall did the trick. She calmed down, even had a pee. She'll be alright now, he thought gratefully.

Ten minutes later he watched Catalino's filly, Harmony Gold, come out of the pack to win by a comfortable margin. It was a good sign, he thought as he painstakingly manoeuvred Moose Rankin's second best sulky into position, careful not to put a mark on it, before snapping it onto Princess's harness.

"Second race, two minutes!" the Paddock Judge barked out. Craig checked his filly's equipment over for the twentieth time. Moose sauntered over, lazily flicking his whip.

"Anything I should know about this one?" Moose asked. Craig wracked his brains, in awe of the leading driver in North America. He felt honoured to have the mighty Moose on board.

"She doesn't like cutting the mile," Craig said at last though he felt sure Moose was already aware of that.

"Any bad habits?" Moose clarified. Craig shook his head.

"None," he replied, giving Princess an affectionate pat on the neck. As the horses filed out, the businesslike tones of the Paddock Judge came over the loudspeaker again.

"There are two claims in the second race. Number One, Barefoot Babe, goes to Tony Hall. Number Two, Harmony Princess, goes to Tom Larson. Will the new trainers please collect their horses directly after the race." For an instant, Craig assumed he must have heard wrong. Even when he realized it was true, he still couldn't take it in.

"Well I'll be doggoned," he muttered to no one in particular, taking his cap off and turning it around in his sweaty hands. After a while, he realized the horses were going behind the gate. The race was about to start. Still in a state of shock, he stumbled out to the viewing area, feeling like a blind man.

"I see they claimed your filly," Dave Bodinski said, sidling up to him.

"Never thought they'd take 'er. Not at this price," Craig replied miserably. "She ain't won a race since May!"

"Ain't life a bitch," Dave agreed. The fillies were coming past the grandstand for the first time. Princess was sitting at the back.

"I bought her as a yearling," Craig said faintly, swallowing hard. "Broke her myself." Moose had pulled Princess out now, but she was going nowhere. There was no flow.

"I'd have claimed her myself if I had the money," Dave confessed. "The one I've got in here is useless! Why'd you put your filly in here if you didn't want to lose 'er?"

"Needed the money," Craig muttered, his eyes glued to his filly. She'd caught up with the leading group.

"Too bad it was Larson that took 'er," Dave remarked sympathetically. As the horses came off the turn, Moose swept her three wide and shook her loose. Craig was certain she'd quit, but he was desperate for her to win.

It made him feel a little crazy. "Claim her back next time," Dave advised. "She'll be right back in for the same price."

"Can't afford it," Craig replied, watching Harmony Princess break free of the pack and get to the front.

"You'd be a fool then. Look at the time." As she came by the wire, the tote board flashed 153.3. "Last quarter twenty-seven flat," Dave whistled. "Pretty good for a fifteen claimer I'd say."

Craig made his way to the winner's circle in a daze. It was a bittersweet moment. "A new life's mark," he heard them say. "Was owned by Craig Brown." But not any more, he thought sorrowfully as he took the lines from Moose Rankin. Despite the win, he felt like the worst sort of loser. They were calling for her to go to the test barn. Somehow he made it back there. As he took the harness off her for the very last time, he wondered how he'd ever imagined he'd get away with it. Those claiming guys were like vultures, always on the hunt for fresh meat. Princess fit the bill only too well. He should've known better, but what else could he have done? If only Izzy had stayed away from those dratted machines, it would never have happened.

"Hey there!" a girl's voice rang out, sounding delighted. Craig swung around. The girl was wearing faded jeans and a hooded sweatshirt. It was Evie Mercer, he realized. He hadn't seen her in quite a while. It wasn't him that she'd hailed, but a tall youth who'd be considered a bit of a "hunk" by today's generation.

"I see your filly win," the hunk said.

"She was A-may-zing!" Evie agreed happily. "She won for fun! Where'd you spring from, Will? Haven't seen you in the longest time!"

"I've been out Trafford way. Lotta people moved there after they closed the backstretch. Stalls are cheap."

"So, why'd you quit Larson?" At this, Craig pricked up his ears.

"Sure you wanna know?" Will asked hesitantly. He wasn't like most kids his age, Craig realized. Not retarded, exactly, but kind of slow. "Remember that black filly...the one with the pretty white heart on her forehead?" Will asked.

"Harmony Valentine? She was gorgeous!"

"Not anymore," Will said. "Larson ruined her." His face crumpled. "He amished her, Evie. An' she was so lame...it near broke my heart." Craig's heart sank. "I couldn't stay after that," Will continued in a husky voice.

"Third race goes out in two minutes. Get 'em ready men," the Paddock

Judge barked out. Craig tried to drag out bathing Princess for as long as he could, putting off the moment when he'd have to part with her. The conversation between the youngsters had moved on.

"You can trust me, Will," Evie was saying quietly.

"I can't even tell Dad," Will replied looking shamefaced.

"We're friends aren't we?" Evie coaxed. "Friends tell each other stuff."

"It was those girls, see. Those grooms that worked on the backstretch before."

"Track rats!" Evie said contemptuously.

"Lotta things went on there, Evie…trainers stashing syringes in their hub caps so's they could shoot up their horses."

"It figures," Evie said unhappily. Will leant down and whispered in her ear. She pulled back. "No? Really?" she asked, looking shocked. Craig had to strain to catch what Will said next.

"They kind of passed me around," Will confessed, blushing scarlet. Jesus! Craig thought, feeling scandalized. A man in a white coat came striding out of one of the stalls.

"Catalino? Your horse is good to go. Gave a beautiful sample," he added approvingly, holding aloft a flask of golden liquid.

"That's me," Evie said, racing to the open stall door, where she was greeted with a single low whicker by the winner of the first race.

Instantly, Princess went crazy. It was all Craig could do to hang on to her. He didn't see what happened next. He was too busy getting his right leg out of the way before it was pulverized by Princess's front hooves. He only cottoned on that she'd snapped the cross ties when she barged past him, plowing into his right shoulder. As he pulled himself up from the floor, he saw the two fillies were greeting each other like long lost friends. They'd been raised together at Harmony Farm, he realized belatedly.

"You okay there, Mr. Brown?" Evie asked in a worried tone. "She gave you a nasty knock." The white coat technician nodded emphatically.

"You should go to the clinic," he said. The two fillies were nuzzling each other's necks now, happy as anything.

"I'll be alright," Craig replied stoically, feeling anything but. He picked up Princess' equipment and slung it over his shoulder, wincing from the pain. But that was nothing compared to the ache in his heart.

"Your turn now, young lady," the man in the white coat said, prising the filly loose from her friend. He disappeared into the stall with her and closed the door. Just like that, Princess was gone. Craig hung around for a bit longer. He knew he should leave but he couldn't. Not yet. A rough looking fellow appeared and led her away.

She didn't look back.

THESSALONIKI, GREECE

After flying overnight from Toronto to Athens Airport, Anya caught an early flight the next morning to the city of Thessaloniki where her parents now lived. After the plane took off, it headed due north, flying high over the blue waters of the Aegean. Just one hour later, it touched down at Thessaloniki Airport. When Anya caught sight of her parents waiting at arrivals, the bad memories she'd harboured about the place melted away. Giddy with relief, she flew into her parents' outstretched arms and held on tight. She'd made it! For now, at least, she felt safe.

In Ano Poli, her parents' neighbourhood, she was greeted by smiling faces everywhere she went. When she asked if anyone had wifi, everyone trooped round to Yanni's house, her mother's second cousin. Excitedly, Anya got on YouTube and clicked on Race Replays from Iroquois Downs. Watching Harmony Gold win was a thrill and a half. The whole family, uncles, aunties, nieces and nephews, cousins and second cousins, watched along with her, cheering and clapping as the filly strode into the winner's circle. Anya got a brief glimpse of Cat's smiling face, before she was swept away for a celebratory lunch at Yanni's uncle's place. There was no chance to call Jeff. But as it was only 6 am in Canada, that hardly mattered. To tell the truth, Anya was glad to have the excuse. The welcome home committee was lifting her spirits. Talking to Jeff would have been a huge downer.

A WINNING COMBINATION

On his way to work on Friday morning, Craig Brown stopped off at the gas station and picked up a jumbo pack of doughnuts to celebrate his win with Harmony Princess. It was the last thing he felt like doing, but it would be expected. Winning a race at Iroquois Downs was something most small trainers could only dream of. Back at the barn, they clustered round him, stuffing their faces, maybe hoping that some of his good fortune would rub off on them. Now Princess was gone, Craig only had two horses left and as Harmony Light was having the day off after some vet work, Craig had plenty of time to talk. Opinions were unanimous that Princess had gone for a sky high price and that the generous purse was an added bonus. Joey Harris, the filly's breeder, called to congratulate him.

"Weird those two winning on the same night," Joey said. "When they were at the farm, you couldn't separate them."

By the end of the morning, Craig was feeling a good bit more cheerful. He'd never had so much attention lavished on him before. He was feeling so buoyed up by it all that he got on the blower to Harmony Light's owner and told him exactly what he thought of the horse's chances in the Merryvale Downs Classic, due to take place in a month's time.

"Harmony ain't near sound enough to race two heats in one day. It'd be suicide," he pronounced. For once, the owner seemed to take him seriously. That's what a win at Iroquois Downs'll do for you, Craig thought feeling pleased.

Soon as he got home, before he could change his mind, he called up the bookkeeper at the track and ordered a cheque for $17,000 in favour of the credit card company. He'd told Izzy at breakfast that she was getting her dream kitchen and no arguments, and at lunch he promised her that he'd buy Crawford a lounge suite for his new place at Meridian Acres, if he'd lend a hand. After he'd done the calculations and the vet bill had been paid, he reckoned he'd have just enough left to pick up a cheap filly at the yearling sale, which was only three days away.

Prices at the sale were crazy. Everyone wanted to join the gold rush ushered in by the Slots. Craig got his filly. She was nice enough looking, but she had no breeding. He didn't like her half as well as he'd liked Princess. In the end though he supposed everyone had got what they wanted. With the possible exception of Princess, of course.

The ache in his heart refused to go away.

IN THE MONEY

It was ten o'clock at night, but Joey Harris could not rest until he'd added up the takings at the yearling sale over a cup of cocoa at the kitchen table.

"Three hundred and seven thousand dollars!" he declared triumphantly. "That's double what we got last year!"

"Brilliant!" Val agreed enthusiastically, cradling their small daughter, who was fast asleep in her arms.

"We got enough to pay two years worth of breeding fees and still have plenty left over. What'd you say to getting a few more broodmares, eh, Mrs Harris?" Val looked thoughtful. This usually meant she didn't agree with him, unfortunately.

"We should switch to trotters," she advised. "That's where the money is. Okay, so Harmony Light's full brother went for a hundred and eighty thousand, but we barely broke even on the rest." Joey thought over what she'd said.

"I guess you're right," he sighed. "We better start paying some of these overdue bills, too."

"Beginning with the feed bill," Val replied in a worried tone. "We owe close to ten thousand dollars. And you know what they say."

"What?"

"Over ten thousand and Reggie Blair sends those guys out to collect."

"The Undertakers? Never!"

"Don't be so sure," Val warned. "It's late," she added as the sleeping child stirred. "I should put her to bed."

"Why do you think trotting yearlings are going for so much all of a sudden?" Joey wondered.

"Catalino doesn't race trotters?" Val suggested. Joey pondered that one silently. Val rose to her feet. "By the way," she said. "I'm pretty sure I'm pregnant again."

"Pregnant?" he shouted, jumping up off his chair.

"I thought I'd wait until after the sale to tell you," Val replied calmly.

"How long have you known?" he asked. "And when is it due?" he added suspiciously.

"Don't worry," she laughed. "Not until after the foaling season." Val's dentistry practice was doomed, Joey realized. With two kids, it'd be impossible.

It was hard enough with one. Maybe though, she'd be able to help with the bookkeeping. The Lucky Seven was a big account but it took up too much of his time. Tired as he was, he wrote out a check for ten thousand bucks to Supreme Horse Feeds. He wasn't taking any chances with Reggie Blair. Perhaps Val was right and whatever Cat Ciardi was using didn't work on trotters, he thought sleepily as he climbed up the stairs.

But why?

FALL OUT

The week after the sale, Craig Brown made the pilgrimage to his local sports bar, along with his pals from Merryvale Downs, all of them anxious to see for themselves how the great Tom Larson would make out with Harmony Princess. She was in against the same bunch of claiming fillies again. Craig hadn't felt so strung up since the creep Tony Hall had stolen his date at the high school prom. At the off, Princess went out for the lead like all the hounds in hell were after her, goaded on by Harry Harper with his usual take no prisoners tactics, stunning everyone watching by opening up fifteen lengths by the half mile point. Craig hung his head and stared intently at his fingernails, feeling sick about it, certain he'd get shown up as a useless trainer. When he dared look up again, the gap had narrowed considerably. Down the stretch, it was obvious to everyone that despite Harry Harper's frantic efforts to rally her, Princess was struggling. Craig watched with concern mingled with relief, as her stride shortened. A dozen feet from the finish, she stopped like she'd hit a wall, barely managing to hang on for fifth. A cheer went up from Craig's end of the sports bar. His fellow B-track trainers had been rooting for Craig to come out smelling like a rose on this one. It looked like the mighty Tom Larson had got the worst of the bargain. Respect for Craig soared. He received a free beer and countless slaps on the back.

There were angry cries from the other end of the bar, however. Princess had gone off at 1-2 and most people had backed her pretty heavy. It was so noisy that Craig missed the announcement on TV but he saw the stark update as it flashed on the screen. "Harmony Princess. Claimed by the Lazer and Lamare partnership. New trainer Keith Lazer". This was not good news, Craig thought anxiously.

"It's like freakin' pass the parcel up there, ain't it?" one of his pals commented jauntily. "They'll be sorry!"

Craig wasn't so sure.

At the end of the week, Harmony Light put in a decent performance at the qualifiers and respect for Craig went to an all time high. That afternoon he hitched his new yearling filly to the jog cart for the first time. She threw herself, shattering both shafts. Ten days later, Princess won in 1.52 flat. She was claimed again, this time by the Lucky Seven Stable. Craig's heart sank. The new trainer was Catalino Ciardi. The next time she raced, Craig watched it at home on TV. Princess was against a better class of fillies this time and was in for a price tag of forty-five thousand. Moose took her straight to the front. She won by five lengths, setting a new record of 150.4. Despite that, she didn't look tired. In fact, she looked like she could easily have gone around the racetrack a second time. The punters were happy. She'd paid 3-1, a high price for a dead cert. She was claimed by Tony Hall, the only trainer foolish enough to take on Catalino. Everyone else had stayed well away.

Speculation was rife as to what Cat could have given Harmony Princess to get her to go that fast. Makes me look like a fucking idiot, Craig thought angrily. She's on her way to winning The Open Mares Race now. His stock in the harness racing world collapsed. Before long he got the call he'd been dreading.

"I've sold Harmony Light to the Lucky Seven Syndicate," his owner declared. "They've made me a fair enough offer. I'd be crazy to turn it down." When Craig expressed astonishment, the owner brushed his protests aside. "You didn't think he'd be any good in that stakes race coming up in October," the owner pointed out. "That was the clincher for me."

Looked like he'd scored an own goal, Craig reflected bitterly. He'd only been trying to look after the horse. To cap it all, his new filly popped the biggest, juiciest curb he had ever seen. Generally, curbs were no big deal but this one was catastrophic. With the two stars of his stable gone, Craig was down to a couple of bad gaited, cheap horses. It had all happened in the blink of an eye. It had been nice having royalty in the barn for a while he reflected, feeling a little misty eyed as he cleared out Harmony Light's stall. Truth was, he was going to miss him even more than Princess. He had a heart as big as a house and it had spoiled Craig for the usual flotsam and jetsam that made up most of Merryvale's race card.

What in heaven's name had Catalino given her? Craig wondered for the umpteenth time as he assessed the damage to his breaking cart. The fact that it was bound to be illegal wasn't much of a comfort. How come Catalino got away with it? He wasn't going to be able to fix the cart, he realized, kicking over the shattered shafts and buckled wheels. How could an honest man make a living with a guy like him on the loose? If only Izzy hadn't forced his hand, getting them into debt like that, he thought, as his new filly cast herself for the second time that week. Damn Catalino!

The fucking guy had fucking ruined his fucking life!

Catalino Ciardi, the man Craig Brown was blaming for the fix he was in, wasn't immune from trouble himself. Up to now, the judge had turned a blind eye to Cat's winning ways. Not this time! They hauled him in the very next morning and demanded an explanation for Harmony Princess' spectacular win. Confident that her blood test would come back negative, Cat protested his innocence. The judges weren't convinced. They issued an ultimatum, along the lines of "Keep this up and you'll be racing out of the retention barn with all your horses!".

Cat took the warning to heart. He wasn't sure how the horses would do without their meds on race day. Ritchie had better have some answers! Half an hour later, he felt a little happier. Harmony Light won his schooler by ten lengths. It would set him up perfectly for the Merryvale Downs Classic, due to take place in two weeks' time. Tonight though, it would be Harmony Gold's turn to shine. As always, she'd be racing "cold". Ever since she had nearly died at two, he'd been scared to give her anything except vitamins and her daily dose of Regumate, which kept her hormones in check. Despite drawing the outside post, she was the favourite in the morning line. Cat was anticipating another easy win, even with the freezing temperatures. Winter arrived early in Canada. Even Thanksgiving happened a whole month earlier than south of the border. In New Jersey, it was still warm and sunny. Not here though! By the seventh race, Cat was shivering, despite his warm jacket. Nevertheless, he left the Race Barn and joined the rest of the horsemen watching the full field of ten line up behind the gate.

As the starting car picked up speed with a full field of ten following along behind it, Cat noticed the drivers jostling for a place on the gate. Harmony Gold was on the extreme outside, so Cat had a perfect close up view of her as she came past him. She was striding out confidently with Moose at the helm, pacing well within herself, even at close to 60 klicks an hour. But worrying, the jostling fillies seemed to be pushing Goldie further and further out. Glancing down, Cat watched horrified, as the wheel of Moose's sulky teetered on the outer edge of the racetrack. Below it was a three-foot drop. Feeling utterly powerless, Cat held his breath, willing the worst not to happen. All at once the wheel lost the battle and slipped off the track, tipping Moose out of the sulky and bringing Goldie crashing to her knees. Cat screamed. The speed of the impact sent Goldie skidding across the rock hard track. An endless time later, she slowly stuttered to a stop and struggled to her feet. Cat reached her a split second before Evie. When he saw blood streaming down his perfect filly's front legs, he felt like killing someone.

"Where's the fucking track vet?" he swore.

"Never mind him. Call Doctor Jay," Evie cried, catching hold of Goldie's bridle. "He'll know what to do," she added, her eyes filling with tears. As she led the filly off to the wash stalls, Cat felt like crying himself.

Back at the Race Barn, Moose was screaming obscenities at the Paddock Judge. A lot of good that would do him. He'd just get days, Cat thought as he steered Moose towards his horse in the eighth, feeling relieved that his driver at least was in one piece. Then he raced back to his filly. Evie had washed off the blood. But the sight of shredded flesh hanging off Goldie's knees made Cat feel like throwing up. A few minutes later, Winterflood arrived. After a shot of tranquilizer, Goldie was soon dozing on the cross ties. Evie and the doc were huddled over her like a pair of boxing seconds after a brutal round inspecting the damage done to their guy. Winterflood squatted down and shone a torch at her knees. The bones in her joints were clearly visible now that the thin layer of flesh had been scraped away. Joey Harris, about the last person he wanted to see, chose that moment to show up.

"Yikes!" Joey exclaimed, when he caught sight of Goldie. "Looks pretty bad eh."

"You don't want to know," Cat replied. "The other two are good. Did you see Princess win?"

"Always hoped she'd be a star," Joey said sounding like a proud father.

"Some idiot claimed her off me," Cat replied. "He'll be sorry!"

"Good luck with her, eh?" Joey said as he left.

"You want the good news or the bad news?" Winterflood asked.

"Go ahead," Cat replied impatiently.

"You got lucky," the vet announced.

"Yeah, right," Cat replied bitterly.

"It looks bad but the joints aren't damaged. However," Cue dramatic pause Cat thought grimly, here comes the real story. "If the lacerations don't receive expert care," the vet continued, "there'll be so much scar tissue, you'll have to give her away."

"I'd rather shoot myself than do that!" Cat declared fiercely. "You take her, Doc, I'll pay whatever it costs."

"That's not necessary," Winterflood replied, the ghost of a smile playing on his lips. How the fuck did he manage to stay so upbeat at times like this?

Cat wondered furiously. "The filly will need twenty-four hour care. The next forty- eight hours are critical. Evie's already volunteered."

"She's my filly," Cat said sullenly. "It's my decision."

"You've got too many other things to do," Evie said.

"What happens now?" Cat asked, wondering if Evie was really up for the task.

"The body's immune response will go into overdrive," Winterflood said. "You've gotta control the inflammation. That's critical. Bute and banamine together will do the job, but you've gotta be careful not to overdo it or she'll colic. Your big problem will be proud flesh. And the more dead tissue, the more scarring you'll get."

"Sounds terrific," Cat said, feeling the exact opposite.

"Looks like Moose won the eighth with your horse," Winterflood remarked. Cat took one last look at Goldie, who was still snoozing gently, and hurried off to the winner's circle.

"How's the filly?" Moose shot at him out of the corner of his mouth, as they posed for pictures. Cat shrugged. "It wasn't my fault!" Moose added defensively. "I'd like to kill that starting car driver. Couldn't even steer straight, the moron. And you know what? The track'll do nothing about it. What if I'd broken every bone in my body? There'd be no compensation, not even an apology. You'll see!"

After a less than stellar night at the races (only one win) Cat was finally on his way home. Goldie had walked into the trailer without faltering, her knees swathed in bandages. Probably glad to get out of there Cat concluded, wondering if his filly'd ever make it back to the races again. By the time all the horses had been put away and the grooms had left, it was one in the morning. The filly was sleeping standing up, her head almost touching the thick mattress of straw Evie had piled up in her stall. As for Evie, she was in there with her, slumped against a pile of hay, tucked up in a blanket, dead to the world. Seeing the two of them together made Cat almost envious. Getting close to the animals was sadly lacking in his own life at present. He had become someone to be feared: the needle man. Most of the horses just rolled their eyes or froze up but memorably, one mare had chased him right out of her stall. He'd passed it off as a joke but it still stung. He actually liked horses. Sensing his presence perhaps, the girl stirred. Cat crept away before she woke up. He needed to get some sleep, keep a little dignity. He had a business to run. Lately, he'd been fantasizing about escaping his gruelling routine for a few days at least. But, with Goldie in trouble, that was now out of the question. He clambered into bed.

Sleep didn't come for a very long time.

THESSALONIKI

She could never live here, Anya reflected as she strolled through the sunlit streets on her way to the bakery in the Ano Poli, or old town, where her parents lived. It wasn't because she didn't speak the language. She understood it well enough, having grown up in Melbourne's Greek community. But though the culture was familiar, it wasn't like Australia. People's attitudes towards women, particularly married women, terrified her. It made Jeff Lamare appear positively enlightened by comparison. Since she'd left Canada, she and Jeff had fallen back into the easy relationship they'd had before she'd moved to Ontario and into his apartment. She wasn't fooled. Jeff was great at long distance relationships but up close and personal where it counted, he was a write off.

Going back to Australia would solve a lot of problems. The threat of André Fontainbleu, real or imagined, would be half a world away. Of course, Pete wouldn't see it that way and what about Cat? She'd felt a connection there, like a key in a lock, that she just didn't understand. She hardly knew him, yet the urge to open up, to trust him was powerful. So powerful that she found herself longing to see him again. How, she wondered, had she become such a closed book? When did it all start? The lies tripped so easily off her tongue nowadays. She'd been so afraid that Jeff wouldn't let her leave, she'd invented a story about her mother being sick. It had worked, but she despised herself for it.

She blamed Jeff, but she also blamed André Fontainbleu. That was when her life had started spiralling out of control. It had left her too weak to fight back, so she'd resorted to using people instead of being honest with them. If she had to do it over, she'd have never talked Pete into leaving Melbourne. He'd come a cropper in Sainte Marie, alright. Maybe if their home town was Sydney, where people were more enlightened, he wouldn't have cared if the video of him and Henri went viral. She wasn't certain about that, though. Some things never changed. Jeff believed anything could be fixed by throwing money at it. She didn't agree. Money was never going to change Fontainbleu's mind. He had too much of it already.

She wished now that she'd taken a chance and told Jeff about her relationship with André, but that ship had sailed a long, long time ago. Besides in some ways, Jeff was a younger, better looking version of Fontainbleu. Of course, he wasn't cruel or ruthless but he had a steeliness deep down, like permafrost. The closer she got to him, the more she felt it. As she walked back to her parents' house, the streets had never looked more beautiful, the bread had never smelled so sweet. She booked a ticket to Toronto anyhow. There was unfinished business to settle there. Not just with Jeff, with Cat, too. Then she checked the race results. Harmony Gold was nowhere. She finally found her name, followed by three stark letters: DNF. She had no idea what that meant. She went on *YouTube* and watched, horrified, biting her knuckles, replaying the clip over and over again. There was no news...no update...no reassuring words. She waited until 2:15 p.m local time, then she called Cat.

LUCKY SEVEN

Cat jerked awake at the first ring of his cell phone. It was 7:15 am. He'd overslept.

"What's the problem?" he asked urgently, fearful that Goldie had taken a turn for the worse overnight.

"Cat? Is that you? It's Anya."

"Anya!" he exclaimed, feeling intense relief that it wasn't Evie with bad news. "I thought you were in Greece."

"I am! I just wanted to make sure Goldie's okay. I saw the replay."

"No! She's not okay," he replied, trying to find his jeans.

"What's DNF mean?" she asked.

"Didn't finish," he said abruptly. "When are you coming back?"

"Soon. . . how's she doing?"

"Look, I gotta go," he said, anxious to see for himself how his filly had fared overnight.

"Wait!" Anya cried. "Have you talked to Winterflood?"

"About what?" he asked impatiently, desperate to get her off the phone.

"About that clipping I gave you from the newspaper."

"Not sure where it is," he replied shoving his feet into his trainers.

"Read it! Please!" she pleaded.

"Okay," he agreed grudgingly. "If I can find it."

"And Cat! Ask the vet about the tea tree oil – it's an old aboriginal remedy… does wonders with infections."

"She's on antibiotics for God's sakes."

"This is better."

"Yeah, okay," he replied hurriedly, ringing off. Then he ran down the stairs.

Generally, the first thing that Cat did every morning was mark up the board, to let the grooms know who was training. Not today! He loaded up two syringes, primed with painkillers and antibiotics and ran over to Goldie's stall. Evie was wide awake.

"Not in here! The stall is her safe place," she chided, leading the filly out into the aisle way. Then she cupped her free hand around Goldie's left eye. Winterflood was right. His filly was in safe hands.

At one o'clock in the afternoon, Evie was still there.

"Go home. Take a shower. Grab a change of clothes. I'll drive you," Cat offered. A worried frown appeared on Evie's forehead.

"I oughta stay. Doctor Jay's coming by later on."

"Doc? I'll be here."

"Okay. I guess," she agreed reluctantly. "I'll have my licence soon," she said, gathering up her things. "I'm getting a car for my eighteenth…"

"Cool," Cat replied quickly, trying to hurry things up.

"Yeah, but Dad's made me promise to finish high school. Didn't want me turning out like Mom, I guess," she added. "So, I'm on home study."

"That's great!" Cat replied distractedly, anxious to get going. He had four horses to pre-race and he needed to do it alone. It bothered him, too, that he had absolutely no idea what he'd done with the newspaper clipping Anya had given him.

When he got back to the farm, Goldie was on the cross ties and Winterflood was down on his knees, putting the last touches on fresh bandages. The timing sucked. He'd have liked to take a closer look at the damage.

"I'll come by tomorrow," Winterflood promised, halfway out of the door already. Cat put Goldie back in her stall and retreated to the tack room. How was he going to pre-race the horses with Winterflood popping in and out all day? He'd nearly been caught by the vet once before, but he'd managed to bluff his way out of it. He couldn't take that chance again, not with the judges breathing down his neck. He saw a flash of green overalls. Winterflood was back. "Forgot my bag," he explained.

"Listen," Cat said. "I need to talk to you." The vet was hovering beside the tack room door, ready to take off again. "This is gonna sound weird but this girl came by about a month ago with a story about you." Winterflood stared at him. "It was in the *Erinsville Echo*," Cat explained.

"Oh that," the vet replied. "A journalist?" Cat shook his head.

"She's Jeff Lamare's girlfriend."

"Well," Winterflood replied. "That doesn't make a lot of sense."

"No," Cat agreed, feeling he had more important things to think about. "What are my filly's chances of a full recovery, Doc?" Predictably, the vet declared it was far too early to tell. Cat concluded he'd have to give the horses their meds at night, after the races. Even Winterflood had to sleep sometime. He explained the problem to Ritchie, who seemed unperturbed.

A few days later, a package arrived with brand new instructions.

"Once a week, 75 hours out" he read in Ritchie's cramped sloping handwriting. Cat had entered uncharted territory. The Merryvale Downs Classic was only ten days away.

Harmony Princess was settling into her new quarters. Life on the road was hard: a new home every week, new neighbours, different food. This place was okay, but there was no sign of her friend here. In Goldie's comforting presence Princess had felt safe, like nothing bad could ever happen. She'd stopped calling for Goldie, but she was constantly watchful, hoping to catch a glimpse of her one more time.

DEVIL'S MOON

André Fontainbleu cast his eyes over the Hermitage's castle like structure, searching its walls for any signs of damage done in the hurricane season. He found none. All was well. As always, the maid Natalie was waiting to greet him after his lengthy absence. He accepted her effusive welcome gracefully, before strolling out onto the deck, drink in hand, to watch the sunset. Sighing with pleasure, he settled back in his lounge chair and gazed out to sea, enjoying the familiar sight of an orange globe slipping into the blue waters of the Caribbean. Glancing up at the cloudless sky, he noticed a bright crescent moon had appeared, shining in the twilight. Astonishingly, it was hanging upside down, looking like the letter "U". André had never seen anything like it before. He gazed at it, transfixed.

Inside the house, the maid, Natalie had seen it too. She walked over to the window, with a deep sense of unease. She saw it once before, long ago, on the night her daughter was born. She stood quietly, thinking of Colette's wild nature which no one had been able to curb. It was easy to believe in witchcraft and black magic on the island of Sainte Marie.

"Natalie! *Viens ici!* Quickly!" Monsieur André called out urgently. He was staring up the sky. She ran outside. The crescent moon was falling from the heavens, tumbling down faster and faster, until it plunged into the sea. For an instant, the two cusps of the crescent were clearly visible on the horizon, sticking up like devils' horns, until they too disappeared from view. "*Qu'est ce qui s'est passe?* What just happened?" Monsieur André asked, his brown eyes troubled.

"It is the Devil's Moon, Monsieur André," she replied. She hesitated. "It brings pain…and trouble." His frown deepened. She watched him as he stood motionless, staring out to sea. Then she went back inside. Whatever was to come in the future, Natalie feared it would not, could not, be anything good.

THE LUCKY SEVEN FARM: MONDAY

It was a clear, still November morning. A few brave leaves still clung to the bare branches of the trees but clearly, winter was on its way. Catalino Ciardi had no time to ponder the passing of the seasons. He was running from horse to horse taking bloods, trying to get it all done before the guys from *Horseman's World* arrived at his barn to do a feature on Harmony Light. Greeting them with a fistful of needles sticking out of his pocket wouldn't give a good impression. It was an open secret that trainers needled their horses, especially among veterinarians who could care less, but still…

"Ask Winterflood to run Harmony's blood off first," he told Evie, handing over a small cardboard box loaded with vials of dark red liquid. The results were generally pretty predictable: nice high RBC counts, decent hematocrit readings and white blood cell counts bang in the middle of the range, a sign of good health. However, as he had injected half the barn with the new style pre-race he'd just received, including Harmony Light, Cat had no idea really what to expect.

Two hours later, when *Horseman's World* finally showed, all the horses had been out except for Harmony Light who had spent the time trying to dig a hole down to China.

"We'll go with the interview first, then we want to get some shots of you and the horse out on the track, okay?" one of them said by way of an opener.

"Harmony Light generally goes out first thing," Cat complained. "He can't wait much longer."

"We'll make it quick," the camera guy promised. That suited Cat just fine. He'd only had the horse for a few weeks. The colt's spectacular two year old season wasn't exactly news anymore. However, Evie Mercer had filled him in on the real story behind Harmony's success: her Dad's brutal training regime, the long exhausting trips to stakes in far flung corners of the province, the horse's constant battles with lameness; Evie had seen it all. Cat was pretty sure *Horseman's World* wouldn't want to hear about that, so he quickly ran out of things to say. Inevitably, things got personal.

"You're now the top trainer in North America. Why d'you think you've been so much more successful since you hooked up with the Lucky Seven Stable?" they asked.

"Better stock," Cat replied promptly.

"What's the difference between you and other trainers?" they persisted.

"I treat each horse as an individual," Cat replied smoothly. It wasn't true. They all got the same dose, the same number of hours out, regardless. Harmony Light was trying to climb over the stall gate now, he realized anxiously. "Put the harness on him, Evie," he called out. "He's going to the sulky, so take the lines up, okay?" Where would he be without Evie? he asked himself. The new kid, Will, was a find too. The rest of the guys weren't bad, but they didn't have a single good idea to string between them.

"Finally, what advice would you give to a young horseman starting out?"

"Get a job working for a top trainer," Cat shot back.

"Like you, for instance?" they suggested, fawning on him, which irritated him beyond belief. "You're practically a household name now." Cat managed an easy grin, relieved that they hadn't asked him about the owners of the Lucky Seven Syndicate. The truth was, he had no idea who the hell they were: not a bunch of little old ladies, obviously, but a group of wealthy businessmen, in for a bit of fun would have been a good fit. Whoever they were, they had money to burn and that had been okay with him. More than okay. Until, that is, Anya had come in with her crime lord theory. Unfortunately, he hadn't been able to totally dismiss it as a possibility. Ritchie didn't exactly have a reputation for moral rectitude.

Harmony Light was hooked up and ready to go. He was pawing at the barn floor, impatient to be off. Big Will had a good hold of the lines and Evie was patting the horse's neck, whispering in his ear, trying to keep him calm. It wasn't working. He should never have put the race bike on him, he realized. Sure, it'd take a better picture but right now, it felt like a dumb idea. As he hesitated, Harmony Light tossed his head and leapt forward, straining at the cross ties.

"Let him loose!" Cat yelled. Grabbing the lines, he jumped onto the sulky. The instant he knew he was free, the horse took off, bounding through the open barn doors. Yet strung up as he was, Harmony Light was still the perfect gentleman, responding politely to Cat's pressure on the bit. After circling the track a few times however, all traces of politeness had disappeared. Harmony Light was all revved up, like a jet on the runway gunning its engines prior to takeoff. It was the race bike and the change in his routine, Cat realized. No wonder he was so hyper. Or was it the pre-race?

The next time he passed by the barn, the *Horseman's World* camera was pointing straight at him. The grooms were out there watching, too. Time to go! Cat swung the horse around but as he did so, out of the corner of his eye, he spotted Winterflood running out of the clinic waving a piece of paper. It unnerved him. Sensing the momentary lapse of concentration, Harmony Light latched onto the bit and took off like a bolt of lightning. Cat lay back in the sulky, exerting as much pressure on the lines as he dared. Harmony Light fought back, his neck bowed. Cat eased up, scared he'd choke the little guy. At the three-eighths pole, right in front of the barn, Cat felt the pressure on the lines ease. But his relief was shortlived. The horse staggered, then lurched to a stop. Terrified, Cat jumped off the sulky, tossing away the useless lines. Harmony Light was breathing hard, his nostrils flapping, his ribcage heaving. More worrying still, the huge vein on his neck was bulging with blood. What was happening to his horse? Scared to death, Cat searched the crowd of onlookers for Winterflood. He had disappeared! Dimly, he was aware that Evie and Will were unhooking the sulky.

"Get Winterflood!" he cried. Frantically, he started loosening the girth, ripping off the harness, anything he could think of to help the horse breathe. As he did so, Harmony Light collapsed onto the racetrack like a pack of cards, his spindly legs stretched out, his slender body in spasm. Gently, Evie prised the bridle loose. Then, careless of the cold, Cat tore off his warm jacket and wedged it under Harmony's head, listening to the sound of the horse's rasping breath. The big eyes were wide open, staring at nothing. How much longer could he keep going like this, before disaster struck? Where the fuck was Winterflood? he thought wildly. Looking about him, he spotted the guys from *Horseman's World* standing around awkwardly. They weren't taking pictures anymore.

Will appeared at a run.

"Doc's coming!" he gasped. Cat heard the screech of brakes and suddenly Winterflood was there beside him, syringe in hand. He didn't say a word. He just stuck his needle into the horse's neck and silently shot the load home.

The seconds crawled by.

"What did you give him?" Cat asked haltingly.

"I'd ask you the same question," Winterflood snapped back, his expression grim, "if I didn't already have a pretty good idea myself." His face burning, Cat looked away. The guys from *Horseman's World* had disappeared. Cat was too busy torturing himself to care. The horse was hardly breathing now. The staring eyes had closed. Damn Ritchie and his fucking drugs! he thought furiously. Why had he ever trusted him? As for Harmony Light, he was unnaturally still. Let him live! Cat implored some nameless unseen force up in the stratosphere, sinking to his knees, knowing it was futile.

Winterflood was moving his stethoscope around the horse's ribcage.

"Is he alive?" Evie sobbed. Cat couldn't tell. He searched the vet's face but Winterflood was giving nothing away. All at once, Harmony Light's eyelids fluttered, then flipped open. "Oh my God!" Evie shrieked.

"Sit on his head!" Winterflood directed crossly. "He's in no state to stand. Not yet!"

Several minutes later, Harmony Light struggled to his feet, looking dazed. The guys from *Horseman's World* reappeared.

"I'll go talk to them," Cat said, jumping up.

"No!" Winterflood snapped. "Will! You go."

"What'll I say?" Will asked in a worried tone.

"Tell them he tripped?" Cat suggested, looking questioningly at Winterflood, who nodded.

"Right!" the vet said. "I'm taking this horse to the clinic. Evie I need you to check out the barn. If any horse isn't acting right, let me know immediately. Cat! You come with me!" Cat was thankful the vet was taking charge. He felt so guilty, he couldn't think straight. He was worse than Evie's dad! he thought. Despite his brutal reputation, Mercer had never even come close to killing a horse. After administering a big bag of fluids by I.V. Winterflood put Harmony Light in a quiet stall. Then he sat Cat down in his office. "What did you do to him?" Winterflood demanded. "Tell me the truth now," he warned.

"I'm not going to lie to you," Cat replied, wilting under the vet's unfaltering gaze. "But I can't tell you because the truth is, I don't know myself." Winterflood thrust a piece of paper at him.

"Harmony Light's blood work," he informed him gravely. "Take a good look at the RBC and the hematocrit. That's just for starters." Cat gulped. The paper was littered with red markers for HIGHS and one or two significant LOWS.

"It's pretty weird," he said shakily. "What does it mean?"

"It means," Winterflood replied, "that this morning, before Harmony Light went out on the track, his system was already overloaded with red blood cells from whatever you gave him." Cat stared at him uncomprehending. "Ever been on the 501 in rush hour?" the vet asked. Cat couldn't get his head around the abrupt change of subject. "Too many cars. No flow," the vet told him. "The medical term for it is increased viscosity. Sludge, to you."

"But he was okay!" Cat protested.

"That was before he got excited," the vet explained. "Then bingo! His spleen dumped a mass of red blood cells into his veins. . .far, far more than he could handle. Now d'you see?"

This time Cat understood. "Traffic jam," he muttered. Winterflood had a faraway look in his eyes. "You fucking saved his life," Cat exclaimed, jumping up off his chair. "How the fuck did you do it?"

"I gave him an anticoagulant," the vet replied calmly. "I'd seen his blood scores, I guessed what the problem was."

"I really messed up," Cat said, as the implications sunk in. "I'll have to take him out of the Classic now, won't I?" Evie burst in. Cat's heart skipped a beat. But it was only to tell him that *Horseman's World* was dropping the story. "Did they say why?" he asked. Not that he cared anymore. Evie shook her head. The expression on Winterflood's face reminded Cat of someone. But he couldn't think who. Wait 'til I get hold of Ritchie, he thought angrily. He'd better have an explanation for this. But he knew if he was going to have any chance of getting at the truth, he'd have to corner the sonofabitch in person. A long buried memory of himself as a boy resurfaced: his father ramming his fedora on his head, his mother, stony faced, his own anguished cry. *Don't leave!* Startled, he realized he'd spoken those words out loud.

"It's okay, no one's leaving," Evie told him with a puzzled frown. As for Winterflood, he acknowledged the appeal with a grave nod. But the expression on the vet's face was unchanged. Cat recognized it, finally. It was the way his father had looked just before he walked out the door, never to return. Regret, sure, but also acceptance that there were no good choices anymore.

Only bad ones.

After Cat left, Jay Winterflood closed his eyes and leant back in his chair. The immediate crisis was over, but he was facing a dilemma. A man is your friend or your enemy, nothing else is possible, the elders had taught him. The problem was that, up to now he had always thought of Cat as a friend. Unlike most trainers who dismissed his advice, Cat had always listened to him. He'd given horses as much time as they needed to recover from illness, or injury, heeding his cry: "Time is the great healer!" Just now, Cat had claimed he knew nothing but how could he be telling the truth? Eventually, Jay raised himself and went back to work, feeding blood samples into a machine so sensitive it picked up every nuance, the slightest departure from the norm. He had no doubt that having it on site had saved Harmony Light's life today.

It was time to check on his patient. Superficially, the horse appeared normal. He was alert and watchful but that was natural. He was in an unfamiliar stall. Only his brown eyes which were cloudy and troubled, hinted at what he'd just been through. Much like Jay's own people, the Cree, Harmony Light was suffering in silence. The horse he had always fondly thought of as the little troublemaker, had finally run into trouble that was not his own making. His run in with the porcupine, his escapade in the village of Indian Falls, even his tricky birth, all belonged in an era of lost innocence. Where were they all now, those colts that the vet had last seen covered in mud and burrs, dehydrated and exhausted yet with no real harm done? Better off than the animal standing in front of him, he hoped. Just thinking about what had happened today made Jay's blood boil. Experimenting on a horse ought to be condemned as a criminal act in his view. Unfortunately, animals didn't have the same rights as people. Cat wouldn't end up in jail for giving a normal, healthy horse a drug that had obviously not been designed for the equine system. Even if he was caught redhanded he'd only get a fine. Of course, he'd lose his trainer's licence too for a while. That was scant comfort.

At six o'clock, satisfied that his patient was no longer in danger, Jay called Cat and told him to collect his horse. Then he drove home. It was almost dark when Helena met him at the front door, rosy cheeked and wrapped up warm. "You're so cold," she exclaimed. "Where've you been? Manitoba?" He wasn't in the mood to talk. "I've just lit a fire in the living room. I'll go get you some hot soup," she added disappearing into the kitchen. He stood beside the huge brick fireplace where half a tree was burning and held out his hands to the roaring flames, feeling like he'd never be warm again. When he had first caught sight of Harmony Light lying prone on the track, his heart had turned to stone. He still felt chilled to the bone. Why hadn't he had the courage to turn Cat in last year? Why had he let Cat talk him into believing that the bottles he'd seen in the tack room were vitamins when plainly they were not? The answers came thudding back like blows to his frozen solar plexus. He'd been convinced, because Cat was telling the truth as he knew it. Was it really possible that Cat genuinely didn't know what he had given Harmony Light, because someone else was pulling the strings? The answer was a resounding "Yes!" As Jay confronted his demons, he understood that the stakes had just got much higher. What if the owners were involved? What if the Lucky Seven Stable lost its licence too?

For Jay, it would mean the end of a dream: his own state of the art equine hospital with hundreds of thousands of dollars worth of technology at his disposal which gave him the ability to diagnose and treat just about any standardbred racehorse ailment going. He could never afford that kind of equipment himself. Going back to trawling the barns, drumming up business, armed only with his bare hands and an old portable X ray machine was something he could hardly bear to contemplate. He drank the soup Helena gave him slowly. With every mouthful, he felt a little warmer, except for a lump of ice somewhere in his chest that remained stubbornly frozen.

"Where's Josh?" he asked.

"Asleep. He started ice hockey today. Must have worn him out." It was the lack of respect, Jay realized. Trudging around the barns was nothing compared with that. Trainers always thought they knew best. Cat had been willing to learn. "What's going on?" Helena demanded.

"Tough day," he mumbled without lifting his eyes from the floor.

"Tell me," Helena asked in a conversational tone. "At what point did you decide that selling your soul might somehow work out?" He looked up, startled. She was staring at him arms akimbo.

"You have no idea," he said.

"Try me," she replied.

That night Cat watched his former pupil, Harmony Princess, race against top conditioned mares. She finished a distant last, thirty lengths behind the leader. Before today, he would have felt contemptuous of her new trainer. Now it bothered him. Tony Hall was no genius but the guy knew how to set a pair of hobbles. Princess had gone from unbelievable to utterly useless in a matter of days. It made so little sense, it aroused his suspicions.

When he got back to the farm, he turned the house upside down, but there was no sign of the newspaper clipping Anya had given him. He trawled through his call records and found her number. He pressed save, not that he had any intention of calling her. Pride had its price. It was past two when he fell into bed. His feet were like lumps of ice.

An hour later, he gave it up and got dressed. There was no chance of him sleeping tonight. The events of the day were preying on his mind. Besides, he needed to know that Harmony Light was still alive and breathing. After he had reassured himself on that count, he went online. December was high season, so flights to Sainte Marie were at a premium. He booked his ticket anyway, determined to confront Ritchie, whatever the cost.

The day before he was due to leave, he called Anya and brought her up to speed with events. He led with Harmony Gold's steady progress. But when he told her what had happened to Harmony Light and his own proposed trip to the island, her mood changed from happy and relieved to horror struck.

"Don't go!" she cried. "You don't know what you're doing, Cat. You're playing with fire."

"I can't carry on like this. I need to know."

"Wait 'til I get to Canada, at least. I'll be there in a couple of days!"

"Too late!" he said.

"They'll kill you!" he heard her cry just before he rang off. She was crazy. That was never going to happen.

After Cat rang off, Anya sat completely still, only vaguely aware of the warmth of the sun and the clear blue sky above her. Two people's lives were now in jeopardy because of her: first Pete, now Cat. Guilty was just a word. It didn't even come close to how she felt. With Jeff Lamare now out of the picture in her own mind at least, she had run out of excuses for letting Pete face the music on his own. Besides, the prospect of something happening to Cat before she'd had a chance to tell him how she felt about him was unthinkable. At whatever risk to herself, she had to go down to Sainte Marie, the sooner the better. Unfortunately, it wasn't that simple. She'd maxed out her credit cards on living and buying her ticket to Toronto. Plus, it was her mother's birthday the next day. She couldn't just up and leave.

A few hours later, she'd calmed down a bit. After all, she'd be back on the right side of the Atlantic in a few days' time. She'd been planning to have it out with Jeff as soon as she got back to Canada. It looked like she'd have to keep up the pretense for a little longer. She'd have to use Jeff's credit card to pay for her flights too, not that she intended to tell him. She hated herself for it, for all the deception, but she couldn't think of another way through. Perhaps she was overreacting. Cat hadn't seemed too worried. Ritchie was his brother after all and it wasn't like Cat had done anything wrong. Maybe her worst fears wouldn't be realized. Maybe things would work out okay.

GOING SOUTH

On a frosty morning in early December, Cat set off for Sainte Marie. Evie Mercer had volunteered to give him a ride to the airport. They had set off early, which was just as well. There was a long line of people waiting to go through Airport Security. Cat had decided it'd be a cool idea to travel light so he'd left his winter gear behind. Other than grabbing a raincoat on his way out the door, he was dressed for the heat.

He was nervous. They'd given him a really hard time in Newark once when he'd packed a razor in his carry on bag. He was no terrorist but as a lone male, he fit that profile all too well. When he checked the pockets of his rain jacket, he discovered an empty syringe and a length of baling twine, both of which he discreetly dumped, together with a piece of newspaper folded up small. He recognized it immediately. He hadn't worn the rain coat since the storm, the day Anya had come out to the farm. All that searching and it had been there all along!

He sailed through security, picked up an Americano and settled down to read the story that Anya had been obsessing about for months. His first response was one of grudging admiration for the guy. Getting seven under-age girls pregnant in a matter of weeks was an achievement of sorts, he thought. As for the headline, THE LUCKY SEVEN ? it was a coincidence, he decided. It had absolutely nothing to do with the Lucky Seven Stable. But then he spotted Winterflood, standing centre stage in the group photo. Someone (it had to be Anya) had put three exclamation marks in blue pen beside the picture of a man called Curly, the so called biological father. It didn't make a lot of sense. Winterflood looked nothing like him. Cat was out of ideas and out of time. Grabbing his stuff, he set off at a run. He only just made it to the plane before the gate closed.

As they took off, he had a fleeting glimpse of a gray Lake Ontario. Then the plane climbed through dense cloud cover, eventually emerging into a clear sunlit sky. They were forecasting snow for the entire Toronto area. Cat wasn't looking forward to confronting Ritchie, but he was happy to get away from winter and the responsibility of running a racing stable for a while. He was giving the horses a week off as well. They could use the break and unlike him, they had nothing on their minds to spoil it. After Harmony Light's brush with death, Princess's dismal performance had scared him. She was due to race again in a day or two. If she collapsed on the track, there'd be no Winterflood around to save her. For a moment, he considered calling Tony Hall to warn him. But what could he tell him, really? Besides, the guy was no sweetheart. He'd probably turn him in to the judges, anything to save his own skin!

The ice clad branches of the trees glittered in the wintry sunlight as Campbell McClaren drove slowly down the unpaved road which led to Catalino Ciardi's farm, keeping a close eye on the van following him and carefully counting fire numbers. This was an official visit, not a social call. When he saw the sign for the Lucky Seven Stable and Veterinary Clinic, he turned off and led the way down the driveway. He parked beside the barn next to a fancy truck and trailer, done up in the stable's colours of black and gold. Then he rolled down his window and sat for a few minutes longer than necessary, enjoying the silence. One day this area was going to be swallowed up by the town of Erinsville but for now it remained a rural idyll, swept clean by the wind and snow, a perfect place to hide out from the modern world... or from prying eyes. He went over to the van, which contained a trio of men from security, plus one woman.

"Give me five minutes," he said. "Then come in." The path to the barn was like a skating rink. Praying that when his security team followed, they wouldn't fall down and break a leg, he slithered his way over to the barn and prised open the barn doors.

"I'm looking for Catalino Ciardi," he announced, squeezing through the gap.

"He ain't here," a heavy set man pushing a wheelbarrow replied gruffly. "Will's around," he added, nodding towards a solid looking young man staring intently at a board, as if he was trying to memorize its contents. Campbell repeated his request.

"You're too late. He's gone down to the islands," Will replied earnestly, looking a trifle worried. So Catalino had left. That wasn't good news. Before he went on vacation, he would have tidied things up. However, the search warrant had an expiration date.

"Some folk have all the luck, eh?" the wheelbarrow man said cheerfully.

"Lots of horses for you to take care of," Campbell remarked, to give himself a little time to think.

"Yeah, well there's generally more of us," Will explained. "Some of the guys left early."

"When the cat's away and all that," the wheelbarrow man put in good naturedly. "That girl's never come in at all. Never trust a woman, eh?"

"Hey! I heard that!" a girl with a blond ponytail exclaimed, emerging from a side door. "It wasn't a fun trip, guys."

"Keep your hair on, Evie," the wheelbarrow man said. "We know you was taking the boss to the airport."

"What's that security van doing outside?" Evie asked curiously. It was time to put a stop to chit chat.

"I'm Campbell McClaren, Head of Security at Iroquois Downs. I have a warrant to search the farm," he informed them, glancing at his watch. Right on cue, the barn doors rolled open. "That'll be security now," he said. The wheelbarrow man looked startled.

"What's this all about?" Evie frowned.

"Illegal substances," Campbell replied bluntly.

"Drugs?" Evie asked anxiously, glancing at the snowy landscape outside.

"You won't find anything," Will declared confidently.

One hour on, it looked like Will was right. A thorough search of the tack room, the trunks, harness bags, the hayloft and even the stalls had turned up precisely nothing. It hadn't been easy to get a search warrant. It would be near impossible a second time. However, Campbell wasn't ready to give up quite yet. Dr. Winterflood's tip off was too good a lead. There had to be something here.

"I need the keys to the house," he said. "No sense in breaking down the door."

"I'll get you the keys to the pickup," Will offered. Campbell moved towards the open barn door, trying to catch a little sun, stamping his feet to keep warm. Next time I'll wear snow shoes, he vowed, as he turned his attention to the big horse trailer sitting outside. Evie hadn't been looking at the landscape, he realized suddenly.

"Wait," he said. "We need to check out the truck and trailer first. Anyone got a crowbar?"

The team from security went through all the usual hiding places, while he jimmied the hubcaps loose. After that, he told security they could stop looking. It was all there, jug hoses, injectables, instructions, the lot. The only things missing were the labels on the vials. Maybe the stuff was relatively innocent, like vitamins. Then again, maybe not. Putting on his gloves,

Campbell loaded the lot into a pouch and carefully sealed it. "I'll need some-one to sign for this," he said.

"Brad's not here." Will said anxiously. "He's the second trainer. He ought to sign."

"You'll do." Campbell said firmly.

Then, he called Al McTavish and gave him the news.

SAINTE MARIE

The sun was shining when Cat touched down at Sainte Marie. The airport was surprisingly modern and cool, but it was hotter than hell outside. There was no sign of Ritchie but Cat was unfazed. It wasn't the first time his brother had showed up late. He quickly discovered his phone didn't work on Sainte Marie, so he hopped into a taxi and picked up a local SIM card. It took him a while to get a hold of Ritchie, but eventually he picked up.

"You can't stay at my place, bro," he said. "It's only a one bedroom and I've got a girlfriend. It'd be much too crowded." Not even for a week? Cat thought, but he didn't say it out loud. What would be the point? He could afford any hotel, even a five star, but finding a room at the last minute, in high season, wouldn't be easy. He shouldn't have made assumptions, he realized. Ritchie had let him down often enough in the past. Why should this time be any different? "I'm working right now," Ritchie added. "Grab a cab and come on over. Tell 'em to take you to the Sunset Bar. It's five minutes, tops."

Ten minutes later, the taxi set him down at the Sunset Bar. The place was nothing fancy but Cat couldn't knock the location between the ocean and the airport runway.

"Let's get you a beer," Ritchie suggested, leading the way to an old converted bus, with all its wheels still on. Apart from the man behind the bar, the place was pretty quiet. However, at three o'clock in the afternoon, it would be that way he supposed, unless Ritchie's business was a total flop. If it was, he'd be the last one to know.

"I'm taking a swim first," Cat said, enticed by the dazzling white sand and turquoise water, a stark contrast to Canada's grey skies and pale sunshine. But even underwater he could hear the roar of the planes as they passed directly overhead.

"You didn't pick the greatest time for your trip," Ritchie announced half an hour later as they both got stuck into plates of grilled tuna and French fries. His brother was heavier than he'd been a year ago by a good thirty pounds, Cat thought. Plus, judging from the bags under his eyes, he was pretty stressed out too. The business? The girlfriend? No sense in speculating. "See, they weren't happy with you taking that horse out of the stake," Ritchie explained.

"Harmony? Hey! You know what happened!" Cat protested. "His blood scores were all over the place…he couldn't race like that."

"Keepin' 'em healthy, that's the trainer's job," Ritchie replied carelessly, plunging his fork into the tuna. "So's keepin' the owners happy."

"Listen," Cat said angrily. "Your fuckin' pre-race totally messed that horse up! What the fuck was it? The owners have a right to know what you're doing to their horses. Who are they anyhow?"

"If I told you that, you wouldn't need me, kiddo," Ritchie replied, patting his chest. "See, I gotta take care of *numero uno*."

"Harmony Light could've died!" Cat said through clenched teeth.

"But he didn't, did he? So everything's cool, right?" Ritchie replied airily. Cat buttoned his lip. Inside, he was seething. But he'd learned from bitter experience never to confront his brother head on.

"By the way," he remarked casually. "Anya asked me to say *Hi* to you."

"Who the fuck is Anya?"

"She and Pete used to come here all the time," Cat replied.

"The Aussies," Ritchie acknowledged grudgingly.

"How come you never told her you had a brother?" Cat persisted. Ritchie shrugged, apparently lost for words. Over the fence, a jet was taxiing down the runway. "She told me to ask you about some guy . . .Fountain Blue. . .I'm pretty sure that was the name. Mean anything to you?" The expression on Ritchie's face was blank, but Cat wasn't fooled. "So?" he challenged. The silence was deafening. Ritchie's cell phone went off.

"Have to take this," he said shortly. The jet took off, its engines roaring, passing so close Cat felt like he could reach up and touch its underbelly. The noise was deafening. Ritchie's lips were moving but Cat couldn't make out a single word. Then Ritchie jumped up, gesturing with his cell phone. "Gotta go!" he shouted. Then he turned tail and ran off.

Ritchie made straight for his car, feeling jumpy as hell. Why the fuck had Anya told Cat about Fontainbleu? he wondered furiously. He sped off, taking his feelings out on the car, crashing the gears, screaming round corners. Halfway home, he came to his senses. Anya wasn't a threat. Not really. All he had to do was practise denial. Everything would be A-OK.

Nevertheless, he pulled over and made a quick call to the boss. No one answered. Back at his apartment, Ritchie did what he always did on a Saturday afternoon: check out the CPTA chat rooms, pick up a few choice bits of gossip and make sure no one was getting too close to the truth behind the Lucky Seven Stable's winning ways. In other words, taking care of *numero uno*.

What he saw there hit him with the force of a triple rum tequila. Holy shit! Cat had been a fucking idiot! Only a total moron would hide stuff in a hubcap! He called the boss again, but he was still AWOL. Ritchie debated with himself for a while, wondering what to do. Eventually, he punched in the number Fontainbleu had given him for emergencies. He recognized the voice instantly. It was the man Ritchie called The Six O'clock Flash. He listened to what Ritchie had to say with interest. He told Ritchie not to worry, that he'd take care of everything.

Afterwards, Ritchie wasn't a hundred percent sure that he'd done the right thing. Cat was his brother after all. However, his own interests lay elsewhere.

It hadn't been a great start, Cat reflected. He'd found out precisely zero so far and he had nowhere to stay. But he'd got his brother on the defensive, which was something. He went for another swim to cool off. As he waded back to shore, he was almost sorry he hadn't listened to Anya. Getting the truth out of Ritchie was going to be an uphill battle. He needed, somehow, to keep up the pressure. Assuming, that is, he got a chance to question Ritchie a second time. He decided to get a beer. . . try to enjoy himself a little. The barman was on the phone, so Cat had to wait. Whoever was on the other end appeared to be doing most of the talking. Eventually the barman spoke.

"*Claro!*" he exclaimed. "*Es Ricardo por usted, senor,*" he said with a dazzling smile, holding out the phone. Cat took it and held it to his ear.

"Something's come up," he heard Ritchie say. "It's a drag but I'm gonna be tied up for the rest of the day. Listen, I checked all the hotels and they're booked solid. Good news is, I've found this great place for you to stay."

"Where?" Cat asked.

"Place called The Hermitage. I've told Pepe all about it. He'll drive you over later."

"Who's Pepe?"

"My barman. Trust me! You're gonna love it!" Ritchie's tone was conciliatory. More to the point, Pepe had a friendly face. Cat decided to go along with the plan. He spent the rest of the afternoon swimming and getting up close and personal with the jet planes which occasionally passed by overhead. The time passed quickly. He ordered tapas, which he discovered were on the house. Afterwards, he told Pepe he was ready to go.

Moments later he was in a jeep, racing up the side of a mountain, with Pepe at the wheel. The road snaked back and forth, so steep in places that the car was practically vertical.

"Where are you taking me? What kind of place is it?" Cat asked anxiously. Knowing Ritchie, the hotel would either be a total dump, or a ripoff. Pepe responded with a volley of incomprehensible Spanish. Cat quickly gave it up. At the crest of the hill, Pepe veered sharp left and they flipped back to the horizontal. Ahead was a floodlit castle, looking like it belonged in Disney World.

"Hermitage!" Pepe declared proudly. Cat dug into his pockets for some cash but Pepe waved it away and took off again immediately. Cat stared at the pair of black iron gates flanked by two statues of golden eagles, their wings spread wide. The place would cost him, he thought. But what did Ritchie care how much he was forced to spend on a bed for the night? He made his way down the long flight of stairs to the front entrance and rang the bell. The doors swung open. Hesitantly, he stepped over the threshold and stopped dead. Giant candelabras hung from a soaring ceiling...gilded columns sprouted from white marble floors. Cat had never seen anything like it...awesome didn't come close to describing it, it was so over the top. It looked like a fucking film set!

"Ah...she is beautiful, yes?"

Cat swung around. A guy dressed entirely in black was standing, or rather striking a pose, directly behind him.

"She?" Cat queried, mystified. The front doors shuddered to a close, operated by an unseen hand. It was creepy.

"*La belle castille...La belle maison.*" Must be French, Cat thought.

"It's stunning," he agreed. The French guy looked flattered.

"Welcome to the Hermitage, *Monsieur*," he said, looking at Cat inquiringly.

"I'm Catalino Ciardi," Cat replied. "My brother Ritchie told me about this place. It's really great!" He smiled. The French guy did not smile back.

"'Enri at your service, *Monsieur*," he replied stiffly.

"Onree?" Cat repeated hesitantly. "Oh, Henri!" he exclaimed.

"Mais, c'est 'Enri," the French guy replied, correcting him.

"Hey, no offence *amigo*," Cat replied putting his hands up and backing away. Henri appeared to recover. He stopped looking down his nose at him anyhow.

"Why you come 'ere, *Monsieur*?" he asked sounding genuinely puzzled.

"I told you, my brother Ritchie…"

"Ah yes," Henri said. He paused thoughtfully, stroking his chin. "Your brother Ricardo," he added, making his dislike and disapproval obvious.

"Hey! What's going on?" Cat frowned.

"Desolé, Monsieur," Henri replied. "But my lips, zey are sealed. You wish to see your room now?" he asked in a hopeful tone. Suddenly, staying at the Hermitage didn't seem like such a great idea.

"You know what," Cat said. "I should just go!"

"Mais, Monsieur Catalino…'ow will you leave? Ze taxi, zey will not come 'ere. You can of course if you wish walk down ze mountain. I do not speak of ze dogs zat bite or ze darkness. I do not say 'ow at ze 'otels, zere are no rooms."

"Then I'll just stay at Ritchie's place," Cat said, giving it one last try. If the doors had been open, he'd have made a run for it. He pulled out his phone and called his brother. There was no reply.

"Desolé, Monsieur," Henri said. *"Mais Monsieur* Ricardo . . 'e is indisposed."

"Indisposed! What's that supposed to mean?" Cat demanded.

"Tomorrow or ze next day," Henri replied affably. "Zen we shall see per'aps. You come now," he ended sensing victory. He was lying, possibly.

"Okay," Cat shrugged. It looked like he'd run out of options. Moving as silently as a cat, Henri led the way swiftly along a wide hallway before descending a long flight of stairs. Hoping they weren't on their way to the dungeons, Cat followed him. When they got there, he had a pleasant surprise. The accommodation included an outdoor pool and jacuzzi. But when he asked for the rate on the room, there was an awkward silence.

"*Mon dieu*," Henri said. "Everything has its price *Monsieur*, but per'aps it is better not to ask." This isn't great, Cat thought, feeling unnerved.

"I don't understand," he frowned.

"I wish you a pleasant evening," Henri replied politely. Cat had a thousand questions he wanted to ask. Before he could ask a single one, Henri disappeared, closing the door behind him. Cat knew it would be locked, but he tried it anyway. Belatedly, he realized that the Hermitage was not a hotel.

He went out to take a look at the pool. Fireflies were flitting in the trees like tiny Christmas lights. But it didn't feel anything like Christmas. As far as he could make out in the twilight, the deck jutted out from the cliff side. He could hear waves breaking on the rocks far below. There was no escape in that direction. When the bats appeared he gave it up, went back inside and called his brother again. Predictably, there was still no reply. Despite his luxurious surroundings, Cat had never felt so vulnerable, or so alone.

He ran through the people in his life: Winterflood, Moose Rankin, Evie and Will, his mother . . . old Uncle Eddie. None of them was in the picture and there wasn't time for long explanations. There was only one person who would understand the fix he was in and she was still on the other side of the world. His worries about Princess seemed laughable right now. He had his hands full with his own troubles. It had been a long stressful day. He stripped down to his boxers and fell into bed, exhausted.

As his eyes closed he slipped into a turquoise sea, alive with fish. Below, the rocks were studded with starfish glinting with gold as the sun caught them. Just one! That's all I want, he thought, taking a deep breath. He swam down until his lungs were bursting, but he was still a long way from the bottom. He breathed out, watching the bubbles of life giving air rising to the surface. Then he kicked up his heels and dived deeper. The starfish looked as far away as ever. Suddenly it hit him. He was never going to reach them. He was way too deep and his lungs were empty. He was going to drown down here. Panicking, he kicked upwards. After what felt like an eternity, he breached the surface gasping for air. He woke up shuddering, fighting for breath. For a moment, he didn't know where he was. Then the truth struck him. He looked at his watch. It was 2 a.m. Cursing, he got out of bed and padded over to the big glass doors. Outside, the sky was bright with stars. He turned on the light and checked his phone but there were no messages. Anya probably hadn't even got his text yet he decided, comforting himself. He tried to stay awake but eventually drifted off.

The next time he woke, it was pitch black. The air was heavy, like breathing treacle. Must be a power cut, he thought sleepily. It happened often enough back in Canada. He lurched over to the French doors and flung them open. It brought no relief. He felt queasy, the result of over-eating and too much sun, he guessed, as he staggered back to bed.

MISSING!

As Sunday morning dawned, Jeff Lamare woke up suddenly and inexplicably. The bed was empty. He walked into the kitchen. The kettle was still warm. An empty cup with coffee dregs lay on the countertop. But Anya was nowhere to be seen. Puzzled, he pulled on some clothes and went down to the garage. The red Fiesta was sitting in its usual parking spot. But of Anya, there was no sign.

Fifteen minutes later, Campbell skidded to a stop outside Jeff Lamare's apartment building. In the passenger seat beside him, Billie jolted back awake. It was snowing: big wet flakes that filled their tracks as they made their way up the steps to the front entrance. That's one of my ideas scuppered, Campbell thought uneasily as he rang the bell to Number 41. Any sign of a struggle, or indeed its absence, were now buried under three inches of snow. As they rode the elevator to the fourth floor, he was hoping to find a simple explanation for Anya's abrupt departure. From the dread look on Jeff's face, it was obvious that her fiancé, at least, was fearing the worst.

"They snatched her right from under my nose! Here in Erinsville of all places…it's unbelievable!" Jeff exclaimed, wild eyed.

"So don't believe it," Campbell replied calmly.

"She only got back from Greece last night," Jeff wailed. "I tell you, she's been kidnapped!"

"Abducted, you mean," Campbell corrected automatically.

"What happens now? A ransom demand? They know I've got plenty of money!"

Campbell shook his head. "You've been watching too many crime shows on TV," he replied steadily. "This is Canada, not the US or Mexico. Things like that just don't happen here. Not as a general rule." He could tell that Jeff wasn't convinced though. "D'you have any reason to think she didn't leave of her own accord?" he asked, trying to bring a note of reality to the situation.

"Her car's still in the garage and she isn't answering her phone!" Jeff said in an anguished tone. "And take a look at this!" he added, beckoning them into the vast living room. Half a dozen silver frames graced the mantelpiece. All of them were empty. "Now do you believe me?"

"Weird," Billie said. She was right, though he wouldn't have put it that way himself, Campbell thought.

"I don't have a single picture of her," Jeff howled. "Not one! I checked my phone, my computer…someone's deleted them all."

"How about Facebook?" Billie asked.

"She closed her account, said it wasn't secure." Jeff replied. Anya had the right instincts there, Campbell decided. But it meant it wouldn't be so easy to post a photo of her now, if she really was missing.

"What about this one?" he asked, pointing to a crisp new cardboard frame on the coffee table, also empty.

"That?" Jeff replied without interest. The emotional roller coaster he'd been on since early morning had evidently taken its toll.

"It looks like a win picture from Iroquois Downs," Billie said.

"Yeah," Jeff replied dully.

"One of your horses?" Campbell prompted. Jeff did not respond. "Try to remember," Campbell persisted.

"One of Catalino's," Jeff said at last. "I never liked him."

"Was Anya in the picture?" Campbell inquired, glancing at Billie who raised her eyebrows at him.

"No!" Jeff replied vehemently. So why has it been taken then? Campbell wondered. He didn't have an answer, but he did have an idea. "Anything else missing, apart from the photos?" he asked. Jeff looked baffled.

"Why don't I check out the bedroom?" Billie suggested brightly. It was still snowing, obscuring the view from the vast glass windows. If this had been an ordinary Sunday he and Billie would still have been in bed, glad to be indoors. But there was nothing normal about this Sunday. Billie started with the wardrobe.

"All her summer things have gone," she reported a few minutes later.

"Wait," Jeff said, perking up a tad. "There was a case in there…she brought it back from Greece…a carry on with wheels."

"Well it's not here now!" Billie stated decisively.

"Cheer up!" Campbell said bracingly. "Kidnappers don't generally allow people to pack a bag!" Jeff did cheer up. But not for long.

"Why didn't she tell me?" he asked plaintively.

"Because she didn't want you talking her out of it?" Billie suggested, not mincing her words.

"I know why she left," Jeff said with certainty, his face chalk white. "She must have gone back to Australia. I knew she wasn't happy here. I should've listened to her!" Like a great many people in crisis, Jeff wasn't thinking clearly. Campbell didn't blame him, but it wasn't helping.

Campbell waited until 9 am to ring an old comrade in arms who owed him a favour. It was Sunday, after all. It turned out there was an Anya Papandreos on a flight to Miami. The plane was sitting on the runway, waiting to take off. So much for Jeff's kidnapping theory. Clearly, Jeff was useless at reading the signs. He felt certain he would have seen it coming if Billie was about to pull a number like that. From Miami, there were connections to just about everywhere but Campbell was betting on Sainte Marie. If Anya wanted to keep a low profile, the last thing she needed was Jeff Lamare posting her photo as a missing person. There was no way to tell if his hunch was correct. The States were beyond the RCMP's jurisdiction, unless a serious crime had been committed. A woman taking an impromptu trip without informing her boyfriend didn't constitute an offence in Canada.

This wasn't Iran.

SAINTE MARIE

The next time Cat opened his eyes, it was broad daylight and he felt like he was about to throw up. He only just made it to the bathroom in time. Was it the tuna? he wondered as he stumbled back into bed, dizzy and weak. Was Ritchie sick too? All he knew was his head was killing him. Gotta get help, he thought, groping for his cell phone, which he'd left on the bedside table. He dialled 911 to no avail. He shouted for help. There was no reply. The house was as silent as the grave. He crawled out through the French doors and called out the only name he knew.

"Henri!" Footsteps on the stairs, a woman's scream...more footsteps...finally, the voice of the Frenchman.

"Some sing wrong, *Monsieur*?" Henri enquired nervously. It wasn't every day, Cat realized, that you came across a guy clad only in his boxers, crawling around like a baby. But right now, he didn't give a shit about Henri's precious sensibilities. He needed help, urgently. He groaned, the universal language of the sick.

"Ah, *vous avez la maladie*?" Henri asked. Nodding made him feel like throwing up again, Cat discovered.

"Nauseous," he explained, aware that he had slurred the words. Henri punched in some numbers on his phone then began speaking so softly that Cat couldn't have made out what he was saying even if he'd been able to understand French.

"*Dîtes-moi*...is it you 'ave pain in ze eyes, ze joints, ze muscles, per'aps?" Cat shook his head.

"Dizzy," he moaned.

"You 'ave ze fever?" Henri asked, placing a hand on Cat's forehead. "*Eh bien, merci. Oui j'arrive*...You 'ave ze luck. It is not ze Dengue Fever... You sleep always like zis...in ze *plein air*? It is not wise, *mon ami*."

"I need help, not lectures," Cat protested weakly.

After Henri left, Cat needed to use the bathroom again, urgently. He finally made it back to bed and collapsed, just as the air conditioning came back on. He'd misjudged Henri, he decided when the guy returned with a packet of pills. He pulled himself to a sitting position, downed a couple and fell back down again.

"Natalie, she stays here," Henri informed him. Risking a brief flutter of his eyelids, he glimpsed a dark, careworn face.

"You sleep now." Surprisingly he did. When he woke up Natalie had gone. A young black girl was sitting next to the bed, filing her nails.

"You okay?" she asked, popping a piece of gum into her mouth. He nodded. The girl jumped to her feet.

"Don't leave," he begged. She left anyhow. Afterwards, he lay on his back listening to the silence for a long, long time. Eventually he gave way to temptation and closed his eyes. The sun plunged into the sea. The moon rose. Stars wheeled across a velvet sky. And still Cat slept on.

It was feeding time at Rivers Training centre. The cheerful red barns were full of horses frantic for breakfast after a long cold night. As Tony Hall bent down to pick up the first feed can, the barn phone rang. He ignored it and carried on.

"Phone!" Gerry Lake shouted. He was sporting a thick red beard. He hadn't shaved since October, when the weather turned cold.

"Tell 'em to wait!" Tony yelled back. Who the hell would be calling at this hour, anyhow? he thought indignantly, turning his back on the phone. Leaving it swinging back and forth on its long cord, he went methodically from one stall to the next, dropping the grain into the beat up feed tubs. His new filly, Harmony Princess, was so enthusiastic that she spilled most of hers on the floor. Then she ran at Tony, baring her teeth. She'd been passed around a fair bit since Craig Brown had lost her. It hadn't done her much harm though. She looked like a million dollars. However, looks could be deceiving. She'd raced like a pig for Tony in her last start. She was in again tonight. He wasn't so much anxious about it as resigned. He had no reason to believe she'd improve a whole lot. The judges had hauled him in last week because the bettors were howling. She'd been the odds on choice and she'd finished last. It wasn't his fault. He'd done nothing.

I'll hay and water after, he thought, hoping it wasn't the owner Jack Dawson, on the phone. But it was! After he'd chewed him out for keeping him waiting while Tony stared at the wall, Dawson moved on to the main agenda: Harmony Princess.

"If that filly of mine quits tonight like she did last time," Dawson said in a threatening tone, "I'm taking her away from you and giving her to Andy Price. McTavish's colt raced a helluva lot better for Price than he ever did for you!" Tony had no doubt he would carry out his threat. It was the thin edge of the wedge. If Princess raced better for Andy, Dawson would take the other five away too. Then Tony would be out of business. He couldn't let that happen!

After thinking it over, he collared Dave Bodinski and offered him a couple of hundred bucks to drench the filly. It was a lot of dough to lay out on his own account, but he knew no vet would do it on a race day and it'd be worth it to save his hide and keep the judges off his back. Dave told him to keep his hair on. He'd be by later on in the afternoon

Cat awoke with a raging thirst and an empty belly. Someone was in the apartment. He threw on some clothes, peered round the bedroom door and laughed with relief. The intruder had been room service! Surprisingly, after a bowl of rice and some sweet tea, he felt pretty good. He showered and shaved. Other than his bloodshot eyes, he looked okay too. He was back!

A rainstorm blew in, sending sheets of water thundering down on the deck. After the clouds cleared, a rainbow appeared, straddling the bay. It took Cat's mind off his troubles for a while. He called Ritchie, but he still wasn't picking up. Neither was Anya. Unbelievably, it looked like he'd slept through an entire day and night. Meanwhile, the outside world had given up on him, including his own brother. The house was eerily quiet. He gathered up his things, intending to pack up and leave, but when he tried the door leading to the stairs, he discovered it was still locked. He tried shifting it, but quickly gave it up. There was no getting past solid steel. He texted Anya another SOS, then he checked out the deck, which was at right angles to the mountainside, teetering on tall wooden stilts. There was no way down from here. It would be suicide to try. He was trapped! All at once, he didn't feel so great. He sunk down on a big comfortable sunbed and closed his eyes, just for a moment. Before he was aware of it, he'd drifted off to sleep.

He was woken by the scream of a siren. Instantly, he was wide awake, listening intently to the sounds of running feet, banging doors, loud curses and the insistent ringing of a telephone, all coming from somewhere directly over his head. After hours of silence, the Hermitage had sprung back to life. He jumped up and ran to the edge of the deck, craning his neck upwards, trying to see what was happening up there.

The siren's wail faltered. An ambulance appeared. Two paramedics in white uniform jumped out and opened the rear doors and a man with close cropped curly hair tinged with gray descended, impatiently brushing aside their attempts to help him down. Cat watched him, taking in the arrogant manner, the intelligent eyes, the cruel mouth…his features were familiar, but why? The answer came almost immediately. Though his curls were tinged with gray now, the guy looked a little like an older version of the guy in the photograph, Curly. Like Curly, he was wearing an earring.

"Monsieur André," Henri cried. "*Bienvenu*," he added, a half beat too late. Just then, Cat's cell phone buzzed. Hoping no one had heard it, he pulled it out of his pocket but the cryptic message, "Look down!" made absolutely no sense to him. Until that is, he heard the blare of a car horn coming from somewhere behind him, halfway down the mountainside. Shit! Cat thought, trying to duck out of sight. The "André" guy was onto it in a flash, his eyes darting swiftly back and forth before locking onto Cat. Cat read surprise in those eyes. Double shit! He had to get out of here, pronto. The sound of heavy footsteps thundering down the stairs sent him scurrying to the edge of the deck. He leaned out as far as he dared. A good hundred feet down, he spotted an open top jeep perched precariously on a hairpin bend. A girl with long dark hair was at the wheel. It was Anya!

"Come down!" she cried.

"How?" he pantomimed with a shrug, gesturing at the sheer drop which separated them. He was scuttling around the edge, trying to locate a toe hold, when a rope came flying up towards him. But as he grabbed it, he heard feet pounding on the deck. He spun around. Three guys were coming at him like avenging demons. The one spearheading the attack was a brute of a man, pumped up on steroids. He picked Cat up as easily as a toy and held him still while the other guys wound the rope around his body. Then they dragged him up the stairs to the grand entrance hall, which was deserted. There was no sign of Henri or any of the staff…no witnesses! Where the fuck was Ritchie, Cat cursed silently as he was bundled into a black vehicle with black tinted windows. Steroid Guy got behind the wheel. Cat ended up jammed between the other two. They stank of garlic! As the car sped down the steep mountain road, he figured out his chances of escape were precisely zero and he had no choice but to accept the situation. When the car finally stopped, his brain had stopped pressing the panic button. However, his heightened perceptions remained.

"Untie his legs!" the Brute on steroids barked out. The harbor looked painfully beautiful after the darkness inside the car. The sight of countless yachts, their tall masts swaying in the breeze, the flapping of their metal stays making sweet music, comforted Cat. But it felt unreal. The two garlic breaths were holding him in a vice like grip and even if he had been able to free himself, he knew he was no match for the Brute. They dragged him along the jetty and halted beside one of the boats.

"Pete!" the Brute roared. "We need a ride!" A blond guy stuck his head out of the cabin.

"Hey, I've got thirty tourists booked," he complained without so much of a glance in Cat's direction. "You can't just treat the Sea Princess like your own personal taxi, not at this time of day!" Pete was an Aussie, Cat realized, feeling a surge of hope. Just how many Aussies named Pete could there be on this island? This had to be Anya's friend. But there was no chance to talk.

"Put him in the hold!" the Brute yelled. The engine stuttered into life. A few minutes later the boat began to pitch and toss like a bucking bronco. It was a relief when they hauled him out and threw him onto the deck of a speedboat riding at anchor. When he twisted his head around, he got a view of the Sea Princess's stern and Pete's cheery wave as he left to pick up his tourists for a fun day out. His own trip, Cat thought bitterly, though free, was a mystery tour which was bound to end badly. The last thing he saw was the speedboat's anchor coming up. Then the world disappeared behind a dark blindfold. He listened to the rumble of chain on the deck, heard the engine roar into life and wondered how many hours he had left.

After what felt like an eternity, the blindfold was ripped off his face. After his eyes had adjusted to the glare of a blindingly blue sea, he caught the glint of a hypodermic. This is it! he thought grimly. The two garlic breaths held him fast, while their boss jabbed him in the jugular vein with the needle until blood was spurting out of his neck. Then they hung him over the side. The water was so clear, he saw every single detail of the big fish that came flocking to the boat, drawn by the taste of his blood. As if to reinforce the point, one of the men threw some fish bait over the side. In less than a second it had disappeared, devoured by vicious jaws.

It'll be me next he decided, bracing himself. There'd be no point in struggling. He'd be better off playing dead. But a dozen sharks against one bleeding human wasn't much of a contest. They were too far from land for him to outswim them, yet he knew he'd have to give it a try. The Brute was staring at him, a malicious smile on his ugly face. The engine throbbed back into life and the boat leapt forward, taking him with it. Along with the relief came confusion. What were they playing at? On the way to shore, the two garlic breaths ripped off his sneakers and tossed them overboard. They were heading for a mass of jagged rocks which stretched as far as the eye could see. It was a bleak vista devoid of all life, like the surface of the moon.

"Iron Shore," the Brute announced with a grimace of sadistic pleasure. "Enjoy," he added, producing a wicked looking knife. The two garlic breaths held him down. Smiling, the Brute went to work on the soles of Cat's feet and the palms of his hands until all four extremities were a bloody mess. Cat's eyes were watering from the pain but he knew if he cried out, he'd only encourage his tormentor. Somehow, he held his tongue.

"Untie him," the Brute growled. "Then dump him." The garlic breaths didn't waste any time. When Cat hit the water, he felt like he'd smashed into a concrete wall. He sank like a stone. He burst to the surface gasping for air and heard wild laughter peeling out as the boat sped away from him. As wave after wave washed over him, each one higher than the last, he was afraid he was going to drown, long before the sharks appeared to finish him off. If he could only catch a wave, he thought, he could ride it to the rocks. Even if he risked ripping himself to pieces, he reckoned it was a chance worth taking. On the third attempt he made it, landing like a fish. Sobbing from the pain, he hauled his body up onto the land, if you could call it that. A thousand needles were digging into him but he forced himself along. Eventually, he collapsed face down, feeling battered and bruised, bleeding from dozens of cuts and scrapes, his hands like raw steak.

He was alive, but right now he didn't feel like celebrating.

What now? he asked himself, balancing himself on his knuckles, getting painfully to his knees, scanning his surroundings for a possible escape route. On one side lay a moonscape with no end in sight. On the other was the dazzling treacherous sea, seething with sharks ready to eat him alive.

His adrenalin high was fading fast. He felt light headed and as weak as a kitten. Nevertheless, he set about the task of assessing the situation, hopeless though it seemed. If there were predators in these waters, he thought, there had to be smaller fish for them to feed on. Maybe he would hit it lucky and a fishing boat would pass by. He decided to keep watch and cling to hope. But as the day wore on, it became harder and harder for him to stay focused.

There was nothing to drink and not a lick of shade. His mouth was so dry his tongue was sticking to the roof of his mouth. His feet ached and throbbed and the sun was beating relentlessly down on his bare head. He kept imagining he was hearing the faint sound of a motor, never coming any closer but always there. In the end, he decided that it was coming from inside his own head. Being delusional was not helpful, he told himself firmly, even as his thoughts drifted away to nowhere.

Tony Hall had known all along there was a chance Dave Bodinski would let him down, even though he had sworn he'd come by that afternoon. It wasn't like Bodinski was a special pal of his. Tony didn't have any friends. He was a loner. He'd searched all the barns, even gone over to the blacksmith's shop. No one had seen Dave and he wasn't answering his phone. Tony had the drench all mixed and ready. He had two choices: race the filly cold and watch her finish up the track or have a go at tubing her himself. How hard could it be? He decided he'd give Dave another few minutes. He was an hour late already but there was still a chance he'd show up.

Cat was startled back into consciousness by a clap of thunder, followed a split second later by a flash of lightning. Storm clouds were racing across the sky. The sea was a muddy grey, splattered by rain, which was bouncing off the waves. It was tantalizing to see and hear water out there, while he lay on a bed of nails, his throat caked dry, his body aching.

Suddenly, the storm was upon him. He hobbled to his knees, standing with outstretched arms, his face tipped skywards, his mouth open as wide as he dared, trying to drink his fill, choking and retching as the torrent bucketed down, forcing water into his lungs nearly drowning him. All too soon it was over.

"I will survive!" he shouted huskily to the horizon. The sun reappeared. After blazing in the sky all day, it was now on a downward path. He stared out to sea but there was no sign of rescue in the vast emptiness before him. Behind him, the sun was low in the sky. Soon it would be dark and no ship would see him then. He steeled himself to accept the truth.

No one was coming.

Tony Hall strode into Princess's stall. He'd made his decision. The filly stopped bouncing off the walls and stood quietly observing him. She allowed herself to be caught and tied up to a ring at the back of the stall. She shied away as he approached her with the length of plastic tubing looped over his shoulder but she allowed him to thread the tube through her left nostril, down her throat, all the way down, feeling for it carefully, the way he'd seen other people do, to make sure it was going into the stomach, not the lungs. She didn't protest as he carefully poured a mug full of the bright orange liquid into the funnel. Emboldened, he picked up the bucket and was getting ready to finish the job, when the filly's deep, rasping cough sent him scurrying backwards. Scared out of his wits, he wrenched the tube out of her nose. She went down to her knees. Violent coughing wracked her body and a tell tale trickle of orange liquid dripped from her nostrils.

He'd put the tube into her lungs, he realized, feeling horror struck. It was only a mug full, he decided, comforting himself. How bad could that be? he asked himself. Thankfully, after a while she stopped coughing. But she was still on her knees, her head resting on the floor of the stall, taking rapid shallow breaths which made the shavings dance around her nostrils. Quickly, he squatted down and shoved them aside. Maybe she'd be okay, he thought as she roused herself. He heaved a sigh of relief. Then she swung her head around and looked at her belly. She was colicking! His heart pounding, he sprinted to the tack room, unlocking the door with shaking hands. A shot of banamine, that's what she needed. He opened his drugs cupboard and clapped a hand to his forehead. He'd given his last bottle to Scotty McCoy that very morning! The bitch of it was, Scotty wasn't around. This was the dead time, the best time for illegal drenching, the worst time if you needed help. He knew he ought to call the doc. Precious minutes were slipping by. But first he needed to dump the evidence. As fast as he could, he rinsed out the length of tubing then stashed it in Scotty's trunk. Next, he broke the end off the largest syringe he could find half filled it with some of the orange mixture and flushed the rest of it down the drain. It was time to call the vet. He had his story ready now. Meecham would be best. He didn't need Winterflood with his sharp eyes, nosing around.

When Tony finally made it back to her stall, Harmony Princess was no longer on her knees. She had collapsed onto her side, her legs stretch out stiffly at right angles to her body, her ribcage heaving. When he tugged on her halter, trying to rouse her, she groaned.

It was time for Plan B, Cat decided. Heaving himself up onto his elbows, he mentally prepared himself for a painful crawl on his knuckles and knees until he reached softer going. After that, he'd find a road and make it to civilization somehow. Gritting his teeth he set off across the Iron Shore, moving forward one slow step at a time. He'd only managed a very short distance when he heard a faint yet unmistakeable sound that sent him scrambling to his swollen feet. Holding his breath, he listened. There it was again! He wasn't imagining it! A few seconds later, he picked up the whine of an engine which broke into a full throated roar as an orange inflatable bounced into view. Cat waved frantically, shouting till he was hoarse.

"Over here! I'm over here!" It was no use. They obviously couldn't hear him over the noise of the motor. But were they blind too? The waves from the boat were breaking on the rocks now. He winced as salt water washed around his ankles, stinging his lacerated feet. Long after the inflatable disappeared beyond the headland, he could still hear the sound of its engine. Eventually, it died away and he was alone again, with only the setting sun for company. Soon, it too had deserted him, sinking down behind the mountains. "Help!" he cried into the silence, cupping his hands. "Help me!" They'd never hear him now. They were much too far away. Night was coming. It'd be impossible to pick his way through the pits and craters tonight. He'd have to try again in the morning, if that morning ever came.

"Help!" Tony shouted into the silence. "For fuck's sake, help!" If she could just hold on until the doc came, he thought, staring down at Princess, his heart in his mouth, visions of the wrath of the judges and the contempt of his fellow trainers torturing him. "I never shoulda tried to drench her," he moaned. "They'll crucify me! Hang on!" he implored the filly. But the shudder than ran through her body as her lungs deflated, the ominous silence that followed, all told him that Harmony Princess had given up the struggle.

It was all over.

In the depths of despair, Cat imagined that he heard his father's voice; the words *Corragio mi filo* rang out, inside his head. If he could only make it through the night, he'd have a chance, he thought. In the cool of the evening, he was finally able to think. He'd have given anything for a hamburger and a soda, but fantasizing about food wasn't going to improve his situation. He needed to try and figure things out. That guy he'd seen at the Hermitage, the one Henri had called Monsieur André, could well be the kingpin behind the whole Lucky Seven Stable operation. There'd been a spark of recognition in his eyes, he remembered. It made sense. After all, Cat had been in the winner's circle a zillion times and the guy didn't have to be in Canada to watch the races at Iroquois Downs. They were posted on YouTube. What if he was using the horses, like Curly had used those young girls years before? Winning would be all that mattered, never mind the consequences. But why all the secrecy? It looked like he'd never get a chance to find out. The worst of it was, he could die out here, but they'd set it up so it would look like sheer bad luck, not murder.

One by one, the stars came out. The moon looked like a New York pizza, he thought hungrily; lashings of cheese on a paper thin crust. But he couldn't eat the moon. He was imagining things again: the faint sound of an engine, coming from a long way off. Then in the distance, a beam of light appeared, shining on the dark water. He peeled off his T-shirt and waved it back and forth like a flag. He took a deep breath and roared for help, over and over again until his voice gave out. All at once the engine fell silent and the light disappeared. It was so quiet, he could hear the waves lapping the rocks. Was he going crazy or had someone answered? Then the engine started up again and he saw a searchlight swinging towards him, wavering at first then shining straight at him, nearly blinding him.

He threw up one arm to shield his eyes and promptly lost his balance, crashing down on his knees. But a few minutes later, the inflatable was bumping up against the rocks, the stars and stripes flying at its bow and he felt a surge of patriotism so intense he could hardly breathe. Were the Americans really here, or was he dreaming?

"Thanks for coming so quick, Doc," Tony said in heartfelt tones when Meecham arrived. It was a relief not to be alone, to hand over the responsibility to someone else. The vet spent several minutes feeling for the filly's pulse, then shook his head.

"I'm afraid I'm too late," he said soberly. "What exactly happened here?"

"I was giving her some vitamins by mouth," Tony lied, waving his syringe and watching the doc's face. "She jus' freaked out."

"All I can do is give her a cursory examination," Meecham said. "The only way we'll really know the cause of death is through an autopsy." The word autopsy made Tony's head spin. If they found his drench deep in her lungs, he was done for.

"She went down like a stone," Tony stuttered.

"It's never nice, losing a horse," the doc said, not unkindly. Tony surprised himself by bursting into tears. Meecham stood there, a puzzled look on his face.

"What d'you think did it?" Tony couldn't help saying, immediately cursing himself for asking such a dumb question.

"She was okay this morning? Not off her feed or anything?" Tony shook his head sorrowfully, remembering the filly wheeling around in her stall, banging her feed tub. Somehow he'd get through this, he told himself. "Standardbreds these days," Meecham said, a trifle wearily. "They're so finely bred now. It doesn't take much to trigger an adverse reaction and bring on an acute case of colic. Then one thing leads to another…the heart gives out and the horse bursts a blood vessel. I'm guessing something like that happened here. Never used to see this sort of thing in the old days. Of course, the breed was much tougher back then." He picked up his doctor's bag. "Pretty little thing," he remarked "What was her name? For the bill," he explained.

"Harmony Princess," Tony replied. A beer, that's what he needed. He'd have to get a few inside of him before he felt brave enough to call the owner and break the bad news. She wasn't insured. But first, he had to tell the judges that Harmony Princess would not be racing tonight or any night hereafter, or he'd get a stiff fine. He already knew they'd tell a whopping lie to the betting public. "Number four in the fifth race, Harmony Princess, has been scratched sick," they'd say. That was almost as sick as what he'd done to her.

No one was telling it like it was. No one!

This was no dream, Cat realized, as a cheery voice hailed him.

"Hang in there, son. We're a comin' to get ya!" Cat tried to answer, but only managed a croak. Up close, he saw the inflatable for what it was: a search and rescue vessel that was all business. His rescuers weren't taking any chances. They put a lifejacket on him and strapped him into a harness. Then they winched him to safety like a fucking sack of potatoes.

"You got some weird looking cuts there, son," one of them said, sounding like he'd never left Texas. "Looka here, Larry." Larry quickly got to work cleaning them up. "We got the call out at noon. Helicopter's bin looking for you too. We must a gone right past you couple o' hours back. Couldn't see a dang thing. Sun was clear in our eyes," the Texan explained.

"Now hold still," Larry warned. "This is gonna sting like the devil." Cat bit his lip while Larry swabbed his lacerated hands and feet with iodine.

"Suck on this," the Texan suggested, proffering a water bottle.

"Slowly now," Larry said. "Don't drink it all at once."

"We was out on a training exercise," the Texan continued. "Suddenly it all got real! What were you thinkin' son, out here all on your own in the middle of nowhere?" Good question, Cat thought silently, unable to come up with a credible answer. As the boat flew over the waves, he realized he wasn't out of the woods yet. Every minute he stayed on this island, he'd be in danger. He didn't intend to give those monsters a second chance to squeeze the life out of him. But he had no money and he'd left his ticket and his passport in enemy territory. If he told his rescuers the truth, they'd check him into a mental hospital. How on earth was he going to get away?

To Cat's astonishment and joy, Anya was waiting at the quayside. She looked exhausted, like she hadn't slept in a week. The Texans had swathed his hands and feet in white crepe bandages. Before he could stop them, strong arms picked him up and, swinging him over the side, delivered him to Anya like a package.

"Where'd you come from?" he gasped as they set him down on dry land. "How did you know . . ?"

"Never mind that!" Anya snapped. "Listen I gotta get the jeep. Wait here, okay?"

"Hey, I'm not going anywhere," he replied, hobbling over to a leaning post and waving farewell to the Texans, who were getting underway already, their mission accomplished. He shouted his thanks, but no words could express what they'd done for him. Even if he had managed to survive somehow, without their help he'd have probably lost his mind.

A few minutes later, he and Anya were speeding away from the harbour. The speedometer needle swung up to 140 kph and stayed there.

"You trying to get us killed?" he protested.

"We got exactly two minutes till the bridge comes up. I don't wanna be a sitting duck, okay?" A tense silence descended. By the time they reached the bridge, the red warning lights were flashing. Anya carried on regardless. The barriers came down, beeping so loudly it made Cat's head spin, but Anya kept her foot firmly on the gas pedal.

"Brake, for God's sakes," Cat cried, bracing himself for a crash.

"Trust me!" Anya said. The gate bounced harmlessly off the roof and they were through, but Anya kept up the breakneck pace.

"Where are we going?" he asked. Not that he cared. He was enjoying the sights and sounds of bright lights and traffic too much. It sure beat being stranded in the middle of nowhere!

"You're flying out of here tonight, if I have to carry you!" Anya said.

"I don't have a ticket, don't even have ID."

"No? Take a look behind you!" A bag was sitting on the back seat which looked a lot like his. "You can thank Henri for that," she said. "He took a huge risk. Huge! What were you thinking?" Anya demanded, swerving to avoid a suicidal biker. "I warned you, didn't I?"

Cat was speechless.

A few minutes later, they pulled up outside Airport Departures.

"I'm gonna need your pin number," Anya said, helping herself to the wallet. "Wait here, okay?" Only three days had gone by since he'd been sitting here waiting for Ritchie to show up, Cat reflected. If felt like half a lifetime. When Anya returned, she was pushing a wheelchair. "Your flight leaves in three hours," she informed him. "They won't let you on the plane looking like that," she added, rifling through his bag. "You'll need a change of clothes."

Several painful minutes later, she wheeled him over to the airport cafe, parked him at an empty table and left him again. The place appeared to be a popular hangout for locals. There were some locals however, that Cat was praying wouldn't show. Anya was back with a sandwich which she fed him, like he was a helpless baby. A waitress with a dark, careworn face began cleaning the table, reminding him of the woman at the Hermitage and suddenly he was back there again, back to the nightmare. Somehow he made it back to the present.

"I don't get it," he frowned.

"You will," Anya assured him. "But first you gotta tell me exactly what happened."

He didn't feel much like reliving it, but he reckoned she had a right to know. Even though he hadn't believed her, she'd tried to rescue him, anyhow. "Listen," she said, when he'd finished telling his story. "There's something I gotta tell you. But you're not gonna like it." His heart lurched. Had one of the horses died? he thought, filled with dread. "They raided your farm Saturday morning, right after you left." Cat gulped. "They found drugs in your hubcaps. Not too clever, was it? It was all over the CPTA chat rooms. Anyone could've picked up on it. You picked a terrific time to go on holidays, Cat."

"Brother! So you really think they were trying to kill me . . .for that?"

"You're still alive," she reminded him. "They just wanted to warn you."

"Seriously? You gotta be kidding right?"

"I'm guessing this whole thing was Boxer's idea," she remarked. He didn't need to ask who Boxer was. He knew.

"Ritchie went along with it," Cat said bitterly. "He dumped me right in it. My own brother!"

"Did you take anything for the pain?" Anya asked quietly. Cat shook his head. No pill was going to blot out what Ritchie had done to him. But he wasn't going to let it eat him up, take it on the chin, like his father. He was going to dump it right back. He just needed to figure out how. "Time to go," Any pronounced, jumping to her feet.

"How much does Jeff know about all this?" he asked, as she wheeled him away. "Your *fiancé*..." he added, into the silence, wishing he could see her face.

"Jeff and I are history," she replied coldly. "I just haven't told him yet." It was a pretty ambiguous statement but he didn't want to push her. "This is as far as I go," she said, beckoning to a man in a peaked cap.

"You're not coming?" he asked, astonished.

"Pete's my oldest friend. I've gotta stick around," she replied.

"You'd be a lot safer in Canada," he argued. She looked troubled. "Hey," he added hastily. "I'm not gonna try to talk you out of it...I'm worried about you, okay?" She didn't say a word, just leant down and kissed him, right on his cracked lips. It hurt like hell, but it left him wanting more. She dropped her voice, so only he could hear.

"Those weren't sharks you saw," she said coolly. "They were Tarpon. They're big, but harmless. . .to people anyhow." Before he could say another word, she was gone.

"Whatever happened to you?" the airline stewardess asked him curiously, after he'd made the painful transition from wheelchair to seat. "Sea urchins got you?"

"Long story," Cat replied. His lips were still tingling from the kiss Anya had planted on them. As soon as he was airborne, he knew he'd done the wrong thing, leaving her there.

Despite her air of bravado, Anya was scared.

Up on the viewing platform, Anya watched Cat's plane take off. She waited until it was a mere speck in the evening sky. Then she drove back to the harbour and the Sea Princess, where Pete was busy hawking a moonlight cruise. She called Jeff from the quayside and set him straight. It was brutal but necessary. She'd had enough of older guys who wanted to control her every move. Cat wasn't like that.

The moonlight cruise was peaceful. Just her, Pete and half a dozen honeymoon couples, not the usual rowdy crowd. Afterwards she and Pete went down to the cabin and split a case of beer. It was almost like the old days.

"Henri's a hero," she remarked appreciatively.

"Isn't he just," Pete agreed.

"I owe you both, big time."

"Listen," Pete said. "Blackmail's one thing. But kidnap and torture! I couldn't be a party to that. I knew it was Cat right away from that win photo you showed me." The Sea Princess was rocking gently in the evening breeze.

"This is nice," she said wistfully. "I've missed this."

"Why'd you come back?" Pete asked suddenly. "It's not safe for you here, you know that."

"It's not safe for you either," she replied quickly. "But I'm guessing you'd never leave without Henri." She'd put herself in harm's way for Cat, without a second's thought. She still couldn't quite believe it. Pete was ruffling his crew cut, a sure sign something was up. "Hey! Don't you hold out on me," she exclaimed.

"Here's the thing," Pete said. "Fontainbleu's fitting out the Shere Kahn. He wants to sail her round the world…If I skipper her…take him wherever he wants to go, in six months. . . a year. . . I'm a free man." It was a knockout punch and it caught her totally by surprise.

"For Christ's sakes Pete!" she burst out. "What's to stop them dumping you over the side I'd like to know!" Pete shrugged.

"What do I have to lose? I can't go on like this."

"Your life," she replied.

"You know what? Right now it's not worth a whole lot."

"Please!" she implored him. "At least tell me you'll think about it."

"Too late. Already signed up. Can't go back on it now, even if I wanted to." Panic…guilt…regret…frustration exploded inside her head like starbursts on Australia Day.

"Okay, when do we leave?" she asked eventually.

"Who invited you?" Pete retorted. "Don't even think about it. You're not coming, okay? It'd only make things worse."

"So what am I supposed to do?"

"Go home," Pete told her.

"I don't have a home. Not anymore. Me and Jeff are done."

"There's gotta be someone somewhere," Pete persisted.

"There is," Anya admitted.

"So what's the problem?"

"It's Cat," she replied, at length.

"Christ," Pete exclaimed. "You can sure pick 'em, can't you."

CANADA

Being in a wheelchair, Cat discovered, did not prevent him from being targeted by Canadian Customs. Making a last minute booking from a Caribbean island had set off red warning lights. The drug squad was waiting for him as he disembarked, complete with sniffer dogs. Quite a welcome! They weren't content until they'd prodded him thoroughly and unwound all four bandages.

"You wouldn't believe the hiding places some people come up with," one of them explained apologetically after it was clear that all Cat was covering up was a mass of cuts and bruises. There was no one waiting for him at Arrivals. A kindly, middle aged couple took him under their wing and wheeled him out to the taxi rank. The cold went right through him and the sight of all that asphalt, the colour of Iron Shore, made him shudder.

"What happened to you?" the cab driver asked. Taking his cue from the stewardess. Cat went for the sea urchin story. The ride to the farm used every last cent of his spare cash. After a struggle with the key, he shouldered open the front door feeling very much alone. Then he sank down onto the floor and tipped out the contents of his bag. There was no sign of his phone. He'd had it just before the Brute and his two sidekicks came for him. But now, who knew? His entire life was in that phone, including Anya's number.

He spotted his computer leaning against the wall, right where he'd discarded it, opting to travel light. Prising it open, he set about freeing up his fingers from the bandages. Then he checked his emails. There was one from Ritchie, informing him that he'd been fired, effective immediately as the Lucky Seven's private trainer, with a copy to the Race Office. Also there was a frosty note from Evie and Will. As Cat wasn't allowed near the Lucky Seven Stable, they had trucked Harmony Gold a few miles down the road to Eddie Clearwater's barn at Meridian Acres. So, Cat thought, trying to ignore the throbbing pain in his hands and feet, he was out of a job, crippled up and probably homeless, too. Of course, it could have been worse. He was alive; he still owned Goldie, and Anya was splitting up with Jeff, or so he hoped. Before the battery ran out, he got on Skype. He needed to talk to someone and old Uncle Eddie was an obvious choice.

"Don't worry about your filly," Eddie said. "She's settling in just fine. Listen sonny, if you need a place to bed down, the door's open. Help yourself. Anytime."

"Thanks," Cat replied gratefully.

"Course, you'll have to help out a bit," Eddie added. Before Cat could explain that he was in no state to help anyone, his computer died. He made it up the stairs on his elbows and knees and fell into bed, comforted by the presence of the bedside phone and figuring he could always call 911 if he was desperate enough. He swallowed a couple of pills, hoping they'd take the edge off the pain. As soon as he was able to get around again, he intended to go and see Winterflood. The vet needed to know the truth about who the owner of the Lucky Seven Stable really was. Then again, maybe he'd be better off keeping quiet about it. Why be the one to give him the bad news?

It was past midnight. Through his curtainless windows, Cat could see the familiar silhouette of the barn and beyond it, on the horizon, a dark plume rising. Before he could figure out what it was, the painkillers kicked in. He lay back on the bed and was soon sound asleep.

FIRE!

Across the valley in Crawfish's hayloft apartment, Bud was curled up in his bed (an extra large carton from The Happy Shopper) dreaming of dog biscuits and salivating gently. One minute he was dead to the world, the next he opened one eye, sniffed the air and was instantly on full alert. He took a flying leap and landed on his master's chest, whining and licking his face.

"Hey, gerroff me!" Crawfish complained sleepily, taking a peek at the luminous dial on his bedside clock. "It's two in the morning!" he exclaimed in outrage. "What's the matter with you?" But the dog didn't back off. 'What's up?' Crawfish wondered, his nose registering the stench of tobacco, or was it burnt toast? Guiltily, he remembered he'd been grilling marshmallows on a makeshift barbecue in front of Andy's barn earlier that evening. "Oh my gawd!" he cried. "I've only gone and set the whole place alight…me and my dratted cooking! We're done for!"

By that time, Bud was barking frantically and scratching at the door to the barn. When Crawfish flung it open, Bud shot through the opening almost as fast as the human cannonball at the travelling circus. Crawfish hurtled down the stairs after him, still wearing his red plaid pyjamas, breathing hard and fearing the worst. "Bless my soul, we're saved, Bud. Saved!" he exclaimed. At first glance everything in Andy Price's barn looked normal. No acrid smell of smoke, no flames licking at the barn door. But the horses were going crazy, circling their stalls like spinning tops. Crawfish smelled a rat. "Something's up!" he declared.

When he ventured outdoors, smoke billowing from the far end of the next door barn sent him flying back inside.

"We gotta get help!" he told Bud, slamming the door shut. He made a dash for the barn phone, the dog snapping at his heels. "Hey, quit it!" he yelled. But Bud was so excited that for once he wasn't paying attention. When Crawfish skidded to a stop, the dog kept right on going. They hit the floor together and crucial moments were lost while Crawfish disentangled himself from the muddle of legs and paws. "This ain't a game!" he warned Bud, as he punched in the number he'd carefully rehearsed in case of an emergency. Andy Price answered on the second ring. Lucky he's one of them insomnia-whatcha-ma-call-its, Crawfish thought gratefully.

"Who the hell is this?" Andy grumbled.

"It's me gov'…Barn's on fire," Crawfish whimpered.

"Which one?" Andy asked urgently. Sounds like he's gonna have a blooming heart attack, Crawfish thought uneasily.

"Ain't me that done it," he said, getting that off his chest.

"Which barn?" Andy demanded, in an exasperated tone.

"Next door's," Crawfish hastened to explain.

"Eddie Clearwater's?" Andy asked. Crawfish nodded silently, forgetting in the present crisis that Andy couldn't actually see him. "I'll take that as a yes," Andy said, impatiently. "You still there? Speak to me man!"

"Present," was the best Crawfish could manage, a throwback to Mrs. Bloomfield's first grade class.

"Listen to me," Andy said, sounding uncannily like Mr. Roberts, the Paddock Judge, now.

"Yes, sir," Crawfish replied automatically, his mind wandering all over the place. Andy proceeded to reel off a series of instructions, rapid fire. A little out of his depth, Crawfish listened intently, anxious not to mess up.

"I gotta go call the fire engine now and wake Eddie up," Andy ended hastily. "Don't forget to take the flashlight. And Crawfish?"

"Yup," he replied expectantly, poised to leave now like a runner on the blocks.

"Where's that dog of yours?"

"Right here!" Crawfish replied promptly, preparing to hand over the phone and stopping himself just in time.

"Those horses ain't gonna leave by themselves. You'll have to use the dog," Andy said before ringing off.

"Fire engine's coming," Crawfish told Bud. "But we ain't got no time to fool around if we're gonna save them horses." Thanking his lucky stars that the electricity was still working, he scooted down the aisleway, yanking leadshanks off their hooks. Grabbing an armful of towels, he dunked them in the nearest bucket of water, which happened to be Harmony Stampede's. The colt looked surprised to see Crawfish, but he quickly went back to checking out next door, like some old busybody twitching at the net curtains.

Oblivious to the cold, Crawfish set off at a run for Eddie Clearwater's barn, clutching the soaking wet towels to his chest and trailing the leadshanks behind him. He'd strung the flashlight on binder twine and was wearing it round his neck. "Sit down Bud!" he ordered, stationing the dog away from danger. Then he wound a wet towel around his face, took a deep breath and went in. |In the end, the flashlight wasn't much of a help. The worst of the smoke was down at the far end of the barn, but even so he had to feel his way along, counting stalls as he went, fumbling with the catches on the gates before flinging them open. Snorts of alarm greeted him from all sides. By the time he got to stall number eight, he was choking half to death. He ran outside coughing and retching, in a vain attempt to clear his lungs. A few minutes later, not one horse had left its stall.

There was no sign of the fire engine.

"Nothing else for it Bud," he said, his voice hoarse. "We gotta go back in. C'mon boy." This time he heard high pitched whinnies. The horses were scared to death but they weren't leaving, even though their stall gates were wide open.

"Wise up!" he told them. "This ain't a good place for you now. D'you hear?" The far end of the barn was ominously quiet, except for the steady lick of the flames. "This is what hell is like I reckon," Crawfish muttered, regretting his many shortcomings. "That's where I'll be going in the end, unless you put in a good word for me, Bud." He was nerving himself up to go back in when he heard the welcome sound of a motor, followed by the squeal of brakes. Old Eddie Clearwater hopped out, leaving the engine running and the headlights full on. Too bad it wasn't Andy...or the fire engine. Still, it was a lot better than nothing and at least Eddie knew the horses. Mutely, Crawfish pointed to the pile of wet towels and leadshanks.

Yelling, "Let's go!" Eddie made a beeline for the horses in the greatest danger, the ones furthest in. The next five minutes were a blur of curses and kicking hooves, against a backdrop of roaring flames and crashing timbers down at the far end of the building. Bud did what he could to help, stationing himself at the back of the stall and barking on command.

"Wot 'bout them horses down the other end?" Crawfish gasped, voicing his deepest fears.

"Left yesterday!" Eddie shouted. He wasn't half bad for an old guy, Crawfish decided, as he and Bud followed in Eddie's wake. "Just two more!" Eddie panted diving into the nearest stall. The first horse walked right out, as good as gold. "This last one's gonna be tough!" Eddie warned. Fearing the worst, Crawfish kept a tight hold of Bud's collar. He got a brief glimpse of a wild eyed chestnut before the flashlight gave out. "Watch yourself! She's a real bitch," Eddie added. Crawfish felt his way to the back of the stall. It was getting hotter by the second. By this time, Bud knew the drill. He produced his best ear splitting bark. Instantly, Crawfish felt a searing pain on his shins. He flew back and crashed into the wall. Bud landed on top of him, howling. Struggling to his feet, Crawfish gave the hussy a boot on the backside.

"Damn near killed us!" he shouted angrily.

"She's out!" Eddie shouted back. With Bud lying limp in his arms, Crawfish hobbled out after them. He was still anxiously looking the dog over when the fire engine arrived, its sirens screaming. Half a dozen firemen jumped out. Eddie slumped down beside him, coughing away. His hair was as black as pitch and his nose was bleeding. Crawfish's new plaid pyjamas were ripped to shreds. They were beyond saving, he realized sadly.

"Get away from the building, it's about to blow!" one of the firemen yelled.

"Move!" Eddie cried, jumping up and hauling Crawfish to his feet. Dazed, Crawfish looked around for Bud. But the dog had disappeared. His eyes streaming, he called Bud's name over and over again. There was no sign of him anywhere. He was running out of places to look, running out of time. Think! he urged himself. Where does he go when he's scared? Smacking himself in the head for not thinking of it sooner, he scooted back towards the burning barn, dodging the firemen, ignoring their shouts of protest. Outside the big doors where stacks of hay were smouldering, he finally got a glimpse of his boy, huddled in a corner looking more dead than alive, too frightened to move.

"Bud!" he screamed, scooping him up and dashing to safety. A camera flashed, then helping hands grabbed the two of them and dragged them towards a waiting ambulance. Eddie was already there, holding a bloody rag to his nose. Crawfish insisted that Bud should be treated right away.

"It's a bit irregular," the ambulance man said uncertainly, looking to his fellow medic for guidance.

"He's a freakin' hero!" Crawfish declared.

"True enough!" Eddie croaked, backing him up.

"Oh well, we're all the same under the skin, I suppose," the medic said, giving Bud a whiff of oxygen. "I've got a dog myself. Heart's strong," he added reassuringly. A short while later, Bud opened both eyes and sat up.

"That gash'll need seeing to," Crawfish piped up, gesturing at the dog's ribcage.

"You're next sir," the medic said firmly. Crawfish gulped. He'd never been called "sir" in his entire life. Reckon there's a first time for everything, he thought, laying back and feeling more exhausted than he could ever remember.

The fire had wore him out worse than the elephants and that was really saying something!

Cat was having a nightmare. His barn had been taken over by clinging vines and as fast as he ripped them off in one place, they sprung up again somewhere else. Through it all, he heard a phone ringing insistently. When he opened his eyes, he discovered he'd ripped the bandages off both hands. The bedside phone was still ringing.

"Yes," he said groggily, wondering where he was and why he felt so cold.

"Your filly's okay," a hoarse voice announced, before breaking up in a fit of coughing.

"Eddie?" Cat asked urgently. The coughing stopped.

"Had a fire in the barn last night. Faulty wiring or something. Anyhow, thanks to Crawfish, we saved 'em all," Eddie wheezed. "Almost forgot! Security was on the phone, wanting to know where you were."

"Go to ER," Cat implored the old timer. "Get 'em to check out your lungs."

"I'll do that. Just as soon as I've got these horses settled. Don't worry about me, I'm a lot tougher than I look," Eddie said huskily before ringing off. Security? Cat thought nervously. Things were happening way too fast! Yesterday had been one hell of a day. It didn't look like today was going to be much better. It took him a full hour to angle his extremities into sweatpants and a T shirt and make his way slowly down the stairs. Then the doorbell rang.

"Be there in a few minutes!" Cat called out, creeping towards the front door, trying not to swear. His feet were killing him. When he finally got the door open, he saw a man standing there, brushing snow off his broad shoulders.

"Catalino Ciardi?" the man asked briskly.

"Who are you?" Cat replied warily.

"I'm not from the press or the police," the man assured him. "I'm Campbell McClaren, Head of Security at Iroquois Downs." Cat groaned inwardly.

"You'd better come in," he said weakly.

"Looks like you've been in the wars," McClaren observed, with a swift glance at Cat's hands and feet. "Need some help?" he added, offering his arm.

"I could kill for a coffee," Cat replied. "But it's a long way to the kitchen."

"Stay where you are," McClaren replied kindly. "I'll make you one. But I warn you, I'm terrible at making coffee. Most people won't touch it!" Cat sank down to the floor. It was a relief to get the weight off his feet. A few minutes later McClaren returned. "Drink this," he said, holding a steaming mug to Cat's lips. McClaren hadn't been joking. The coffee wasn't like anything Cat had ever tasted. Hoping it wasn't going to poison him, he gulped it down. Afterwards, McClaren carried him into the living room and settled him onto the sofa.

"Now," he said. "I wanna hear your whole story."

An hour later, Cat leant back against the sofa cushions and closed his eyes, feeling pretty rough.

"You sure you've told me everything?" McClaren asked. Cat nodded. "Then I just might be your guardian angel."

"What are you talking about?" Cat asked, coming out of his torpor.

"The results have come back from the lab," McClaren informed him. "It practically guarantees you'll lose your trainer's licence."

"Great! So what can you do for me?" Cat replied mutinously.

"Your fingerprints were plastered all over the place," McClaren continued. "Besides, there's other incriminating evidence: the horses' blood tests. You're better off co-operating."

"So! What d'you want from me?" Cat asked impatiently. It sounded hopeless. When was McClaren going to get to the point?

"The charges against you are serious, Mr Ciardi. Class One drugs. You could even end up serving time, not to mention the huge fine they're going to slap on you."

"Jail?" Cat exclaimed, feeling terrified. "No one said anything about that!"

"Maybe we can help each other," McClaren suggested. "Are you certain you can't identify any of the owners of the Lucky Seven Syndicate?"

"I only ever talked to Ritchie," Cat replied somewhat evasively, keeping his suspicions about the André guy to himself. He had no proof. Maybe the guy just liked watching the races on TV.

"It's definitely Ritchie's handwriting on the instructions for the pre-race? You're sure of that?"

"Of course!"

"Because I don't want to have egg on my face," McClaren said sternly.

"I swear it is!" Cat replied.

"Okay. This is what's going to happen. I'm taking you to ER. I'm guessing those cuts will need stitches. But first I'm going to pack up your stuff, if you're sure Eddie Clearwater will take you in. You can't stay here on your own. Then sometime today, we'll have to stop off at the OPP station."

"What?" Cat exclaimed, horrified.

"Just to put together photo fits," McClaren hastened to reassure him.

"Oh! Of the Brute," Cat said, feeling relieved.

"The Brute and his two friends," McClaren confirmed. Cat realized this was probably his last chance to say anything about Anya's crime lord theory. But it was Anya's idea, not his.

"Okay," he agreed. "But can we stop off and pick up some breakfast on the way?"

"How about the gas station? Will that do?" McClaren replied. "As long as you don't try and give me the slip," he added sternly.

"Fat chance," Cat replied bitterly.

SAINTE MARIE

Later that morning, Pete had news.

"Heard from Henri," he told Anya, as she stuck her head out of the cabin. Up above, puffy white clouds were floating in a pure blue sky. "He's just dropped Fontainbleu off at the airport," Pete informed her. "Won't be back for a couple of weeks. The Shere Khan'll be ready to go by then. If you wanna hang around for a bit, it's okay by me."

"What about Cat?" Anya countered.

"What about him? You're not the greatest nurse Anya, believe me. He's gonna need some time to heal up, get back to normal."

"He's still not answering his phone," Anya reported a short while later.

"Don't chase him," Pete advised. "Give him some room."

"Okay," Anya agreed. "I'll try him again tomorrow. Where'd Fontainbleu go anyhow?"

"Took a plane to Miami," Pete replied. With André out of the way, it would be safe for her to stay on, Anya decided. Cat could wait. It looked like it would be the last time she'd get a chance to hang out with Pete for quite a while.

The story of the fire made the front page of the *Erinsville Echo* and featured a picture of Crawfish, Bud and half a dozen grinning firemen. The story was picked up by a local TV station and then by the *Toronto Times*. Overnight, Crawfish and the dog became celebrities. Under doctor's orders to take it easy for a few weeks, owing to a cracked rib, Crawfish toured local venues, showing Bud off and retelling the story of the part they'd played in the rescue of ten standardbreds. Most people had never heard of harness racing but a horse is a horse, whatever it does for a living and for animal lovers all over Ontario, it was a compelling story which held their interest long after Bud's gash had healed over. However, when Cannon's Pet Foods wanted to take Bud on to advertise a new brand of dog food, Crawfish turned it down flat. Giving Bud big ideas, like he was a film star or something, wouldn't have been good for him. Skipping his next doctor's appointment, he and Bud returned to active duty at Andy

Price's barn with a mutual sigh of relief. The only one who wasn't happy was the new guy.

He'd been let go again.

THE PARTY

It was the season of goodwill. Christmas was fast approaching. Eddie Clearwater had lost all his equipment in the barn fire and the harness racing community was rallying round. Nearly everyone bought tickets to the fundraiser, not only the drivers and trainers but people on the periphery of the business: the tack shop lady, cooks from the track canteen, the carrot man, Harvey the travelling hot food vendor, the hay man, the guy who floated the horses' teeth, the family who mended blankets and harnesses, the herbalist, the physio, even the girl who made cakes and pies and brought them round on Wednesdays.

Eddie was popular; he paid his bills on time. For the grooms, the party was a fine excuse for a shindig. For everyone else, it was a rare opportunity to socialize outside of work, especially since Val and Joey Harris had thrown open the doors of their comfortable farm house for the event. Campbell McClaren had arranged a discreet security presence, in case the party got out of hand. He and Billie arrived just in time to witness a grateful Eddie Clearwater make a dignified speech of thanks, before taking himself off home to bed. After that, Joey Harris ramped up the volume on the stereo and the real fun began. Crawfish Brown was having the time of his life. Horsemen were lining up to buy him a drink from the cash bar and hear about the barn fire, first hand.

"You'd think he'd be tired of telling that story by now!" Joey Harris remarked.

"Never! He'll be telling it to his grandchildren," Campbell laughed.

"Fat chance of that, poor sod," Joey replied. "He doesn't even have a girlfriend, so far as I know. He wasn't best pleased when I told him he couldn't bring his dog to the party. They're joined at the hip, those two." Wondering where Billie had got to, Campbell made his excuses and set off to find her, glancing at the bevy of rapt grooms swigging beer and hanging on Crawfish's every word. He was about to wander on past them when he heard something far more interesting than the story of the fire.

"Hell yes! It was him, I swear it!" Crawfish was insisting loudly. "Theo Vettore! Large as life. Leastways his ghost! Gave me the heebie jeebies!" Campbell waited to hear more. The crowd stopped joking around and fell silent. "Looked right through me he did!" Crawfish continued. "Didn't give no sign he knew me." He paused dramatically. "'Cause he was dead see." Everyone starting talking at once. There was a chorus of questions. But, having said his piece, Crawfish seemed to be regretting his loose tongue. His eyes darted this way and that, evidently searching for a way out. Campbell pushed his way through the pack of sozzled grooms.

"Don't feel so good…I wanna go home," Crawfish declared, lurching to his feet and spilling his beer all over Val's rug.

"Not in this state you're not," Campbell said firmly, taking Crawfish's arm, envisaging him flying through the air on his motorbike after crashing into a tree. "You don't want to go making Bud into an orphan," he added. That appeared to do the trick.

"Where'd you spring from anyhow?" Crawfish asked suspiciously, swaying on his feet.

"C'mon," Campbell replied, grabbing him by the collar and hauling him through the crowd. Unfortunately, on the way, Crawfish lurched into a table, sending a lamp crashing to the floor.

"I'll deal with it," Joey said in a resigned tone. "Better get him into the kitchen and sober him up. Val's put some coffee on."

After two black coffees, Crawfish wiped his mouth on his sleeve and declared he was fit to travel.

"Not until I've asked you a few questions."

"You ain't the police," Crawfish replied grumpily.

"No," Campbell agreed. "But I've paid you a ton of money! So far I haven't got a lot to show for it."

"It ain't easy with a dog under me feet all the time," Crawfish replied. I ain't fuckin' invisible no more, see." Campbell did see.

"Tell me about Vettore," he suggested. "It'd be a way for you to even the score."

"I don't know nothin'," Crawfish declared brazenly, his standard response when pushed too far. Campbell decided to let it go for now. "Got any grub?" Crawfish inquired. "I ain't had a bit to eat since breakfast."

"How about some toast?" Val offered, casting her eyes up to the ceiling, a gesture which went right over Crawfish's head.

"Capital!" he replied enthusiastically. Then his face fell. "My prize!" he wailed, jumping to his feet and nearly keeling over. "Someone's took it."

"Sit tight," Campbell said, pushing him back down. "I'll find it. Don't worry." Someone had dimmed the lights in the living room but eventually he found what he was looking for: a red dog collar with Bud's name on it and a cheap, silver plated cup which he had no doubt Crawfish would treasure for the rest of his days. On his way back, he spotted one or two couples entwined who clearly did not belong to each other, judging from the glowering expressions on the faces of the onlookers. It was only a matter of time before a fight broke out. He rounded up the two security guards and alerted them to the problem. On his way back he ran into Billie.

"You're not gonna believe what I just heard," he told her as they entered the safe haven of the kitchen where Val was calmly buttering toast. The domestic scene was quite a contrast to the den of iniquity he'd just left.

"Try me," Billie suggested.

"Vettore may be alive," he replied.

"According to who?" she asked coolly.

"Crawfish Brown."

"Crawfish!" she exclaimed. "You expect me to believe *him*?"

"Yes," Campbell replied quietly. After all, he reasoned, Crawfish hadn't steered him wrong yet.

"Wow," Billie breathed. "But where...how?"

"That's what I'm hoping to find out," Campbell said, nodding at Crawfish, who was making maddeningly slow work of his food. "But I'm not going to get any sense out of him tonight."

"Wonder why Catalino never showed up," Val remarked.

"Looks like he took my advice and stayed away," Campbell replied, feeling relieved. "And a good thing too! The last thing that kid needs now is trouble."

"Heard the latest?" Val asked. "The Lucky Seven are getting out of the business. All their horses are up for sale. What'll happen to Cat now?"

"He'll lose his licence for sure," Campbell replied.

"He's already lost his job and his place to live. Isn't that punishment enough?" Val asked plaintively.

"Hey," Campbell said. "Whose side are you on?"

"There are worse trainers than Catalino," Val replied. "Tony Hall for one...look what happened to Princess...and no one's taken *his* licence away."

"What did happen to Princess?" Billie asked nervously.

"We haven't had the report back yet," Campbell replied carefully, not wanting to upset Billie unnecessarily.

"What report?" Billie frowned.

"They're doing an autopsy on her," Campbell explained, glancing at Val.

"She died!" Billie exclaimed, looking grief stricken.

"I can't carry the weight of the world on my shoulders," Val said defensively, "Joey went into the breeding business with his eyes wide open. He has to accept the consequences."

"Which are?" Billie prompted.

"Seeing horses we've raised from babies, and who've learned to trust people, get into the wrong hands," Val replied. A moment later Joey appeared, carrying a small child clad in a pink sleepsuit and much to Campbell's relief, the conversation was over. Judging that Crawfish had sobered up enough to drive, Campbell said his goodbyes and he and Billie left. The loud party music was soon drowned out by the roar of Crawfish's motorbike. Billie had insisted on doing up the buckle on Crawfish's helmet.

"I pray he's able to get it undone again," she said fervently as they followed Crawfish down the laneway. "He'll be sleeping in it tonight otherwise." To his surprise, she broke up laughing. The idea of Crawfish rolling around in bed with his helmet on didn't strike Campbell as particularly funny. Once Billie had started, she couldn't seem to stop. The laughter turned to helpless giggles and then to tears. Hearing her ex boyfriend could be alive and kicking, when she had assumed he was dead, had come as a shock, Campbell imagined. He pulled over onto the side of the road and tried to comfort her, stroking her hair. After a while she calmed down. But he'd got it all wrong. She wasn't remotely interested in Vettore.

"Don't you dare go looking for him!" she said, clearly on the warpath now. "He'd never do that for you."

"Why d'you think I'm so anxious to find him?"

"Because you feel responsible, I assume," she replied.

"It's not just that," Campbell hastened to assure her.

"Then what? I'm freezing by the way." He started up the engine, but cranked open the window. No sense in being asphyxiated. He knew it wasn't supposed to happen in modern cars, but why take the chance?

"It's because I know Vettore is the only one who'll have the guts to tell me what he knows."

"About the Scorpion?" Billie asked.

"That's right," Campbell replied.

"So...put out a nationwide search for him."

"Easier said than done. But yes," Campbell replied. "It's a good idea. However, right now I'm much more worried about Catalino."

"Because…"

"One of his attackers sounded a lot like the man who was hanging around the airport in Sainte Marie the day I left. If it comes out that Cat went to the Provincial Police, it could be dangerous for him, even here in Ontario."

"He's lucky he didn't end up like Vettore," Billie remarked soberly.

"He has Anya to thank for that," Campbell replied, pulling out onto the silent, icy road.

"D'you ever feel Anya knows a lot more than she lets on?" Billie asked.

"About what?"

"About everything!" she replied. As they drove along in silence, snowflakes began drifting down onto the windscreen. "You're sure he'll get home okay?" she added nervously.

"Don't you worry about Crawfish," he replied, patting her knee reassuringly. "He knows how to take care of himself!"

Riding out in the open air had cleared Crawfish's head. He didn't own a watch, but he guessed it was pretty late. Bud wouldn't be happy, left all on his ownsome. His boy wasn't used to it. Long before he reached the barn, Crawfish realized something was up. He'd only left one small lamp burning, yet the hayloft apartment was a blaze of lights. He abandoned his precious motorbike and slunk towards the barn, his heart hammering in his chest. Shitface and Pervert must have caught up with him at last! It was small wonder. He and Bud were famous now. The terror he'd felt at their hands, hanging upside down from the flyover, staring down at the highway a million feet below, was still vivid. The thought of Bud all alone with those monsters scared the shit out of him.

Inside the barn, the familiar sound of the horses quietly munching hay steadied him. He reached for the key to Andy's tack room which was in its usual place just above the door. Then he crept in and took down the heavy flashlight from its hook on the wall. He had a weapon now and he intended to use it. He wasn't going down without a fight, like last time. He was ready! He climbed the stairs, his ears out on stalks. Shitface and Pervert were keeping quiet, the crafty buggers. When he finally reached the top, he stopped for a moment. Bracing himself, he took a deep breath. Then he kicked open the door of the apartment and took a running jump, brandishing Andy's flashlight and yelling at the top of his lungs. Immediately, harsh barking broke out mixed with high pitched screams that sent chills down his spine. A slip of a girl was slumped on the brown couch his dad had given him, sobbing her heart out. Bud was growling at him, baring his teeth. Then the dog padded over and stood guard over the girl, barking defiantly. Imagine! Crawfish thought, shaking his head in disbelief. His own dog turning against him!

"Bud!" he cried, throwing aside the flashlight and sinking to his knees. "It's me, Crawfish!" To his relief, Bud wagged his tail. But the dog quickly turned back to the girl and took to licking her hands, which were covering her face. Deciding she wasn't much of a threat, Crawfish checked out every last corner of the hayloft apartment. He felt pretty foolish when he discovered it was empty. When he returned, the girl was dabbing at her eyes with a tissue. She had a bruise on her cheek which was turning yellow, matching her spiky blond hair, and black bruises around her throat. Her hands seemed okay, but goodness knows what else was wrong with her, hiding under her jeans and long sleeved shirt. It made him shudder to think about it. Whoever had done this to her could come back for him!

"What's going on?" he hollered. Seeing her flinch, he added hastily. "I ain't gonna hurt you. See I thought it was burglars before...I was worried about my dog!"

"He's a good boy," she replied shakily, pulling Bud's ears. That voice! He'd heard it so many times in his dreams. But it couldn't be her, could it? Bud jumped up on the couch and sat himself down next to her, which was strictly not allowed. However, Crawfish felt it wouldn't be right to enforce the rules. Not tonight.

"What's going on?" he repeated.

"You don't remember me," the girl replied forlornly. Oh but he did! He just hadn't wanted to be right, for her sake.

"I couldn't never forget you, Tammy," he said, his voice rough with emotion. This brought on a fresh bout of crying, while Bud whined and thrashed his tail. "Down boy," Crawfish said quietly. The dog obeyed, but he rested his head on the girl's knee and gazed up at her, a picture of devotion. Crawfish couldn't help but feel just a tiny bit jealous.

"Remember that night?" she asked, speaking so softly he had to strain to hear her. "That time I ran away."

"Remember?" he exclaimed. "O' course I remember!"

"You helped me once," she pleaded. "I'd nowhere else to go..." He couldn't bear to see her like this, brought down so low.

"Who did this to you?" he demanded, his voice breaking, as a boiling rage rose in his throat and threatened to choke him.

"Nobody," she replied quickly. "I did it to myself." He didn't believe her.

"Swear to me you won't go back to the son of a bitch. Because if that's wot you're thinkin' you may as well leave right now and don't go makin' excuses for 'im neither!" he cried. The girl looked at him blankly. "I'll make something to eat," he said, his anger subsiding. "Then you can talk about it. But only if you want to. There ain't gonna be no interra-whatcha-macall-it."

He made oatmeal and two mugs of strong tea with plenty of sugar. Between spoonfuls of porridge, she told him the story: how she and the Candy Floss Kid had hooked up with a circus out west. "Did he do this to you?" Crawfish asked doggedly. Her eyes went all dreamy for a bit, then they hardened.

"Him? No, it wasn't him. But what's the difference? He wasn't interested in me...just like my father, really. Dad always whopped me when he was drunk...not where it showed of course." Feeling sick to his stomach, Crawfish resolved there and then to give up the drink. When he'd pictured them together, it hadn't been like this. She'd been like a bright star, up in the sky. Now she had fallen to earth. But he discovered that he loved her even more, seeing she was made of real flesh and blood. His heart swelled with pride that of all people he could have gone to for help, she'd chosen him.

"Tell me what happened," he begged. "I ain't gonna judge you."

"I fell," she said simply. "Off the high wire. They'd strung the safety too tight...I bounced...over and over like a freakin' trampoline. It hurt like hell." She buried her face in her hands. "In front of all them people...I must a passed out. When I woke up, I was in the hospital. I couldn't go back. I never felt scared, ever, before. But now...I lost my nerve, see. Lost what bit of money I had, too. I been travellin' for days. I hitched rides from them big trucks that go up and down the highway..." She lay back against the couch, her face as pale as a ghost except for the big bruise on her cheek. "I seen you on TV. That's how come I knew where you was."

She closed her eyes. He covered her with one of the horse blankets he'd pilfered from Andy. Then, very quietly so as not to wake her, he went to his own bed. Halfway through the night, she joined him, huddling closer for warmth. It was pretty nigh impossible for him to get any sleep, with the girl of his dreams lying beside him. He was thankful tomorrow was Sunday.

He wasn't ready to go back to the real world. Not yet.

A LUNCH APPOINTMENT

It was one of those glorious, still January days, with the temperature hovering at minus ten degrees, the sky a cloudless blue and the snow sparkling in the sunlight: a day when it was good to be alive. Al McTavish thanked God and his surgeon that he was still around to enjoy it. He had been intrigued when Phil had called and suggested they meet up for lunch. He hadn't seen Phil in months. There had to be an agenda. There always was. As he pushed open the door of the Old Mill Restaurant, he was surprised to see that Phil was already there. That was a first!

"Hey! Lookin' good, pal," Phil said cheerfully, grasping Al's hand and pumping it up and down. Sadly, Al could not return the compliment. Somewhere along the way, Phil's perma tan had faded. There were lines on his face that Al didn't remember noticing before and a lot more grey in his hair, too.

"You okay, Phil?" he enquired, with a puzzled frown.

"Had to give up the sun lamp," Phil revealed as they took their seats at the table, beside a roaring fire. "Better safe than sorry, eh?" he added with a wink, his blue eyes as bright as ever.

"Lot of bad publicity in the press about them," Al agreed.

"I got us the best table and a magnum on ice," Phil replied, smiling at him. "I thought we deserved a small celebration."

"Great," Al replied. "What are we celebrating?" he asked wistfully. Harmony Stampede had raced abysmally in his last start.

"You've pulled off quite a coup, my old friend, catching the top trainer at Iroquois Downs with illegal drugs...I have to hand it you!"

"Oh, that," Al replied modestly. "More luck than anything, I'm afraid."

"Really? That wasn't what I heard!"

"We did have a little help!" Al admitted.

"Sounds like your guys did a thoroughly professional job," Phil replied.

"We found quite a haul," Al conceded, opening up a notebook and handing it to Phil. "Take a look yourself!" Phil ran his eyes down the page.

"I've heard of that last one," he said, his voice dropping an octave. "Here! Take it," he added, sliding the notebook back across the table.

"Erythropoietin, you mean?" Al asked. "It's a cancer treatment, apparently. But it can kill a horse."

"Imagine that," Phil said.

"Of course, with a scandal like this, the handle's gone down," Al remarked sorrowfully.

"Every racetrack's nightmare," Phil replied sympathetically.

"Exactly the kind of publicity we don't want! The papers had a field day. It was even on TV."

"What happens next?" Phil inquired, pouring the champagne.

"Catalino Ciardi's up in front of the judges tomorrow. I have a feeling after that, the Lucky Seven Syndicate will need to find themselves another trainer," Al said.

"So you're not penalizing the owner?"

"We don't generally do that," Al replied stiffly. Phil had once been a trusted friend. However, things were different now and it wouldn't do to be indiscreet.

"Who are these people anyway?" Phil asked.

"I wish I knew," Al replied. "But I don't."

"Nothing at all?" Phil asked, sounding surprised.

"No idea. Could be almost anyone," Al confessed, feeling embarrassed by his lack of knowledge.

"Truly?" Phil frowned.

"As things stand at present, there's no legal obligation for a syndicate to reveal the names of the individual owners," Al revealed unhappily.

"That's astonishing!" Phil replied.

"I think...I assume...in the light of the present scandal that CPTA will have to change the rules," Al said. "In future, syndicates will have to reveal the identity of the individual owners. Otherwise we'd be condoning hidden ownership...," he trailed off.

"Let's order," Phil suggested, glancing at the waiter who was hovering nearby. "I hope the soup's good and hot! I'm freezing my toes off here. The chicken's pretty good, I seem to remember...What a day," he sighed after the waiter left.

"Isn't it just?" Al responded enthusiastically. "Glorious!"

"You think?" Phil asked, looking at him askance. "Feels like the arctic to me. Must be getting old!"

"You grew up in Vancouver," Al said. "You got spoiled."

"Vancouver?" Phil frowned. Then he chuckled. "You should try living there...rains all the time. Worse than here, I'd say."

The soup arrived.

"No," Phil continued. "I'm seriously thinking of getting out of the cold once and for all. I'm flying down to Florida next week to take a look around."

"You're deserting us?" Al asked.

"Somewhere quiet, on the Gulf Coast," Phil continued. "South of Orlando. Tarpon Springs is beautiful, I'm told. I could afford a pretty nice place down there."

"Of course you could," Al replied warmly.

"You and Sofia would be welcome to come and stay of course," Phil said unconvincingly. Aware of how much Sofia disliked Phil, Al wracked his brains for a suitable response.

"We'd miss you," he said finally.

"Nonsense!" Phil replied briskly. "But that wasn't the reason I wanted to meet up with you today. I've had an idea for the backstretch at Iroquois Downs and I think you're gonna love it!"

"Go ahead," Al said, feeling hopeful. Ever since its closure, the empty barn and unused space had been on his conscience.

"Just last week, I heard that Theme Parks Canada were looking for a site for a new animal park with a Wild West theme in Ontario, somewhere within easy reach of Toronto. Iroquois Downs would be an ideal location! No one could object because there are animals there already!"

So that was why Phil had wanted them to meet, Al thought. "Great idea! It could really work!" he replied enthusiastically.

"Let's hope so. You're gonna need it," Phil confided, leaning in conspiratorially. "You may not have the income from the casino for too much longer."

"What?" Al gasped.

"'Fraid so. I've been hearing a lot of talk from my pals at City Hall about pulling the Slots out from under the racetrack." So this was the real reason he'd invited him to lunch, Al realized.

"It would a disaster for us financially," he stated.

"It would," Phil agreed.

"Could they really do it? Pull the rug out from under us? Just like that?!"

"There's a rumour going around that the politicians want to disassociate themselves from Iroquois Downs, if you get my drift," Phil said quietly. "In the circumstances, especially in the light of the present drug scandal, I can't really blame them."

At that moment in time, Al wished he had never heard of Iroquois Downs.

"Maybe it's just an excuse…" Phil continued. "City Hall getting greedy, who knows? There's an idea on the table to allow video terminals in bingo halls…same thing really, but it doesn't sound like gambling and City Hall would get a much bigger slice of the pie. Maybe that's what it's really all about. Just wanted to give you the heads up."

"To tell you the truth," Al said, "if the track didn't need the revenue so badly, I'd be happy to be rid of them. I worry about the addicts and there's been a lot of bad publicity…in some ways it would be a relief."

The chicken arrived. Phil topped up their glasses with champagne. For several minutes, silence reigned.

"We've been on a merry chase all these years, haven't we?" Phil said fondly. "It's kept us both on our toes, especially Iroquois Downs. It'd be a shame if it had to close."

"You've been itching for an excuse to get your hands on that land for years," Al retorted. He hadn't intended to sound so bitter but he'd had a shock. A big one.

"Well, let's not throw the baby out with bathwater," Phil replied enigmatically. "But things are changing. There are plans in the works for a major expansion to the west of the town…of course zoning will have to be altered. If so, land prices in the area will sky rocket. Be a pretty good investment, I'd say."

Why was he telling him all this? Al wondered. "You are coming back aren't you?" he asked.

Phil snapped his fingers at the waiter. "We'll have a couple of black coffees," he said. "Too bad Vettore disappeared," he added thoughtfully. "That guy had charisma. He was really something wasn't he?"

"He was," Al agreed. Phil hadn't answered his question. But Al knew there was no sense in pressing him. There never was. The rest of the meal passed pleasantly enough in a flurry of reminiscences buried in the mists of time, some of which Al hardly remembered anymore. But despite his claim of getting old, Phil's brain seemed as sharp as ever, his blue eyes lighting up at long forgotten incidents.

"Well I've gotta get going," he said at length. "I gotta say, Al, I'm proud of you, nailing Catalino Ciardi! How'd you do it eh? You can tell me!" he added pushing back his chair and getting to his feet.

"Oh, it was Jay Winterflood," Al replied, looking up at him. A spasm of pain appeared on Phil's face for a fleeting instant. Just as quickly it was gone. "What's wrong?" Al frowned.

"Nothing! Old ski injury," Phil replied dismissively, rubbing his knee. "You were saying?"

"Yes, it was the Lucky Seven's own vet who blew the whistle," Al repeated. "Dr. Winterflood."

"Good for him!" Phil said heartily, reaching over and shaking Al's hand. "He stood up for what he believed in! What do you believe in, Al McTavish?"

"I believe in you," Al replied simply. Despite what had happened between them recently, he was telling the truth.

"Don't get sentimental on me, pal," Phil said, slapping him on the back. "I'll see you around."

"Have a good trip," Al replied forlornly. Phil looked back and saluted him. That was a first, too.

Phil Harman glanced at his watch. Goodbyes were never easy. He doubted he would see Al again in this world or the next. Theirs had been an unequal friendship. He had tried to look out for Al in the early days. Lately that hadn't been possible. He had an appointment at 4 p.m at Erinsville General. It would be tight, but he had just enough time to check out the Lucky Seven Syndicate's farm. He had often passed by it on his way to Indian Falls and wondered what it was like. He couldn't resist taking a look around today. He was unlikely to have another chance.

Ten minutes later, he was driving down the farm's laneway. It was bordered on both sides by neat paddocks which were blanketed in snow. He pulled up beside the training track, and cast a professional eye over the property. The land was as flat as a pancake and there was easy access from the road, which would make real estate development a breeze. However, from an aesthetic perspective the farm was not attractive. There were few trees gracing the fields and nothing to break the wind. Nevertheless, the place had real potential. Well heeled families who loved the great outdoors would be lured by its proximity to Erinsville. Out of habit, his mind clicked into gear. The entire concept, luxury homes, country cottages, hiking and skiing trails, sprang to life, appearing on the bleak landscape in his imagination at the blink of an eye.

There was a tap on the car window. Phil jumped. A man with dark, unkempt hair and shadows under his brown eyes was standing there. Cautiously, Phil rolled down his window.

"I noticed your brights were on," the man said. The car heater was blowing out cold air, Phil realized. When he tried to start up the engine, nothing happened. "Are you okay? You look a little lost," the man added.

"Battery's dead," Phil said ruefully. "I'm Phil Harman," he added extending a gloved hand.

"Jay Winterflood," the man replied earnestly, returning the handshake. He was tall. And there was something very familiar about his face, though for the moment, Phil couldn't quite place it. Then he knew. The Cree were a tough breed. The man's hands and head were bare. Evidently, Jay did not feel the cold. Yet he barely recognized him from his picture in the *Erinsville Echo*. Back then, he had looked relaxed and prosperous. Not now. "Harman! I know that name!" Jay suddenly exclaimed. "You're that friend of Al McTavish's...the one he's always talking about...keeps on saying what a great guy you are."

It meant the world to Phil to hear that.

"Al and I go back a long way," he smiled.

"It's too bad I don't have my truck with me today," Jay said apologetically. "I'd have given you a boost. But there's bound to be some jumper cables around here somewhere."

"How about the barn?" Phil suggested.

"Good thinking," Jay replied, walking over and rolling open the doors. The barn was like a city but it was full of racehorses, not people. Seeing them all close up like this overwhelmed him for a moment.

"Wonderful creatures," he murmured.

"I prefer them to humans myself," Jay declared, heading off down the aisleway. Phil followed, coming to a stop beside a horse with a startling white star on his forehead and a slim athletic body. But it was the burning eyes that captivated him. "Nothing here," Jay pronounced, returning a few minutes later. "That's Harmony Light," he added. "Fastest horse in the barn...but also the most fragile." Despite his heavy coat, Phil shivered. "You'd better come to my office," Jay offered. "It's the warmest spot in the place. I can call AA towing from there."

He led the way to the veterinary clinic. The office was tiny. X-rays occupied the whole of one wall. But as promised, it was warm.

"Take a seat," Jay suggested. Phil perched himself on a chair while Jay made the call. "So," Jay inquired. "Tell me, Mr. Harman, what were you doing here today?"

"I'm a property developer, and please call me Phil." Jay looked alarmed.

"Is that why you've come? Are they selling up? Already?" he asked.

"Not at this stage," Phil replied reassuringly, ducking the question.

"So, it's not definite, right?" Jay asked with the air of a man clutching at straws. Like many a whistle blower, he was paying the price for truth telling. That much was clear.

"No," Phil confirmed. A haunted expression appeared on Jay's face.

"How much do you know about all this Mr. Harman…Phil? If you're a friend of Al's, he must've told you something."

"He did," Phil replied in what he hoped was an encouraging tone. It dawned on him that the troubled soul before him was agonizing over whether to unburden himself to someone he'd only just met. It didn't make much sense. But perhaps it did. Perhaps it was the most natural thing in the world. He thought he knew what was coming next. But he was in for a surprise.

"Come and look at this," Jay said suddenly, ushering him into the next room: a vast gleaming space. "State of the art animal hospital," he declared, throwing his arms wide. "The owner's spent hundreds of thousands of dollars on the latest equipment: digital X-ray, ultrasound, shock wave therapy, infra-red, scopes with cameras the size of your little fingernail, blood machines… it's all here!"

"Impressive," Phil remarked, wondering where all this was leading.

"Yes! I can diagnose and treat almost anything that's wrong with a race-horse. What an opportunity!"

"It is indeed," Phil agreed.

"But there's a problem," Jay said. "Actually two," he confessed.

"Go on," Phil urged.

"You're sure you're interested in this?" Jay asked uncertainly.

"Please," Phil replied, nodding encouragingly, wanting to know more, despite his intention of keeping his distance.

"A racehorse's system is a delicately balanced mechanism, you see," Jay explained. "Just like the engine of a racing car, really. Give it the wrong fuel and…" He paused.

"It blows up?" Phil suggested.

"Exactly! That's what happened to Harmony Light a couple of weeks ago. I'm not sure whether he'll ever make a full recovery, but at least he's alive." Phil couldn't think of a suitable reply. "These young trainers don't have any idea what they're doing," Jay continued. "They're playing with fire. The problem is, it's the horses that get burned. Cat Ciardi got caught, but that's just the tip of the iceberg. And there's another problem," Jay added, his face plunged in gloom.

"There is?" Phil asked uncertainly.

"I can only advise," Jay replied unhappily. "I can't compel a trainer to give a horse time."

"Time?" Phil frowned. "Time for what?"

"To heal!" Jay exclaimed, a fanatical gleam in his eyes. "Time is the great healer!"

"You honestly believe that?"

"I do!" Jay replied fervently.

"There are some things surely that even time cannot heal," Phil countered gravely. "The wrongs done to your people spring to mind."

"How'd you know I'm Cree?" Jay demanded.

"It's written all over your face," Phil replied with a smile. "D'you have brothers and sisters? Parents still alive?"

"I never knew my father. My mother…"

"Yes," Phil said eagerly.

"She died…" Jay replied. Regret filled the tiny room, bouncing off the X-rays…creeping into the walls.

"I'm sorry," Phil said. "That's too bad." That didn't even come close to expressing how he really felt. For a moment he was so overcome by emotion, he could hardly breathe.

"I actually liked Cat," Jay confided. "He's a good kid but I had to put the horses first."

"Of course," Phil replied, thankful they were off the subject of death.

"I could lose everything, you see…probably will. I don't expect you to understand. I could just quit, I suppose…it wouldn't be the end of the world."

"Don't do it," Phil replied decisively. "The racehorse community needs people like you!" Before Jay could respond, there a loud knock on the door.

"AA Motors!" a man, red cheeked from the cold, announced cheerily. Phil was almost relieved. The conversation was getting too intense for his liking.

"Thanks for your help," Phil said, taking off his gloves and shaking Jay's hand warmly. "It's been interesting talking to you, Dr. Winterflood."

"Please call me Jay," the vet said. "Actually it's Blue Jay, but that's a little over the top for most Canadians." A wintry smile lit up his gaunt features for an instant.

"Well Jay," Phil replied. "I'll leave you with this thought, something I learned along the way: there is a great deal more to life than money!"

"Well, you can't eat it!" Jay agreed. Phil laughed. He followed the red cheeked mechanic to his waiting car. While the man was working on it, an SUV came slowly past.

"All done sir," the mechanic declared shortly. "That'll be seventy-five dollars. You'll need to give her a run, okay?" Absently, Phil handed him a hundred-dollar bill...his eyes on a striking looking woman with flowing dark hair who had emerged from the SUV.

"Keep the change," he said. She was holding a child with a solemn face by the hand. It was a boy, Phil realized. Suddenly, Jay appeared beside them, smiling, transformed. The boy was jumping up and down.

"Daddy!" he cried. It was so cold that ice crystals were forming in the air. A breeze sprang up. Snowflakes came floating down from a darkening sky, swirling around the little family, encircling them in a world of their own. The woman was pregnant, Phil realized, swallowing hard, unable to explain away the lump in his throat. The boy was looking at him curiously. Phil stared back. The scene was searing itself into his brain with the ferocity of surgical steel.

"Be seeing you all," he cried. Then without further ado, he jumped into his car and sped off down the laneway onto the icy road, fighting back the tears. And he knew then that nothing would ever be the same for him.

How could it be?

SAINTE MARIE

Anya was sunbathing on the deck of the Sea Princess when Pete arrived unexpectedly.

"Got something for you," he announced.

"What is it?" she asked, reluctant to move. She was much too comfortable.

"You'll really want to see this," Pete added, holding up a dusty, battered looking phone. "The gardener found it this morning. There are a whole lot of messages on it. Mostly from you."

"That's private!" Anya cried, jumping up.

"I'm guessing you'll want to go back to Canada now," Pete said. "There's nothing to keep you here anymore."

THE HEARING

The morning of the hearing, Cat pulled on a pair of work boots. The cuts on his hands and feet had healed cleanly. At least he would look presentable when he was up in front of the judges later that day, he thought. But it was depressing after winning so many races for the Lucky Seven Stable, to be back at the bottom of the heap, shacking up with old Uncle Eddie with only one horse to train: Harmony Gold. The way things were heading, he wouldn't even be allowed to train her for much longer. On the upside, Anya had finally got in touch. She'd even found his lost phone. She was flying in from Sainte Marie today. They'd agreed to meet up at the Cherokee Inn, right after the hearing, which was at 5:30 p.m. Apparently, Ritchie, as the Lucky Seven Syndicate's agent, had been asked to attend the hearing as well. Cat didn't expect Ritchie to show. He hadn't seen or heard anything from him since the island. Did his brother know or care if he was alive or dead? Campbell's advice to keep his distance from Ritchie had been easy to take.

To Cat's surprise, that afternoon he got a text from Ritchie, suggesting that they meet up at the Cherokee Inn at 4:30 p.m. Not knowing what to expect, Cat met his brother in the bar. One hour to go before Armageddon, he thought nervously, sitting down at the table. Ritchie's hair was slicked back and he smelled of laundry soap, a picture of the all American boy. Yet the mutinous expression in his eyes reminded Cat of the way he had looked years before, when he'd been forcibly cleaned up and sent off to school which he had clearly despised.

"I can't believe you showed up," Cat said.

"I didn't have much choice," Ritchie muttered.

"What the fuck were you playing at, on the island?" Cat retorted. He would have said more but he remembered Campbell's advice. He needed to stay cool.

"Let's not talk about it, okay? I'm in as much trouble as you, bro'," Ritchie replied. Cat let it go. Ritchie was as slippery as an eel. He'd never get the truth out of him, anyhow. "Listen, we'll get through this okay if we pull together," Ritchie stated confidently, his eyes pitch black like the gateway to hell. "Gonna need to replace you, little brother, after this," he added. Cat didn't trust himself to speak, he was so angry. "Come on!" Ritchie cajoled. "Give me some ideas, bro'." So he hadn't heard the rumors about the Lucky

Seven selling up, Cat realized. Maybe it was just a rumor or maybe Ritchie was out of the loop. Meanwhile he was just using him, like always.

"No decent trainer is gonna give up on his owners and go work for peanuts," Cat replied resentfully.

"You did!" Ritchie pointed out. "And you're forgetting the five percent."

"True," Cat acknowledged reluctantly. The horses had made so much purse money he was going to end up with over a hundred thousand bucks, even after allowing for Revenue Canada's insane taxes. He hadn't decided what to spend it on yet. It wasn't enough to totally change his life, but it was way too much to fritter away. Anya would have some cool ideas, he thought. But why even think about that? He'd be getting a massive fine. It'd probably clean him out. He realized Ritchie was still waiting for an answer. "Most trainers want to be left alone to do their thing. That wouldn't suit the Lucky Seven guys, right?" Cat said.

"Right!" Ritchie agreed lazily. The only owners he'd attract after this, Cat figured, would be the sleazy kind, out for a quick fix and a fast buck.

"It's five fifteen," he said. "We need to go." Ritchie got to his feet and smoothed his hair down. Then they were on their way to purgatory.

They were early at least, Cat thought with relief as they approached the Judges' Room. To his dismay, Judge Jewells was standing at the door, looking pointedly at his watch. Cat had been up in front of the judges before (who hadn't?) but he'd been hoping to avoid a run in with Jewells. The guy had quite a reputation. He reminded Cat of a turkey: a purple nosed, blotchy faced, gimlet eyed, dog eared old bird way past its sell by date. Stay with that, he told himself. It'll make him seem less scary.

"You're late, boys!" the Judge snapped, ushering them into a large room with a heart stopping view of Iroquois Downs Raceway. The infield was buried in snow. Winter! Cat had had enough of it already and it was only January.

"I apologize, Your Honor," Cat said nervously.

"Sit down!" Judge Jewells barked. No one spoke. After listening to the judge drumming his fingers on the boardroom table for nearly five minutes, Cat felt ready to scream. At 5:30 p.m. precisely, a tall grey haired man kitted out in a smart suit, marched in without knocking like he owned the place. Two paces behind him was the Head of Security, Campbell McClaren, carrying a clipboard. He gave no sign of knowing Cat. Cat took the hint and acted dumb. "Ready when you are, Director McTavish," Jewells said, consulting his watch again.

Wasting no time, the director announced that the hearing would have to be delayed by half an hour in order to clear up some unresolved ownership issues. That was news to Cat! Judge Jewells, looking more like a turkey than ever, scowled at the breach of his authority. Apparently undeterred, Campbell handed Ritchie a paper to fill out and sign. Then Director McTavish began questioning Ritchie about who was behind the Lucky Seven Syndicate. For once, his brother was stuck for an answer.

"You're licenced as an agent for the Lucky Seven Stable. You must know who the owners are," McTavish insisted.

"Just give us the names," Campbell said softly, his tone nevertheless conveying a veiled threat. Ritchie was squirming in his chair. If he hadn't felt so angry, Cat could have pitied him.

"This is about hidden ownership," McTavish said significantly glancing at Judge Jewells, who inclined his head. Ritchie was staring into space, like they'd given him a math problem that was way too hard for him to solve. Jewells sensed it and honed in on him, like a vulture that had scented a fresh kill.

"I can't tell you who the owners are," Ritchie said at last, looking scared.

"What about you, Mr. Ciardi?" McTavish asked. "Have you ever spoken to the owners of the Lucky Seven?"

"No sir," Cat replied, glad that he hadn't had to lie. "Your Honor," he added, fearful of Judge Jewells' gimlet like stare.

"Sir will do," the Judge said curtly. But Cat could tell he was flattered. For the first time since he'd arrived back in Canada, he felt a glimmer of hope. That hope evaporated in a heartbeat when the spotlight switched from Ritchie to him. He decided to admit to everything. It was far easier than making stuff up. Plus, in a weird way, it felt good to get it off his chest. He knew he was talking way too fast, but there was so much to explain: the packages that arrived every week, the unlabeled bottles, the reservations he'd had, the unanswered questions, the worries that had kept him up at night... it all sounded so unlikely.

"So you really didn't know what you were injecting?" Director McTavish asked, sounding skeptical, not the greatest sign.

"No sir," Cat sighed. "But I should have. Ritchie told me it was some kind of supercharged vitamin. As it didn't seem to do the horses any harm, I went along with it. Until Harmony Light collapsed."

"Collapsed?" Judge Jewells frowned.

"It's all in Dr. Winterflood's report," McTavish informed. So Winterflood had turned him in, Cat realized. It figured.

"How did you know what to give and when?" Campbell asked. It was a leading question. Ritchie shot him a warning glance.

"Oh, Ritchie took care of that," Cat replied easily. "He wrote down everything I had to give each horse every time they raced and when to give it."

Like an idiot, Ritchie exclaimed, "You've got no proof!" Realizing he'd goofed, he added lamely. "It's not true." Out of the corner of his eye, Cat saw Judge Jewells writing furiously.

"Oh, I think you'll find it is true," McTavish said calmly, taking the clipboard from Campbell and releasing several scraps of paper which Cat recognized as Ritchie's pre-race instructions. "We can call in an expert, but I think you'll have a hard time denying that the handwriting matches yours, Mr. Sanchez. Take a look, John," he added, handing them to the judge together with the form Ritchie had been foolish enough to fill in. Ritchie, Cat was interested to see, was now looking like he'd just swallowed battery acid.

"As their agent, Mr. Sanchez, I am assuming you were acting on direct instructions from the owners," Judge Jewells pronounced gravely. "Is that correct?" Ritchie looked like a deer caught in the headlights.

"I'm taking the fifth amendment," he mumbled eventually.

"You're not in the US, Mr. Sanchez," Campbell informed him. "You don't have to answer, but we will draw our own conclusions, which may not be to your advantage." Cat thought he understood. Ritchie was caught between incriminating himself or the owners. Cat knew what he'd have done in his place. McTavish cleared his throat.

"I believe we have enough evidence here to argue that the owners were involved in the illegal pre-racing of standardbred horses. I shall be appealing to the PRC to treat the Lucky Seven Syndicate and their trainer as equally culpable. In other words, any suspension of their trainer's licence in Canada, and therefore the US, will equally apply to the Lucky Seven's licence to own horses. But as Director of Iroquois Downs," he added severely. "I must inform both of you that whatever decision is made here today, no horse owned by the Lucky Seven Stable will be allowed to race at Iroquois Downs for a period of at least one year. After that time, the situation will be reviewed. Meanwhile, the syndicate's purse account at the track has been frozen."

"This meeting is adjourned," Judge Jewells said. "Mr. Ciardi, you will stay for your hearing. Everyone else is dismissed." In any conflict, Cat realized, you had to take sides. McTavish had just declared war and Cat was on the losing side. It sucked.

"Need to talk to you after," Ritchie told Cat before he left.

"I never want to see you as long as I live," Cat replied fiercely.

"It's about your dad."

"What?" Cat exclaimed, wild hope mingled with black despair overwhelming him.

"Later bro," Ritchie replied.

The hearing lasted precisely thirty minutes. Cat gulped when he heard the sentence. The judges were taking away his licence for five years. Half a decade! The time opened up like a chasm. He'd be twenty-eight by then. He'd be old! What was he going to do? He'd work in a bar. It'd be okay, he told himself, building a rosy picture of himself and Anya living somewhere warm like Miami, party town.

"Lastly," Judge Jewells said, cutting across Cat's fantasy. Here comes the fine, he realized, imagining his bank account showing only zeros. "In view of your youth and inexperience," Jewells said, "and because this is your first offence, the panel has decided that a fine of just twenty-five thousand dollars will be imposed. Make yourself scarce, Mr. Ciardi, before I change my mind. You are dismissed."

Good old Eddie was waiting for him outside Judge Jewells' office

"How's the enforcer?" Eddie enquired. "Did he try and eat you alive?"

"Gave me five years!" Cat replied miserably. "Can I stay with you while I figure out what to do?"

"So long as it's not against Jewells' rules," Eddie replied kindly. "Now that I know what really happened, I'd like to help you. It's Ritchie I'm mad at, not you. Sure wish you'd come to me sooner, sonny."

"Listen," Cat said. "I have to find Ritchie. It's about Papa."

They rode the elevator to the ground floor. Post time for the first race was an hour away, but a few diehards were already there, noses buried in race programs, snacking on beer and pizza. There was no sign of Ritchie anywhere. How'm I gonna find him? Cat wondered. In the end it was pretty easy. Predictably, Ritchie was propping up the bar. On the counter behind him were three empty shot glasses and a half full bottle of liquor. He stank of alcohol. Cat's heart sank.

"You fuckin' little shit!" Ritchie hissed, picking up the liquor bottle and advancing on him menacingly. "I'm gonna take you apart for this! All you had to do was keep your fucking mouth shut. But you couldn't do that! What were you thinkin' huh?" His face was only inches away from Cat's now. "Huh?" he repeated. Aware of Eddie watching nervously from the sidelines, Cat didn't dare say a word. "He'll destroy me! Understand?" Ritchie continued in anguished tones. "I'll have nothing! He'll take my bar…my apartment…even my car. They'll all be gone! Why couldn't you just play along, you little shit? You were gonna lose your licence anyhow! Why'd you have to drag me down with you? Fuck you!" Despite his deep tan, Ritchie's face was flushed red. His mouth twisting with rage, he turned his back on Cat, raised his right arm and brought it down hard on the bar. The sound of splintering glass, followed by the sickly sweet smell of liquor, filled the air. When he turned back to face Cat, Ritchie was brandishing a shard of glass, more lethal than any knife.

"Get security!" Cat shouted at Eddie.

"You and your precious principles," Ritchie sneered, waving his improvised weapon in Cat's face, utterly terrifying him. "Think you're so high and mighty, huh?" he snarled. "Well, let me tell you something, moron! Right from the horse's mouth! You're dead meat! The Undertakers are on their way for you right now, little brother!" Mesmerized by Ritchie's threat, Cat didn't see the kick coming. He landed howling on the bare floor, doubled up in agony, listening to Ritchie's maniacal laughter, flashing back to scenes in the room he and Ritchie had shared as kids, wondering why on earth he had ever let his brother back into his life.

Boxer lived by the maxim: Actions speak louder than words. Occasionally, that had to be accomplished by proxy. His good friends the Undertakers didn't come cheap, but they would get the job done on Catalino Ciardi. Unfortunately, they'd be shutting the barn door after the horse had bolted, but a little violence and intimidation never did any harm. The boss might disapprove, but he had flown to Miami, leaving Boxer in sole charge. If he had been given the green light to go back to the Iron Shore and administer the *coup de grace* to Ciardi, it would have saved everyone a great deal of trouble.

Boxer helped himself to a cold beer and walked out onto the deck of the beach house. Visitors admired the views over Half Moon Bay. Boxer was unmoved by its beauty. He was puzzled by the change in André

Fontainbleu recently. Was the Australian bitch to blame? The whore had certainly got her claws into him. It felt like a long time since they'd had their bit of fun with Ritchie Sanchez. For months now, André had seemed preoccupied. All he cared about was some crazy plan to sail the Shere Khan to Australia. Then that had suddenly been put on hold. Now, André had given up on the horses too. They were all going up for sale to the highest bidder. Boxer had no idea what was going on. But he'd given up trying to figure out André Fontainbleu a very long time ago.

When the pain in Cat's groin finally eased, he unwound himself and looked up. The faces gazing down at him, full of concern, belonged to two people that he had learned to trust: Uncle Eddie and Campbell McClaren. A pair of powerful arms hoisted him to his feet just in time to see Ritchie being led away by two uniformed guards. The crisis was over, for now.

"Who...who are the Undertakers?" Cat stuttered. The question had an electric effect on Campbell. "Ritchie said they're on their way here now," Cat added fearfully.

"We gotta get you out of here," Campbell said, grabbing him by the shoulders and hurrying him away. "Call the Provincial Police. Tell 'em to get over here right away," he told Eddie. "And don't go home tonight. Stay somewhere safe, like the Cherokee Inn, okay? I'll take care of the boy!" Then he marched Cat off down a passage and opened a door marked *Security*. "This ought to fit you," he said, ripping a uniform off its hanger. "But for heaven's sakes, be quick about it! Gimme your things, including your wallet," Campbell added.

"Hey," Cat protested.

"They'll be safe enough in here," Campbell replied calmly, stuffing everything into a locker. "Anyone asks, you're Pete Burgess, okay? Now, how fast can you run?"

"Fast enough!" Cat replied confidently. But as they sprinted through a maze of corridors, he was barely able to keep up. Finally, Campbell pushed open a fire door and they were out!

"Staff parking lot," Campbell announced. He pointed his keys at a blue saloon and jumped in. Cat followed suit. As they slipped out of a side exit, Cat spotted a black hearse speeding in through the main gates. They had had a narrow escape. "They're not idiots, those guys," Campbell warned. "And they carry a lot of firepower, these days. Pull your cap down and buckle up!"

When they hit the highway, Campbell put his foot to the floor, totally dissing the speed limit. Thankfully, traffic was light. But then they came up against a wall of Beco Bananas trucks, riding three abreast. Campbell hit the horn, but the trucks kept right on going. "Hang on tight!" Campbell exclaimed, swinging right, onto the hard shoulder. The truckers immediately speeded up, making overtaking on the inside a slow business. The exit sign for Erinsville appeared, hanging from a bridge spanning the highway. Campbell braked hard and swerved back onto the main road. When Cat looked back, he got an eyeful of a yawning chasm where the hard shoulder should have been. They could have been killed! Cat realized. "Close," Campbell muttered under his breath, as they left the highway. Had those truckers been playing games? Cat wondered. The alternative was something he didn't even want to think about! Before he could decide, the phone on the dashboard vibrated. "Answer it, please," Campbell said, executing a sharp right turn onto Erinsville's main street. Cat picked up.

"Campbell, it's me," a woman's voice announced breathlessly. "Dad called. He said you just disappeared. Where on earth are you?" Cat did his best to explain. "Okay, tell him it's Billie and to come to Laurel Drive," she replied, sounding a lot more businesslike. He passed on the message.

"Change of plan," Campbell said, apparently unfazed. "I was going to take you to my apartment but maybe it's for the best."

A few minutes later, they drew up at 210, Laurel Drive. The house was lit up like a Christmas tree. A woman with long wavy hair burst out of the front door and came running down the icy path to meet them.

"Billie! Take Cat down to the basement," Campbell said tersely. "And please, open the garage. This car needs to disappear. Now!"

"What's going on?" Billie frowned, looking thoroughly alarmed.

"The local heavies are after Cat and it's only a matter of time before they put two and two together and come here."

"Kill the lights," Cat muttered.

"The kid's right," Campbell agreed. "Kill the lights!"

"I hope Eddie's okay," Cat said, worried about the old guy.

"It's you they're after, not him," Campbell replied firmly.

Cat wasn't in the least bit reassured.

Snow was falling as Anya's plane touched down at Toronto Airport. By the time she set off in her rental car, it was dark. The Cherokee Inn was a homely place with comfortable chairs, a roaring fire and a low beamed ceiling. Its only concession to the modern world was a TV screen, set to the racing channel.

There was, as yet, no sign of Cat.

THE UNDERTAKERS

Eddie Clearwater collared the first security guard he came across. The man seemed ignorant of the Undertakers' fearsome reputation. Evidently, he had led a very sheltered life. However, he agreed to call the Provincial Police, albeit reluctantly. Counting on McClaren to keep Cat out of trouble, Eddie hurried off to the Race Barn. He had a horse in the first race. Her British owners, Kip and Caroline Davies, were staying up until 12:30 a.m. UK time, to watch their trotter go and Eddie did not intend to disappoint them. He had left Harmony Fire tethered to the cross ties, smothered in coolers. She'd probably worked herself up into a frenzy by now, Eddie decided with gloomy resignation. She was too high strung to make a top trotter. He'd have never picked her out himself. Being a chestnut, and a mare to boot, Harmony Fire had always been a little crazy. Two years on, she was still crazy, despite his best efforts to calm her down. However, tonight he had put a Pelling pacifier on her and plugged her ears. She would see little and hear nothing, unless a bomb exploded in her face!

Mercifully, when the race started, she behaved herself. He managed to find her a nice spot along the rail and he stayed put until the three-quarter pole. Then he sneaked her up to third place and waited for his chance, hoping a spot would open up between horses. Sure enough, with an eighth of a mile still to go, he got lucky! He slipped through a gap on the inside rail and gave her a quick tap with his whip. As if she'd been waiting for it all along, Harmony Fire responded with a surge of speed. Past the wire, Eddie let her roll on and let her stretch her legs a bit. She took the turn sweetly, not a hint of a break in stride. The stress lines in her right knee which could have ended her career before it had even begun were a distant memory now. The win was a training and driving triumph! Eddie decided. He might be seventy seven years old, but he could still run rings around those young whippersnappers that called themselves horsemen, teach 'em a thing or two about waitin' on a horse. Guessing the cameras would still be on them and knowing Caroline and Kip would be watching, he gave the mare her head and grandstanded it, like he was a mere passenger, along for the ride. The judges were calling for a photo but he wasn't worried, not in the least.

In the winner's enclosure, he did a thumbs up for the benefit of Kip and Caroline, who were an ocean away and grinned and waved at the camera. All that patience had finally paid off! Outside the Race Barn, he pulled up short, his elation ebbing away. There was blood everywhere, scuffed up by horses' hooves, staining the snow bright red. Eddie's stomach turned over. There was no sign of a body, but with all that blood, it looked like someone had been murdered. He drove Harmony Fire into the Race Barn at top speed.

"What the hell's happened?" he yelled at Scotty McCoy, as the trainer came rushing past.

"Can't talk. I'm getting the doc," Scotty replied. Whoever it was, they might still be alive, Eddie surmised hopefully. He hustled the mare to the test area and gave her a bath. No one there knew anything about a murder. Mystified, he handed Harmony Fire over to a white coated urine collector, then took up the bloody trail. It led to number five in the third race, Gerry Lake's horse. Worriedly, Eddie pushed his way through the crowd of horrified onlookers. Gerry's driving colours were daubed with blood, so was his face, which now matched his flaming red hair. The source of the blood was a grey colt, who looked for all the world like he'd been in a knife fight at the Hot Tamale. Eddie's relief that no one had been killed was quickly overtaken by concern for the poor horse, whose name was Harmony Storm. After Gerry had washed the blood off him, Eddie realized that the colt hadn't been attacked by the Undertakers. He was a bleeder. Though the blood was pouring from his nose, Eddie had no doubt it was coming from somewhere deep down in his lungs.

"Bled through lasix," Gerry confided to Eddie. "They'll never let 'im race again, not here. He'll be worthless!" The solid figure of Scotty McCoy reappeared, with the vet in tow. Eddie left them to it and went to pick up his mare. McClaren had advised him to stay over at the Cherokee Inn, but they didn't take horses there. Harmony Fire needed to go back to her own stall at Meridian Acres, first. Buoyed up by his win, Eddie didn't see anyone sinister following him out of the racetrack and onto the highway, only an old blue sedan. But when he pulled up outside his own barn, an ugly looking black hearse was waiting for him, blocking his way. The single light shining down from the barn roof illuminated some wicked looking tackle welded onto its frame. Eddie shivered as a giant of a man, all in black, emerged from the cab carrying a gun. No prizes for guessing what they wanted with him, Eddie thought nervously. He locked the doors from the inside and rolled down his window an inch. Behind him, he could hear Harmony Fire kicking, expecting to be let out of the trailer.

"Can I help you?" Eddie croaked.

"Where's Catalino?" the man demanded. "He's not in your house, not anywhere. You better tell us, or you'll be sorry." The hell I will! Eddie thought angrily. A second man appeared, bigger than the first, swinging a huge club, with a machete stuck in his belt. The hair on Eddie's neck rose. Both men were wearing ski masks.

"Tell us," the second man said menacingly. "An' we might let you live, you little shit!"

"I don't know where he is, but I wouldn't tell you if I did," Eddie replied stubbornly. Bang! Smash! The windscreen shattered, letting in a blast of freezing air and showering Eddie with glass like confetti. But this wasn't a wedding!

"Lose the seat belt or I'll blast you to all hell, you fuckin' moron!" the gunman screamed, brandishing his weapon. A huge hand reached in through the shattered windscreen and hauled Eddie over the hood. "Now you'll talk, you little bastard!" the gunman shouted, pointing the gleaming barrel of his gun at Eddie's head. "You wanna have your head blown off?" he screeched. "Put your fuckin' hands up in the air!" Eddie did so, praying that Harmony Fire would keep quiet. If they so much as raised a hand to her, he knew his knees would turn to jelly and he'd tell them everything he knew to save her. The whine of a siren in the distance got his hopes up, but it immediately fell silent. Where the hell was Crawfish Brown? he wondered, risking a swift glance at the next door barn. But there was no sign of life. The place was plunged in darkness. With no hope left, Eddie decided to count his blessings. If he died tonight, he'd be going out on a high: with the most surprising win of his life under his belt and the best damn trotting mare he'd ever had in the barn, an' her only a four year old. The man with the club was scowling at him.

"Stop your grinnin' you old fool. You won't feel so happy when you hear what we're gonna do to you if you don't tell us what we need to know!"

"Why?" Eddie replied bravely. "What've I ever done to you?"

"Why?" the gunman repeated mockingly. "Seven grand is why! An' I'm buggered if I'll let an idiot like you stop us collecting on it!" This was the pair Reggie the feedman sent out to scare his late payers, Eddie realized. They hadn't killed anybody yet, not in Ontario so far as he knew. But there was always a first time. Had he imagined it, or had a twig snapped? The Undertakers had heard it too. They swung their black, balaclavaed heads around, staring out into the darkness.

"Get in the limo, now!" the gunman growled, grabbing Eddie by the neck and shoving him into the back. "Go-go-go!" he cried to the man in the driver's seat. Craning his neck, Eddie looked back. A swarm of men appeared out of the shadows, brandishing submachine guns. He heard the rat-a-tat of gunfire. The limo shuddered and sank down, its tires blown to shreds. Praying they weren't being attacked by some rival gang, Eddie lay low. When the dust settled, Eddie peered nervously out of the hearse. The two giants were trussed up like turkeys at Thanksgiving. It looked like the Mounties had saved the day! However, there was an ominous silence coming from the horse trailer. Eddie had a sudden, terrible thought. Had Harmony Fire caught a stray bullet? If so, it would break his heart. How would he ever explain it to Caroline and Kip? This wasn't supposed to happen, not in Canada. Trembling, he tottered over and threw open the trailer doors. Then, he pulled down the ramp and stared inside. It was pitch black and deathly quiet in there. At least she wasn't suffering, he thought.

"Anyone got a flashlight?" he called out.

"This do ya?" a familiar voice enquired. Crawfish was holding the biggest flashlight Eddie had ever seen. "It's Andy's but never mind that! Who ya got in there eh?" Crawfish asked, squinting inside.

"Harmony Fire," Eddie replied. "She won tonight, won big!" With some trepidation, he shone the torch on her. To his astonishment, she appeared unharmed.

"Hey! Ain't that the one that fuckin' near killed Bud?" Crawfish asked in an outraged tone.

"Forgot to take her earplugs out!" Eddie exclaimed, laughing with relief. "Where's that dog of yours?" he added.

"Gone to dog trainin' with Tammy," Crawfish replied. "She's teachin' 'im all kinds of tricks. Hear that?" he added, at the wail of sirens. "I called 'em out. Took 'em long enough to get here, eh?" An ambulance appeared, followed by the Provincial Police. Somehow, he hardly knew how, Eddie got Harmony Fire back to her stall, aided by Crawfish. The events of the night had finally caught up with him. He felt knackered.

"You okay there?" a voice called out cheerfully a few minutes later. It was Campbell McClaren. He had a red welt on his cheek and his arm was in a sling.

"What the hell happened to you and where's Cat?" Eddie asked anxiously.

"He's safe enough!" McClaren replied reassuringly. "Never tackle an

Undertaker!" he grimaced. "I brought him down, but he made me pay," he added ruefully. "Lucky I decided to tail you, eh."

"The blue sedan."

"Was it that obvious?" Campbell grinned. "I called for backup, once I saw who you were up against. Hey, Crawfish, what's up?"

"Shitface and Pervert got their comeuppance, didn't they?" Crawfish said, rubbing his hands with glee. "What'll happen to them now? Hope it's something horrible." McClaren acknowledged Crawfish's remark with a modest smile.

"Well," he said. "Illegal possession of lethal weapons, attacking police officers, resisting arrest, kidnap, attempted murder...should be enough to keep them behind bars for the rest of their lives."

"I don't envy the other prisoners," Eddie remarked.

"Me neither," Crawfish declared with feeling.

"After the medics have looked you over, I'll get someone to drive you home," McClaren told Eddie. Eddie started to protest, but in the end he accepted the ride. It had been one hell of a night! When his head finally touched the pillow, he relived his win with Harmony Fire. A mare like that was what made life worth living. He had fully expected to die tonight. As it was, he aimed to hang on for a fair bit longer yet.

By 10:45 p.m., when there was still no sign of Cat, Anya was at her wits end. The only number she had for him was Eddie Clearwater's landline which wasn't answering. Her emotions had run the gamut in the last few hours: excited, anxious, disappointed, angry and finally hysterical. By now she felt thoroughly unnerved. She was still waiting in the bar of the Cherokee Inn. She didn't know what else to do.

"Is there an Anya Paparotti here?" the barman called out.

"I'm Anya Papandreos," Anya said, getting to her feet.

"There's a Mr. McClaren on the line for you. You can take the call at reception. Go on through."

"Campbell?" Anya asked, holding the phone to her ear.

"Are you sitting down?" he replied.

"What's going on?" she asked, her heart pounding.

"It's a long story," Campbell began, before launching into a whole saga. Anya was only half listening.

"Where's Cat now? I need to see him!" she said impatiently.

"Why is that?"

"I don't have to tell you!" Anya exclaimed.

"No," Campbell agreed. "But there are things you do need to tell me. Until then, why should I help you?"

"You're not being fair," Anya declared eyeing the receptionist, who could hear everything she was saying.

"All's fair in love and war," Campbell replied enigmatically. "You need to sort things out with Jeff by the way. At least go and see him."

"Okay," she agreed eagerly.

"That's not part of the deal," Campbell clarified. "It's just common decency."

"What have you done with Cat?" she hit back.

"Nothing yet. But he needs to drop out of sight for a while. . . and so do you."

"Well, I'm not going into any witness protection scheme!" Anya declared forcefully.

"Neither is Cat," Campbell hastened to reassure her. "I'm acting on my own here. Theo Vettore disappeared nearly two years ago. Help me find the son of a bitch who wrecked up his life. I need a name."

"A name?"

"Pete wouldn't tell me...Cat won't talk either, I'm guessing out of loyalty to you."

"I only knew him as André," Anya replied, deciding to give away as little as possible.

"Where is he now?" Campbell asked.

"He could be anywhere, anywhere in the world."

"You can do better than that," Campbell replied steadily.

"No! He's gone travelling...Pete's gone with him," Anya said, feeling the familiar jolt of guilt whenever Pete's name came up.

"Okay, here's what's going to happen," Campbell began in businesslike tones. "Tomorrow morning you're going to give me the description of this guy and everything you know about him. After that, you'll get Cat's address. But don't even think about going anywhere without telling me, either of you."

"It's a deal," Anya replied hurriedly, before Campbell changed his mind. She handed the phone back to the receptionist and booked a room for the night.

After all the excitement, Caroline and Kip Davies were finding it impossible to sleep. They met up in the kitchen.

"How about some hot chocolate?" Kip suggested, switching the kettle on.

"Wasn't she wonderful?" Caroline said dreamily. "Isn't Eddie terrific? I can't wait to see her again!"

"It's 4 am!" Kip complained.

"Let's watch her race again. Just once more!" Caroline said. "Then I promise we'll go back to bed."

"Hardly worth it," Kip replied. "I have to be up at five!"

An hour later, Campbell was also having trouble sleeping, though it was only midnight in Canada. The makeshift bed in the McTavishes' basement didn't make for the greatest night's sleep, especially with his injured shoulder. The Undertakers were no longer a threat, but Campbell didn't want to take any chances. This time tomorrow Cat would be safely tucked away in a Toronto suburb, staying with Sofia's Italian relatives until he was sure that the coast was clear. The arrest of the Undertakers was a step in the right direction in the hunt for the Scorpion, but as they were mere foot soldiers, at the bottom of the chain of command, Campbell wasn't expecting any major breakthroughs. He wasn't getting his hopes up about Anya either. Everyone but Theo's cousin, Lara Vachon had given up on Theo Vettore but Campbell couldn't shake off the feeling that Vettore was out there, somewhere, still alive, holding the key to the Scorpion's identity. With Crawfish's help, the Provincial Police had put together a photo fit of Theo Vettore wearing a black cowboy hat and leather chaps. It was currently being posted all over Alberta. So far, there had been no response.

The next afternoon, Anya was on her way to the town of Lakeview. The roads were icy and the fields were ankle deep in snow. What a country! she thought. The sooner I'm out of here, the better. She had fudged her description of André, leaving Campbell with nothing that stood out. Luckily he had accepted her version of the truth. She arrived in Lakeview just as the sun was setting. Cat's street was lined with trees, their bare branches reaching out to a colourless sky.

Inside the house, Cat was waiting eagerly for her. She'd hardly set her bag down, when he started kissing her.

"Hey," she said, placing a hand on his chest. "Take it easy, Cat!" He immediately backed off.

"Have I got this all wrong?" he asked with a worried frown. She shook her head.

"Just not here," she explained. "Where d'you sleep?"

In the bedroom, she removed her watch, tucking it into the pocket of her jeans. Then she took them off as well. They landed on the bed together, rolling over and over until she was on top.

"It's okay," she told him, as he fumbled in the drawer of the bedside table, looking for a condom. He hesitated. "Trust me," she added gently. André had been violent in bed. Jeff predictable. Cat was neither. An hour went by in a flash. Young men were tireless when it came to love, she discovered. As for her, she couldn't get enough of him.

Two days later, though he knew there was scant chance of success, Campbell went to see Ritchie Sanchez who was still being held by the Provincial Police. Ritchie had been unable to make bail, which had been set at twenty-thousand dollars. So far, no one had come to his rescue. The prisoner was both sober and clean shaven, a pleasant change from the last time Campbell had seen him when he'd looked like a bull on the rampage. Campbell came straight to the point.

"You've got yourself into a pretty good mess, haven't you, Mr. Sanchez?" he said.

"For fighting with my brother? C'mon!" Ritchie replied contemptuously.

"Time you woke up to reality, Sanchez. The charges against you are serious."

"What charges?" Ritchie mocked.

"Incitement to violence…actual bodily harm. If I were you, I'd start talking. Unless you'd enjoy three to five in the penitentiary." The big vein in Ritchie's neck began pulsating. "Coming clean on the ownership of the Lucky Seven Syndicate might make things easier for you. I might even put in a good word for you myself," Campbell offered.

"Oh yeah? Like I'd really believe that!" Ritchie spat out.

"Why don't you tell me what you know about André?" Campbell urged. The colour drained out of Ritchie's face.

"If I tell you that, I'm dead," Ritchie muttered, turning away. "What kind of fool do you take me for?"

"I'm trying to help you here."

"We're done," Ritchie said abruptly, nodding at the guard.

"I'll be back!" Campbell replied. He wasn't sure he meant it, though. What would be the point? However, the look of dread on Ritchie's face had confirmed Campbell's suspicions about the owner of the Lucky Seven Syndicate. Taken together (intimidation, drugs, high stakes and big money) everything pointed to an operator like the Scorpion. But with only the name André to go on, he had no way to find him.

Snow clouds were looming overhead as he made his way home.

A blizzard had Ontario by the throat. Even the races had been cancelled. A new arrival was standing in the aisleway of Keith Lazer's barn. He was as slender as a whippet, not an ounce of fat gracing his lean frame. Surveying his latest acquisition with a jaundiced eye was Keith Lazer himself. He cursed the Slots, Cat Ciardi and the Lucky Seven Stable in equal measure.

Nothing was the same anymore.

Since Cat's demise, Keith Lazer was back at the top of the trainer's table, back where he belonged. But the months spent pinned down in second place had left their mark. Now Cat was out of the picture, the Moose had returned to driving duties, slinking back to Keith with his tail between his legs. But, like a wife coming back home after fucking another guy, things were never going to be like they were before. Theirs was an uneasy truce. Any finesse Moose had ever possessed as a driver had vanished, thanks to his spell with Catalino Ciardi, when all he'd had to do was go to the front and stay there.

So much had changed at Iroquois Downs! The good times, when all Keith had had to give a horse was a shot of Human Growth Hormone, had gone forever. They had a test for that now and for almost everything else, it seemed, including EPO. Still, every problem threw up a new opportunity. Keith was going to give Cobalt a try. It did the same job as EPO, but there was as yet no test for it. The dealer who sold it to him had called it *Blue Magic*. Lazer badly needed a little magic right now. As he looked over at the former star performer, Harmony Light, he was seized by a familiar sinking feeling. After four days' stall rest, the gelding still looked strung up, used up and worn down. Cringing inwardly, Lazer walked over and ran his hands over the horse's legs. They felt like fragile pieces of china, as if they could shatter at any moment. Occasionally, Lazer envied his second trainer, Bob Summers, his carefree life.

This was one of those times.

Constant vigilance was Lazer's only defence against tragedy's bite: bones fractured on the rock hard track in winter, tendons sprung and ligaments ruptured in the spring mud, the speedfest of the summer season which knocked down young horses like ninepins, leaving a ragged column to limp through the fall. What hope did any horse have, really? When it all got too much, Lazer lit up another cigarette.

As Bob led Harmony Light back to his stall, Lazer watched intently, his steely grey eyes focused on the horse's legs, listening out for the telltale sound of a break in the rhythm. It never came. Lameness wasn't the problem. It was too bad. Lazer did most of the vet work himself. Injecting joints was child's play if you knew what you were doing. He despised the way some veterinarians carried on: charging sky high fees for simple procedures and jacking up prices on injectables, too lazy or too inept to get the diagnosis right the first time around. Dr. Jay was the exception who proved the rule. Keith had guessed from the price the Lucky Seven were asking that there had to be something wrong with Harmony Light. So far, he had failed to find it. With his own money down, the safest course would be to price Harmony Light and race him in a claimer. The horse wasn't robust enough to compete at the top level as a four year old and Keith couldn't afford to get caught holding the baby. The decision made, he turned his cell phone back on. He'd missed two calls and the Porn Guy, of all people, had left a voice message. Apparently he had a colt he wanted to give him to train.

"Hey Bob!" Keith called out. "We're gettin' another horse!" His thoughts returned to Harmony Light. He and Theo Vettore...they'd made a good team, once upon a time. Vettore had never asked the horse for more than he could give.

Time had moved on, for both of them.

LOST VALLEY RANCH, ALBERTA: MARCH

At sun up, storm clouds glowing blood red appeared in the wintry sky. After weeks of subzero temperatures, it felt like spring. By noon the ranch hands, their chores done, were kicking their heels outside the horse barn. Scarecrow joined them. The chinook was blowing: a warm dry wind that was melting the snow, like a blow torch set on high. Scarecrow didn't understand it, but it hardly mattered. There were so many other things about his current situation that he couldn't explain: how it was he'd fallen onto a mountain ledge in the middle of nowhere, why he'd woken up with no idea of who he was, where he'd come from and what his life had been before. The mystery of the chinook paled in comparison. His fellow cowhands were growing restless, eyeing the white capped mountains which stood like sentinels, hemming them in. There was little for them all to do, these days. The steers had come down from their summer pastures in the foothills months ago. They were stabled just a short tractor ride from their winter fodder: the big round hay bales that would keep them alive until spring.

"Snow's melting!" one of the men remarked, stating the obvious. The clouds had returned to a normal dull grey, but the temperature had jumped from minus twenty to plus fifteen. It felt like summer!

"Let's have us some fun," one of the hands declared roguishly, peeling off his jacket.

"Like a rodeo, eh?" another asked, grinning delightedly.

"How 'bout that new bull o' Wayne's, eh?" a rough cut individual, his chin covered in stubble, suggested. There was a chorus of "Yeah, let's draw straws! Short straw wins! C'mon Wayne!"

"Think I'm gonna let you guys wreck up my new rodeo bull? He ain't even broke in yet!" Wayne replied firmly. "But I got somethin' for you!" he promised, turning on his heel and heading for the horse barn.

"What? Tell us boss!"

"Jus' you wait 'n see," the headman said.

The men formed a tight circle, talking excitedly. Scarecrow stood with them, shoulder to shoulder. Wayne reappeared, leading a long legged, loose limbed thoroughbred, already saddled and bridled. The men parted to let them through.

"This do you? Ain't bin outa the stall all winter," Wayne declared proudly, jerking the reins and forcing the animal to a halt. "No straws," he added, aiming a thumb at Scarecrow. "The new guy gets to ride him." They were a tight knit bunch. After a year and half, he was still the new guy.

The horse was trembling.

Amid cries of "Aw, gee boss…it ain't fair!" Scarecrow stepped inside the circle, settling his black Stetson firmly on his head. Tall as he was, the horse was taller. Wayne tossed him onto the flimsy saddle and jammed the toes of his boots into the stirrups. They were set too short for his long skinny legs but there was no chance to change them. The animal was prancing now, bouncing him up and down in a jerky trot. Scarecrow leant down and hurriedly gathered up the reins, looking out over the tops of the men's heads to the wide, open grasslands beyond. Scenting freedom, the thoroughbred tossed his head and broke into a long, loping canter, scattering the onlookers and sending Scarecrow's black Stetson flying. After they went through the open gate, the animal took off in a rhythmic gallop, ratcheting up a gear every dozen strides.

"Whoa!" Scarecrow cried, his ears singing, his jacket flapping in the wind. The runaway paid no heed. He simply put his head down and went faster, slicing a path through the soft, melting snow. Desperate to stop him, Scarecrow stood up in the stirrups and, perched precariously on the horse's back, jerked the reins grimacing with the effort. It was no use. Instead of slowing down, the horse got mad. He bucked, twisting his body this way and that like a rodeo bronc. Scarecrow lost first one stirrup, then the other. His long legs dangling, he threw aside the useless reins and grabbed a handful of the horse's mane as they raced towards a stand of fir trees.

"Stop! You son of a bitch!" he yelled, crouching low on the horse's neck as they dived into the wood. He felt branches scraping his back and he was soon covered in pine needles but somehow he clung on. When they broke out into the open again, there was nothing between them and the distant mountain peaks but a vast expanse of wilderness. The horse pulled up short, almost unseating him and let out a loud whinny.

There was no reply.

Again and again the stallion called, high stepping in a staccato walk. Scarecrow took advantage of the lull by sneaking the reins back into his hands. If he could get the horse turned around, he thought, while he had his mind on others things and point him towards home, he'd be okay. More than okay. He'd get a hero's welcome from the ranch hands and they'd all go down to the chow house to celebrate. His spirits rose. Trusting to luck, he kicked with his dangling left foot and pulled the right rein. But this was no cow pony! The thoroughbred reacted instantly, wheeling around, throwing him off balance. Scarecrow lurched sideways, saving himself by snatching at the reins. But, to his dismay, the horse reared, his front legs flailing at empty air. Endlessly, it seemed, the horse teetered at the tipping point. Scarecrow clung on with his knees, delaying the inevitable for as long as he could but the reins slipped from his fingers and he was falling…falling…plummeting towards the ground. The last thing he saw was a mass of blazing orange storm clouds sweeping across the sky. It looked like the end of the world.

Then everything went black.

Theo Vettore woke up in bed. It was early morning. The sun was peeping through the curtains. He'd been having this weird dream, but it kept slipping away from him. He half opened his eyes. Where on earth was he? Probably at some girl's house, he decided. He felt pretty hung over. Must have been some wild party last night. The odd thing was, he couldn't remember a thing about it. Someone was trying to rouse him, none too gently. Hope it's not the boyfriend, he thought, sniggering to himself. Where on earth was Ginny? Then he remembered he'd broken up with her. No, that wasn't right. They'd got back together again.

"Wake up!" It was a man's voice. Reluctantly, he opened his eyes. A total stranger wearing a cowboy hat was staring at down at him. What the hell? He thought. Above him, livid yellow storm clouds loomed in the darkening sky. Nothing, but *nothing* made any fuckin' sense. He heard the sound of galloping hooves then a chorus of "Is he okay?" No I'm not okay, he wanted to shout but he couldn't speak, not yet.

"Can you feel your legs, young fella?" the cowboy was asking now, prodding them.

"Leave me alone," he replied irritably, sitting up. He stared, dumbfounded, at the wild country, at the sun setting behind the mountains and the men on horseback. His head throbbed. "What's going on?" he asked shakily.

"You took a bad fall off Wayne's horse, Scarecrow. C'mon, we gotta get you up on your feet now."

"Who the hell's Wayne?" Theo asked.

"Hey, c'mon Scarecrow. Get a grip." Theo felt more confused than ever. "Don't you know your own name?" the cowboy asked, looking frightened.

"Of course," he replied indignantly. "I'm Theo Vettore!" Cries of disbelief came from the men.

"Hey we better go catch the horse or Wayne'll be gutted!" someone said.

"What was the last thing you remember, Theo Vettore?" the cowboy asked. Theo frowned, pictures flashing in his head: Ginny lying on the bed beside him…white powder in the palm of his hand…the thrill of driving a winner…a needle coming at him…the leer on the man's face. He pushed it all aside and plucked a single image, clear as a bell out of the mayhem.

"I won a big stake at Cree Horse Park," he said. The look on the cowboy's face floored him.

"Well I'll be doggoned," the man whistled softly. "Hey!" he shouted. "One of you get the doc on the blower and bring the jeep. We gotta get 'im back to the ranch somehow and he can't ride in this state! Took us an age to find you," the cowboy confided. "But you looked pretty good on that horse of Wayne's. You a jockey or somethin'?"

"No! I'm not a jockey, damn you!" Theo declared angrily. "I'm the best friggin' harness horse driver in Canada!" The cowboy looked thunderstruck. "I set a new track record just yesterday afternoon with a two year old colt!"

"This colt," the cowboy said awkwardly. "You don't happen to know its name, eh?"

"Of course I know it! He's the fastest two year old in North America!"

"And his name?" Theo stared at the cowboy for a long moment.

"Harmony Light," he declared. Then a shooting pain in his head made any more talk impossible.

ONTARIO

Midnight in the dead of winter…the solitary figure of Tom Cowboy Larson standing in the horse barn, his thumbs stuck in his braces, his head bowed. Three hours had passed since he'd won the booby prize. Ten claims there'd been for Harmony Light this night. Ten greedy owners who couldn't wait to get their sticky fingers on a top colt at a cut price. But, see, this wasn't your Walmart or even your Zellers, where there were guarantees, returns if not fully satisfied etc. Oh no! This was the racetrack. It was buyers beware here, goods sold in an "as is" condition, like the used cars on Erinsville's East Side. Eighty-two thousand dollars plus HST was a good deal of money to waste on a gamble. It wasn't like the horse had even won. He'd tailed off badly and finished a poor fifth. But Tom was stuck with him anyhow. Because he'd had to go and win the toss, hadn't he?

"How many 10-1 shots ever come in? I ask you?" he muttered, raising his eyes to the heavens. "Would it have been too much?" he implored the rafters, "to arrange for me to lose like usual? There's many a good claim I missed when someone else got lucky. Why now? Why this one? Eh?" He got no answer from the twenty-five standardbreds quietly getting on with their lives.

Gentle, willing creatures, nervous optimists, fearful of strange noises and the unexpected appearance of unusual man made objects, the horses in Larson's barn welcomed the attentions of the barn cat, a fat ginger tabby who made the rounds nightly, hunting the rats which fed on the grain doled out to the inmates three times a day. They were searching their stalls now for any wisps of hay left uneaten, preparing for the long night ahead, warily watching the human who was standing lost in thought outside the new horse's stall.

All at once, the wait was over. The man wheeled round and marched off. Sighs of relief followed in his wake. But a few minutes later, he was back. Whickers of alarm travelled up and down the aisleway. A bay gelding bobbed up and down, snorting. A coal black stud with a ragged mane reared, pawing the air. The others caught the whiff of danger and panicked, kicking futilely at the walls that contained them.

"Be quiet there!" the man growled. "You'll break a sesamoid. Then it's straight to the killers for you." The horses froze. A handsome chestnut stood trembling, his coat dark with sweat, showing the whites of his eyes. The new horse, Harmony Light, a sleek bay with a white star on his forehead and a long flowing mane and tail, looked around curiously, his nostrils dilated, sniffing the air. The man kept right on walking until he reached his stall.

Clipping a leadshank to the horse's halter, he tied him up tightly to the back wall. He was holding something that Harmony Light had never seen before. What was it? he wondered, as the man edged his way past his power- ful hind quarters. Harmony Light's ears flickered back and forth. He wasn't too sure about this. He heard the buzzing sound a split second before the searing pain coursed through his body. The ugly jagged sounds of Harmony Light's screams tore through the clean, freshly swept barn. His kicks reached the top of the wooden partition separating him from his neighbours. He tried to bite his tormentor, but the man danced just out of reach, darting in and out like some gigantic horse fly.

A ripple of fear flowed through the horses in the barn like water down a river. They felt his pain. . . his agony. They were united, one herd, held together by a terrible secret: the cattle prod that plagued their nights and stalked their dreams. There were many who left, never to return and the frequent newcomers who experienced their first moment of pure terror at Larson's hands. Nothing, not the weaning nor even the breaking process, had prepared Harmony Light for this. He was wrapped up in it, subdued by it, desperate to flee from it.

Suddenly, it was over: the leadshank unclipped...the stall slammed shut... footsteps getting fainter. Lights out. The barn door closing.

Silence.

Harmony Light stayed awake until the dawn feeding. Then at last he lay down and slept.

ALBERTA

It was four in the morning. Theo Vettore was wide awake. In the dimly lit hospital ward, the only signs of life were the flashing lights of the monitors and the hum of the air conditioning. They held no answer for him. His vital signs were normal. There was no hint in his blood pressure or his heart rate of the turmoil inside his head. He'd been knocked out before…but he'd always come to, either on the racetrack, in the ambulance, or at Erinsville General. Not in the middle of nowhere surrounded by strangers.

Dawn brought a new crew of nurses to the ward and talk of a foot of snow which had fallen overnight. That blew Theo's mind! Snow in summer? Where the fuck was he? The Great White North? The window blinds were pulled down and he was hooked up to a drip, so there was no easy way to check. He didn't want to alarm anyone and risk being sedated…or sectioned.

Breakfast arrived.

"What's the name of this hospital?" he asked trying to sound normal.

"Fort Douglas," came the reply. "Best hospital in Alberta!" That explained the snow in summer, he thought. It wasn't unheard of in Alberta. But why was he here at all?

"And the date?" he enquired hesitantly, trying to get his bearings.

"March 2nd. Now eat your breakfast!" Staring down at his toast and orange juice, he fought the urge to scream out loud. March second? It made no sense. No sense at all! Six whole months had gone by and he couldn't remember a thing about it! Had he been abducted by aliens? he wondered wildly. Was he insane? His mind reeled…then began to split in two. One half was back at Cree Horse Park on a glorious summer day, the other was leaping through space and time, landing out west in the middle of winter. Between them was a dark yawning chasm about which he knew nothing. Sitting alone in his hospital bed, his breakfast tray untouched, Theo tried to hold it together. Weird stuff had happened, he remembered, when he'd taken drugs. But he didn't feel high. Apart from the throbbing in his head, his body appeared to be in excellent shape. He wasn't paralyzed. He hadn't broken anything. Just his memory. There had to be an explanation for those missing months. But he'd have to wait for a doctor, someone who could give him answers to his burning questions. There was a sudden commotion outside in the corridor. He heard a familiar voice.

"Lara!" he cried. A moment later, his cousin came storming in, ignoring the nurses' protests that it was outside visiting hours.

"Theo!" he heard Lara gasp. "Thank God!" There were dark shadows under her eyes. She looked so much older. "I been travelling all night...I start ze moment I hear. I never give up on you. Never! Zey say you are dead. Me, I did not believe it!"

"Dead?" Theo asked faintly, feeling more confused than ever.

"Didn't zey tell you? You 'ave been gone for so long, Theo. After you win ze General Custer, *tu es disparu*! It has been one year and a half since I see you!"

"No way!" Theo cried. Eighteen months! It was far too much to take in. His brain rebelled at the overload. It began to shut down.

"Very soon we leave ze 'ospital," Lara was saying in reassuring tones. "The doctors, zey say it will be better for you at home," she added. Theo didn't feel in the least bit reassured.

"Where's Ginny?" he demanded suddenly. "She oughta be here!" An expression flitted across Lara's face. Was it pity?

"For now, it is only me," she replied softly. "But Campbell McClaren, 'e is flying down this afternoon. 'E tell me, 'e need to talk to you."

"No way!" Theo exclaimed, panic stricken. He knew perfectly well who Campbell McClaren was!

"What is ze matter, Theo?" Lara frowned. Theo couldn't speak. Memories were flooding back with terrible clarity: Room 115...the discovery of cocaine in his car...the prospect of prison...his yielding to pressure. It had all led irrevocably to this moment in time...Had he betrayed the Scorpion for nothing? Was Campbell McClaren coming to arrest him anyway?

"Don't let him send me to jail!" he cried.

"What is zis, Theo?" Lara replied, looking confused. "You will not go to jail. You 'ave done nothing wrong, Theo!"

"That's not true," he replied slowly. "As hard as it is to say it, I brought this on myself." Suddenly he couldn't hold back the floodgates any longer. He broke down and told his cousin everything. Lara acknowledged his confession with a heartfelt sigh. She sat down beside the bed and covered Theo's hand with her own. Theo closed his eyes, exhaustion overwhelming his desire to understand his predicament. The long night's vigil was finally taking its toll. He stayed awake as long as he could, grasping Lara's hand like a drowning man thrown a lifeline. Then he went under.

By the time Campbell McClaren reached the hospital, Vettore was in a medically induced coma. As there were strictly no visitors, except close relatives, Campbell's questions had to wait.

ONTARIO

Harmony Light's spectacular win a week later hardly raised a ripple in the Race Barn. There were only two claims on him. Tony Hall won the toss.

No one cared.

The only thing anyone wanted to talk about was Theo Vettore, who was in intensive care, dead to the world. The way Lara told it, Theo had acted pretty normal for a few hours, before losing consciousness. None of the horsemen knew the medical term *lucid interval* but a few of the drivers had experienced it first hand. Theo's parents were in Alberta, sitting by his bedside. Lara was back in Ontario, clinging to hope as she went about her daily routine. She called the hospital every day, only to be told there was no change.

THE SCORPION

A turquoise ocean...blending imperceptibly with an azure sky on the distant horizon...a light breeze filling the white sails. André Fontainbleu relaxing on the deck of the Shere Khan, brown as a berry, his head bare...his eyes closed...dreaming of times and places...in the future... in the past.

It is too hot to think. An era has ended...filled with violence, passion and greed. There is no need for that anymore. Pictures of the past crowd into his mind. The city of Quebec, basking in the evening sun...snow on the rooftops...skaters on the frozen river...Cree girls with long hair and laughing eyes...children he never knew...his frantic, grieving parents... Philippe...shot in mistake for him.

"Dolphins!" a voice cries out. "Come and see!" The crew rush up to the bow. Only Pete remains at his post, holding a steady course. Dependable, but gullible...wanting to believe he has little to lose. He is wrong! That era is nearly over, André reminds himself. But it is a habit that is difficult to break. Was he always like this? he wonders lazily, closing his eyes again. He and his brother Philippe looked so much alike, aside from a small difference in height, and the colour of their eyes. The differences were not so evident, but they were profound. Philippe possessed the soul of an optimist, gregarious, easy going and carefree. André joined the gang in tenth grade. It suited his melancholy character and his cynical view of human nature. They were all amateurs...but hungry to prove themselves.

He has seen the dolphins before, many times on this southern ocean. Surfing on the bow wave...so healthy and so sure of their place in the world. Yet even for them, the tuna fish nets are waiting.

Consequences run through his restless mind. Twenty-five thousand cash is a great deal of money to teenagers. How could he have been so foolish as to imagine that his lie about being robbed would be believed? Boxer alone remained loyal. Without waiting to see whether Philippe had survived , they took off with the cash and fled those streets, where death lurked round every corner. That money seeded his empire. But it was paid for with his brother's blood. It is not easy to forget that ugly fact.

He pulls a faded piece of newsprint out of his pocket. It has travelled with him, for a very long time. Once more, he searches the faces, trying to find anything that reminds him of his brother or himself. He grimaces at the irony that it was Jay Winterflood who sabotaged his racing operation: his own son! He's torn between pride and disappointment, thinking of the grandchildren that he will never speak to, never know.

The sun dips westwards. The breeze drops. The sea is as still and quiet as Lake Ontario on a summer evening. Where did all that rage come from? Revenge has always been uppermost in his mind, frustrating his efforts to live the kind of life his brother would have wanted for him. Violence, or the threat of it, has served him far too well. The arrest of the Undertakers is no disaster. Others will rush to fill the void. But they will not be working for him.

He has always given his victims a chance. At times, it has been a struggle to rein in Boxer's aggressive loyalty, but he has, as far as he is aware, succeeded. The drug addicts, the gamblers…they sealed their own fates. As for traitors like Theo Vettore, André did not orchestrate the final, fatal blow. He gave even him a tiny chance at life…for the sake of Philippe, who had no chance at all. *If only*. Two words, so small yet so powerful. They pull at his heartstrings.

Dusk. Sharks congregate: simple killing machines going about their business. They remind him of Boxer, so easy to understand.

That night he dreams of Philippe again. They are swimming with the dolphins, play fighting as they used to do, diving beneath the waves. When a dark silhouette appears above them and he sees the dorsal fin, he knows exactly what is going to happen next. He wakes himself up before it does. He lies awake in his bunk, rocked by the waves, cursing fate. He has travelled so far, experienced so much, lived half a lifetime. Even so, he cannot forget her. If he had met her first…before the others, who were mere playthings…who knows? She was older than the rest. Wiser too.

Leaving her was the hardest thing he has ever done, though he was not aware of it at the time. That came later, after he was out of danger, when she refused to leave the tribe and join him. Now she is dead.

Only cats, it seems, have nine lives.

HARMONY LIGHT

Maybe it was the freak thaw which had transformed the hard, frozen track of Iroquois Downs into a quagmire. Maybe it was because the new set of hopples Tony Hall had put on Harmony Light had stretched. Perhaps though, it was an accident waiting to happen. Because a horse can only race every week with a fragile body and a big heart, before something truly calamitous occurs. Exactly one month after winning in spectacular fashion for Tom Cowboy Larson, Harmony Light made a catastrophic break down the backstretch, catapulting his trainer into the limelight for all the wrong reasons. The driver eventually made it back to the Race Barn, a painful five minutes after everyone else.

"Put a fuckin' head pole on him next time! I couldn't even steer him he was on the line so bad!" Moose Rankin said, before storming off. There was no next time. A few minutes later, Tony's owner came striding into the Race Barn. Nattily dressed in casual sportswear, looking clean and well rested, Jack Dawson stuck out like a sore thumb amongst the horsemen, most of whom, like Tony were covered in mud from the track.

"I'm taking all my horses away from you and giving them to Price," Jack announced brutally. Tony Hall carried on with the business of unclipping the sulky from his steaming horse, without uttering a word. "How'd you expect me to pay the damn bills, Tony?" Jack raged. "First, that mare dies and now this! I paid nearly a hundred thousand for that damn animal! I needed him to win tonight, not finish dead last." Tony remained stubbornly silent. "I did this for a bit of fun. Losing isn't fun! What d'you have to say for yourself, eh?" Jack asked, sounding totally exasperated. Aware that the horsemen nearby were listening intently, Tony tried to salvage something of his reputation and recover his hurt pride.

"Take your damn horses!" he declared loudly, wrenching his cap off and throwing it on the floor in a gesture of defiance. Jack Dawson turned on his heel and strode off. Tony stayed put, staring off into space. It was a while before he registered that there was something terribly wrong with Harmony Light's left hind leg. "Must've broken somethin'," Tony moaned. "Oh God!" he exclaimed. "Where's the fuckin' vet when you fuckin' need 'im?!"

"Fourth race, get ready!" the Paddock Judge barked out.

"Better move it, Tony," Scotty McCoy advised as he walked past swinging a bucket of soapy water to and fro, reminding Tony horribly of the drench that had killed Princess. "Jesus Christ!" Scotty exclaimed, catching sight of Harmony Light and staggering to a stop. "Want me to get the doc?"

Tony nodded speechlessly, numb with shock and disappointment. He'd seen legs swell up plenty of times, but he'd never seen parts of them dragging along the floor like that. It looked like it had exploded.

"I'm putting him on the vet list, long term," the doc told Tony unhelpfully after he'd given Harmony Light a shot for the pain. I could use a bit o' that myself, Tony thought, pitying himself.

"You're having a bad run o' luck," Scotty commiserated. "But things'll turn around. You'll see."

"Always do," Dave Bodinski agreed. At Dave's words, fury welled up in Tony's chest, making it hard for him to breathe. If Dave had drenched Princess that day, instead of letting him down, none of this would've happened. Everything had gone wrong after that. He hadn't been able to keep his mind on anything. Jack Dawson was the only owner he had. He was out of business.

Andy Price's man, Crawfish Brown, came and took Harmony Light away. The horse was so lame, he couldn't hardly walk, but Crawfish, who'd been a total cripple before, was now as sound as a bell. It didn't make no sense and it wasn't fuckin' fair, Tony thought miserably.

Andy Price waited ten days to call Jack Dawson and put him in the picture about Harmony Light. The old saying that bad news travels fast didn't apply to the horse business. Most trainers kept their heads down, continued charging the daily rate and hoped the problem would go away. Sometimes it did! Andy generally blamed track conditions, the driver, the previous owner or sheer bad luck for horse disasters. This time, he blamed all four.

"Doc Meecham says he'll never race again," he told Dawson. "He said the kindest thing would be to put the horse to sleep." Dawson reacted like most owners to bad news: disbelief and denial, followed by an unrealistic hope that the animal could somehow be salvaged by some treatment or other they'd heard about. "I agree with the vet," Andy added firmly after Dawson had calmed down a bit. "He's never going to race, not with that leg, wouldn't even make a trail horse." There was a loud sigh at the other end of the phone, which Andy took to be the last stage: resignation.

"Can't you sell him? He's got to be worth something," Dawson asked, giving it one last try. "He's only had one bad race!"

"Maybe," Andy replied doubtfully.

"I'll sign the papers and bring 'em over later," Dawson said. "Do whatever you want with him. But no more bills after today, okay?"

"Doc Meecham charges three hundred dollars to put a horse down," Andy responded. Jack Dawson was silent. "Two hundred and fifty, if you pay cash," Andy said, pushing his point home. He didn't add anything to the cost, as he generally did. He felt under the circumstances that it wouldn't have been playing fair. Even he had some principles.

Next morning, at the Schoolers, he dutifully asked around, hoping someone would take the horse on before he had to ship him out to Doc Meecham's clinic. His efforts were met with incredulous stares. No one had missed seeing the horse self destruct. Spotting Tony Hall waiting around by the exit, Andy's heart sank. He'd been side stepping him all morning. Ex-trainers were often bitter and angry, just like some ex-wives. Separation, like divorce, never came easy. He wouldn't have blamed Tony for being jealous of him. In the end though, Andy got a pleasant surprise. Apparently, Tony had decided to go into the shipping business and was offering his services for a reasonable price.

"I've got one for you," Andy said immediately. "Be at my barn, two o'clock sharp." It took Harmony Light almost an hour to hobble into the trailer. Tony insisted on taking the papers, as well as a signed statement from Andy that the horse was to be destroyed.

"Don't want no trouble from no one," Tony explained. "I got enough problems. Dawson did me in proper." After he left, Andy walked over to the coffee shop with a lighter step. That was one thing over with at any rate, he thought thankfully, as he dove into his apple pie.

No one asked him where Harmony Light had gone the next day, except Crawfish's girlfriend, the acrobat girl, who had turned out to be a dab hand at harness cleaning and stalls.

"Gone to horse heaven," Andy replied shortly.

It was a week before Meecham came to the barn again. Neither of them mentioned Harmony Light. He was just one more fallen soldier.

André Fontainbleu was lying down in the Shere Khan's cabin, his eyes closed, thinking about the plan he had made. The final act in the drama was imminent, leaving one less player preying on humanity's greed and fear. The news had reached him that the traitor, Theo Vettore, was

apparently back from the dead. It mattered little now. André Fontain-bleu roused himself. He climbed up onto the Shere Khan's deck and halted for a moment, gazing out at the white sand dazzling in the sun, fringed by waving palms. Then he stepped ashore, carrying a suitcase. Its contents were worth hundreds of millions. After months at sea, it felt strange to be on dry land. His legs buckled and he cursed his weakness. Boxer was there to meet him...right on time. They were heading for a hotel in Clearwater Springs, where Phil Harman had booked a room.

Up to now, Phil Harman had been useful in Ontario, essential for André's business interests there. He had played his part perfectly, with only two lapses, when his bonhomie slipped and his true nature seeped through. It could have been disastrous, but André did not give up on him because without Phil, his life would have been so much more diffi-cult and so very banal. However, now it was time to say farewell to Mr. Harman once and for all. He would not be needed anymore. He had one last service to provide. Afterwards it would be all over for Phil Harman. André did not regret his decision. Though he contemplated it with just a *soupçon* of trepidation, he felt no remorse.

The world would be a better place without him.

Remorse was for sentimental fools!

GULF COAST, FLORIDA

Campbell McClaren parked the rental car outside the Tampa Bay Morgue. An ashen faced Al McTavish was in the passenger seat beside him. Twenty-four hours ago Al had called him into the office and told him that Phil Harman had been found dead in a hotel room in Florida. Campbell was praying that Al was equal to the job of identifying the body of his oldest and dearest friend. Apparently the Tampa Bay Police Department was treating Phil's death as suicide. There had been no sign of a struggle in the modest hotel room where he had been found, no personal possessions either: just an empty suitcase and Phil's last will and testament, laid out neatly on the bedside table. Al had been named as executor.

That was all Campbell knew, so far. At the morgue, he waited while Al went about his grim task. A TBPD officer, a grizzled veteran who gave the impression of having seen it all, was waiting there with him.

"Who are you, a relative?" the officer enquired in a bored tone. Campbell shook his head.

"RCMP," he replied, deciding to keep things simple.

"So, you're one of us!" the officer said in a more animated manner. Campbell nodded noncommittally. "Let's see your ID then…" Campbell produced it. "Listen," the officer said quietly. "When you get him back to Canada." He jerked his head in the direction of the mortuary. "You might wanna check some things out…"

"Okay," Campbell replied, wondering what this was all about.

"It looks like a suicide…" the man paused. Intrigued, Campbell waited for more. "Don't mean it is though, right? You just wanna be sure, right? I mean… The guy was shot through the heart at point blank range. That takes a lot o' guts!"

"I didn't know," Campbell frowned. It sounded more like an execution to him than a suicide.

"Yeah, well, males usually blow their brains out. Females…they take pills," the officer stated.

"You're not convinced," Campbell suggested tentatively.

The man shrugged. His skepticism was making Campbell uneasy. He owed it to Al to get to the bottom of this.

"Would it be possible to see the room where Phil died?" he asked carefully. "He was a close friend of Al McTavish's and…"

"Probably rented out again by now," the officer replied dismissively.

"What about CCTV footage from the hotel?" The door to the morgue swung open and Al reappeared, looking haggard.

"It's definitely Phil," he pronounced in an anguished tone. "But I don't understand it! We talked on the phone…just last week! He had it all figured out. He said he'd never have to endure another Ontario winter. He loved it here. He sounded so happy. He had everything to live for!"

"I'll drive you back to the hotel," Campbell offered. "You can rest up. It's been a long day."

"I could use a lie down," Al agreed soberly. "But there's so much red tape… so much to arrange."

"I'll deal with it," Campbell said firmly.

"I'm on duty for another two hours," the officer revealed, with a meaning-ful glance in Campbell's direction.

"I'll be back," Campbell replied, shepherding Al away.

Dead people do not travel in the hold, with the rest of the baggage. They are carried in the cargo area, at the rear of the plane. After a harrowing two days, Campbell was airborne again, on his way back to Ontario. As the plane took off, Al McTavish kept glancing anxiously behind him. At least someone had cared about the man, Campbell reflected. There was no sign of any griev-ing relatives. A copy of the CCTV footage from the hotel was safely stowed in his carry on bag, sealed and signed for. After trawling the footage for half the night, Campbell had yet to pick up on anything significant, unless he counted Phil Harman checking in, carrying a small suitcase.

"Mind if I take a look at that will?" he asked Al, hoping it might shed some light on Phil's state of mind.

"Go ahead," Al said dully, glancing at the overhead lockers. "It's up there somewhere." As the plane soared above the Florida beaches, Campbell settled down to read. There were a number of small bequests to people he had never heard of. Then he caught sight of a familiar name. He glanced over at Al. His eyes were closed. After the strain of the last forty-eight hours, he was catch-ing up on some much needed sleep but this really couldn't wait. He reached over and gently shook his shoulder. Al opened his eyes.

"Listen to this," Campbell said. "I leave the remainder of my estate to my son, Jay Winterflood, residing at Sunnyvale Farm, Puslinch County, Ontario.

"What?" Al cried. He tried to leap to his feet, but the seat belt stopped him. "Damn this thing," he complained, unbuckling it. "Read that again, will you?" Campbell did so. "Phil never breathed a word about this." Al said in an anguished tone. "And his estate must be worth millions."

"As executor, you have every right to request DNA testing," Campbell pointed out.

"Yes," Al replied. "Good idea. But I still have no idea why Phil is dead. I simply can't understand it!"

"I could arrange for an autopsy, if you want," Campbell suggested. "But they might find nothing. Also, it could delay the funeral for several weeks, depending on what they find."

"Go ahead," Al replied. "It would set my mind at rest."

NIGHT RAIDER

At Toronto Airport, another passenger returned home, also travelling cargo class: the standardbred stallion Night Raider, back from servicing a hundred mares in Queensland, Australia. In stark contrast to Phil Harman, he was very much alive. Theo Vettore was there as the horse was unloaded from the plane. He listened to the stallion calling out over and over again, on the way to Ferme Victoire. He watched him take possession of his stud quarters, his head erect, his demeanor regal, apparently eager to begin another breeding season, this time in the northern hemisphere. After being released from hospital, Theo had spent his waking hours in a daze, unsure who he was anymore. Seeing Night Raider again cracked open the door to the past and let in a chink of light that grew brighter as every day passed.

A week later, Theo woke up and remembered Harmony Light. To his dismay, no one seemed to have any idea where the horse was. After breaking down, Harmony Light had apparently disappeared off the face of the earth, a story not unlike his own, Theo concluded a little wistfully. Finding him seemed suddenly crucial to his own recovery. But where was he to start?

The phone was ringing in Al McTavish's office on the fifth floor at Iroquois Downs. After the trip to Florida, Al had gone straight back to work. The only outward sign that anything had changed was a new framed photo of Phil and himself in their younger days which now had pride of place on his desk. Al picked up the phone.

"Director of Racing," he said.

"This is the autopsy department. I need to speak to Alastair McTavish."

"This is he," Al replied nervously.

"First, apologies for taking so long. There was a mix-up and it ended up being filed in a drawer."

"Okay," Al said doubtfully, surprised that they had such a cavalier attitude to a man's death.

"We found nothing in the gut, no sign of any displacement of the intestine, but we did find some minute grazing in the throat and a small amount of yellow liquid in the lungs. The cause of death..." The man paused.

"Yes," Al prompted eagerly.

"It's definitely tubing I'm afraid. The mare was perfectly healthy in every other respect."

"The...mare?" Al stammered.

"Harmony Princess," the man confirmed. "It's the last thing you wanted to hear, I imagine, but we could find no other explanation."

"Thanks," Al said, feeling the exact opposite.

"Report's in the mail."

"Thanks," Al repeated, feeling he'd now reached rock bottom. The story would set the media alight and the flames would sweep through the race-track, leaving no one unscathed. The sudden reappearance of the cocaine addict Theo Vettore had created plenty of bad publicity already. Now this!

This time there would be no Phil Harman to help him.

It was snowing again. Snowflakes were alighting on frozen tire tracks and muddy footprints, made during the brief thaw. Campbell McClaren had retreated to base camp, a modest room next to Al McTavish's office. He was staring down at the depressing scene below him, his head spinning. There were far too many questions and no real answers. Listing them had only made him feel worse. He had been given one chance to put pressure on the elusive Anya, one opportunity to run the Scorpion to ground and he had blown it. Anya was a master at half truths, innuendos and, if those failed her, downright stonewalling. The only other person who might have been able to help, Theo Vettore, had been effectively neutralized, his memory of crucial events a complete blank.

The one positive note was the fact that Phil Harman's dental records had checked out, so Campbell had been able to lay to rest any doubts over Phil's identity. However, there was still a big question mark about the owner of the Lucky Seven Stable, something Judge Jewells and Al McTavish were both anxious to uncover.

Winter lost its grip on Ontario. The gloom of dark evergreens was relieved by the pale green of willow and silver birch. Shrill cries of Canada Geese filled the air. And everywhere, in fields and woods, new life was appearing as rac-coons, deer, coyotes, red foxes and race mares dropped their young. Theo Vettore woke up early and, as usual, he spent the first half hour torturing himself, trying to recall the eighteen lost months of his life. Since being discharged from hospital, he'd been sleeping in his old room at his uncle's farm. He wasn't cut out for the breeding business, but it was better than staying at his parents' suburban box outside Toronto, where he felt like a fish out of water.

The foaling season was in full swing, but after it was over, there'd be nothing for him to look forward to but months of mind numbing boredom. Yet when he thought about returning to his old life as a driver, he knew it was out of the question: not because of the risk associated with re-fracturing his skull, though his doctors had issued dire warnings about that. No! It was the cocaine inducing nervous tension. There had to be a way to make a living that fell somewhere in between suffocating routine and life on the high wire, didn't there? But where? How? He had absolutely no idea.

He threw back the covers, leapt out of bed and drew back the curtains, breathing in the cool air and listening to the sound of birdsong. It brought to mind the morning he had set off for Cree Horse Park to drive Harmony Light. On second thoughts, it was better not to dwell on that: his missing car, the confrontation with McClaren…and worse, much worse to come. Still, the memory of winning the General Custer with Harmony Light was almost the only thing that brought a smile to his lips these days. But where was the horse now? No one could give him a straight answer…not even his cousin Lara. If he wanted to find out, he was going to have to do it himself. He decided that any excuse to leave the farm was a good one. He'd been hiding out for long enough. It was time he faced the world again. After a quick cup of coffee, he jumped into his truck (fast cars didn't feature in his life these days) and headed east towards Meridian Acres where Lara was stabled. He found a spot in the horsemen's parking lot and walked the rest of the way.

His sudden appearance created a minor sensation. Lara's barn was soon crowded with people, all wanting a piece of him. He had forgotten what it was like, being a famous driver. The problem was, that wasn't what he was about anymore. Sensing his unease, Lara came and stood protectively beside him. Gazing out at the sea of people, he spotted some familiar faces, but there were plenty of new ones too like Will, Lara's assistant trainer and one or two like Evie Mercer who he barely recognized. He remembered her as a giggly teenager. Now she was a seriously desirable young woman. How had that happened so fast? Not that fast, he reminded himself. It had been nearly two years. There was no sign of Tony Hall, the man still listed as Harmony Light's trainer. No one knew where Tony was these days. He had been given a lifetime ban for tubing. Apparently the unfortunate horse hadn't lived to tell the tale.

At length, the familiar figure of Reggie Blair appeared pushing his way through the throng, a bulging feed sack balanced on his shoulder. What the feed man didn't know about Iroquois Downs and its inhabitants wasn't worth knowing. Once, a long time ago, Reggie had saved Theo's life. Could he save him again?

"Tony Hall?" Reggie asked, setting down his sack. "Easy! It's the last Thursday of the month. He'll be on his way to the abattoir. I saw him earlier, picking up one from Gerry's barn. Near killed 'em both loading 'im!"

"It wasn't a grey colt, was it?" Evie inquired anxiously, a look of dread on her face. Reggie scratched his head.

"Reckon it was," he replied.

"Not Storm!" Evie gasped.

"Could well be," Reggie conceded.

"*Mais c'est incroyable!*" Lara murmured, reverting to French, as she always did when her emotions got the better of her.

"Storm going for meat!" Evie cried. "No!"

"Well, we'll have to just stop him, won't we," Reggie declared. "I got room for two more," he offered, striding for the exit. Evie ran after him. Theo hesitated. A chance to talk to the elusive Tony Hall was too good a chance to miss but...

"Go!" Lara said decisively. "You call me, yes?"

"Hey, what about my feed?" Andy Price demanded in an outraged tone, following them outside as the three of them piled into Reggie's van. It was a tight fit.

"Later!" Reggie shouted, as he drove off. The racehorses on their way to the killers would be packed like sardines too, Theo thought grimly. Where those animals were headed, no amount of cuts and bruises would matter to anyone. Beside him, Evie was sitting bolt upright, rigid with fear.

"Hey," he said. "We'll get there in time." She shook her head.

"No chance. Tony left hours ago," she replied.

"Hang on tight! I'm taking a short cut," Reggie warned, swerving left and lurching down an unpaved road. Two kilometres on, they ran into trouble. The highway department was hard at work, repairing the ravages of the previous winter. After what felt like an eternity, the huge machines finally moved aside and let them through.

"We're not going to make it," Evie stated in a tone of despair.

"It'll be okay," Theo replied with a certainty he didn't feel.

"Good to have you in the cab this time, Vettore!" Reggie remarked cheerfully, as they hurtled along. "'Stead of back there!" Theo shuddered. The way Reggie was driving now, Theo reckoned he'd been lucky to get to ER in one piece that day. They were going so fast, the countryside was a blur. In his past life, he wouldn't have cared. But danger no longer thrilled him.

"This is it! There's Tony's truck," Reggie said, jamming on the brakes. It was far too quiet, Theo realized, as he jumped down from the van. There wasn't a horse in sight, just a mountain of discarded halters which told their own harrowing story. But it was the stench of dead flesh that really got to him.

They were too late!

Steeling himself, he walked over to Tony's truck, let down the ramp and flung open the doors. It was empty! A broken halter lay on the floor. When he saw the name plate on it, his heart sank. Hoping there'd be some explanation, praying that the worst had not occurred, he hurried on, determined to find Tony and confront him. Round the back of an old brick building, he came across a door marked Office. Behind him, he heard Evie screaming Storm's name. A moment later, she came flying towards him, a look of anguish on her face. The office door swung open. Tony Hall waltzed out, waving a freshly cut cheque: the day's takings, Theo realized, his stomach churning.

"Murderer!" Evie cried fiercely. Tony stopped in his tracks.

"How come you're here?" he frowned.

"What did you do to him?" Evie demanded furiously, her eyes flashing. "Where's Storm?" Tony took a step backwards.

"The grey colt," Theo explained.

"Oh, him. He's gone," Tony said.

"Gone. Gone where?" Evie asked. Tony jerked a thump in the direction of the abattoir. Evie burst into tears. "No!" she sobbed. "Please, no!"

"I tried to find 'im a home, honest," Tony said. "I promised Gerry, see. But no one wanted him," he faltered. "I went to all the training centres. And the riding stables."

"You never came to Meridian," Evie said in a strangled voice.

"No! Cos no one there would've wanted a cheap horse like him," Tony replied.

"Tammy would have!" Evie said. "She loves grey horses!" Silence fell. Tony looked downcast. No doubt he was thinking of the extra money he could have earned, Theo though cynically. But it wasn't Tony's fault. Not really.

The truth was, there were too many horses bred and too much wastage. It was impossible to find homes for them all. Theo had never had to face the problem first hand before. The horses he had driven were always in their prime.

"Little bastard got loose in the van," Tony said. "Broke his halter...wanted to go with the others. I couldn't have stopped him even if I'd wanted to."

"Is that what you did to Harmony Light, Tony?" Evie burst out. Tony looked shifty. It was impossible to guess what he was thinking.

"Well, is it?" Theo pressed, dreading the answer.

"You never took him to the vet, did you Tony?" Evie persisted. "Lara checked with Meecham."

"I don't understand," Theo said uncertainly.

"They were going to put him to sleep," Evie explained. It looked like the search was over. The knowledge went like a knife through Theo's heart. No wonder Lara hadn't wanted to tell him.

"Hey!" Reggie boomed.

"Over here," Evie called out. Reggie came around the corner, his face one big question mark.

"No good," Theo muttered with a quick shake of his head.

"We were too late. We're trying to find out what he did to Harmony Light," Evie said. Reggie turned to Tony, the expression on his face positively murderous.

"Keep your hair on!" Tony whined, brushing himself down even though Reggie hadn't laid a hand on him.

"Start talking," Reggie snapped. Start talking...the phrase took Theo back to the day his life began to unravel, the day he'd made a deal with McClaren. He hadn't been prosecuted for possession of cocaine, but he'd ended up paying a far greater price than ruining his reputation, thanks to the punishment the Scorpion had doled out.

"Andy told me to ship 'im to the doc," Tony conceded, wilting under Reggie Blair's furious stare. "Give me the cash 'n' all. But I figured a horse like 'im...'e'd be worth something if 'e ever sounded up."

"He's alive?" Theo exclaimed, his heart doing a backward somersault. Right away, doubt set in. If the vet had decided to put Harmony Light down, his injuries must have been pretty catastrophic. Probably the owners had already collected on the insurance. He decided to rein in his expectations.

"I could take you to 'im if you like," Tony offered. "But it'll cost you. It's a fair ways...out in Mennonite Country."

"Okay," Theo agreed with alacrity. "What about you, Evie?"

"I'm in!" she replied without hesitation.

"Well, I best get back to work," the feed man said, turning on his heel. "Good luck eh."

After the wild ride with Reggie, Tony Hall seemed like a model driver.

"I guess Storm finally ran out of luck," Evie sighed. "He almost bled to death once. Lost a ton of blood."

"Bust an artery," Tony concurred. "I heard 'bout that. Everyone was talking about it."

"Then he got really sick…nearly died," Evie said, "An old man from Alberta bought him. I thought he'd be safe, but then he showed up here again…"

"Alberta," Theo frowned. "I didn't know they even raced out there." A shred of memory was teasing him, dancing just out of sight.

"They have County Fairs," Evie replied. "In Saskatchewan."

"D'you have any pictures of him, maybe?"

"Somewhere," Evie replied vaguely. Theo glanced out of the window, hoping for inspiration, but all he saw was bare fields, with the occasional glimpse of winterwheat poking its green shoots through the earth. "You know," Evie continued. "Until a few years ago, my room was plastered with win pictures, some of Harmony Light but mostly of you. All, of you, actually." Theo reached over and silently squeezed her hand. "When you disappeared, I took them down. I thought you were dead. Everyone did."

"Everyone except Lara," Theo said softly.

"You were so remote back then, so…"

"Arrogant?" Theo suggested. Evie nodded.

"I like you better now. Don't change, okay?"

"No danger of that," Theo replied bitterly. "Looks like I'll always be what I am now."

"And what's that?"

"A has-been," Theo replied.

"That's crazy," Evie declared. "You're only, what, twenty-eight?"

"That's nearly thirty," Theo said heavily. "And you know the worst of it? I have absolutely no idea how that happened to me."

"Thirty! That's nothing!" Tony pronounced. "Wait 'til you're forty!"

Half an hour later, Tony pulled over and parked by the roadside. They had arrived.

"We'll have to leg it from here. Mennonites don't hold with motors," Tony warned. They walked down the laneway, serenaded by the buzz of crickets. There was a lot riding on this, Theo thought. If he found Harmony Light, he might just find himself. That was the theory anyhow. They passed a boy herding pigs under an old gnarled oak. As the farm house came into view, a pair of white geese waddled across their path, pursued by three little girls in long dresses. It was a quite a contrast to the cut and thrust of Iroquois Downs. How would he have fared in the Mennonite world? he wondered. Would he have ended up as a farmer, a blacksmith or a horse trader? The choices were almost as limited in the racing game. But what if he'd never heard of harness horses? How would he have made his living then?

"He'll be in there," Tony said, pointing to a tall weather beaten wooden barn which dominated the farmyard. After wandering around in the semi darkness and finding only empty stalls and stacks of hay and straw, they eventually came across a horse. He was standing with his head out of a narrow window, gazing out at the fields, where a team of plow horses was plodding patiently along. Above, a sparrowhawk hovered: a scene as old as the ages. "That leg of his, it ain't gonna be pretty," Tony warned as they approached. "Fair dragging on the ground it was…" At the sound of Tony's voice, Harmony Light whinnied shrilly. It triggered a flood of images in Theo's head: a tall leggy thoroughbred, a vista of snowcapped mountains and a circle of men standing shoulder to shoulder. He could see their faces clearly.

It all felt so real! Evie unlatched the stall gate and walked inside. The scene was still playing in his head. Was it a memory or just a waking dream?

"Harmony!" she whispered, burying her face in the horse's neck. With an effort, Theo switched back to the here and now. The expression in Harmony Light's eyes was a little deeper, a little wiser but otherwise he appeared unchanged: same tumbling mane and forelock, same startling white star. Theo gave the horse's legs a cursory glance. Then he caught sight of the left hind. He'd expected to find a cripple. What he saw made him far, far angrier. If it hadn't been for Tony, Harmony Light would be six foot under, put to death on one man's say so. Before he'd realized what he was doing, he'd grabbed Tony in a fierce bear hug. Tony backed away, looking terrified or mortified. It was hard to tell which. "You know what?" Evie said. "That leg doesn't look so bad."

"So, what happens now?" Theo asked.

"He's yours if you want 'im," Tony declared loftily. "For a price."

"Of course I want him," Theo started to say. Evie stopped him.

"Tony didn't pay for Harmony Light," she pointed out. "He sneaked off with him, right Tony?"

"Dawson's signed the papers," Tony replied sullenly. But no money had changed hands, Theo realized.

"We're going to have to call Dawson," Evie said. "Better to clear it up before…" She hesitated. Before what? Theo wondered. The horse was probably never going to race again, but at least he'd have a life. "What if Dawson's already collected on the insurance?" Evie asked.

"'E never took any," Tony assured them. "Too damn mean."

"If Dawson knows you're involved, Theo, the price'll sky rocket," Evie said.

"You call him," Theo replied immediately.

"Wot do I get outa this, eh?" Tony asked glumly, as he handed over his phone. Theo tried not to listen to the conversation between Evie and Jack Dawson. There was too much at stake. As the minutes crawled by, he vowed he'd find some way to prize him loose from Dawson, no matter what it took.

Evie had stopped talking. He held his breath. The signs weren't great. She was looking so serious.

"Twenty-five hundred cash," she said. "I'm meeting him in the grandstand before the races."

"Thank God," Theo gasped.

"I'm glad things worked out for you," Evie stated quietly. She hadn't been as lucky as him today, Theo realized.

"Want to go partners on him?" he offered.

"Really?" she asked, her face lighting up. "But I couldn't afford to pay much," she warned.

"I'd need someone to take care of him," Theo said. "So…job's yours if you want it!"

"Okay," she agreed.

"Wot 'bout me?" Tony demanded.

"We'll work something out," Theo assured him. "But how do we move him? I don't want to leave him here."

Tony shrugged helplessly.

"Don't worry, I know what to do," Evie said confidently. "Winterflood showed me, years ago."

Half an hour later, his leg swathed in a mass of old T-shirts, held together with two red bandages, Harmony Light stepped into Tony's rattle trap of a horse trailer, evidently pleased to get out of there. Neither one of them was cut out for life on a farm, Theo concluded, smiling at the thought.

"Meridian Acres or bust?" Evie asked. It didn't come anywhere close to expressing how he felt. But with Tony listening in, he wasn't about to divulge his innermost thoughts, never mind his conviction that his and Harmony Light's fates were inextricably linked.

Where he led, Harmony Light always seemed to follow.

Back at Meridian Acres, Evie settled Harmony Light into an empty stall in Lara's barn. No one else was around. Theo had left, tailed by Tony, who wasn't letting him out of his sight until he'd been paid his money. If Harmony Light hadn't been a star two year old, he would be dead too, just like Storm, Evie reflected bitterly. As the silence pressed in around her, she couldn't shake off the image of the grey colt's body dangling from a meat hook in the abattoir or worse, lying in pieces on the abattoir floor. Grief, guilt, anger washed over her in quick succession and a wordless cry, like an animal in pain, burst from somewhere deep inside her. Blindly, she made for Lara's tack room, desperate for a place to hide away. All too soon, there was a loud knock at the door.

"Go away!" she screamed. The door swung open. When she looked up, Will was standing there.

"What's going on?" he asked, in a worried tone. If only she could cry, she thought. Maybe she'd feel better, get some relief.

"What are you doing here?" she demanded angrily. Will looked startled, but he answered the question.

"They were running three hours late at the clinic. Doc was called out on an emergency," he explained. Of course, she realized. None of this was Will's fault. "What's happened, Evie?" he frowned.

"You really wanna know?" she asked, sinking down onto a chair.

"We're friends, right?" Will said. "Friends tell each other stuff. That's what you said, Evie, remember?" She did remember. It was the night Goldie had won her first race, the night Princess had been claimed. Now Cat was out of the picture and Princess was dead. And Storm...Storm was dead, too. The dam broke. The tears flowed. After an age, she told Will the whole story.

When she was done, Will was silent for a long moment. "I know you liked him a lot," he said carefully. "But Storm was nuts, Evie. He could've got someone hurt bad."

"He was only four years old!" she replied angrily.

"He was never gonna change. Near tore my shoulder off its hinges that day we tried to hitch 'im to the cart. Hurt like the devil for the longest time."

"You never told me that."

"Yeah, well. No sense complaining, eh. Anyhow, in the end, the doc shocked it for me. It was okay after that."

"Winterflood? He gave you shockwave therapy?" she asked, feeling astonished. "I never knew that!"

"So, when are you gonna get around to telling me what Harmony Light is doing in our barn?"

"It's complicated," she countered, reluctant to go into it all again.

"But it's gotta be good, right?"

"Yes," Evie agreed, feeling a little more cheerful.

"Six o'clock already. I gotta feed," Will declared.

"I'd give you a hand, but I've gotta go get ready."

"Ready? For what? We don't have anything racing tonight."

"I'll tell you tomorrow," Evie said, feeling a tiny bubble of excitement at the prospect of her and Theo's name down as joint owners of Harmony Light.

"Okay," Will replied, tossing grain into the feed tubs.

It looked like she was going to have to face the fact that she had let Storm down, Evie thought sadly, without totally beating herself up for it. She had saved Jetson. But no one could save them all. Not even her.

It was 7:39 on the tote board clock. With just one minute to go before the first race went off, Theo Vettore was watching the familiar scene, drinking it all in. He was now the proud owner of a half share in a former star performer. He was also flat broke with no clear way of making a living. Beside him, Evie was climbing the rail and leaning over it to get a better view. Surprisingly, his protective instinct kicked in; he wanted to warn her that it wasn't safe. But who was he to tell her that? The thunder of hooves, when the horses went by brought on a rush of emotion. It wasn't anything like watching it on TV. The sights and sounds brought everything back: the highs, the lows. How could he have forgotten all this? Why on earth had he stayed away for so long? Harness racing was a drug. Everyone involved was an addict. He watched, spellbound, as a powerful trotter emerged from the pack and took over the lead.

"She's gonna win!" Evie screamed. As the horses flashed past, she peeled herself off the rail and grabbed Theo's arm. "Let's go!" she cried. A fiery chestnut, appropriately named Harmony Fire, came flying into the winner's circle with old Eddie Clearwater grinning like an idiot on board. A smartly dressed young couple ran up. Must be the owners, Theo realized.

"Kip! Caroline!" Evie exclaimed. Shrieks of delight, hugs and handshakes followed, while Theo stood on the sidelines, out of the party. Eddie, who had to be pushing eighty, was still driving horses, while he was washed up at twenty-eight! It wasn't fair! he thought, as the cameras flashed. Out of habit, he followed the procession into the Race Barn. On the way, one of the owners fell back and joined him.

"I'm Kip," he said. "We watched you win the General Custer with Harmony Light. You aced it!" Theo acknowledged the compliment with a smile. He decided not to tell this well meaning stranger that his days as a driver were over. Was he imagining it, or were people cheering? He was aware that Eddie Clearwater was a living legend, but even so . . .

"Wave!" Evie hissed in his ear. Reluctantly, he did so. The cheering intensified, followed by the sound of applause. His heart full, he finally understood that the horsemen of Iroquois Downs were welcoming back one of their own.

"Second race leaves in two minutes, men!" Mr Roberts barked out. "Get ready with the One horse!" Instantly, everyone went back to work. But it made Theo realize that for better or worse, this was still his world, warts and all. Somehow, he'd have to find his place in it, or his life would simply not be worth living anymore. But how?

"Vettore!" a voice boomed. Jim Mercer came striding towards him, his ruddy face wreathed in smiles. "Thank God you're back, you son of a bitch! I got a two year old colt for you to drive that..." Theo cut him off mid flow.

"Haven't got my licence back yet."

"Well go get it!" Mercer said heartily, slapping him on the back, before marching off. It wasn't that simple, Theo wanted to say, but he let it go. He knew one thing though. Life without harness racing would be a total waste of time.

"Dad was pretty happy to see you," Evie said, looking surprised.

"Nothing personal. Just looking for a driver," Theo replied. "Hey Crawfish!" he shouted, anxious to get off the subject of driving. "How's it going?"

"Ain't talking to you," Crawfish said, looking scared to death. Not everyone was pleased to see him, Theo realized.

"Just look at Gerry!" Evie cried furiously, pointing to a man with flaming red hair carrying a load of blankets. "He's got some nerve, showing up here tonight, after what he did. He's not even sorry!" This was all about Storm, Theo realized. "I'm not gonna let him get away with it," Evie added vehemently, breathing hard, her fists clenched.

"We need to leave," Theo said firmly. "You can go see him tomorrow if you want. Not here. Not now. Trust me." Evie didn't move a muscle. "Let's go to the Cherokee Inn," Theo suggested. "We'll get something to eat there, okay?" Slowly, reluctantly, Evie allowed him to shepherd her away. "I'd really like to see a picture of Storm," he added, purely to take her mind off things.

At the Cherokee Inn, Evie pulled out a photo of Harmony Storm hitched up to the sulky, out on the racetrack.

"He went a big mile that day," she said.

"Where'd you take this?" Theo asked, staring at the picture.

"Rivers Training centre. It was freezing that day!" That made no sense to Theo. He was certain he'd seen the colt before. But where? It wasn't just Storm's unusual colour, it was his unique silhouette. He never forgot a horse. But where had he seen him? Certainly not at Rivers Training centre in the middle of winter. But what about Saskatchewan? Hadn't Evie said they had County Fairs there? A bell rang in Theo's head. He was dimly aware of the clink of glasses, the background chatter at the Cherokee Inn, but his mind was far away, watching a grey colt coming from last place to win by a whisker. . .hearing the roar of the crowd. Suddenly everything went deathly quiet.

"Hey, you okay?" he heard Evie ask hesitantly.

"I need to go home," he replied.

"I don't think that's such a great idea," Evie said. "You look kind of weird."

The room was spinning! Images of people, of places were coming at him so fast that he felt like he was going to throw up. He cradled his head in his arms, trying to fend them off but the bombardment continued. The images felt sickeningly familiar, like a dream he'd had many, many times. At last, the action slowed dramatically. A close up view of a needle appeared out of nowhere, then disappeared into the blackness. A harsh voice grated in his ear: "That'll teach 'im to fuck with Fontainbleu!"

When he came to, he was lying on the floor, surrounded by a sea of faces.

"I'm calling 911," he heard Evie cry.

"No!" he replied firmly. "I know who did this to me! It was Fontainbleu!"

"That makes absolutely no sense," Evie said, sounding bewildered. He brushed her concerns aside. Finally, he had a name. Nothing else mattered. He was terrified he'd forget it. "You need to go to ER," she added.

"Need to see someone first," he replied. There was only one man alive who'd take him seriously.

"Who?" Evie asked, helping him to his feet.

"Constable Campbell McClaren of the RCMP," he said. She pulled out her phone. "Hey! What are you doing, Evie?"

"Campbell McClaren," she explained. "Is the Head of Security at Iroquois Downs."

Anya's cell phone was ringing. When she saw Jeff's number come up, she almost didn't answer it. But guilt, and if she was honest, curiosity, won the day. After the awkward "how are you's" were safely out of the way, her ex-boyfriend explained why he'd called. Apparently a package had arrived for her.

"Feels like there's a set of keys in there," Jeff said. "Have you lost any?"

"No! Open it for me, okay, Jeff?" A rustling sound was followed by a silence so profound she wasn't sure Jeff was even there. But eventually he got back on the line.

"You never told me you were moving back to Australia," he said in a baffled tone.

"I wish," she replied.

"Oh yeah? Then what are you doing with the deeds to a house in Sydney? I'm guessing these keys open the front door." Anya sat down, her heart racing. "There's something else, a card…with a heart on it and there's a message inside," he said.

"Don't open it, Jeff," she said tersely. But it was too late.

"Fond memories of times past," he read out, before she could stop him. "'Adieu cherie, André Michelangelo'…who's André Michelangelo?" he asked haltingly. "And what's this? Wealth warning! D'you want me to read it out to you?"

"No! Where are you? I'm coming right over," Anya replied immediately. After she'd rung off, Jeff picked up the card, his imagination running riot. He was tempted to rip it up. Then he had a better idea. He called Billie and told her everything.

"I have to go over to Jeff's," Billie said, shaking Campbell awake.

"What time is it?" Campbell asked sleepily, squinting at the clock. He had been up half the night with Theo Vettore, who, once he had started talking, couldn't seem to stop.

"10 a.m. Something's happened."

"What? Tell me!"

"No time!"

"Give me five minutes and I'll come with you..." he offered.

"Okay, but hurry! I'll explain on the way," Billie replied impatiently.

It was raining as they ran up the steps of Jeff's building. Jeff greeted them at the door of his apartment, his face purple with rage.

"Is Anya here?" Billie asked immediately.

"Been and gone," Jeff said angrily.

"That's unfortunate," Campbell replied. "I wanted to question her. It was important."

"Important to who?" Jeff asked through clenched teeth. "I never want to see or hear about her ever again! Imagine what she had to do to be given a house on Sydney harbour?" he ranted. "It's like she's some sort of prostitute or something. She never told me, never breathed a word about it. I can't believe I wanted to marry her. I feel like an idiot!" Suddenly his face went chalk white.

"Jeff!" Billie cried out, helping him over to the sofa, where he sat down hard.

"He's had a shock!" Campbell said, reproaching himself for missing the signs. "Is there any brandy in the house?"

"Fat chance!" Billie replied in an exasperated tone. "He's a health nut!"

"Check out the kitchen..." he suggested. "Hey!" he shouted, waving his hands in front of Jeff's face. "Wake up!" When he tried to take his pulse, Jeff fended him off. "Found anything?" Campbell called out.

"Not yet!" Billie called back. "Only carrot juice! Wait, what's this?" A couple of minutes later, she returned holding a glass of orange liquid. "I found a bottle of something called *Stress Buster*," she said. "What d'you reckon?"

"Sounds okay," Campbell conceded.

"Ugh," Jeff spluttered as he gulped it down. "What d'you give me? It tastes disgusting!"

"You'll feel better in a minute," Billie assured him. But Jeff didn't feel better. He looked positively goggle eyed.

"Water!" he said thickly.

"Whatever did you give him?" Campbell asked.

"Nothing. Just carrot juice! And the stress buster of course," she replied, handing over a small glass bottle. He squinted at the contents.

"It's a hundred percent proof! How much of this did he have?"

"The whole thing!" Billie gulped as the implications of giving Jeff pure alcohol sunk in.

"Make him some strong coffee," Campbell advised.

"There's only decaff," Billie reported a short while later, sounding close to tears. "I've got a bar of chocolate. Would that be any use?"

"He needs water first," Campbell replied, joining her in the kitchen.

Jeff drank the water; then he polished off the chocolate. "I'm fine. What's all the fuss about?" he asked groggily.

"Safest place for you is bed," Campbell said.

"I'll stay with him," Billie offered. "He needs me."

"He does," Campbell agreed. "I'll swing by later."

"Where are you off to in such a hurry?" she asked.

"Me? I can't wait to get started," he said. Billie looked at him blankly. "André Michelangelo Fontainbleu," he added. "At last I have the full name of the Scorpion, thanks to Vettore…and Jeff of course."

"Hey! Don't do anything stupid. No heroics, okay?" she pleaded, following him out to the elevator. "Jeff will probably break out in hives from the chocolate," she added glumly. "That's if the alcohol doesn't finish him off… I'm going to jail for sure!"

"Don't worry…I'll pull a few strings. Get you out in a day or two!" Campbell assured her with a broad smile.

"Great! That's really made my day!" he heard her say fretfully as the elevator doors slid shut.

Theo Vettore and Evie Mercer were standing outside Harmony Light's stall, admiring their new purchase. Despite having had no sleep the night before, Theo was feeling better than he had in months.

"So what next?" Evie asked.

"Ultrasound," Theo replied. "Need to know the story with that leg."

"I meant, what's next for you?"

"No idea," he confessed.

"Too bad we're not in the UK."

"The UK? Why would I want to go there?"

"The racing channels over there are always on the look for ex-jockeys to join the team. . . as presenters, apparently. That's what Kip and Caroline told me, anyhow…Harmony Fire's owners," she explained.

"Well, this isn't the UK," Theo stated.

"But why not do that here?" Evie suggested eagerly. "People know you… they'd talk to you. You could do interviews, features…it'd be brilliant. The show they put on at Iroquois Downs puts everyone to sleep. Besides, it's only about betting! There's so much more to racing than that, right?"

"It's an idea, I guess," Theo replied dubiously.

"A great one!" Evie said enthusiastically. "I'd jump at the chance to talk about the horses and what they go through, what happens to them after they're done racing."

"That'd be pretty controversial."

"What's wrong with that? Things need to change."

"We could talk to someone about it, I guess," Theo conceded.

"Like Al Mactavish?" Evie said.

"Maybe. But I want to take Harmony Light to Winterflood first."

"It's a deal," Evie replied happily.

Campbell drove back through the sodden countryside to base camp. On his way there, he mulled over the events of the past twenty-four hours. The house in Sydney, Australia had come with a wealth warning. True to his character, André Michelangelo Fontainbleu had made it clear that accepting his generous gift would not be risk free. That ought to give Anya some sleepless nights. Was it worth it? Not in Campbell's book. But he had concluded long ago that the potential for criminality existed in nearly everyone, simply waiting for the right circumstances, or a single life changing event to bring it out. With her secretive nature, he was fairly sure Anya would decide to move into that house, even with the wealth warning that came with it.

But, if everyone had a breaking point, what had triggered André Michelangelo's fall from grace? It was lunchtime but Campbell didn't feel in the least bit hungry. He decided to start at the very beginning. Knowing André was French Canadian was a big help. He logged on to the national register and quickly discovered that André had been born in Quebec City. He got on the website of the *Quebec Quotidien*, Quebec City's daily newspaper, and keyed in the name Fontainbleu with no particular expectations. After a few false starts, a headline popped up which screamed out at him: TRAGEDIE DE LES DEUX FRERES FONTAINBLEU!

"Tragedy of the two Fontainbleu brothers," Campbell murmured. He knew enough French to understand the headline, at least. A photo of two teenagers, arm in arm, gazed out at him across the years. The taller of the two had straight dark hair which flopped over his forehead. The other boy sported a crop of dark curls. Eagerly, Campbell clicked on *Translate* and began to read.

"On the same day that Philippe Fontainbleu, 19, was shot in the chest, his younger brother, André, 16, has vanished, leaving the family devastated and desperate for news. Philippe Raphael Fontainbleu (named after the famous Renaissance painter) is currently in hospital, in intensive care. The family suspect the attack may have been intended for the younger brother. The two boys look very much alike, except for a slight difference in height and the colour of their eyes. Philippe's eyes are blue. André's are brown. Doctors have described Philippe's condition as critical…"

Phil Harman's middle name was also Raphael. A coincidence? Campbell didn't think so. Just how many Canadians named after Renaissance artists could there be? Had Philippe somehow survived? Had he fled to Vancouver, needing to put as much space as possible between him and his attackers? Had he changed his name for the same reason? If so, Phil Harman was the Scorpion's brother? Unbelievable! Unthinkable! Concluding he was getting light-headed from lack of food. Campbell went to lunch.

Every day, as he drove to the Lucky Seven's farm, Dr. Jay Winterflood fully expected to see a For Sale sign erected beside it. It had to happen sometime. After all, apart from his veterinary clinic, the place was deserted. The horses had left; the barn was empty. But no one had locked Jay out yet, so he was carrying as normal, hoping for a miracle. He was looking forward to seeing his last patient of the day: the one he always thought of as the little trouble-maker. Harmony Light seemed to be in good spirits and didn't look lame, though his left hind leg was swathed in bandages. After the bandages came off, Jay ran his hand down the leg. Disappointingly, he felt heat and inflam-mation. Clearly the injury was not yet fully resolved.

"Don't look so worried. I'll ultrasound it," Jay told Evie Mercer. "Where's Theo?"

"Waiting outside, in the truck," Evie explained. As Jay rolled out his ultrasound machine, he wondered as always, how much longer he would continue to have access to it. "What do you make of it?" Evie asked anxiously, before he was halfway done.

"There's a great deal of damage here," Jay replied at length. "Both old and new. Some healing has already taken place, which is a good sign. His problem appears to be limited to the suspensory ligament, but I'll need to take a few X-rays to be certain."

"What are his chances?" Evie asked.

"Of making a full recovery? Difficult to say at this point. If a mare had an injury like this, I'd suggest retiring her to the broodmare ranks."

"He's not a mare," Evie replied steadfastly. "He's a gelding." She patted his neck affectionately. "I wouldn't care if he never raced again but Theo . . . I know he's hoping he'll make it back to the races."

"I'll drop by with the results of the X-rays in a couple of days," Jay said. "In the meantime, keep him quiet and don't take him out of the stall. Let's hope for the best, okay?"

After a hearty lunch, designed to keep hunger at bay for several hours, Campbell set to work digging up facts about Philip Raphael Harman. He remembered Al had told him that Phil had grown up in BC. He found out that much was true, at least. The birth certificate showed Philip had been born on Victoria Island. He went to school there too. Campbell probed further. Pretty soon, he wished he had left well alone.

Philip Raphael Harman had died thirty-five years ago, aged nineteen, in a skiing accident.

Jay Winterflood stopped his car beside his mailbox at the end of the drive. There was a package inside. Deliveries of equine supplies arrived several times a week, so Jay didn't give it much thought. He tossed it onto the passenger seat and drove on down the laneway to the house.

When he opened the package, he found an envelope full of what felt like photographs and a letter.

Dear Jay, he read. *By the time you see this, I shall have left this world. But I wanted you to know that your mother was the love of my life. I thought about her often. I always hoped I would see her again. But it was not to be. By now, you will have guessed the truth. I am the father who deserted you both all those years ago. There were many compelling reasons for my actions, but I shall not go into them now.*

"After I saw your picture in the Erinsville paper surrounded by your half brothers and sisters, I wished only to go back, to live my life again, to be there when you were growing up. But when I met you for the first and only time, I understood something. Despite my absence, you had, after all, received a precious gift. The genetic heritage that your mother and I passed on to you had combined to create a powerful individual in harmony with himself. A matter of chance, you may say but perhaps also a reflection of the relationship your mother and I enjoyed, if only for a brief time.

You have your own family now: a beautiful woman, a son and another child on the way. Your future is bright and I have no doubt, as the chief beneficiary of my will, you will put the many millions that are at your disposal now to good use. Through you, I shall achieve things I could only dream of. Adieu, mon fils. Perhaps I shall now finally find peace.

Philip Raphael Harman.

Stunned, Jay read the letter several times. At last, he turned his attention to the contents of the envelope. As the photographs tumbled out, he noticed a scrap of paper flutter to the floor.

If only he had known! If only Phil had told him, he thought, blinking back the tears. Now it was too late. Bending down, he retrieved the scrap of paper, hoping for something, anything really, to distract him from what he was feeling now. The combination of consternation and sorrow, mingled with relief was difficult to handle. All his financial worries were over, but what a way for it to happen! The heading on the typewritten sheet caught him completely unawares.

WARNING, he read. *Any person or persons discovered receiving cash or goods obtained wholly or in part from illegal activities can be tried in a court of law and, if found guilty, will be subject to fines, imprisonment or a combination of the two.* The words erupted in his head, impossible to ignore or explain away. The implications were extraordinary but undeniable. Phil Harman was not the respectable citizen he had appeared to be. Jay's mind was in turmoil. He needed to talk to Helena, urgently.

"Jay!" he heard her say. "My waters just broke."

Thunderstruck, Campbell sat staring at the screen for a full five minutes, his head buzzing with the implications. If he was right, Philippe had somehow survived and had taken on a dead man's name. What other possible conclusion could there be? There was only one way he knew to the get to the bottom of this: facial recognition software. He printed off the photo of the two boys in the *Quebec Quotidien*, then he marched next door, into Al's office. Al was still at lunch but the photo of Phil Harman was sitting in full view on the desk. For the first time, Campbell noticed how extraordinarily blue Phil's eyes were. Philippe Raphael Fontainbleu had also had blue eyes, he realized according to the *Quebec Quotidien*.

Campbell helped himself to the photo and hurried off, convincing himself that it wasn't really stealing, since he intended to return it: the poor excuse of many a burglar, he realized, guiltily. He ran up the stairs to the fifth floor and knocked on a door marked *Technology Services and Support*. He had his cover story ready: a lie about wanting to post a photo of Phil as a young man onto his memorial website. Lying, stealing. How many other commandments was he going to break before he was done? he wondered uncomfortably.

Pete was sitting on the stern of the Shere Khan, drinking a beer, watching the sun go down and cursing André Fontainbleu. He'd been gone over a week and he still hadn't shown up. It was typical of the guy, Pete thought bitterly. He'd kept his side of the bargain, skippering the son of a bitch wherever he'd wanted to go. But when it came time to cough up, the bastard had done a runner. Now what? Pretty soon, he'd have to go ashore, load up with supplies. He was running out of beer for starters.

"Hey, is this the She R Can?" a voice called out cheerfully. Cautiously, Pete made his way to the bow and looked down.

"This is the Shere Khan," he replied.

"Got a package for someone called Pete."

"That'd be me," Pete confirmed. Mystified, he took the package and went down into the cabin, turned the lights on and ripped open the envelope. It contained the exact location of the two hidden cameras in the Hermitage, one of which had captured him and Henri making love. The fear of it going viral online had tortured him for years. That fear had turned him into a puppet, dangling helplessly while Fontainbleu pulled the strings. He dialled Henri's number. In a few hours, the camera records would be erased and they would both be free.

As for Fontainbleu, let him rot in hell!

Playing around with facial recognition software was the Department's idea of a treat, Campbell discovered after handing over the photographs to the boffins who provided technical support at Iroquois Downs. He settled down and prepared himself for a wait. The results came back much more quickly than he'd expected and they were a complete surprise. Phil Raphael Harman and Philippe Raphael Fontainbleu had scored high enough to indicate a close family tie, probably siblings. But Philip Raphael Harman and André Michelangelo Fontainbleu had scored a hundred percent. They were a perfect match, so perfect there was only one possible conclusion. André and Phil were not two separate people; they were one and the same. It took Campbell quite a while to fully understand that the hunt for the Scorpion was over. The Scorpion was no longer alive! Campbell's first thought was that no one would believe him. He wasn't sure he believed it himself. He had been wrong plenty of times in the past.

Back at base camp, he put in a call to Erinsville Morgue asked to be put through to the autopsy department, hoping it might provide some answers. He was put on hold. Eventually, a woman got on the line. It looked like she could set Al's mind at rest on one point at least. They had uncovered a motive for suicide. An aggressive form of cancer, originating from an undetected melanoma on the sole of his foot, had taken over Phil's body. He had had mere weeks to live. Killing himself with a simple shot through the heart would have required nerves of steel, something the Scorpion would have possessed in great measure, Campbell imagined.

"Anything else I should know?" he enquired, hoping for clues to his theory.

"Not really. There were a couple of things we noticed. They didn't seem important and I'm not sure they'll even be in the official report."

She hesitated.

"Go on," Campbell said.

"His left ear lobe was pierced, but there was no earring in it and we couldn't find it anywhere on the body. Also…" she paused again.

"Yes," Campbell prompted.

"The hair doesn't actually grow after death, but it appears to," she revealed, a little awkwardly. "The victim's natural hair type was curly, not straight. And he was wearing contact lenses, which were coloured blue. His natural eye colour was brown." Barely able to contain himself, Campbell thanked her and rang off. The puzzle was finally solved! After his initial feeling of satisfaction had ebbed away, Campbell was truly sorry about it. It had ruined everything! Al McTavish would have a rude awakening when he discovered who his best friend and mentor really was. And how would Winterflood feel about a man like that being his father?

Campbell asked Billie to marry him that afternoon. They met up beside the Speed River.

"Let's take a walk," Billie suggested, linking arms with him. Together they followed the trail beside the river, strolling along in companionable silence, a silence broken only by the quacking of ducks. The whole scene was bathed in the mellow light of late afternoon. Billie's response to his proposal wasn't exactly what he had hoped for.

"Aren't you supposed to go down on one knee when you say that?" she asked playfully. Rarely had the two of them been in such disparate states of mind. Her elation at the sale of Fence Sense for a top price, his gloom at the Scorpion's cold fingers reaching out from the mortuary slab. "What's going on?" she demanded. "And why are you even mentioning the 'm' word? You're not pregnant are you?" she added in mock disapproval. She had got him to smile. In the present situation, that was quite a feat. "Seriously," she added. "What about the Scorpion? We agreed to wait...until you collared him. It seemed to be all you cared about." This was Campbell's cue.

"The Scorpion is dead," he pronounced. "I got positive confirmation of that about three hours ago."

"Oh my God!" Billie gasped. "How? When?"

"It's a long story," Campbell hedged. "Are you sure you want to hear it? You may wish you didn't afterwards."

"No secrets," she replied without hesitation. "Not between us, anyway," she clarified.

"André Fontainbleu, later known as the Scorpion, was born and grew up in Quebec City. By the age of sixteen, he had a criminal dossier as long as your arm."

"That makes sense!" Billie replied.

"His brother Philippe was shot right outside his parents' home. André may well have seen it happen. In any case, within hours, he had fled the city. He probably thought they were coming for him next."

"Oh my God!" Billie said again.

"Fontainbleu shows up again at the Cree Reserve, outside Montreal. No doubt he was hiding out there until things cooled down. The Cree ran him out of the reserve when they discovered that a number of young Cree girls were pregnant and were naming him as the father."

"What a total low life!" Billie burst out.

"I'm guessing that his next point of call was Vancouver. He took the identity of Philip Raphael Harman, a nineteen- year-old who had died in a skiing accident."

"What? That's unbelievable!"

"Phil flew under the radar for about ten years. It's a fair assumption that he was setting up a drug smuggling network during that time, across Canada."

"Go on," Billie said.

"He popped up again running a fledgling business as a property consultant in Ontario."

"Why Ontario?" Billie queried.

"He couldn't stay in Vancouver and he didn't dare go back to Quebec. Ontario was the logical choice."

"But. . . Erinsville?" Billie asked, sounding sceptical.

"Who knows? In any case, his timing was perfect. During the next two decades, Erinsville grew from an insignificant town into a small city."

"But what about the Scorpion?"

"You mean André Fontainbleu? Or Phil Harman? They're the same person, Billie. He was leading a double life, one in Sainte Marie where he was free to indulge all his appetites, the other in Erinsville, a gregarious well liked fixer, a lot like his brother had been, from what I've been able to find out." Maybe it was André's way of keeping his brother's memory alive, Campbell thought, however unlikely that sounded. Philippe had graduated from high school with top honours.

"I should have known," Billie said.

"Known what?"

"That day at Cree Horse Park. It was just before I met you for the first time. Phil was drunk that day...I sensed something. His mask must have slipped just for a moment and I saw...it was the look in his eyes," she finished with a shudder.

"You saw the Scorpion," Campbell stated.

"He made me question Dad's integrity. That was cruel. Beyond cruel!"

"Sadistic?" Campbell suggested.

"He wanted to make the world pay, I suppose," she said. "His brother took a bullet that he must have known was meant for him." A silence fell between them, broken only by the sound of the river. Campbell folded her in his arms and held her close, ignoring the curious stares of Canada Geese swimming by.

"For richer, for poorer," he whispered in her ear. "In sickness and in health. 'Til death do us part."

"Where's the ring?" she asked, pulling away.

"I've seen one I liked," Campbell replied. "One with three red stones but I thought we could choose it together."

"Rubies?" Billie said thoughtfully. "Three rubies. D'you know what that means to me?"

"Something good?" Campbell replied hopefully.

"It means...you'll love me always, now and forever," Billie declared.

"Sounds about right," he replied with a broad smile.

"We can't tell Dad," Billie said. Campbell raised his eyebrows. "About Phil," she clarified. "It would kill him. But, what about Winterflood? Phil left him all the money, right? Wouldn't we be breaking the law if we didn't say anything?"

"Perverting the course of justice, you mean? Probably," Campbell acknowledged gloomily.

"What about Anya? What d'you think she'll do?"

"That's for Anya to decide."

"And Winterflood? You want to see him behind bars?"

"Of course not!" Campbell protested.

"Then you can't stay silent, can you?"

"Not sure. What about you?" he countered.

"It's curious, isn't it?" she said. "Phil didn't leave Dad anything in his will. I know Dad was really put out by that. Now I realize Phil was doing him a favour."

"Your father was probably the only person the Scorpion really cared about," Campbell agreed.

"No," Billie said. "Not the only person. He must have cared about his brother too. What a sad, sad life he must have led. I pity him."

"Tell that to Theo Vettore," Campbell replied.

Jay Winterflood was gazing at his newborn daughter, barely three days old, as Helena rocked her gently back and forth.

"D'you think she's gonna have blue eyes?" he asked.

"Too early to tell," Helena replied.

"Phil's eyes were so blue. It'd be nice if she had something of her grand-father."

"Don't bank on it. We both have brown eyes."

"It's a recessive gene. It could happen."

"Finding out who your father was, really means a lot to you, doesn't it?" Helena said softly.

"It's crazy," Jay replied. "All this time I thought my father was a drifter...a wastrel called Curly...and then I discover he's living the life of a model cit-izen."

"They did check Phil Harman's DNA against yours right?" Helena asked. Jay nodded. "Makes it all more curious that he never contacted you...or your brothers and sisters."

"I guess he was worried about his reputation," Jay replied.

"Makes sense..." The baby whimpered. Helena put her to her breast. "Have you decided what you're going to do?"

"About the money? Phil even left me the Lucky Seven farm...and the clinic...everything."

"Including the bingo halls," Helena reminded him disapprovingly. "And what about the wealth warning? You can't just ignore that, Jay."

"I suppose...back in his past...Phil may have broken the law," Jay con-ceded. "He was trying to protect me."

"Trying to warn you, more like." Helena said. Jay sighed. If only...but it was too late for that.

"The Phil Harman Charitable Foundation?" he said at last. "It has a good ring to it, yes?"

"Sounds like a plan," Helena agreed. "But you'd have to distance yourself from it entirely. You can't benefit, Jay, not financially. It's too risky. We don't know anything about Phil Harman, not really."

"I'd like to name her after him," Jay said. "It'd mean a lot to me."

"Philippa?" Helena asked, sounding horrified.

"His middle name was Raphael. How about Rafaella, with an "f"?"

"I could go for that," Helena replied, smiling at the baby, who was sucking vigorously.

"Well, I gotta go. Gotta give a report on some X-rays I took."

"Anyone we know?"

"Yeah, Harmony Light. You'll never believe who owns him now."

"Who?"

"Evie Mercer and…Theo Vettore!"

On a dazzling white sand beach, on the Gulf coast of Florida, Boxer was reading a letter.

Mon cher Boxer.

Pendant tou ma vie (for my whole life), *tu mas protégé de tout* (you have protected me from the consequences of my actions). *Mais, mon ami, la mort, elle vient pour tout le monde* (But my friend, there is no escaping death) *et maintenant, c'est mon tour* (now it is my turn). *Je te donne le Shere Khan.* (I want you to have the Shere Kahn.) *Vive en paix, mon ami. Le travail, c'est fini.* (Live in peace, my friend. Your work is finished*) Ne regrette rien!*

Adieu,

André.

There was something else in the envelope. Boxer shook it. A single gold earring shaped like a horseshoe fell onto his huge, outstretched palm. He didn't notice the slip of paper fall onto the sand. With a heavy heart, he gathered his things together and began to walk up the beach.

"Hey, mister!" a shrill voice called out, "You dropped somethin'!" Boxer ignored it. André was gone. Nothing else mattered. His purpose in life was over. He heard footsteps. Someone was scampering after him. Reluctantly, he turned around, shading his eyes from the glare of the sun. A small boy handed him a scrap of paper. "You're supposed to put it in the bin," the boy said, reprimanding him. Boxer took it, read it and immediately crumpled it up into a ball and dropped it on the sand. He had never paid attention to threats or warnings. Now was not the time to begin. He was only dimly aware of a beach guard blocking his way.

"No litter! Pick it up!" the man said. Boxer felled him with a single blow to the chest, leaving him sprawled out on the sand. Then, he kept on walking, past the lifeguard station, through the swaying palms. He reached the parking lot and saw a police car with its lights flashing.

"That's him!" someone cried out. "That's the guy." Four men descended on him like hounds of hell, clubs at the ready. Blindly, Boxer hit out at all four at once, their blows bouncing harmlessly off his head and body. He never heard the gunshots that killed him.

On a cool, sunny morning, Al trudged off to Phil Harman's funeral feeling like he wanted to die himself. Campbell had broken the news about Phil's cancer as gently as he could, but it didn't make the truth any easier to bear. Phil had died alone, opting to kill himself in a strange hotel room. He had kept his illness a secret from everyone, even from Al.

It was heartbreaking.

During the service, Al couldn't help thinking about the very last time he and Phil had met. In retrospect, there were so many clues that all was not well with his friend: his pallid complexion, his greying hair, his recognition of the medication, erythropoietin, which Al had since learned was a treatment to combat anaemia after chemo: the reminiscences, the spasm of pain which had gripped Phil for a fleeting instant and finally the salute.

Al had missed it all.

Jay Winterflood was in the front row, standing quietly, gazing intently at Phil's coffin. Al forgot his own troubles for a moment, imagining how Jay must be feeling now: never knowing who his father was until he was dead. What a tragedy. Al had expected to be asked to give the eulogy. To his surprise, one of Phil's pals at City Hall delivered it instead. Phil had been popular. The church was full of mourners. It made Al feel a little less alone Yet painful as it was for him to face the truth, he knew he had let Phil down. Phil had always been there to help, whenever Al had had a problem. Phil was the ultimate fixer. Yet Al had not returned the favour. He finally understood why Phil hadn't been in touch for months. It was because he was fighting for his life! How badly he had misjudged him. Why oh why, hadn't he just picked up the phone and reached out to his friend when he had the chance?

One week after the funeral, Theme Parks Canada called. They expressed an interest in purchasing the backstretch of Iroquois Downs Raceway, in order to construct a tourist attraction, focusing exclusively on horses. The phone call cheered Al greatly. A Horse Park would benefit the racetrack in so many ways: not just financially, but by increasing its footprint, too. Even though his friend was dead, Phil's influence was still alive. It was like a precious, parting gift.

That same day, Al found out that, just as Phil had predicted, the government was planning to take away the Slots revenue from Iroquois Downs, as part of a major reorganization. The intention was to place horse race betting under the Gaming Commission which would take over the role of policing the industry. To Al, this was akin to removing the local police patrol, who knew the neghbourhood and shunting the job to somewhere further up the line. Though he had known it was coming, the speed of the decision shocked Al to the core. Quebec had already lost its premier racetrack after installing slots in a *bait and switch* operation. It looked like that could happen in Ontario, too. With Phil gone, he realized the politicians were free to do whatever they wanted. Phil's influence must have been huge. Al missed him in so many ways. What a man!

A week later, Al received a bland email from the Gaming Commission informing him, amongst other things, that gambling on virtual reality horse racing would soon be introduced at all its casinos to "stimulate interest in harness racing". Al wasn't fooled. He was certain that their real intention was to make live racing redundant. His great fear was that left to its own devices, Iroquois Downs would begin a long, slow slide to oblivion. He found himself identifying with the captain of the Titanic, as the ship hurtled towards certain disaster. If the racetrack closed, it would change so much for so many people, himself included. Racing Harmony Stampede at small tracks wasn't what he'd had in mind when he paid up for him at the yearling sale and he had sold McTavish Construction. What would he do every day? And what about Sofia? Ironically, since the caffeine scandal, followed by his own health crisis, the two of them were getting along better. She seemed equally keen to solve the problem of illegal drugs at the racetrack and had come up with an interesting solution, based on her unique perspective as a pharmacist. That would go to waste if the track closed. What was going to happen to his Head of Security and future son in law? Al wondered anxiously. Would Campbell have to go back onto the mean streets of some major Canadian city, miles from Erinsville, with his life at risk on a daily basis? How would Billie feel about that?

Of course, all that was nothing compared to the fate of the horses, he imagined. The best ones would go south of the border; others would pull Mennonite buggies. But far too many horses would end up at the killers and throughout Ontario, everyone associated with harness racing would be put out of work – not just trainers and grooms, but blacksmiths, feedmen, breeders . . . veterinarians. His heart went out to Doctor Jay Winterflood.

His thoughts turned to the two young hopefuls that had come to see him in his office recently with a plan to liven up the pre-game show. Theo Vettore appeared to be genuine in his desire to turn over a new leaf and make a better life for himself. Purely to take his mind off his troubles, Al clicked on the link they had sent him. He spent the next four hours glued to the computer screen, transported to the glories of Cheltenham Gold Cup Day in the UK. The horses weren't pulling carts; they were jumping fences. There was none of the glamour of thoroughbred racing. But as Al saw the wall to wall crowds and the tens of thousands of fans thronging the grandstand, he realized what was possible. It gave him hope. This is what he wanted for Iroquois Downs. If he failed, he would have to bow out gracefully, knowing that he had done everything possible to carry out Phil's mandate: to clean up Canada's flagship Standardbred Racetrack.

That night he was unable to sleep. He lay still, trying not to wake Sofia, with Walter the cat sitting on his head purring loudly. The next morning, anxious to get someone else's take on things, he asked Campbell McClaren to come into the office. After he replayed the running of the Cheltenham Gold Cup, Campbell told him that it reminded him of Charlottetown Driving Park on Cup and Saucer day. This encouraged Al no end. If they could pull that off in PEI, why not in Ontario? He tentatively laid out some of his ideas for reforming Iroquois Downs, the fiasco of the Retention Barn still fresh in his mind. Phil had tried to put him off the idea, he remembered. If only he had listened!

After listening to everything Al had to say, Campbell advised him to test run the plan on the horsemen. With Phil gone, Campbell reasoned, obtaining support from the grassroots for any future changes would be vital. Knowing he was under time pressure, Al scheduled an open meeting in the grandstand of Iroquois Downs for July 15th, the start of the stakes season, when everyone was sure to be around. Next, with Campbell beside him, he set off on a tour of local farms and training centres, drumming up support and garnering ideas. On his travels, he was struck more and more by how many honest, decent people there were in this business: men and women who genuinely loved the sport and had a healthy respect for the animals they worked with every day. It was heartwarming! Yet it was these same people who told him the real story, anxious for harness racing's dark secrets to be exposed.

Watching old timers harnessing up young colts in dingy, cramped barns, Al learned that everyone was in too much of a hurry these days, speed being all that mattered. People didn't care if a horse was lame so long as it could go fast. It was a curse hanging like a dark cloud over the industry. Washing down horses, girl grooms came close to tears as they complained that trainers never listened to them, even when they were sure something was wrong.

Sheltering in run-in sheds from April showers as breeders doled out hay to their horses, Al listened to stories about cynical commercial outfits who bred mares with crooked legs to speedy fragile sires, not thinking about the consequences, but counting on rich owners to throw fortunes at those babies just because they looked good on paper. To make things worse, the current crop of young horse trainers, apparently, were ruining promising horses by going too fast, too soon. Patience had gone out the window.

Under clear blue skies alive with the cries of Canada geese, Al heard horse-men complain about claiming trainers who were little more than chemists, sending honest trainers to the poor house and drivers desperate to win at any cost barrelling out to the front of the pack at lunatic speeds, oblivious of the destruction they caused to young bones. Horses, Al realized, were falling victim to the throw away culture and the commoditization that was sweeping the western world. No wonder fans had abandoned harness racing in droves!

After allowing everyone to have their say, Al made a shopping list of changes that he thought horsemen and Iroquois Downs Management would support. Most of the changes could be done in house but there were some things he could not do on his own. He had spent the last two decades living in Phil's shadow, depending on his friend to point him in the right direction. Curiously, Phil's absence made Al feel surer of himself. It was time to step out into the sunlight, to trust his own judgement for a change. With this in mind, he picked up the phone and called his opposite numbers at Merry-vale Raceway and Cree Horse Park intending to rustle up support for major changes in the stakes schedule for young horses, especially two year olds. To sweeten the deal, Al suggested entering into a mutually beneficial agreement: all stakes races would be regularly screened at all three racetracks simulta-neously, increasing interest, participation and naturally, the betting handle.

Then he walked upstairs to Judge Jewells' office, high up in the grand-stand and told him what he needed the soon to be defunct Provincial Racing Commission to do. With less than a month to go before the meeting with horsemen, Al was understandably nervous; it was a race against time. Judge Jewells' response was, as usual, short, sweet and to the point.

"Three months ago, I wouldn't have given you the ghost of a chance!"

Jewells declared. "But Bill is hopping mad!" Al knew Bill Johnson. He was the head of the PRC and he was being airbrushed out of existence along with everyone else in the organisation. "He might just relish the chance to take a parting shot at the Gaming Commission by loading them up with a whole set of new rules!" Jewells added, a gleam in his eye. "Leave it with me. I'll try to talk Bill into it. They won't have to face the consequences of passing this. They'll be long gone. What do they have to lose?"

What indeed? Al thought.

JULY 15TH 2:30 P.M.

The sun was shining as Al McTavish cast his eyes over the large crowd of horse people that had gathered in the grandstand, hoping that they hadn't just come for the free pizza. He knew most of them by sight now and many of them by name. Al was taking a huge gamble. His own future, as well as the future of Iroquois Downs hung in the balance this afternoon. He picked up the microphone and took a deep breath.

"Welcome everyone. Thanks so much for coming. Find a seat anywhere you can." Out of the corner of his eye, he saw Jay Winterflood coming in at the back. Good timing, he thought, feeling pleased. A hush fell over the grandstand and a sea of faces turned in Al's direction. He had their attention. Good! He took a last look at his neatly typed speech before tossing it aside. He had done his homework. The facts were all in his head and he intended to speak from the heart.

"We're here today to discuss the future of Iroquois Downs Raceway," he began. "You all know that we are going to lose the revenue from the Slots. That's bad news," Al conceded. "But every problem is an opportunity!" he added loudly, wanting to put a stop to the groans and complaints about the injustice of it all. "The good news is that it means for the first time since I took over as Director, we'll have much more say in managing our own affairs." Clearly this came as a let down to most people present. "When I took on the job six years ago," Al continued. "My aim was to clean the place up by getting rid of the bad apples. I wanted to create a more level playing field, both for horsemen and the bettors." He paused. "I tell you now, honestly, that I have failed." His confession was met by silence. In the front row, Tom Larson scowled, his trademark cowboy hat hiding his eyes. "I have failed because I was so intent on catching the bad guys that I forgot all about the victims: the decent, honest trainers…"

"Right on!" Bob Summers called out.

". . .owners with a love for a sport," Al continued. "And let's not forget the horses, who all too often are treated as pincushions by the unscrupulous trainers among us. You will know who you are," Al added gravely. A few heads turned in Keith Lazer's direction. So he had been right about Lazer all along, Al thought, feeling vindicated.

"The system as it is operating now is fundamentally flawed," Al said boldly.

"It's a system that turns a blind eye to horses being treated like commodities. It's a system that's happy for horses to put on the show and attract thousands of bettors and fans, but which abandons them when they need help. Not one cent of the purse money horses make is available to them by right. Slavery's been abolished in the free world, but if you happen to be a standardbred racehorse no one's listening!" He couldn't believe how angry he sounded. "It doesn't have to be like that," he added, dropping his voice and trying to stay calm. "There are plenty of decent people out there, people who've been driven to the edge of extinction by trainers using drugs like EPO, capturing the lion's share of the purse money by illicit means, receiving plaudits and awards, until, at the end of the day, after the fact, they're finally caught. Does that seem right to you?" A murmur of approval ran through the grandstand. Encouraged, Al continued. "The public is staying away from an industry that is seen as tainted and inhumane. It's not enough to change racing's image by clever marketing. We need to change the reality...go back to the days when harness racing was a sport, beloved by fans all over North America. Richer purses and high priced claiming races attract the wrong kinds of people: trainers who will do anything to win and owners who put up big bucks and expect a big return. Horses are dying," Al said, his voice breaking. He was still grieving for Phil, he realized. No wonder he was emotional. "Some of them from the stress of racing. That's bad enough, but far too many deaths are directly caused by illegal drugs. These brave athletes deserve better!"

"Tell it like it is!" a man in grey overalls called out. It was Craig Brown, Al realized. Then a girl with dark hair raised her hand.

"We don't have claiming races in the UK," she said. "It doesn't stop thousands of fans coming to the races to watch the horses and have a fun day out."

"You're absolutely right," Al replied, smiling. "We don't need claiming races to bring in the crowds at Iroquois Downs, either." Cries of disbelief greeted his statement. "And that's not all," Al continued. "Our young horses are getting a raw deal, too. Some trainers are incapable of judging whether a youngster is mature enough or sound enough to race as a two year old. I'm told these trainers carry on regardless, with some vague theory of survival of the fittest. The fact is that only a fraction of the yearlings sold at public sales go on to win stakes the following summer. Far too many of the rest end up crippled by injury. The breakdown rate is just not acceptable. No wonder the Race Secretary can hardly fill the race card!"

"Well that's a goddamn lie!" Moose Rankin shouted. Al ignored him.

Lara Vachon rose to her feet. "You zink you 'ave all ze answers 'ere in Ontario," she said. "But in Vancouver, ze stakes for two year olds, zey do not begin until September."

"That'd be suicide for the trainers!" Jim Mercer cried, jumping up from his seat.

"Not if Iroquois Downs changed their stakes schedule," Al replied firmly. To his relief, Mercer sat down again. "I realize now," Al continued, moving swiftly on, "that banning all medications for horses on race day is positively dangerous." A gasp swept the grandstand. "Let me explain. A few months ago, one of the trainers at Iroquois Downs was so desperate to stay in business that he tried to tube a horse on race day." He paused. "That mare died."

"Jesus," a little guy high up in the grandstand exclaimed, clapping his hand to his mouth. It was Dave Bodinski.

"We already have a lasix program, which operates on the day of the race to prevent bleeding. But what about the other ailments suffered by our equine athletes? Ulcers, allergies, tying up, to name just a few, are not so visible as a horse bleeding from the nose or the lungs, but they are just as distressing to the horse and often more painful too.

"I want to make a clear distinction here between illegal performance enhancing drugs and beneficial remedies commonly prescribed by veterinarians to their equine patients. Banning these treatments on race day isn't kind. It isn't fair. Human athletes don't have to put up with that. Why should horses?" There was a smattering of applause. "We need to encourage trainers to take the legal route to success," Al said, driving his point home. "But at the same time, I promise you that we shall be cracking down on the use of illegal drugs with every means available to us, including mass spectrometry, which can pick up the most minute particles of any illegal substance. A list of all treatments allowed to be given on race day, under controlled conditions, will be made available to trainers. Anything *not* on that list will be automatically banned." The crowd was hushed, taking it all in. Al pressed on.

"So, today I am proposing the following: *One!* The abolition of the retention barn." This was greeted enthusiastically. "*Two!* The introduction of a *Prep* barn, offering therapeutic treatment on race day by qualified veterinarians. These will be published on the race program beside each horse's name. *Three!* Pre-race testing for all horses two hours before post time. Those found with blood results which are suspect will be scratched from the race, without penalty *Four!* I am further proposing the introduction of a membership system for everyone who wishes to participate at Iroquois Downs. Membership rules will include owners and trainers giving their consent for spot testing of any of their horses currently racing at Iroquois Downs, at training centres or private farms, wherever they are stabled, without notice."

"There are private property laws in Ontario, Mr. McTavish," Keith Lazer interrupted in an irritated tone. "What you're proposing is illegal!"

"Already covered! My lawyers have gone into that point thoroughly," Al replied dismissively. "*Five!*" he continued. "The Race Secretary will not be writing any more claiming races for older horses." Howls of disbelief followed this announcement.

"You're out of your mind, McTavish," someone yelled from the front row. Al soldiered on.

"We all know that claiming races attract the wrong kinds of owners and trainers. Using the excuse that more money is bet on claiming races just isn't good enough anymore. People used to bet a great deal of money on cock fighting once upon a time. Doesn't make it right! However," he added calmly, "a few claiming races will still be offered for three and four year olds with large allowances who have not yet made much purse money." Most people looked relieved. "*Six!*" Al continued. He was on a roll now. "Penalties for racing a lame horse. Any trainer caught racing a horse lame will face a stiff fine. Three strikes and you're out! Horses should never be brought to the Race Barn on race night unless they are sound. It's not fair to the horses and it's not fair to the betting public." Was he imagining it, or was there a hint of respect on Lazer's face?

"*Seven!* I had a call from the Provincial Racing Commission this morning. The dates of all provincial stakes races have been changed. Two year olds won't race until the fall, starting September first." From the middle of the grandstand Eddie Clearwater spoke up.

"I never dreamt I would see this in my lifetime. Hats off to you Mr Mctavish!" he said, taking off his cap and throwing it up in the air. Al acknowledged the compliment with a wave.

"There will be a new program of stakes for four year olds who didn't race at two, to reward owners who are willing to wait." Hearing scattered applause Al got encouraged. His next point would be a tough sell, but it was crucial. "*Eight!* To remain eligible to Ontario stakes, two year olds will have to be thoroughly vet checked by May first, to ensure their suitability to begin training down. *Nine!*" he continued, raising his voice to be heard over the noise of the crowd. "To protect the welfare of our young horses in training, statistics will be published on the percentage of young horses that individual trainers succeed in bringing to the races. This will help owners make an intelligent choice." This last point was met with complete silence. Al didn't know what to make of that but at least they hadn't lynched him yet, he thought, counting his blessings. "*Ten!* Pensions! How many people in this room think it's a good idea for everyone to have a pension when they can't work anymore?"

Every hand in the room went up.

"Good! I'm glad you agree," Al said, pausing for effect. "Yes! Everyone deserves a pension, including the standardbred racehorse! Therefore, from January first next year, I propose to set aside one percent of the purse money towards a retirement fund for our ex-racehorses! And I understand that Dr. Jay Winterflood, of the recently established Phil Harman Charitable Foundation, intends to earmark a matching grant for that purpose."

Up at the top of the grandstand, Jay saluted, in a gesture that reminded Al painfully of his last memory of Phil. For a moment, he wasn't sure he could go on. Then Evie Mercer stood up.

"I'd like to suggest a big bunch of carrots for the winning horse," she said. "They deserve a reward for their hard work." Al heard scattered applause mingled with laughter.

"Finally," he said, beaming. "I've got a piece of really good news for you. Last night, Iroquois Downs signed an agreement with Theme Parks Canada to build a horse park on the backstretch of Iroquois Downs, an amenity which will draw crowds from all over Ontario. Some of that money will be used to give Iroquois Downs a much needed facelift, and make it a more attractive and, dare I say it, a more exciting place for the public at large. Let me stop there and let the rest of you have your say. I'll leave you in the capable hands of Bob Summers and Jim Mercer, your Horsemen's Representatives!" Everyone started talking at once. Al had set the cat among the pigeons. It was time to make a graceful exit. But that was not to be! There were too many people crowding around him, wanting to talk about the proposals. Keith Lazer got to him first.

"I got something to say. Most trainers have no idea their horses are lame. What are you going to do about that, McTavish?" Lazer demanded.

"If you feel that way, why don't you come and run a workshop on lameness?" Al suggested.

"What? Help the competition?" Lazer asked, his contempt obvious. "Want some free advice, McTavish? Tell your idiot trainer to get your colt's hocks done!" He left before Al could think of a rejoinder. There were more than a few grumbles in the background about the pre-race testing and especially the membership rules. That was no great surprise! He couldn't expect to change things for the better without stepping on a few toes!

Then Theo Vettore rushed up to him and shook his hand.

"I'm with you all the way," he said enthusiastically. That meant a great deal to Al. Theo Vettore had all the markings of a reformed character and he had plans for him.

After the meeting, Theo climbed into his truck and drove off. It had been a mind blowing couple of months, but he was slowly regaining his equilibrium. His memories of the missing eighteen months in his life had been getting clearer all the time. In the fall, he was hoping to visit Lost Valley Ranch, with Evie. He took the road south, through the village of Indian Falls, past the church where Harmony Light had paid an impromptu visit to the congregation, then on to Harmony Farm, where the colt had been raised. On his way, he passed by Jay Winterflood's place, the man who had come to the horse's rescue countless times to hear Jay tell it, starting with the night he had been foaled. Then Theo turned west towards Ferme Victoire, where Harmony Light's story had really begun, when the stallion Night Raider had leapt into Heart of Darkness' stall on a wintry January night. That, Theo realized, smiling to himself, was totally down to him. His carelessness had created a precious being, a creature to treasure.

As he drove, he thought he had never seen the countryside look more beautiful: the giant round hay bales lying out in the fields, ready to be gathered in, the horse barns and paddocks, the lakes and streams, the dense forests, the green corn standing tall, the dirt roads…it was all so achingly familiar. After what he had endured, after all that he had lost, he had succeeded in making it back home. He was finally free of the Scorpion. The Undertakers were in jail.

All was right with his world.

In the darkness, just before dawn, Harmony Light lay dreaming. He dreamt of the land of his birth, Harmony Farm. They were all there, all the colts in his group. The strong bay with the white face, the slender grey, the chunky little black colt, smaller than the rest. Together, they thundered across the wide green meadow, coming to a breathless stop at the white fence. The meandering stream beckoned and the grass tasted so sweet. Petty rivalries, bites and kicks, posturing and play fights. All were forgotten at the end of the day when, safe from the night, noses buried in good clean oats, they huddled together in the run in barn that sheltered them from the hot summer sun and the icy blast of winter. Harmony Light's legs moved gently. His breathing grew deeper and deeper. He was running, running over the hills, kicking up his heels, chasing the leader who was always just ahead of the pack…

The noise from the feed room woke him. It was a new day. Evie Mercer was feeding breakfast.

A BETTER PLACE

Three years on, Al McTavish feels proud to be Director of Iroquois Downs Raceway. The sea of grey asphalt has been replaced by green tarmac and paved walkways lined with cherry and crab apple trees. The casino is long gone. In its place is a virtual reality playground, where state of the art optics make it possible for young people and their families to take a dare devil ride on a roller coaster, fly a plane, snowboard down a mountain, sky dive, even drive in a horse race and feel that they are actually there. The hodge podge of snack bars at the racetrack is a distant memory. The new, earlier race time of 6–9 pm attracts an after work crowd who get together for a meal at one of the many national restaurant chains now operating at Iroquois Downs. On Friday and Saturday nights throughout the summer, a program of top rate popular entertainment is held after the races with an enticing line-up of well known artists, drawing in crowds of people in their teens and twenties.

Thanks to Billie's ideas and Jeff Lamare's high tech expertise, the racing experience is something everyone can enjoy now, not just inveterate gamblers. Surround sound and wifi devices on drivers' helmets ensure that the thunder of hooves, the screams of drivers and the rattle of sulkies are delivered directly to the grandstand, thrilling all who hear it. Expert camerawork zeroes in on the action from multiple angles, making it a great spectacle to watch, too. The stirring notes of Aaron Copland's Fanfare for the Common Man greet every winning horse in the specially designed winner's circle, reverberating through the grandstand. Throughout the race program, Theo Vettore provides lively commentary and broadcasts special features. There is nowhere that Theo isn't prepared to go to get his story: training centres and farms, the winner's circle, the Race Barn, even the drivers room! Meanwhile, the aptly named Indian Falls Horse Park, built on the backstretch, is bringing in new people all the time. Most are merely looking for a fun night out, but they are happy to put a few dollars on the driver or trainer with the most wins of the night or even the number pad winning the most races. Anything goes!

Al McTavish has achieved his dream of creating a level playing field for all participants at Iroquois Downs. The proposal he put forward three years ago in the grandstand was adopted by the board in its entirety and it seems to be working. There are no more suspicious horse deaths. There are no more claiming races for older horses, either. Far fewer horses are on lasix these days. Perhaps that's because the racetrack now closes for three months every winter, to give everyone, including the horses, a much needed break. The handle is up twenty-five percent in the last year alone. Al is thinking of retiring soon. If so, he will be going out in a blaze of glory.

Sofia McTavish has opened an unusual kind of pharmacy, specializing in giving expert advice on natural remedies and on using food as medicine. She and Al now live in a townhouse with a small garden in the historic quarter of Erinsville. Walter the maine coon cat has settled in well and is getting to know his new neighbour, an orange tabby.

Lara Vachon has won the new award "Young Horse Trainer of the Year" twice now, ably assisted by Will, her second trainer. Because the two year old stakes races do not start until the fall, she is able to compete on an equal footing. She has found love with Jean Claude's younger brother, who moved down from Quebec when Hippodrome de Montreal closed down. She and Evie are great friends. They agree on everything, even about Theo!

There is a brand new retraining centre for retired racehorses on the backstretch of Iroquois Downs, currently run by Evie Mercer. One of the first of many graduates was Harmony Jet, who pulls a specially adapted cart for disabled drivers along the trails and bridleways that weave through Indian Falls Horse Park.

Harmony Light has recovered from his catastrophic injury. Exactly one year ago, he won the Phil Harman Memorial Pace, beating Harmony Stampede, finally getting even with his boyhood rival. He has since retired from the racing scene but he proudly leads the post parade on Canada Day. Evie visits him regularly at Harmony Farm, where he is living out his retirement in Joey's second best paddock.

Harmony Light's sire, Night Raider has hung up his horseshoes. His son, Perfect Harmony, who is Harmony Gold's full brother, was a World Champion at three and has now taken over stallion duties at Ferme Victoire.

Joey and Val Harris have switched to breeding trotters. The only pacing mares on their farm now are Heart of Darkness and Gold Digger, who they kept out of sentiment. The new rules introduced for commercial breeding farms have not affected them. They have always chosen fillies with good conformation as broodmares.

Bob Summers doesn't work for Keith Lazer anymore. He has gone back to training young horses. One day, he knows, patience will pay off and he will get his champion. Harmony Stampede is back in Bob's barn, racing in the preferred class at Iroquois Downs. He gets his hocks injected regularly.

Harmony Gold is enjoying life in Australia, where it seems to be always summer. She's given birth to a fine young colt. Being a mother suits her. But she keeps a look out for her friend, Harmony Princess, in hopes of seeing her again, one day. It's too bad that will never happen.

In Australia too, are Cat and Anya. They live in the house André Fontain-bleu bought for Anya in Sydney Harbour before he died. Pete and Henri are renting an apartment on the north end of Bondi Beach. The two couples get together often.

Pam Mercer still works at the Hot Tamale. Jim Mercer, her ex-husband, pops in to see her from time to time. At least they're on speaking terms!

Campbell and Billie have been married for two years now. Billie's new company, Business Innovations, keeps her lively mind fully occupied. She and Campbell visit PEI a few times a year and they never miss the Cup and Saucer, the highlight of the racing calendar there.

Tom Cowboy Larson has given up racing horses and is only using his cattle prod on cattle now.

Stinker the groom has taken over Crawfish's hay loft apartment. It's a big improvement on sleeping in Mercer's tack room!

Crawfish Brown insists on being called Crawford now. He wears a shirt and tie to work every day at Winterflood's clinic, where he is a veterinary assistant. He, Tammy and Bud live in the old farm house, where Cat once made spaghetti bolognese for Anya Papandreos on a stormy summer day.

Jay and Helena Winterflood haven't touched a penny of Phil Harman's vast fortune. Jay pays a commercial rent on the clinic to the Phil Harman Charitable Foundation, which has established retraining centres for harness horses all over the province. Jay still believes that time is the great healer. He often thinks of the few precious hours that he and his father spent together. When Rafaella is old enough to understand, he will tell her who she is named after and what a generous man her grandfather was. Unfortunately, she didn't inherit Phil's startling blue eyes. In fact, she has a shock of dark brown curls. Where in the world, Jay sometimes wonders, did that come from? Helena is, and always will be, the love of his life.

Theo Vettore's life has turned completely around. His show, Harness Racing Live, is a hit. Theo's dark good looks have young fans tuning in all over North America, some of whom had never heard of harness racing before. His in depth interviews, and human interest stories about the colour-ful characters both equine and human at Iroquois Downs, have captured the public's imagination.

Judge Jewells threatens every year to quit and move to Arizona. He hasn't left yet, though. Mr. T. Roberts barks commands at the horsemen in the Race Barn each evening. Some things never change!

Reggie Blair finally broke down and bought a new truck. Business is booming. A colt out of Heart of Darkness, by Mr President, is being sold in this year's yearling sale. Reggie is determined to buy him, come what may. He's going to give him to Bob Summers to train. Ginny is still an outrider at Iroquois Downs. She sees Theo all the time, but she is certain that she made the right decision, giving up on him. Life with Theo would never have been an easy option. Besides, she and Reggie Blair are getting along like a house on fire!

The Undertakers have recently been transferred to a maximum security prison, near Sudbury. Apparently, they started too many fights that led to serious injuries amongst the other prisoners. They are currently in solitary confinement, for their own protection.

Scotty McCoy is back at Erinsville General working as a janitor. His rich owner upped and died on him, so he is out of horses and out of luck for the time being. Dave Bodinski has gone straight. The PREP barn has been his salvation.

Though in his eighties now, Eddie Clearwater is still training and driving horses. His dearest wish is to drop dead in the sulky after winning the Trot-ting Classic. He is still racing Harmony Fire, who will be seven years old this year.

Caroline and Kip are back living in the UK again but they spend a few weeks in Ontario every summer on a busman's holiday.

Andy Price had no idea what he was going to do after claiming races were abolished. However, he soon landed on his feet, opening up a tack shop in the village of Indian Falls. He has lost fifty pounds in weight, astonishing his doctor.

Harmony Valentine is a star broodmare. Every year she produces a strong black colt or filly, with no white markings. They are in great demand from the Mennonites for their willing nature, their dark colour and their ability to pull heavy loads.

Campbell's role as Head of Security of Iroquois Downs has been greatly expanded. He now oversees pre-race testing and spot checking of horses. It's his job to stay ahead of the latest attempts to foil Al's reforms. He read recently that a laboratory in the US detected a new synthetic designer drug, as potent as morphine, especially compounded to thwart the testing process. This was progress. He and Billie have never told Al who Phil really was. They both felt there was no need for him to know.

Keith Lazer has been spending a lot of time on the internet lately, researching articles about synthetic biology, genetic engineering and nanotechnology. These are the tools, he believes, that will be necessary for any trainer who wants to stay at the top of the standardbred game in future. As they will form part of a horse's genetic make-up, Lazer hopes they will be impossible to test.

Time will tell.

Enjoyed this book? Email Tina on horseflesh85@gmail.com or go on the facebook page www.facebook.com/tinasugarmanauthor.

LAST WORD

Take me back
To the winding track,
To the old farm house and barn
When the log fire's burning
And leaves are turning
To crimson brown and gold.
Over the hill where the trees grow tall
And the harvest moon shines bright in the fall,
Geese flying high
In a darkening sky,
Colts shivering from the cold.

Coyotes howl at the setting sun.
The Ontario winter has begun
And snow will fall like a beating drum.
Yet spring will surely come.

www.ingramcontent.com/pod-product-compliance
Lightning Source LLC
Chambersburg PA
CBHW020819030726
47496CB00001B/2